TELL ME
WHO
I AM

Julia Navarro is a journalist, a political analyst, and the internationally bestselling author of seven novels, including *The Brotherhood of the Holy Shroud*, *Tell Me Who I Am* and *Story of a Sociopath*. Her fiction has reached millions of readers all around the world through translations sold in over thirty countries. She lives in Madrid.

www.julianavarro.es
 Julia.Navarro/Oficial

JULIA NAVARRO

TELL ME WHO I AM

Translation by
James Womack

GRUPOIII
IIIBOOKS

Penguin
Random House
Grupo Editorial

Grupo Books is an imprint of Penguin Random House Grupo Editorial, S. A. U.

©2010, by Julia Navarro
©2014, 2020 by Penguin Random House Grupo Editorial, S. A. U.
Travessera de Gràcia, 47-49. 08021 Barcelona, Spain
English translation ©2014 by James Womack
Originally published in Spanish in 2010 by Penguin Random House Grupo Editorial
as *Dime quién soy*

ISBN: 978-1-64473-320-2

Printed in USA

∎

For my mother,
without whom I would not be here.

For my grandparents Teresa and Jerónimo,
for their kindness and generosity,
and for all I learnt from them.
Their memory will be with me always.

And for my dear friend Susana Olmo,
for the laughter we share.

Acknowledgements

I would like to thank Riccardo Cavallero for his support and trust in my novels. He makes difficult things look easy.

And, as always, thanks to the team at Penguin Random House for making this novel possible. Thanks to everyone for their help, and to Cristina Jones for her patience.

And thanks to Fermín and Álex for always being there.

GUILLERMO

1

"You're a failure."

"I'm a normal, decent person."

My aunt looked up from the sheet of paper she held in her hands. She had been reading it as if the information it contained were new to her. But it was not. It was a CV, which summarized my brief and disastrous professional life.

She looked at me with curiosity and continued reading, although I knew there was not that much left to read. She had called me a failure not out of any desire to offend me, but simply as if she were confirming something self-evident.

My aunt's office was oppressive. Well, what really made me feel uncomfortable was her attitude, superior and distant, as if her success in life gave her permission to look down on the rest of her family.

I did not like her, but I had never been her favorite nephew either, which was why I had been surprised when my mother told me that her sister wanted urgently to see me.

Aunt Marta had become the family matriarch; she even dominated her brothers, my uncles Gaspar and Fabián.

Everyone asked her advice about everything, and nobody made a decision without her giving the go-ahead. In fact, I was the only one who avoided her and who, unlike all my cousins, never sought her approval.

But there she was, proud of having saved and even tripled the value of the family business, a company that dealt in and repaired machinery: something she had managed to do, among other reasons, because of her opportune marriage to her good-hearted husband, Uncle Miguel, for whom I felt a secret sympathy.

Uncle Miguel had inherited a couple of buildings in the center of Madrid, and got a good amount of rent each month from the tenants. He used to meet with the building administrator once a month, but otherwise he had never worked. His only interests were collecting rare books, playing golf, and taking every opportunity to escape from the vigilance of my Aunt Marta, to whom he had gratefully ceded the monthly meetings with the administrator, knowing that she had the intelligence and the drive to succeed in everything that she did.

"So you say that a failure is a normal, decent person. So people who succeed are abnormal? Indecent?"

I was about to answer yes, but that would have gotten me into trouble with my mother, so I decided to give a slightly smoother reply.

"Look, in my line of work being decent usually means that you end up unemployed. You don't know what it's like being a journalist in this country. You're either on the Right or you're on the Left. You're nothing more than a conduit for transmitting the slogans of one side or the other. But if you try to simply describe what's happening and give a truthful opinion, then you end up marginalized and out of work."

"I've always thought you were on the Left," my aunt said ironically. "And now the Left's in power..."

"Yeah, but the government wants their reporters to shut their eyes and mouths as far as their own errors are concerned. If you criticize the government, that means isolation. They stop thinking that you're one of them, and of course, you're not one of the others, so that leaves you in no man's land, or unemployed, like me."

"It says here on your CV that you're working for an internet newspaper at the moment. How old are you?"

The question annoyed me. She knew very well that I was in my thirties, older than any of my cousins. But this was her way of showing me how little she was interested in me. So I decided not to tell her how old I was because it was clear that she already knew the answer.

"Yes, I write literary criticism for an online newspaper. I haven't found anything else, and at least I don't need to ask my mother for money to buy cigarettes."

My Aunt Marta looked me up and down, as if seeing me for the first time, and appeared to hesitate before deciding to make her offer.

"Okay, I'm going to give you a job, a well-paying one. I trust that you can live up to my expectations."

"I don't know what the offer is, but my answer is no; I hate company press offices. If I'm here it's because my mother asked me to come."

"I'm not going to offer you a job in the company," she replied, as if the idea of my working for the family firm were crazy.

"So..."

"So I'm going to ask you to do something for the family, something more personal. Something private, in fact."

My aunt carried on looking at me as if she were still not sure if she was making a mistake.

"I want you to investigate an old family story, having to do with your great-grandmother, my grandmother."

I didn't know what to say. My great-grandmother was a taboo topic in the family. No one spoke about her; my cousins and I knew almost nothing about this mysterious person, about whom it was forbidden to ask questions and of whom not a single photograph existed.

"My great-grandmother? What do I have to investigate?"

"You know that I have almost all the family photographs. I wanted to give my brothers and sister a present for Christmas. So I started sorting through the old photos and choosing some to make copies. I also looked through my father's papers, because I remembered seeing some photos mixed in with them as well, and I found some photos and... Well, there was a sealed envelope, which I opened and found this..."

My aunt turned back to her desk and picked up an envelope, from which she took a photo. She gave it to me doubtfully, as if she thought I was clumsy and that the photo would not be safe in my hands.

The photograph had torn edges and had turned yellowish with time, but the portrait, of a young woman in a wedding dress, smiling and holding a bunch of flowers, was still intriguing.

"Who is it?"

"I don't know. Well, we think it could be our grandmother, your great-grandmother... I showed it to your mother and my brothers and we all agreed that our father looked a lot like her. We've decided that the time has come to investigate what happened to our grandmother."

"Just like that? You've never wanted to tell us anything about her. And now you find a photo that you think could be of one of our relatives and you decide you want to find out what happened."

"Your mother's told you something about her, surely..."

"My mother's told me the same as you've told your kids: practically nothing."

"But we don't know that much; our father never spoke about her, he couldn't get over losing her even after a long time."

"As far as I know, he never knew her. Didn't she abandon him when he was a newborn baby?"

My Aunt Marta seemed to be vacillating between telling me all she knew and throwing me out right away. I suppose she was thinking that I might not be the right person to deal with the business at hand.

"What we know," she said, "is that our grandfather, your great-grandfather, imported and sold machinery, above all from Germany. He traveled a great deal, and tended not to say when he was going, much less when he was thinking about coming back, something that his wife can't have liked very much at all."

"It's impossible that she wouldn't have known. If he was packing, I suppose she must have asked him where he was going, that's how these things work."

"No, he wasn't like that. Your great-grandfather used to say that he carried his suitcase in his wallet, that it was enough for him to take money with him. So he didn't have to get anything ready, he just bought whatever he needed. I don't know why he behaved like that. But I suppose it must have been a source of conflict in their marriage. Like I told you, your great-grandfather was an entrepreneur and his business was always getting bigger, he didn't just sell industrial machinery but also repaired it, and Spain needed a lot of both at that time. One day he headed off on one of his trips. While he was away, she had the kind of lifestyle that was normal for people of her position in those days. As far as we know, she would go to visit friends, you know that back then visiting people was an innocent and above all cheap form of entertainment. You'd go and visit some friends or relatives one afternoon, they'd come and visit you a few days later, and the drawing rooms of these houses turned into meeting-places. At one of these meetings she met a man, we don't know who he was or what he did. Once we heard a rumor that he was in the Argentinean navy. And it looks like she fell in love with him and ran away with him."

"But my grandfather had already been born; she had a son."

"Yes, and he was very young. She left him with her nurse, Águeda, who was the woman who your grandfather thought was his real mother until he found out the truth when he was older. Your great-grandfather shacked up with Águeda and had a daughter with her, Aunt Paloma, your grandfather's stepsister; you know about that side of the family already."

"Not really, we've never been that keen on knowing each other, I've only seen them at some funerals," I replied insolently, to provoke her.

But my aunt wasn't the kind of person to rise to a provocation if she didn't want to be provoked, so all she did was look at me with a flash of annoyance and decide to carry on talking as if she hadn't heard me.

"Your grandfather decided to get rid of his mother's surname, that's why he's named Fernández. When you change your name, you have to change it to one that's common."*

"I've never found out what he was really named," I replied, bored of this conversation.

"We don't know, we've never known." My Aunt Marta sounded sincere.

"And where does this interest in your grandmother's history come from?"

---

* Spanish people have two surnames, the first taken from one's father and the second from one's mother. For example, if your father is Javier Gómez Obeso and your mother is María Sierra Borrachero, then your surname would be Gómez Sierra. [*Translator's note.*]

"This photo I've shown you has caused us to make the decision. I've made copies; I'll give you one to help with the investigation. We think it's her, but even if it's not it doesn't matter: It's time to find out about these things."

"What things?" I liked trying to irritate her.

"To find out who we are," my aunt replied.

"I don't care what happened to my great-grandmother, it doesn't matter, I know who I am and that's not going to change, whatever this woman did so long ago."

"And I don't care that you don't care. If I'm asking you to do this it's because we don't know what we're going to find out, and I'd like the dirty laundry, if there is any, to stay in the family. That's why I'm not hiring a detective. So I'm not asking for a favor, I'm offering you a job. You're a journalist, you know how to do research. I'll pay you three thousand euros a month and expenses."

I said nothing. My aunt had made me an offer I knew I could not refuse. I had never earned as much as three thousand euros a month, not even when I worked as a television reporter. And now that I was in a woeful professional situation, making almost nothing by writing literary criticism for an online paper that couldn't even pay me five hundred euros a month, along came my aunt like the snake that tempted Eve. I wanted to say no, she could stuff her money, but I thought about my mother, how every month she had to lend me money for the mortgage on my apartment that I had bought but could no longer afford. Well, I thought, there wasn't anything dishonorable in looking into my great-grandmother's history, nothing wrong with getting paid for it. It would be worse to have taken a job puffing up this month's politician.

"A couple of months should be enough, shouldn't it?" Aunt Marta wanted to know.

"Don't worry, I don't think it'll take too long to find out about this woman. I don't know, I might even find out all I can in a couple of days."

"But I want something more," my aunt said in a threatening voice.

"What?" I asked hopelessly, as if I had suddenly woken up from a dream: Nobody pays three grand a month to find out what happened to their grandmother.

"You have to write my grandmother's story. Write it like a novel, or however you want, but write it down. We'll get it bound and it'll be my present to the family next Christmas."

I interrogated my mother, exhaustively, to find out what she remembered about her father, my grandfather. She spent some time praising him to the skies and I tried to remember what I could as well. I remembered him as being tall, thin, standing very straight, taciturn. One day they'd told me that my grandfather had been in a car accident that kept him in a wheelchair until he died.

Every Sunday when I was a child I would go to my grandfather's house with my mother. We'd have a family meal with lots of chatting at the dining table and I would get very bored.

Grandfather would watch us all in silence as he ate, and only every now and then would he say something.

Aunt Marta was the youngest of her brothers and sisters. She was single and lived with her father, and that's why she'd taken control of my grandfather's company, just as she'd become the owner of that enormous dark house. So my memories offered me no clue about my grandfather's mother, that mysterious figure who had disappeared one day, leaving my grandfather in the arms of the nurse.

I must admit that I started my investigation without much enthusiasm, I suppose out of an extreme lack of interest about what might have become of one of my relatives.

I started searching in the obvious place: I went to the Civil Registry to ask for a copy of my grandfather's birth certificate.

Of course, the names of both parents appear on a birth certificate, so this was the best way to find out the name of my grandfather's mother. I asked myself why Aunt Marta might not have done this herself, instead of paying three thousand euros for me to go to the Registry.

A very kindly civil servant dashed my hopes by telling me that it was impossible to issue a birth certificate for someone who had died.

"And why would you want a birth certificate for Javier Carranza Fernández?"

"He's my grandfather, well, he was my grandfather, I told you he died fifteen years ago."

"Okay, but I'm asking why you might want his birth certificate."

"I'm drawing up our family tree, and the problem is that my grandfather changed his surname, the maternal half of his surname, because of a family problem. He wasn't really named Fernández, and that's what I'm trying to find out about."

"Ah, well, you can't do it."

"Why not?"

"Well, because if your grandfather changed his name, then his file's kept in the Special Registry, and you can only consult the information there if it's your own file or if you get a court order."

"Obviously he can't ask anything about his own file," I replied crossly.

"That's true."

"Look, he was my grandfather, he was named Fernández, and I don't know why. Don't you think I've got a right to find out what my great-grandmother was named?"

"I don't know what your family problems are, and I really don't care. I'm just doing my job: I can't give you any birth certificate related to your grandfather. And now, if you'll excuse me, I've got a lot of work to do..."

When I told my mother about this, it was clear that she wasn't surprised at all by the scene with the civil servant. But I have to admit that she gave me a clue about how to get started.

"Just like us and like you, his grandchildren, grandfather was baptized in the church of San Juan Bautista. He got married there, and we got married there, and I hope that one day you'll get married there."

I didn't answer, because at that moment my only relationship was with the bank that had given me my mortgage. I had signed up to pay them back over the next thirty years.

The church of San Juan Bautista urgently needed to have its dome repaired; at least this is what I was told by Father Antonio, the old parish priest, who decried the apathy of his congregation in the face of the church's ruinous state.

"People are giving fewer and fewer donations. You always used to be able to find a benefactor to help with these problems, but now... Now rich people prefer to set up foundations to decrease their taxes and cheat the treasury, and they don't give a penny for these kinds of things."

I listened to him patiently because I liked the poor old man. He had baptized me, given me my first communion, and if it was up to my mother would also officiate at my wedding, but I thought he was a bit old to have to wait so long.

Father Antonio complained for a while before asking me what it was I wanted.

"I'd like to see my grandfather Javier's baptismal certificate."

"Your grandfather Javier was always a good friend to the parish," Antonio remembered. "Why would you want to see his baptismal certificate?"

"My Aunt Marta wants me to write a family history and I need to know a few things." I had decided to tell almost the whole truth.

"I don't think it will be easy."

"Why not?"

"Because all the older documents are in the basement archive; they went through the parish records during the war and now they're all disordered. We'd have to reorganize everything that's down there, but the archbishop doesn't want to send me a younger curate who knows about archives and I'm not as young as I was and can't think about organizing so many papers and documents, and of course I'm not going to let you just rummage through them all."

"I'm not promising anything, but I could ask my Aunt Marta to see if she might want to help the parish and hire a librarian or an archivist to help put things in order..."

"That's all very well, but I don't think your Aunt Marta would care very much about the parish documents. Anyway, we hardly see her round here."

"Well, I'll ask her, there's no harm trying."

Father Antonio looked at me thankfully. He was a gentle man, one of those priests whose kindness justifies the existence of the Catholic Church.

"God bless you!" he exclaimed.

"But I would like you to let me look for my grandfather's baptismal certificate in the meantime. I promise I won't look at any document that doesn't have anything to do with what I'm looking for."

The old priest looked at me intently, trying to read the truth of my assertions in my eyes. I held his gaze while I composed my face into its best smile.

"All right, I will let you go into the cellar, but you must give me your word that you will only look for your grandfather's baptismal certificate and not start poking around... I trust you."

"Thank you! You're a wonderful priest, the best one I've ever met," I said thankfully.

"I don't think you know that many priests, you don't come to church that often either, so the odds are in my favor," Father Antonio replied ironically.

He took the keys to the cellar and led me down a staircase that was hidden beneath a trapdoor in the sacristy. A bulb hanging from a wire was the only light in this damp place, which needed, like the dome of the church, a thorough restoration. It smelled like some shut-up place and it was cold.

"You'll have to show me where I need to search."

"It's a bit of a mess down here... When was your grandfather born?"

"I think 1935..."

"Poor child! Right on the eve of the Civil War. A bad time to be born."

"Well, no time is great," I replied, just to say something, but I immediately realized I had said something stupid because Father Antonio gave me a severe look.

"Don't say that! You, of all people! Young people today don't know how lucky they are, you think it's normal to have everything... That's why you don't appreciate anything," he grumbled.

"You're right... I said something stupid."

"Yes, my son, you said something stupid."

Father Antonio went from one side of the room to the other look-ing at archive boxes, rummaging through boxes lined up against the wall, opening trunks... I let him look around and hoped he would tell me what to do. In the end, he pointed out three boxes.

"I think that this is where the baptismal records of those years are kept. Of course, there were babies who were baptized a long time after they were born, I don't know if that's the case with your grandfather. If you don't find it here, we'll have to look in the boxes."

"I hope I'm lucky enough to find it..."

"When are you going to start?"

"Straight away, if you don't mind."

"Well, I have to go and prepare for midday Mass. When it's over, I'll come down to see how you're getting on."

I stayed alone in that mournful cellar, thinking that I would more than earn Aunt Marta's three thousand euros.

I spent the whole morning and part of the afternoon looking through the baptismal record, a book yellow with age, but found no sign of my grandfather Javier.

By five in the afternoon my eyes were unbearably itchy; also, my stomach was rumbling so loudly that I couldn't ignore it any longer. I went back to the sacristy and found a lay sister who was folding the altar cloths, and asked for Father Antonio.

"He's resting in the rectory; there's no Mass until eight o'clock. He told me that if you turned up then I should tell you. If you want to see him, go out through this passage and knock at the door you come to. The church is connected to Father Anto-nio's quarters."

I thanked her for her directions, although I knew the way very well already. I found the priest with a book in his hands, but he appeared to be dozing. I woke him up to tell him that my search had been a failure, and asked his permission to come back early the next day. Father Antonio told me to be there at seven thirty, before the first Mass of the day.

That night I called Aunt Marta to ask her to make a donation to the church of San Juan Bautista. She got cross with me for asking, angry that I didn't have more consideration for the way the family's money was spent. I tricked her by saying that I thought Father Antonio was vital to the investigation and that we needed to keep him happy in order to make him collaborate. I thought that the poor priest would have been upset to hear me talk like that about him, but there was no other way I could have convinced Aunt Marta. She cared little about Father Antonio's goodness and the difficulty he was having keeping his church afloat. So I convinced her that she should at least make a donation to help repair the dome.

It was not until four days later that I found my grandfather's long-sought baptismal certificate. I was upset, because at first I thought it was not what I was looking for.

Even taking into account that my grandfather had changed his maternal surname to a more common one, Fernández, it took me some time to realize that this Javier Carranza was the man I had been searching for.

It is true that the names Carranza and Garayoa are not very common, even less so in Madrid, but even so I nearly overlooked it because of the name Garayoa on the certificate. But now I knew that my grandfather's mother was named Amelia Garayoa Cuní.

I was surprised that she had one Basque and one Catalan surname. A strange mixture, I thought.

I took the photograph that Aunt Marta had given me out of its envelope, as if the image of the young woman could confirm, somehow, that she was indeed that Amelia Garayoa Cuní who appeared on my grandfather's baptismal certificate as his mother.

That young woman in the photograph was very attractive, or maybe that's what I thought because I had already decided that she really was my great-grandmother.

I read the entry in the register of baptisms several times until I had convinced myself that it was what I was looking for.

"Javier Carranza Garayoa, son of Santiago Carranza Velarde and Amelia Garayoa Cuní. Baptized on November 18, 1935, in Madrid."

Yes, there was no room for doubt, this was my grandfather and this Amelia Garayoa was his mother, who had abandoned her husband and her son to run away, or so it seemed, with a sailor.

I felt pleased with myself, and told myself that I had now earned my aunt's first three thousand euros.

Now I had to decide whether to share my discovery with her or to carry on with my research before I revealed our relative's name to my aunt.

I asked Father Antonio to let me photocopy the page on which my grandfather's baptism was recorded, and after promising faithfully that I would return the book as soon as possible, and in perfect condition, I left.

I made several copies. Then it was I who exacted a promise from Father Antonio that he keep the original book under careful guard, but easily accessible in case I should need it again.

I knew my great-grandmother's name: Amelia Garayoa Cuní. Now I had to find out something about her, and I thought that the first thing to do was to look for a member of her family. Did she have brothers? Cousins? Nephews?

I had no idea whether the name Garayoa was very common in Basque country, but I knew that I should go there as soon as possible. I would call all the Garayoas I could find in the phonebook, but I hadn't yet decided what I would tell them... If they answered the phone, that is.

But before I left, I thought I should look at the Madrid phonebook. After all, my great-grandmother had lived here, had married a man from Madrid. Perhaps she had family...

I didn't expect to find anything, but to my surprise I found two Garayoas in the Madrid phonebook. I wrote down their phone numbers and addresses while I thought about how to proceed. Maybe I should call them. Maybe I should just turn up at their houses to see what would happen. I decided on the second course of action, and was determined to try my luck with the first address the next day.

2

The building was in the Barrio de Salamanca, the rich part of Madrid. I spent a little time walking up and down the street, trying to get every detail of the building into my mind, and above all to see who was coming and going, but all I managed to do in the end was attract the attention of the doorman.

"Are you waiting for someone?" he asked aggressively.

"Well, no... or yes, I suppose. Well, look, I don't know if the Garayoas live here."

"And who are you?" he wanted to know, and his question made me realize that there must be some Garayoas here.

"A relative, a distant relative. Could you tell me which of the Garayoas live here?"

The doorman looked me up and down in an attempt to convince himself that I was the kind of person to whom he could give this information, but I didn't manage to dispel his doubts by my appearance alone, so I showed him my identity card. The man looked at it and handed it back straight away.

"You're not named Garayoa..."

"Garayoa was my great-grandmother, Amelia Garayoa... Look. Maybe you could talk to the Garayoas who live here and if they're willing for me to go up and see them I'll go up, and if not then I'll go."

"Wait here," he ordered, and I could tell from his tone of voice that he didn't want me even to come into the doorway.

I stayed impatiently in the street, asking myself who might live in this house, if it was an old nephew of my great-grandmother, or her cousins, or just some Garayoas who had nothing at all to do with my family. Maybe Garayoa was as common a surname in Basque country as Fernández was in the rest of Spain.

Eventually the doorman came out to see me.

"She says you should go up," he announced, sounding a little uncertain.

"Right now?" I asked in bewilderment, because I hadn't really expected that anyone would agree to meet me, thought rather that the doorman would tell me to get lost.

"Yes, right now. You need to go up to the third floor."

"Is it the apartment on the right side or the left?"

"The ladies' apartment occupies the whole floor."

I decided to take the stairs instead of the elevator, to give myself time to think about what to say to the people in the house, but my decision made the doorman even more unsure of himself.

"Why don't you take the elevator?"

"Because I like to get exercise," I replied, disappearing out of his curious field of vision.

A woman was waiting by the open door; she was middle-aged, wearing a gray dress, and had short hair. Her look showed even less confidence in me than the doorman's had.

"They will see you now. Please come in."

"And who are you?" I asked with interest.

She looked at me as if my question had somehow intruded upon her privacy. She glared at me before replying.

"I am the housekeeper, I look after the house. I look after the ladies. You will wait in the library."

Just as the doorman had, she spoke about "the ladies," which made me draw the obvious conclusion: There were at least two women who lived here.

She led me into a spacious room with ancient mahogany furniture, the walls covered with books. A dark brown leather sofa and two armchairs occupied one end of the room.

"Please sit down, I'll tell the ladies that you are here."

I didn't sit down, instead I started to poke around among the beautifully bound leather volumes. It struck me that apart from the books there was nothing else in the library, no ornaments, no paintings, nothing.

"Are you interested in books?"

I turned around, a little embarrassed, like a child caught putting his hand in the jam jar. I stammered out a "yes" while I looked at the woman who had spoken to me. From her appearance it was impossible to tell her age: She could have been fifty or seventy.

She was tall and thin, with dark chestnut hair, and she wore an elegant trouser suit; a diamond ring and diamond earrings were her only accessories.

"I'm sorry to bother you. My name is Guillermo Albi."

"Yes, the doorman said. You showed him your identity card."

"It was to calm him down, make him see... well, make him see that I'm not a madman."

"It is a little strange for you to come looking for the Garayoa family, claiming that Amelia Garayoa is your great-grandmother..."

"Well, it might seem strange, but it's true. I'm Amelia Garayoa's great-grandson, or at least I think I am. Do you know her?"

The woman smiled widely and looked at me in amusement before replying.

"Yes, I know Amelia Garayoa. She's me, and it's quite clear that I'm not your great-grandmother."

I didn't know what to say. So, this woman, who suddenly reminded me strongly of Aunt Marta, was Amelia Garayoa, and of course she couldn't be my great-grandmother.

"You're named Amelia Garayoa?"

"Yes, anything wrong with that?" she asked ironically.

"No, no, nothing, sorry, it's just... well, it's very complicated."

"To start with, I'd like to know what you're talking about when you say 'it's very complicated,' and also, who are you? What do you want?"

The housekeeper came into the library before I could answer and announced solemnly:

"The ladies are waiting for you in the drawing room."

Amelia Garayoa looked at me as if wondering whether to take me to this room where the other ladies were apparently waiting.

"My aunts are very old, they're both over ninety, and I don't want them to be upset..."

"No, no, I won't upset them, I have no intention of upsetting them, I... I'd like to explain to them why I'm here."

"Yes, some kind of explanation is in order," she replied drily.

She left the library and I followed her in a trance. I felt as if I were an uninvited guest about to make a fool of himself.

The drawing room was large, with two wide balconies. But what first caught one's attention was the imposing marble fireplace where a log fire was crackling. There was an armchair on each side of the fireplace and a black leather sofa facing the fire.

Two old women who appeared to be twins were sitting in the armchairs. Each had white hair drawn up into a chignon. They wore identical black skirts. One was wearing a white sweater, and the other was wearing a gray one.

Both of them looked at me curiously without saying anything.

"Allow me to introduce my great-aunts," Amelia said. "This young man is Guillermo Albi."

"Good afternoon; I am sorry for intruding, you are both very kind to see me."

"Sit down," ordered the oldest woman, the one wearing the white sweater.

"We have decided to see you because my aunts have agreed to it. I was not keen on speaking to a stranger," Amelia interrupted, making it clear that if the choice had been hers then she would have sent me packing without further ado.

"I understand, I know it's not very normal to turn up at someone's house saying that you have a great-grandmother called Garayoa and asking about her. I apologize, and I do not want to intrude too much."

"What do you want?" the old woman in the gray sweater asked.

"Before I start, it's probably best for me to say who I am... My family has a small firm, Carranza Machinery, run by my Aunt Marta; I'll leave you the address and the telephone number so that you can confirm that I am who I say I am. I can go away and will come back when you have confirmed that my intentions are good and that there's nothing strange about my visit..."

"Yes," Amelia said. "You give me your address, that's the best thing, and your phone number, and..."

"Don't be impatient, Amelia," the woman in the gray sweater interrupted. "And you, young man, tell us what you want and who you're looking for and how you came to this house."

"My name is Guillermo Albi, and it appears that I have a great-grandmother named Amelia Garayoa. I say 'it appears' because this woman is a mystery, we know little or nothing about her. In fact, we did not know her name until yesterday, when I found it on my grandfather's baptismal certificate."

I took a photocopy of my grandfather's baptismal certificate out of the pocket of my jacket and held it out to the old woman in the white sweater. She picked up some reading glasses from the table and read the document eagerly, shot me a steely glance, and made me think that she was reading my innermost thoughts.

I couldn't hold that gaze, so I looked at the chimney instead. She gave the document to the woman in the gray sweater, who also read it with care.

"So you are Javier's grandson," the old woman in the gray sweater said.

"Yes, did you know him?" I asked.

"And what was Javier's wife named?" continued the old woman in the gray sweater, without answering my question.

"My maternal grandmother was named Jimena."

"Carry on," the old woman in the white sweater said.

"So, my Aunt Marta, my mother's sister, found a photograph a while back and thought that it could be a picture of this mysterious vanishing grandmother. Because I'm a journalist, and because I'm going through a bit of a rough patch at the moment, I'm practically unemployed, she decided to hire me to investigate what happened to Amelia Garayoa. In fact, neither my mother nor my uncles knew until yesterday what their grandmother was really named. Their father changed his name from Garayoa to Fernández, and apparently he never spoke about his mother; it was a taboo topic in the family. For some time he thought that his mother was Águeda, the nurse, with whom his father had another child. I suppose it must have been very hard for him to realize that his mother had abandoned him. None of his children ever dared to ask him what had happened, so we have no information at all."

"And why does your Aunt Marta want to find out about her father's mother?" asked Amelia Garayoa, the old ladies' grandniece.

"Well, like I said, she found a photo and thought that it could be a picture of Amelia Garayoa, and she thought that I could write a history, the history of this woman. My aunt wants to give it to her family as a Christmas present. It will be a surprise. I don't want to lie to you: I really don't care what my great-grandmother did and the reasons that made her do it, but as I said, I'm going through a bad patch in my career, and my aunt is paying generously for this story. I've got a mortgage, and I'm ashamed to be always asking my mother for money."

The three women looked at me without speaking. I realized that I had been in this house for more than half an hour and that I hadn't stopped talking, hadn't stopped explaining who I was, while I knew absolutely nothing about them. Silly me, I had been so open it was almost ridiculous, like a teenager trying to talk himself out of a difficult situation.

"Do you have the photograph your aunt found?" the old woman in the white sweater asked in a trembling voice.

"Yes, I have a copy with me," I replied and took it out of my jacket pocket.

The old woman broke into a wide smile when she saw the picture of this young woman dressed as a bride.

The other two women drew close to look at the picture. None of them said anything, and their silence made me uneasy.

"Do you know her? Do you recognize the woman in the photo?"

"Young man, we'd like to be left alone now. You would like to know if we knew this Amelia Garayoa, who appears to be a relative of yours... It's possible, although Garayoa is not an uncommon name in Basque country. If you could leave us the photo and the copy of the baptismal certificate... it would be very useful," the old woman in the gray sweater said.

"Of course, there's no problem. Do you think she might be a relative of yours?"

"Why don't you leave us your telephone number? We'll be in touch with you," the old woman in the gray sweater went on, without answering my question.

I agreed. There was nothing else I could do. Amelia Garayoa got up from the sofa to say goodbye. I bowed my head to the two old women, murmured "Thank you," and followed the elegant woman who had led me to this room.

"What is a real coincidence is that you've got the same name as my great-grandmother," I plucked up the courage to say as I took my leave.

"I don't think so, there are a lot of Amelias in my family; I've got aunts and cousins and nieces with that name. My daughter is also named Amelia María, like me."

"Amelia María?"

"Yes, to tell the difference between all the Amelias, some are just called Amelia and some are Amelia María."

"And those two ladies are your great-aunts?"

Amelia wondered whether to answer my question. Then she spoke.

"Yes. This is the family home; when I lost my husband I came here to live with them, they're very old. My daughter lives in the United States. We're a very close-knit family: aunts, nephews, grandchildren... We love each other and look after each other."

"That's good," I said, to say something.

"They're very old," she insisted. "They're over ninety, even though they've still got their health. We'll call you," she said as she shut the door.

When I got down to the street I felt lightheaded, like I'd been punched in the jaw. The scene I'd just been through seemed surreal to me, although Aunt Marta's request was also odd, as was presenting myself at the house of some unknown people and asking if they knew anything about my great-grandmother.

I decided not to tell my aunt anything, to at least wait and see whether the women would call me or see me again, or would close their door on me forever.

I spent a few days waiting for the phone to ring, and the more I thought about them the surer I became that I had found a clue; I just didn't know where it would lead me.

"Guillermo Albi? Hello, I'm Amelia María Garayoa."

I hadn't got up yet, it was eight a.m. and the telephone had woken me up with a jerk, but I was even more surprised to hear Amelia Garayoa's voice.

"Good morning," I stammered without knowing what to say.

"Did I wake you up?"

"No... no... Well, yes, I was up late last night reading..."

"Right. Well, it doesn't matter. My aunts want to see you, they've decided to talk to you. Can you come this afternoon?"

"Yes. Of course I can."

"Alright, we'll be waiting for you at five o'clock."

"I'll be there."

She didn't hang up the phone. She seemed to be waiting to speak. I heard her breathing on the other end of the line. In the end she spoke. Her voice had changed tone.

"If it were up to me, you'd never set foot in our house again, I think you're only going to bring us problems, but my aunts have made up their minds and I have to respect their decision. So let me say now that if you try to cause us any trouble I will make sure you regret it."

"What?" I said, shocked by the threat.

"I know who you are, an unlucky journalist, a troublemaker who's had problems wherever he's worked. And I am telling you that if your behavior goes beyond the boundaries of what I consider acceptable, I will do whatever it takes to make sure you never find work again as long as you live."

She hung up without giving me a chance to reply. Now I knew that Amelia María Garayoa had been investigating me while I'd been waiting for a phone call instead of looking into the lives of these strange women. I told myself that this was a real disaster for an investigative journalist, and then, as I like to be kind to myself with regard to my faults, I also told myself that investigative journalism had never really been my thing, I was more used to covering politics.

I went to eat at my mother's house, and ended up having an argument with her about my immediate future. My mother didn't think it was bad that I'd taken Aunt Marta up on her offer, because it meant earning three thousand euros a month, but she reminded me that this was a salary with a time limit on it, and that once I'd found out things about my great-grandmother and written the account, then I would have to go back to earning money at my own trade, and apparently I was wasting time not looking for a better job than literary critic for an online newspaper.

My mother thought that online newspapers were less than nothing, because she would never dream of turning on the computer to read the newspaper online; what I did seemed irrelevant to her. She wasn't entirely misguided, but I was too much on edge to listen to her complaints, and I didn't want to own up that I was going to see the old women that afternoon. I was sure that she wouldn't have been able to keep my secret and would have spoken to Aunt Marta about it.

At five to five I went into the entrance of the Garayoa's building. This time the doorman didn't make any trouble.

The housekeeper opened the door, and with a brief "Good afternoon," followed by "Please come in, the ladies are waiting," she accompanied me into the room with the fireplace that I had seen the last time I was there.

The two old women greeted me with serious faces. I was surprised not to see their great-niece Amelia María, so I asked after her.

"She's working, she'll probably finish late. She's a broker, and there's usually a lot of deals to be done with the New York Stock Exchange at this time of the day," one of the old women explained.

This time, the one who appeared to be older was wearing a black dress, and the other one was again wearing a gray sweater, but a darker one than last time, and she was also wearing a pearl necklace.

"We will explain why we decided to talk to you," the old woman in black said.

"Thank you," I replied.

"Amelia Garayoa is... well, was a relative of ours. She suffered a great deal when she had to leave her son, Javier. She never forgave herself. You can't turn the clock back, but she always felt that she needed to make reparations. She couldn't, of course, she didn't know how. But we must say that there was no moment in her life when she didn't think about Javier."

She seemed to think for a moment before continuing.

"We will help you."

I heard with amazement these words coming from the old woman dressed in black. She spoke in a tired voice, as if it were difficult for her to say these words, and I don't know why, but I felt that rummaging through the past was going to cause them a great deal of pain.

The old woman in black stayed silent, observing me, as if looking for strength to continue.

"I'm very grateful that you've decided to help me... ," I said, without knowing very well what to add.

"No, don't thank us; you are Javier's grandson, and we are going to impose certain conditions," the old woman in gray replied.

I realized that their great-niece, Amelia Garayoa, had not told me their names; she had never introduced us, and this was why I identified them by the color of their clothes. I didn't dare ask them now, given the air of solemnity that they were giving to this moment.

"Also, it will not be easy for you to find out your great-grandmother's story," the old woman in black added.

These last words confused me. First they told me that they were going to tell me my relative's story, and then they told me that this knowledge would not be easy, but why?

"We cannot tell you things we do not ourselves know, but we can give you clues. It would be best for you to rescue Amelia Garayoa from the past, to follow her footsteps, wherever they might lead, to visit people who knew her, if they are still alive, to put her life back together from the foundations upwards. That's the only way you can write her story."

The one who was speaking was the old woman in gray. I had the impression that the two women were turning me into their puppet. They moved the strings, they were going to tell me the conditions I would have to obey in order to approach my relative's life, and they were giving me no other option than to accept their wishes.

"Of course," I said unwillingly. "What do I have to do?"

"Step by step, we'll go through it step by step," the old woman in gray continued. "Before we start, you'll have to agree to certain things."

"What would you like me to agree to?"

"First of all, that you will follow our directions without complaining; we are very old, and we have no desire, or even time, to waste trying to convince you of things. So, you will follow our suggestions and you'll find out what happened. Second, we will retain the right to decide what you can or cannot do with the text you end up writing."

"But I can't accept that! It makes no sense for you to help me investigate Amelia Garayoa if you won't let me give whatever I write about her to my family."

"She wasn't a saint, but she wasn't a monster either," the old woman in black murmured.

"I have no intention of judging her. It might seem astonishing for you that a woman decided, more than seventy years ago, to leave her home and to place her son under the care of her husband, but there would be nothing at all strange about it nowadays. We can't think a woman is a monster for abandoning her family," I protested.

"These are our conditions," the old woman in gray insisted.

"You aren't giving me much of a choice..."

"We're not asking for anything very difficult..."

"Okay, I accept, but I would like you to answer a few questions yourselves. What was your relation with Amelia Garayoa? Did you know her? And who are you? I don't even know your names...," I protested.

"Listen, young man, we come from a generation where a man's word was law, so: Do you give us your word that you accept these conditions?" the old woman in gray insisted.

"I have already said I do."

"As for who we are... As you have guessed, we are direct descendants of Amelia Garayoa, and therefore indirect relatives of yours. In the past we shared her worries, her decisions, her mistakes, her regrets... You could say that we are the guardians of her memory. Her life ran its course parallel to our own. The important thing is not who we are but who she was, and we are going to help you find out," the old woman in black declared.

"As far as our names are concerned... call me Doña Laura and call her," the old woman in gray said, pointing at the other old woman, "call her Doña Amelia."

"Amelia?" I said in confusion.

"My niece has already told you that there are lots of Amelias in our family... ," Doña Laura replied.

"May I ask why there is such an affinity for the name Amelia?"

"It used to be common for daughters to have the same name as their mother, or their grandmother, or the godmother, so our family has lots of Amelias and lots of Amelia Marías. My sister was called Amelia María, although we have always called her Melita to tell her apart from my cousin Amelia, isn't that right?" Doña Laura said, looking at the other old woman.

At least I now knew what the two old women were called, who as far as I could tell were sisters.

"I'm sorry for insisting, but I'd like to know what the exact relationship is between you and my great-grandmother. I think you're her cousins..."

"Yes, and we were very close, that's certain," Doña Laura replied.

"Well, now that we've reached an agreement, the best thing is for you to get down to work. We are going to give you a diary, it will help you start to know your great-grandmother," the old woman in black said.

"A diary? Amelia's diary?" I said in surprise.

"Yes, Amelia's diary. She started to write it when she was an adolescent. Her mother gave it to her as a present when she was fourteen, and she was happy, because she dreamed of being a writer. Among other things."

The old woman in black smiled as she remembered Amelia's diary.

"A writer? So long ago?" I asked in surprise.

"Young man, I suppose you know that there have always been women who have written, and when you talk about 'so long ago' don't do it as if you were talking about prehistory," Doña Laura said, sounding angry.

"So Amelia, my great-grandmother, wanted to be a writer..."

"And an actress, and a painter, and a singer... She had a great desire for life and a certain amount of artistic talent. The diary was the best present she was given on that birthday," Doña Melita said. "But we've said that you have to go finding things out step by step. So, read this diary, and when you've finished it come and see us and we'll tell you the next step."

"Yes, but before you read the diary we should explain to you what the family was like, how they lived...," Doña Laura said.

"Sorry, but let me get things straight. You are Doña Laura, and should I call you Doña Amelia María like your great-niece, or Doña Melita?" I asked, interrupting Doña Laura.

"However you wish, it's not important. What we want you to do is read the diary," Doña Melita protested. "In any event, young man, ours was a well-off family of businessmen and industrialists. Educated, cultured people."

"It's necessary so that you can give some context to what happened," Doña Laura insisted, irritated.

"Don't worry, I'll know how to do that..."

"Amelia was born in 1917, a turbulent time in world history, the year the Russian Revolution triumphed, and the First World War was not yet finished. There was a coalition government in Spain, and Alfonso XIII was king."

"Yes, I know what happened in 1917..." I was scared that Doña Laura would start to give me a history lesson.

"Young man, don't be impatient, people's lives make sense if you explain them in context, the reverse is difficult if you don't understand anything. As I was saying, Amelia, and I myself, grew up during the dictatorship of Primo de Rivera, we were there for the Republican victory in the municipal elections of 1931, and the famous declaration of the Republic and Alfonso XIII's departure into exile. Then came the center-left governments, and the ratification of the Statute of Catalonia, Sanjurjo's attempted coup d'état, the triumph of the right-wing CEDA groups in 1933, the revolutionary general strike in 1934..."

"I can see that you lived through some difficult times," I said, trying to cut short the old woman's speech.

At this moment, Amelia María, the great-niece of the old women, came into the room. I was getting confused by so many Amelias. She barely glanced at me, then kissed her aunts and asked them how they had spent their day.

After an exchange of pleasantries, which I listened to in attentive silence, Amelia María deigned to speak to me.

"And you, how are things?"

"Very good, and I'm extremely happy with your aunts' decision to help me. I have accepted all their conditions," I replied with a certain irony.

"Wonderful, and now, if you don't mind, my aunts need to rest. The housekeeper has told me that you've been here for more than two hours."

I was annoyed by the rapid way in which I was being thrown out, but I didn't dare argue. I got up and nodded to the two old women. This was when Doña Melita held out two clothbound books, cherry red but faded with time.

"These are Amelia's diaries," she explained as she held them out to me. "Be very careful with them, and come back to us when you've read them."

"I shall, and thank you once again."

I left the house exhausted, without well knowing why. Those old women, in spite of their apparent imperturbability, displayed a strange kind of tension, and their great-niece, Amelia María, didn't hide her dislike of me, most likely because she was convinced I was upsetting her aunts' peace and quiet.

When I got back to my apartment I turned off my mobile so as not to have to answer any calls. I was keen to bury myself in my great-grandmother's diaries.

3

How happy I am! My birthday party was a success. Mama is unsurpassed when it comes to organizing parties, and what's more, she gave me the best present: this diary. Papa gave me a pen and my sister some gloves. But I had a great many other presents as well, from my grandparents, from my aunts and uncles, and my friends have also been very generous.

My grandmother Margot insisted to Papa that Antonietta and I spend the summer with her in Biarritz. I would be so happy! All the more so because they say that my favorite cousin Laura is invited as well. It is not that I am uncomfortable with my sister Antonietta, but Laura and I share everything...

Laura says we are very lucky to have a French grandmother, because she would be as happy as I am to spend a summer in Biarritz. I think the truly lucky thing is to have a family like ours. I shudder when I think that I could have been born in some other family. Papa has told grandmother that we shall go spend some part of our holiday with her.

Now I am tired, today has been so full of emotion, I shall continue tomorrow...

Amelia's was the diary of an adolescent in a well-off family. As far as I could make out, Amelia's father, my great-great-grandfather, was Basque on his father's side and French Basque on his mother's. He was in commerce and traveled all over Europe and North America. He had a brother who was a lawyer: Armando, the father of Melita, Laura, and Jesús, my great-grandmother's cousins.

Amelia and her sister Antonietta had an English governess, although their guardian fairy was their nurse, Amaya, a Basque woman to whom they were devoted, and who had stayed with the family after the girls had left the nursery, helping the family in other ways.

My great-grandmother had been a dedicated student. It seems that what she most liked was playing the piano and painting, she dreamed of being famous for either of these skills, and she had a natural ear for languages. She shared all her girlish secrets with her cousin Laura. She was two years older than her sister Antonietta, but for Amelia this was an eternity.

It appears that Amelia's father insisted that his two daughters study and have good educations. They both studied with the Sisters of St. Teresa and took piano lessons and French classes.

My great-great-grandfather must have been a rather special person, because from time to time he took trips outside of Spain with his family. Amelia wrote down in her diary her impressions of Munich, Berlin, Rome, Paris... All stories told by a girl who was full of life.

I thought the diary was quite boring. I wasn't at all interested in Amelia's daily life, and apart from its revealing that her favorite cousin was called Laura and that one of her grandmothers was French, the rest of it was a syrupy story that I found tedious. That's why I decided to turn my phone on again, and to call a female friend so we could go out for a drink to take my mind off things. I left the second diary for the next day.

I have tuberculosis. I've been in bed for several days and the doctor won't allow me to have visitors. Laura came today, taking advantage of the fact that Papa is away in Germany and Mama always goes to Mass at nine in the morning. Laura brought me a diary as a present, just like the one Mama gave me when I was fourteen.

I didn't let her come close to the bed, but her visit made me very happy. Laura is more to me than just a cousin, she's like a sister, she understands me better than anyone else, much better than Antonietta. And I was touched by her present: this diary. She told me that it would help me be less bored, and would make the time pass more quickly. But what will I be able to put down here if I can't leave my bed?

The doctor came to see me, and it annoyed me that he treated me as if I were a child. He said that I need to keep taking rest, but that I should also breathe pure air. Mama has decided to send me to the country, to Amaya's house. They had thought to send me to grandmother Margot's house in Biarritz, but grandmother has had a series of persistent colds, so she's not in the best of health to look after a patient with tuberculosis. Also, Dr. Gabriel has said that pure mountain air is the best.

Mama is getting everything ready for us to go to Nurse's farm. Amaya will look after me, Mama has to stay with Antonietta and wait for Papa to come back from Germany, but she will come to see me from time to time. I prefer leaving to remaining here in this room; if it wasn't for Laura's visits then I think I should go mad. Although I am scared that maybe I will infect my cousin. Nobody knows she comes to see me, just Nurse, but she says nothing.

Nurse allows me to get up. She does not insist that I stay in bed. She says that if I feel strong enough then the best thing is for me to go outside and breathe pure air like Dr. Gabriel said. Here, up in the mountains, pure air is something we have a great deal of.

Nurse's parents are old, it's difficult for me to understand them because they speak Basque the whole time, but Amaya's oldest son Aitor is teaching me. Papa says I have a gift for languages, and the truth is that I am learning quickly.

I get on well with Aitor, and I also get on well with Edurne, Amaya's daughter, who is the same age as me... well, a few months older. Aitor and Edurne are very different, just like Antonietta and me. Nurse wants Edurne to come back with us to Madrid, to work in the house. I've promised her that I will convince Mama. Edurne is very quiet, but she always smiles and she tries to do everything I need.

Papa has provided a reference for Aitor to work in one of the offices of the Basque Nationalist Party, the PNV, in San

Sebastián. He is spending the whole week there. He says he is very happy with his work, he carries messages, he looks after visitors, and he also does little jobs round the office, such as addressing envelopes. Aitor is three years older than me, but he does not treat me like a child.

Nurse looks after him a lot, she's very proud of her son. The poor thing has really never lived with them, she came to our house when I was born, and I see now that it must have been very difficult to look after us instead of her own children. She must have missed them so!

We went into San Sebastián to call grandmother Margot, she is a little better and has promised to come to see me.

Aitor was surprised that I speak French with my grandmother, but we have always done so. Grandmother Margot also speaks in French with Papa. She speaks in Spanish only with Mama, but Mama is not very good with languages, and although she speaks French she speaks it only when we are in Biarritz.

I have gone out with Aitor to walk up in the mountains. Nurse told me not to tire myself out, but I do feel better, and I insisted that if we climbed a little further then we would be able to see France.

I think about grandmother Margot. I would like to see her, but I am still convalescing. As soon as I am better I will go to Biarritz.

Aitor knows a way to get into France without going past the customs post. He told me that there are many roads that lead to France, and that all the people round here know them, especially the shepherds. His grandfather showed him. Apparently, his grandfather and other shepherds have even earned a few pesetas by smuggling. Aitor made me promise not to tell anyone and I won't, I don't want to think what my father would say.

Aitor has told me that he does not want to stay in the village forever. He studies at night, when he gets back from work. He's only three years older than I am. And he is learning French now; I'm teaching him in exchange for him teaching me Basque.

Aitor says that I am Basque as well. And he says it as if it were something special. But I don't feel special, I don't care if I'm Basque or from some other place. I cannot feel the same way he *does, and he says it's because I don't live on the land. I don't know. I feel proud to be called Garayoa, but because it is Papa's name, not because it is a Basque name. No, whatever Aitor says, I can't think that I'm special simply for being half Basque.*

Now I speak in Basque with Aitor, and also with Amaya and her parents. I like doing it. Everyone in the village speaks in Basque and they are very surprised to hear me. I am really not bad at it. Aitor's French is getting much better. His mother says that it won't help him at all, that it would be better for him to learn how to milk a cow properly, but Aitor isn't going to stay here, he's sure about it. When he comes back from San Sebastián he brings the newspaper with him. He says that the political situation is bad. Mama says that things have gotten worse since the king left, but Papa doesn't feel the same way, he supports Acción Republicana, Manuel Azaña's party. Aitor doesn't seem to feel any sympathy for Alfonso XIII either. Of course, Aitor dreams of Basque independence. I ask him what he would do about all the people here who aren't Basques, and he says that I shouldn't worry, that I'm a Garayoa.

At supper he told us that there is a group that has formed, CEDA, the Spanish Coalition of Right-Wing Groups, and that it will run in the elections. I am not sure if this is a good or a bad thing, I will ask my parents when they come to see me in a few days. I miss them so much! Antonietta will not come because I am still not fully cured.

It has been very difficult for me to leave my parents again. When the car started to move I began to cry just like a little girl. Dr. Gabriel has said that I am still not fully cured and that I will have to stay in Nurse's house a while longer, but how long is that? No one will tell me and I am frantic.

I have convinced Mama to allow Edurne to come with us to Madrid; I have said that she could be a good maid, and that we should do this for Amaya who has been such a good nurse for Antonietta and me. She resisted for a while, but eventually she gave in and I am very happy, because she says that she will have Edurne look after Antonietta and me.

Papa has come back worried from Germany: He told us about the new chancellor there, a man named Adolf Hitler. According to Papa, Hitler makes speeches that stir everyone up, and my father is worried, and doesn't trust him. Probably this is because Hitler does not like the Jews, and Papa's business partner there, Herr Itzhak Wassermann, is Jewish. Apparently Jews have started to have problems. Papa has offered Herr Itzhak the chance to come and set himself up in Spain, but he says that he is a good German and should have nothing to fear. Herr Itzhak is married and has three daughters, they are very nice, Yla is my age. They have spent a few summers with us in Biarritz, and Antonietta and I have been to their house in Berlin as well. I hope that this Hitler gets over his dislike of Jews. After Laura, Yla is my best friend.

My parents have come back and we have gone to San Sebastián. We were invited to tea at the house of one of Papa's friends, one of the leaders of the Basque Nationalist Party, and he and Papa spent the afternoon talking politics.

My father said that if things go on like this, so uncertain, then President Alcalá Zamora will have to call early elections. Papa explained that the people on the Right are scared by some of the decisions that the government has been making, and the people on the Left do not believe that the president is instituting the social changes they were hoping for.

I stayed the whole afternoon listening to Papa, even though Mama and our hostess tried to insist that I go speak with them in the drawing room. I was more interested in what my father and his friend were saying. I do not understand much, but I like politics.

One of Amaya's childhood friends is married to a fisherman. This is good, because one Saturday they invited us out in their boat. It is little, but Amaya's friend's husband handles it well. We took sandwiches and ate on the high seas. We laughed a lot because we were always crossing over into French waters. But there are no borders in the sea. The fisherman showed Aitor and me how to handle the boat. His son Patxi, who is the same age as

Aitor, is a fisherman like his father, and goes out with him at dawn every morning to go fishing. I think that if I didn't study then I'd love to be a fisherwoman. I feel so at home on the sea!

I spent all morning reading my great-grandmother's second diary and I have to admit that the second volume was more enjoyable than the first. I found out that Amelia had spent almost six months on her nurse's farm before the doctor gave her the all-clear, and although she wanted very much to go home, it was difficult for her to leave Aitor.

This young man spoke to her about politics and tried to inspire her with the same love for the "Basque homeland" as he himself felt, he spoke about an idyllic past and a future in which the Basques would have their own state.

My great-grandmother didn't really care what happened to the Basque country; what was important for her was Aitor's company.

It was not difficult to say goodbye. Aitor asked for the day off work and we spent it walking together on the hillside. I now know four different paths that lead to France; some of them are used by smugglers. But everyone knows each other here, and whatever they do, no one reports their neighbors.

I wonder if I will come back soon, and above all what Aitor will do when I am gone. I imagine he will meet a girl and they will get married, it's what his grandparents want. They have brought him up to take charge of the farm.

Although he does not say it out loud, what he would really like to do is to dedicate himself to politics; he is ever more involved in work for his party, and his bosses have faith in him.

A few days ago I went with Amaya and Edurne to San Sebastián, we went shopping and then we went to the PNV office where Aitor works. Amaya was very proud to see how much confidence everyone had in her son, his bosses were very proud of him, and said that he had a great future ahead of him.

I am pleased for him, but... well, I must say it: I know that I will not be a part of that future and that hurts me.

I am leaving early tomorrow. Aitor will take us to San Sebastián station.

Amaya is sad. If it were up to her then she would stay on the farm, but she says that she has to continue working to support her parents and her children. She has a dream that Aitor will become a politician and that Edurne will fit into our family and will stay with us as a maid, but then who will take care of the farm? I think that what Amaya wants is for Edurne to take her place and for her to go back to be with her parents.

Aitor's parents have never left these mountains, the furthest they've ever traveled is to San Sebastián. They say they're not interested in finding out about other places, that their world is here and that it's the best of all possible worlds.

Papa says that there are two types of Basques, those who set out to conquer the world and those who believe that there is no world beyond the mountains. He is one of the first kind, Aitor's grandparents are the second type. But they are good people. To begin with they seemed withdrawn and reserved, they don't trust those of us who come from outside. But when they got over their shyness, you realized that they are very sensitive people.

Some nights, after supper, we would sit by the chimney and Aitor's grandfather would sing songs that at first I did not understand, but I thought were nostalgic. Now I can sing them as well, and I know that Papa will be very surprised when he hears me singing in Basque.

This diary is running out of pages, I don't know if I will write another one. I have said it: I am going home tomorrow, and I think that I have grown up during my time here. I feel as if I were a thousand years old.

I did what we had agreed to and phoned the old women to tell them that I had read the two diaries and to ask them when I could come and see them again. I wondered what they might have prepared for me to help continue my "apprenticeship" in the study of my great-grandmother's life.

I couldn't speak with them directly, but the housekeeper arranged that I would come three days later. I decided to spend this time sketching out the first draft of my great-grandmother's life, although I had found out nothing extraordinary up to this point.

Doña Melita and Doña Laura were like two statues. They were always seated in the same armchairs, meticulously dressed in black and gray, the hair of each in a chiffon, with pearls or diamonds in their ears and an air of apparent fragility that was belied by the vigor with which they manipulated me.

That day they were accompanied by another woman as old as they were. I thought that she was a friend or some relative. They did not introduce me, but I approached her to shake her hand, and I found it was trembling.

The woman, also dressed in black, but without jewelry and with a more wrinkled face, seemed nervous. I thought she was older than Doña Laura and Doña Melita, if age has much meaning after you reach ninety.

I saw that Doña Melita took her hand affectionately and clutched it tightly, as though to encourage her.

They asked me for the diaries, which I gave to them without hesitation, and they wanted to know what I made of Amelia.

"Well, the truth is she doesn't seem very special, I suppose she was the typical daughter of a well-off family from that period."

"Nothing else?" Doña Melita wanted to know.

"Nothing else," I replied, trying to think what I had missed, what was special about the two youthful accounts she had written.

"Well, now you have some kind of an idea about the sort of person Amelia was as an adolescent, the time has come for you to know how and why she got married," Doña Laura explained, looking at Doña Melita out of the corner of her eye. "The best thing is for you to be told by someone who lived with her, without leaving her side, throughout these crucial years of her life. Someone who knew her very well," Doña Laura continued, looking at the old woman whom she had not introduced and who had not yet said a word. "Edurne, this is the great-grandson of Amelia and Santiago," Doña Laura said to the old woman.

My heart gave a leap. Edurne? Edurne the daughter of the nurse, of Amaya? I said to myself that it was impossible to have so much luck.

The old woman they had called Edurne raised her tired eyes to meet mine, and I read a certain amount of fear in them. I saw that she was uncomfortable. She looked deathly, like a person who was not only old, but unwell to boot.

"You are the daughter of the nurse, of Amaya?" I asked her, keen to hear what she would say.

"Yes," she muttered.

"I am pleased to meet you," I said sincerely.

"I know that it will be a great effort for Edurne to talk to you. Her memory is good, as if all these things happened yesterday, but... She is ill... We're so old that we spring leaks everywhere. So listen to her and don't tire her out too much," Doña Laura ordered me.

"Can I ask questions?"

"Of course, but don't waste time with questions, the important thing is what Edurne has to tell you," Doña Laura said again. "And now, please go to the library, it will be quieter there for you to speak."

I nodded. Edurne looked at the old women and they gave her a barely perceptible sign, as if encouraging her to speak to me.

The old woman walked with difficulty, leaning on a stick; I followed her step by step into the library.

Edurne started to unwrap her memories...

SANTIAGO

1

When we got to Madrid, Doña Teresa, the mistress, said that from now on I should look after her two daughters, Doña Amelia and Doña Antonietta.

My work consisted in looking after the children's clothes, keeping their room clean, helping them to get dressed, accompanying them on visits... My mother taught me how to do all these things. I had a bad time to start with, in spite of the immense piece of luck that I was sharing a roof with her.

The mistress put another bed in my mother's room. The house was big, but we were the only ones to live with the family, the other servants slept in the attics. I suppose this was our privilege because my mother, who had been the girls' wet nurse, always had to be close to them to feed them. Then, after they were weaned, she kept her room and did all kinds of work for them. She cleaned and helped in the kitchen; she did whatever they asked her to.

My mother wanted me to learn how to become a ladies' maid, to leave me well set up in the house, and for her to be able to go back to the village to be with her parents for their final years.

I had never seen a house like this, with so many bedrooms and drawing rooms, and so many valuable objects. I was afraid of breaking something, and would walk with my skirts and my apron lifted up so as not to brush against the furniture as I walked past.

Because I already knew Doña Amelia, the work wasn't as hard as it might have been. Although the situation had changed: When she was at the farm she was just another one of us, and here

I didn't dare call her by her name, for all that she insisted I not call her "Doña."

What she liked was for us to talk in Basque. She wanted to annoy her sister, although she said to me it was so she wouldn't forget the language. Don Juan, the master, didn't want to hear us speaking Basque, and he would tell her off; he said it was the language of peasants, but she didn't obey him.

In the mornings I used to take Doña Antonietta to school. Doña Amelia had classes at home because she was still convalescing. In the afternoons, when Doña Antonietta came back, they let me sit in the corner of the schoolroom while a teacher who helped them with their homework made them speak in French and play the piano. I liked to listen to the lessons because it helped me learn. When she got better, Doña Amelia began to study to be a teacher, like her cousin Laura.

Nineteen thirty-four was not a good year. The master's business started to go badly. Herr Itzhak Wassermann, his partner in Germany, was suffering from Hitler's attacks against the Jews, which were carried out by the SA, the Nazi paramilitary group. Business got even worse, and he had awoken on several occasions to find his shop windows broken by these devils. It got more and more difficult to travel to Germany, especially for people like the master, who hated Hitler and didn't mind saying so out loud. The master started to lose weight, and the mistress worried about him more every day.

"I think that Papa is ruined," Doña Amelia said to me one day.

"Why do you say that?" I asked in a fright, thinking that if the master was ruined then I would have to go back to the farm.

"He owes money in Germany, and things aren't going very well there. My mother says it's the fault of the left-wingers..."

The mistress was a very Catholic woman, a monarchist, keen on order, and she was scared by the disturbances stirred up by certain left-wing parties. She was a good person and treated all the people who lived in the house well, but she found it impossible to understand that people were in great need, and that the right-wing ruling parties were incapable of facing up to the problems of Spain at that time. She did good works, but she did not know what social justice was, and that was what the workers and peasants were demanding.

"And what will my mother and I do?" I wanted to know.

"Nothing, you'll stay with us. I don't want you to go."

Amelia sent letters to Aitor. Whenever he wrote to my mother and me, my brother would always include a sealed envelope with a letter for Amelia. She would write back to him in the same way, giving us a sealed letter that we in turn would put into our next letter.

I knew that my brother was in love with Amelia, although he would never dare to tell her so, and I also knew that she was by no means indifferent to Aitor.

One Monday afternoon, the master came back earlier than usual and locked himself in his office with Doña Teresa. There they talked until after nightfall, without allowing their daughters to interrupt them. That night Amelia and Antonietta had supper alone in the schoolroom, asking themselves what was going on.

The next morning, the mistress called together all the servants and told us to clean the house from top to bottom. The family was going to host a dinner party that weekend, with important guests, and they wanted the house to shine.

The girls were very excited. They went out shopping with their mother and came back laden down with parcels. They were going to have new clothes.

That Saturday the mistress seemed nervous. She wanted everything to be perfect and although she was normally so friendly, she got angry if things weren't to her taste.

A hairdresser came to the house to prepare the mistress and her daughters, and I got them ready in the afternoon.

Amelia had a red dress and Antonietta had a blue one. They looked lovely.

"It's been so long since we've had guests!" Amelia exclaimed while the hairdresser twisted her hair into ringlets and held them together at her neck with a comb.

"Don't exaggerate, we have visits every week," Antonietta replied.

"Yes, but that's to have tea, not to have supper."

"Well, they didn't used to let us join in because we were too little. Mama says some friends of Papa are coming with their children."

"And we don't know them! Papa's new friends... How exciting!"

"I don't understand how you can enjoy meeting new people. It will be boring, and Mama will be keeping an eye on us to make sure that we behave properly. The dinner is very important for Papa, he needs new partners in his business..."

"I love meeting new people! Maybe there will be some nice-looking young man in the group... Maybe you'll get an admirer, Antonietta."

"Or maybe you will, you're older than I am, so you have to get married first. If you don't hurry up you'll get stuck on the shelf."

"I will marry when I want and who I want!"

"Yes, but do it soon."

Neither of them suspected what would happen that night.

The guests arrived at eight o'clock. Three married couples with their children. A total of fourteen people were seated around the oval table, exquisitely decorated with flowers and silver candelabras.

The García family, with their son Hermenegildo. The López-Agudo family, Francisco and Carmen, with their daughters Elena and Pilar. And the Carranza family, Manuel and Blanca, with their son Santiago.

Antonietta was the first to notice Santiago. He was the most handsome of all the guests. Tall and thin, with light brown, almost blond hair, and green eyes. And very elegantly dressed: It was impossible not to notice him. I also looked at him, secretly, from where I was hidden behind the curtains.

He must have been about thirty years old, and he seemed very sure of himself.

The other unmarried female guests buzzed around him. I knew Amelia well and knew what her tactics would be to get herself noticed.

She was very friendly when she greeted her father's guests and stood next to her mother listening to the ladies talk as if she were interested in what they were saying. She was the only young woman present who seemed immune to Santiago's magnetism, and she did not even look at him.

Doña Antonietta, along with Doña Elena and Doña Pilar López-Agudo, tried to capture Santiago's attention: He had become the hub of the conversation among the younger guests. Not just because he was the oldest among them, but also because he was friendly. I couldn't hear what he was saying from where I was hidden, but he had the women under his spell.

The maids served the aperitifs and I was sent to the kitchen to help my mother and the cooks, but as soon as I could I went back to my hiding place where I could watch the party, which filled my senses with the scent of perfume and cigarettes coming from the ladies and the gentlemen.

I wondered what Amelia's next step would be in attracting Santiago's attention. He had realized that the only young woman who was not taking part in the general conversation was the oldest daughter of his host, and he started to throw sidelong glances at her.

The mistress had put name-cards at the place settings, and Amelia was sitting next to Santiago.

She was so pretty... She began by paying no attention to Santiago, but spoke instead with young Hermenegildo, who had been seated to her left.

It was not until halfway through the meal that Santiago could no longer support Amelia's manifest indifference, and struck up a conversation with her in which she participated with a certain degree of reluctance.

When the meal was over, it was clear that Amelia had achieved her objective: She had Santiago on a string.

Once the guests had left, the master and mistress stayed in the drawing room with their daughters to discuss how the evening had gone.

Doña Teresa was exhausted, so great was the tension that had built up over the course of the week, as she strove to make sure that everything was perfect. My mother said that she had never seen her so nervous, and this was strange because Doña Teresa was accustomed to having guests.

Don Juan appeared more relaxed; the evening had served its purpose, we discovered later; he was trying to go into partnership with Carranza to save his business. But the person who saved the family fortunes was, in fact, Amelia.

I heard what they said, for all that Doña Teresa told them to keep their voices down.

"If Manuel Carranza is interested in the business, and it seems he is, then we're saved..."

"But Papa, are things so bad?" Amelia asked.

"Yes, dear, you are both old enough and should be allowed to know the truth. The business in Germany is going very badly, and I'm worried about my good friend and colleague Herr Itzhak. The warehouse where we store all our goods for export to Spain, all the machinery, has been sealed by the Nazis, and I can't get to it. All our money was there, invested in the machinery. They've also appropriated our bank accounts. Herr Helmut Keller, our employee, is very worried. He's under suspicion anyway for having worked with a Jew, but he's a brave man and he tells me it would be best to wait; he tells me that he'll try to save what he can from the business. I've given him all the money I could find, which isn't much given the circumstances but I can't leave him abandoned to his fate..."

"And Herr Itzhak, and Yla?" Amelia asked in alarm.

"I am trying to bring them out here, but they are resisting; they don't want to leave their house. I have been in touch with Sephardi House, an organization that exists to create connections within the community of Sephardic Jews."

"But Herr Itzhak isn't Sephardic," Doña Teresa exclaimed.

"I know, but I've asked their advice, there are lots of important Spaniards who support them," Don Juan replied...

"Lots? I wish you were right," Doña Teresa protested in a tense voice.

"I've also been in touch with a group called 'Ezra,' which means 'Help'; they are dedicated to helping Jews, especially the ones who are trying to escape from Germany."

"Can you do anything, Papa?" Amelia asked sadly.

"It doesn't depend on your father," the mistress corrected her daughter.

"Manuel Azaña is sympathetic toward the Jews," Don Juan replied. "But it looks like the world is going mad... Hitler has declared that his party, the Nazi Party, is the only one that can actually get things done in Germany. And Germany has left the World Peace Conference. This madman is getting ready for war, I'm sure of it..."

"War? With whom?" Amelia asked.

But Don Juan could not reply, as Doña Teresa asked in her turn:

"And what's going to happen here? I'm scared, Juan... The left-wingers want to have a revolution..."

"And the Right is against the Republican regime, and does whatever it can to make sure the Republic fails," Don Juan replied in annoyance.

Their marriage had political differences, because Doña Teresa came from a family of monarchists, and Don Juan was a steadfast Republican. Of course, back then women didn't let their politics go very far, and in general the master of the house's opinion was the one that held sway.

"And what are you going to do with Carranza?"

Antonietta's question surprised her parents. Antonietta was the younger daughter, fairly quiet and thoughtful, very different from her sister Amelia.

"I'm going to try to buy machinery from North America. It will be more expensive, because of the ocean, but what with the situation in Germany I don't think we have a choice. I have given a very detailed study to Carranza and he is interested. Now my problem is to get a loan so that I can officially create a limited company... I think he will be able to help me. He's well connected."

"With whom?" Amelia asked.

"Bankers and politicians."

"Right-wing politicians?" she insisted.

"Yes, but he also has quite a lot of connections with Lerroux's Radical Party."

"That's why this meal was so important, wasn't it, Papa?" Amelia continued. "You wanted to make a good impression, and you wanted him to see the house looking beautiful, and your family... Mama is so beautiful and elegant..."

"Come now Amelia, don't say such things!" Doña Teresa said.

"But it's the truth, anybody who knows you realizes that you are a real lady. Carranza's wife is not as elegant as you," Amelia insisted.

"Doña Carranza belongs to an excellent family. Tonight we discovered that we have friends in common," Doña Teresa announced.

"His son Santiago is more difficult to convince," Don Juan muttered.

"Santiago? Why do you need to convince him?"

"He works with his father, and his father listens to him a lot. Apparently Santiago is a good economist, very sensible, and advises his father well. He has doubts about whether the business is viable; he says that it's an investment that is much too large, and that he'd prefer to keep on buying machinery in Belgium, France, England, even in Germany. He says it's safer," Don Juan explained.

I couldn't see her face, but it was not hard for me to imagine that at that moment Amelia was making a decision: She would be the person to overcome Santiago's resistance in order to save her family from its economic problems. Amelia was very keen on novels, and saw herself as the heroine of every novel that she read, and her parents were, without realizing it, giving her a chance to act this role.

Two weeks later, the Carranza family invited Don Juan and his family for Sunday lunch in a house that they owned on the outskirts of the city.

This time Don Juan did not hide his nervousness, because Manuel Carranza was starting to show signs of uncertainty about the idea of going into partnership to bring machinery from America. The political situation was getting worse as well, Spain appeared to be ungovernable.

Amelia had spent several days thinking how to dress for the occasion. This Sunday lunch was a great occasion to pull a little on the string that she had fastened round Santiago's neck, because she was sure that the Carranzas' invitation derived at least in part from the interest that she had awoken in Santiago. Don Juan had said that in spite of Santiago's reservations about the project it had been his idea to invite Don Juan to spend Sunday with them, insisting that he be accompanied by his enchanting family.

I know, because Amelia told me so, that this was a key day in what she called her "program of salvation."

No one else was invited to the lunch apart from the Garayoa family, that is, Don Juan and Doña Teresa, Amelia, and Antonietta, and right from the start Santiago showed his interest in Amelia.

She used all her ruses: indifference, friendliness, smiles... everything! She was a great seductress.

That Sunday Santiago fell in love with her, and I think she fell in love with Santiago. They were young and beautiful and elegant...

He, who looked as if he were going to develop into a bachelor, with no formal wife, had let himself fall for a young woman who impudently expressed her political ideas: She insisted that women should gain the rights that they had thus far been denied; she said, to the horror of her mother, that she had not the least intention, when she married, of becoming a simple housewife, and that she would help her husband in all things, as well as working as a teacher, which she said was her calling.

All these revelations and more were revealed with the wit and friendliness that came naturally to her, and, as Antonietta told me later, the more Amelia talked, the more Santiago ceased resisting.

They began to see each other as people of that time did. He asked Don Juan's permission to "speak" to Amelia, and her father gave it with pleasure.

Santiago would come to the house every afternoon to see Amelia; they would go out every Sunday together, accompanied by Antonietta and myself. Amelia allowed him to take her by the hand and smiled as she leaned her head on his shoulder. Santiago bent down to look at her. She had beautiful hair, a light brown that was almost blonde, and large almond-shaped eyes. She was thin, and not very tall, but women back then were not very tall, not as tall as they are now. He was tall, at least a head taller than her. She looked like a doll standing next to him.

Santiago succumbed to Amelia, which meant that Don Juan was saved. The Carranzas provided a guarantee for him to obtain his loan, and they went into partnership with him, as minority partners, in the new company that Don Juan intended to use to buy and import machinery from America.

Don Juan and Santiago ended up becoming closer, because the young man was connected to Azaña's political party and was a steadfast Republican, like my master.

"I'm getting married! Santiago has asked me to marry him!"

I remember as if it were yesterday Amelia going into her parents' room.

I had not gone with them that Sunday because I had a cold, and it had been Antonietta who had been their chaperone.

Don Juan looked at his daughter in surprise, he had not expected Santiago to ask for her hand so soon. They had been walking out together for barely six months, and Don Juan intended to travel to New York the following week to begin visiting factories.

Amelia hugged her mother, who seemed, by her expression, to be not entirely happy with this piece of news.

"But what foolishness is this?" Doña Teresa said with displeasure.

"Santiago has told me that he does not want to wait anymore, that he is of an age when he should marry, and he is certain that I am the woman for whom he has been waiting. He has asked me if I love him and if I am sure of my feelings toward him. I have said I am, and we have decided to get married as soon as possible. He will tell his parents this evening, and Carranza will call on you to ask for my hand. We could get married at the end of the year, there won't be time to get things organized before then. I do so want to get married!"

Amelia chattered away without pause, while her parents tried to calm her down in order to speak to her more tranquilly.

"Come on, Amelia, you are still a girl," Don Juan protested.

"I am not a girl! You know that most of my friends are either married or about to be married. What's wrong, Papa? I thought that you would be happy that I got engaged to Santiago..."

"And I am happy, I have nothing to complain about with the Carranza family, and Santiago seems to me a fine young man, but you have only known each other for a few months and it seems a little soon to be talking about a wedding. You don't know each other well enough yet."

"Your father and I were engaged for four years before we got married," Doña Teresa said.

"Don't be old-fashioned, Mama... This is the twentieth century, I know that things were different back in your day, but times have changed. Women work, and go out alone into the street, and not all of them get married, even, some people decide to live their own life with whoever they want to... By the way, I am not going to take a chaperone anymore when I go out with Santiago."

"Amelia!"

"Mama, it's ridiculous! Don't you trust me? Do you think badly of Santiago?"

Amelia's parents felt crushed by the runaway force of their daughter's will. There was no way back: She had decided to get married, and she would, with or without their permission.

They agreed that the wedding would be celebrated when Don Juan returned from America; in the meantime, Doña Teresa and Santiago's parents would organize the details of the wedding.

Although Amelia had always shown an interest in politics, perhaps it was a result of Santiago's influence that during those months she seemed more worried than ever by what was happening in Spain.

"Edurne, President Alcalá Zamora has asked Alejandro Lerroux to form another government, and they will have three ministers from the CEDA. I don't think it is the best solution, but is there any other way?"

Of course, she didn't want to hear my reply. At that time Amelia spoke about everything with herself; I was the wall against which she threw her ideas, but nothing else, even though

I knew how easy she was to influence. Many of the things she said were a mishmash of things she had heard from Santiago.

At the beginning of October 1934, Santiago came to the Garayoa house in a very odd mood. Don Juan was in America, and Doña Teresa was arguing with her children about Antonietta's desire to go out by herself.

"The General Workers' Party has called a general strike! Spain will be paralyzed on the fifth!" Santiago cried.

"Good Lord! But why?" Teresa was upset by the news.

"Madam, the left doesn't trust the CEDA, and with good reason. Gil Robles doesn't believe in the Republic."

"That's what the left-wingers say to justify everything they do!" Doña Teresa protested. "They're the ones who don't believe in the Republic, they want to have a revolution like the one in Russia. Lord save us from that!"

I and another maid were serving light refreshments as we listened to this conversation.

It wasn't that Santiago was a revolutionary, in fact quite the opposite, but he firmly believed in the Republic, and didn't trust those people who reviled it and took advantage of it at the same time.

"You wouldn't like what happened in Germany to happen here," Amelia said.

"Be quiet, child! What does this Hitler have to do with our right wing. Don't fall for the left-wingers and their propaganda, it won't bring Spain any good," Doña Teresa complained.

Amelia and Santiago remained in the sitting room, while Doña Teresa and Antonietta took their leave by giving some imaginary excuse. The mistress had no desire to argue with Santiago, and it had been agreed that at this stage in proceedings the two young people could be together without a chaperone.

"What's going to happen, Santiago?" Amelia asked worriedly as soon as she was alone with her fiancé.

"I don't know, but something big is brewing."

"Can we still get married?"

"Of course! Don't be silly, nothing will get in the way of us getting married."

"But there are only three weeks to go until the wedding."

"Don't worry..."

"And Papa is still not back..."

"His ship will come in a few days."

"I miss him so much... especially now that everything is so confused. I feel lost without him."

"Amelia, don't say that! You have me! I'll never let anything happen to you!"

"Of course, you're right, sorry..."

For the next few days we were all on edge. We couldn't imagine what might happen.

The government responded to the call for a general strike with a declaration of martial law, and the strike was not a success, at least not everywhere. That evening my mother told me that the Nationalists were not going to support it, and neither were the Anarchists.

The worst that happened was that in Catalonia the president of the Generalitat, the Catalan Parliament, Lluís Companys, proclaimed a Catalan state in the Federal Republic.

Amelia was ever more worried about her wedding, because the Carranzas had business in Catalonia, and one of Don Manuel's business partners was a Catalan. Doña Teresa was also affected; she was half Catalan and had relatives in Barcelona.

"I have spoke to Aunt Montse and she is very scared. They've arrested a lot of people she knows, and she's seen people fighting in the Ramblas from her balcony. She doesn't know how many deaths there have been, but she thinks a great number. I thank the Lord that my parents don't have to see this."

Doña Teresa's parents were dead, and all she had left were her sister Montse and a good handful of aunts, cousins, and other relatives, spread out through Catalonia as well as in Madrid.

Amelia asked me to call my brother Aitor in the Basque country to try to find out what was happening. I did so, and she impatiently snatched the telephone out of my hands.

Aitor told us that his party had kept to the sidelines during the strike, and that the flame of revolution had really spread only in Asturias. The miners had attacked the Guardia Civil, and had taken control of the principality.

Meanwhile, back in Madrid, the government asked generals Goded and Franco to take care of the rebellion, and these two suggested that the Moroccan Regulars would be the key to suppressing it.

They were uncertain days, until the government quelled the rebellion. But this was just a rehearsal for what was to come...

This was when Amelia met Lola. This girl affected her, marked her forever.

One afternoon, in spite of Doña Teresa's protests, Amelia decided to go out into the street. She wanted to see the impact of events with her own eyes. Her excuse was that she was going to visit her cousin Laura, who had been sick for several days.

Doña Teresa ordered her not to go out, and my mother begged her to stay at home, and even Antonietta tried to convince her to remain. But Amelia insisted that she had a duty to visit her favorite cousin when that cousin was ill, and went out into the street in defiance of her mother, with me following her. I did not want to go, but my mother ordered me not to leave Amelia alone.

Madrid looked like a war zone. There were soldiers everywhere. I followed her unwillingly to her cousin's house, which was this one, the house we are in at this moment, and which was only a few blocks from Amelia's home. We were just about to arrive when we saw a young girl running like a madwoman. She dashed in front of us as quick as a flash and hid in the doorway of the house we were heading to. We looked back, thinking that maybe someone was chasing her, but we saw nobody. But two minutes later two men came around the corner, shouting "Halt! Halt!" We stopped dead, waiting for the men to catch up with us.

"Have you seen a girl run past here?"

I was going to say yes, that she was hiding in the doorway, but Amelia answered first.

"No, we haven't seen anyone, we're just on our way to visit a cousin of mine who is sick," she explained.

"Are you sure you haven't seen anyone hiding in a doorway?"

"No, sir. If we had seen anyone we'd tell you." Amelia replied in the voice of a prudish young lady, a voice I hadn't heard her use before.

The two men, who must have been policemen, seemed unsure whether to believe us, but Amelia's appearance persuaded them. She was the very image of a bourgeois woman from a good family.

They ran off, arguing among themselves about where the girl could have got to, while we went into Doña Laura's house.

The doorman was not there, and Amelia smiled in satisfaction. The man must be upstairs helping a neighbor with something, or else out on an errand.

With firm footsteps, Amelia headed toward the back of the entrance hall and opened a door that gave onto the patio. I followed her in a fright, because I could guess who she was looking for. And so it was: There, among the rubbish bins and tools, was the girl who had run away from the police.

"They've gone, don't worry."

"Thank you, I don't know why you didn't turn me in, but thank you."

"Should I have? Are you a dangerous delinquent?" Amelia smiled, as if she found the situation amusing.

"I'm not a delinquent, and as for being dangerous... I suppose I must be dangerous for them because I fight against injustice."

Amelia was immediately interested by this reply, and although I grabbed her arm to try to make her come along up to Doña Laura's apartment, she ignored me.

"Are you a revolutionary?"

"I am... Yes, I suppose you could say I am."

"And what do you do?"

"I'm a seamstress."

"No, I mean what kind of revolutionary are you?"

The girl looked at her with mistrust. It was clear that she didn't know if she should reply, but in the end she was sincere with Amelia, even though she was a stranger.

"I work with a few comrades in the strike committee, I take messages from one place to another."

"How brave! I'm Amelia Garayoa, how about you?"

"Lola, Lola García."

"Edurne, go out to the street and have a look round, and if you see something suspicious come back and tell us."

I didn't dare protest, and I went trembling toward the door that let out into the street. I thought that if the police saw me then they might suspect something and arrest the three of us.

I calmed down when I saw that the doorman was still not there, and I barely stuck my head out of the door to look to the left and the right. I didn't see the two men.

"There's no one," I told them.

"It doesn't matter, I think it's better if Lola doesn't go out quite yet. Come with us to my cousin's house. I'll tell her you're a friend of Edurne's and that we met you on the way. They'll give you something to eat in the kitchen while I'm with my cousin, and then when we go enough time will have passed for those men to have stopped looking for you round here. Also, my Uncle Armando is a lawyer and if the police do come looking for you then he'll know what to do."

Lola accepted this offer with relief. She didn't understand why this bourgeois woman would help her, but it was the only option she had and she took advantage of it.

Laura was bored in bed while her sister Melita gave a piano lesson, and her mother had a visitor. As far as her father, Don Armando, Amelia's father's brother, was concerned, he still had not come back from his office.

A housemaid took Lola and me to the kitchen, where we had a glass of milk and some cookies, and Amelia stayed with her cousin to tell her about this latest adventure.

We were in the house of Don Armando and Doña Elena for two hours visiting Laura, two hours that seemed eternal because I imagined that at any moment the police could knock on the door, looking for Lola.

When Amelia eventually decided to go home, Don Armando arrived. As he was worried about the idea of us being alone in the street, given the tumultuous situation in Madrid at the moment, he offered to accompany us home. There was little more than four blocks between the two houses, but Don Armando insisted on accompanying his niece. He was not at all surprised when Amelia said that Lola, whom she introduced as a good friend of Edurne's, would be coming with us. I looked down at the floor so that Don Armando would not see how nervous I was.

"Your father would be cross with me if I let you go out alone with all this chaos. What I don't understand is how he let you go out in the first place. It's not a time to go happily out into the street, Amelia, I don't know if you're aware of it, but Asturias has unleashed a real revolution, and here, even though the strike was a failure, the left has not resigned itself to letting things remain as they were, there are a lot of fanatics..."

Amelia looked at Lola out of the corner of her eye, but her face was impassive, and she looked down at the ground like I did.

When we got home, Doña Teresa was sincerely grateful to her brother-in-law for having accompanied us.

"I can't do anything with this child, and ever since she's decided to get married she seems even more thoughtless. I want her father to come home, Juan is the only person who can deal with her."

When Don Armando left, Teresa turned her attention to Lola.

"Edurne, I didn't know you had friends in Madrid," Doña Teresa said, looking at me with curiosity.

"They know each other from meeting when Edurne goes out on errands," Amelia said quickly, and it was a good thing she did, because I wouldn't have been able to lie with such ease.

"Well, if you're not going to offer this young woman anything, then we'd better go in to dinner, your sister Antonietta is waiting for us," Doña Teresa concluded.

"No, I really should be going, I'm very late already. Thank you very much, Doña Amelia, Doña Teresa... Edurne, let's see each other soon, alright?"

I nodded, hoping that she'd go and that we'd never see each other again, but my wishes were not going to come true, because Lola García would again cross Amelia's path, and mine.

2

As if the emotions stirred up by the day before were not enough, the next morning also brought surprises with it.

Santiago had arranged to come see Amelia, but he didn't appear the whole day.

Amelia was first worried and then furious, and asked her mother to call Santiago's parents house under the pretext of speaking to his mother about some detail of the wedding.

Doña Teresa resisted, but in the end gave in, as Amelia was threatening to go to Santiago's house herself.

That afternoon Amelia found out something about her future husband's personality that she could not have imagined.

Santiago's mother informed Amelia's mother that her son was not at home, that he had not been home for lunch, neither had he telephoned, and she did not know if he would be there for supper. Doña Teresa was surprised that Santiago's mother was not alarmed, but she said that her son often disappeared without saying where he was going.

"It's not that he's going somewhere he shouldn't, quite the opposite, it's always for his work; you know that my husband has charged him with making the purchases for the company, and Santiago has traveled to France, Germany, Barcelona... wherever he has needed to go. Santiago always goes without saying anything, I was scared to begin with, but now I know that there's nothing wrong," Doña Blanca explained.

"But you must realize that he's going because he takes a suitcase," Doña Teresa said, a little scandalized.

"My son never takes a suitcase."

"But how is that possible? These journeys are so long... so many days... ," Doña Teresa exclaimed.

"Santiago says he takes his baggage in his wallet."

"What?"

"Yes, he gets on the train and when he gets wherever he's going he buys what he needs, he's always done it like that. I'm telling you, I used to be worried, and his father would scold him, but we've gotten used to it. Calm yourself, Amelia, please, Santiago will be back in time for the wedding. He's so much in love!"

Doña Teresa, without hiding the fact that Santiago's behavior was very strange to her, told her daughter about the conversation she had had with Doña Blanca. But far from calming down, Amelia became even more nervous.

"That's such a stupid excuse! How are we meant to believe that he heads off on trips with no suitcase and without telling his parents? And what about me? Why didn't he say anything about this to me? I'm his fiancée! Mama, I think Santiago's had a change of heart... He doesn't want to marry me anymore. Ay, Lord! What are we going to do?"

Amelia burst into tears, and neither Doña Teresa nor Antonietta were able to console her. I observed them from where I was hidden behind the door to the room, until my mother found me and took me to the kitchen.

That night Amelia did not sleep, or at least her light was on until dawn was already breaking. The next day she woke me up at seven; she wanted me to get dressed quickly in order to go to the Carranzas' house to deliver a letter. She had been writing it all through the night.

"When Santiago gets back from his trip, if he really is on a trip and isn't betraying me, then he'll know that he can't do these things to me. And if he wants to leave me, then I would rather be the one to take the first step, I'd be terribly embarrassed if our friends were to find out that he had left me. Go straight away before my mother wakes up. She'll be cross when I tell her that

I've sent a letter to Santiago announcing the end of our engagement. But I will not allow myself to be humiliated."

I got dressed hurriedly, and hardly had time to get washed, being urged on all the time by Amelia. When I reached the Carranzas' house the door to the street was closed, and I had to wait for the doorman to open it at eight. He thought it was strange that anyone should want to go up to the Carranzas' home so early, but as I was dressed in my maid's outfit he let me go up.

Another housemaid, as tired as I was, opened the door. I gave her the envelope and told her to deliver it to Santiago, but she told me that Santiago had gone off on a trip, that Don Manuel was having breakfast, and that Doña Blanca was resting.

When I returned home, Amelia was waiting for me with a new task: I had to return to the Carranzas' house with a packet containing all of Santiago's letters, the love letters they had exchanged, along with the engagement ring. She ordered me to give the ring to Doña Blanca personally.

I started to tremble when I thought about what Doña Teresa would say when she found out, and before going out I went to find my mother to tell her what was happening. My mother, showing her good judgment, told me to wait until she had spoken to Doña Teresa and Doña Amelia herself. As Doña Teresa had not yet come down from her room, my mother went to look for Amelia.

"I know that I am not in a position to say anything, but don't you think you should think a little bit more about what you are about to do? Just suppose that Santiago has an explanation for what has happened and that you're breaking off the engagement without giving him a hearing... I think you are being a little hasty..."

"But Amaya, you should be on my side!"

"I am on your side, how could I not be? But I don't think that Santiago wants to break your engagement, he must have an explanation beyond what his mother has given you. Wait for him to come back, wait to hear what he has to say..."

"But what he's done to me is unforgivable! How can I trust him? No, no, no. I want your daughter Edurne to go and give him his letters and his ring and to make it clear that everything is finished between us. And this afternoon I will go and take tea with my friend Victoria, where there will be lots more of my friends as well, and it will be me who decides to announce that I have chosen to break off my engagement with Santiago because I am no longer sure how I feel toward him. I won't let him be the one to break things off and humiliate me..."

"Amelia, please, think about it! Speak to your mother, she'll be able to give you better advice than I can..."

"What's going on here?" Doña Teresa came into Amelia's room, alerted by the hysterical edge to her daughter's voice.

"Mama, I am going to end things with Santiago!"

"What do you mean?"

"Doña Teresa, I... I am sorry that I have come to talk with Doña Amelia about this family affair, but it was because she was going to send my Edurne to take the engagement ring back to the Carranzas..."

"The ring! But Amelia, what are you going to do? Calm down, don't do anything you may regret later."

"That's what I told her," my mother added.

"No! I am going to break things off with Santiago, it's what he wants. I am not going to let him make me look ridiculous."

"For goodness' sake, Amelia, at least wait for your father to come home!"

"No, because by the time Papa comes home, I will already be the laughingstock of all Madrid. I will go and take tea with my friend Victoria this afternoon, and I will tell her and all my friends that I have broken things off with Santiago. And you, Amaya, tell Edurne that she should go the Carranzas' house straight away. And that if she will not go, then I will."

Antonietta also came into Amelia's room, brought there by the sound of voices, and she added her pleas to those of her mother and me to try to make Amelia change her mind. It was Antonietta who came up with a possible solution: Doña Teresa should call Doña Blanca again to communicate to her Amelia's distress and her decision to break things off with Santiago if he did not return immediately to explain his actions.

More nervous than pleased by this suggestion, Doña Teresa rang Doña Blanca. She promised that she would call her husband straight away and make him try to find her son, wherever he might be, something, she swore, that she herself did not know; but she also asked that Amelia show a little patience, and above all that she trust Santiago.

Amelia accepted this compromise reluctantly, but even so she went to take tea with Victoria that afternoon, along with several other friends their age. There, in an atmosphere of laughter and secrets, she let it slip that she was not entirely sure that she had not been a little hasty in rushing into an engagement with Santiago, and she said that she was doubtful about whether to get married. They spent the whole afternoon analyzing the pros and cons of matrimony. Amelia felt satisfied when she left Victoria's house: If Santiago did break up with her, she could always say that it was really *she* who had wanted to break things off with him.

Little could we imagine that this storm in a teacup would eventually turn into a real tempest that would sweep up everyone who came into its path. When Santiago, who was in Antwerp, called his father a few days later to discuss some details of the business trip, his father immediately urged him to come back to Madrid as soon as possible, because Amelia had taken his disappearance badly and was threatening to break off the engagement. Santiago came back at once. I still remember how frantic he was when he got back to Amelia's house.

She met him in the drawing room, flanked by her mother and sister.

"Amelia... I am sorry for upsetting you, but I can't believe that my absence on business could lead you to want to break our engagement."

"Yes, I am upset. It was truly inconsiderate of you to leave without saying anything to me. Your mother has said that this is something usual on your part, but you must understand that this behavior is more than strange on the very eve of your wedding. I don't want you to feel obliged by the promise you have made, so I am freeing you from your engagement."

Santiago looked her up and down, uncomfortable. Amelia had recited a paragraph that she had been rehearsing in her mind ever since Santiago had telephoned to announce his visit. The presence of Doña Teresa and Antonietta, both of them very nervous, did nothing to help the pair be sincere with each other.

"If you truly want to break off our engagement, I have no other option than to accept it, but I call on God as my witness that my feelings toward you have not changed, and that I want nothing more than... than for you to forgive me, if I have offended you in any way."

Doña Teresa sighed in relief, and Antonietta gave a nervous giggle. Amelia did not know what to do: On the one hand, she still wanted to play the role of the offended woman, a role she had started to enjoy, and on the other hand she wanted to put everything behind her and marry Santiago. It was Antonietta who permitted the lovers to sort things out.

"I think that they should have a chance to talk alone, don't you, Mama?"

"Yes... yes... If you are still willing to marry Amelia, all I need to say is that you still have our blessing..."

When they had been left alone they spent a few minutes without saying anything, merely casting sidelong glances at each other, without knowing how to begin. Then Amelia burst out laughing, which disconcerted Santiago somewhat. Two minutes later they were chatting as if nothing had happened.

Both families breathed a sigh of relief. They had feared the worst, a scandal mere weeks before the wedding, when the banns had been read and the first presents had arrived at the Garayoas' house, and the reception, which was to take place at the Ritz, had been reserved and paid for by the two families.

With the excuse of Don Juan's return from America, the two families met at the Garayoas' house; they could see that Santiago and Amelia seemed as much in love with each other as before. Or even more so, if such a thing were possible.

Don Juan had been impressed by what he had seen in America. He had admired the efforts of the citizens to escape from the

Great Depression, and compared American society with that of Spain. They spoke a great deal about politics at the dinner, even though Doña Teresa had forbidden it as a subject of conversation.

"The Americans are very clear about what they want and how everyone should pull together to get out of the crisis, and they *are* getting out of it: The collapse of '29 will soon look like nothing more than a bad dream."

"My dear friend, we spend a lot of time getting in each other's way here, these two years of the Socialist Azañist government is a good example," said Don Manuel.

"I don't understand what the trouble is with Manuel Azaña," Don Juan replied. "He's a politician who knows where we need to get to, who thinks that the state needs to be strong in order to allow the necessary democratic reforms to be made."

"But you see where his politics have taken us. I don't think that it was a success for him to give Catalonia autonomy in '32, and of course the Basques, the PNV, are moving in the same direction. It's a good thing that Catalan autonomy has been put on hold after the October revolution."

"Papa, you have to respect people's opinions; they have a very strong sense of national identity in Catalonia. The best thing is to do what Azaña has always tried to do, which is to channel these sentiments. Manuel Azaña has always been in favor of a united Spain, but we have to find a way that we can all feel comfortable here."

Santiago was trying to be conciliatory to prevent his father from getting annoyed because of politics.

"All? What do you mean, all?" Don Manuel said in irritation. "Spain has a shared culture and above all a shared history, but all this nonsense about autonomy means that it will stop being so, mark my words."

Doña Teresa and Doña Blanca tried to introduce other topics so that their husbands would stop talking about politics.

"I think that they are going to produce *Blood Wedding* in Madrid again," Doña Blanca said in a sickly voice. "García Lorca is very daring, but he is a great dramatist."

However, both women failed in their attempt to move the conversation into other areas. Neither Don Juan nor Don Manuel were willing to stop talking about the things that worried them.

"But you would agree with me that the victory of the Right in '33 hasn't calmed things down at all in Spain. They're undoing all that the previous governments did," Don Juan interrupted.

"Don't tell me that you think it's fair to expropriate someone's lands simply because they happen to be a member of the nobility..."

"Not anybody's lands, no. You know that the government in '31 wanted to put an end to feudalism," Don Juan replied.

"And what about your beloved Azaña's military reforms? If he's not careful we'll end up with no army. He's got rid of more than sixty-five hundred officers and talks a lot about reforming the army while reducing the defense budget," Don Manuel replied.

"They've also done some positive things, the religious and education reforms, for example... ," Santiago interjected.

"But what are you saying, Santiago! Good Lord, anyone who didn't know you would think you were one of those Socialist revolutionaries!"

"Papa, it's not about being a revolutionary, just about looking at the world around us. When I travel around Europe it makes me sad to see how backward we are by comparison..."

"And that's why they interfere with the poor priests and nuns who help out in our society, entirely disinterestedly. You, you think you're a democrat, will you claim that it's democratic to forbid religious orders from teaching children? And kicking a cardinal out of Spain because they don't like what he says? Is that democratic?"

"Papa, Cardinal Segura is someone you need to watch out for, I think we all feel better now that he's no longer in Spain."

"Yes, yes, all of these left-wing excesses are what have made your hated right wing make great steps forward," Don Manuel said angrily.

"And I think there is cause to be worried by what's happening with the right wing in general, not just in Spain. Look at Germany, this Hitler is a madman. I'm not surprised that people on the Left are very worried," Don Juan replied. "I myself am an indirect victim of Hitler's fanaticism. His anti-Jewish policies have suppressed the legal and civil rights of the Jews, and made their economic activity impossible. I am victim of this policy because my partner Herr Itzhak Wassermann is a Jew. We have lost all our business. You know that they've broken the windows in our warehouse more than four times?"

"What Hitler wants to do is throw the Jews out of Germany," Santiago said.

"Yes, but the German Jews are as German as the rest of them, you can't stop them from being what they are," Doña Teresa added.

"Don't be naïve, woman. Hitler is capable of anything," Don Juan said. "And poor Helmut, our employee, has to take care just because he used to work with a Jew."

"Yes, what's happening there is terrible, but what's happening here has nothing to do with Germany, my dear friend. I am sorry about what has happened, but there's no comparison, none at all... What we should be worried about are the threats from some Socialists who talk about putting an end to bourgeois society. Even moderates like Prieto have spoken about revolution."

"Well, it is a way to try to stop the most controversial right-wing plans. They cannot undo everything that came before them. Prieto is giving them a warning to make them think a little before acting," Santiago said.

"Son, don't you realize that what happened in Asturias was an attempted revolution that could provoke a real catastrophe, if the same thing happened across Spain?"

"Our problem," Santiago continued, "is that the forces of the Right and of the Left are mistreating the Republic. Neither side believes in her, nor has tried to settle down in her."

Santiago had a different view of politics. Perhaps because he spent a lot of time traveling outside of Spain. He was not right-wing, and although he sympathized with the left wing, he did not refrain from criticizing them. He was an Azañist, he was a fervent admirer of Manuel Azaña.

The wedding took place on December 18. It was very cold and it was raining, but Amelia was radiant in her dress of white silk and taffeta.

At five in the afternoon, on the dot, in the church of San Ginés, Amelia and Santiago were married. Theirs was one of those wedding that is reported in the society pages of the Madrid press, and people came from far and wide to attend, as Manuel Carranza and Juan Garayoa each had, because of their business dealings, colleagues, and contacts in cities all over Spain.

Doña Teresa was more nervous than Amelia, and Melita and Laura were as nervous as she was; along with Antonietta, they were the bridesmaids.

Three priests, friends of the family, conducted the ceremony. And later, during the reception at the Ritz, Amelia and Santiago danced the first dance.

It was a beautiful wedding, yes... Amelia always said that it was the wedding she had dreamed of, that she could not have imagined it any different from how it was.

When they said goodbye to their guests at midnight, Amelia embraced Laura in tears, the two of them had always been so close. That night they knew that Amelia's life would change, that she would at the very least stop being the girl who was permitted to make all kinds of mischief, and would now become a woman.

Edurne stopped speaking. She had been talking for a long time, and I hadn't even moved, so caught up had I been in the story.

I started to see the sort of person my great-grandmother must have been, and I must acknowledge that there was something about her that intrigued me. Perhaps it was the way Edurne had described her, or just that she had known how to awaken my curiosity.

My great-grandmother's elderly maid seemed exhausted. I suggested that we ask for a glass of water, but she shook her head. She was there talking to me because the Garayoas had ordered her to do so, the link that she maintained with the family was based on each person having a clear role: They ordered and she obeyed. That was how it had been in the past, and that was how it would be in the present; neither of them could hope to have a future.

"What happened then?" I asked, ready to stop her from breaking her story.

"They went to Paris on their honeymoon. They went by train. Amelia had three suitcases. They also crossed the Channel to go to London. I think that the crossing was terrible and that she got seasick. They did not come back until the end of January. Santiago used the journey to see some of his partners."

"And then?" I insisted, because I couldn't imagine that the story would finish like that.

"When they got back they moved into a house of their own, a wedding present from Don Manuel to his son. It was near here, at the beginning of Calle Serrano. Don Juan and Doña Teresa were furnishing it, and had everything ready for when the newlyweds returned from Paris. I went to work in Amelia's house. Don't think that it wasn't hard for me to leave my mother, but Amelia insisted that I go with her. She didn't treat me like a servant, she treated me like a friend; I suppose that the months together at the farm must have helped make a special bond between us. Santiago was surprised by the familiarity between us, but it was a familiarity in which he ended up participating as well. He was a great person... Amelia asked him to allow her to finish her teaching qualification, and he readily accepted; he knew his wife and he knew how difficult it would be for her to dwindle into a housewife. As far as I was concerned, Amelia made me study, made me have ambitions. You see how she was. But Amelia was also greatly influenced by Lola García, and this convinced her to send me to get instruction in a spot run by the Spanish Young Socialists. They taught everything there: reading, typewriting, dancing, sewing..."

"Lola García, the girl who ran away from the police?"

"Yes, the very same. She was a vital figure in Amelia's life... and in mine."

Edurne was very tired, but I didn't want her to stop talking. I guessed that what she was going to tell me next would be the most interesting bit. So I insisted that she drink some water.

"Forgive the question, but how old are you, Edurne?"

"Two years younger than Amelia, ninety-three."

"So my great-grandmother would be ninety-five..."

"Yes. Shall I continue?"

I nodded gratefully while I wondered what would happen if I lit a cigarette. But I was scared that the housekeeper of the old ladies' niece could appear at any moment and I decided not to tempt fate.

They had only just got back from their honeymoon in Paris when Amelia met Lola García again. It was an accident. Three afternoons a week Lola went to do the laundry, mending, and ironing at the house of a marquis who lived in the Barrio de Salamanca, very close to where Don Armando lived. One afternoon when Amelia went to have tea with Melita and Laura, she bumped into Lola. Amelia was extremely happy, and for all that Lola resisted, she eventually agreed to go with Amelia to her new home.

Amelia brought Lola home with her as if they had been friends all their lives, asking her how things were going, and in particular about her political opinions. Lola answered her questions doubtfully, she could not understand this bourgeois girl who lived in luxury in the Barrio de Salamanca and who kept on asking about the workers' demands and the causes of social unrest.

They took coffee in the drawing room, and Amelia invited me to sit with them. I felt as awkward as Lola did, but Amelia did not seem to notice.

Lola explained that she went to study in one of the Socialists' People's Houses, that she had learned to read and write there, that they taught her about history and theater, that she had even learned to dance. Amelia seemed interested, and asked if they would let me join or if I had to be a member of the Young Socialists. Lola did not know, but promised to ask.

"I'm sure they'll let her in. In the end, Edurne is a worker... but wouldn't you like to join the party?"

"I... Well, I've never been much interested in politics, I'm not like my brother," I replied.

"You have a brother? What party is he a member of?" Lola wanted to know.

"He's in the PNV, and works in one of the party offices..."

"So, he collaborates with the conservative Nationalists."

"Well, he's a worker and I think the Basques are different," I said in alarm.

"Right? Different? Why? We all need to be equal, to have the same rights wherever we are. No, you're not different, you're a worker like I am. How are you different from me? By the fact that you were born on a farm and I was born in Madrid? No one will ever give us anything, we will only be what we are capable of becoming by ourselves."

Lola was an avid Socialist and spoke about rights and equality with a passion that ended up infecting Amelia. I was to study at the People's House, and Lola was to take me. That very afternoon, my fate, as well as Amelia's, was decided.

3

Lola's visits to Amelia's house grew ever more frequent, until one day Amelia asked Lola to take her to a meeting of the Spanish Socialist Workers' Party—the PSOE—or the Workers' General Union, the UGT.

"But what will you do in one of our meetings? We want to destroy the conservative order of things, and you... well, you are a bourgeois, your husband is a businessman, your father as well... I like you because you are a good person, but Amelia, you are not one of us."

Lola's words wounded Amelia. She did not understand why she was being rejected in this way, why she was not considered one of them. I did not know what to say, I had been studying at the People's House for two months and I was happy with my progress. They were teaching me how to type, and I was worried that if Lola and Amelia fell out then I might have to leave.

But Amelia did not get angry, she just asked what she needed to do to become a Socialist, to be accepted by those who had the least and who suffered the most. Lola promised that she would speak to her superiors and find out.

Santiago knew of Lola's friendship with Amelia and never criticized it, but they did argue when Amelia announced that she would join the Socialists if they accepted her.

"They'll never think that you're one of them, don't fool yourself," Santiago argued. "I am not affected by these injustices, and you know what I think of the radical governments. The right-wing movements we have are not up to the circumstances, but I don't think that revolution is the answer. If you want, I'm going to a meeting of the Republican Left; they're the group that best represents us, them, not Largo Caballero or Prieto. Think about it, I don't want them to use you, or even less, to hurt you."

In 1935, the right wing had launched a smear campaign against Manuel Azaña. Santiago said that it was because they were afraid of him, because he was the only politician capable of getting Spain out of the jam in which it now found itself.

Amelia didn't get as far as to ask for membership in the PSOE, but she helped Lola whenever she could, and most especially shared with her the opinion that all these continual ministerial crises and collapses of government were proof positive that neither Lerroux's radicals nor Gil Robles's CEDA had the solution for Spain's problems.

Lola was a member of the most revolutionary wing of the PSOE, Largo Caballero's group, and she was a passionate admirer of the Soviet Revolution. One day she gave in to Amelia's pressure and took her to a meeting where various prominent Socialists were appearing.

Amelia came home excited and scared. Those people had a magnetic force about them, they spoke to the hearts of people who had nothing, but at the same time suggested alternatives that could lead to revolution. So Amelia had contradictory feelings about the Socialists.

Santiago, worried about the influence which Lola was having on Amelia, started to take her to meetings where Manuel Azaña appeared. Amelia struggled with the profound admiration and disconcertedness that she felt when she came into contact with politicians of such different ideas, so far apart on the political spectrum, but similarly convinced of the healthiness of their proposed policies.

Amelia met Socialist worker friends of Lola as well as Communists, or Azañistas, like the majority of Santiago's friends. She began to live in two worlds: her own, into which she had been born and married, the world of a bourgeois; and the world of Lola, who was a seamstress who wanted to do away with the established bourgeois regime, and in particular the privileges enjoyed by people like Amelia.

I used to go with Amelia to the political meetings Lola took her to, but not always, because Amelia did not want me to abandon my studies at the People's House.

At the beginning of March, Amelia started to feel ill. Her pregnancy brought with it nausea and vomiting. Santiago was happy, he was going to be a father, and he also thought that the pregnancy would calm Amelia's political worries, but in this he was mistaken. Pregnancy did not stop Amelia from accompanying Lola to many different meetings, in spite of the protests of her husband and her parents, for Don Juan and Doña Teresa asked their daughter to leave aside her political commitments during the pregnancy. But it was useless, even Laura couldn't make her see reason, and Laura had always been the person with the most influence on Amelia.

And one day it happened again. Santiago disappeared. I think this was back in April 1935. Amelia had gone to teach in the morning, and to her cousins' house in the afternoon; she still saw them regularly. Laura was still her best friend. She was as interested in politics as Amelia was, but his ideas were all more or less Azañist.

When Amelia came back that night she waited for Santiago to come and eat, but he had not got back by eleven, and no one was answering in the office. Amelia was worried; disturbances were not rare in Madrid, especially not between various political parties, to the extent that there were right-wing groups that attacked left-wingers, who responded in kind.

We managed to keep our cool until the evening, and the next morning Amelia called Santiago's father.

Don Manuel said that he did not know where his son was, but that he could be sure that he was traveling, because he had set off to meet a supplier in London.

Amelia had an attack of rage. Throwing herself on the bed, she shouted and swore in tears that she would never pardon her husband for this affront. Then she seemed to calm down, worrying that maybe he had suffered an accident or she was judging him too hastily. We had to call Doña Teresa, who came immediately with Antonietta to take charge of the situation. Laura, aware of her cousin's reaction, also came to find out what was happening.

Santiago took two weeks to come back, and in those two weeks Amelia changed forever. I can still remember a conversation she had with her mother, her sister Antonietta, and her cousins Laura and Melita.

"If he has been capable of abandoning me when I am pregnant, what else might he be capable of? I cannot trust him."

"Come now, you mustn't say that, you know what Santiago is like; Doña Blanca has told you how he is, she's his mother and she suffers greatly whenever he disappears, but it's his business, he doesn't do it to annoy people."

"No, he doesn't want to annoy people, but he has to be aware of the harm he does. Amelia is pregnant, and to upset her like this... ," her cousin Laura said.

"But Santiago loves her," Antonietta, who was strongly in favor of her brother-in-law, insisted.

"It's a fine way to show it! To upset me so much it nearly kills me!" Amelia replied.

"Come on, cousin, don't exaggerate," Melita said. "Men aren't as sensitive as we are."

"But that's no excuse for them to do whatever they want," Laura said.

"You have to put up with a great deal from men," Doña Teresa said in a conciliatory fashion.

"I doubt that Papa has ever done to you what Santiago has done to me. No, Mama, no, I'm not going to forgive him. Whoever said that they have the right to do what they want with us? I won't let him!"

From that moment on, Amelia's interest in politics (or rather, Socialism) was redoubled. She never went to another meeting held by Azaña's party, and in spite of Santiago's insistence, and fears about her pregnant state, Amelia became a generous colla-

borator with Lola in all her political activities, although she discovered that her friend did not have the same trust in her.

One afternoon in May I went with Amelia and her mother to the
doctor. When we came out, Doña Teresa invited us to have tea in
Viena Capellanes, "the Viena," Madrid's finest patisserie. We
were going to celebrate the doctor's assertion that the pregnancy was entirely normal. We were just about to go into the shop
when we saw Lola on the pavement in front of it. She was walking fast, holding by the hand a child who must have been about
ten or eleven years old. It looked like she was scolding him, because the boy had a crestfallen expression. Amelia let go of her
mother's arm and was about to ask Lola to join us.

Lola did not disguise her discomfort at seeing us. But we were
more surprised when the boy said, "Mama, who are these ladies?"

Lola introduced her son unwillingly.

"He's called Pablo, after Pablo Iglesias, the founder of the
PSOE."

"I didn't know that you had a son," Amelia replied, upset
because her friend had kept secrets from her.

"And why should I tell you?" Lola replied grumpily.

"Well, I would have liked to know. Would you like to have tea
with us in the Viena?" Amelia suggested.

Pablo immediately said that he would, and that he'd never
been in such a fancy teashop, but Lola seemed uncertain. Doña
Teresa felt uncomfortable and I was worried about what the consequences could be of finding out about Lola's son. Lola finally
accepted, seeing that it was a chance for her child to eat in such a
famous place.

"I did not know that you were married," Doña Teresa said, to
start a conversation.

"I'm not," Lola replied, to Doña Teresa's astonishment.

"You're not married? So... ?" Amelia asked.

"You don't need a husband to have kids, and I didn't want to
get married. Pablo came along without us looking for him, but
there you go."

"But he must have a father..."

"Of course I have a father!" Pablo said angrily. "His name is Josep! I'm half Catalan because my father is Catalan. He's not here now, but he'll come and see us when he can."

Lola looked daggers at her son, and we could see in her gaze that once the two of them were alone Pablo wouldn't escape a good telling-off for talking too much. But Pablo decided to ignore his mother and carry on.

"My father's a Communist. What are you?"

Without us being able to stop it, Lola slapped her son and told him to shut up. Doña Teresa had to intervene to calm the child's tears and the mother's anger.

"Come, come! Drink your chocolate... and Lola, don't hit your child, he's little and the only thing he's done is to say that he's got a father whom he's proud of, which is no reason for you to scold him." Kindhearted Doña Teresa tried to calm Lola's anger.

"I've told him that he's got to keep his mouth shut, that he shouldn't tell anyone about me or his father; there are people who are scared of the Communists and the Socialists, and they could make things awkward for us."

"But not us! I'm your friend," Amelia insisted, feeling hurt.

"Yes... yes... but even so... Pablo, finish your chocolate and your bun, we've got to go."

The next afternoon, when Amelia and I were at home sewing, Lola came to see Amelia. I made a move to leave the room, but as Amelia did not tell me to go, I preferred to stay and see what Lola was going to say.

"I didn't tell you that I've got a son because I don't want to tell my life to everyone who comes along," Lola said.

"But I'm not just anyone, I thought that you trusted me, and, well, I thought you were my friend."

Lola bit her lip. It was clear that she'd thought a lot about what she was going to say, and she didn't want her emotions to carry her away.

"You are a good person, but we're not friends... You have to understand, you and I are not equal."

"But we are, we are equal, we're two women who like each other; you've convinced me of certain things, you've made me see that there's a life beyond these walls, you've made me see my privilege and feel guilty about it. I try to help your cause because I feel that it is just, because it's not right that I should have everything and others should have nothing. But maybe that's not enough, and, you know what, Lola? I'm not going to apologize. No, I won't apologize for having marvelous parents, a loving husband, and a supportive family. As far as money is concerned, my father has been working his whole life, just like my grandparents did and their parents before them... And Santiago, you've seen how much he works, how he spends all his time in the factory, how he looks after the people who work there for him. Even so, I admit that we have more than we need, that it's not fair that others have nothing while we have so much. But you know, Lola, that we don't exploit anyone, that we help others as much as we can. But I see that this isn't enough for you and that you'll never trust me."

They argued, and though in the end they reconciled with each other, Amelia realized that there was a barrier between her and Lola, the boundary of Lola's own prejudices, and that it would be a very difficult barrier to cross.

Even so, Amelia got even more involved in political activities, if that were possible; she volunteered to work in the People's House, she did secretarial work for Lola's party, and did whatever was asked of her.

Amelia's political activity developed in parallel with Santiago's; in that year of 1935, Don Manuel Azaña made many appearances between May and October and gained the support of large sections of society, and Santiago was present at many of these meetings of the Republican Left. He was sure that the solution for Spain's problems was for Manuel Azaña to take charge of the country, which was sinking ever deeper in an economic and institutional crisis.

Things were no better in the rest of the world. The whole of Europe was worried about Hitler.

One April night when Amelia's parents had come to visit their daughter and son-in-law, Don Juan said with satisfaction that the League of Nations in Geneva had condemned Germany's rearmament.

"It looks like they're finally starting to do something about this madman... ," Don Juan said to his son-in-law.

"I wouldn't be so optimistic. Lots of people in Europe are very worried about what's happened in Russia, they're afraid of being contaminated by the Soviet Revolution," Santiago replied.

"You may be right, it seems as if the whole world has gone mad, people are saying that Stalin is strongly opposed to the dissidents," Don Juan said.

Amelia burst in angrily, surprising her father and husband.

"Don't believe the Fascist propaganda! What's happening is that some people are scared, scared of losing their privileges, but Russia for the first time is becoming aware of what dignity is, is building a Republic of workers, of men and women who are equal and free..."

"Why, my dear, what things you say!"

"Amelia, don't get upset, remember you're pregnant!" Doña Teresa was anxious on her daughter's behalf.

"You know, Amelia, I'm worried when you say these things, you're letting yourself get taken in by the Communists and their propaganda," Santiago appeared angry.

"Come, come, let's not argue, it's not good for the girl," Doña Teresa hated for Amelia to get caught up in political arguments.

"We're not arguing, Mama. It's just that I don't like Papa to say that things aren't going well in Russia. And you, Santiago, you should be hoping that something like the Russian Revolution happens in the rest of Europe, people can't wait forever to be treated with a little justice."

That night Amelia and Santiago had an argument. As soon as Don Juan and Doña Teresa left, Amelia and Santiago began a fight that ended up being audible throughout the rest of the house.

"Amelia, you have to stop meeting with Lola! She's putting these ideas in your head..."

"What do you mean, she's putting ideas in my head? Do you think I'm an idiot, that I can't think for myself, that I don't notice what's going on around us? The right wing is leading us into a catastrophe... You complain about the situation, you and my father... You know the difficulties my family is facing..."

"Revolution is not the solution. Lots of injustices are committed in the name of revolution. Do you think that your friend Lola would have mercy on you if there were a revolution?"

"Mercy? Why would she have to have mercy? I would support the revolution!"

"You're mad!"

"How dare you call me mad!"

"I'm sorry, I didn't mean to offend you, but I'm worried, you don't know what's happening in Russia..."

"You're the person who doesn't know anything! I'll tell you what's happening in Russia: People have enough to eat, for the first time there's food enough for everyone. There are no poor people, they've got rid of the bloodsuckers, the capitalists, and..."

"Don't be naïve, my girl!"

"Naïve?"

Amelia left the salon sobbing, slamming the door behind her. Santiago followed her up to her bedroom, worried that their argument could affect the child she was carrying.

Amelia was ever more filled with Lola's ideas, or rather the ideas of Josep, Lola's partner and Pablo's father. Because Amelia had finally met him.

One afternoon that Amelia and I went to Lola's house, Josep was there, recently returned from Barcelona.

Josep was a handsome man. Tall and strong, with black eyes and a savage aspect, although he tried to appear friendly as well as cautious; he did not seem as mistrustful as Lola had.

"Lola's spoken to me about you, I know you helped her. If they'd caught her she'd definitely be in prison. You don't know how these disgusting Fascists treat women. It was a pity that we couldn't make the revolution happen. We will be better prepared next time."

"Yes, it was a shame things didn't go better," Amelia replied.

Josep monopolized the conversation for two hours, and this is how it would be on all the other occasions that we saw him. He told us how things were changing in Russia, how people had gone from being serfs to being citizens, how Stalin was cementing the foundations of the revolution by enacting all that the Bolsheviks had promised: Social classes had been done away with, and the people had enough to eat. They were putting their plans for development into action, and the rural workers were enthusiastic.

Josep described a paradise, and Amelia listened to him fascinated, drinking in his words. I was fired up by what he said, and decided that I would write to my brother Aitor to persuade him to open his mind to the new ideas that were coming from Russia. We were workers, not landowners, people like Josep. Of course I knew that Aitor would pay me no attention, he was still working and campaigning for the PNV, dreaming of a Basque homeland, although he didn't yet say so out loud.

At that moment I did not know why, but Josep seemed to become interested in Amelia, and sent Lola to come and find us regularly during the time he was staying in Madrid.

Amelia was excited because a man like Josep was taking her seriously. Josep was a Communist leader in Barcelona. He was the chauffeur for a bourgeois Catalan family. He took his employer to his textile factory in Mataró every day, as well as accompanying his employer's wife on her visits, or taking the children to school. He had previously been a bus driver. He had met Lola once while his employers were on a trip to Madrid, and they had had Pablo, without either of the two wanting to get married, or at least that's what they said, although I always suspected that Josep had been married before meeting Lola. They had a curious relationship, because they saw each other only when Josep came to Madrid with his employer, something that happened about every six weeks, as his employer sold his fabrics throughout Spain and had a partner in the capital. Apart from their intermittent relationship, Lola and Josep appeared to get along well, and of course Pablo adored his father.

From what he said, Josep was well connected, and not only with the Catalan Communists.

Amelia felt flattered that a Communist militant of his importance would show interest in her opinions, and would listen to her. Above all, Josep dedicated a large period of the time he spent with us to our indoctrination, using us for his own purposes, convincing us that the future would belong to the Communists and that the Russian Revolution was only the beginning of a great world revolution that no human force would be able to hold back.

"Do you know why the revolution will triumph? Because there are more of us, yes, we are more numerous than ever. There are more of us who have a great treasure in our control, the force of our labor. The world cannot turn without us. We are progress. Who will make the machines turn? The rich bosses? If you knew how they live in the Soviet Union, the advances they've made in less than twenty years... Since April Moscow has had underground trains, a metro that runs for eighty-two kilometers; although this is important, it's more important that the stations are decorated with works of art, with chandeliers, with paintings and frescoes on the walls... and all of this put in place for the workers, who have never had the chance to see a painting, or stand under the light of these fine crystal lights... This is the spirit of the revolution..."

Amelia didn't dare take the next step, but I did, and asked Josep to support me in my application to join the Communists. What else could a girl like me do, a girl born in the mountains, who had been a worker ever since I'd been able to think?

One afternoon Lola left a message for us in her house that we should meet with her and Josep and some Communist comrades that evening.

Amelia didn't know how to tell Santiago that she'd be out that night, especially as the fighting in the street between the left and the right was continuous, and always resulted in someone being wounded, if not killed.

"I should never have gotten married," Amelia complained. "I can't go anywhere without asking Santiago."

In fact, her husband was not party to her political investigations, but going out alone at night was more than could be permitted. But she had always been very obstinate, so that when Santiago came home she declared openly her decision to go to Lola's house to meet some of her and Josep's Communist friends.

They had an argument, which Santiago won.

"But what are you thinking? Do you think that with everything that's happening I'm going to let you go out past the bullring to Lola's house with people we don't know? If you don't care about me, if you don't even care about yourself, at least think about our child. You have no right to put him in harm's way. Some friends this Lola and Josep are, to invite a pregnant woman out into Madrid at night!"

Santiago did not give way, and although Amelia tried to change his mind, first with blandishments and caresses, then with tears, and finally by shouting, she did not in the end dare to leave the house without her husband's approval.

The political situation got worse by the day, and for all his efforts, Niceto Alcalá Zamora, the President of the Republic, could not create any kind of consensus between the CEDA and the parties of the Left.

Joaquín Chapaprieta, who had been the Treasury Secretary, ended up being asked by Alcalá Zamora to form a government, which failed like the others.

I remember that we went to dine at the Carranzas' one Sunday. I think that it was in October, because Amelia was already in the last stages of her pregnancy, and she was upset to see herself fat and clumsy.

Don Manuel and Doña Blanca had invited all of the Garayoas, not just Amelia's parents but also Don Armando and Doña Elena, so the cousins were there as well: Melita, Laura, and little Jesús.

If I remember this meal it is because Amelia very nearly went into labor.

Don Juan was more worried than usual because he had received a letter from the man who had until recently been his employee, Herr Helmut Keller, in which he explained in detail what the September 1935 Nuremburg Laws meant. Helmut was worried, because according to the new laws, only those who had "pure" blood were deemed German; everyone else was no longer considered a German citizen. Marriage was forbidden between

Jews and Aryans. Keller also thought that the time had come for Herr Itzhak Wassermann and his family to leave Germany, although he had not managed to persuade them to do so, even though there were many Jewish families who had emigrated out of fear of what was happening. Keller begged Don Juan to try to convince Herr Wassermann.

"I've thought I should go to Germany. I have to get Itzhak and his family out of there, I'm scared for his life," Don Juan said.

"It could be dangerous!" Doña Teresa exclaimed.

"Dangerous? Why? I am not a Jew."

"But Herr Itzhak is, and look at what happened to your business, they ruined it, you've been without any German company buying or selling material from you for months, they've even accused you of fraud." Doña Teresa was very scared.

"I know, my dear, I know, but they haven't been able to prove anything."

"But even so they've closed the warehouse."

"You must understand that I have to go."

"If you'll allow me to speak, I think your wife is right." Don Manuel's powerful voice broke into the argument between Don Juan and Doña Teresa. "My friend, you must resign yourself to the loss of your business in Germany; you've paid the price for having a partner whom the new regime does not like. I don't think you'll sort anything out by going there, they should try to leave Germany on their own."

They got into a debate in which Amelia supported her father so forcefully that she ended up insisting that she herself would accompany her father to rescue Herr Itzhak and his family, and that it was a cowardly act to leave them to their fate. She got so worked up that she ended by feeling indisposed and we worried about her state.

Javier was born at the beginning of November. Amelia went into labor early in the morning of November 3, but did not bring her son into the world until the following day. How she cried! The poor girl suffered terribly, and this was with the constant assistance of two doctors and a midwife.

Santiago suffered with her. He beat furiously against the wall to find some kind of outlet for the impotence he felt at being unable to help his wife.

In the end it was a forceps birth, but Amelia was nearly killed. Javier was wonderful, a healthy baby, large and thin, who came into the world extremely hungry and who bit his fists in desperation.

Amelia lost a lot of blood during the birth and took more than a month to recover, for all that everyone spoiled her, especially Santiago. Nothing was too much for his wife, but Amelia appeared sad and indifferent to everything that was going on around her; she cheered up only when she saw her cousin Laura or Lola. Then it seemed that the light came back into her eyes and she became interested in the conversation again. In those days Laura had become engaged to a young lawyer, the son of some friends of her parents, and all the signs pointed to a wedding. As far as Lola was concerned, whenever she came to visit Amelia insisted that they be left alone together, something that Santiago accepted so as not to go against his wife's wishes.

Lola brought news of Josep and other comrades whom Amelia had met. And Amelia asked her how the preparations for the revolution were progressing, that great revolution Josep had spoken about and in which Amelia wanted to participate.

As time went by, Lola seemed to trust more in Amelia, and let her in on little secrets about Josep, and his important position among the Catalan Communists.

"And why are you a Socialist and not a Communist?" Amelia asked her, not understanding why she did not share Josep's political militancy.

"You don't have to be a Communist to realize the achievements of the Soviet Revolution; anyway, I'm a Socialist by tradition: My father was one, he knew Pablo Iglesias... and I am a supporter of Largo Caballero, he also admires the Bolsheviks. What's happened is that Prieto and the other Socialist leaders are opposed to Largo Caballero; they aren't workers like he is, and they can't understand what we want..."

These were fragments of a conversation that I overheard while I was serving them their tea. I was the only one who could interrupt them, not even Águeda was allowed to go into Amelia's room.

Ay, Águeda! She was Javier's wet nurse. They brought her down from Asturias because Amaya, my mother, could not find a Basque wet nurse, like Doña Teresa or even Amelia herself would have wanted.

Águeda was a ruddy-faced woman, tall, with chestnut hair and eyes the same color. She was not married, but a guy from the mines had left her pregnant, and she had had the great misfortune to lose her child when he was very young. Some friends of Don Juan recommended her as a nanny for Javier, and she arrived in our house barely a week after burying her son.

She was a good woman, caring and kind, who treated Javier as if he were her own son. Silent and obedient, Águeda was like a beneficent ghost in the house, and all of us grew fond of her. It was a relief for Santiago to see his son so well cared for, given Amelia's apathy: Not even her son could cheer her up.

Given Amelia's weakness, Christmas that year was celebrated at the home of Don Juan and Doña Teresa. Santiago's family understood that this was best for Amelia, who was in no state to be the hostess of such an important event.

Amelia and Santiago's house was only three blocks away from the Garayoas', so it was no great effort for Amelia to go to her parents' house.

It made you envious to see all the Garayoas, Don Juan's brother Don Armando, his wife Doña Elena and their children, Melita, Laura and Jesús, along with the Carranza family, Santiago's parents.

With my mother's help, Doña Teresa took great pains with the meal. That Christmas was special for me as well, it was the last one I spent with my mother. It had been decided; she would go back to the farm after Christmas, and her departure meant that I would be alone in Madrid.

My brother Aitor's work was going well, and he insisted that my mother should stop looking after other people and should instead look after our grandparents and our little plot of land. Land was as important for my mother as it was for Aitor; at that time I felt myself to be sufficiently Communist as to be able to look at the world with a little more perspective, seeing it as a place where everything was everybody's for the use of everyone, and no one apart from the People owned the land, and it did not matter where you were born, because one's property was the whole world, and one's family was the workers of the world.

But to go back to that dinner... They sang carols, they ate and drank all those things that never end up on the tables of the poor, although those of us who served in this house couldn't complain: We always ate and drank what our employers did.

I still remember that we ate turkey with chestnuts... And as always happened when the two families met, people spoke about and argued about politics.

"It seems that Alcalá Zamora is ready for a new government to be formed by Manuel Portela Valladares," Don Juan commented.

"What he needs to do is call elections," Santiago replied.

"How impatient you young people are!" Armando Garayoa responded. "Don Niceto Alcalá Zamora doesn't want to give power to the CEDA; he doesn't trust Gil Robles."

"And right he is!" said Don Juan.

"I don't see a way out of this situation... I don't think that the elections will solve anything, because if the left wins, Lord help us!" Don Manuel Carranza, Santiago's father, lamented.

"What do you want? That these right-wingers, incapable of solving Spain's problems, end up in government?" Amelia looked angrily at her father-in-law.

"Amelia, dear, don't get cross!" Amelia's mother tried to intervene.

"It's just that I'm furious that there are still people who believe that the CEDA can do any good. People are not going to put up with this situation much longer," Amelia continued.

"Well, I'm afraid of a left-wing government," Don Manuel insisted.

"And I'm afraid of a right-wing one," replied Amelia.

"There needs to be authority. Do you think that the country can move forward if there are strikes all the time?" Don Manuel asked his daughter-in-law.

"What I think is that people have a right to eat and not have a terrible life, which is what happens here," Amelia replied.

Santiago always supported Amelia, even though he felt the need to qualify her political positions. He, as I've said before, was an Azañist, he didn't believe in revolution even though he didn't support the right wing either.

Apart from Amelia, who said that she was tired and who stayed with her son Javier, who was sleeping calmly in Águeda's arms, at midnight the family went to the church to hear Mass.

4

President Alcalá Zamora was unable to deal with the situation of conflict between the left and the right, and general malaise was increasing throughout Spain, so he had no option other than to call a general election for February 16, 1936. None of us could imagine what would happen next...

From the PSOE, Prieto insisted on the necessity of forming a grand coalition of the Left, while Largo Caballero fought for a united front with the Communists, but he didn't know how to get his opinion heard; also, I don't know if you know, but the Communist Party was advised from Moscow to ally itself with the bourgeoisie on the Left against the right-wingers and Fascists. This was a much more realistic position. And so the Popular Front was born.

"Amelia, Amelia! They've formed a Popular Front!"

Santiago came joyfully home on January 15, 1936, knowing that his wife would be extremely happy with the news. Santiago also thought that the fact that the Republican Left would be in this grouping with the Communists and the Socialists would bring him closer to his wife, who was ever more infused with the ideology of her friends Lola and Josep.

"Great! That is good news. And what do you think they'll do if they win the elections?"

"Some friends from the Republican left have told me that they'll try to bring back the policies they implemented in '31 and '33."

"That's not enough!"

"What are you saying, Amelia? It's the right thing to go down that path. I don't like to go against you, but I am worried by the ideas that Lola and Josep are putting in your head. Do you really think that Spain's problems can be solved by a revolution? Do you want us to kill each other? I can't believe that you could be so thoughtless..."

"Look, Santiago, I know that it upsets you that I don't agree with your ideas, but you should at least respect mine. I'm sorry, it just doesn't seem fair that we should have everything and others... Sometimes I think about Lola's son, Pablo. What sort of a future can he look forward to? Javier will never lack for anything, and I feel comforted by that, but it's not fair. No, it's not fair."

The discussion was interrupted by Águeda, who was worried by Javier's nonstop crying.

"I don't know what's wrong with the child, but he doesn't want to eat, and he won't stop crying," the nurse explained.

"How long has he been like this?" Santiago asked.

"He had a bad night, but he started crying this morning and I think he's got a fever."

Santiago and Amelia went immediately to the child's room. Javier was crying inconsolably in his crib, and his forehead was burning.

"Amelia, call Dr. Martínez, something's wrong with Javier, or else, no, we'd better go to the hospital, they'll treat him better there."

Amelia wrapped Javier in a shawl and went to the hospital with Santiago, holding the baby tight.

It was nothing serious. Javier had otitis, and the pain in his ears was what made him cry. But the fright had its effect on Amelia, who had been unconcerned about Javier until this point, and had let Águeda do everything, from bathing him to feeding him.

"Edurne, I am a bad mother," Amelia confessed to me, sobbing, that night, while she looked at her child in the crib.

"Don't say that..."

"It's true, I've realized that sometimes I am more worried about what's happening to Pablo, Lola's son, than I am about Javier."

"It's normal, you know that your son wants for nothing, while Pablo, the poor mite, doesn't have a thing."

"But he has something more important: his mother's continual love and attention." It was Santiago's voice.

We started. He had come into the room so slowly that neither of us had realized.

Amelia looked at Santiago desperately. What her husband had just said had wounded her deeply, above all because she thought he was right.

She left the room in tears. Santiago came to his son's crib and sat down next to it, ready to spend the night in vigil over his son. I offered to stay up with Águeda looking after Javier, but Santiago did not want us to, so we both went to bed.

"A sick child needs his parents; anyway, I wouldn't be calm enough to stay away; I couldn't sleep thinking that the boy was crying because he was in pain."

I went to sleep, but the next day I discovered that Águeda had got up in the middle of the night to be by Javier's side. Santiago and her had watched over the boy in silence, listening to him breathe.

Amelia woke up with her eyes red and swollen with so much crying, and she cried even more when she realized that her husband and Águeda had stayed up all night by the child's crib.

"Don't you see that I'm a bad mother, Edurne?"

"Come on, don't blame yourself..."

"Santiago was up the whole night with our son, and so was Águeda, who has nothing to do with... She's... she's just..."

I know that she was going to say that Águeda was just a maid, but she held back because she knew that to say so would have compromised her revolutionary ideals.

"Águeda is the child's nurse," I consoled her, "and it's her duty to look after Javier."

"No, Edurne, it's not her duty to look after the child when he's ill, it's the mother's duty. What is wrong with me? Why can't I give the best of myself to my husband and my son?"

Amelia was right. Her behavior was extraordinary: With strangers she would go out of her way to be of use to them, and she paid less and less attention to Santiago and Javier, her son, a newborn child.

I didn't dare ask her if she still loved Santiago, but at this moment I thought that Amelia was crying for just this reason, because she didn't feel capable of loving her husband or of feeling the tenderness that a mother should feel toward her children. But I did not judge her because at that time I too was filled with revolutionary ideas, and thought that what happened to her or to me was nothing compared to what would happen to the whole of mankind, and the important thing to do was to build a new world, of the kind that Josep told us was being built in the Soviet Union.

"The child is better. I fed him this morning and he didn't reject it. He's not vomiting anymore and he is much calmer."

Amelia looked at Águeda as she put Javier to bed. It was clear that the woman loved this child and that she was using him to make up for the loss of her own son.

On February 16 the Popular Front won the elections, although by a smaller margin than expected over the CEDA and the other right-wing forces. It was the PNV, Alcalá Zamora's centrist party, and the Lliga Catalana that won the rest of the votes.

With results like this, it was difficult for Manuel Azaña to restore the calm that the country needed so much.

People were sick and tired of living badly, of being exploited, and the rural workers began to occupy farms in Andalusia and Extremadura; there were strikes that put pressure on the new government, and as if that weren't enough, people from the newly created Falange dedicated themselves to trying to destabilize the Popular Front.

Azaña reestablished the autonomy of Catalonia, and Lluís Companys became its president. And then there was an attempt to expel Alcalá Zamora... And the Socialists, well, Largo Caballero's group, vetoed Prieto to stop him joining the government... It was a mistake... No... They didn't do things well, but we can say this now that time has passed; we were living through it back then, and we didn't have a moment to think about want we were doing, much less about its possible consequences. Do you know something, young man? No, we didn't do things well, all of us who had our high ideals, who were in favor of progress, who were always right, we also didn't do things well.

"I think that you should go with the child to your grandmother's house for a while," Santiago suggested to Amelia. I don't like how things are, and you will be much calmer in Biarritz. Why don't you ask your sister Antonietta to go with you?"

"I'd rather stay. What are you scared of?"

"I'm not scared, Amelia, but there are things I hear that I don't like and I'd prefer it if Javier and you were away for a while. You've told me that when you were a girl you always waited for the summer so you could go and stay with your grandmother Margot."

"That's true, but things are different now, I'd rather stay, I don't want to miss what's going on."

"It just means bringing your holidays forward a little, nothing more, and I'll come and meet you when I can. I'm worried, things aren't going well, and your father's business is also not working out as he planned. The imports from the United States are extremely expensive, and we cannot keep on helping him to bring machinery and spare parts from there, it's too expensive."

"You're going to stop being in business with Papa?" Amelia asked in alarm.

"It's not about stopping the business, we just have to close down this channel of imports. It's not worth it."

"This comes from your father! You know very well that my father had to close his businesses in Germany, and for all the sales he made there, the Nazis took everything... and your father's only interested in money."

"That's enough, Amelia! Stop accusing my father of all the wrongs of the world. My family loves you, and we've shown our affection to you and yours in spades, but we can't keep on losing money, things aren't going well for us either."

"So, just now, when the Popular Front is in charge and things are going to get sorted out, just now is when you give up on my father..."

"No, Amelia, it does not look like the Popular Front is going to be able to sort things out. You know how much I admire Don Manuel Azaña; I know that if it depended on him alone... But things are never how we like them to be, and Azaña has lots of problems to face up to. The strikes are bleeding us dry..."

"The workers are right!" Amelia protested.

"They're right about some things, but in others... In any case, you can't sort out in a few months problems that have been building up over centuries, and this is what's happening, what with impatience on one side and the boycott on the other, we're heading toward an impossible situation."

"You're always so calm!" Amelia said angrily.

"I try to see things as they are, realistically." There was a tone in Santiago's voice, a tone of tiredness with these constant arguments with Amelia.

"My place is here, Santiago, with my family."

"Do you really want to stay here because of us?"

"What are you trying to say?"

"You spend more time with your Communist friends than you do at home... Ever since you met Josep you have changed. If we were really so important to you, if you really were only thinking about Javier, then you'd agree to go for a while and be with your grandmother Margot."

"How dare you tell me that I don't care about my son?"

"I dare because the truth is that Águeda spends more time with him than you do."

"She's his nurse! Do you think I love him less because I go to political meetings? What I want is to build a new world where Javier will never face any injustice. Is that such a bad thing that you need to scold me for it?"

These arguments exhausted both Amelia and Santiago, and were driving them apart. It must be acknowledged that Santiago had the worst of it, because he suffered due to the situation he lived in, while Amelia was living her own life through politics. Santiago was making superhuman efforts to save their marriage.

Their arguments were ever more frequent, and the Garayoas and the Carranzas were both aware of the deterioration of the relationship between their children.

Doña Teresa reproved Amelia, saying that she wasn't behaving like a good wife, but Amelia said that her mother was "old-fashioned" and did not understand that the world was changing and that women no longer had to be submissive.

The Carranzas, Don Manuel as much as Doña Elena, tried not to interfere in the problems of the marriage, but they suffered in seeing their son so worried.

One of the ever rarer occasions when the two families gathered together to eat was on March 7. I remember because Don Juan arrived late and Amelia was upset to have to delay the meal.

When he finally arrived, he came with news that seemed to have particularly upset him.

"Germany has invaded the Rhineland," he said in a tired voice.

"Yes, we heard on the radio," Don Manuel replied.

"I've been trying to speak to Helmut Keller all day and I finally managed to... He's in despair, and ashamed by what's happening. You know that Helmut is a rational person, a good man..."

Don Juan talked incoherently. His luck had gone sour the day Hitler came into power, and since then he had followed events in Germany as if it were his own country. He was also desperate to get Herr Itzhak out of Germany, but Itzhak kept on saying that this was his country and that he wouldn't leave his homeland for anything.

"Hitler has broken the Treaty of Versailles," Santiago said.

"And the Treaty of Locarno," Don Manuel added.

"But what does he care about international treaties? One day the powers that be will regret not having stopped him earlier," Don Juan complained.

The day after that meal, March 8, Santiago went away again without telling anyone. He did not come back for several days, apparently he had been to Barcelona to talk with the business' Catalan partners.

Amelia got extremely annoyed, and on the second day of Santiago's absence she decided that she no longer needed to obey any social conventions.

"If he can come and go whenever he wants, I'll do the same. So get ready, Edurne, because we are going to Lola's house this evening, there's a meeting and some of Josep's comrades will be there."

I was about to tell her that we should not go, that Santiago would be furious, but I held my peace. Santiago was not there, and by the time he found out it would be some days later.

Amelia went to Javier's room to give him a kiss before we left.

"Look after him, Águeda, he's my most precious treasure."

"Don't worry, Madam, you know he's fine with me."

"I know, you look after him better than I could."

"Don't say that! I just try to give him all he needs."

Águeda was right: She gave Javier everything he needed, especially the love and constant presence that Amelia did not provide. I don't think I'm judging her, she just did what she thought best. We were all convinced that we had to do whatever we could, however small, to make the world a better place. We were very young and very inexperienced, and we were convinced of the worth of our ideals.

There were more people than usual in Lola's house that night. And he was there, Pierre.

We were not expecting Josep to be there, because he had left a fortnight ago, but apparently it was urgent that his employer return to Madrid.

"Come in, come in... Amelia, I'd like you to meet Pierre," Josep said, as always extremely deferential toward Amelia.

At that time, Pierre must have been about thirty-five years old. He was not very tall, but he had dirty golden hair and steel-gray eyes that seemed to be able to read your innermost thoughts.

Josep introduced him to us as a half-French comrade, a bookseller by trade, in Madrid on business.

I would be lying if I said that I didn't notice the immediate attraction between the pair of them, Amelia as much as Pierre. Although Pierre was giving a talk that evening on the situation in the Soviet Union, and the reason why European intellectuals were supporting the revolution in ever greater numbers, he did not stop seeking Amelia with his eyes, as she listened to him in fascination.

"Why don't you come with me to Paris?" he asked her when he had taken her to one side.

"To Paris? Why?" Amelia asked, ingenuously.

"The revolution needs women like you, there's a great deal of work to be done. I think that you could help me, work with me. Lola has said that you speak French, and even some English and German, isn't that right?"

"Yes, my paternal grandmother is French, and my father used to have business in Germany, my best friend is German; I learned English from my nurse, although I don't speak very well..."

"I repeat my invitation, although it's actually a job offer. You could be very useful to me."

"I... I don't see how."

Pierre looked at her fixedly, and his gaze was filled with words that only she could understand.

"I'd like you to come with me not just for work. Think about it."

Amelia blushed and looked down. A man had never propositioned her like this before, so directly. As I was standing nearby, ready if Amelia needed me, and had heard Pierre's invitation, I went to her immediately.

"It's late, Amelia, we should go."

"Yes, you're right, it's late."

"Do you have to go already?" Pierre wanted to know.

"Yes," she murmured, but without moving. It was clear that she had no desire for us to go.

"Will you think about what I said?" Pierre insisted.

"About going to Paris with you?"

"Yes, I will be in Madrid for a few days, but not many, and I don't know when I will return."

"No, I cannot go to Paris, I'll see you some other time," Amelia said with a sigh.

"What's stopping you from coming with me?"

"She has a husband and a son," I replied, although I immediately regretted interrupting, especially given the look of rage that Amelia turned on me at that moment.

"Yes, I know that she's married and has a son. Who isn't? Who doesn't?" Pierre answered tranquilly.

"No, I cannot come with you. Thank you for the invitation."

We left Lola's house in silence. Amelia was angry because of my interruption, and I was worried that this would provoke, more than anger, a loss of her trust in me.

We did not speak until we got home. I was about to go to my room, when she grasped me by my arm and said very low:

"If someone has to know something about me I will be the one who tells them. Bear that in mind."

"I'm sorry, I... I didn't want to get involved..."

"But you did."

She turned on her heels and left me there in the hall, crying my eyes out. It was the first time she had got annoyed with me since we'd met, the first time that I felt that I was not her friend, but only a stranger.

The next day Amelia got up late. The chambermaid said that she had asked not to be disturbed, and although it was my privilege to be able to go into her room, I did not dare do so after what had happened the night before.

I did not see Amelia until midday; she looked like she was running a temperature and she complained of having a headache. Her mother, who had come to have lunch with her and to see the baby, ascribed this illness to the distress Amelia felt at Santiago's absence, but I guessed that her husband was not the cause of this febrile situation, rather it was the sudden appearance of Pierre in her life. In *our* lives, for he would change both our lives.

Antonietta came at six to look for her mother, and Amelia said goodbye to them with relief, because that afternoon neither her mother nor her sister had been able to take her mind off what was bothering her.

Around seven o'clock Lola came to the house. As soon as I saw her I guessed she must have been sent by Pierre, because she asked to see Amelia alone. I do not know what they talked about, but it is easy to guess, because half an hour later Amelia called me to say that she was going out to a political meeting at Lola's house and that she did not want me to go with her. I protested: Santiago did not want her to go out without me, but above all I felt sad to be left out.

Amelia went to Javier's room. The child was in Águeda's arms, and she was singing to him. He smiled and lifted his arms up to the nurse's face. Amelia kissed her son and left quickly, followed by Lola.

I sat in the hall, waiting for her to come back, which she did not do before midnight. She came in with her face red, sweating, and seemed to be shaking. She was not pleased to see me there, and sent me up to my room.

"Amelia, I want to talk to you," I begged.

"At this time of night? No, go and rest, I'm not feeling well and I need to sleep."

"But Amelia, I am worried, I've spent all day with a pain in my breast... I want you to forgive me for last night... I... I didn't want to offend you, or get mixed up in your business... you know... Well, I only have you, and if you didn't want anything to do with me then I don't know what I would do."

"But Edurne, what things you say! What do you mean, you only have me? What about your mother, or Aitor, or your grandparents? Come on, don't be silly and go rest."

"But will you forgive me?"

Amelia hugged me and stroked my back lovingly; she had always been very generous and could not bear to see anyone suffer.

"I don't have anything to forgive you for, last night was nothing, a trifle, I had a sudden attack of grumpiness, but don't worry about it."

"But you went without me tonight... and... well... It's the first time you've gone out without me. You know you can trust me, that I'll never say anything or do anything to hurt you."

"And what could you say?" she said in annoyance.

"Nothing, nothing, there's nothing but good to say about you." I started to cry, worried that I had really made things worse.

"Come on, don't cry! We're both very sensitive, it must be the times we live in, the political situation; things aren't going well, I'm worried about the government of the Popular Front."

"Your mother is very worried because the workers are occupying farms in Andalusia and Extremadura," I replied, just to say something.

"My mother is very good, and because she treats everyone well she thinks that the whole world is equal, but there are people living in terrible conditions... And we're not trying to give people charity, but to promote justice."

"Are you going to go?"

I don't know why I asked this, I'm still asking myself today. Amelia got very serious and I saw her hands trembling and how she was trying not to lose control.

"And where do you think I would go?"

"I don't know... Pierre asked you to go with him to Paris yesterday... Maybe you have decided to go and work there..."

"And if I did go, what would you think?"

"Could I go with you?"

"No, you couldn't. I would have to go alone."

"Then I wouldn't want you to go."

"How selfish!"

Yes, she was right, I was selfish, I was thinking about me, about what would become of me if she were to leave. I lowered my head and felt ashamed.

"If we want the revolution to triumph all over the world, then we cannot think of ourselves, we have to offer ourselves up as a sacrifice."

"But you're not a Communist," I babbled.

"Can you be anything else?"

"You've always sympathized with the Socialists..."

"Edurne, I was as ignorant as you, but I've opened my eyes, I've realized how things stand, and I admire the revolution, I think that Stalin is a blessing for Russia and I want the same for Spain and the rest of the world. We know it's possible, they've managed to do it in Russia, but there are lots of interests at stake, the interests of people who don't want to give anything away, who defend their old privileges... It will not be easy, but we can do it. Now, thanks to the people of the Left, women are taken into account; we used to be worthless, but it's still not enough, we must struggle for true equality. In Russia there is no difference between men and women, everyone is equal."

Her eyes were shining. She seemed to have attained a state of ecstasy while she talked to me about Stalin and the revolution, and I knew that it was a matter of time, of days, of hours, before Amelia would leave, but at the same time I tried to convince myself that it was impossible, that she would not dare to leave Santiago and abandon her son.

5

For several days Amelia continued regularly meeting Pierre at Lola's house. She allowed me to go with her, but sometimes when we reached the house she would send me on some errand or other in order to be alone with him.

Santiago's parents came by one afternoon to see their grandson and decided to wait until Amelia came home. As we were late, and it was past ten o'clock, Águeda and the other maids had no choice other than to admit that sometimes we came back after midnight.

Don Manuel and Doña Blanca were scandalized, and Águeda told us that Doña Blanca had told her husband as they were leaving that they needed to speak with Santiago as soon as he got back, before his marriage collapsed entirely.

Meanwhile, Don Manuel decided to speak with Amelia's father, and tell him that he had to make his daughter behave herself.

Don Juan and Doña Teresa sent a message telling Amelia not to leave the house, as they were going to pay her a visit.

"Why are they getting involved in my life?" Amelia complained. "I'm not a child!"

"They are your parents and they love you." I tried to calm her down.

"They should leave me alone! It's my in-laws' fault, they ruin everything. Why did they come round to see Javier without warning?"

"Doña Blanca called you," I reminded her.

"It doesn't matter, they're meddlers all the same, not only don't they help my father, but they ask him to talk with me as well. But who do they think I am!"

Don Juan and Doña Teresa came round at tea time, and while Doña Teresa looked after Javier, Don Juan took the opportunity to speak to Amelia.

"Dear, Santiago's parents are worried and... well, so are we. I don't want to get involved in your business, but you must understand that it's not good for you to go in and out of people's houses as if you had no obligations to anyone. You are a mother, Amelia, and this means that you cannot just do the first thing that comes into your head, you have to think about your husband and your son. You must realize that you're making a fool of Santiago with your nocturnal visits."

"And how does Santiago make me appear, with his disappearances? He left ten days ago and I don't know where he is. Doesn't he have obligations to me, or to his son? Is he allowed to do everything just because he's a man?"

"Amelia, you know that this is Santiago's way of doing things; he goes on journeys with no warning, even his mother scolds him for it. But whether you like it or not, it's not the same for you; he is a man and he's not endangering either his reputation or your own."

"Papa, I know that you can't understand this, but the world is changing, and women will eventually have the same rights as men. It's not fair that you can come and go as you please without having to explain your actions, and we are subject to gossip."

"It may not be fair, but it is how things are, and you should be careful at least until things change, out of respect for your husband, for your son, and for us. Yes, your behavior is damaging for us as well."

"How can it hurt you if I go to a political meeting?"

"I think that you are getting too involved, and what's worse, involved with the Communists. We have always defended justice, but we do not share the Communists' ideas, and you don't know what you're getting involved in."

"I am not a child!"

"Yes, Amelia, you are. You are married and you have a child, but you are not yet nineteen years old. Don't think that you know everything now and that you are immune to the influences of others, you are still a little naïve, as one should expect of someone your age, and I think that Lola is taking advantage of it."

"She is my best friend!"

"Yes, I am sure that she's your friend, but do you really think that she thinks you are her best friend? What about your cousin Laura? You used to be inseparable and now you can scarcely find time to see her. Why?"

"Laura has a fiancé."

"I know, but that doesn't explain why you have stopped going to your uncle's house and spending time with your cousins like you always used to; you don't even come home to see your sister Antonietta, and you are never in when she comes to find you. It hurts me to have to say this, but I don't think you are being a good mother, you put your politics in front of your son, and that, Amelia, does not make any woman appear in a positive light."

Amelia burst into tears. Her father's last words had wounded her. She had an uneasy conscience because she was unable to give to her son what she gave to her political activism.

"Come on, don't cry! I know that you love Javier, but your son spends more time with Águeda than with you, which is not good."

Amelia's sobbing grew more intense because she knew better than anyone that she was not a good mother and this made her sad, even though she thought it was something she could not solve.

Sometimes she would go into Javier's room, take him from his crib and kiss him and hug him as if she wanted to make him understand how much she loved him, but she only made the child scared and start to cry, she felt like a stranger, and she would throw up her hands and look for Águeda.

Doña Teresa also took her daughter to one side and repeated her husband's arguments, but she made no more of an impact than her husband had, she only made Amelia feel guilty and unable to stop crying. When they left, I heard Doña Teresa say to her husband: "I think Amelia is ill, it's like she's been bewitched... This Lola is a bad person, who's taken our daughter away from us."

Two days later, Amelia sent a message to her cousin for her to come and see her, and Laura did not need to be asked twice and came at once. The two cousins sill loved and confided in one another.

I was sewing, sitting by the balcony, and as they did not ask me to leave I heard their conversation.

"What's happening, cousin dear?" Laura asked.

"I am in despair and I don't know what to do... I need your advice, you're the only person who can understand me."

"But what's happened?" Laura was alarmed, especially to see Amelia much thinner and in such a feverish state.

"I have fallen in love with another man! I am so wretched!"

"Good heavens! But how is it possible? Santiago adores you and you... well, I thought you were in love with your husband."

"I thought I was, but it is not so, he is the first man I knew, the first man who didn't treat me like a girl, and also... Well, you know already, because I told you, I liked Santiago but I also wanted to help Papa, he has not gotten better since losing all his business in Germany."

"I know, I know... but you told me that you loved him, that you were getting married to Santiago to help your father but that you loved him as well."

Laura was in agony to discover so suddenly that her cousin did not love her husband; she sympathized with Santiago, it was difficult not to take his part, Santiago was such a gentleman, always attentive and gallant and well-mannered, and so handsome...

"I don't know what I'm going to do, but I must make my mind up."

"Make your mind up?"

"Yes, Laura, the man I love has asked me to go away with him. He doesn't know that I'm in love with him, he has only asked me to help our cause, to help Communism triumph, and thinks that I could help him... I, who am nobody... But he believes in me..."

"Does he love you?"

"He hasn't said anything, but... I know he does... I know it from how he looks at me, because he shudders just like I do if we accidentally brush against each other, I read it in his eyes... But he is a gentleman, don't imagine that he has tried anything with me, quite the contrary."

"If he were a gentleman, he wouldn't ask for you to abandon your family and go and foment revolution," Laura protested.

"But you don't understand. To be a Communist is... is... is like a religion... You can't attain paradise without making sacrifices, and us believers don't have the right to put our personal interests in front of the interests of humanity at large."

"For God's sake, Amelia, the things you say! Look, charity begins at home..."

"This isn't charity, this is justice! We should use all our strength to support the revolution, we have to make the world into the homeland of the working man, we have to follow the example of Russia."

"I know that you don't like the right-wingers and that your parents like mine are supporters of Azaña. Who is working for the country to be a better place, but Communism... I asked Papa to explain to me what he knows about the Communists, and, Amelia, I don't think that revolution would really be such a good thing."

"How can you say that! It's because they can't see the good that Communism could bring us. Look at what's happening in Germany with Hitler."

"But it doesn't have to be one thing or the other, you've always exaggerated so. Anyway, tell me who he is."

"He's named Pierre, he's French, his parents own a bookshop near Saint-Germain, and he helps them, and writes for some left-wing newspapers. He is extremely involved in Communist circles and comes to Madrid from time to time to meet with comrades here, to find out how things are, to evaluate the situation. He goes to other places as well, and uses the opportunity to buy books for his father's shop, special editions, bibliographic treasures... But he is a Communist above all."

"Yes, you've told me he's a Communist. And what does he want from you?"

"To help him, to travel to visit comrades in other countries. Learn about their difficulties, their needs, prepare information for the Communist International, work to bring the revolution everywhere we can..."

"And you need to leave your husband and your son for that?"

"Don't put it like that! I can't bear it for you too to reproach me, not to understand me. I am in love, so much I cannot say. I count the minutes until I am with Pierre."

"Amelia, you cannot abandon your son!"

Every time Javier was mentioned, Amelia burst into tears. But that afternoon I had heard enough to realize that despite her tears Amelia had already decided to leave her house, and Santiago and her son, to be with Pierre. The same fever that appeared never to have left her had nothing to do with an actual illness, but rather the passion she felt for this man. Her fate was decided, and so was mine.

Although Laura asked her to think again, she swore to her cousin that whatever happened Amelia could trust her. Amelia calmed down once she realized that her cousin would never abandon her.

"Is he married?" Laura wanted to know.

Amelia was shocked. She had never considered the possibility that Pierre might be married. She had never asked him and he had never said anything about it.

"I don't know," Amelia said, barely in a whisper.

"You must ask him, although I hope for your sake he isn't. You know what? I have always been afraid that you would fall in love with Josep and that this would destroy your friendship with Lola."

Amelia looked down, ashamed. Laura knew her well and had realized that there had indeed been a moment when Amelia had felt attracted to Josep.

"I admire Josep, but I have never fallen in love with him."

"I think that you have a special attraction toward Communists. I don't know what they say to you, but you can't fool me, they really fascinate you."

"I will never be able to fool you, and yes, you're right, I am attracted to them, They are so strong, so secure, so certain about what it is they need to do, ready to make any sacrifice... I don't know how you don't feel the same..."

"I've never met one who really made an impression on me, the ones I've known... well... The truth is I can't imagine marrying the mechanic who fixes Papa's car. What do I have in common with him?"

"You think that you are better than the workers?" Amelia asked.

"Not better or worse, just that we don't have anything in common. I'm not fooling myself, Amelia, I want the world to be a fairer place, but that does not mean that I need to marry the car mechanic. Of course I want him to live well, not to lack for anything, but..."

"But he goes his way and you go yours, right?"

"Yes, more or less."

"One day social classes will disappear, we will all be equal, nobody will earn more just because of having gone to university, of coming from a bourgeois family, we will make the bourgeoisie disappear, make all our differences disappear."

"You're as bourgeois as I am."

"But I have realized that the existence of social classes is a perversion, and I want to renounce all my privileges, I don't think it's fair that there are people with more opportunities than others, I think it's unfair that we are not all equal."

"I am sorry, Amelia, but I cannot accept your ideas. Of course I think that we should all have the same opportunities, but you know what? All men will never be equal."

"That is how things have been up until now. Stalin has shown that it is possible to have a society in which everyone is equal."

"Well, well, let's not talk about politics. Take me to Javier's room, I want to give him a kiss before I leave."

That night Amelia went to Lola's house, or at least that is what she said, because she would not let me go with her. She assured me that Pierre would meet her on the street corner and that she would not have to walk through the streets alone. She did not come back until dawn was already breaking. I don't know what happened that night, but when she came back she was no longer the same.

She spent the whole morning in a very agitated state, and she got very cross when her mother rang to tell her that she and Antonietta were going to come to lunch to see Javier.

She seemed absent over lunch, and at five o'clock she asked her mother and sister to leave, claiming that she had to go and pay a call. I was surprised when suddenly she hugged them both tightly and could barely fight back her tears.

When Doña Teresa and Antonietta had left, Amelia locked herself in her room for half an hour. Then she left and went to Javier's room. The child was asleep, with Águeda next to him, crocheting.

Amelia took the child in her arms and woke him up, and he started to cry while she whispered, "My child, my dear child, forgive me, my son, forgive me."

Águeda and I observed her without speaking, both of us feeling rather disconcerted.

"Look after Javier, he is my dearest treasure," Amelia said to Águeda.

"Yes, Madam, you know that I love him like my own son."

"Look after him, treat him well."

She left the room and I followed her, knowing that something was going to happen. Amelia went into her room and came out with a suitcase, which she could barely carry.

"Where are you going?" I asked her, trembling, although I knew what the answer would be.

"I am leaving with Pierre."

"Amelia, don't do it!" I started to cry as I begged her.

"Shh! Be quiet, or the whole house will find out. You are a Communist like I am and you can understand the step I am about to take. I'm going where they need me."

"Let me come with you!"

"No, Pierre doesn't want you to come, I have to go alone."

"And what will become of me?"

"My husband is a good man and will let you stay. Come, here's some money which I have set aside for you."

Amelia pushed a bundle of notes into my hand, as I tried not to take it.

"Edurne, don't worry, nothing will happen to you. Santiago will look after you. And you will always be able to rely on my cousin

Laura. Come, I want you to take her this letter. I've told her where I am going and what I am going to do and I'm asking her to take care of you, but don't give it to anyone who isn't her, promise me this."

"And what will I say when you don't come back? They'll ask me..."

"Tell them that I went out to pay a call and that I told you I would be back late."

"But your husband will want to know the truth..."

"Santiago is still on his journey and when he comes back tell him to talk to my cousin Laura, she will explain it all. I've put in the letter that I want Laura to tell the whole family that I have gone forever."

We hugged each other, crying, until Amelia pulled away and, without giving me a chance to say anything, opened the door and left, shutting it quietly behind her.

It would be a long, long time before I saw her again.

Edurne sighed. She was tired. She had spoken without pause for three long hours. I had stayed motionless, caught up in a story that interested me more the more I heard of it.

I was surprised, lots of the things I had heard seemed unbelievable to me. But then again, here was this old woman, her gaze lost in the place where her memories lived, a grimace of sadness over her features.

Yes, Edurne felt sad to remember these days that changed her life, even though she had not told me how her life had changed afterwards.

I realized that I could not force her to speak much more, she was too tired, both physically and emotionally, for me to insist that she clear up some points about her story.

"Would you like me to take you somewhere?" I said, just for the sake of saying something.

"No, there's no need."

"I'd like to help you..."

She locked her tired eyes on me as she shook her head. She wanted me to leave her alone, not to force her to carry on squeezing information out of that part of her memory where the ghosts of her youth lived.

"I will go and tell them that we have finished. You cannot know how grateful I am for everything you have told me. You have been a great help for me. Now I know much more about Amelia, my great-grandmother."

"Really?"

Edurne's question surprised me, but I did not reply, I only managed to smile. She was very old, I realized that she had that bluish pallor that can come before one's final journey, and I began to feel scared.

"I will go and tell the ladies."

"I will come with you."

I helped her get to her feet and waited for her to support herself against the stick that she held in her right hand. I couldn't imagine what Edurne must have been like in the past, but now she was an extremely thin and fragile old woman.

Amelia María Garayoa was with her aunts. She appeared worried, and when we came in she leaped up from the sofa.

"About time, haven't you realized that Edurne is very old? If it had been up to me you wouldn't have been allowed to keep her so long."

"I know, I know..."

"Was the conversation useful?" Doña Laura wanted to know.

"Yes, I am really surprised. I need to think, I need to get everything that Edurne told me in order... I couldn't have imagined that my great-grandmother was a Communist."

They were silent and made me feel awkward, something that had become a habit of theirs.

Amelia María helped Edurne to sit down while Doña Laura looked at me expectantly, and the other old woman, Doña Melita, seemed caught up in her thoughts. Sometimes she seemed not to understand what was going on around her, as if she weren't interested in what she was living through.

I was also tired, but I knew that I should talk with them in order to continue my investigations.

"Well, you said that you would guide my steps. What is the next step to take? Although of course, Doña Laura, I need to talk with you so that you can explain what happened when..."

"No, not now," the old woman said, "it's late. Call me tomorrow and I will tell you how to carry on."

I didn't argue, I knew that it would have been useless, especially since Amelia María was telling me with her look that if I did argue then she would throw me out of the house without any ceremony.

When I got home I wondered if I should call my mother to tell her everything I had found out about my great-grandmother, or if I should not say anything at all until I had the whole story. In the end I decided to go to sleep and leave the decision for the next day. I felt confused; my great-grandmother's story was proving more complicated than I had expected, and I did not know if it would end up as a romance novel or if there were still more surprises to come.

I fell asleep thinking about Amelia Garayoa, and how this mysterious relative of mine had been a temperamental romantic, a woman desperate for experiences who was restricted by the social conventions of her time; she was incautious and obviously had a clear fascination with the abyss.

The next morning I called my mother over my first coffee of the day.

"Great-grandmother's story's a real soap opera!" I said as a greeting.

"So you've already found out what happened..."

"Not everything, no, but a part of it, yes, and she was a very strange woman for those times. She had no respect for anything."

"Tell me..."

"No, I'm not going to tell you anything, I'd rather finish the research and write it up, like Aunt Marta told me to."

"I think it's good that you're not telling anything to Aunt Marta, but I am your mother, and let me remind you that it was me who gave you your first clue, telling you to talk to Father Antonio."

"I know that you're my mother, and I know you so well that I am sure you won't be able to resist the temptation to tell your brothers and sisters everything, so I'm not going to tell you anything."

"So you don't trust me!"

"Of course I trust you, you're the only person I trust, but only for important things; this is not important, so I prefer not to say anything, at least not now, but I promise you will be the first to know the whole story."

We argued a little, but she didn't have any other option than to accept my decision. Then I called Aunt Marta, more than anything so as to tell her that I wasn't spending her money without doing any work.

"I want you to come to the office and tell me how things are going."

"I'm not going to tell you anything until I give you the written document you asked me for. I've told you that I've found traces of my great-grandmother, your grandmother, and that the family will find out what happened, but I need to work according to my own rhythm, with no pressure."

"I'm not pressuring you, I'm paying you to research this story and to tell me how you are spending my money."

"I assure you that I haven't wasted any of your money, and I'll even give you the receipts for the taxis I've taken; but for the time being, however you react, I am not going to tell you anything. I'm starting my research and all I wanted to do was to tell you that it has already had some results; I am on the trail of Amelia Garayoa. I don't think it will take too long to finish things up, and then I will write the story and give it to you."

I did not tell my aunt that I had met her grandmother's cousins, and that I had come to an arrangement with them: their help in exchange for reading my manuscript and approving of it before I handed it over to my family. I would deal with this problem when I came to it.

I had also promised that my mother would be the first to know the whole story of our relative, so when the time came I would have to decide who would be the first to find out; until then, what I needed was to be left in peace.

Aunt Marta accepted reluctantly. Then I called my mother again, because I was sure that my aunt would call her with a list of complaints about me.

PIERRE

1

Over the next few days I tried to get everything that Edurne had told me down on paper in a orderly fashion. I was waiting for the old Garayoa women to call me, because I couldn't really continue my research without their help.

It occurred to me that I should try to find Lola, but she would be dead by now; as for Pierre, he was a figure who really intrigued me. "He's a sly dog!" I thought. "You've got to be pretty sneaky to steal someone's wife in the name of the revolution."

It was unlikely that Pierre was still alive, unless he was more than a hundred years old, something that was pretty near impossible. Edurne had told me that when he first met Amelia he was several years older than her. She was eighteen and he was over thirty; so the chances of Pierre being alive were practically zero.

When Amelia María Garayoa called me I breathed a sigh of relief; the truth was that I had started to worry if the old women hadn't regretted their offer and had decided to block any continuation of my research.

"My aunt wants to see you," she blurted out as a greeting.

"Which aunt?"

"My Aunt Laura."

"And your Aunt Melita?"

"She's got a bad cold and doesn't feel well."

"Just one question: Are Doña Amelia and Doña Laura sisters? It's just that I read in my grandmother's diary, and Edurne told me as well, that Amelia's best friend was her cousin Laura. I'm just a little confused," I said, trying to be friendly.

"Maybe all this is too much for you," she replied, emphasizing once again what little confidence she had in me.

"I think that the existence of so many Amelias would surprise anyone," I said in my defense.

"Not really. One of my aunts' great-grandmothers was called Amelia, she was a woman who was very beautiful and who was loved by the whole family; they loved her so much that her grandchildren decided to call their daughters Amelia if they had any. And that's what Juan and Armando Garayoa did, call their firstborn daughters Amelia."

"You see, it is confusing!"

"Maybe for you, but in our families things are pretty clear."

"As far as I am aware I also have something to do with your family..."

"That's a may be."

"But I showed you my grandfather Javier's baptismal certificate!"

"Look, I have my doubts about you; and anyway, even if you are Amelia Garayoa's son's grandson, why would you suddenly show up with this stupid story about having to write a book about your great-grandmother?"

"I didn't say I'm going to write a book, just that I'm writing an account, which my Aunt Marta will wrap up and give to my family as a Christmas present."

"How moving," Amelia Garayoa said in an ironic tone that I found very annoying.

"Listen, I understand that you're reluctant, but I have been open with you right from the start and in any case, we're family."

"No. You're wrong there. You and I have nothing in common, for all that you try to look for connections. You don't think that suddenly the Garayoas and the Carranzas are going to get back together as if this were a trashy romantic novel?"

"No, you're right, my great-grandmother's story does have a bit of a whiff of the romantic novel about it... But no, I'm not going to suggest that we spend Christmas together."

"Don't even think about getting the two families together."

"I have no intention of doing that, I've got enough to cope with with my own family, without adding another one that's got you in it."

"How rude you are!"

"No, I just want to say that I agree that the past should remain in the past."

"Let's stop this useless conversation. My aunt will be waiting for you at midday tomorrow. Be on time."

Amelia Garayoa hung up without saying goodbye. She really didn't like me.

The next day I arrived on time, with a bunch of red roses. The housekeeper led me through to the library where Doña Laura was waiting for me.

She was sitting down, with a book open on her knees.

"So you're here... Sit down," she ordered, as she pointed to an armchair next to hers.

"How is your sister?" I asked as I offered her the flowers. "I brought these flowers..."

"My sister?" she said in a slightly confused voice.

"Amelia María told me yesterday that Doña Melita had a cold..."

"Oh yes! Of course, she has a cold, but she's better, she hasn't had a temperature since yesterday. We're both very old, you know? And everything affects us... and there's been a lot of flu this year. But she's better. I'll tell her you asked after her."

She waved to the housekeeper to get her to take the flowers, and asked her to bring coffee for the two of us.

"So, what do you think about Edurne's story?" she asked me without preambles.

"Your cousin seems like a fairly flighty young woman, who was keen on becoming some kind of heroine," I summed up.

"Yes, there was a bit of that about her, but it's not everything. My cousin Amelia was always a clever, anxious woman, but born in the wrong century; if she'd been born today, she would have become a well-known woman, she would have been able to display all her talents to their best advantage, but in those days..."

"But running away with Pierre out of the belief that she should sacrifice herself for the revolution... It just seems a fairly childish excuse to me. She went with him because she fell in love, and she would have gone whatever, revolution or no revolution," I concluded, in the face of Doña Laura's shocked expression.

"Young man, it seems to me that you have understood nothing. You seem fairly keen to judge Amelia. Maybe you don't understand... or else you're not the right person to write her story..."

It was clear that I had put my foot in it. Who asked me to blurt out my opinion of my great-grandmother, just like that? I tried to sort out things as best as I could.

"Don't get me wrong! Sometimes journalists are just impulsive like this, we say things straight out, but I assure you that when the time comes to write the story I will be calm and kind, after all, she was my great-grandmother."

I was afraid that she would ask me to leave, but she said nothing. She waited for the housekeeper, who had just come in, to serve the coffee.

"Well, you said you had a few questions to ask us. What else would you like to know?"

"Really, it's you who should tell me which threads I need to tug. I can see that it will be very difficult to get to my great-grandmother's story without your help. I would also like you to tell me what happened when Santiago my great-grandfather got home."

"Don't feel sorry for him. Santiago was a rough-hewn man who suffered, yes, from losing Amelia, but who knew how to control himself with great dignity."

"Well, I would like to know about this, because you were Amelia's closest family."

"Alright, I'll tell you something, but don't take it for granted that it will be us who give you information; that's not the agreement we made. Also, there are things that we couldn't tell you even if we wanted to because we don't know them. But we do know, as you say, which threads you need to tug. I have a couple more interviews arranged for you."

I settled myself in my chair, ready to listen to Doña Laura, who had fallen silent, as if she were trying to find the right place to begin...

The day after Amelia's flight, Edurne brought me the letter my cousin had written. It was a Sunday at the end of March 1936 and we were all at home. I have it here to show you. Amelia wrote that she had fallen in love with Pierre, that she could not bear the idea of his leaving and her not seeing him again, that she would rather die than lose him. She also begged me to explain to her parents and to Santiago her disappearance; she insisted that the true cause was not Pierre, but his revolutionary ideas. She begged everyone's pardon and asked me to do all that I could to make sure that her son did not hate her; she also said that she would come back one day to find Javier. And she asked me to look after Edurne, because she was afraid that Santiago might dismiss her.

You can imagine how worried I was when I read this letter. I felt abandoned, lost, even betrayed, because Amelia was my best friend as well as my cousin. We had shared everything, even our most trivial confidences, and were closer to each other than we were to our sisters.

Edurne was terrified. She thought, and not without reason, that she might end up unemployed, that she would have to return to the farm. She sobbed and begged me to help her. I felt overwhelmed by the situation, because I was just eighteen, and in those days, you can imagine how little we knew about the world, and my cousin had fled, leaving me with a responsibility I was not prepared for. The first thing I did was to try to calm Edurne and to promise that nothing would happen to her, and I told her to go back to Amelia's house, and if anyone asked for Amelia she was to say that she did not know where she had gone. Then I went to see my mother, who was in the kitchen giving instructions to the cook: We were to have guests that night.

"I need to speak with you."

"Can't it wait? Don't imagine it's easy organizing a meal for twelve guests."

"Mama, it's very urgent, I need to speak with you," I insisted.

"How impatient you young people are! Grown-ups have to drop everything to attend to your whims. Alright, go to the small salon, and I will come straight away."

Even so, my mother took her time in coming to find me; by the time she did come, I had bitten all my nails.

"What is it, Laura? I hope it's not another of your sillinesses."

"Mama, Amelia has gone."

"Your sister? Of course she's gone, she went to see her friend Elise."

"No, not my sister Melita; my cousin."

"If you haven't found her at home she must have gone to her parents' house or maybe to see that Lola..."

"She's gone for good."

My mother fell silent, trying to process what she had just heard.

"But what are you saying? What ridiculous story is this? I know that she's cross with Santiago because of his last trip... The truth is that Santiago should be more considerate and not just go off without telling anyone... but Amelia knows what her husband is like..."

"Mama, Amelia has left Santiago."

"But what are you saying? Stop being ridiculous!"

My mother had flushed red. It was difficult for her to take in what she was hearing.

"She has gone because... because she believes in the revolution, and she is going to sacrifice herself for a better world."

"Good Lord! I cannot believe that Lola has brainwashed your poor cousin to such an extent! Look, tell me where she is, I'll call your father, we have to go and find her immediately... I suppose she will have gone to see that Lola."

"She has gone to France."

"To France? What? Tell me what has happened, how can you say that Amelia has gone to France?"

My father came into the room, alerted by my mother's cries. He was startled to see her walking from side to side and gesticulating wildly.

"But what's going on here? Elena, what's happening? Are you unwell? Wait; I hope you haven't upset your mother, Laura, especially not tonight. We have guests!"

"Papa, Amelia has gone to France. She has left Santiago and her family, even though she says that one day she will come back for Javier."

I told him everything, without beating around the bush.

My father was silent, and looked at me fixedly, as if he did not understand what he was hearing. My mother had broken into inconsolable tears.

In fits and starts I told them the story of Amelia's flight, trying not to betray her, never mentioning Pierre.

My father could not believe that his niece, flighty as she might be, had gone to France to pursue the cause of revolution.

"But which revolution?" my father insisted.

"You know, *the* revolution. You know that the Communists want to promote the revolution all over the world... ," I replied without very much conviction.

My father asked me questions for more than an hour without letting up, while my mother talked and talked about Lola's influence.

"We must call Juan and Teresa. How upset they will be! And you, Laura, show me that letter Amelia wrote you," my father ordered.

I lied to them. I swore that, in the heat of the moment, I had torn it to pieces. I could not give it to them, because in it Amelia told the truth, which was that she had fallen in love with Pierre.

"I don't believe you!" my father said, insisting that I give him the letter.

"I swear that I tore it to pieces without thinking," I protested, in tears.

Uncle Juan and Aunt Teresa arrived at my house barely half an hour later. My father had insisted that it was urgent that they come. It was a great torment for him to have to tell his brother that their daughter had run away.

My father asked me to tell them everything I knew, and I told them what I could, crying all the while.

Aunt Teresa fainted and my mother had to look after her, which allowed my father, Uncle Juan, and me to hide ourselves away in my father's study, where both of them told me to tell them all I knew.

I did not allow them to twist my arm, and I insisted that the revolution was the prime cause of my cousin Amelia's flight.

"Alright," Uncle Juan agreed, "in that case we will go to the house of this Lola, who has been the cause of Amelia's getting all these extremist ideas into her head. She will know where she is, and I don't think that Amelia will have had time to get to France; in any case, she will have to tell us where to find her. But first we will go to Amelia's house and make sure that the servants don't find out what is happening. I hope that Edurne has kept her mouth shut."

While my mother looked after Aunt Teresa, I went to Amelia's house with my father and my uncle. But this was not our lucky day, and when we got to Amelia's house we found that Santiago had made a surprise return that morning.

Santiago was speaking with Edurne, or rather, Santiago was speaking and Edurne was crying.

She was surprised to see us, and I started to shake. To stand up in front of my uncle and aunt and my parents was one thing, but to stand up to Santiago...

Uncle Juan was just as nervous. It was not going to be easy for him to tell Santiago that his wife had run away.

"What happened?" Santiago asked icily.

"Can we speak in private?" Uncle Juan asked.

"Of course. Come with me to my office, and you, Edurne... We'll speak later."

We followed him to his office, with me praying under my breath, asking God to perform a miracle and make Amelia suddenly appear. But that day God did not listen to me.

Santiago asked us to sit down, but Uncle Juan was so nervous that he stayed standing.

"I am so sorry for what I am going to tell you... I am distraught... and I am sure I don't understand it, but..."

"Don Juan, the sooner you tell me why you have come, the better," Santiago cut him off.

"Yes... of course... I'm sorry for what's happened... but I have to tell you that Amelia has run away."

I grasped my father's hand as if to take shelter, because there was boundless rage on Santiago's face.

"She's run away? Where? Why?" Santiago tried to control himself, but it was clear that he was about to explode.

"We don't know... Well, we do... Apparently she has gone to France."

"To France? What madness is this?" Santiago's voice was raised.

"Amelia wrote to Laura to explain herself," my father managed to say.

"Ah, is that so? Well, let us read this letter." He looked straight at me and held out his hand for Amelia's missive.

"I don't have it," I muttered. "I tore it up in shock..."

"Right! You think I'll believe that?"

"It's the truth!" I realized that in spite of my insistence Santiago did not believe me.

The truth is that I have always been a bad liar.

"And what has Amelia asked you to tell us?" Santiago was still making an effort to control himself.

"She has gone to France to help the revolution, they are better prepared there to spread the Soviet Revolution."

I said all this in a rush, I had learned my lesson.

"Laura, who did Amelia go with?" Santiago's tone was harsh and cutting.

I bit my lip until I drew blood, and tears came to my eyes.

"Answer him, daughter," my father asked me.

"I don't know..."

"Yes, yes, you know. You and Edurne know exactly what's happening, when and with whom she left," Santiago insisted.

Don Juan and my father looked at each other in shock, while Santiago stared at me so fiercely that I hung my head in shame.

"Laura, you are not helping Amelia by hiding the truth from us. Your cousin, acting on very bad advice, has made a mistake, but if you tell us anything then maybe there is still time to fix it," my father insisted.

"She's gone to join in the revolution... ," I repeated, almost sobbing.

"Don't talk nonsense!" Santiago interrupted me. "Do you take us for idiots? It was my fault for allowing Amelia to go to those Socialist Youth meetings with Lola. And it was my fault for thinking it funny that Edurne should take her militant beliefs so seriously. Amelia, a revolutionary? Yes, a revolutionary who travels with a maid, because a young lady shouldn't even have to make her own bed."

"Amelia has not taken Edurne with her," I protested, finding some degree of courage somewhere.

"No, she didn't go with her because she wasn't allowed to. Edurne has told me that she wanted to go with her mistress, but Amelia said that she was not allowed to travel with anyone. Well, you've come to tell me what I already knew, that Amelia has run away. When I got home this morning I asked for my wife and nobody knew what to say to me, and Edurne burst into tears. She's only managed to give me the same ridiculous story as you, Laura, that Amelia has gone to France to join the revolution."

Santiago suddenly appeared tired, as if all the anger that he was holding within himself had turned into resignation.

"Santiago, we're with you, ready to help however we can, but we'd like you to forgive my niece, she's just a little girl without any bad intentions." My father's words seemed to stir up Santiago's anger again.

"Help me? How would you help me? Don't fool yourself, Don Armando. If Amelia has gone, then she has gone... with another man."

"Impossible!" Uncle Juan stood offended in front of his son-in-law. "I will not allow this lack of respect toward my daughter. Amelia is a child, yes, she's made a mistake, but to go off with another man? Never! I don't want to blame you for anything, but your disappearing acts have not been the best way to have a well-cared-for marriage."

Santiago clenched his fists. I believe that if it had not been for his excellent manners, and above all because he was a man who knew how to control himself, he would have punched Uncle Juan.

"I want to think that it is only a grand passion that could cause Amelia to abandon her son and me. Abandon Javier for the revolution? No, you don't know Amelia. It may be true that she has never behaved like a caring mother with Javier, but I know that she loves him; as far as I am concerned... I believe that she loves me too."

"We had thought about going to Lola's house," my father said. "I hope you will come with us."

"No, no, Don Armando, I will not go with you. I will not go looking for her. If she has left, then she will know why and she will have to face the consequences."

"But she is your wife!" Uncle Juan protested.

"A wife who has abandoned me."

"But you have just returned from a journey, on which you left without saying goodbye!"

Santiago shrugged his shoulders. It was entirely natural for him to come and go without explaining himself, as if it were a prerogative that he did not have to excuse.

"We would like you to come with us to Lola's house," my father insisted.

"I have already said no, Don Armando. And you, Laura..."

He said nothing more, but he made me feel like a wicked woman.

We felt terrible as we left Santiago's house. We had not been able to speak to Edurne, and I was glad, because I do not know if we would have been able to keep our story straight had we both been interrogated at the same time.

I showed them where Lola's house was. We walked quickly to Calle Toledo until we reached the apartment that Lola shared with Josep and where she lived with her son Pablo.

Lola lived in an attic that we reached via a dark staircase. I had been in this house only once before, accompanying my cousin. I did not like Lola much, and she did not like me, so we were cold toward each other, something that upset Amelia. She would have liked us to be friends, and especially for me to have accompanied her on her adventures with Lola.

The doorbell did not work, so Uncle Juan beat on the door. Pablo opened it. The child had a cold, and it also looked like he had a temperature.

"What do you want?"

"Pablo, we're looking for Amelia," I managed to say before my uncle or my father could speak.

"But Amelia has gone off with Pierre, they left last night on the train," he replied.

Uncle Juan turned pale when he heard what the child said.

"May we come in?" he asked, pushing the child to one side and walking in.

Pablo shrugged and looked at me in bewilderment.

"My mother's not here, neither is Josep."

"Who is Josep?" Uncle Juan asked.

"My father."

"And you call him Josep?" My uncle's question did not seem to surprise the child.

"Yes, we all call him Josep, and sometimes I call him Dad, depending on how I feel."

By this point in the conversation we were in the little room that was a living room and also on occasion Pablo's bedroom. The attic only had two rooms: The one we were in, and the other, even smaller, where Lola and Pablo slept when Josep was not there. There was also a tiny kitchen that let onto a small interior patio. There was no bathroom; just like the rest of the residents, they had to use a small water-closet on the landing.

Uncle Juan looked around for a chair to sit on. My father and I remained standing, while Pablo sat in the other chair and waited for us to say what it was we wanted.

"Well, tell us exactly where Amelia is," my uncle ordered.

"I've told you, in France with Pierre."

"And who is Pierre?" my uncle insisted.

"Amelia's fiancé... Well, I don't know if he's her fiancé, because Amelia's married, but if he's not then he's something similar. They love each other and Amelia is going to help him."

Uncle Juan started to sweat, while my father, shocked by what Pablo was saying, decided to sit down.

"Pablo, don't say such things... Amelia and Pierre are just friends... Amelia is going to help him with the revolution," I said, staring in anguish at Pablo, trying to tell him with my eyes that he shouldn't say anything else.

"Shut up!" My father's words and tone of voice stopped me dead. "You, child," he added, "tell us everything you know."

Pablo seemed to get scared all of a sudden, and realized he had said more than he should have.

"I don't know anything!" he said, terrified.

"Of course you do! And you are going to tell us." My father

had got to his feet and stood in front of the child, who looked at him in fear.

"The sooner you tell us, the sooner we will leave," Uncle Juan pushed.

"But I don't know anything! Laura, tell them to leave me alone!"

I looked down in shame. I could say or do nothing, neither my father nor my uncle would allow me to interrupt and stop the child from talking.

"My mother says that I am not a slave, that I don't have to humiliate myself in front of the damn capitalists," Pablo said, trying to pluck up his courage.

"If you don't tell us what you know, then we will take you down to the police station, the police will look for your mother, and then who knows what might happen," my father threatened.

Pablo, whose eyes were shining ever brighter from fear and from his illness, started to whimper.

"My mother is a revolutionary, and the Fascists are not in charge here." This was Pablo's last attempt.

"Well, let's go down to the police station; as far as I know, your mother might have some unfinished business with the police, and however revolutionary she may be, the law is the law for everyone," my father said.

Pablo looked again for me and for help, but I couldn't say anything to him, even though I prayed that Pablo would not give any clues that might stop Amelia's escape.

"Amelia came to the house last night, Pierre was waiting for her. They said that they were going to catch the train, to go to Barcelona and then to France."

"To Barcelona?" asked Uncle Juan.

"Pierre has to see some of my father's friends," Pablo managed to say.

"Where does your father live?" Uncle Juan wanted to know.

"In one of the streets in the new district."

"What is your father's name?" my uncle insisted.

"Soler."

"Tell me, who is Pierre?" My father was speaking calmly now, trying to calm Pablo.

"He is a friend of my parents, a revolutionary from Paris. He works to take the revolution across the world, and he is helping us."

"Is he Amelia's fiancé?" My father asked this question without looking either at Uncle Juan or at me.

"Yes," Pablo whispered. "When Amelia arrived yesterday they kissed each other. She cried a lot, but he promised that she would never regret going with him. Pierre was kissing her the whole time, and she was kissing him. They kissed like my parents kiss each other, and Amelia said that she would follow him to the death."

I started to cough. It was a nervous cough, the only thing I wanted was for Pablo to stop talking, not to say a single word more, for my father and my poor Uncle Juan not to carry on hearing these things.

Uncle Juan was pale and so stiff that he looked like a corpse. He was listening to Pablo with his eyes wide open, and there was not only suffering in them, but shame and stupor as well. How could he imagine Amelia kissing a man who was not her husband? Was it possible that she had promised herself to another man until death? It was as if what he was hearing were impossible, that it was a tale told of a stranger, not his own daughter. It was as if he suddenly realized that he did not know her, that the woman they were talking about had nothing to do with his first-born daughter, the light of his life.

My father approached my uncle and suggested that we leave. Uncle Juan got heavily to his feet. He was like an automaton. My father took him by the arm, leading him to the door. They left without saying goodbye to Pablo.

"I'm going to Barcelona tomorrow," the child said to me in farewell.

"To Barcelona? And will you see Amelia?" I asked in a low voice.

"I don't know, but my mother says that we are going to live with my father. She is very happy. I am sad to leave Madrid, even though we have no one to keep us here. Well, there's my grandmother, but my mother doesn't get along with her."

"If you see Amelia, tell her... tell her... tell her to be very happy and that I love her a lot."

Pablo nodded without saying anything, and I left hurriedly, to catch up with my father and Uncle Juan.

When we got back home, my Aunt Teresa was still crying. My mother had given her two cups of tilleul and a glass of mineral water, but they had had no effect on her. My mother had called for my cousin Antonietta, who was sitting in the room, very serious and silent.

"Did you find her?" my mother asked impatiently.

My father told her without offering many details that we had been with Santiago and later to Lola's house, and that apparently Amelia had gone to Barcelona, although her final destination was France.

When she heard our account of the last few hours, Aunt Teresa cried all the more, and all she could do was ask for them to bring her daughter back.

We did not know what to say or what to do; it was the longest day of my life.

In mid-afternoon my father, Melita, and I took my uncle and aunt and cousin back to their house. We were in mourning, but my mother had decided that it would be impossible to cancel that evening's dinner, because there was a married couple among the guests who were bringing their two sons, one of whom was going out with my sister Melita, and we knew that this was the night when he would officially ask for her hand.

I would have been happy to stay with my uncle and aunt, but they preferred to be alone.

The dinner was a nightmare. My father was distracted, my mother was nervous, and my sister was upset by what had happened and scarcely paid any attention to her beloved. Although it is true that the young man was not upset by the unusual atmosphere and, with his father's support, asked my father for permission to woo my sister. My father gave it without any show of enthusiasm. Years later we told Rodrigo what had happened that day.

Although it is not relevant, I will just say that Rodrigo did marry my sister Melita, shortly after the outbreak of the Civil War.

The next morning Edurne came to my house with her suitcase. Santiago had given her a generous sum of money to go back to the farm with her mother and her grandparents.

"I cannot go back, Doña Laura; my mother will kill me if she finds out that Santiago fired me."

"But what happened wasn't your fault; your mother will understand," I said uncertainly.

"They need my wages back at home, the farm doesn't give them enough to live off, and my mother is putting together my trousseau in case I get married one day."

"The trousseau can wait," my mother interrupted, "and you can always work on the farm. And your brother Aitor has a good position with the PNV; my sister-in-law Teresa tells me that they think a lot of him."

"But Doña Elena, you don't know my mother! You don't know how cross she's going to be. She asked me to behave like she always had with the Garayoas, and look at what I've done."

Edurne cried disconsolately and grasped my hand, begging me not to abandon her. I debated doing what my cousin Amelia had asked, that I look after Edurne, and thought about the weight of responsibility that would entail. My loyalty to my cousin won.

"Mama, may I speak with you alone for a moment?"

My mother looked at me suspiciously; she knew me well and knew what I was going to ask for, and so pretended naïveté.

"I don't know, Laura, we can't lose any more time, so much has come up..."

"Just a moment!" I begged.

We left the room and went into my bedroom. My mother's mood had gone very black.

"Laura, you have to be sensible," she began, but I interrupted her.

"What's your problem with me? How have I disappointed you?"

"No problem, nothing, my darling, but you must understand that we cannot take on Edurne, and that is what you are going to ask me."

"But Mama, she cannot go back to the farm! You know that Amaya had a temper..."

"Amaya was always a loyal servant. I wish Edurne had been like her mother, then she wouldn't have got into problems, and wouldn't have filled her head with chaff about the revolution."

"I'm begging you, talk to Papa!"

"We are not rich, we cannot take on another mouth to feed. Haven't you realized what the situation is? Politics is tearing everything apart: There are strikes, disorder, some madmen are even attacking convents; I don't know what's going to happen... Your father is a saint, he supports Don Manuel Azaña just like his brother Juan, but I don't think that Azaña will sort out the situation..."

"I don't care about politics! What I want to do is help Edurne! And don't tell me that we can't make room for her at home. She can sleep in your maid's room, Remedios won't mind, it will be good for her to have someone to help her."

"No! No, I don't want a Communist for a maid, I don't want troubles in my house. It's enough what happened to your cousin Amelia."

My father knocked gently on the door. He had heard my mother's raised voice.

"I'm going to my office, I will be back for lunch. But what's wrong?"

"Your daughter wants us to take Edurne in; Santiago has dismissed her."

"Oh Papa, please!"

"Look, what we can do is speak to your uncle and aunt, I will go to speak with Teresa myself and explain the situation. It should be they who take care of Edurne. Edurne is Amaya's daughter, after all, and Amaya worked for them for many years. They'll know what to do."

My mother was stubborn as a mule.

"I don't think that's a good idea," my father said, to both my mother's surprise and mine.

"Why not? Tell me, Armando, why not? Edurne is not our problem."

"Amelia is my niece, and what she has done has consequences for us, and we can't just wash our hands. Look, Elena, it would be difficult for my brother and Teresa to have to take in Edurne. Of course they would do it out of a sense of responsibility, but her presence would be a permanent reminder of the situation they have been presented with. No, I don't want to cause my brother and sister-in-law any more pain, and Laura is right, we cannot abandon this silly little girl."

"She's a Communist," my mother replied, and she spat out the word.

"Do you really think that Edurne knows what Communism is? And even if she does, why shouldn't she be one? What has her life given her that she should be anything else?"

"She should be grateful to your family for everything they have done for her. They've treated her like she was one of them, they've done the same for her mother..."

"Thankful? No, Elena, the world's not like that. They've treated her like a human being, and no one should be thankful for being treated like what one is. Edurne has done her job well, just like Amaya did; they don't owe us anything."

"How can you say that! Sometimes I think you're a Communist as well!"

"Come on, Elena! Don't get Communism mixed up with justice. That's what hurts this country so badly, that's why the things that are happening are happening. People have been kept in a state of slavery, and lots of you are terrified because they are finally reclaiming what is their own."

"And that's why they need to burn down churches? Does that justify the peasants occupying farms? It's not their property!"

"Look, let's not argue, I have to go to the office, and I want to go and see my brother Juan. What's happening with Amelia is a tragedy for them, and we have to give them a hand."

My father's firm tone vanquished my mother.

"What do you want us to do?"

"For the time being, let Edurne stay, at least provisionally. Put her wherever's convenient for you and give her something to do."

"I don't want my daughters to be contaminated by her ideas..."

"Elena, don't argue, and do what I tell you," my father interrupted. "And you, Laura, I hope that you will be sensible. I know how close you were to your cousin, but you must see that she has behaved very, very badly toward everyone: toward her husband, toward her son, and also toward you. I don't want you to go anywhere with Edurne without your mother's express permission. There have been enough disappointments with politics in this family."

"I promise, Papa, you will have nothing to complain about."

"I hope so, and your sister Melita is more sensible. She has the same name as her cousin Amelia, but perhaps the extra María, Amelia María, makes her different."

"What do you mean, what do names have to do with behavior?" my mother said.

The result of my parents' argument was Edurne moving into our house, and her stay, although it was provisional to begin with, quickly became permanent. Edurne has been with me ever since.

Doña Laura sighed. Her memories seemed to worry her, and she passed her hand over her forehead as if trying to shoo them away.

"Maybe you can find out from your family what happened to Santiago after that point. After all, he is your great-grandfather. Santiago broke off all ties with the Garayoas."

"He never saw them again?" I asked in confusion.

"He didn't want to know anything about us. I imagine that seeing us would have been a permanent reminder of Amelia's abandonment. He never allowed us to visit Javier, none of us, not even my aunt and uncle, who were the child's grandparents."

"That's tough. And Don Juan and Doña Teresa accepted it?"

"What could they do? They felt ashamed, and they blamed themselves for Amelia's behavior. They didn't want to contribute to Santiago's suffering, and in fact they did not dare impose themselves. Santiago cut off all business ties with my Uncle Juan, and this was a terrible blow for him. My aunt and uncle had been almost ruined when their business in Germany was closed, so losing the support of the Carranzas was a blow from which Uncle Juan never recovered. After this came the war and everything got worse. They were tough times for everyone... Anyway, I have another meeting arranged for you, so that you can continue your investigation."

"Right. With whom?" I asked, without hiding my interest.

"With Pablo Soler."

"Lola's son?"

"Yes, Lola's son. But you're a journalist, you'll know who Pablo Soler is."

"Me? Never heard of him. Why should I know?"

"Because he's a historian, he's written several books about the Civil War, and he has been in several debates on television over the last few years, as well as writing articles for newspapers."

"Yes, the name does ring a bell, but I've really never had much interest in the ins and outs of the Civil War. So many books have been published, so many arguments... It was an atrocity, and I really try to steer clear of atrocities."

"That's a stupid attitude."

"Goodness, Doña Laura! You don't mince your words."

"Do you feel better not knowing your history? Do you think it never happened just because you don't know about it?"

"At least I can stay on the margins."

"That's an incomprehensible attitude for a journalist."

"I've never said I was a good journalist," I defended myself.

"Let's leave it at that. Here you are, here is Pablo Soler's phone number; I've spoken to him and he's willing to see you. You will have to go to Barcelona."

"I'll call him straight away, and go as soon as he's willing to see me."

"Alright, then there's nothing more to say for the time being."

Doña Laura got up with difficulty. I thought that she was getting older by the day, but I did not dare offer to help her stand up. I knew that she would reject my help. I realized that in spite of their advanced age, the Garayoa women liked to feel independent, autonomous.

2

When I got home I started to write down everything Doña Laura had told me. It was all fresh in my memory and I did not want to forget a single detail.

Laboring with a good bottle of whisky at my side, I was still writing as dawn began to break. It was fairly light out when I got into bed, and I slept like a baby until the music of my mobile phone, which I had left on my bedside table, pulled me back to reality.

"Hello, how are you?"

"Mom, couldn't you call me some other time?"

"But it's two o'clock. You weren't asleep?"

"Yes, I was, I worked late. They told me a lot of things about great-grandmother yesterday and I didn't want to forget any of them."

"That's what I wanted to talk to you about. Look, Guillermo, I'm worried about you. I think you're taking Aunt Marta's job too seriously, and you're letting the professional side of things slip. I know that your aunt's paying you generously; it's alright to write about great-grandmother for fun, but I don't want you to get sidetracked and stop looking for real work."

My head felt like it was stuffed with cotton wool, but I knew that nothing would stop my mother from delivering a sermon, so I decided in advance to give in.

"I'd love to get a good job. Do you think I'm not looking everywhere for one? But there's no job's going, Mom. The right doesn't trust me because they think I'm a red, the left doesn't trust me either because I don't support them uncritically, so I don't have many options."

"Come on, Guillermo, it can't be as bad as all that. You're a good journalist, you've got perfect English and French, and your German's quite good as well, it's impossible that they're not offering jobs to a gem like you."

"Mama, I might be a gem for you, but they don't look at it like that."

"But the news agencies don't belong to the politicians."

"No, but it's as if they do; some support one side, others support the other. Don't you listen to the radio? Don't you watch TV?"

"Guillermo, stop being stubborn and listen to me!"

"I am listening to you! I know that it's tough for you to understand how bad the journalism business is, but trust me, that's how it is."

"Promise me you'll carry on looking for a job."

"I promise."

"Good. When are you coming to see me?"

"I don't know, let me get up and get sorted, and then I'll call you, okay?"

Once I'd got through the conversation with my mother, I got into the shower to wake myself up. My temples were throbbing, and I felt a knot in my stomach. The whisky had done its work.

I looked into the fridge and found a carton of juice and a yogurt. It was enough to give me a bit of energy back before I called Pablo Soler. Of course, I went online to look up things about him, and found to my surprise that Professor Soler was a reputable historian, who had taught at Princeton and who had come back, laden with honors, in '82. He had published more than twenty books and was considered an authority on the Civil War.

I looked for the phone number that Doña Laura had given me.

"Don Pablo Soler?"

"Speaking."

"Don Pablo, my name is Guillermo Albi Carranza. Doña Laura Garayoa gave me this number, I think she's spoken to you about the research I'm doing."

"That's right."

The man didn't seem very talkative, so I carried on speaking.

"If it's no trouble, I would like to meet you to clear up some things about Amelia Garayoa, I don't know if Doña Laura told you, but she was my great-grandmother."

"She told me, yes."

"Right, well, when can I come and see you?"

"Tomorrow at eight sharp."

"Eight p.m.?"

"No, eight a.m."

"Ah! Well... alright... If you give me your address I'll be there."

I cursed my luck. I would have liked to have gotten over the lack of sleep and the whisky, but there was nothing to do except put a couple of items in a bag and to go to the airport to get the next flight to Barcelona. A good thing that Aunt Marta wasn't scrimping on the extras, because I would have to sleep there, and in the state I was in, nothing less than a four-star hotel would do.

Pablo Soler was a tall old man, thin, very upright for his age, which was over eighty, although he was still surprisingly agile. He himself opened the door to his top-floor apartment in a residential area of Barcelona.

"Some Communist!" I thought as I went into the large and elegantly decorated apartment. I recognized a Mompó, two drawings by Alberti, a Miró... Anyway, doing the place up must have cost a mint.

"Are you interested in painting?" he asked me, seeing my eyes returning to the pictures.

"Yes. I trained as a journalist, but I was wondering about whether to study fine arts."

"And why didn't you?"

"I didn't want to starve. I know I don't have the talent to produce a great work, although journalism isn't going so well for me either at the moment."

Pablo Soler led me to his office, which was lined from floor to ceiling with bookshelves. A portrait occupied the only free space on the walls. My attention was drawn to it; it was a portrait of a young black woman.

"My wife," he said.

"Ah!" was what I came up with.

"Well, let's get started. Speak."

"Doña Laura has told you..."

"Yes, yes," he interrupted, "I know, you're trying to find out about Amelia's life."

"Yes, that's the idea. She was my great-grandmother, but my family doesn't know anything about her, she has always been a forbidden topic. Look, I've brought a copy of an old photograph with me. Do you recognize her?"

Pablo Soler looked slowly at the picture.

"She was a very beautiful woman," he murmured.

He picked up a little bell and rang it. A Filipina maid, perfectly dressed, came in at once. I had taken him for a revolutionary, and was surprised. He asked her to bring us coffee, which I was grateful for: Eight a.m. is not my best moment of the day.

"Where would you like us to begin?" he asked without further ado.

"I thought I'd ask you if you saw Amelia here, in Barcelona, when she ran away with Pierre. From what Doña Laura told me, it was at exactly that time that your mother brought you to live here. And, well, if you could tell me who Pierre really was..."

"Pierre Comte was an agent of the INO."

"What's that?" I had never heard that acronym.

"The Foreign Department, a branch of the NKVD, which itself evolved from the Cheka, which Felix Dzerzhinsky founded in 1917. Do you know what I'm talking about?"

Pablo Soler looked at me curiously, as his revelation had left me gobsmacked. I had just discovered that my great-grandmother had run off, lightly, just like that, with a Soviet agent.

"I know who Dzerzhinsky was, a Pole who was in charge of Lenin's security service, and who ended up founding the Cheka, which was a police force designed to root out counterrevolutionaries."

"Well, if you want to put it like that... The Cheka went on getting stronger and taking on more responsibilities, and it turned into the GPU, the State Police Directorate, and then the OGPU, the Unified State Police Directorate. And then it was incorporated into the NKVD in 1934. But the KGB will be a more familiar name for you, which is what the force was called after '54. The NKVD was organized like a ministry, everything depended on it: The political police, the border guards, the external spy service, the gulags, and the INO were inside the NKVD, a shadow army that acted all over the world. Their agents were formidable."

"And my great-grandmother got mixed up in all this?"

"When Amelia ran off with Pierre, she had no idea that this was what he did. Neither Josep nor Lola had told her anything about him, apart from the fact that he was a bookseller in Paris, and a Communist; they didn't know that Pierre was a Soviet agent. And Josep and Lola were also committed Communists, ready to do whatever the party asked."

"I thought your mother was a Socialist."

"She was, to begin with, but she ended up joining the Communists; she didn't like to do things by halves. Lola had a very strong character."

"I'm surprised that you call your parents by their first names..."

"It's always good to try to put some distance when you are talking about historical facts, but I started to think of them as Josep and Lola when I reached adolescence. And they were committed Communists, nothing and no one could make them change their convictions. They were formidable. I have never stopped admiring them for their faith in the cause, for their honorableness, for their sense of loyalty and sacrifice, but I've also never stopped reproaching them for their blindness."

"I'm sorry, professor, I'm going to ask you what may seem an impertinent question. Are you a Communist?"

"Do you think I could have given classes at Princeton if I had been? I had enough with my parents... No, I am not a Communist, I never was one of them, it's a puerile idea of paradise. I rebelled against my parents like children are supposed to do; in my case it was for personal reasons, above all my relationship with my mother, but back then I was a child who adored his father and who felt a limitless admiration for him. If you want to know what I think, I can summarize it as follows: I abhor all 'isms.' Communism, Socialism, Nationalism, Fascism... Anything that carries the germ of totalitarianism within itself."

"But you must have some ideological position..."

"I am a democrat who believes in people, in their initiative and their capacity to progress without being led by politics or religion."

"So your parents must have been bummed out..."

"I'm sorry?"

"It's a colloquial expression. I suppose children must always disappoint their parents, we're never what they dreamed we would be."

"In my case I can guarantee that to be the truth."

"I'm sorry, I won't interrupt you again."

Pablo began to speak.

Josep admired Pierre. I think that, although he did not know about Pierre's being a Soviet agent, he realized that because of his comings and goings and his collaboration with the Communist International, Pierre must be important, especially because he was engaged in information gathering. He was interested in everything, from how the Spanish Communists were organized, to the Trotskyite movements or the strength of the CNT, to the Socialists, to Azaña's government. Sometimes he would let slip in conversation that he had spoken to some left-wing politician, or had dined with an important journalist.

Pierre's alibi was ideal: a bookseller, specializing in rare and antique books. His bookshop in Paris was an important point of reference for anyone looking for a rare volume, an incunabulum, or a banned book. This allowed him to travel the world and to meet people connected with culture, who are always nervous and open to new experiences, including new ideologies. So nobody was surprised when this bookseller turned up in Spain, and moved between Barcelona and Madrid, as well as visiting other provincial capitals.

I was a child when I met him. I thought it was funny that he spoke Spanish with a French accent; he spoke English and Russian as well. His mother was a Russian who had married a Frenchman. Pierre's father shared his son's ideological positions, but his mother thanked God that she had escaped the revolution, because many of her family members had disappeared without a trace as a result of Stalin's repressive policies.

This was Pierre, a man who was irresistible to women because of his gallantry, and above all because he listened to them, which was something rare in a time when men, even revolutionaries, were not as sophisticated as they are today. But Pierre had made listening to people into an art, there was nothing that he found uninteresting, nothing that was a tale of minor importance. It seemed that he found a use for everything that he was told, he kept it in his brain and waited for it to come in handy. Sometimes my mother chided Josep for not being able to listen to her as Pierre did, and my father was actually a good listener, something that had enabled him to convince Amelia of the benefits of the revolution.

Amelia fell in love with Pierre without wanting to. He was very handsome, and he was different. He dressed carelessly but always with elegance; he was always sympathetic and in a good mood, and he was very well educated, without being pedantic.

And you were right, I did meet Amelia and Pierre in Barcelona at the beginning of April 1936. My mother and I arrived two days after they did.

My father had decided that we should go live with him. He had found a job for my mother as a seamstress in his employer's house.

My father's attic was much more spacious than the one in which we had lived in Madrid. It had three rooms and a kitchen, it even had a little room with a sink, which was a luxury in those days. It was on the top floor of the house of my father's employer; he had made it available to my father in order to have him always at hand at day and at night, in case he had to go out suddenly or take his wife somewhere. Before he had been given so much space, my father had slept in an attic room with the butler, but my father explained to his employer that he would like to live with his family and he needed space for them, without which he would have to leave his job and look for another.

His employer gave them the attic, but asked my father not to tell his wife that he was not married, that Lola, my mother, was not his lawfully wedded wife, because it could cause problems for the pair of them. He himself did not mind about my parents' civil situation; he was a pragmatic businessman who enjoyed having his chauffeur available twenty-four hours a day, especially as my father was a discreet man, who drove his employer every Thursday afternoon to a certain house where a young woman lived, whom my father's employer kept. There were occasions, when they traveled to Madrid on business, that this woman would journey with them. They reached an agreement: the large attic, but a smaller wage.

A few days after arriving in Barcelona I went to Doña Anita's house with Lola. Amelia was there. Doña Anita was the widow of a bookseller from whom she had inherited his bookshop and his Communist convictions, and it may have been that he got them from him. Doña Anita, before people began to call her "Doña," had taken on ironing, and the bookseller's family members were among her clients. Back then she already worked with the Communists. She was a clever girl and managed to get the son of the family to fall for her, and then she married him, but his health was fragile and he died young from a heart attack. She fought tooth and nail with her in-laws to remain in charge of the bookshop that had been her husband's, and in the end was victorious. She started to organize what she called "literary evenings," and managed to gather together a great number of intellectuals, aspiring writers, journalists, and left-wing politicians. In one of my books, on Alexander Orlov and the Soviet presence in Spain in the years before the Civil War, I mentioned Doña Anita's bookshop: It was a place where people left messages, shared information, and even organized clandestine meetings between agents and their controllers.

Doña Anita's bookshop had an interior staircase that led up to her home, on the second floor of a building near the Plaza de San Jaime. That is where we met Amelia.

"Lola, Pablo, what a pleasure to see you!" Amelia seemed happy to see us.

"How are you? Is everything going well?" Lola asked.

"Yes, yes, I'm very happy, but I can't stop thinking about my son and..."

"Don't speak! You've made the right decision. You and Pierre have a mission to complete, and... you love each other. Amelia, you have decided to be a revolutionary, and you need to revolutionize your silly bourgeois life as well."

Lola did not stand on ceremony where Amelia was concerned. Over time I have realized that she felt a secret envy for her. Amelia was beautiful, elegant, pleasant, cultured, and had the air of someone who has grown up surrounded by beautiful things: books, pictures, furniture... Lola had been a skivvy and then had done ironing and sewing, and that is what she was: a proletarian full of illusions, convinced that the hour had come for people like her who had nothing.

"I can't help it! I love Javier so much! I hope that one day my little boy will understand what I have done, even though Pierre has told me that I will be with my son again, that this separation is only temporary..."

Amelia wanted to fool herself, but Lola would not let her.

"Your son won't lack for anything, like your cousin Jesús, who's the same age as my Pablo and... There are millions of children who will never have half what your child has; you need to sacrifice yourself for these children. Forget about yourself and your petty bourgeois egotism."

There were not many people at Doña Anita's house that evening, and Doña Anita herself made a face when she saw me. For all that I was the son of Lola and Josep, she did not like children, and she made no bones about saying so.

"There's no room for the kid."

"I don't have anywhere to leave him and Josep said that he should come here to meet us."

Lola recognized Doña Anita for the proletarian she had been, in spite of her well-made dress and silk blouse, her pearl earrings and well-groomed hair. A woman like Doña Anita did not impress her.

"Important people are coming to see Pierre this evening and I don't want anything to disturb him," Doña Anita insisted.

"Pablo won't disturb him, my son's been a Communist since the day he was born, and he's used to political meetings. Anyway, he knows Pierre well. Tell him yourself, Amelia."

"Don't worry, Doña Anita, the child is very good and won't be a nuisance."

Josep occupied an important position among the Catalan Communists; he was not a boss, but he was the confidant of bosses. He worked as a "postman," thanks to his job as a chauffeur and his frequent journeys to Madrid.

For a child, this was not a fun afternoon. Sitting on a chair, not allowed to move, I could do nothing but observe what was happening. When Pierre arrived, Amelia went anxiously up to him.

"It's taken you a long time," she complained.

"I couldn't come earlier, I had to see some comrades."

"And you couldn't see them here?"

"No, not these ones. And now let me speak to the gentlemen who have just entered; I will introduce them to you later. One of them is the secretary to a member of Catalonia's Executive Council."

"And he's a Communist?"

"Yes, but his boss doesn't know. Now keep quiet and listen. You have to get used to these meetings. Above all, listen, and then tell me what you hear, I've told you I want you to remember anything, no matter how insignificant it might seem. Look, try to talk to the people in this group, the ones on the right are two journalists who have a lot of influence here in Catalonia, and the man they're talking to is a higher-up in the Socialists. I'm sure that what they're saying is of interest. Ask Doña Anita to introduce you to them and behave as I said, speaking little and listening much. You are very sweet and very pretty and they will not mistrust you."

Pierre was grooming her to be an agent. An agent who would work for him. Amelia was a young lady, distinguished, educated, who could fit into the most select environments without calling attention to herself. Pierre had realized her potential and meant to use it to his advantage. Of course, he had not the least intention of being truthful with her, of explaining that he was an agent of the INO. He had told her half-truths: that he was a part of the Communist International, that he sometimes represented them on some of his journeys running errands to comrades in different countries... And he explained his activities in such a way that they seemed innocent, especially to the ears of an inexperienced woman such as herself.

Amelia went to Doña Anita and told her in a low voice that Pierre wanted her to be introduced to the gentlemen who were conversing animatedly at the far end of the room.

Doña Anita agreed and took her by the arm, chatting of trivialities while they went toward the journalists and the Catalan Socialist.

"My dear friends, have I introduced you to Amelia Garayoa? She is a friend from Madrid who is visiting Barcelona for a few days. She told me how much unrest there is in the capital, isn't that so, Amelia?"

"Yes, there are lots of people who are hoping that the government will show some kind of decisiveness in the face of these disturbances and the far right's provocations."

"Yes, they have to be stopped," the Socialist acknowledged.

"And what do they say about Alcalá Zamora?" one of the journalists asked.

"Whatever they want. At the moment all attention is focused on Manuel Azaña."

The three men looked at each other as if they thought that Amelia knew more than she was letting on, but she had only said this to get out of a hole. Little did she know that Alcalá Zamora would be forced to resign as president of the Republic two days later. And there was a political movement afoot to install Manuel Azaña as president, something that these three men knew about.

To begin with they spoke cautiously in front of Amelia, but later with greater confidence. She limited herself to listening, agreeing, smiling, but above all paying a great deal of attention to every word they said, which made them feel that they were the center of the world.

This was a quality that Amelia successfully cultivated her whole life, and it was this quality that Pierre knew how to discern, mold, and develop.

Josep arrived late with two trade union officials whom Pierre wanted to meet. So the evening spread out until after ten o'clock. We were the last to go, and I remember that Amelia kissed me as she hugged me with affection. She was lodging with Pierre in

Doña Anita's house. Pierre did not want to stay in a hotel, as he had no desire to put Amelia in a compromising position by sharing a room with her. He knew that he had to be careful and move slowly so as not to make her regret the step she had taken, and not for anything in the world would he humiliate her. Doña Anita's house was large enough for them to stay without getting in the way of their hostess, and they spent their first few days there, and many more in future visits. It was in Doña Anita's house that they would spend the first few days of the Civil War.

It is not difficult to imagine what Amelia Garayoa and Pierre Comte spoke about that night.

"So," Pierre asked. "What did the journalists say?"

"They criticized Alcalá Zamora for dissolving parliament on two occasions, because there is no provision for that in the constitution. And the Socialist said that it was not out of the question that Prieto would end up forming a government. Then Josep and the trade unionists from the UGT came along, and one of them said that Largo Caballero would never let Prieto get what he wanted."

"It's difficult to make Largo Caballero see reason, he doesn't understand that even if this is not the moment for a government of the Left, it is still important to make connections with the part of the bourgeoisie that is not Fascist."

"But that seems a contradiction..."

"No, it's just a question of learning to deal with the different circumstances that each moment throws up. We cannot deliver the definitive blow to the bourgeoisie before it's time because one runs the risk of losing everything. The non-Fascist bourgeoisie cannot make a move without us."

"And can we move without them?"

"Yes, yes we can, although the cost will be greater. Let's let Azaña's Republican government carry on, at least for a while..."

I saw Amelia again the next day when she came to our attic to talk with Lola. She was always kind to me, and she brought me a packet of coffee-flavored caramels that tasted wonderful. She seemed happy, this was because, as she told my mother, Pierre was teaching her Russian.

"I have a gift for languages," she admitted.

Amelia and Lola spent a good part of the afternoon talking about the divine and the human; I listened to them carefully, because adult conversation fascinated me. Also, I was accustomed to being silent and unobtrusive during the meetings my parents had with their comrades.

"Josep has convinced me to leave the Socialist Youth. I regret it, because I like what Largo Caballero says, but Josep is right, we can't each of us be on one side of the question, we have to share everything, and it's a very delicate moment, there are things that he wouldn't be able to tell me if I were in another party."

"It's the right thing to do, Lola. It's such a beautiful thing to share everything with the man you love! And Largo Caballero isn't that far removed from the Communists, is he, when all's said and done?"

"Yes, there are differences of course, but not as many as there are between Prieto and the Spanish Communist Party. Prieto is too soft on the bourgeoisie."

"Santiago liked Prieto... He said he was a gentlemen, and he worried about Largo Caballero's power."

"Forget about your husband! It's all water under the bridge, you have another life now and you shouldn't look back."

"If only it were so easy... What I feel for Pierre is so intense that it feels like I am burning from the inside, but I can't stop thinking about Santiago and little Javier... I love them, in my own way, I suppose, but I do love them. I have had nightmares ever since I left them, I sleep badly. As soon as I close my eyes I see Santiago's face, and as soon as I fall asleep I wake up because I think I hear my son crying. I cannot get over my bad conscience..."

"Conscience is something dreamt up by the Church! It's an easy way to have control over people. If they control your conscience then they control you because you cease to be free. From the day we are born, priests tell us what's good and what's bad according to their own opinions, and then they convince you that if you don't do the right thing you'll go straight to hell. But hell does not exist, it's a story for idiots, to keep the poor under control. They want us to suffer on earth in order to enjoy the heavenly paradise up in the sky, but no one's ever come back from the dead to tell us that it exists. And you know why? Because there's nothing, after death there's nothing. The rich made up God to control the poor."

"What things you say, Lola!"

"It's the truth! Think about it, think where you see God. Does God do anything for the poor? If He's omnipotent, why does He allow so much injustice to exist? Why does He allow so many innocent people to suffer?"

"Don't think you can judge God, even less understand Him! He knows why He puts us to the test, and we have to accept it."

"Well, even if God does exist, I assure you that I will not accept that my son will be less than your son, that he will lack the education that your son will receive, eat worse food, have fewer opportunities. Why do your son Javier and your cousin Jesús have to have advantages over Pablo? Tell me, why?"

Lola raised her voice and looked defiantly at Amelia, whose smile had turned into a grimace of pain. Amelia suffered in seeing all the hate that Lola contained within herself, and how a part of that hate was directed toward her.

"I have given up everything to fight for those weaker than I am. I have given up my son and my husband, my house, my parents, my sister, my family, my friends, and I have done this because I don't believe that the world is just and that no one has any right to have any more than anyone else. Does this seem like nothing to you?"

"You think we have to thank you for taking this decision? Would you have done it if you hadn't fallen in love with Pierre?"

Amelia leaped up, her eyes filled with tears. Lola had struck below the belt; she had said what everyone knew, what Amelia herself knew, that until Pierre had appeared she had only flirted with revolutionary ideas.

I was scared to see Amelia and Lola looking in silence at each other. Lola looked angry; Amelia was stunned. Eventually she swallowed, took a deep breath, and seemed to recover the calm that she had temporarily lost.

"I think it's best if I go. Doña Anita has invited some friends to dine and I think it would be best if I were there to help her."

"Yes, it's a bit of a trek back to her house from here."

Amelia kissed me and tenderly stroked my face. Then she left without saying anything. Lola sighed. Josep would be cross when he found out that she had argued with Amelia. If Pierre had chosen Amelia it was because she had a special value for the sacred cause of Communism, and it was better not to contradict her, better that she not risk regretting having left her husband and son. But Amelia annoyed Lola, who had never felt any affection toward her.

Although this wasn't the first argument they'd had, it was the quarrel that most affected Amelia, so much in fact that we did not see her at all over the next few days, and it was Josep who announced one evening when he got home that Pierre Comte and Amelia had gone to Paris.

"Is she still in a mood with me?" Lola asked.

"I don't know, I don't even know if she told Pierre about your argument. He hasn't said anything to me, and she's been just as charming as ever. You know you put your foot in it," Josep complained.

"Me? Says you! I'm sick of that two-faced bitch, she's leading you all along, you too; if Pierre hadn't come along she'd have made a play for you. You think I didn't see her looking at you and licking her lips? And you preaching Communism to her as if you'd been doing it all your life."

"Come on, Lola, don't play the jealousy card! I don't like it."

"Oh, right. Well, if sir will just tell me how he likes me, I'll do my best to make him happy. Would sir like me to look down, to blush when he speaks to me?"

"Don't talk nonsense!"

They ended up shouting at each other, paying no attention to me. It was not the first time they had fought, but it had never been like this before. Lola dripped with rage. That was the logical thing. She was a brave woman, capable of making great sacrifices for her ideals, and did not know how to use her feminine wiles in dealing with men. She treated them as equals, and in that society, for all the talk by men on the Left about equality between men and women, everyone had been brought up under the same rules, and the men she dealt with were used to women sacrificing themselves, not being equal.

Lola had fought for the respect and the consideration of her comrades, she had shown self-possession and bravery in the disturbance caused by the general strike in October '34. She was a true revolutionary, by conviction and by provenance and because her reason told her that this was the path toward liberty for women such as her. She was irritated by, felt a deep disdain for men who did not give way to women such as her, and who could not shrug off the impression made on them by women such as Amelia. Lola was strongly in favor of equality, she had won the right to be treated equally, but in her heart of hearts it provoked her that men forgot that she was also a woman, and not just a comrade.

3

A melia did not settle down all that well with her new family in Paris. How do I know? Well, as I told you, I undertook exhaustive research into spies during the Civil War in order to write what I consider one of my best books. And Pierre was a very special agent; he appeared to be working with the Communist International, which allowed him to establish contact with its agents all over the world, but in fact, as I said, he was with the INO.

Don't imagine that it was not hard to reconstruct his life in order to contextualize its importance to the revolutionary movement and its role in the Civil War. I spent several months in Paris interviewing people who had information about him; some people had known him, some had second- or third-hand knowledge. Of course, his liaison with Amelia was no secret, and there are documents that prove the presence of *la belle espagnole* in Paris at that time.

Pierre's mother, Olga, unwillingly took her in. She did not like that her son had become involved with a married woman. As a good Frenchman, Pierre's father, Guy, accepted the situation more philosophically. Also, he knew his son well and understood that there was nothing that would affect his son's revolutionary obligations, not even his relationship with *la belle espagnole*. Guy Comte knew that his son worked for the Communist International; if Pierre was a Communist it was thanks to his father's influence. But Guy did not know that his son had become a Soviet agent.

"So you have abandoned your family for my son," Olga said bluntly, once Pierre had explained the situation to her.

Amelia blushed. She had felt Olga's disapproval as soon as she had crossed the threshold to the apartment that Pierre shared with his parents.

"Please, mother, treat our guest with a little courtesy!"

"Our guest? Your lover. Isn't that what they call married women who lose their heads and run away from their homes to have an affair with no future?"

"Don't speak like that, woman! If Pierre loves Amelia, she's welcome into our family, welcome to join us. And you, don't be afraid of my wife, she's like that, she says what comes into her head without thinking, but she's a good person, you'll see, she'll end up loving you." And, turning back to Olga, he added: "It's Pierre, your son, who's chosen her, and we should respect his decisions."

"I love Pierre, if I didn't... if I didn't I wouldn't have been able to do what I've done... and... I believe in the revolution, I want to help... ," Amelia babbled, her eyes flooded with tears. She felt humiliated, and this might have been the first time that she realized how her decision had turned her into a pariah in the eyes of the world.

"Mother, Amelia is with me, and if you don't accept her then we will go straight away, you decide. But if you'd like us to stay, you will treat her with the respect and the consideration which a woman deserves who has shown herself to be brave and who has sacrificed a comfortable and unproblematic life to fight for world revolution. I don't only love her, I respect her deeply, too."

Pierre looked angrily at his mother, and Olga realized that if she wanted not to lose her son then she would have to accept this mad Spanish woman. She would once more have to resign herself, just as she had when she discovered that her husband and son were raging Communists.

Olga had met Guy Comte when she was a companion to an old Russian aristocrat, a duchess, who used to spend seasons in Paris. The old lady was an incorrigible reader and liked to buy her books in person, so she became an assiduous client of the Rousseau Bookshop on the Boulevard Saint-Germain, on the Left Bank of the Seine, owned by Monsieur Guy Comte.

Olga and Guy traded sidelong glances. Then Guy started to speak with her while the duchess browsed the bookshelves. Even later, Guy, with the duchess's permission, arranged a meeting with Olga. If matters had been left in Guy's hands, this would have been no more than a simple seduction, but the duchess was not willing for her companion's reputation to be ruined, and so, when she discovered that Olga was pregnant, she urged them to marry. She was the young woman's maid of honor and gave her a large amount of money.

Maybe it was the years she had spent with the aristocracy, maybe it was an inherent dislike of revolutionaries for the threat they offered her bourgeois life with her bookselling husband, but Olga never let herself get carried away by ideas that, as she put it, could lead goodness knows where. So, for Olga, Amelia was nothing more than a silly girl who had let herself get carried away by Olga's attractive son, who would abandon her once he had grown tired of her. That was how all stories of forbidden love came to an end: She knew this well, having read all of the Russian classics. Tolstoy, Dostoevsky, and Gogol were her guides in these matters.

Pierre had two rooms in his parents' house; one was his bedroom and the other his office. Amelia spent more time in this office than in the drawing room so as not to meet Olga. The two women treated each other coldly and tried to avoid one another.

Amelia could see Pierre's great attachment to his parents, the way that, despite the continual fights between mother and son, they were connected by a great bond of affection.

For Amelia, this was a different Paris from the city she had known traveling with her parents. This time she did not spend her days visiting her great-aunt Lily, her grandmother Margot's sister; neither did she go to museums, as she had with her father and mother and her sister Antonietta. She would have liked to go see her great-aunt, but how to tell her that she had abandoned her family? Aunt Lily would not have understood, would surely have reproached her for her decision. Pierre seemed to be in a hurry for Amelia to meet his friends, and above all for her to take the pulse of the political activity in this fascinating city, which appeared to have revolutionaries on every corner. Even so, she still found time to take the Russian classes that she found so inspiring.

A few days after arriving in Paris, Pierre supported her bid for membership in the Communist Party, in the face of the chary reaction of certain comrades, who thought it a little hasty to welcome this little-known Spaniard into their ranks.

Jean Deuville, a poet friend and coreligionist of Pierre, was one of the people who opposed most firmly Amelia's entry into the French Communist Party.

"We don't know who she is," he argued before the Paris committee, "for all that Comrade Pierre vouches for her."

"Isn't my guarantee enough? You will recall that it was enough to get you admitted into the Party," Pierre counterattacked.

Perhaps because of a certain polite pressure from the Soviet Embassy, or else because Deuville did not want to compromise his friendship with Pierre, Amelia Garayoa was admitted into the French Communist Party. She, a foreigner, with no credentials other than being the lover of a man valued by the Soviets who was convinced that this Spanish woman could be extremely useful. What Amelia did not know was that, weeks earlier, Pierre's controller had sent him the most recent orders from the head of INO operations in Moscow: Pierre was to travel to South America to support and help expand the Communist networks that were being set up there with local agents.

The head of INO operations had warned him of the occasionally explosive temperament shown by South Americans, and had insisted that he be careful in choosing his collaborators.

Since then, Pierre had not stopped thinking of his approaching mission, and how he would need a more convincing alibi than that of a bookseller in search of bibliographic rarities; that made sense in Europe, but not in that part of the world, which seemed to him both distant and unknown.

When he met Amelia, he began to think that the young woman could be of some use. Not only was she delicately beautiful and graceful, but she was also a complete innocent, pure clay in his hands, incapable of seeing beyond her own emotions.

To set up in Mexico or Argentina as two lovers fleeing an abandoned husband would lend verisimilitude to their alibi for setting themselves up abroad. And with her being Spanish, the alibi would be all the stronger.

Bear in mind that Pierre was a Soviet agent, a man who lived only for the revolution, and his blind dedication to the cause was such that the human beings who stood in his path were no more than pawns, to be used and discarded for a superior idea. Amelia was no exception.

Ever since he decided to include her as part of his South American plan, Pierre had been careful not to make any mistakes with Amelia, to whom he had appeared as a seducer fallen into love's clutches.

To reinforce Amelia's dependence on him, Pierre made her go with him to all the meetings of his friends where it was likely that he would meet one of his former lovers, with whom he would exchange significant glances in order to make the Spanish woman uncertain.

This was why Amelia had been caught up in a whirlpool of political meetings from her first day in Paris, interspersed with meals with Pierre's friends, some of whom commented behind his back that they could not understand why a man of his convictions and value had surrendered himself to such a beautiful yet insubstantial and naïve creature.

All people were talking about in those days was Léon Blum, and the consequences of the dissolution of the Action Française, whose militants had attacked Blum in February 1936 as he followed Bainville's funeral cortège.

It was during a dinner at La Coupole, in celebration of Pierre's birthday, that Amelia first met Albert James.

Albert James was an American newspaperman, of Irish descent, who was freelancing for various North American newspapers and magazines. Tall, with chestnut hair and green eyes, he was good-looking and very successful with women. He liked to behave like a bon vivant, he was a virulent anti-Fascist, but he had not fallen for Marxism. He was a friend not of Pierre's but of Jean Deuville's, so he came to their group to say hello, attracted by Amelia above all.

He drank a glass of champagne with their little group and managed to get next to Amelia, whom he noticed appeared out of place.

"What's a young girl like you doing in a place like this?" he asked without preambles, taking advantage that Pierre was greeting another friend who had come to join the group.

"Why shouldn't I be here?"

"Well, it's clear that this is not your normal milieu, I imagine you sitting in a window, embroidering, waiting for your handsome prince to come and rescue you."

Amelia laughed at Albert James's notion; she found him friendly at first sight.

"I am not a princess, so it would be hard for me to have the time to wait, embroidering, for a prince to come along."

"French?"

"No, Spanish."

"But your French is perfect."

"My grandmother is French, from the south, and we always spoke in French; we spent our summers in Biarritz."

"You sound nostalgic."

"Nostalgic?"

"Yes, as if you were very old and remembering bygone times."

"Don't let Albert reel you in," Jean Deuville interrupted. "He may be an American, but his father was Irish, and he's learned the art of seduction from us French; as normally happens, the pupil is better than his master."

"Oh, but we weren't talking of anything in particular!" Amelia excused herself.

"Also, although it doesn't seem that way, Pierre is jealous, and I would not like to have to be the second at a duel between good friends," Deuville joked.

Amelia blushed. She was not accustomed to these relaxed jokes. It was difficult for her to play the role of the lover that she had taken on among these apparently unprejudiced men and women who nevertheless scrutinized her and murmured behind her back.

"Are you Pierre's fiancée?" Albert James asked with interest.

"More than his fiancée, she's the woman who has stolen his heart. They live together," Jean Deuville said, so as not to leave the American any room for doubt that he should not try to go any further with Amelia.

She felt uncomfortable. She did not see why Jean had needed to be so explicit in positioning her in a situation in which she felt clearly inferior.

"I see, so you are a liberated woman, something that surprises me, as you're Spanish, although they've told me that things have changed in Spain, and thanks to the government of the Left, women have started to have a significant role in all areas of society. Are you a revolutionary as well?" Albert James asked ironically.

"Don't tease me," Amelia said, breathing a sigh of relief to see Pierre approaching.

"What are you telling these two scoundrels?" Pierre asked, pointing at Albert and Jean. "By the way, that was a very good article in the *New York Times* about the danger of Nazism in Europe. I read it when I got back from Spain, and I must say I am frankly surprised at your perspicacity. You say that you are sure that Hitler will not stay happily inside his frontiers, that he will want to expand, and you suggest that his first little mouthful will be Austria, and that Mussolini will do nothing to stop him, not just because he's a Fascist too, but because he knows that he is bound to lose anything he stakes against Germany."

"Yes, I think so. I spent a month traveling around Germany, Austria, and Italy, and that's how things are. The Jews are Hitler's principal victims, but one day it will be the whole world."

"It's not that we should fight against Nazism because they persecute the Jews, but because they're a blot on the whole of humankind," Pierre replied.

"But you cannot avoid what's happening to the Jews."

"I am a Communist and my only aim is revolution, to free all men from the capitalist yoke that holds them down without allowing them to be free. I don't care if they're Jews or Buddhists. Any religion is a cancer. You should know that."

"You have to have an idea of God not to believe in Him," Albert shrugged.

"If you believe in God you will never be a free man, you'll let your life be ruled by superstition."

"And if only I became a Communist... Do you think I'd be freer? Wouldn't I have to listen to what Moscow wanted? In the end, what Moscow wants to do is to save mankind from capitalism, and lots of you end up making Communism your religion. Your faith is greater than that of our parents when they recited the

Bible. I don't know if you'll be so keen on my next report on the Soviet Union; I'm hoping to go very soon. You know that the Soviet Minister of Culture has organized a tour for European and American writers and journalists to see the achievements of the revolution; you know me, my problem is that I analyze and criticize everything that I see."

"That's why nobody likes you." Pierre's reply showed just how much Albert was annoying him.

"I've never believed that journalists should be likeable, quite the contrary."

"Well, you're doing a good job."

"Boys, boys, boys!" Jean Deuville interrupted. "Look how upset you get over nothing. Don't pay them any attention, Amelia, they're like that, as soon as they meet they argue and there's no one who can stop them. They carry the seeds of argument around with them. But it's your birthday, Pierre, so let's celebrate. That's why we're here, right?"

Albert took his leave, abandoning Pierre to his bad mood and Amelia to her surprise. She had listened to the argument in silence, without daring to speak. The two men seemed to be fighting some duel that they had begun a long time ago.

"He's a poor devil, just like the rest of the Americans, he cannot abandon capitalism," Pierre pronounced.

"Don't be unfair. Albert is a good person, he just hasn't had his road to Damascus moment yet; it's our fault, we haven't been able to convince him to sign up for our cause, although he's not against us either. But in one thing he is very close to us, he hates the Fascists," Jean Deuville replied.

"I don't trust him. He has a lot of friends who are Trotskyites."

"And who in Paris doesn't know a Trotskyite?" Jean Deuville said. "Let's not be paranoid."

"Look who's defending the American!"

"I'm defending him from your arbitrariness. The pair of you are unbearable whenever you try to be right."

"Don't compare me with him!"

There was something ferocious in Pierre's tone, and Jean did not reply. He knew that if he carried on speaking then they would end up having an argument, and they had already had one a few weeks ago about Amelia, which was why Jean wanted sincerely to show that he meant no offense.

"Come on Amelia, there's nothing that a glass of champagne won't cure," Pierre said, taking Amelia by the arm and leading her to the table where the rest of the group was seated.

Pierre was cautiously organizing the trip to South America that Moscow had ordered him to make. Their first stop would be in Buenos Aires, where the Communist Party seemed to have great prestige among the cultural strata of the Argentinian capital. From a strategic point of view, this was not a vital area for Soviet interests, but the head of the INO wanted to have eyes and ears everywhere. During his Moscow training, Pierre's INO instructors had made much of the fact that it was important to know how to listen to and gather all kinds of information, however insubstantial they might seem; it happens that vital information is sometimes gathered thousands of kilometers from where it might have an effect. They had also drummed into him the importance of having agents who moved within the most influential spheres of the country of operation. It was not useful at all for them to have enthusiastic activists who worked a long way from the centers of power.

Moscow had a "resident" in Buenos Aires, but they lacked well-positioned agents capable of transferring them information of interest.

Amelia did not want to leave Paris, and insisted to Pierre that they wait a little longer, that she was not yet mentally ready to leave her child so far away. It was not that she was intending to return to Spain, but when she thought about Buenos Aires the distance seemed to her unbearable.

Extremely patiently and with great caution, Pierre tried to convince her that it was better to begin a new life in a place where nobody knew them.

"We need to know if our love is truly valuable. I want us to be alone, where no one recognizes us, just you and me. I am sure that no one and nothing will manage to separate us, but we have to put our love to the test, without any interference, without any family, without any friends."

She asked for more time, time to get used to the idea that the best thing was to start a new life on the other side of the ocean. Pierre did not want to force her, afraid that she would decide in distress to return to Spain.

At times he despaired of Amelia's attitude, because she could swing from euphoria to despair in seconds. He regularly found her weeping, lamenting that she was such a bad mother and that she had abandoned her son. At other times she seemed happy and care-free, she would encourage him to come out for a while and have fun, and they would get lost in the corners of Paris like lovers.

His mother, Olga, did not make things easier, convinced that she had lost her son because of this Spanish woman.

"You're going to throw your life away for this woman! She doesn't deserve it! What will we do with the bookshop if you don't return? You father is suffering, even though he doesn't tell you," she reproached her son.

In fact, Guy Comte accepted Pierre's decision to go live in South America with resignation. He trusted his son implicitly, and was convinced that if Pierre had made a decision, then it was the right one. In his heart of hearts, however, he asked himself how it was possible for his son to sacrifice so much for a woman like Amelia, whom he found beautiful but bland.

On June 4, 1936, Léon Blum became the premier of a Popular Front government. Don Manuel Azaña had already become the president of the Spanish Republic after a vote in which the Right abstained. Indalecio Prieto could not accept the government because of the veto applied by the bloc supporting Largo Caballero in the PSOE.

Amelia followed the news from Spain with anxiety, and knew that the situation was much more uneasy than it had been when she had left.

Pierre's friends said that anything could happen in Spain, as long as the right wing did not step back from its policies of terror and provocation.

Pierre had intended to leave for Buenos Aires at the end of July. They would travel in a luxurious first-class cabin on a liner that was leaving from Le Havre.

"It will be our honeymoon," he assured her as he tried to overcome her last resistance.

At the beginning of July, Pierre met with his controller in Paris. Igor Krisov looked like something he was not: an affable British Jew of Russian origin, dedicated to antiques.

In reality, Igor Krisov ran agents in the United Kingdom, France, Belgium, and Holland.

Kristov came to the Café de la Paix and looked for Pierre. Pierre was reading a newspaper in an inattentive way and drinking coffee. He sat down at the table next to Pierre's and ordered a cup of tea.

"I see you got my message."

"Yes," Pierre replied.

"Well, Comrade, I have instructions for you. Moscow wants you to go to Spain before you head off."

"To Spain, again?"

"Yes, the situation there is getting worse by the day, and we want you to speak with some people. This envelope contains the instructions. We really would like for it to be you to undertake this mission: It's only for a few days."

"I have a problem. You know that I have a 'cover,' a Spanish woman; she's not very convinced about the journey we're going to make. If I leave her alone for a few days, she might get cold feet..."

"I thought you were more persuasive with the ladies," Krisov replied ironically.

"She's just a kid. I've spent a lot of effort and patience on her. I think that she'll end up being a good agent, 'blind' but useful."

"Don't make the mistake of telling her what you really do," Krisov warned him.

"That's why I said she'd be a 'blind' agent; she'll work for us without knowing what she's really doing. She's an inveterate romantic and she's convinced that my only desire is to spread Communism throughout the world."

"Isn't it, Comrade?"

Krisov's ironic gaze upset Pierre.

"Of course it is, Comrade."

"We've approved your use of the Garayoa woman. Given her characteristics, we believe, as do you, that she could prove useful, but don't confide in her."

"I won't, Comrade."

"Well, we'll see each other when we return from Spain."

On July 10, Pierre and Amelia arrived in Barcelona; they stayed once again at Doña Anita's house. It was helpful for Pierre's peace of mind to be able to count on the widow's hospitality, as she looked after Amelia while he was at his meetings. He had first thought to leave Amelia in Paris with his parents, but he abandoned the idea, as he realized that his father would not be able to do anything if Olga and Amelia came face to face. Also, Pierre was starting to worry, because with every day that passed Amelia seemed to regret the step she had taken, and this meant that he could not let her out of his sight.

Amelia was overjoyed to hear that they would be returning to Spain. She had asked if she could go to Madrid to try to see her son, and Pierre decided not to say no directly, even though he had not the slightest intention of allowing this to happen.

"Well, well, well, here's the happy couple again!" Doña Anita said by way of welcome. "How many days can we expect to enjoy your presence here this time?"

"Three or four. I have to see a client who says that he has found a volume that I have been looking for for years. If things go well, then we might even be able to go to Madrid," Pierre replied.

"And you, Amelia, will you see your friend Lola García? She was here a few days ago with Josep; he's a good man, and so proud of his little brat of a son."

Amelia agreed without much enthusiasm. After their argument she had no desire at all to see Lola. She was starting to feel repelled by her old friend, whom she blamed for the sudden transformation that had taken place in her life.

The next day, when Pierre had said goodbye and gone off to carry out his tasks, Amelia told Doña Anita that she was going off to buy some items that would be necessary for her on her journey to Buenos Aires. The widow wondered if she should let her go off alone, as Pierre had told her that Amelia needed to be watched, but an order of books had come in that morning, and although there was a boy who helped her she did not want to leave the bookshop, so she allowed Amelia to go alone.

"But don't be too long or I'll be worried," she warned Amelia.

"Don't worry, Doña Anita, I won't get lost. I'm sure I'll find all the fabrics I need in the neighborhood."

"Yes, the English Silkworks is just two blocks away, and you can find all the fabrics you need there."

In fact Amelia had another plan, to go to the Central Telegraph Office and call her cousin Laura. She wanted to have news of her family, and of little Javier. Since her flight she had not been in touch with Laura, and she had not even dared send her parents a letter begging their forgiveness.

She had not dared call from Paris for fear that Pierre would stop her. She realized that for the first time since her escape she had some time to herself, alone.

She left Doña Anita's bookshop and started to walk, knowing that she was about to break the trust that Pierre had in her. But she was sure that, just as he had his secrets, she would have hers.

Little did Amelia know that luck was not to be on her side. When she was in the office, she went up to an employee and asked him to connect her with her uncle and aunt's house in Madrid. She did not realize that this man was looking at her in surprise. She did not remember him, but he remembered her. In her previous stay in Barcelona, Amelia had gone with Pierre to a meeting of the local party, and among the attendees was this man, a well-situated local activist. The man was surprised to see her alone and so agitated.

Amelia twisted her hands anxiously as she waited to be put through, and the man convinced his colleague behind the desk that she should take a break, as it looked like it would take a while to establish the connection.

"Don't worry, I'll take care of it."

"Thanks, I've needed to go to the bathroom for an hour."

The man had decided not to miss a word of Amelia's conversation, so he passed her call through his own telephone.

Then, when the Madrid operator confirmed that a connection had been made, he told Amelia to go into a booth where she could speak. She still seemed extremely anxious.

"You can speak now," the Madrid operator said.

"Laura? I'd like to speak with Laura," Amelia muttered.

"Who shall I say is calling?" the maid who'd answered the phone asked.

"Amelia."

"Señorita Amelia?" the maid asked in alarm.

"Please, hurry up! Tell my cousin, I don't have much time."

A couple of minutes later Amelia heard the voice of her Aunt Elena.

"Amelia, thank God! Where are you?"

"I don't have much time to explain... Where is Laura?"

"At this time of the day she's in class, you know that very well. But what about you? Where are you? Are you going to come back?"

"I... I can't explain... I'm sorry about what happened... How's my little child? How are my parents?"

"Your son is well. Águeda looks after him like she was his mother, but we haven't seen him again. Santiago... well, Santiago has cut off all contact with the family. Your parents call Águeda to find out about the child."

"And my father? What about my father? Does he know anything about Herr Itzhak?"

"Your father... Well, he had a heart attack when you left, but don't worry, it wasn't anything serious, the doctor said it was his blood pressure, he's better now."

Amelia burst into tears. Suddenly she realized the consequences of what she had set in motion with her departure. She had not wanted to think about all she'd left behind, she preferred to think that everything would remain as it had been, that nothing would change. And now she found out that Santiago had stopped her parents from seeing Javier, that her father had suffered a heart attack... and it was all her fault.

"My God, what have I done? You'll never be able to forgive me!" she said between sobs.

"Why not come home? If you come, then everything will be sorted out... I am sure that Santiago still loves you, and if you ask his forgiveness... You have a son... he can't refuse to forgive his son's mother. Come back, Amelia, come back... Your parents will be so happy, they miss you every day, as do we. Laura has been ill as well, from the shock... I am sure that no one will blame you if you come back. Do you remember the parable of the prodigal son?"

"And what about Edurne?" Amelia managed to ask.

"She's with us, your cousin Laura insisted that she stay here... Santiago did not want to have her..."

"What have I done? What have I done?"

"It wasn't your fault, it was the company you got mixed up in. That Lola, those Communists... Leave them, Amelia, leave them and come home."

The man decided to cut the connection. He realized that this young woman, Comrade Pierre's lover, was about to give in to her aunt's appeals. The best thing was to stop them from talking and to call Doña Anita immediately. She would know what to do.

"Hey, I've been cut off!" Amelia called, trying to attract his attention.

"One moment, Madam, I'll see if I can get it set up again, stay in the booth."

But instead he called Doña Anita, to whom he explained quickly what he had heard.

"Keep her there, I won't be a minute. These bourgeois women think that life is just a game."

Amelia stayed impatiently in the booth waiting for the line to her aunt's house to be set up again. She would have preferred to have spoken with Laura, but her aunt had been loving and understanding. If she went home... maybe they'd forgive her.

Suddenly she felt cold eyes drilling into her. Doña Anita headed toward the booth that held her.

"Amelia, darling, what a coincidence! I had to go out on an errand and I thought I saw you from the street. Who were you waiting to talk to, my dear?"

She wanted to run away, to escape, but Doña Anita had already seized her arm.

"I wanted to talk to my family," she said, in tears.

"Of course, of course! Well, I'll wait while they make the connection."

"No, don't worry, there are problems with the line, and I'll call again."

"But you don't have to come all the way here, there's a telephone in the bookshop, it's one of my few luxuries."

"It was so as not to bother you... ," Amelia offered as an excuse.

"You? Bother me? Impossible, you and Pierre are both welcome in my house. We have common goals. You don't know how lucky you were when Pierre fell in love with you. How many woman wanted to be the chosen one! And he's so kind and such a gentleman with you... Take advantage of what life offers you and don't give up this great love... Listen to me, I know what I'm talking about."

Amelia paid for the phone call and left the Central Telegraph Office with Doña Anita, who still held her arm tightly.

"Now I'll come with you and buy your fabric, is that alright? And stop crying, you've made your nose as red as a pepper, and your eyes are all shrunken. What a shock if Pierre were to see you like this! Come on, we'll go and see your friend Lola this afternoon, she'll know how to cheer you up."

Doña Anita did not leave her alone for another minute. She hid the annoyance she felt in having to be the "guardian" for the "little bourgeois girl," which was how she thought of Amelia, and spent the rest of the day accompanying her on a pointless ramble through the city. When they met Pierre in the afternoon, Doña Anita hid her annoyance with great difficulty, and Amelia made no effort to hide the depression that had overcome her since her conversation with her aunt.

Pierre had already been informed by the telegraph office employee about the conversation between Amelia and Doña Elena.

"How was your day?" he asked, feigning ignorance.

"Very good, we went shopping, Amelia needed some things for your trip to Buenos Aires," Doña Anita replied.

"Well, I'd like to invite you to dinner. I met Josep and he will bring Lola and Pablo with him. The best thing after a day of work is to eat with friends. Come on Amelia, wipe away that frown and tidy yourself up a bit; I need to speak with Doña Anita about the book I came here to buy: I need her expert opinion."

Amelia obediently shut herself up in the room she shared with Pierre. It was difficult for her to think about seeing Lola, especially when she was so downcast. But she did not dare to contradict Pierre, so she opened the wardrobe and looked for something to wear. Meanwhile, Pierre and Doña Anita spoke in the bookshop, far from Amelia's ears.

"I know what happened, Comrade López told me the same time he told you. As far as I can tell, it was an unimportant conversation," Pierre said.

"He wasn't able to tell me exactly what they were talking about, but the girl has spent all day whining and moaning about her son. I don't know, I think you'll have problems with her. She's very young, and I think she regrets leaving her family," Doña Anita replied.

"If she becomes a problem I'll send her back to Madrid myself."

"Oh, you seemed to love her so much!"

Pierre did not reply. It annoyed him to lose control over Amelia. He was sick of pretending to be head over heels in love, sick of having to pretend to be a great seducer, sick of having to pay attention to every single one of her grimaces. He was almost hoping she would say that she was returning to Madrid. If he hadn't already planned his cover in Buenos Aires with her, he would have left her there, in Barcelona, to make her way back to Madrid as best she could.

Amelia came down to find them and everything about her suggested apathy: her gestures, her walk, her absent attitude.

They walked to the Barrio Gótico, where there was a little restaurant owned by a comrade, and where Josep, Lola, and Pablo were already waiting for them.

"You're late," Lola complained. "We've been here for half an hour already. Pablo is starving."

We sat down at a table a little distance from the rest of the customers, and Pierre, making an effort, tried to liven up the meeting a little. But neither Amelia nor Lola wanted to play along, and Doña Anita was a nervous wreck after spending the whole day with Amelia.

Josep tried to help Pierre in his distress and made great efforts to cheer everyone up. In the end, the two men decided to give way to the women, and they got involved in a conversation about the latest political events, in particular the evidence, growing stronger by the day, that a sector of the army wanted to bring the Republican experiment to an end. Everyone was talking about General Mola.

Amelia scarcely touched a mouthful; Lola and Doña Anita always had good appetites.

When the meal was over, Josep offered to accompany them part of the way back to Doña Anita's house. Pierre and Amelia walked in front, and even though they spoke in low voices I was able to hear parts of their conversation.

"What's wrong, Amelia, why are you sad?"

"No reason."

"Come on, don't try to lie to me, I know that something's getting to you."

She burst into tears and covered her face with her hands while Pierre put his hand on her shoulder in a protective gesture.

"I love you, but... I think I've been very selfish, I've only thought about myself, about how I want to be with you, and I haven't behaved well, I haven't behaved well," she repeated.

"Where does all this come from, Amelia? We've spoken about this before. You yourself said that you can't make an omelette without breaking eggs. I know that it's not easy to break with your family, you think I don't understand that? You don't get on well with my mother, but she's my mother and I love her, and I think we should give ourselves the chance of starting a new life: Just as you abandoned your family, so I have left mine, as well as leaving my business and my future."

"But you don't have a son!"

"No, I don't have a son, but I would like to have one as soon as our relation is firm and permanent. Nothing would make me happier. It is my sole regret, that you cannot bring Javier with you, at least for now, but let's not set aside the idea that we may be able to have him with us in the future."

"That will never happen! Santiago will not allow it; he won't even let my parents see the baby."

"How do you know that? Have you spoken to your parents?"

Amelia blushed. She realized that she had let the cat out of the bag, but then she thought that Doña Anita would have told Pierre anyway.

"I have spoken to my Aunt Elena. I called to speak to my cousin Laura but she was not there, and my aunt took the call."

"That's good, you shouldn't lose touch with your family. I know that you will be calmer if you know how things are with them," Pierre said, hiding the fact that he felt the exact opposite. "Tell me what your aunt said."

"She knows from Águeda, the nurse, that Javier is well. Santiago doesn't want to have anything to do with my family and won't let them see the child. My father fell ill when I left, his heart... my fault... He could have died."

"This I cannot permit! I will not allow you to blame yourself for your father's illness. Be rational, nobody gets heart disease from shock; if your father had a heart attack, you were not the reason for it. Insofar as your husband won't let them see your son, that seems to me cruel, it doesn't speak well of him, and it doesn't seem fair to punish your parents in this way. No, Amelia, your husband is not behaving well."

Pierre's words made Amelia sob all the more, as she tried to justify her husband's behavior.

"He's a good man and he's not unfair, it's just that seeing my parents reminds him of me, and he has his reasons for wanting to forget me. I behaved so badly! Santiago did not deserve to be treated like that!"

Pierre spent that night consoling Amelia, trying to soothe the pain of the open wound in her conscience.

The next day was July 13, which would turn out to be a key date in Spanish history: José Calvo Sotelo, leader of the monarchist Right, was assassinated.

Pierre decided to go to Madrid, even though he did not have specific orders to do so; this was a sufficiently serious occurrence for him to go to the capital and make contact with some of the comrades who regularly gave him news about the Azaña government. Although there were *rezidentura* agents in Madrid, Pierre wanted to evaluate the situation himself and send an accurate report to Moscow.

Amelia was overjoyed to hear that they would travel to Madrid. Pierre deceived her by saying that he had decided to travel because of the pain she was obviously feeling. The truth was that he did not dare to leave her with Doña Anita, and Lola and Amelia were distant with each other for the time being, something that he would have to work out the reasons for in due course.

The train journey seemed to last forever. When they finally reached Madrid, they found the capital buzzing with all kinds of rumors. Pierre decided to set up base in La Carmela, a boarding-house on Calle Calderón de la Barca, near the parliament. The owners of La Carmela kept a clean house, and looked after their guests very well. They were proud that these guests had even included a member of parliament or two. They only had four rooms, and Amelia and Pierre were lucky that one of them happened to be available.

"Don José left yesterday, you know him, the commercial traveler from Valencia who comes once a month. I think your paths might have crossed once or twice," said Doña Carmela, the landlady.

"Yes, I think so," Pierre replied, without much desire to talk.

"I didn't know you were married," Doña Carmela said.

"Well, you see... ," Pierre answered ambiguously.

Pierre worried about what to do with Amelia during their stay in Madrid. He could not take her everywhere with him, he had to meet agents and have private conversations, which would be impossible with Amelia present. But if he left her alone he was sure that she would end up giving in to her desire to see her family, and who knows what the consequences of that might be. So he decided to take the initiative, to set up the meeting himself and to be there when it happened.

"Maybe you should talk to Doña Laura. She can tell you better than I can what happened during those days in Madrid. Then come back and we can carry on talking," Pablo Soler concluded with a satisfied smile.

Pablo Soler smiled at me in satisfaction. He had been speaking for more than four hours and not once had I opened my mouth. I could not overcome my surprise: My great-grandmother had run away with a Frenchman, a Soviet agent, and she had joined the French Communist Party. Such a sweet-seeming thing, and then all of a sudden she turns out to be a budding Mata Hari.

"Did you see Amelia again?"

"Yes, of course, when they came back to Barcelona. But I've already told you that one of my best books is about the Soviet agents of that time, and Pierre was one of them. So I had to investigate everything that happened to him. He was an interesting man, a fanatic, although he didn't seem like one. I think you should read my book, it will be very useful for you."

"Do you mention my great-grandmother in it?"

"No."

Pablo got up and took a fairly thick book from a shelf. I thanked him for the present and said that I would be sure to call on him again.

"Yes, do, I don't have so much going on these days, I've just sent a book off to the printer, so I'm practically on holiday."

He accompanied me to the door, and his wife came out to meet us on the way.

"Won't you stay for lunch with us?" she asked with a smile.

"Ah, Charlotte, I haven't introduced you. This is Señor Albi."

"Pleased to meet you. I am Guillermo Albi."

"Señor Albi, I have to thank you for keeping my husband entertained; he doesn't know what to do when he's not writing, and he had no option other than to stop writing now, given that he's just finished a book. So you came at a welcome moment."

"Thank you very much, I hope I won't have to intrude too often, although Don Pablo has given me permission to come and see you again soon."

Although she was older, Charlotte was clearly the woman from the painting that had attracted my attention. She seemed to be North American, although she spoke good Spanish with a soft southern accent. I thought that Don Pablo's wife was very friendly, and must have been very beautiful in the past, she still had traces of her former beauty.

I went to the hotel so I could call Doña Laura at my leisure. I was starting to enjoy this job my Aunt Marta had employed me to do. I was going from surprise to surprise, and I could just imagine the scene when my family sat down to read the story next Christmas. My Aunt Marta, a real right-winger, was going to have kittens when she discovered that her grandmother had been the lover of a Soviet agent.

I turned on my mobile on the way back to the hotel. I had an urgent message from the head of the culture section on the online newspaper I worked for. I called him straight away.

"Guillermo, what's going on? You should have given us the Pamuk review yesterday. You've really screwed things up for us, we had ads running from the publishing house and they've rung us up to ask what's going on."

"I'm sorry, Pepe, I got sidetracked, I'll send it to you right away, give me an hour."

"An hour? This is an online newspaper, and I've got to upload the article now. Where the hell are you?"

"In Barcelona, I came to meet a historian, Pablo Soler."

"Wow! Soler's one of the big names, his books on the Civil War are some of the most serious and balanced ones there are. He's an authority in the North American universities."

"Yes, I know, he's the real deal. Well, I got the chance to meet him and... Well, I didn't do the Orhan Pamuk review, but I read the book and it won't take me any time at all to write the article and send it to you. Let me get back to the hotel, I'm on my way now."

"Well, just this once... and hey, now that you know Pablo Soler, ask for an interview; it'd be a real coup, he doesn't like journalists and he never gives interviews."

"Alright, I'll try, let's see what he says."

"Give it a go, at least it'll stop the boss from being so cross with you. Oh, and get me the article in the next half hour."

My mother had been right: I was getting so caught up in my great-grandmother's story that I was forgetting my own reality, a rubbishy job at an online newspaper where they paid me a hundred euros per article. It had been months since I'd earned more than four hundred euros, enough to pay for cigarettes and bus fare, but not much else. If Pablo Soler agreed to give me an interview, then maybe the director of the newspaper would think that I was good for more than just writing book reviews. They paid more for interviews. Of course, it was a bit embarrassing to go back to Professor Soler's house and ask for an interview; it was one thing for him to agree to talk about my great-grandmother, and quite another for him to agree to talk to the press. But I would try. I wasn't in any financial position to allow myself delicate feelings, even with Aunt Marta's support during the investigation into Amelia Garayoa.

4

I had not read the whole of Pamuk's book, but I was practiced enough at my job to be able to bluff my way through a review, which is what I did. I called Pepe to ask him if he'd gotten the review, and after that was done I felt calmer. He insisted that I interview Professor Soler, and I promised I would try. Then I called my mother.

"But where are you? I've been calling your mobile all morning but it was turned off."

"I'm in Barcelona, I've been meeting with a man who knew great-grandmother."

"He knew her? He must be as old as the hills, because your great-grandmother would be over ninety now, if she were still alive."

"Well, he was a kid when he knew her, but he's pretty old, yes."

"Who is he?"

"I'm not going to tell you, I'm not going to say anything until I've finished the investigation, but I will tell you that my great-grandmother had a pretty busy life, and that you'll be surprised."

"Your Aunt Marta has been ringing me to complain: She says that you won't tell her how the investigation's going, and that she doesn't know if you're really working or just living the high life at her expense."

"Your sister's a real charmer."

"Guillermo, she's your aunt and she loves you a lot!"

"Me? Well, she must have taken acting classes, because she's very good at hiding it."

"Guillermo, don't be silly."

"Well, I won't deal with Aunt Marta any more than necessary. Well, I'm ringing to see how you are and if you'll have me round for dinner this evening."

"Of course, I want to see you."

"Well, I'll be at the door at ten on the dot."

I hung up and thought about how my mother had infinite patience with me.

Then I called Doña Laura; I wanted her to tell me what had happened in those days before the Civil War, or else to tell me who could give me that information, because it was clear that this was the only lead I had to follow.

The housekeeper seemed to vacillate when I told her who I was and asked if I could speak to Doña Laura or Doña Melita. She left me waiting and it was only after several minutes that I heard the voice of Doña Laura, which seemed less lively than on previous occasions.

"I'm not well, I've had hypoglycemia," she said in what was little more than a whisper.

"I don't want to bother you, but Professor Soler told me that Amelia was in Madrid two or three days before the Civil War broke out and that she was trying to get in touch with her family. The Professor told me that you might be able to let me know what happened during those days, before he tells me the rest of his story. But if you're not well, I suppose... I could wait or else you could give me the name of someone else to talk to."

Doña Laura told me again that she was not well and that the doctor had told her to keep to her bed. As for Doña Melita, she wasn't well either, so maybe it would be best for me to talk to Edurne.

"It was Edurne whom Amelia saw in those days. She was only with me for less than an hour. Come tomorrow morning, but try not to tire her out too much, she's very old and this is a big effort for her."

"I'll try to keep the conversation as short as possible, I promise."

I realized that all my sources were old people who were entering the last leg of their lives. I would have to work fast, or else

I might find that they'd vanished overnight. I decided to concentrate on my investigation and just sleep less so as not to lose my job with the online paper.

When I got to the airport, there were only business-class tickets back to Madrid. I wondered if I should wait for the next flight, but then I thought that Aunt Marta wasn't going to go bust just by paying a little more for a flight.

When I got back I took a taxi. I was headed home when my mobile buzzed and pulled me out of my reveries.

"Guillermo, handsome, where've you gone to? You haven't called me for more than a fortnight."

"Hello Ruth, I'm in Madrid, I just got back from Barcelona."

"I wondered if you'd like to have dinner with me, I've got a great foie gras I bought in Paris yesterday."

I didn't hesitate. I called my mother to apologize; an evening with Ruth was much more exciting, especially if we started to look deep into each other's eyes over the liver. Ruth was a flight attendant for a low-fare airline, and did the Paris run a lot, so I could be sure that the foie gras would be accompanied by a fine Burgundy. So it looked like a great night.

My mother grumbled, but she didn't get cross. The truth is that when she told me what she'd cooked, I became even more sure that I wanted to eat with Ruth. My mother was convinced that I ate badly, so whenever I went to see her she would insist that I have salad, followed by grilled fish without salt.

It was a memorable evening. I had forgotten how much I missed Ruth until I saw her again. She was extremely patient with me and wasn't trying to hurry me into marriage. She gave me space, I don't know whether this was because she only wanted to use me from time to time or because she realized that I wasn't mature enough to make any kind of commitment. But whatever, it was an ideal relationship.

I arrived at the Garayoas' house at eleven in the morning. The housekeeper told me that Doña Laura was still in bed and that Doña Melita was at the doctor's, having some tests done. Amelia María had taken her.

Edurne was sitting in the library waiting for me. She was not happy to see me.

"Didn't I tell you enough?"

"I promise I won't bother you too much, but I want to know what happened when Amelia came back to Madrid with Pierre. It must have been about the fourteenth or fifteenth of June in '36. Doña Laura told me that you saw her."

"Yes, I saw her," Edurne said in a very faint voice. "How could I forget..."

Amelia and Pierre had been in Madrid for a couple of days. He'd asked a couple of friends, a married couple, to look after Amelia and not to leave her alone. Although she tried to get out of being accompanied, she had no option but to accept, but the loss of liberty and the lack of trust shown by Pierre were such that she started to think about leaving him. But Amelia really only felt confused, and the idea of leaving Pierre evaporated when she saw him appear smiling, with a rose in his hand.

One day he realized that there was no way of delaying Amelia's encounter with her family any longer, that he could not tell her any more stories. On the morning of the seventeenth, with Pierre by her side, Amelia telephoned Laura. Laura was not at home, she had gone out with her sister Melita and her brother Jesús and her mother, Doña Elena. Don Armando was not there either. Amelia, in desperation, asked for me. She wanted to see her parents, but she didn't dare turn up at their house without knowing who would be there, or if they would agree to receive Pierre.

I was so happy when I heard her voice, and she asked me to go to La Carmela, the boardinghouse where she was staying. I got there in less than ten minutes, and you can't imagine how fast I ran, because it was quite a long way.

We saw each other and began to weep. We hugged for a long time before Pierre could separate us.

"Come on, stop crying! Were you so keen to see each other? Well..."

Amelia asked me to tell her how her family was.

"Don Juan is better, he has recovered well from the heart attack; Doña Teresa won't leave his side. Your mother had a terrible fright, she was with Don Juan when he had the attack. At least she had enough presence of mind to call the chauffeur and get him to take Don Juan to hospital right away. That's what saved his life. But your father is sad, he's not been the same since you left. Doña Teresa has grown old suddenly, but she hasn't given way; she's the main support for the whole house. Antonietta took it badly as well; she was crying for weeks."

"Do you think my parents will forgive me if I go to see them?"

"Of course! They'll be so happy."

"And what will they say about Pierre?"

"But... is he going to come with you?"

"Yes, Pierre is... is... well, he's like my husband."

"But he isn't your husband!"

"I know, but it doesn't matter. As soon as I can I am going to get divorced and marry him, it's only a matter of time."

"But your parents are still extremely shaken by what happened, is there no way you can go by yourself?"

Amelia would have liked to do this, but Pierre was not ready for her to meet her family without him being present. He was afraid of losing her. And he was in fact very close to losing her.

"And what about my son? How is Javier?"

"We only hear about him via Águeda. Don Santiago doesn't want to know anything about your family. He has said that he prefers to establish a distance between them, and that we will see in the future if he will allow them to see your son. But he's a good man, he allows your parents to call and see Águeda when he's not there to ask about the child."

"Have you seen my son?"

"No, I haven't dared to go. But you have no need to worry, Águeda is looking after him very well, she loves him as if he were her own child."

Amelia burst into tears; she felt indebted to Águeda for looking after her child, but at the same time it hurt her greatly that she was playing the role of the baby's mother.

"But he's my son! He's mine!"

"Yes, he's your son, but you are not here."

These words were worse than a slap in the face. She looked at me in angry pain.

"I want my son!" she shouted.

Pierre held her, afraid that she would have a fit, which wouldn't look good in La Carmela, where people thought they were a married couple.

"Calm down, Amelia, nobody is saying that Javier is not your son, and we will get him back, just you wait, but all in good time. We will start divorce proceedings from Buenos Aires, and then you can come back for Javier."

"Are you going to Buenos Aires?" I asked.

"I don't know! I don't want to go anywhere!"

You could see that Pierre was fed up with the situation, and I think he was just about to tell me that I should take Amelia, and good riddance.

"You don't have to come if you don't want. I just wanted to start a new life, far away from our past, and if you don't love me..."

"Yes, yes, I love you! But I think I'm going mad!"

"It's best if you go, Edurne, you know where we are. Tell Amelia's aunt and uncle, and if they think it's a good idea we can go to their house, or to Amelia's parents' house. I want to beg pardon from Don Juan and Doña Teresa for the damage I have caused them, and to let them know that I love Amelia more than life itself and only want her to be happy."

I went home in a state of extreme surprise. I had admired Pierre ever since I had seen him in Lola's house. He was so commanding, seemed so sure of himself... I was sure that he was completely in love with Amelia. Although I realized that she wasn't happy, that she regretted the step she had taken, and that if she could undo the actions she had taken, then she would do it in an instant. But I did not know how to help her, I felt as confused as she did.

Doña Elena and her children did not get back until midday, and when I told them that Doña Amelia was in Madrid, seemed very unhappy, and wanted to see them, Laura did not hesitate.

"We'll go see her at once!"

"But we cannot go to that boardinghouse, where she is staying with that man!"

"Why not? Don't you see that she doesn't dare come here?"

"She's welcome to come here, but not with that man. That's what Edurne has to say to her. We want to see her and we will go with her to her parents' house, but she has to come alone. It would be a disgrace for her to present herself here with that man. Your Uncle Juan would die of shock. Amelia has to understand that."

"Don't be like that, Mama!" Laura protested.

"I will not have that man in my house! Never! He is shameless, he has taken advantage of Amelia's innocence, and I don't want to deal with people like that."

"Mama, Amelia is in love with Pierre!"

"Right, so now you tell us that she ran away for love, and not to start a revolution... Santiago was right."

"But, Mama..."

"That's enough, we will do as I say. Edurne, go and see Amelia and tell her that we will wait for her. As for that man, she must understand that no decent family can receive him. Your father is about to arrive and he will agree with me."

I ran back to La Carmela without realizing that Laura was following close behind me. She had decided to disobey her mother in order to see Amelia; she was afraid that Amelia would refuse to come see them if she could not come with Pierre. She caught up with me just as I was about to go into the building. We went up together to the boardinghouse, which was on the second floor. Amelia and Pierre were having lunch in the little dining room. I can remember even today that they were having fried eggs and peppers.

If Amelia had cried when she saw me, it was nothing next to the flood of tears she shed when she saw Laura. The two cousins hung together in an endless embrace.

Pierre felt uncomfortable, especially as Doña Carmela did not miss the chance to come into the dining room to see what was going on. He suggested that we go out into the street to someplace where we could talk without being seen. He took us to a café in the Plaza de Santa Ana, and the four of us sat down.

"Amelia, you have to come home, Mama will call your parents and we will all go to see them together, but you have to come alone. You have to understand that you are not welcome for the time being, perhaps at some point in the future... ," Laura said, addressing this last sentence to Pierre.

Amelia seemed prepared to allow her cousin to convince her, but Pierre's reaction prevented this.

"I will do whatever Amelia wants, but I must say that it was not easy for my family to accept my relationship with a married woman, and, much as I love my mother, I have made it clear to her that if I do have to choose between her and Amelia, then my choice will be Amelia."

When she heard this, Amelia felt obliged to take his side.

"If you don't want him to come with me, then I will not go," she said in tears.

"But Amelia, you have to understand! Your father has had a heart attack, and if you appear with Pierre who knows what will happen to him? And you could hurt your mother as well... It's better to take things slowly, let them see you and then you can convince them that they should receive Pierre. You can't ask for your parents to accept a man who isn't your husband, just like that; and you know that your father likes Santiago a lot..."

Pierre held Amelia and stroked her hair.

"All shall be well!" he said in an impassioned voice. "Don't worry, all shall be well, but we have to show the whole world that our love is true."

Amelia disengaged herself and dried her tears with Pierre's handkerchief.

"Tell your parents that I will not go anywhere if it is not with him. I want to divorce Santiago and become Pierre's wife. If you can willingly manage to help my parents receive me, I will be the happiest woman in the world; if you cannot, then I am happy that I have at least managed to see you and embrace you. I am sure that you will be able to convince them but if it is not to be... then at least promise me that you will never forget me, and will try to forgive me one day. Now, go home with Edurne and try to do what I have asked you."

They embraced again, again in tears, and Laura promised that she would try to convince her parents.

"At least I hope that Papa will help us; he is more understanding than my mother. Neither she nor your mother are in favor of divorce, but I am sure that if they know that you are going to get married then they will soften their stance a little."

Who could have known that when we got home it would be to find Don Armando in a highly agitated state, upset by the news that had just reached him from North Africa, where a group of soldiers had apparently rebelled.

The news was confused during the first few hours, and people said that there could have been an insurrection led by the generals Mola, Queipo de Llano, Sanjurjo, and Franco.

"Papa, I need to talk to you," Laura said to Don Armando.

"I can't talk now, I need to get over to Parliament, I am meeting a deputy there, I'm his lawyer; I want to know what's going on."

"Amelia is in Madrid."

"Amelia? Your cousin?"

"Yes, your niece is here, Armando, and Laura has run off to see her. I was going to tell you but you gave me no time, you were so upset about this rebellion... ," Doña Elena added.

The news upset Don Armando severely. This was the worst of all possible days to face a family drama. The country was falling to pieces and the family had to think about Amelia.

"We must tell her parents. Sort it out, Elena, we have to go to my brother's house. Where is this madwoman?"

"In the La Carmela boardinghouse, with Pierre."

"That scoundrel! Well, let's go for her. Good God! She had to come today, didn't she!"

"For goodness' sake, Papa, the important thing is that she is here!" Melita, his oldest daughter, said.

"The important thing is that we don't know if there's a coup d'état going on, with all the terrible consequences it will bring. Well, let's do what we have to do, let's go and find her."

"No, Papa, we can't do it unless you are ready to accept Pierre," Laura declared.

"Accept that scoundrel! Never!"

"Papa, Amelia says that she will only agree to come here or to her parents' house if she comes with Pierre, and if not..."

"But how dare she set conditions? No, we will not receive that man, I will not open my house to him," Doña Elena insisted.

"Explain yourself, Amelia," Don Armando said extremely seriously.

"Either we receive the pair of them or Amelia will not come here or to her parents' house, she was very clear about that. Papa, I beg you to accept Pierre, if you don't then we will lose Amelia forever. Edurne has said that he is planning to take her to Buenos Aires. I think that if we go to her and pretend that we accept him, then we might be able to convince her to stay; if we don't then we'll lose her for good."

Don Armando felt overwhelmed by events, political as much as familial.

"Listen, after what Amelia has done she cannot set any conditions. This house will always have its doors open for her, and I am sure that my brother would say the same if his daughter were ever to knock on his door. But she cannot insist that we accept a man who has brought so much scandal on the family. And I don't dare go to your uncle's house and upset him by giving him the dilemma that if he wants to see his daughter then it has to be with this Pierre. It would be cruel to him."

"I know, Papa. I tried to reason with Amelia, but it was impossible. It's... it's like she's lost her free will. Pierre has carried her away."

"What are we going to do?" Doña Elena wanted to know.

"Edurne will go back to the boardinghouse and explain that if Amelia wants to come then it will have to be without that man. Then we will take her to her parents' house," Don Armando declared.

"And if she refuses?" Laura said in a very small voice.

"We will be in a very difficult situation. I will have to go see my brother and tell him what has happened, and I'm afraid that it will give him such a shock that it might affect his health."

"Papa, why don't you go see Amelia?" Laura begged.

"Me? No, it's not right that I should see that man, who deserves only to be challenged to a duel for what he's done."

Just as they told me, I went back to the boardinghouse, but I couldn't find Amelia or Pierre. The landlady told me that they had hurried out because a young man had come to the house to tell Pierre that there was a military uprising taking place in North Africa. The landlady told me that she was shocked by the news of the uprising, but even so she had no qualms in asking me what was going on between Amelia and Pierre, and why Amelia wouldn't stop crying. I didn't answer her, I only asked if she knew where they had gone or when they would come back, but she couldn't tell me and so I went home.

That night Amelia telephoned Laura. Don Armando and Doña Elena had gone to Don Juan's house and they had not yet returned. Laura tried to convince her cousin to see her family without Pierre being present, but it was no use. Amelia said that they would be going back to Barcelona the next afternoon and from there to France. She did not know if they would see each other again.

Edurne fell silent, looking into the distance, just as when we had spoken the last time. It was as if these memories hit her hard and she did not know how to control them.

"Is that everything?" I asked.

"Yes, that's it. Amelia left. Doña Teresa and Antonietta went to La Carmela the next day, but she had already gone. It wasn't easy for Doña Teresa to go to a boardinghouse, looking for her daughter, but she had decided that she needed to drag Amelia out of Pierre's clutches; her love for her daughter was stronger than any social or familial convention. She didn't tell Don Juan, she just made her decision and asked Antonietta to go with her, but they were too late. She cried a lot and blamed herself for not having acted sooner and gone earlier, or even the previous night. I suppose Pierre thought that it was better for them to leave earlier, before Amelia's family came to take her away."

I took my leave of Edurne and thanked her sincerely for all that she had told me, saying that I hoped I would not have to bother her again. I was upset by all that I had heard, and asked myself what had happened next with Amelia. It was clear that I would have to talk to Pablo Soler again.

I met Amelia María and her Aunt Melita downstairs. All these Amelias!

"I'm just leaving," I said, before Amelia María could make a face.

"Yes, I knew you were coming today."

"And how are you?" I asked the old woman, who was walking extremely slowly, with a nurse and her great-niece helping her.

"I'm on my last legs, my dear, but I'll hang on until I read your story," she said with a smile. "I think I'm a bit better today, and the doctors say they can't find anything; as if old age weren't an illness, but it is, my dear Guillermo, it is. The worst of it is that you lose your memories."

"Come on, Auntie, you need to rest. Help my aunt to the elevator," Amelia María said to the nurse.

Amelia María stayed for a few moments watching her great-aunt get into the elevator with the nurse.

"Well, Guillermo, how's your story getting along?"

"It's full of surprises, I think my great-grandmother had a very exciting life."

"Yes, I'm sure. What else?"

"Nothing special, your Aunt Laura is helping me a lot and giving me a lot of leads. What did the doctor say to Doña Melita?"

"She's alright; her health is good, which is a miracle given her age. I hired a nurse a few days ago to be in the house and help the pair of them. I'm not happy to leave them alone when I go to work. If something does happen the nurse will know what to do."

"That's the right thing to do. Well, lovely to see you, Auntie."

"What?"

"We are related, even if you're not happy about it, and you must be something like my aunt several times removed, right?"

"You know what, Guillermo? You're not as funny as you think you are."

"I wasn't trying to be funny."

I liked to annoy her because she reminded me a lot of my Aunt Marta.

I went to my mother's to eat the salad that I knew I would not be able to escape, then I went to the editor's office at the online newspaper to pick up my modest check, and then I went straight to the airport. Pablo Soler had agreed to see me the next morning. He was a man who liked to get up early: the meeting, once again, was scheduled for eight a.m.

5

Charlotte opened the door and went with me to her husband's office.

"I'll make some coffee," she said in a maternal voice.

A few minutes later the door opened and a maid came in with a tray on which stood a coffee pot, a jug of milk, and a plate of toast. Don Pablo served coffee for both of us, but he made no move to take a piece of toast, and so I did not either, even though I would have liked to have one, thickly spread with jam and butter.

"So, what did Doña Laura tell you?" he asked me.

"I couldn't see her, she's a bit out of sorts, but I spoke with Edurne, you know who she is."

"Good old Edurne, of course. Doña Laura is very fond of her. I spoke to her last night and she says she's feeling much better. As far as Edurne is concerned... she was an exceptional witness to everything that happened. Lola held her in very high regard, much higher than she did Amelia; she thought of her as an equal, a worker. Lola used to say that the Garayoas were being charitable, and that was why they treated Edurne well, but she herself supported the idea of social justice."

"Well, she was right," I replied.

"Yes, that time, although Lola's judgments were fairly arbitrary."

"It wasn't easy for her," I suggested.

"No, it really wasn't. But let's get back to our business."

I explained what Edurne had told me, and he listened to me carefully, and even, to my surprise, took notes. Then, after drinking the last sip of coffee, he took up his story where he had left it at our last meeting.

Pierre decided to return to Barcelona, where he wanted to make contact with one of his informants and then go immediately to France and meet up with Igor Krisov. The military upheaval put the government in a difficult position. Taking into account that he was an agent who traveled everywhere, but also that he had valuable contacts in Spain, Pierre did not know if his Moscow bosses would decide to suspend the planned trip to South America. The ship was to sail at the end of July and Pierre arrived in Barcelona on the nineteenth, on what would turn out to be the first day of the Civil War.

I remember as if it were yesterday the night that Lola and Josep took me to Doña Anita's house for a meeting: There were Communists and guild leaders, journalists and union bosses, about twenty people all told.

Amelia gave me a loving hug. I remember her pallor and her reddened eyes. Doña Anita scolded her for having lost so much weight in so few days. Josep started to summarize the situation.

"People are worried because they think that the army might rise up here as well. It seems that the rebellion has had success in Galicia, in Castile, in Navarre, in Aragón, in a few Andalusian cities and in Asturias; they say that it is also finding success in the islands, the Balearics and the Canaries. But these are unconfirmed reports, everything is too confused. And everything points to the air force staying loyal to the Republic."

"And Companys, what will he do?" Pierre wanted to know.

Marcial Lluch, a journalist who sympathized with the Unified Socialist Party of Catalonia and was also a friend of Pierre's, answered.

"He will try to get the army on his side, he's speaking with them, but as far as I know he's not sure if he can trust even those who say they'll stay loyal to the legal Republic."

"And what are we doing?" Pierre asked Josep.

"Our people went to their offices asking for instructions. We don't have much that we can use to defend ourselves, but we do have something. The CNT is better organized and they don't seem to have problems getting weapons. But why doesn't Lola tell you, she's seen some of the fighting."

Pierre looked at Lola with interest. He saw in her someone as hard as flint, the type of person the revolution needed. She did not hesitate.

She swallowed before starting to speak. She was someone who preferred action to words.

"In the morning a group of soldiers came from the Pedralbes barracks, and they had a big fight in University Square. Luckily the Assault Guards joined up with the militia, but we couldn't stop them taking the Central Telegraph Office, the Army and Fleet Headquarters, and even getting as far as the Columbus Hotel. We were very badly armed."

"And you were there?" Pierre asked in surprise.

"I went out into the street with a group of comrades."

"General Llanos de la Encomienda has said that he is opposed to the uprising," Marcial Lluch said.

"Yes, but he has no authority over the rebels," Doña Anita asserted.

"But his attitude is a good sign for those who are still vacillating," the journalist insisted. "The best thing is that the rebel troops were forced out of the university's central building by midday; they were also thrown out of Plaza de Cataluña, and the Central Telegraph Office was recaptured."

"They say that Buenaventura Durruti led the assault," Doña Anita said.

"That's right," Marcial Lluch, the journalist, confirmed. "And he didn't need anyone's help, it was just him and the CNT militiamen. He's got guts, alright. And the latest news is that the Military Command put out a white flag this evening at six. I think the militiamen wanted to shoot General Goded, but some higher-ups stopped them."

They talked for hours, analyzing the situation and the decisions the Communist bosses had made.

Pierre was worried, as was Josep; Lola on the other hand seemed euphoric. It was as if she thought that only armed conflict could do away with the hated Fascists. She was longing for a paradise where the angels would be proletarians like her. Josep, on the other hand, had not participated in any of the skirmishes because he had only arrived in Barcelona an hour before; his employer was now living in Perpignan. Josep and Lola had argued because she had left me alone in the house to go out and fight. Lola said that she had done this so that I could be a free man one day, and that nothing and no one would stop her fighting the Fascists. She even threatened to leave him if he stood in her way. I think that this was the day when Josep realized that my mother's only passion was Communism, and her only aim was to destroy Fascism; everything else was merely circumstantial, including him and me.

Lola seemed like a different woman, sure of herself, relaxed, as if the fighting had allowed her true nature to come to the surface. She spoke forcefully, and everyone noticed that she had changed.

While we helped Doña Anita to serve a snack, I asked Amelia if she had seen her family in Madrid.

"I was with my cousin Laura, but my family doesn't want to know anything about Pierre, and so I haven't seen my parents or my aunt and uncle," she replied, trying to hold back her tears.

"They are bourgeois and conventional, that should only have been expected. It's one thing to say that you believe in freedom, and another very different thing to show it. Your family doesn't want you to use your freedom as you want to use it," Lola said.

"It's not that, my father and my uncle are supporters of Azaña, but they think I made a mistake by leaving my son and my husband. My father always spoke to me about the responsibilities of freedom..."

"Responsible freedom! What's that when it's at home? You have to do what suits other people? You have signed up to be with a revolutionary, and he thinks that you have a lot to offer our cause. Maybe that's true. In any case, you are privileged, because you can show that you're not like the right-wing rabble, all those hypocrites who speak about the rights of others but refuse to lose their own privileges."

"My parents aren't like that! I'm sorry for what you've suffered, for the way life has abused you, but that stops you from seeing the reality of things. You judge everyone by the same criteria, divide the world into the good and the bad, and you can't put yourself in anyone else's skin. Anyone who has anything is bad in your eyes, but everything my parents have they have earned by their own efforts, their own work, they haven't exploited anyone."

"I understand that you defend your family, it shows you in a good light, it really does, but things are as they are, there are exploiters and exploited in the world and I am trying to get rid of this division and have everyone treated equally, to make sure that no one has an advantage for having been born into any particular family. My mother gave birth to me by herself, with only my sister to help her. Do you know how old my sister was? Eight, she was eight years old. And my mother had to leave me that same day so that she could go and clean the house of some bourgeois family for whom my mother meant less than nothing. My father had died two months earlier from tuberculosis, leaving my mother with two daughters. We were living in a tiny room, we even had to share a mattress. My mother had to go to the spring to fill two buckets if we wanted to wash; even so, she made us wash every day, even in winter when the water was freezing. Do you know when I started to work, the same as my sister, I was eight when I went to help my mother clean. She went to a house every day and did the hardest work: She washed the floors, cleaned the windows, emptied the chamberpots... We were never able to go to school, we didn't even have time to go to catechism class. Look at my hands, Amelia, look at them and tell me what you see. They are the hands of a cleaner. I grew up feeling envious, yes, envious of the houses where my mother went to clean, and where children of my age played peacefully and happily with dolls the likes of which I couldn't even dream about. Once a woman gave me her daughter's doll. She didn't want it anymore, she'd torn off one of her arms and one of her eyes was missing, but she was a treasure for me. I looked after her and cared for her as if she were a creature made of flesh and blood, and I made sure that no one hurt her like this rich girl had hurt her. I held her at night to keep her warm, and sometimes I even gave her my little corner of mattress so she could be comfortable, even if that meant I had to sleep on the floor. Have you seen my knees? I've got calluses from so much cleaning; you don't know how long I've spent on my knees washing floors, waxing floors, terrified that it wouldn't be shiny enough and that the ladies of the house would scold me, or would pay me less for my work. One Christmas, at one of the houses where we went to clean, they gave my mother the head and the feet of the chicken they had just killed for their meal that evening. Not the legs, Amelia, the feet. Those little thin feet with their three hard nails on them. That, and a loaf of bread. Can you imagine the party we had? When I was thirteen, the oldest son of the family got interested in me, so I had to put up with his wandering hands, still scared that they would sack my mother and me if I fought back. My older sister had died of tuberculosis by then, like my father before her. My mother was a believer and she told me that we had to accept what God sent us, but I asked what we had done to be treated like this. I felt guilty for a very long time, I was sure that we must have done something terrible to be condemned to poverty, but in the end I decided to rebel. The priest came to see my mother to tell her that I had become proud, that when I went to confession the only thing I did was to blame him for our situation, that I needed to learn to accept with joy whatever God sent. I went from feeling envious to feeling furious. I stopped feeling envious of the ladies in their fine houses and started to hate them. Yes, to hate them. There they were, living happy and cosseted, and their only task was to find a husband who would keep them in the style to which they were accustomed, comfortable, unworried. My mother insisted to the priest that the lay sisters who did good works in the parish, who showed the poor children how to sew, should also teach me. So, when I finished cleaning, I went to learn to sew. My poor mother dreamed of my becoming a seamstress, of not having to clean anymore. Apparently, I had a certain degree of talent for sewing, unlike my sister, who had to remain content with cleaning. I put up with the lay sisters until I had learned to sew, and then I told the priest that he would never see me in church again, not in the church of that God who punished us without our having done anything. You can imagine how upset he got. My mother begged me with tears in her eyes not to try to understand God's ways, that He knew what He was doing, but I had made a decision and was never going to change my mind. One day I met Josep; he was honest with me, and told me that he had been married, but that he and his wife had drifted apart. He taught me what Communism was, how to channel my rage in useful directions, how to fight for those who had nothing, people like me. He taught me to read as well, he gave me books, he treated me like an equal. We fell in love, Pablo was born, and here we are. I am fighting to make sure that my son is no less than yours. Why should he be? Tell me, why should he be?"

Amelia stayed watching me in silence. She couldn't find any answers to Lola's questions: Why should I, Pablo Soler, be any less than her son, Javier Carranza? Why was his future assured and mine not? Amelia was a very good person, and innocent, so even though Lola's questions tore her apart, she admitted that Lola was right, even though this meant putting distance between herself and the people she loved the most, her family.

"When are you leaving?" Lola asked, changing the subject brusquely.

"I don't know, Pierre hasn't told me. But our boat leaves Le Havre on the twenty-ninth of July, so we cannot stay much longer, unless he changes his plans."

"And why should he change them?"

"I don't know, but what's happening here is significant, even if we don't know the extent of the military uprising yet."

"It's the best that could happen, it will be them or us, and right is on our side, so we will get rid of fascism once and for all and found a workers' republic. We know it's possible, they've done it in Russia."

"And what will you do to the people who aren't Communists?"

Lola fixed her black eyes on Amelia and seemed to hesitate for a moment.

"They will have to accept reality. We will do away with classes: Your son Javier will be no greater than Pablo."

Amelia looked at me fondly. I was sitting on a chair near them, very quiet. My childhood took place in silence, with me not getting in the way, while my parents dreamed of revolution.

Lluís Companys, the president, told General Goded to make a broadcast to the rebel troops, telling them to give up their rebellion immediately. The general, who was the rebels' figurehead in the city, had no option other than to accept, although he did so with little enthusiasm. He was executed.

Armed conflicts continued throughout the night, and the news, which spread like wildfire across the city, signaled the triumph of the forces loyal to the Republic. The CNT fought like tigers, and their achievements were essential during those first few days.

On Monday, July 20, Barcelona was apparently calm again. The CNT militias patrolled the city. Catalonia's government, the Generalitat, sent down a decree the next day that allowed for the formation of the Citizen Militias, whose aim was to fight against Fascism and defend the Republic. From this moment on, the militias were a genuine power, and the Generalitat could do nothing without their help.

The Citizen Militias were controlled by the Central Committee of Anti-Fascist Militias, which contained representatives of all the parties and unions. Lola joined the militias, just as Josep did, but the truth must be told: She was a woman of action, whereas he was a good administrator, so he started to work with the Central Committee, organizing the work carried out by the patrols, while Lola became a militiawoman with a pistol on her belt, a member of one of the patrol squads whose aim was to keep order in the city, arrest suspects, search shops and houses looking for any sign of insurrection.

I still remember her with her black hair combed backwards, tied up in an improvised bun. I liked Lola's black hair. When I was little and ran to be comforted in her arms, I smelled her lavender smell. That's why I cried when she cut it off. One morning before she went out on patrol, I found her in front of the mirror, cutting off her long ponytail with scissors.

"What are you doing!" I cried.

"I need to be comfortable, and this is not the time to worry about hair. It gets in my way, the hairpins keep on falling out; it'll be better like this."

It was hard for me to recognize her with her hair cut so unevenly, so short it didn't even cover her ears.

"I don't like it, Mommy!" I said angrily.

"Pablo, you're not a little boy anymore, so don't make me waste my time. Your mother is fighting for you," she said, giving me a kiss and hugging me tight. Although in fact she was fighting for herself, for the childhood she had not been allowed to have.

Doña Anita invited us to a farewell dinner that she had arranged for Pierre and Amelia. It was just us, because Pierre and Doña Anita thought that Lola and Amelia were the best of friends, and that we were now the nearest thing Amelia had to a family.

Amelia seemed resigned to leaving, but she did not hide her apathy and lack of enthusiasm, even though Pierre preferred not to take the hint. He had thought up a plan for his time in South America, and Amelia was an alibi he was unwilling to renounce. But he was obviously trying to keep things bottled up, as if he were already disgusted by her.

Amelia and Pierre arrived in Paris on July 24, and they had another meeting there with Ivan Krisov, who wanted a first-hand account of Pierre's impressions of Spain.

Krisov wanted Pierre to bring Amelia with him, and arranged to meet them two days later in the Café de la Paix. They would run into each other in a seemingly fortuitous meeting, and he would introduce himself as a nationalized English antiques dealer, a false identity that he had sometimes used when he went to the Rousseau Bookshop.

On the afternoon of July 26, Pierre invited Amelia to take a walk with him around the city.

"We're going to Le Havre tomorrow, it will be our way of saying goodbye to Paris."

Amelia accepted indifferently. She didn't care; she felt like she was an object in the hands of fate, before whose whims she had to bow down.

They walked casually toward the Café de la Paix, where Pierre suggested they drink something. They had been there for ten minutes when Ivan Krisov appeared.

"Monsieur Comte! How are you? I was thinking only recently that I really should come by the bookshop again."

"How nice to see you, Monsieur Krisov, allow me to introduce Mademoiselle Garayoa. Amelia, Monsieur Krisov is an old client of the bookshop."

Igor held out his hand to Amelia and could not avoid feeling an immediate sense of pity for her. Maybe it was her youth, or her beauty, or her air of helplessness, but the experienced spy was captivated by Amelia.

"May I invite you to have a coffee with me? It is the first moment all day when I have been able to enjoy a little calm, and some company would be pleasant."

"Of course, Monsieur Krisov," Pierre accepted.

"Are you Spanish?" Krisov asked.

"Yes," Amelia replied.

"I don't know your country very well, I have only visited Bilbao, Barcelona, and Madrid..."

Krisov led the conversation. Amelia was cold and distant to begin with, but the Russian overcame her defenses until at last he made her smile. They spoke in French until Amelia let it slip that she had studied English and German. Krisov switched to English and then to German, jokingly trying to find out if this young woman really knew these languages as she said she did, and he was surprised to find out that not only was she relatively skilled, but her accent was also good.

"My father always insisted that we study English and German, and we spent some summers in Germany, at the house of one of his partners, Herr Itzhak Wassermann."

The Russian asked her to tell him about Herr Itzhak, and Amelia spoke at length about scenes from her childhood in Berlin, and her friend Yla.

"Of course, Hitler's coming to power has been a hard blow for my father's business. They have been taking everything from the Jews. My father has been insisting that Herr Itzhak leave Germany, but he's resisting, he says he is German. I hope that he pays attention to my father eventually, I don't want to imagine Yla in that repressive and hateful environment being treated like a criminal."

"If I agree with Monsieur Comte on one thing it is that Hitler is a danger for the whole of Europe, the worst face of Fascism," Krisov said.

"Oh, he's worse than Fascism, I can be sure of that," Amelia said ingenuously.

An hour later Pierre cut the meeting short, saying that his parents were waiting for them to have dinner.

"I hope we will meet again," Krisov said to Amelia as she left.

"My dear friend, it will be difficult, we are leaving for Le Havre tomorrow, out boat is waiting to take us to Buenos Aires," Pierre said.

That night, after dinner, Pierre claimed to have an unavoidable meeting with some comrades.

"My mother can help you finish packing..."

"No, I'd rather do it myself. Will you take long?"

"I hope not, but now that we're leaving for Buenos Aires I want to know if I can be useful for our cause. You know that I work with the Communist International."

Amelia accepted Pierre's excuse without any quibbles; she almost preferred to be alone.

Pierre met Ivan Krisov, his controller, in front of the door of the church of Saint-Germain.

"So, what did you think?" he asked Krisov.

"Sad and charming," he replied.

"Yes, it's not easy to be with her."

"Well, I envy you, my friend, she's very pretty. She'll be useful where you're going, her innocence is a good disguise. But be careful, she's no fool, and if one day she shakes off her lethargy and melancholy..."

"Who's going to deal with my Spanish contacts?" Pierre wanted to know, worried about the military uprising.

"Don't worry, they've got all the information about what's happening in Moscow. Just concentrate on your job."

"I'm not arguing with my orders, but wouldn't I be of more use in Spain, given the situation?"

"My friend, I can't tell you that. The department has decided to expand our intelligence service in South America, and that's what we need to do."

"Yes, but given the circumstances, I insist that I would be more useful in Spain."

"You need to be where Moscow decides you shall be. We are not doing this job for our own satisfaction, but in the service of a great idea. There are things it's better not to think about: You have your orders, obey them. That's the golden rule. Ah, I know you have to get in touch with the Soviet Embassy, but take your time about it, everything has to seem casual. You can't go to the embassy or call them. I won't tell you how you have to do it, you're a professional and will find a way."

"With all due respect, Comrade, I still do not understand the significance of my mission."

"It is significant, Comrade Comte, it is. Moscow has to have ears everywhere. Your mission is to develop agents who are well positioned, close to the bastions of power, preferably in the Ministry of Foreign Affairs. People whose jobs are secure, civil servants who don't depend on the vicissitudes of politics. You will be able to work at your ease in Buenos Aires, because the great powers don't think that it's an important field for their operations. But messages arrive at the Ministry of Foreign Affairs every day from all over the world, messages that uncover little secrets, conversations between the higher-ups of the countries where they are accredited, analyses of the situation. All this material can be useful sources of information for our department. Neither the United States, nor France, nor Great Britain, nor Germany have any strategic interest in the area at the moment, so it should be easy to move your mission forwards. Battles are won not only at the front."

Amelia enjoyed the first few days of the crossing. They were staying in an elegant first-class cabin and shared their evenings with a group of people that included commercial travelers, businessmen, families, and even an opera singer, the bel canto diva Carla Alessandrini, who became the center of attention for the passengers and crew right from the start of the voyage.

It was on the third day of the journey that Amelia struck up a conversation with Carla Alessandrini. The Italian diva was a woman of about forty, large without being fat, tall, with blonde hair and intense blue eyes. She had been born in Milan to a Milanese father and a German mother, to whom she owed her transformation into a great opera star, as it was she who in the face of storms and torments, opposing the will of her husband, had fought for her daughter to make her way in the world and become the diva that she now was.

Carla Alessandrini was traveling with her agent, who was also her husband, Vittorio Leonardi, a sly Roman who was dedicated exclusively to maximizing the income generated by his wife's voice.

Amelia and Carla were standing very close to one another, leaning on the railing, looking into the distance lost in thought, when Vittorio shook them out of their respective reveries.

"The two most beautiful women on the ship! Here, silent and alone! It cannot be!"

Carla turned to her husband with a smile, and Amelia looked with curiosity at this carefree Italian.

"You feel so insignificant, when you look at the sea...," Carla said.

"Insignificant, you? Impossible, my darling, even the sea bows down before you, we've been at sea for three days and haven't seen a single wave, it's as if we're traveling over a lake. Isn't that so, Signorita?" he said to Amelia.

"Yes, the sea is calm and we're lucky, even though we still feel seasick," she replied.

"Vittorio Leonardi, at your service."

"Amelia Garayoa."

"This is my wife, the divine Carla Alessandrini," Vittorio said. "Are you traveling for pleasure, to see your family, for business?"

"Come, Vittorio, don't be so nosy! Don't mind him, my husband is terribly indiscreet," Carla interrupted.

"Don't worry, I don't mind him asking questions. I suppose I'm traveling to begin a new life."

"How so?" Vittorio continued, unabashed.

Amelia did not know how to reply. She was embarrassed to say that she was running away with her lover, that the future held nothing for her.

"Please, Vittorio, stop upsetting the young woman! Come on, let's go back to our cabin, the wind is getting up and I don't want my voice to be affected. Please forgive my husband, and please don't imagine that all Italians are as intrusive as he is."

The diva and her husband went back to their cabin, and Amelia heard Carla affectionately scolding her husband, who looked at her penitently.

That night the captain held a cocktail reception to welcome the first-class passengers, and, to Pierre's surprise, Carla Alessandrini and her Vittorio came over to Amelia. She introduced them, and Pierre was extremely friendly, aware that this couple could be useful to him. They chatted until the dinner gong was struck, and Vittorio suggested that they share a table.

From that day on they became inseparable. Vittorio, who was a *bon vivant* above all things, felt an immediate pull toward Pierre, who seemed to share his taste for the finer things in life. Carla, who had a well-developed sense of drama, was impressed by the story of Amelia and Pierre's love, which had led them to flee halfway across the world to make their lives anew.

The diva intended to spend a month in Buenos Aires, as she was booked to star in *Carmen* at the Teatro Colón, which fit in well with Pierre's plans, as he thought that Carla and Vittorio could open lots of doors for him.

When they arrived in Buenos Aires it was midwinter there. The last few days of the voyage had not been pleasant. The waves washed over the deck, and the majority of the passengers, suffering from seasickness, had been forced to remain in their cabins. Unlike their partners, neither Carla nor Amelia found themselves affected by the strong waves. Vittorio cursed his fate and assured Carla that he was about to die. Pierre stayed in their cabin without eating anything, except when Amelia insisted. This meant that the two women's friendship flourished even more, so that when they reached Buenos Aires Amelia thought that she had found a second mother in Carla, and Carla considered Amelia the daughter she had never had.

"Well, Guillermo—will you allow me to call you Guillermo? Now that we've got so far, I think the best thing is for you to talk to Francesca Venezziani and Professor Muiños," Pablo Soler said.

"Who are they?" I asked in disappointment.

"Francesca Venezziani is the world's greatest authority on opera. She has written several books on the world of opera and its principal figures. She talks about Amelia Garayoa's friendship with Carla Alessandrini in the biography she wrote of the singer. There are even photographs of the two of them together."

The shock of this revelation must have shown in my face.

"Don't look so confused, I've already told you that Francesca Venezziani is an authority on everything to do with opera. I've spoken to her on a couple of occasions, trying to find out if Carla ever suspected that Pierre Comte was a Soviet spy, but she's never found anything in Carla's letters or in the reports of people who knew her. If I were you, I'd go to Rome to talk with Francesca Venezziani, and then to Buenos Aires to talk with Professor Muiños."

"And who is Muiños?"

"Well, you can tell from his name that he's of Galician origin. Don Andres Muiños is emeritus professor at the University of Buenos Aires; I knew him at Princeton, where he taught Latin American history. He has published several books, and two in particular are essential. One is about the Nazi community in exile in Latin America and the other is about Soviet spies."

"And which side is he on?"

"You seem to be a bit too worried about other people's ideologies..."

"It's so I know who I'm speaking to, so I know how to treat what he tells me."

"You have a lot of prejudices, Señor Albi."

"No, I'm just prudent; when you live in this country, you feel the weight of ideology fairly heavily. Here you're either on one side or the other, or else you're nothing, and of course, history isn't told the same way from each side. You should know that better than anyone, you're a historian and you were also a witness to our last civil war."

"Professor Muiñoños is an erudite man, I am sure that you will find what he has to say interesting. Doña Laura agrees with me that it is vital for you to speak to him. I took the trouble to call him myself last night after speaking with Doña Laura, and he would be only too pleased to talk to you."

Pablo Soler gave me a card with phone numbers and addresses on it: Francesca Venezziani's in Rome, and Professor Muiños's in Buenos Aires.

"I haven't spoken to Señora Venezziani yet, but I shall, never you worry."

While Pablo was talking to me, I was weighing in my mind whether I dared ask him for the interview my editor at the online newspaper had suggested, and although I was afraid he'd send me away with a flea in my ear, I plucked up my courage.

"I'd like to ask you a favor, but of course, there's no obligation..."

"Young man, I don't feel any obligation to anyone at this stage in my life, so ask away."

"Well, you know that I'm a journalist, and... Well, would it be too much for you to grant me an interview to talk about your books, especially the one that you've got coming out?"

"Ah, journalists! I don't trust them all that much... and I don't give interviews."

"Well, I had to try," I said with a laugh.

"Is it so important for you to get an interview with me?"

"Yes, it is, really, I'd get good marks with my boss and it might help me keep my job. But I mustn't abuse your kindness, and you're helping me so much with all this about my great-grandmother, which is why I'm here after all."

"Send me a list of questions and I'll answer whatever you put to me; I won't answer at great length, but you have to promise not to cut anything or change a single comma. If your boss accepts this condition, then I'll answer your questions as soon as you send them to me."

I didn't know if I should kiss him after shaking his hand, but it is a fact that I will always be grateful to him for that interview.

When I left Don Pablo's house I called Pepe at the newspaper to tell him that the interview was on, as long as we didn't change a single comma. I insisted that he tell the boss this, as I didn't want any problems with Soler.

"Look, Pepe, I only know him because of some family contacts and I don't want to get on the wrong side of him. You know he doesn't give interviews and it'll be a coup for us, but it's got to be how he wants and I don't want to take any chances."

Pepe put me through to the boss, who assured me that even if he sent fifty pages they wouldn't cut a word of the interview.

"If you really get it, we can talk about your future here," he said as bait.

"The first thing we have to talk about is how much you're going to pay, because don't think you'll get this for a hundred euros."

"No, sure, if you get it I'll pay you three hundred for the interview."

"In that case, no. They'd give me at least double that in any supplement or Sunday newspaper."

"How much do you want, then?"

"I won't do it for less than six hundred."

"Okay, send it when you've got it."

Half an hour later I sent him the questionnaire by e-mail, and Pablo wrote back to promise that he'd have the answers for me soon.

I called Aunt Marta to tell her that I would need more money, as I was going to Rome and then to Buenos Aires.

"What do you mean you're going to Rome and Buenos Aires? As if you were just jumping on the metro... You have to give me some explanation."

"Your grandmother Amelia, my great-grandmother, had a very eventful life, and if you want me to write the story I've got no option other than to follow where the trail leads me. Don't think that this is a walk in the park."

"A pretty expensive walk in the park."

"Look, you were the one who wanted to find out about your grandmother; I really don't care. If you want me to drop it, I will."

Aunt Marta weighed whether to tell me to get lost, and I crossed my fingers that she wouldn't: I really didn't want to lose the chance of finding out what happened to Amelia Garayoa.

"Alright, but tell me why you have to go to Rome and Buenos Aires."

"Because I have to see the world expert on opera in Rome, and a professor who knows all there is to be known about Soviet and Nazi spies in Buenos Aires."

"What nonsense!"

"She didn't spend her whole life doing embroidery, and she got caught up in some pretty impressive events."

"You're not making them up to pull my leg?"

"No, I'm really not; I don't have enough imagination to invent the things that happened to my great-grandmother. She was quite a lady!"

Aunt Marta agreed to put some more money into my account, after threatening me that if I were making things up I wouldn't know what hit me.

"I'm going to talk to Leonora to tell her that I'm not going to let you get away with anything."

"You should speak to my mother, because she wants me to drop the whole thing; she thinks I'm wasting my time."

My mother was worried when I told her that I was going to Rome and Buenos Aires.

"But this is nonsense. Tell Aunt Marta to keep her money, and look for a proper job."

"Aren't you curious about what happened to your grandmother?"

"What can I say? Yes... but not if you're going to lose job opportunities."

6

I arrived in Rome that same night and checked into the Hotel d'Inghilterra, in the heart of the city, a stone's throw from the Spanish Steps and the Spanish Embassy to the Vatican.

The hotel was extremely expensive, but Ruth had recommended it to me. I don't know if my friend used it a lot, given that the low-fare airline for which she worked was not precisely renowned for its generosity in putting its personnel up in quality hotels. I thought about calling her to find out what she was doing at that moment, but decided in the end not to, as it would be behaving too much like a paranoid and jealous boyfriend. As they always say, what the mind doesn't know, the heart doesn't grieve over.

When I called Francesca Venezziani the next morning, I arranged to meet her the same afternoon. Professor Soler had called her and spoken about me.

I was ready to be surprised, and the truth is I *was* surprised when I saw Francesca: She was extremely beautiful, tall, dark-haired, about thirty-five years old, and dressed in Armani. The skirt suit she was wearing must have cost a fortune. She met me at her home, a beautiful loft in the Via Frattini, close by my hotel.

"So you're investigating Amelia Garayoa..."

"She was my great-grandmother," I said, to justify myself.

"How interesting! And what do you need to know that a stranger can tell you?"

"Well, it might seem strange, but we don't know anything about her in my family, she upped and disappeared and left us all one day, including her son, my grandfather."

"I can only tell you about Amelia Garayoa's relation with Carla Alessandrini. Your great-grandmother has only really been interesting to me to the extent that Carla treated her like a daughter."

"Well, if you would be kind enough to tell me what you do know, then I would be extremely grateful."

"I'll do better, I'll give you my book about *la Alessandrini*. Read it and if you have any questions, ask me."

"That seems fine, but given that I've come to Rome, I wouldn't like to leave emptyhanded…"

"You'll have my book. Is that too little?"

"No, no, it's great, but couldn't you tell me something about the relation between Carla and Amelia?"

"I'm telling you, it's all written down in the book. Look, there are even some photos of Carla with Amelia. You see? There's this one in Buenos Aires, then this one in Berlin, and here, Paris, London, Milan… And Amelia read a poem at Carla's funeral. Carla Alessandrini was an exceptional woman, as well as being the most extraordinary opera singer of all time."

"Why did she take Amelia in?"

"Because the only thing that Carla did not have was a child. She sacrificed everything for her career, and when she met Amelia, she was at that age, past forty, when women begin to ask themselves what they have done with their lives. Amelia made her feel a strong sense of protectiveness; she was the daughter that Carla could have had and she was so defenseless that Carla adopted her, emotionally speaking. She protected her, she gave her help at various moments of her life, and she never asked for anything apart from what Amelia gave her, love and sincere affection. Carla always held out her hand when she saw Amelia about to run aground. She became a safe refuge for Amelia, and Carla, a generous woman, never asked questions that Amelia couldn't answer. She didn't want to know anything other than what she saw in this young Spanish woman."

"And what about Vittorio Leonardi, Carla's husband, what did he think about this mother-daughter relationship?"

"Vittorio had no illusions, he was a good person but he had no illusions about himself. He was handsome and friendly as well as smart. He was Carla's manager, he knew how to look after her interests, he mollycoddled her and knew her well. He knew that there were some points where it was useless to try to stand up to her. So he accepted Amelia without asking questions, just as he shut his eyes to some of his wife's love affairs as well. Vittorio was not well-off when he met Carla and he suddenly went from being a gossip-columnist who found it hard to make ends meet to living surrounded by all kinds of luxury at the side of a woman who was desired and adored by everyone. He went from nowhere to the very top of things in an instant and never risked his relationship with Carla: He, at least, was always faithful to her."

"And what did Carla Alessandrini think about Pierre Comte?"

"That's just what Professor Soler wanted to know when he called me a couple of years ago: He was working on a second edition of his book about Soviet spies in Spain. I felt very flattered that an authority like Professor Soler might be interested in my opinion. Well, I answered his questions, I said that Carla did not like Pierre Comte very much, and she helped Amelia when she decided to break with him. I think she didn't trust him, and I've read in some of Professor Soler's books that he was nothing more than a Soviet spy. Of course, Carla never knew this, or at least there is no document or witness that makes us think that she did know this. She didn't sympathize with him, not because he was a Communist, but because Amelia was unhappy; I don't know if you knew that Carla Alessandrini was a great woman who not only stood firm against Mussolini but also always spoke out against Hitler in public. There was one occasion when she sang at the Berlin Opera and Hitler wanted to come and congratulate her in her dressing room, and she refused to receive him, pleading a headache. As you might guess, that was a time when no one stood up to Hitler no matter how much his head ached. What Carla did know was what Amelia did years later. Not because Amelia told her, but because she figured it out; she was a clever woman."

"And what did Amelia do years later?" I asked, a little annoyed.

"Aha! You'll have to find that out for yourself. Professor Soler has told me that you need to find things out step by step, that's what you were told, and what he was told. I don't know what all this is about, but apparently someone wants you to put together the puzzle that was Amelia Garayoa's life yourself. And anyway, as I said, she is only of tangential interest to me; my main interest is Carla Alessandrini. Do you like the opera?"

"I've never been in my life, and I don't even have any operas on CD."

"A pity! It's your loss."

"And how come you are so interested in it?"

"I wanted to be a singer, I thought I could be a new Carla Alessandrini, but... well, I didn't have her voice or her talent, nowhere close. It was difficult for me to accept, but in the end I decided that if I couldn't be the best then it was better not to continue. I studied musicology at the same time that I took my singing lessons, and was in the chorus on one or two occasions, but not to any great effect. My thesis was on Alessandrini, and various little-known aspects of her life. My thesis supervisor had connections with various publishers, and he was convinced that my thesis could be turned into an interesting book. And that's what happened. Now I write about music, above all about opera, both books and newspaper articles. I'm somebody now, which is what it's all about, anyway. Well, you know almost everything about me, tell me something about yourself."

"I'm a journalist, out of work because of the way politics functions. I don't know what things are like in Italy, but in my country if you want to write about politics you're either on the Right or on the Left, or a nationalist of some kind, or else you're unemployed. And I'm the latter."

"You don't have any opinions?"

"Well, I think I'm on the Left, but I've got this nasty habit of thinking for myself, not wanting to churn out other people's slogans, which makes me a bit untrustworthy."

"I don't think it's that different in Italy... If I were you I'd write about something that wasn't politics."

"I'm trying, but I've got a bit of a reputation, and they don't even trust me to write about culture."

"Well, you're in a bit of trouble, then."

"Yes, I am."

Francesca took pity on me and invited me to eat with her that evening to carry on talking about Carla and Amelia.

"They met on the voyage to Buenos Aires. Tell me, what happened when they got there?"

"Well, you can imagine the reception they got when the boat got into port. Dozens of journalists waiting impatiently for Carla Alessandrini. She never let her fans down, so she came out of the boat in a sable coat, holding the arm of her husband, handsome Vittorio. They took a suite in the Hotel Plaza, and she spent the next four days rehearsing, giving interviews, and attending social events. The Italian ambassador held a reception in her honor, which was attended by all the most important people of the city, as well as by diplomats from other countries, and Amelia and Pierre were invited also, at Carla's request. I've said that Carla did not approve of Mussolini, but whenever she traveled abroad she tended to accept the homage offered her by the various Italian embassies. You really have to read my book. I think that Professor Soler has recommended that you travel to Buenos Aires to interview Professor Muiños, and I think that between my book and what Muiños will tell you, you will have enough to write your own story."

I took Francesca's suggestion.

My mother woke me from a deep sleep at eight in the morning.

"But Mom, what kind of a time... ," I protested.

"I couldn't sleep for thinking about you. Look, I think you need to stop this ridiculous investigation into grandmother's past. I'm sure it's interesting, but you are losing chances with your career."

"What career would that be?"

"Don't be so stubborn! You're very proud and you think that everything should just fall into your lap, but things aren't like that, so you have to go and knock on people's doors to find work."

"It's eight in the morning, I'm in Rome, I got to bed late and I've told you a thousand times already that my knuckles are bleeding from knocking on so many doors!"

"But..."

"Look, let's talk later, I'll call you."

I hung up in a bad mood. My mother wouldn't give me any breathing space about finding a job. I decided to go to Buenos Aires that very day, at least she'd bother me less because of the cost of transatlantic phone calls.

I plugged in my computer and looked to see if I had any e-mails I had to answer. I was surprised to find Professor Soler's answers to my questions. I told myself that the day hadn't started all that badly, in spite of my mother's phone call. So I wrote an introduction and a conclusion to the interview, gave it a lede and sent it to Pepe, the head of the cultural section at my online newspaper, with a note reminding him of the promise he'd made to Professor Soler.

I fell in love with Buenos Aires on the way from the airport to my hotel. What a city! I was going to have to say thank you to Aunt Marta for asking me to do this job, because I was having a most interesting time meeting surprising people and visiting a city like this one that opened up to me on that Southern Hemisphere autumn morning. Summer was arriving in Spain just as Buenos Aires was gearing itself up for the autumn. But the morning of my arrival was bright and warm.

The travel agency had reserved me a room in the central part of the city. Once I had unpacked I called Professor Muiños, who had already been in touch with Professor Soler. He arranged to meet me the next afternoon, and I was grateful for this as it allowed me to get past my jetlag a bit and see a little of the city.

With a map that they gave me at reception as my only guide I set out into the street, keen on discovering the best parts of the city. The first place I went to was the Plaza de Mayo, which I had seen so often on television: Here was where those brave women, the Grandmothers of the Plaza de Mayo, met to protest the disappearance of their sons and grandsons during the military dictatorship.

I spent a while in the square, soaking it all in, feeling the strength of those women with their white headscarves who had peacefully set themselves, in the most effective way, against that bunch of murderers who formed such a large part of the military junta.

Then I went to the cathedral, and then I let the human tide of the Buenos Aires streets carry me around until the jetlag kicked in at about six in the evening and I could go no further. I hailed a taxi and went back to my hotel, went to bed and did not wake up until the next day.

The first thing I did was to call my mother, sure that if she had no signs of life from me then she was entirely capable of calling Interpol to report my disappearance. These are the downsides of being an only child, of having grown up without a father, as my father died when I was a child.

Professor Muiños's house was a two-story building in the elegant Palermo district. As soon as I opened the door I smelled waxed wood and books, which were piled on shelves all over the walls: The whole house was one enormous library.

A Bolivian housekeeper shyly opened the door and then took me straight to the professor's study.

You could tell that Andres Muiños was a professor just by looking at him. He was dressed informally, in a knitted cardigan, his white hair was combed back and he had a scholar's distracted air, as well as the friendliness proper to someone who had seen everything and who could no longer be surprised by anything.

"So you're the Spanish journalist!" he said in greeting.

"Yes... Thanks a lot for agreeing to see me," I replied.

"Pablo Soler asked me, and he's a good friend and colleague. We were together at Princeton."

"Yes, Don Pablo told me."

"If you are looking for extraordinary lives to write about, then Pablo Soler is a good choice, but we're here to talk about Amelia Garayoa, your great-grandmother, if I'm not mistaken."

"Yes, Amelia Garayoa was my great-grandmother, but we know very little about her in the family, practically nothing."

"That's as may be, but she was an important woman, far more important than you can possibly imagine; her life was full of adventure and danger, like a John Le Carré novel."

"It's true, I'm discovering one surprise after another. But I should say that what I'm finding out about her so far doesn't turn her into an interesting woman, rather she was someone who let events move her without having any control over them."

"As far as Pablo Soler has told me, you know about Amelia's life until she came to Buenos Aires with Pierre Comte. She was twenty years old then: I don't know about you, but there's no one that age who's interesting. I don't even know anyone interesting who's your age, thirty-something."

Well, that was the professor! He didn't mince his words. He was telling me, with a smile, that he wouldn't have chosen to have this conversation with me. But now was not the time to get offended, so I didn't say anything.

"I think you met Francesca Venezziani as well, is that right?"

"I've just come from Rome, from her. She gave me her book about Carla Alessandrini."

"I've met *la señora* Venezziani a couple of times, she's interesting, and bright; she knew she would never be a great singer, and she's managed to make a name for herself writing stories of the great bel canto divas. Her books aren't bad, she's done her research. Have you read her book about *la Alessandrini*?"

"Not all of it, I started it on the plane."

"Carla Alessandrini was a remarkable woman, aside from her talent at singing. She was strong, brave, decisive, one of those people who upset all kinds of social conventions, but because she wanted to, not like your great-grandmother, who let herself be stolen away by Pierre Comte. Look, I don't have much to do, so I've put together a list of places to visit that are connected with your great-grandmother; you'll get to know her time in the city better this way, and you'll see a bit of Buenos Aires, the city my parents immigrated to as soon as the Civil War ended. My father was a captain in the Republican Army, and he escaped as soon as the war ended. A good thing too! They'd have shot him otherwise. I was only five years old back then, so I feel like I'm from here even though I was born in Vigo. But let's get down to business. Where shall we start?"

"I'd like to know what happened when Pierre and Amelia arrived here."

"Alright," Muiños said with a smile as he watched me turn on my recorder.

They took up lodgings at the Castelar, on the Avenida de Mayo. We should go and have a look, because that's where Lorca stayed as well, from October 1933 to March 1934.

It was a comfortable hotel where artists and writers tended to stay on their way through Buenos Aires. Pierre Comte had no intention of spending too much time in the hotel; he wanted to look for a house he could use for his double business as bookseller and spy.

Perhaps you don't know this, but Buenos Aires at the beginning of the twentieth century was a glamorous city that had taken its lead from Paris, inspired by Haussmann. There was no artist worth his salt who would refuse to act at the Teatro Colón. An Italian impresario had built it, working with several architects until its completion in 1908. The Teatro Colón has seen true legends pass through its doors: Caruso, Toscanini, Menuhin, Maria Callas, and, of course, Carla Alessandrini. Lots of the great artists claim that, leaving aside La Scala in Milan, the Teatro Colón has the best acoustics in the world.

So at that time it was entirely logical that an artist like Carla Alessandrini should appear there.

Pierre thought that the friendship that seemed to be forming between Amelia and Carla was a great stroke of luck. The singer's mere presence opened every door in the city, which paid homage to *la gran Alessandrini*.

Our man lost no time and the day after their arrival he was already looking for a house. He had several trunks of rare books and special editions in his luggage, things that would doubtless be of interest to book lovers. He had bought many of them in Spain as he started to develop his plan of using Amelia as his cover for setting himself up in Buenos Aires.

Moscow was not stingy toward its spies, but neither did it let them spend money like water; they had to account for every penny they spent, and were expected not to be extravagant. The people's money could not be spent on vain show.

The second day, Carla sent them a reminder that they were invited to a cocktail party that was to be held in her honor at the Italian Embassy. Pierre could not be any happier about how things were progressing, and asked himself if he had in fact not made a mistake bringing Amelia with him.

Even though Pierre was fifteen years older than her they made a good couple. She was so slim, almost ethereal, blonde and dainty. He was a man of the world who carried himself elegantly.

Carla embraced Amelia when she came into the embassy.

"Why didn't you call me? I've missed you, I haven't had anyone to speak to."

Amelia said that they had been house-hunting, and that it was not proving easy for Pierre to find what he wanted.

"But I can help you! Can't I, Vittorio? I'm sure we can find someone who can find you what you need. Leave it up to me."

The guests at the reception, the whole of Buenos Aires high society, took note of Carla's affection for Amelia.

If *la gran Alessandrini* had this couple under her wing, then it must be because they were important. That night Pierre and Amelia received invitations to dinners, suppers, concerts, and horse races. Pierre deployed all his French charm, and more than one woman was taken with this gallant man whose gaze promised so much.

Pierre and Amelia were both desperate for news of Spain, and almost all their questions were answered by a bullish Neapolitan, Michelangelo Bagliodi, who was married to one of the secretaries at the Italian Embassy.

"Franco hasn't entered Madrid yet, but he will any day now. You have to remember that the best generals are at the forefront of the uprising: Sanjurjo, Mola, and Quiepo de Llano. I am sure that they will triumph for the good of your country, Señorita Garayoa."

Pierre grabbed Amelia's hand to stop her from making an angry reply. He had taught her the advantages of watching, listening, and holding one's tongue, but she was so upset that it was difficult for her to keep calm.

"And do you think that Italy and Germany will work with the army forces that have set themselves up against the Republic?" Pierre asked.

"My dear friend, how can you doubt that they have the fullest sympathies of Il Duce and Der Führer! And if they are needed... well, I am sure that Germany and Italy will help our great sister nation, Spain."

Michelangelo Bagliodi was extremely pleased to be the object of attention of this couple, who had been introduced to him by Carla herself. What's more, they appeared to appreciate what he had to say, which he found only natural, as he was a man who knew all the vicissitudes of the political sphere thanks to his marriage to the ambassador's secretary, his dear sweet Paola. He, who had emigrated several years before from his native Naples, had worked hard to turn himself into a successful merchant, and then had moved a few rungs up the social scale by his marriage to an employee of the embassy, something that brought him new business contacts and gave him, above all, the chance to rub shoulders at embassy dinners and parties with people from the highest echelons of Buenos Aires society.

"And what is President Azaña doing?" Amelia asked.

"He's a disaster, Madam, a disaster. The Republic is allowing civilians to take up arms in its defense, because more than half the generals are with the rebels. The experts say that the forces are very well matched, but in my opinion there's no comparison between the bravery and military skill of the two sides. Also, how on earth are Republicans and Socialists and Anarchists and Communists and all those left-wing types ever going to agree on anything? They'll end up fighting among themselves, you mark my words. I foresee a happy ending to this struggle: Franco's triumph, the best thing that could happen to Spain."

The Neapolitan, pleased with his conversation with Pierre and Amelia, offered to help them with anything they might need.

"You have just arrived in the city, and you do not yet know it well, so please do not hesitate to take advantage of my help for anything you need. My wife and I would be extremely honored to invite you to our house, we could organize a dinner party... ," Bagliodi dared to suggest.

"We would be delighted to attend," Pierre said.

Bagliodi gave them his card and made a note of the hotel where Pierre and Amelia were staying, promising to tell them as soon as he had organized the dinner party.

"He's an idiot!" Amelia said as soon as he had left them. "I'm not going to go to that Fascist's house! I can't understand how you could accept his invitation!"

"Amelia, if we told everyone our true beliefs the first day we came to the country then we'd become vulnerable. We don't know anyone here, and we need doors to be opened for us. I've told you that I sometimes work with the Communist International, and it really doesn't hurt to know how the enemy is thinking."

"Don't act like you're a spy!" Amelia exclaimed.

"What silly things you say! It has nothing to do with spying, it has to do with keeping your ears open, because what your enemies say unguardedly allows us to be prepared, to keep one step ahead of them. I want there to be a worldwide revolution, I want to get rid of the privileges certain people have, but of course they won't let us just take them away, and that's why we need to know how they think, how they move..."

"Yes, you told me that already. Even so, I am not going to spend any time with that unbearable man and his insipid wife."

"We will do what needs to be done," Pierre decreed, upset by Amelia's bad mood. "Anyway, who better than this man to keep us up to date with the situation in Spain? I thought that you wanted accurate news from your country."

The next day Amelia had a call from Carla inviting her to take tea at the Café Tortoni.

"But come by yourself, so we can talk at our ease. I finish my rehearsals at about six. I think you'll find the café without any problem: It's in the Avenida de Mayo and everyone in Buenos Aires knows it."

Pierre made no objection to the arrangement and spent the day looking for the ideal apartment, which up to that moment existed only in his imagination.

Amelia found Carla nervous: She was always nervous before a first night because she didn't let people's praise turn her head.

"They're all very nice, but if I hit a wrong note then they'll crucify me and turn their backs on me just as easily as they butter me up today. I can't make a mistake: They want me to be sublime, and that's what I have to be."

The first night, at Carla's invitation, Pierre and Amelia were seated in a box. Amelia was extremely beautiful, according to the next day's gossip columns, which all referred to her as "*la gran Carla*'s best friend."

Carla was sublime, if we trust the same newspapers. The audience gave her a standing ovation of more than half an hour and she had to take several curtain calls.

Vittorio had arranged a dinner for after the performance, with some of Buenos Aires' most important society figures, people from the cultural sphere and the editors of the major newspapers, and naturally Pierre and Amelia were present as well. Luck smiled on Pierre that evening, as a gentleman with a strong Italian accent asked them where they were staying, and Pierre explained that he was looking for a place where he could both live and have a small shop for his bibliographic rarities.

The man introduced himself as Luigi Masseti, the owner of a number of buildings and shops in town, and offered to help them find the right place.

"I have just the thing for you. It's in the basement of an old building in a very good location, in the Calle Piedras. Even though it's in the basement it has very good light because it has a large window onto the street. The problem is that it is not really a family house, and not really a shop, but it would be perfect for a couple and a small business selling books. Why not come to my office tomorrow and I'll get one of my employees to show it to you?"

Pierre accepted gratefully. For her part, Amelia was surrounded by a fair number of gallants. It was now well known, because

Pierre had made it so, that they had run away from their respective families, that she had abandoned her husband and son and he had left a promising business because of their passionate romance. Some of these men thought that the Spanish woman would be easy prey for their amorous attentions and tried to take liberties that surprised and hurt Amelia in equal measure.

Carla Alessandrini, when she realized what was happening, had words on a couple of occasions, making it clear that anyone who upset her friend was offending her.

Pierre preferred to ignore the situation, because his aim was to make as many contacts as possible in the closed and highly refined world of Buenos Aires high society. And the people here were the crème de la crème. He couldn't have had a greater stroke of luck.

Carla introduced them to a couple who seemed to be old friends of hers.

"Amelia, I want you to meet Martin and Gloria Hertz. They're the best friends I have in Buenos Aires."

Martin Hertz was a German Jew who had arrived three years previously, looking for a place where he could escape the Nazi pressure. He was a throat specialist, and had met Carla years ago in Berlin, when the diva had a problem with her voice two days before appearing at the Opera. Martin took care of her and made it possible for her to get up on stage and perform brilliantly once again. Ever since then, Carla had been unconditional in her support of this young German doctor; for his part, soon after his arrival in the city, he had fallen in love with Gloria Fernández, a young *porteña* woman of Spanish origin, and had married her.

Amelia was immediately attracted to the Hertzes. Martin's face was so cheery that it inspired confidence from the first, and Gloria exuded friendliness and strength of personality.

"You have to come to my art gallery," Gloria invited them. "I'm exhibiting a young Mexican painter at the moment, and I predict great things for him. I want my gallery to be a reference point for new painting, a place where young people have a chance to exhibit."

Pierre immediately agreed to visit the Hertzes' gallery. And he reminded himself once again of how useful a key Amelia was to Buenos Aires high society.

"My best friend is German, from Berlin," Amelia said, "although I do not know if she's in New York at the moment. I hope so! Yla is Jewish, and her father Herr Itzhak Wassermann is a business partner of my father's, but the Nazis have intruded to such an extent that their business has gone to pot. My father spent a long time trying to convince Herr Itzhak to leave Germany, and... well, before I came here, he told me that they were thinking of immigrating to New York."

"The Nazis don't leave us many options, they are stealing from us, stripping us of our possessions, and the SS are spitefully coming after us all the time. First they took some of our rights as citizens away from us, and then the Nuremburg Laws turned us into outcasts. I left in '34, because I knew that even if the Jewish communities want to believe otherwise, the Nazis are not just some flash in the pan. In March of 1933 I was a witness to that shameful and terrible act, the public book-burning, books written by Jews, books that belong to the whole of humanity... That was what made me decide to leave, because I knew that they would keep on persecuting us, which they have. My parents did not want to come with me, I have an older brother, who is married with two children, who also did not want to come. I pray for them daily, and my blood boils when I imagine them being bullied by their neighbors."

"Come, Martin, we're at a party... ," Gloria said, trying to change her husband's mood.

"I'm sorry, it was my fault... I shouldn't have..."

"Don't say that! I am happy to know that you are a sensitive person who can feel for the situation that others are in," Martin replied, "but Gloria is right, we cannot get upset here, at Carla's party, she wants us to have a good time."

On the way back to the hotel, Pierre was extremely kind and solicitous with Amelia. Anyone seeing them would have thought that this man was madly in love with the fragile young woman who walked at his side.

One week later, Amelia and Pierre moved into the basement that they had rented from Luigi Masseti. Pierre thought it was perfect: The way in was via a huge front door giving out onto the street. Then a short hall led into a fifty-square-meter salon, which was lit by a huge window looking out on the street. At the other end of the salon were two bedrooms, a little kitchen, and a bathroom, and this was the space that would be their home. The windows in this part of the house gave onto a shared patio.

Amelia cleaned the apartment from top to bottom. Pierre showed his skills as a carpenter by buying wood and making bookcases for all the walls of the salon. As far as the rest of the apartment was concerned, they spent very little on decoration, they bought only what was truly necessary.

"Let's see how things go, we'll get the sort of furniture you deserve in the future," Pierre said to Amelia.

Things did not go badly for them. Buenos Aires was a cosmopolitan city that opened itself up to the Europeans who came to it seeking refuge. And Pierre was French, and Amelia was a delicate and beautiful woman, so they had no problems in gradually making all the doors of the city open to them. The only thing that truly surprised Amelia was that Pierre insisted on cultivating his relationship with Michelangelo Bagliodi, the husband of the Italian ambassador's secretary. Pierre and Bagliodi seemed to have hit it off, and it was not unusual for them to have lunch together, or for the four of them to spend Sunday in Pierre and Amelia's house.

If Martin and Gloria Hertz were their gateway to the city's intellectual sphere, then Bagliodi, via Paola his wife, made sure that they were invited to several of the events organized by the Italian Embassy, events where Pierre rubbed shoulders with ambassadors and diplomats from several other countries.

Amelia seemed to adapt well to her new situation, and was not at all unhappy, although she was always worried about the civil war in Spain. The worst for her was Carla Alessandrini's departure. The diva had finished her engagement in Buenos Aires and had to return to Europe, where she would start the season in September at Milan's La Scala with *Aida*, a difficult and ambitious opera. Before she left she met up once again with Amelia to have a *tête-à-tête* in the Café Tortoni, which had become the favorite haunt of both of them. They loved to share confidences there, at the oak and green marble tables.

"I will miss you, *cara* Amelia... Why are you not coming back to Europe? If you want I could help you..."

"And what would I do? No, Carla, I made a decision that I have at times regretted, but now it is too late for me to turn back. My husband will never forgive me, and as far as my family is concerned... I have hurt them a great deal, what would they do with me if I came back? I only pray that Franco loses the war, and that peace returns. I'm scared for them, even though Madrid is still holding out..."

"But what about your son? Don't you realize that if you don't go back then you will lose him... He's still small, but one day he'll want to know what happened to his mother, and what will they be able to tell him? Amelia, I can take you back to Europe..."

But Amelia seemed now to reaffirm the decision that she had regretted so often. Also, at that time she would not have dared to confront Pierre. She shuddered to think of his reaction if she were to tell him that she was abandoning him.

"I have lost my son and I know that I will never forgive myself. I am the world's worst mother, maybe he'll even be better off for my absence," Amelia said, unable to contain her tears.

"Come now, don't cry, everything has a solution; all you have to do is want it. You have my address and the address of Vittorio's office, and you can always send me a message, or else they will know where I am and how to find me. If you need me don't hesitate to write, I will do everything in my power to help you."

Pierre worked hard, but sometimes he too was overtaken by melancholy. By October he had regular contact with his controller, the secretary to the Soviet ambassador, to whom he would pass the information that he had picked up in his intellectual circles, and also from among the tradesmen and the city's upper classes. His reports were detailed and left nothing out, however insignificant something might seem.

And he would submit Amelia to intense interrogation every time she went out with her new friends to take tea, or if she spoke to some important person at a cocktail party, or at a reading or a wedding dinner.

He was a disciplined agent with a mission to fulfill, but he believed that his true place was not in Buenos Aires, where he had "placed" an agent in the Ministry of Foreign Affairs, just as he had been ordered to do, within the first six months of his being there. Miguel López was an employee at the ministry, leaning communist in his opinions but not affiliated with any party. He disapproved of Buenos Aires high society and regretted the poverty-stricken state in which many of his compatriots outside of the capital found themselves. Even in the capital, there were those who could only stand on the sidelines and observe the city's glamour.

Miguel López had gotten his office job thanks to one of his uncles, who worked for the ministry as a porter. He was an affable type who had spoken out one day in his young nephew's favor, praising his knowledge of typing and shorthand and even basic accounting. Also, Miguel had a gift for languages, because he had taught himself French without any formal course of study. This must have been a convincing pitch, because Miguel López was given a job as an office boy and, because he was smart and discreet, he was made the secretary to the head of communications. He spent his free time studying law; his dream was to become a lawyer, which also added to the positive opinion his employers had of him.

Amelia felt friendly toward Miguel López, and was surprised to find the friendship growing between him and her husband. For her the friendship was a blessing; he kept her up to date with the news from Spain, for it was he who dealt with the coded messages that came from the Argentinian ambassador in Madrid.

One night, when Miguel came to dinner with Amelia and Pierre, he told them that the situation was getting more serious by the minute.

"It seems," he said, "that the Fascists' rearguard are committing all kinds of atrocities, shooting the leftist militants and showing no mercy to the Republican leaders. But the most important thing is that the workers have organized a functional resistance to the Fascists, and there are popular militias as well as the Republican Army. The Abraham Lincoln Battalion is now taking part in the struggle, and people are arriving from all over the world to join the International Brigades. Of course," he added, "the trip taken to Mexico by the women's antifascist delegation has started to bear fruit. From a propaganda point of view things could not be better, most newspapers are attacking the rebels and have sided with Azaña's government. And we're here and unable to do anything! I feel so ashamed of our politicians!"

López felt a strong satisfaction in having transformed himself into a Soviet agent, and dreamed of the moment when they would call him to the "workers' homeland" in recognition of his services, and let him stay there forever.

Pierre had explained to him that he should not draw attention to himself, that he should trust nobody, and that he should above all continue in his dull state job.

Even though Miguel López had told Pierre that one of his female work colleagues seemed to feel the same hatred of the regime that he did, and had even made negative comments about Fascism, Pierre forbade Miguel from confiding in her.

But although Miguel was a great achievement, Pierre needed another agent in the Ministry of Foreign Affairs, or even in the office of the president himself, because this was what his controller had asked for.

However, as luck seemed to have been on his side ever since their arrival in Buenos Aires, Amelia told him one afternoon that she had been to Gloria's gallery and had been introduced there to a friend of Gloria's who was going through a rough patch.

"You can't imagine what the poor girl has to go through, working in Government House and being such a strong anti-Fascist. According to Gloria, Natalia is a Communist."

Pierre didn't seem very interested, but he insisted on inviting Martin and Gloria Hertz to have dinner with them a few days later, and brought up what Amelia had said.

"Oh yes, poor Natalia! It's very difficult for her to work in Government House. She's not got a very important job, she doesn't work directly with the president; she's in the Translation Department. She spends her day translating letters and documents and all kinds of stuff from English. And if the president needs an interpreter, then of course they use her. Natalia speaks perfect English: Her father was a diplomat, and she lived in England, and then in the United States, and later in Norway and Germany. She was five when her father was sent to England, and stayed there till she was nine; her father's next posting was to Washington, so English holds no secrets for her."

Pierre displayed a sympathy for Natalia that seemed sincere, and he suggested they invite her the next time they came round.

It was a month later, and by chance, that Pierre met Natalia Alvear at the launch of an exhibition in Gloria's gallery.

Natalia was around fifty years old, of average height, elegant and with chestnut-brown hair, but by no means a great beauty. She was single and bored, and spent time in intellectual and artistic environments, where she met a lot of people of the Left. Her work in Government House was boring, and her lack of prospects for her personal life made her bitter.

From the first moment he saw her Pierre realized that he might be able to turn her into an agent, and that this might be what could give his life its ultimate meaning. But he decided to go slowly until he was sure that this single woman was able to take on such a responsibility.

Two days later, he passed by the front of Government House and arranged to bump into her just at the time that she had said she normally went out to eat lunch.

"Natalia, dear! What a surprise!"

"Yes it is, Señor Comte..."

"You don't have to call me Señor Comte, I think we can use each other's first names, don't you? I was coming from a client nearby, and I was looking for somewhere to have a light lunch in the area: I've got another meeting nearby in a bit. And what about you, where are you going?"

"The same as you, to have lunch."

"If you don't think it's too forward of me, I would be happy to invite you to join me."

"Oh no! I couldn't accept."

"Do you have another engagement?"

"No, no, it's not that, but I think that I shouldn't."

"Isn't it the custom in Buenos Aires for two people who know each other to have lunch together?" Pierre asked innocently.

"Well, if they are friends, then I suppose so."

"You are Gloria's friend, the Hertzes are some of our closest friends, so I don't see the problem... Come on, please let me invite you to lunch. Amelia will be cross if I tell her I'd met you and wasn't polite enough to invite you to lunch."

They went into a nearby restaurant, and Pierre deployed all of the savoir faire that marked him out as a man of the world. He made her laugh, and even flirted a little with her to make her think that she was desirable.

Natalia was too lonely and tired of her gray little life to resist a man like Pierre.

This was not the only occasion when he organized a meeting and she allowed herself to be invited to lunch. Little by little a relationship sprung up between them that, to the eyes of an innocent bystander, would have seemed nothing more than a simple platonic affair between two people whose sense of duty would not allow them to take matters any further.

Pierre hid himself behind the fact of Amelia, who had abandoned her husband and son for him. Natalia admired him all the more for this, although she secretly could not avoid hoping that Pierre would decide to be disloyal.

Pierre confessed to Natalia that he was a Communist and that only she could understand the importance of his cause.

Without her realizing it, he convinced her little by little that she could not simply stand by with her arms folded while the Fascists went on with their work, and one day he asked her to give him any information that could be useful for the "cause," which he would then pass on to the relevant authorities.

Natalia was doubtful to begin with, but Pierre took one more step and one afternoon they became lovers.

"Lord, what have we done!" Natalia lamented.

"It was meant to happen," he consoled her.

"But what about Amelia?"

"I don't want to talk about her, allow me to enjoy this moment, this is the happiest I have been in a long time."

"But what happened is wrong!"

"Could we have avoided it? Tell me, Natalia, haven't we tried to avoid this moment for as long as we could? Don't tell me you regret it, for I wouldn't be able to bear it."

She did not regret it, and was only worried about the future, if there could be a future for the two of them.

"Let's live for today, Natalia, that's what we've got; as for the future... Who knows what may happen? It is not the ties of the flesh that bring us together, but the ties of an idea, a great and liberating idea for the whole of humanity. This sacred idea is more important than anything else. What happens to us does not matter, we will always be together because we share a cause."

Natalia did not know about Miguel, and he did not know about her. They were both controlled by Pierre, who was controlled in turn by the ambassador's secretary.

7

Moscow seemed happy with Pierre Comte's work. At least, this was what his controller told him. In little more than six months he had established two collaborators in strategic sites, and both promised to be mines of information.

Amelia suspected nothing of Pierre's affair with Natalia and kept up a friendly relationship with her. Natalia would often come to dinner at the couple's house, or else would go with them to exhibitions at Gloria's gallery, or on holidays take daytrips with them out of Buenos Aires.

They became an inseparable trio, and Pierre was stimulated by the thought of walking out with his two lovers, one on either side of him.

"I feel sorry for Amelia," Natalia would say. "She's so innocent. How come she cannot see that it is me whom you really love?"

"It has to be like this, my darling, I am not strong enough to abandon her, at least not now; we have been in Buenos Aires for such a short time, and after bringing her all the way here... You must understand, I need time."

What Pierre really needed was Amelia. The young Spanish woman had a natural ability to be accepted wherever she went; she opened all kinds of doors for Pierre, and he could not forget that most of their new friends came to them via Carla Alessandrini. If the diva discovered that he had abandoned or betrayed Amelia, then it was a certain proposition that she would call on her friends in Buenos Aires to turn their backs on him. So Pierre had urged that Natalia be discreet and not to let on that they were lovers.

Neither had Pierre given up on his friendship with Michelangelo Bagliodi and his wife, Paola. They were also an excellent source of information. Natalia would come and have lunch at the Italians' house, and they were delighted to host a woman who worked so closely with the President of the Republic. Also, under Natalia's guidance, Paola started to take care of her appearance, wearing elegant but attractive clothes, changing her hairstyle and plucking her eyebrows.

At one of these lunch parties Bagliodi explained to Pierre the reasons why Hitler and Il Duce supported General Franco.

"You have to understand that, notwithstanding their ideological affinities, Der Führer cannot allow there to be a pro-Soviet regime in place in Spain, quite apart from having the French Popular Front on his doorstep. That's why Franco knew from the start that he could rely on having the Junkers-52s that Hitler sent to Tetuán, as well as the Condor Legion, and you can be certain that with the help of the German army victory is assured. There is no other army like the German army."

"Ah Pierre! I've got *Divini Redemptoris* here for you, Pius XI's encyclical in which he condemns Communist atheism," Paola interrupted, handing Pierre a file.

"How are Azaña and the Popular Front Communists going to win the war if they don't have God on their side!" Michelangelo Bagliodi exclaimed, to expressions of exasperation from Amelia and smiles from Natalia.

"Do you think that God is on the side of the Fascists?" Amelia asked without being able to stop herself.

"Of course, my dear! Do you really think that God would be on the side of people who spit on Him and burn churches? Paola told me a few days ago that the far-left militants are shooting priests and monks and burning churches."

"Not only that, dear, but there are groups of militiamen who turn up in villages simply to assassinate people with property, Catholics or militants or right-wing sympathizers."

"But Franco hasn't taken Madrid," Amelia blurted out, trying to control the anger she felt.

"He will, my dear, he will, he just doesn't want to fight useless battles. It's true that they've stopped him at the Jarama, but for how long?"

"General Miaja has a great reputation," Amelia replied.

"Ah! The man who thinks he's the savior of Madrid," said Bagliodi.

"He's in charge of the National Defense Council, and they say that he's a skilled soldier," Pierre said.

"But the government is a barrelful of monkeys with Largo Caballero at the head of them, and then the Anarchists and the Communists... Do you think they'll really be able to agree among themselves? He's let Prieto take charge of the navy and the air force, but what does Prieto know about war?"

These luncheons were a nightmare for Amelia, and she would later hurl recriminations at Pierre.

"I don't know how you can bear them, what they say about Communism is offensive, but you don't say anything, as if I weren't with you and we weren't Communists. Have you forgotten that that's what we are?"

"And what do you want me to do? It would be useless to engage in dialogue with them, but they are a good source of information and we're finding out through them what's happening in Spain."

"The newspapers write it up as well."

"Yes, but Michelangelo and Paola have more information."

"And why do we need their information? The Soviet Union is helping the Republic, so they know very well what the situation is. There's nothing we can tell our comrades that they don't know already," Amelia reasoned.

One evening in April, Miguel López came to Amelia and Pierre's house unexpectedly. She was taking dictation from Pierre. He was still giving her daily Russian lessons.

Miguel was upset and keen to speak, but Pierre made a sign that he should not say a word until Amelia had left them.

"Darling, why don't you make us some supper? Miguel and I will have a drink and a chat. I'm tired of teaching for the day, so you are giving me just the opportunity I need to take a break, my friend."

Amelia went to the kitchen. She liked Miguel, so she did not object to his staying for supper.

"What's up?" Pierre wanted to know.

"We got a communiqué from our Madrid embassy this afternoon: The Condor Legion has bombed Guernica; it's been totally destroyed. It's not yet official; I don't think the papers will report it tomorrow."

"Guernica is the Basques' spiritual home," Pierre mused.

"I know, I know, and it's been flattened... ," Miguel said.

"Guernica will become a symbol, and that, my friend, will be a strong incentive for those who fight for the Republic."

"General Miaja has Soviet planes and troop transports and, according to our ambassador, the two brigades made up of International Brigade volunteers are fighting successfully."

"What's happening with England and France?"

"According to our Madrid embassy, they prefer not to intervene officially; they don't want the conflict to become international, they don't care that Italy and Germany have been supporting the insurrection from day one. Franco is getting diplomatic recognition as well."

"What is your embassy's opinion on how the war is progressing?"

"They say that Franco has the upper hand."

Miguel gave Pierre copies of certain dispatches that had been received from other embassies. They were valuable documents that would ensure that the Soviet *rezidentura* in Buenos Aires would receive congratulations from his superiors in Moscow.

Amelia called them to supper in the kitchen, and they shared some leftover meat from lunch along with salad and a bottle of Mendoza. They spoke about this and that, and Amelia asked Miguel, as she always did, if he had any news from Spain; Miguel looked at Pierre before answering.

"You know that they've been bombing the Basque Country since March 31; Vizcaya has suffered a great deal and... Well, it is not official, but the Condor Legion has destroyed Guernica."

Miguel could see the effect this news had on Amelia, who paled and pushed her plate away.

"Amelia! It's war, you know these things happen." Pierre tried to calm her down, as she was trembling.

"I am a Basque, and... you don't know what Guernica means," she said in a faint voice.

"You are a Communist, and your country is the world; for all your Basque names, how important is this really? We want to build a world free of nations and nationalities, don't you remember?"

"No, I have not forgotten, but I don't want to abandon who I am or where I come from. My father told me when I was a girl that being Basque was a feeling, an emotion..."

In July it started to be very cold in Buenos Aires. It was a year ago that Pierre and Amelia had left Spain for the Argentinian capital. For Amelia this seemed like an eternity, but Pierre claimed to be satisfied and said he felt no nostalgia. The many trunks filled with books that they had brought with them formed the basis of his business, and he had built it up by buying editions of Argentinian books and those from other South American countries. His father sometimes also sent books from Paris. It wasn't a large business, but it was enough for them to live comfortably and to maintain the cover that Pierre had designed for them.

Amelia still suspected nothing of the relationship between Natalia and Pierre until one afternoon, when she was taking tea with Gloria Hertz in the Ideal cake shop, Gloria said something that gave her an uncomfortable feeling in her stomach without her being quite sure why.

"Don't you think it's a bit overwhelming, Natalia being around all the time? I've already told her that she should give you a bit of breathing space, she's always between the two of you, like a third wheel. I don't know, it might be a good idea to put a bit of distance between you and her, I like her a lot, but I couldn't bear for her to be between me and my husband all the time."

Amelia didn't know what to say, and clenched her fists.

"Well, don't worry about what I say," Gloria said, trying to calm her down, "you know I'm a very jealous person, I'm too much in love with Martin."

From that moment on Amelia paid close attention to Natalia and especially to how Pierre behaved toward her. After a few weeks she concluded that she had nothing to worry about. Natalia was a woman who suffered from loneliness and who had found a refuge with them, and Pierre seemed none too impressed with Natalia, who was, although elegant, not particularly physically attractive.

But Pierre and Natalia carried on their romance away from everyone and had become extremely skilled at lying.

At the end of August Pierre received a communiqué from Moscow congratulating him for the work he had done and telling him that he would soon receive new instructions.

One day, as he was leaving Natalia's house, Pierre met Igor Krisov in the doorway.

To begin with he did not know how to react, but the Russian's ironic smile led him to give his friend a hug.

"You look like you've seen a ghost!" Krisov said.

"But you are a ghost! Where have you come from? I put you a thousand miles from here, with an ocean between us."

"And I imagined you in love with dear Amelia," the Russian replied, slapping him on the back.

"Well, it's not what you think... ," Pierre tried to explain.

"Yes, yes, it is what I think. You have another lover, her name is Natalia Alvear, she works at Government House and she's one of your agents. You're sacrificing yourself for the cause," Krisov said, laughing.

"Well, something like that; but tell me, what are you doing here?"

"It's a long story."

"A long story? What happened? I received congratulations from Moscow a little while back, they're happy with the information I am gathering..."

"Yes, that's what they would have said. Where can we talk?"

"Well... I don't know... Let's go home, we can talk at ease there and Amelia will be having tea with one of her friends at this hour."

"Does she still not know the truth?" Krisov asked.

"The truth? Ah! No, of course she knows nothing. But she's a gem, a real jewel, everyone opens their doors to her, and the most important people squabble to have her as a guest. I knew she was a sure thing."

They got home and Pierre was surprised to find Amelia there.

"Goodness, I thought you'd be with your friends!" he said reproachfully.

"I was going to go out, but you had forgotten that there were some clients coming today about that eighteenth-century edition of *Don Quixote*."

"It's true, I had forgotten!" Pierre said.

"I think I know you," Amelia said to Krisov, smiling and holding out a hand.

"It's true, Señorita Garayoa, we met in Paris."

"Yes, one day before we left France..."

"You sound regretful."

"Yes, I miss everything we left behind. Buenos Aires is a splendid city, very European, it's not hard to feel comfortable, but..."

"But you miss Spain and your family, that's only natural," Krisov said.

"If you don't mind, Amelia, I've got some business to discuss with Señor Krisov..."

"I'll try not to get in your way, but I'd prefer to stay, I don't feel like going out anymore."

Pierre was annoyed at Amelia's decision but said nothing, and Igor Krisov seemed pleased at her presence.

The two men remained alone in the room that served as the bookshop.

"Well, what's happened?" Pierre wanted to know.

"I have deserted." Krisov's face screwed up in pain as he admitted this.

Pierre was upset by the news. He didn't know what to do or what to say.

"Are you really surprised?" Krisov asked.

"Yes, really. I thought you were a committed Communist," Pierre said at length.

"I am, I am a Communist and I will die a Communist. No one will ever be able to convince me that there is a better idea for making this world a better place than that we should all be equal and that our destiny should not depend on chance. There is no cause more just than Communism, I am sure of it."

Igor's announcement surprised Pierre even more.

"In that case... I don't understand."

"They called me to Moscow two months ago. We have a new chief, Comrade Nikolai Ivanovich Yezhov. He's the man who has taken over from Genrikh Grigorievich Yagoda as the head of the NKVD. They are two men who are difficult to choose between when it comes to cruelty."

"Comrade Yagoda was always efficient, but I think he went a bit off the rails recently... ," Pierre dared to say.

"Look, I haven't been to Russia in eight years and I found out that Yagoda, Genrikh Grigorievich Yagoda, has been much worse than they had told me."

"Comrade Yagoda, head of the NKVD, had the complete trust of Comrade Stalin... ," Pierre scarcely dared to reply.

"It's not strange that Yagoda should rise so high, receiving as he did direct orders from Stalin and turning himself into his strong right hand, but in the end he was the victim of his own medicine. He could not escape from the terror that he himself instigated. He has been arrested, and I am sure he'll end up confessing what Stalin wants him to confess."

"What are you trying to say?"

"That he's in prison undergoing the same type of interrogation that he personally ordered for enemies of the revolution and people whom Stalin found awkward. After the crimes he has committed, I will not mourn his fate."

"Criminals need to be brought to justice, and people who betray the revolution are the worst," Pierre replied.

"Come on, Pierre, don't play the innocent with me, you know as well as I do that there are purges being carried out in the Soviet Union against all those whom Stalin declares to be counterrevolutionaries, but the real question is, who are those who are truly betraying the revolution? The answer, my friend, is that the biggest traitor of them all is Stalin himself."

"But what are you saying?"

"Are you shocked? Stalin has ordered lots of his former comrades assassinated, people who were in the front lines with him fighting for the revolution. Suddenly, previously untouchable people have turned into nuisances for Stalin, who doesn't want anyone to threaten his absolute power. Any criticism or even contrary opinion is punished by death. You've heard about the trials of supposed counterrevolutionaries..."

"Yes, trials of people who have betrayed the revolution, who felt nostalgia for the past, bourgeois who didn't adapt to the new situation, who couldn't face losing their privileges."

"I thought you were smarter than that, Pierre, too smart to swallow all this propaganda. I must say that I saw it like that as well to begin with, but it has become impossible for me to accept that this brave new world which we were going to build was going to end up doing anything other than transforming Russia into a ferocious dictatorship, where life was worth even less than under the czars."

"Say it isn't so!"

"First of all I found out about friends of mine who had disappeared, good Bolsheviks who were arrested at dawn by the NKVD in their houses, accused of being counterrevolutionaries. Comrade Yagoda carried out the job of commissioner for Internal Affairs with especial brilliance. Everyone Stalin wanted to get rid of was visited by Yagoda's goons."

"Lots of the people who were arrested confessed to plotting against the Soviet Union."

"I don't know what you would end up confessing to if you'd been tortured to a pulp for days on end."

"But what are you trying to say? I would never be a traitor."

"Neither would I, I would never betray my ideals, everything I have been fighting for. I am much older than you, Pierre, I could almost be your father, and I was devoted to the cause as a young man, when I fought in the revolution. I killed and I risked my own life, because I thought that we were building a better world. It is Stalin who has betrayed everything we were fighting for."

"Shut up!"

"The purges have reached all strata of society, no one is free from being declared suspicious, not even the highest officials in the Red Army are safe. Nikolai Ivanovich Yezhov is as bloody as Yagoda, and he will end up like him, because Stalin doesn't trust anyone, not even those who kill in his name. Yezhov is getting rid of everyone who worked with Yagoda. I'm telling you, trust no one. You and I have both worked for Yagoda."

"No! I work for the NKVD, names don't matter, what matters are the ideas, I serve the revolution."

"Yes, that's what it was about, Pierre, serving a higher cause, but things aren't like that, Pierre, and we are working for psychopaths. Do you know who was shot recently? General Berzin, a brilliant soldier and head of the Soviet military intelligence agency GRU. You might ask what his crime was: The answer is that there was no crime, none at all. Lots of his friends, his comrades, have been shot, the ones who were less lucky were sent first to the Lubyanka, others have been sent to punishment camps to be 're-educated'... Moscow is a city ruled by fear, where no one trusts anyone else, where people speak in whispers, where friends betray friends in order to win themselves a single more week of life. Intellectuals are suspicious, you know why? Because they think, and they think that they can express themselves freely, that this was why they fought in the revolution. Artists have to follow the dictates of Stalin: Artistic production can be considered counterrevolutionary if it does not hitch itself to his criteria. Do you know, my friend, that homosexuals are considered scum, perverse beings that society should get rid of?"

"That's your specific problem?" Pierre asked bluntly.

"Yes, I am a homosexual. I don't tell everyone, but I don't hide it either, there's no need. In the new world that we will build no one can be discriminated against for his race, for his sexual orientation, for his beliefs... When I fought in 1917, no one asked me who I was, we were all comrades with the same dreams. Being a homosexual did not stop me from fighting, from feeling hungry, from feeling cold, from killing and preparing to be killed; it's a miracle that I am alive, a bullet went through my shoulder, and I have the scar from a bayonet that went through my leg as a souvenir."

Ivan Krisov lit a cigarette without asking permission. He didn't care what Pierre might say to him, he saw him shrunken somehow, as if he were being beaten up, or as if he were a child who had suddenly discovered that Father Christmas did not exist.

Without taking pity on him, Krisov continued.

"Moscow is filled with fear, fear imposed by people such as Yagoda and now Yezhov, strong-arm men for Stalin's madness. Your mother is Russian, and as far as I know she has never sympathized with the revolution, but she must still have family and friends in the Soviet Union. Have you asked her if they're still alive?"

"My mother thinks that all of us revolutionaries are mad, she was a petty-bourgeois, an aristocrat's paid companion," Pierre said, mildly censorious.

"So you probably prefer not to know what has happened to her family in Russia and accept that they got what they deserved... Don't disappoint me, I thought that you could think for yourself."

"Tell me what you want."

"I've already told you that I met Yezhov and he treated me coldly, with disgust. Do you know what his nickname is? The Dwarf, yes, Yezhov is a dwarf, but this would be no problem at all if he were a different kind of person. He asked me to give him a list of all my agents, people who have been working with me all these years for the NKVD. He wanted to know names, addresses, cover stories, who their friends and family were... Everything, absolutely everything. And he criticized me for the fact that my reports had not been more complete about my agents' personalities, that I should have been less concise when explaining who our collaborators were. He insisted that I find out down to the last detail about everyone who has collaborated over the years with the NKVD, even as a 'blind' agent. You know that I have controlled a group of direct agents such as yourself, but also occasional collaborators, people whom I would never have accepted as agents but who were occasionally useful in the cause of the revolution. Moscow still has no precise information about these people or about the 'blind' agents, and this in particular was what Yezhov was asking me for. Ask yourself why. Yezhov told me that he was thinking of a new posting for me, in Moscow. I could tell from his look, from his gestures, from the cruel smile he was unable to hide that I was done for, that as soon as he had what he wanted he would send me to the Lubyanka where I would be tortured until I confessed whatever they wanted. I had to play for time, so I told him that all the personal details about my agents were in a safe in a London bank; some of these agents were known to Moscow only by their nicknames and the positions in which they were infiltrated. A capitalist bank is the safest place to hide Communist secrets, I told Comrade Yezhov. He didn't believe me, but he could not risk what I was saying turning out to be true, so he changed his approach and started to be friendly in a very cloying way. He invited me to have lunch with him, and suddenly asked about you. This didn't surprise me, because you are already a veteran agent of the NKVD. You started to work with us when we were still the OGPU. Not even Yezhov questioned that you were a valuable agent. Your cover as a bookseller has allowed you to travel all over Europe and to get in touch with the intellectual elites and collaborate usefully with them, but above all the information you provide is trustworthy. There are very few people like you who know Spanish politics in such detail."

"What did Comrade Yezhov want to know about me?"

"Nothing in particular, but I was surprised by his interest in you, especially since he asked me if your Communist beliefs were solid or merely the result of intellectual dilettantism. I'll give you my opinion: Yezhov does not like you. Later I met an old comrade, Ivan Vasiliev, who had been sidelined into one of the administrative departments of the NKVD; he was one of Yagoda's trusted workers and he had been shunted off to one side, but he was happy not to have been shot. This friend had been the recipient of your messages from Buenos Aires until his transfer, and he said that you were making waves there because you'd managed to insert two agents right into the heart of the state apparatus, so there was no obvious reason for Yezhov to have set his sights on you. But it is impossible to understand the mind of a murderer."

"I think you're trying to alarm me without any basis. I think it's normal that Comrade Yezhov should ask about his agents, your job is to report to him."

"Pierre, you are not one of my agents, you are here in Buenos Aires and you have another controller. Two days later this friend of mine confirmed what I had guessed: Yezhov wanted to 'tidy things up,' get rid of me, put one of his trusted men in charge and get rid of anyone who seemed half-hearted in his zeal. My friend said that Yezhov didn't like the bourgeoisie, however revolutionary they could make themselves out to be, and so you may have fallen into disgrace, just as I have done.

"Yezhov allowed me to return to London, but I found an old colleague waiting for me at the airport when I arrived, a man with whom I'd had serious arguments in the past. His orders were clear, I had to give him all the information I said I had in the London safe and then go back to Moscow. This agent was ordered not to separate from me by day or night until I was back on the plane, and he moved into my house until that moment should arrive."

"But you are here..."

"Yes, I've been doing the job for too many years not to think about what I should do if I needed to leave in a hurry, whether because the British intelligence services found out I was a Soviet agent or else because I lost the trust of Moscow, as has happened to other colleagues. You don't have to believe me, but I swear to you that a lot of the comrades I fought alongside with in 1917 are now dead, victims of Stalin's terror. Others have been sent to labor camps, and some were so scared that they didn't dare talk to me and instead shut the door with tears in their eyes, begging me to leave and not to compromise them with my presence. So, before I left Moscow, I started to put my plan for desertion into action. I managed to slip away from the agent Yezhov had sent to watch me; I'll tell you how I did it, I put a powder in his glass of wine. I was about to have to drink it myself, because he seemed to mistrust me when I proposed a toast to the glorious Soviet Union and Comrade Stalin. Once he was deep asleep I tied him to the bed and gagged him. I spent what was left of the night getting in touch with my agents and telling them to be prepared for what might happen. Early in the morning I went to my bank, asked for the safety deposit box where I kept money, false passports, and documents, and went to France, where I did the same as you, and headed off to Buenos Aires. I was at risk in dear old Europe, sooner or later they'd manage to find me, but the New World is immense and we still do not have very solid networks in place here, so Latin America was the best place for me to lose myself."

"Where will you go?"

"That, my friend, is something I am not going to tell you. If I am here at all it is because I still have some of my integrity as a man and a Bolshevik, and I feel obliged to tell you that you might be in danger. I owe a debt of loyalty to those comrades who worked with me, who have given the best of themselves to spread the revolution and the idea of Communism. Men such as yourself who have given up comfortable existences because they believe that all men are created equal and deserve the best. When you fight a war you know how important it is to be loyal and to be able to trust your comrades. You are nothing without them, and they are nothing without you, so I have fulfilled my obligation by coming here. I know you well, and I believe that you would not have trusted a letter. I've already told you that during the long night before my departure I got in touch with my agents in London who were most in danger, who would feature sooner or later on Yezhov's blacklist. I told them about the situation so that they could choose what they should do. Before I caught the boat I asked another agent to go to my house and untie Yezhov's homunculus. Well, here I am. I think that you will get an invitation from Moscow some time soon; if I were you I would not go, and even less would I take Amelia Garayoa with you. In Moscow they know her as a 'blind' agent, but as far as I am aware they only think of her as a petty-bourgeois caprice, an excuse that lets you have an adulterous relationship with a woman. Amelia is worthless for them, so I would not put her in the way of Yezhov's mental lucubrations."

"Are you saying that you've come to Buenos Aires simply to tell me that I have to desert?"

"I'm not telling you to desert, I'm explaining what the situation is, I'm giving you information and now you need to decide what to do with it. I've done my duty."

"You're not trying to tell me that you deserted but you felt the need to come and warn me before disappearing. That's just puerile," Pierre said, raising his voice.

"It is an inconvenient thing to have a conscience, and I have one, my friend, for all that I've tried to get rid of it. I'm an atheist, and I've got rid of all the stories my parents told me when I was a kid, as well as the ones the priest insisted that we take as gospel truth. No, I don't believe in anything, but I've got a conscience hidden away in some corner of my brain; I assure you that I would have liked to have been able to get rid of it, because it's the worst companion a man can have."

Pierre was walking up and down the salon. He was beside himself, scared and irritated in equal measure. He did not want to believe Igor Krisov, but neither could he bring himself not to.

Suddenly the two men realized that Amelia was standing on the threshold, silent and pale, with her eyes full of tears.

"What are you doing here?" Pierre shouted at her. "Nosy! Always cropping up where you shouldn't!"

Amelia didn't answer, didn't even move. Igor got up and hugged her as one hugs a child, trying to make her feel calm and safe.

"Come on, don't cry. Nothing's happened that can't be put right. How long have you been here?"

But Amelia said not a word. Igor helped her sit down and went to the kitchen to get a glass of water while Pierre scolded her for eavesdropping. In the end she told them that she had come to say dinner was ready and that she had been unable to avoid hearing a part of what Igor had to say.

"It's horrible! Horrible!" she repeated through sobs.

"Enough! Stop being a little girl. I didn't lie to you, it was you who wanted to be lied to," Pierre said, scarcely able to contain the anger that Krisov's revelations had stirred up.

"You should calm yourself; I can see that you're not ready to face a crisis, I thought you had more control over yourself," Krisov said to Pierre.

"Don't you start preaching!" Pierre shouted.

"I'm not preaching. I've fulfilled my obligations, I'm leaving. Do what you have to do... I'm sorry for you, Amelia, I know that you fell for the Communist idea full of hope, don't let this idea be beaten down within you by the bad name that some men are giving it. But look after yourself and learn to rely on yourself, take control of your life."

"Where are you going?" Amelia asked, trying to control her tears.

"You must understand that I cannot tell you. For my safety and for your own."

"Go now, before I turn you in!" Pierre threatened.

"You will, I know you will, I'm sure that you'll get in touch with the *rezidentura*; if you are going to carry on working for them it's what you have to do. If you decide to think about what I've said, then it's probably better that they know nothing. But the decision is yours."

Igor Krisov kissed Amelia's hand and left the house without saying anything further. He was soon lost among the first shadows of the night.

"I don't want you to blame me," Pierre warned Amelia.

She rubbed her eyes to try to control her tears. She felt stunned by what she had heard. She didn't know what to say or what to do, but it felt clear that she was waking from a dream, and the reality that now faced her was terrifying. They sat for a while in silence, trying to become calm enough to talk to one another. It was Pierre whose words broke the silence that had grown between them.

"Nothing has to change; all that's happened is that you've realized the extent of my collaboration with the Soviet Union; just by knowing it, you are now exposed to more danger. You have to forget what you've heard this afternoon, for your own safety, you can't tell anyone, we shouldn't even talk about it between ourselves. That's the best."

"Just like that, so easy?" Amelia asked.

"Yes, it can be that easy, it all depends on you."

"In that case I'm sorry to tell you, but it will be impossible, because I cannot forget what I've heard today. You want me not to give any importance to the fact that you have lied to me, and manipulated me, that you're a spy, that your life, and mine, depends on some men in Moscow. No, Pierre, what you want is impossible."

"It's what has to happen, or else..."

"Or else, what? Tell me, what will you do if I don't accept what you want me to do? Whom will you tell? What will they do to me?"

"That's enough, Amelia! Don't make things more difficult than they already are."

"I'm not responsible for this situation, you're the guilty one. You have tricked me, Pierre, and you know, I would have followed you just the same, I wouldn't have cared who you were, I would have abandoned my husband and my child for you even if you had told me that you were the devil himself. I loved you so much!"

"You don't love me anymore?" Pierre asked in alarm.

"Right now I don't know, to tell the truth. I feel empty, incapable of feeling anything. I don't hate you, but..."

Pierre felt panicked. The only thing he had never planned for was for Amelia to stop loving him, for her to stop being the beautiful young woman, obedient, who always showed him absolute devotion. He had grown accustomed for her to love him and the idea of losing her seemed unbearable. At that moment he realized that he loved that young woman who had followed him to the end of the earth and whom he could not imagine not spending the rest of her life with him. He went up to Amelia and hugged her, but her body was rigid, and she rejected his tenderness.

"Forgive me, Amelia! I beg you to forgive me. My only intention was to keep you out of danger..."

"No, Pierre, you didn't care about that. I still don't know why you have brought me here, but I know it was not because you felt a love for me such as I felt for you," she replied as she extricated herself from his clutches.

Pierre realized that this was the night on which Amelia had truly become a woman, and that the person standing before him was unknown to him.

"Don't doubt that I love you. Do you think I could have asked you to abandon your family and come with me if I didn't love you? Do you think I don't care about what my parents think? And even so..."

"It was I who loved you, and what I thought was that you loved me with the same passion. Tonight I have discovered that our relationship is based upon a lie, and I wonder how many other lies you have told me."

"Don't think that you are not important to me!"

Amelia shrugged indifferently; she felt that there was now nothing to tie her to this man for whom she had sacrificed so much.

"I need to think, Pierre, I have to decide what I am going to do with my life."

"I will never leave you!" he said as he tried to embrace her again.

"It's not just what you want but what I want, and this is what I am going to think about. If you don't mind sleeping on the sofa, I will sleep here, or else I'll ask Gloria to let me stay with her for a few days."

He was tempted to deny her this, but he did not, knowing that he could not oppose her in anything at the moment without losing.

"I am sorry for hurting you and I only hope that you can forgive me. I will sleep on the sofa and I will try to bother you as little as possible. All I ask is for you to realize that I love you, to know that I cannot imagine life without you."

Amelia left the room and shut herself in the bedroom. She wanted to cry but could not. To her surprise, she fell asleep immediately.

From that night on, they established a routine that was filled with silence. Although Pierre was extremely humble, he tried to avoid her.

One of the few conversations they had was when Amelia asked him if he had informed on Igor Krisov.

"It was my duty to inform the authorities of his presence here, he's a deserter."

She looked at him with contempt and he tried to justify himself.

"If I hadn't informed on him then we would have become suspects, collaborators! I will never be a traitor!"

"Krisov was always kind to me," Amelia murmured.

A few days later Natalia turned up at the house, worried because Pierre had stopped visiting her, or even calling her, and she could not avoid a secret thrill when she saw the crisis that was affecting the couple.

"I am sorry for coming without warning, but I missed you," she said when Amelia opened the door.

"Come in, Natalia, Pierre is working in the salon. Would you like a cup of tea?"

"I would appreciate it, it's cold. How are you? You didn't come to Gloria's house for lunch, we missed you."

"Like I told her, I have a bit of a cold."

Natalia noticed that Amelia did not seem to have any symptoms, but she said nothing; on the other hand, Pierre's icy greeting did worry her.

"We didn't expect you. What are you doing here?"

"Well, I missed you, I haven't heard anything from you for a week and everyone was asking me what had happened to the 'inseparable trio'..."

Pierre didn't say anything, and looked annoyed when Amelia said she was going to the kitchen to make some tea.

"I don't want anything, I've got work to do," he said without trying to hide his bad mood.

"I won't be here long," Natalia said, getting ever more uncomfortable.

As soon as Amelia had left the room she looked at Pierre, wanting to ask for an explanation.

"Do you want to tell me what's happened?"

"Nothing."

"What do you mean, nothing? I have important information to give you and you haven't been in touch. Also... well... I missed having you near me," she whispered.

"Shush! I don't want you to say anything here, I'll call you."

"When?"

"When I can."

Amelia came in with a tray bearing a teapot and three cups, as well as an apple pie that she had bought in El Gato Negro, a Spanish-owned shop where you could buy anything.

For all that Natalia tried to enliven the conversation, neither Amelia nor Pierre seemed prepared to help her. She saw the tension between them and how they avoided speaking to one another. Natalia decided that it was better to leave them alone. But before she left, while Amelia went to find her coat, she indicated to Pierre that it was important they should see each other. He nodded but said nothing.

When Natalia left, Amelia came into the room and sat in front of the table where Pierre was working.

"I've made up my mind, and I think that the sooner I tell you the better for us both. Our friends are calling and want to know why we don't accept their invitations, and even Natalia comes to the house, worried about us."

"Natalia is a bit of a busybody," Pierre replied.

"No, she's not, she was right, she was always with us, and she doesn't understand what's going on. If you don't mind, I think the time has come for us to talk."

Pierre closed the account book he was working with and prepared to listen to Amelia. He had no desire at all to argue with her. He had told himself over these past few days that he was lost without her.

"I am going to go back to Spain. My country is at war, sunk in a terrible civil war, and I don't want to live with my back turned to everything that's happening there. I haven't heard anything about my family since we arrived here, and I can't bear the idea that something might have happened to them. I know that they will never forgive my behavior, which was flighty and vain, but even if they decide never to speak to me again I will be happy to be near them. I don't imagine that my husband will let me see my son, but I would be happy to see him even from a distance: I need to see him grow up, to see him run around, to see him laugh, to see him cry... and maybe I will be able to go up to him one day and beg his forgiveness..."

"You can't go," Pierre murmured, his face tense.

"If you're worried about what I know, don't be; I won't ever tell anyone that you're a Soviet spy. I will keep that secret. I won't ruin your life, I just want to go home."

"I can't let you go..."

"What will you do? Denounce me to the Soviet Embassy? I'm not an agent."

"I'm sorry, Amelia, but you have been an agent without knowing it, you're what we call a 'blind' agent, someone who works for us without knowing that that's what she's doing. I brought you here as an alibi to set myself up without anybody being suspicious. It was easier for people to be willing to open their doors to a couple who were deeply in love. Moscow approved of my plan, and it was a success. Thanks to your friend Carla Alessandrini, and the contacts that she provided for us, we have been able to get to know people who are very useful for our cause. And... well, my mission was to set up a network of agents, that takes time, but thanks to you I have managed to set one up in a very few months. You heard Igor Krisov: They value my reports in Moscow, they value the information my agents provide."

"You're a rat!" Amelia burst out.

"I am, and I am sorry. The only thing I can say is that I love you, and more than using you, the important thing is what you mean to me. I love you, Amelia, much more than I thought I did. You cannot go, we are united by a cause, you are part of Moscow's plan for Buenos Aires. They won't just let you leave like that."

"Not even Moscow will stop me going, unless they kill me," Amelia replied, and got to her feet.

8

Amelia was firmly decided that she would leave Pierre, though she had no money of her own and was entirely dependent on him. This circumstance made her realize the importance of having her own source of income in order to take control of her own life. She had gone from the care of her family to that of her husband, and from that of her husband to that of Pierre. She had never been lacking for anything, but neither had she had anything that was specifically hers, and she understood that to follow Krisov's advice to take control of her life there was nothing for her to do but to work. Pierre would not give her the money to buy a return ticket to Europe, and she did not feel capable of asking to borrow the money, so she decided to work.

The day after their conversation, Amelia went to Gloria Hertz's gallery.

"I need to work. Can you help me?"

"What's wrong? Is the bookshop not going well?"

"Quite the opposite, it's going extremely well, better than Pierre had imagined, but this isn't about the bookshop, it's about me, I want to be independent and have my own money."

It was not difficult for Gloria to realize that this request came as the result of a crisis between Amelia and Pierre.

"Have you quarreled with Pierre?" Gloria asked.

"I want to leave him and go back to Spain, and to do that I need to work," she replied simply.

"I don't want to get involved in something that is none of my business, but are you sure that this isn't a passing quarrel? After all you've been through together..."

"I want to go back to my country. I can't get the war out of my head, how my son is, what's happened to my family."

"Have you stopped loving Pierre?"

"Perhaps... In fact, when I look back I am surprised that I decided to run away with him, that I fell in love with him. But I can't regret things that happened in the past, I have no control over them, but I am the mistress of my future."

Gloria was impressed to hear Amelia talk this way; she suddenly seemed to have become a mature woman, not the sweet and friendly girl whom everyone wanted to spend time with.

"And what does Pierre say about all this?" insisted Gloria.

"He doesn't want me to go, but it's a decision that doesn't depend on him but on me. And it's a decision that has been made, I just need the money to go home."

"And he... well... he doesn't want to help you?"

"Pierre will not help me to return, so I have to rely on myself. I need a job. Can you help me find one?"

"It's not easy... But perhaps we could lend you the money."

"No, not that. I don't want to be in anyone's debt. I prefer to work."

"Well, what can you do?"

"Whatever, I don't mind, I only want to earn enough money to pay for my ticket."

"I'll speak to Martin, maybe he'll be able to think of something... but... Are you sure? All couples fight at times, I've wanted to separate from Martin in the past, but what's important is love, in the final analysis, if a couple loves each other, then nothing else matters."

"You're right, there has to be love, and I don't feel enough love to be sure of wanting to continue with Pierre. I want to go back to Spain," Amelia insisted.

She spent the rest of the morning walking through the city looking for anything that could be a job offer. When she was headed home, she came across a sign in the door of a cake shop that said help wanted, and she said a little prayer.

Amelia didn't think twice and walked in. The cake shop was small, decorated simply but in good taste, and its owners were an old couple. They were both Spanish. They had emigrated from Lugo at the end of the nineteenth century and had worked hard to get their little shop, which made them proud because it was the fruit of their own efforts and sleepless nights. They had no children, and although Doña Sagrario had been sad about this for a while, in the end she accepted what she saw to be God's will. As far as Don José was concerned, he truly missed having no children, but he never said this to his wife.

Don José was sick, he had suffered two heart attacks, and the last one had also affected his brain, leaving the left side of his body paralyzed. Doña Sagrario had no time to look after her husband and their business, so they had decided to employ someone to take charge of the cake shop.

The two women felt an immediate connection, and Doña Sagrario was pleased to discover that Amelia was a good cook and knew something about baking.

"You can help me to make the cakes and tarts as well as sell them," the good old woman said.

The salary was not very high, but Amelia calculated that a few months would be enough for her to save up enough money for a passage on any boat going to France, and from there to make her way back to Spain. She didn't mind the idea of traveling in third class, without luxuries or comforts.

Doña Sagrario suggested that she start immediately, and Amelia accepted with pleasure. She worked behind the counter, and when there were no clients she went into the kitchen that was just behind the shop to help Doña Sagrario with the cake batter. Don José looked at them silently, but Doña Sagrario assured Amelia that he was happy that they had hired her.

It was growing dark when Amelia returned home, where Pierre was waiting for her nervously.

"But where have you been! I've been worried about you! Gloria called me a while back to say that she might have found a job for you. What's all this about working? You haven't asked me, and let me tell you: Don't even think about it."

But Amelia was not the sweet young girl whom Pierre had once known, and she defended herself sharply, justifying her recently initiated journey toward independence.

"You do not own me. As far as I know, you don't approve of private property, so there's no way you are going to own a human being such as me. I have decided to work, to earn money and to buy a ticket on any boat that will take me back to France. I asked Gloria if she knew of any jobs, but I've been lucky and found one by myself, in fact I have already started working."

Pierre listened to her in silence, and every word was like a blow to the stomach.

"Amelia, I have asked you to forgive me... I have explained to you why I couldn't let you know, for your own safety... What else do you want? Isn't it enough that I love you? You said that this was the only thing that was important to you, that I love you..."

"You have to realize that things have changed, that I have changed. You can't expect to betray me as you have betrayed me and for nothing to happen. Do you really think so little of me, Pierre? Of course... you must have your own motives for thinking of me a fool. You have manipulated me like a puppet, I have followed you blindly, without thinking, but I am awake now, Pierre; your friend Krisov has brought me back to reality, and I blame myself as much as you for what happened. I hate myself for what I have done, so you must understand that I hate you for it as well."

"And what about our dreams, our ideals? We were going to change the world."

"They were your dreams and your ideals, never mine, not mine, Pierre; my only dream now is to go back to my country and to be with my people. I know that neither my father nor my uncle will have supported the rebels against the Republic, and I fear for them, just as I fear for Santiago and for my son."

"Don't leave me, Amelia," Pierre begged.

"I'm sorry, but as soon as I can I will go."

Gloria and Martin insisted on inviting them to dinner. They were worried about the couple and were convinced that their problems were only temporary. Amelia resisted but in the end gave in, and one night after her work at the cake shop was done she met with Pierre and the Hertzes.

Amelia liked talking to Martin because they always spoke in German. He insisted that they speak the language so they would not forget it.

"I'm surprised by how good an accent you have," Martin said.

"That's what my friend Yla said, but I'd forget it all if it weren't for you."

"I've got a letter from an uncle of mine who has managed to make it to New York. If you'd like I can tell him to look for Yla and her parents, but I'll need some details to start the search."

"I don't know, Martin, I don't know; my cousin Laura only told me that Herr Itzhak had yielded to the evidence of the danger that Hitler posed to the Jews, and that he was preparing for Yla to go to New York. I hope he managed it!"

They spoke about everything and about nothing, but in spite of the Hertzes' efforts to animate the discussion, neither Pierre nor Amelia were in the mood to hide the huge chasm that there was between them.

Little by little, Pierre was growing accustomed to the new routine that Amelia had imposed upon them. They slept apart, he on the sofa and she in the room that they had shared until the night that Igor Krisov came around.

Amelia was up with the dawn, left Pierre's lunch ready for him, and went to the cake shop, where Doña Sagrario was teaching her everything she knew about baking. There were occasions when Amelia had to take charge of the shop all by herself, either because Don José was not feeling well or even, as had happened on a couple of occasions, because they had had to take him to hospital.

When she got home she greeted Pierre but she made no effort to enter into conversation with him, she didn't even ask him how his day had been. She was normally exhausted and only wanted to rest.

For his part, Pierre continued his affair with Natalia. He saw her more often now that he and Amelia slept apart.

He told Natalia that his relationship with Amelia was not going well, and Natalia took care to provide everything that Amelia was no longer offering. She also took ever greater risks removing documents from Government House, to show Pierre that she was willing to perform any act of madness for him.

Miguel López was still a source of privileged information, as he now dealt with the ciphers coming into Argentina from its embassies all over the world.

Pierre's controller, the ambassador's secretary, congratulated him from time to time, assuring him that Moscow was happy with his work, and although they had not suggested again that he go to Russia, Pierre could not help worrying that they would, as Krisov's warnings had filled him with fear.

It was not until Christmas 1937 that major new changes arose in Pierre and Amelia's life.

Amelia exchanged letters with Carla Alessandrini, and kept these letters as though they were precious jewels. The diva spoke about her successes or else complained about the inconvenience caused by her busy schedule, but especially she gave her opinion of the civil war in Spain, a country where Carla had many friends.

Amelia had asked in her last letter for her to try to get in touch with her cousin Laura Garayoa in order to find out about her family.

Pierre, without Amelia's knowledge, read these letters when Amelia went out to work. He was afraid of losing complete control over her, and justified his behavior to himself by saying that if he read Carla's letters it was to protect Amelia, to stop her from telling the diva something she should not.

He always waited for Amelia to read them before hunting them out from the chest of drawers where she kept them.

Gloria and Martin invited them to dinner on December 24 to celebrate Christmas. Although Martin was Jewish, he had also incorporated Catholic festivities into his daily life, and joked with his wife to the effect that they had more parties than other people.

Although Amelia had no desire to celebrate Christmas, she did not want to disappoint her friends and agreed to dine with them and Pierre.

The Hertzes had invited a dozen friends, including Doctor Max von Schumann, a childhood friend of Martin's and a doctor as well.

"Amelia, I would like you to meet Max, my best friend," Martin said, introducing Amelia in German.

She replied in the same language and the three of them sparked up a conversation that seemed to annoy Pierre, who could not understand a word.

"Who is your friend?" the Frenchman asked Gloria.

"Our dear Max... Baron von Schumann. Martin has known him since they were children, and they studied medicine together; Max is a surgeon, and the best there is, according to Martin."

"So he's an aristocrat..."

"Yes, he's a baron and an army doctor by family tradition. But most importantly he's a wonderful person."

"And his wife?"

"He hasn't yet married, but it's only a matter of time. He's engaged to the daughter of some friends of his parents, the Countess Ludovica von Waldheim."

"And what's he doing in Buenos Aires?"

"Visiting Martin. Max did everything he could to help him leave Germany, and has helped his family, and his many Jewish friends, as much as he could. They are like brothers, and it is a great joy for us that he has come to visit."

Pierre did not let Amelia out of his sight. She seemed charmed by Baron von Schumann, and Pierre was annoyed when Gloria, offering the excuse that the two of them could speak in the Baron's language, sat Amelia next to the German during the meal.

The Baron was impressed by Amelia. Her fragility and the sadness that seemed to come from her moved him deeply.

They spent the whole dinner talking, and Gloria was pleased to see her friend so lively, and above all to see her laugh, but she felt that it was her obligation to warn Amelia.

"I haven't seen you this happy for a long time," she said in a low voice when Martin called Max away for a moment.

"You know, I didn't feel very much like coming, but now I'm glad I did," Amelia said.

"Do you like Max?" Gloria asked, smiling to see how her friend blushed.

"What things you say! He's very nice and friendly, and... Well, he makes me feel good."

"I'm so happy. But... well... I should remind you that he's about to get married to Countess Ludovica von Waldheim. Martin says she's a beautiful young woman and that they make a very handsome couple."

Gloria did not want Amelia to feel attracted to Max and to be disappointed again, so she preferred to set things straight from the start.

"Thank you, Gloria," Amelia said, a little annoyed by her friend's warning.

"Just something for you to bear in mind... well... It looks like you and Max have formed a connection."

"You sat me next to him because I spoke German, I tried to be nice."

"I don't want you to suffer!"

"I don't see why I'm going to suffer because I sit next to a friend of yours," Amelia said sharply.

"Max belongs to an old Prussian family and has a very strong sense of duty."

"Yes, I got that from the conversation we had over dinner."

Max and Martin approached the two women and immediately began a new conversation about the difficult situation in Germany.

"It's Christmas, and we should talk about happier things!" Gloria said.

"So many of our friends have disappeared! From what Max says, the country is getting dragged further and further into Hitler's madness... ," Martin lamented.

"The worst is that Chamberlain is following a policy of appeasement with regard to Hitler and Mussolini, and this makes the Führer feel ever more secure."

"But the English can't support the Nazis," Amelia said.

"The problem is that Chamberlain doesn't want problems, and this lets Hitler's dreams grow ever bigger," Max said.

"How can you serve in Hitler's army?" Amelia asked, not bothering to hide a certain annoyance in her voice.

"I do not serve in Hitler's army, I serve in the German army, like my father, and my grandfather, and my great-grandfather... Mine is a family of soldiers, and it is our duty to continue the tradition."

"But you told me you hated Hitler!" Amelia said in a complaining tone.

"I do. I feel nothing but contempt for this Austrian corporal whose delusions of grandeur may lead who knows where, and I am scared for my country."

"So leave the army!" Amelia insisted.

"I have been educated to serve my country above all things. I can't leave just because I don't like Hitler."

"You yourself told me about the persecution of the Jews..."

The conversation made Max uncomfortable and Martin decided to change the subject.

"Amelia, sometimes we are obliged to do things we do not like but we are nonetheless unable to escape, we can't do anything else no matter how much we might want to. Everybody's life is filled with patches of light and patches of shade... Let my friend Max enjoy Christmas, or else he might never again want to spend it with me."

"I'm sorry, but I just hate Hitler so much," Amelia said.

"The weather's lovely, and I thought that we could go for a trip out of the city; if you and Pierre want to join us tomorrow we'd be extremely pleased," Gloria interrupted.

Amelia and Pierre did not go on the excursion that Gloria had planned because when they returned home at dawn they found a note under their door. Pierre's controller required Pierre to get in contact with him immediately.

At nine in the morning Pierre left home to go to the Kavanagh Building, a thirty-story skyscraper built in 1935 that the citizens of Buenos Aires were especially proud of.

Behind the building, a little passage opened up onto the Calle San Martín, where the Church of the Holy Sacrament was to be found; here it was that Pierre was to meet his controller.

The Russian was seated in the last row of pews and seemed to be reading a breviary, given that Mass was at that moment being celebrated by a young priest in front of about thirty communicants, whose faces all showed the excesses of the night before.

Pierre sat next to his controller and waited to hear what he would say.

"You have to go to Moscow," the Russian announced.

"When?" Pierre's response displayed a little fear.

"Soon, the Ministry of Culture is organizing a congress of European and North American intellectuals in order to introduce them to the glories of the Soviet Union. You will be a part of the organizing committee. This is a very important event, you know that there are Fascist groups dedicated to attacking the honor of the revolution. Our best allies are the European intellectuals."

"And what can I do?"

"You know lots of French intellectuals, Spanish, British, even a few Germans... You have always been a part of those circles. We need personal information about them... Everyone has a weak spot..."

"A weak spot? I don't understand..."

"They'll tell you in Moscow. Get ready for the journey."

"And what will I say to the people here?"

"Your agents will pass their information directly to me, and as for your friends... you'll think of something, and anyway, you've always traveled looking for special editions."

"And Amelia?"

"She will go with you."

"But maybe she won't want to... She's been very worried lately about the war in Spain. She suffers for her family..."

"A Communist doesn't think about his or her personal desires, but rather about what is best for the revolution, for our cause. I thought that she was a good Communist..."

"She is! No doubt about it!"

"So there should be no problem with Comrade Garayoa. She will go with you. It will be an honor for her to get to know Moscow."

When Pierre arrived home, Amelia was sitting with a cup of coffee, waiting for him. Before he even said anything she could read the panic in his expression, the tension in the smile he gave her.

"What did they say?" she asked, without waiting for Pierre to sit down.

"They've ordered me to go to Moscow. I have to go in two or three weeks."

"Krisov said..."

"I know what that traitor said!" Pierre's voice displayed his worry and fear.

"Why do they want you to go?"

"They're preparing a congress of artists, intellectuals, they're going to invite people from all over the world. Intellectuals are the best propagandists for the revolution. They have moral authority in their home countries. They want me to go to Moscow to be on the organizing committee."

"Right. They're going to take you out of Buenos Aires, where you have set up a spy network, and they want you to go to Moscow to be on a committee... Pierre, don't go."

"I can't not go."

"Yes you can, just tell them you're not going and... Stop all this, get your life back."

"My life? Which life do you mean?"

"Tell them you don't want to be an agent anymore, that you're tired, that you've done enough..."

"Do you think it's so easy? No, Amelia, you don't just go in and out of this when you want. Once you're in you have to go all the way to the end."

"You have the right to live another life."

Pierre looked at her tiredly, he felt old, weighed-down.

"I've dedicated my life to Communism. I've never had any other ambition than to serve the revolution. Amelia, I don't know how to do anything else."

"Krisov warned you about what might happen if you went to Moscow."

He shrugged. He didn't feel capable of doing anything other than face up to the destiny that he himself had chosen.

"They want you to come with me," he muttered.

"Yes, I suppose they would. They don't want to leave any loose ends."

"But don't come. I've been thinking about this, I'll make them think that you're coming, but you'll get ill the day we're meant to travel, appendicitis or something, and I'll get you admitted to the hospital. I'll tell them that you'll meet me later. I'll give you money so that you can go back to Spain or wherever you want; perhaps you'll be safer with your friend Carla, at least for a while. My Moscow bosses will be upset that you're not coming and..."

"And they might decide to eliminate me, right?"

"I don't know what might happen to you in Spain, you know that there's a Soviet force there helping the Republic."

"Krisov gave me a piece of advice which I've followed devotedly since the day he came to this house. From now on it's me who has control of my own life."

"I don't want anything to happen to you, I love you, Amelia. I know you don't believe me, that you don't want to forgive me, but at least allow me to help you."

"I will decide, Pierre. I will make my own decisions."

Over the next few days Pierre decided to meet with Natalia and Miguel to tell them of his voyage to Moscow and about how they should get in touch with the Soviet controller.

Natalia had a nervous attack when Pierre told her that he had to go to Moscow and that he might be gone for months.

"You can't leave me!" she said. "I want to go with you!"

"I wish you could, but it's impossible. You have to understand this. I won't be gone for more than five or six months..."

"And what am I going to do?"

"The same as you do now. You won't have any problems passing the information you gather to the controller."

"I don't trust anyone, only you. What if they follow me? They might suspect me if they see me with a Russian..."

"I've told you how to avoid being followed, and I've also told you that there's no need for you to see each other except in extraordinary circumstances. When you have something useful to pass on, you put this pot of geraniums in the left side of the window. Leave it there for three days. On the third day put your report between the pages of a newspaper and go have lunch in the zoological gardens. Sit down on a bench near the birdcages, watch the birds and leave the paper behind when you go."

"And if someone takes it who shouldn't?"

"That won't happen."

It was not easy for Pierre to convince Natalia to keep on working with the Soviets. Her interest in the revolution was directly proportional to the proximity of her lover.

He spent more time than ever with Natalia, and Amelia carried on working, and spent her few moments of free time with the Hertzes.

Gloria and Martin could see the attraction that Amelia and Max felt for each other, and they were worried that they might be encouraging a relationship that they could see was impossible. Amelia was married; in Spain, yes, but it was still a binding marriage, and she also lived with her lover. And Max von Schumann was the kind of man who would prefer to die rather than to leave a promise unkept or to stain what he termed his "family honor." However much he was in love with Amelia, he would never break his engagement with the Countess Ludovica von Waldheim, so his relationship with the young Spaniard had no future. Pierre reached the same conclusion, after having initially been worried by the obvious attraction that the German doctor and Amelia were incapable of hiding.

However, Pierre did try to go with Amelia when she dined with the Hertzes, even though she did not always tell him about these meetings.

On one evening when Pierre had to go to have supper with Natalia, because she had rung him in a flurry of tears, Amelia took the opportunity to accept Max's invitation.

"I am going to leave in a few days, and I would like us to eat alone together at least once; I don't know if this is correct or if it will cause problems with... with Pierre, but if you could...," Max had asked her.

When her day's work in the cake shop was done, Amelia said goodbye to Doña Sagrario more hastily than was her normal habit. The older woman realized that Amelia's eyes shone more than was usual.

"I can see you're happy. Is it a special celebration with Pierre?"

Amelia smiled but made no reply. She did not want to lie to the good old woman, who had been so understanding when she realized that Pierre was not her legal husband, but neither did she wish to tell her that she was meeting another man, as she worried what Doña Sagrario might think.

Max was waiting for her in the Café Tortoni, and from there they went to dine in a restaurant.

If Amelia was nervous, Max was not much less so. Both of them knew that this meal meant that they were crossing a line that neither of them could step back over.

"I am happy that you agreed to dine with me. I am leaving in a week, I cannot spend any more time in Buenos Aires."

"I know, Gloria told me that you need to join your unit."

"I'm a privileged man, Amelia, to have had this long holiday with my best friends, but my family's influence does not allow me to stretch my time here any further," Max said, laughing.

"Why did you come to Buenos Aires? Just to see Martin?

"Is that odd?"

"A little, yes..."

"You wouldn't go to New York if you knew where to find Yla? You told me that she and your cousin Laura were the closest friends of your childhood."

"Of course I would go!"

"Well, that's what I did, come to see my best friend, who has had to leave our country on account of some madmen. I needed to know that he was well, that here... Well, I wanted to see that he was happy. It isn't easy to leave your homeland, your house, your friends, to stop breathing the air you have always breathed... You can understand this; you left your country as well."

Amelia grew sad. In the last few months, every time she had thought about Spain she had felt an empty sensation in her stomach that gave way to pain.

"But let us not be sad! I don't want the only chance we will have to be alone together to turn into a wake."

"Don't worry, I won't be sad."

They went to have dinner and made an effort to lead the conversation along uncontroversial lines, but by dessert Amelia could not resist asking Max about his future with the army.

"Tell me, how can you accept obeying the orders of someone who thinks that there are different categories of human beings, who persecutes the Jews and takes everything they have?"

"We've talked about this already..."

"Yes, but... I just can't imagine you under orders from Hitler."

"He is chancellor now, but he won't be chancellor forever, and Germany will always be Germany. I don't serve Hitler, I serve my country."

"But Hitler controls Germany!"

"Yes, and that's a terrible shame and embarrassment, but what would you have me do? He won the elections."

"Even so..."

"I'm a soldier, Amelia, not a politician. And now I want to talk about something else, I know I shouldn't, but I am going to anyway."

"Please, I'd prefer you not to..."

"Yes, it would be the right thing to say nothing, but I have to. I have fallen in love with you and I swear that I have made every effort not to let that happen. I didn't want to leave without telling you."

"I think the same thing has happened to me. But I'm not sure... I'm very confused..."

"I think that we are in love, and that's the worst thing we could have done, because we have no future together."

"I know," whispered Amelia.

"I cannot break off my engagement with Ludovica, and... well, the wedding is arranged for when I return. And you have sacrificed a great deal to be with Pierre... and I don't want to lie to you, even if I broke off my engagement with Ludovica, my family would never accept you; you would always be a married woman to them."

Amelia felt her face burning. She felt ashamed, as she had never felt when she abandoned her family to be with Pierre.

"I didn't want to upset you... I am sorry... I want to be honest with you, even if I have to be blunt," Max apologized.

"It's better to be clear about things," Amelia replied, and smoothed her skirt with an automatic hand, as if this gesture would lessen the shame that she felt at Max's words.

"I need you to understand me, for you to tell me what you think, and if you think that there's any other way out."

"No, Max, no, there isn't. The truth hurts, but I prefer truth to lies. I wouldn't have been able to bear it if you had given me hope and then... I know who I am: a married woman who has abandoned her husband and her son, her family, to run away with another man. In the eyes of the rest of the world this turns me into a disreputable woman, and I understand that your parents would never be able to accept me. I don't ask for you to break your engagement with Ludovica, I know that your sense of honor would suffer so badly that you would never be able to forgive me for breaking your word, even if you never made mention of this to me again. Let's leave it at this. We have shared some very special days together, but I have always known that you were going to have to leave and that I would play no role at all in your future. It is just... Well, you have given me back my desire to live. I wanted to leave work so that I could meet you and the Hertzes, I waited for the telephone to ring and for Gloria to invite me to spend some time in the country. I will always be grateful to you for these days, because, don't you see, I thought I was dead."

He took her home. They walked next to one another without touching, in silence.

"We will see each other again before I leave," Max said.

"Of course, I know that Gloria is preparing a farewell party for you."

To the relief of Martin and Gloria, Max and Amelia did not see each other alone again. Amelia did not come to Max's farewell party, but sent a note to wish him luck.

This brief and barren relationship with Baron von Schumann left a deep mark, one more deep mark, on Amelia. She lost the happiness that she seemed to have found at Max's side, and her friends found her ever more taciturn and pensive.

February 5 was the day planned for Pierre to begin his journey to Moscow. As the date approached, he grew ever more nervous. Krisov's warning had taken root so strongly in his mind that he was almost unable to sleep, seeing himself in dreams being inter-rogated and tortured by his comrades. Some nights he woke up screaming, and Amelia would come to calm him down and offer him a glass of water. He held her hand like a desperate child.

Pierre's fears awakened Amelia's protective instinct. She began to worry about him as if he were indeed a child. When she finished her day's work at the cake shop she would hurry home to be with Pierre. They did not share a bed, but she looked after him affec-tionately. Amelia was so caring that their friends thought that they had reconciled. He, the sophisticated man of the world, allowed himself to be controlled by her and looked at her gratefully; he also got nervous when she was not at his side. A special bond grew between them during these days.

Although Pierre had told Amelia that she would not travel with him, and insisted on his plan of having her fall ill on the day of their departure, they had both announced to all their friends that they were going to travel in Europe, and would most likely pass through Moscow. Nobody was surprised that Pierre wanted to visit his parents in Paris and to go hunting for those special editions that he later sold for so much.

The day before his departure, Pierre looked at the care Amelia was taking with the luggage.

"I'll miss you," he said in a low voice, thinking that she wouldn't hear him.

"I don't think so," Amelia said, and looked him straight in the face.

"Yes, I will miss you, you're a part of me, the best thing I've ever had in my life even though I haven't seen it until it was too late," Pierre said with regret.

"You're not going to miss me because I'm coming with you."

"What are you saying! You can't, it's impossible."

"Yes, I can. I don't think you'll be able to face up to what you are going to have to deal with."

"What do you mean?"

"That you're scared, and with good reason. And when you scream at night even I get scared. You don't know what you're going to have to deal with in Moscow, and you need someone by your side."

"Yes, I am afraid of what might happen. They say terrible things about Comrade Yezhov."

"They said the same things about Comrade Yagoda."

"You don't have to take any risk for me, you've sacrificed enough. It's your chance to go back to Spain, to be free."

"You're right, it is my chance, but I'm not going to leave you alone. I'll accompany you, we'll see what happens in Moscow, and if Igor Krisov told us the truth, then at least I'll be by your side; if he was wrong, then I'll go back to Spain as soon as possible."

"Amelia, I can't ask you to do this."

"You're not asking me, I've decided for myself. I'm just postponing my plans for a month or so. I have loved you a lot, Pierre, in spite of the pain you've caused me, and I cannot bear to see you in this state. I will go with you tomorrow and I hope to God that Krisov was mistaken and that we will both be able to return..."

Professor Muiños fell silent, lost in his thoughts. His silence brought me back to the present.

"My great-grandmother! Who'd have thought it?" I said in surprise, realizing as I did so that the phrase was becoming a bit of a cliché.

I had spent three days going backwards and forwards all over the city with Professor Muiños; he had shown me all the places my great-grandmother had visited. He hadn't given me any time to breathe, even.

"Well, we've reached the end of this part of the story, you need to go to Moscow," the professor said absentmindedly.

"To Moscow?"

"Yes, my dear boy, to Moscow. I've told you everything I know about Amelia Garayoa's time in Buenos Aires, but if you want to know more then you'll have to carry on with your investigations, and that means Moscow."

"I thought that you might be able to tell me the whole story."

The professor laughed unfeignedly, as if I had just said something funny.

"I see that not even my good friend Professor Soler has all that much information about Amelia Garayoa. Young man, you have only just started to find out what happened to her. I'm telling you that this woman's life was passionate and difficult, difficult above all else. I'm afraid that if you want to find out more then you will have to go to Moscow."

"To Moscow?"

"Yes, I told you that your great-grandmother followed Pierre Comte to Moscow. Don't pull faces. I have arranged for you to meet with Professor Tania Kruvkoski. She's an important person and an independent historian, an expert on everything to do with the Cheka, the GPU, the OGPU, the NKVD, and the KGB. Professor Kruvkoski is the right person for you to see if you need to know about Amelia's stay in Moscow. She's one of the very few people who has been allowed to see some of the KGB archives, although with restrictions and only after having promised not to speak about certain topics. She has been allowed to look at material from the thirties and forties, all the way up to the end of the Second World War. The KGB was the skeleton on which the new state was built, so they haven't let her see anything from any later period, anything after 1945. I called her this morning, and although she does not want to meet you she has agreed to do so because of her friendship with Professor Soler and me. I suggest that you are careful in your dealings with her; Tania Kruvkoski has a devilish temper and if you don't win her respect than she'll send you packing."

I went back to my hotel thinking about what to do. It was obvious that Professor Muiños thought that his conversations with me were done, and what's more he had arranged for me a meeting in Moscow in two days' time.

I decided to call my mother, the newspaper, and Aunt Marta, in that order, to know whether I could take the flight to Moscow.

I was tired. In less than a week I had passed through Barcelona, Rome, and Buenos Aires, but if Aunt Marta gave me the go-ahead I'd find myself on my way to Moscow.

As I had expected, my mother scolded me. I hadn't called her for four days and she said that she had been so worried that she got a stomachache, and that it was my fault.

The conversation with Pepe, the editor of the newspaper, was equally unflattering.

"Guillermo, where the hell are you? One thing is getting an interview with Professor Soler, another is thinking that you're going to get the Nobel Prize. I've sent you three books for urgent review and you haven't shown any signs of life at all."

"Look, Pepe, don't get upset with me. The review can wait, because I've got something better for the newspaper. I told you I had to go to Buenos Aires, and it's the Book Fair here now, the one that's the most important in Latin America alongside the one in Guadalajara in Mexico."

"Look at you! So you're in Buenos Aires."

"Yes, and I'll send you some articles about the Book Fair, and a few interviews with authors, and I won't charge you expenses, but I'd like you to pay more than you do for the reviews, alright?"

Pepe grumbled for a bit but accepted in principle, but only if I got him the first article within the hour.

I didn't promise anything, and called Aunt Marta, who greeted me with her habitual ill-humor.

"Are you living it up over there?" she asked ironically.

"Yes, yes I am. Buenos Aires takes your breath away, you really should come here for your vacation one year."

"Stop talking nonsense and tell me what you're doing!"

I summarized my investigation without going into much detail, which made her even more annoyed, so much so that when I said I was going to Moscow her response was abrupt: She hung up on me.

I decided to take a break and think about what to do, and also to go to the Book Fair in order to send the reports I had promised. The difficult part would be getting an author to give me an interview. I had no accreditation and nobody was scheduled to see me.

I must have a guardian angel, because when I got to the convention center where the Book Fair was being held I met a couple of young Spanish authors, who had been invited to participate in a round-table discussion on current literary developments organized by the fair. I stuck to them like a limpet, attended the discussion, and asked each of them a dozen or so questions, which was how I got my interviews done; then I ran the risk of having them think me a sponger by not leaving them alone, so I ended up meeting four Argentinian writers, an editor, a couple of literary critics, and a few journalists like me.

When I got back to the hotel I had a "harvest" that was large enough to keep me on good terms with the newspaper and to win me some time, if indeed I eventually went to Moscow.

I called my aunt again.

"Do you know what time it is here?" she shouted at me.

"No, what's the time?"

She didn't tell me, she merely hung the phone up. So I decided to wake up my mother and ask her for a loan to go to Moscow myself, but she wasn't keen to help me either, because she still blamed me for her stomachache.

End of the road, I said to myself. I was quite upset, because the story of Amelia Garayoa was starting to become an obsession with me, not just because she was my great-grandmother, I couldn't care less about that, but because she was turning out to be a great story.

I let a few hours go by so as not to wake up anyone in Spain, then I called Doña Laura.

The housekeeper made me wait for almost ten minutes and I breathed a sigh of relief when I heard the old woman's voice on the other end of the line.

"Tell me, Guillermo, where are you?"

"In Buenos Aires, but I need to give you some bad news: I can't carry on with the investigation."

"What? What's happened? Professor Soler told me that you were being given the steps you need to follow and that you had a meeting arranged in Moscow."

"That's the problem. My Aunt Marta doesn't want to pay for my research anymore, so I won't be able to go to Moscow. I'm sorry, I just wanted to tell you. Tomorrow or the day after I'll go back to Spain, and if you don't mind I'll come around in the next few days to thank you for all the help you have given me. The truth is that I wouldn't have been able to do anything without it."

Doña Laura seemed not to have heard me. She was silent, even though I thought I could hear her excited breathing over the phone line.

"Doña Laura, can you hear me?"

"Yes, of course. Look, Guillermo, we'd like you to continue your investigation."

"Yes, I'd like so too, but I don't have any funds, so..."

"I'll pay for your trip."

"You?"

"Well, both of us. At the beginning you were... Well, you didn't make that much of a positive impression on us, but someone has to do what you are doing, and now we think that you're the right man for the job. You have to continue. Give me the number of your bank account and we'll transfer the money you need. But from now on you are working for us; that is, the story you write will not be for your Aunt Marta nor will it be read by her or any other member of your family."

"But... well, I don't know what to say... I don't think it's right that you should pay for this investigation. No, I wouldn't feel comfortable."

"Don't be silly!"

"No, Doña Laura, I can't accept, I'm very sorry but I just can't."

"Guillermo, it was you who came to our house asking us for help to write about Amelia. It was difficult for us to make the decision, but once we made up our minds to trust you we haven't stopped helping you, in fact... Well, as you said, you wouldn't have found out anything without us. What you don't know is that you have started a process that cannot now be stopped. So you should accept working for us, writing what you find out about the life of Amelia Garayoa, and then forget about her forever."

"But why are you so interested that I should investigate your cousin's life? You should already know what happened..."

"Don't ask me questions. Answer me: Will you work for us or not?"

I hesitated. The truth was that I did not want to give up on the investigation, but neither did I want to have to accept money from the Garayoas.

"I don't know, let me think."

"I want an answer now," Doña Laura insisted.

"Alright, I accept."

I wrote an e-mail to Aunt Marta telling her that I was going to continue the investigation with another "patron," and, as might have been imagined, she rang me up a few minutes later in a fury.

"Are you mad? You've flipped! Do you think that I'm going to let some unknown person pay you for investigating my grandmother's life story? Guillermo, let's put an end to this. I had an idea that turns out to be more complicated than I had imagined; come back to Madrid, tell me what you've found out, and I'll think about what to do, but I can't pay your world tour, you have to see that."

"I'm sorry, but I've promised some other people that I'm going to carry on with the investigation, and I'll give them whatever I find out."

"But who are these people? I'm not going to let the family's dirty linen be aired in front of devil knows who."

"I agree with you, but Amelia Garayoa, as well as being your grandmother, had relatives who are just as interested as you are to find out what became of her, so it won't go out of the family."

My mother rang me to tell me that I was ruining her life. She had just argued with her sister about me. But I had also made a decision and had come around to thinking that working for Doña Laura and Doña Melita was the best thing, as I wouldn't have taken a single step forward if it hadn't been for them. Anyway, I was fed up with having to beg for every euro I needed from Aunt Marta.

9

I don't know what the temperature was like in Moscow in the spring of 1938, but it was freezing in 2009.

I was happy to be in a city that seemed full of mysteries. As Doña Laura had, to my surprise, called me to say that she had made a deposit in my account and had reserved a room for me in the Hotel Metropol, it seemed that everything would run smoothly.

"There's swank for you!" I thought as I entered the Metropol. The city I had seen through the windows of my taxi did not need to envy New York, Paris, or Madrid, and I had seen more Maseratis and Jaguars in a few minutes than in my entire life. "These ex-Communists haven't been slow to get up to date with how capitalism works!" I said to myself.

Once I was in my room I decided to do my "homework" and call Tania Kruvkoski.

The professor spoke English, thank goodness, and we understood each other immediately, even though I got a surprise when she said that if we wanted we could speak in Spanish. We arranged a meeting for the next morning at her house; she explained that it was not far from the Metropol, and I could easily reach it on foot.

I spent the rest of the day being a tourist: I went to Lenin's Mausoleum, strolled in Red Square, visited Saint Basil's cathedral, and lost myself in the lively streets that were filled with bars and restaurants and high-end clothing boutiques.

I had no idea about what Moscow must have been like before the fall of the Berlin Wall, but now I perceived it as the quintessence of capitalism. It was nothing like the city my mother had described to me: gray, poor, and sad. She had taken a trip to the Soviet Union back in the Communist days, and I think that if she could have seen it now, she would have flipped out.

Professor Kruvkoski's apartment was small but comfortable, with wooden shelves laden with books, cretonne curtains, a sofa, a couple of green velvet armchairs, and a dining table covered in papers. The professor was as I had imagined her, a hefty woman getting on in years, with her white hair tied back in a chignon at the nape of her neck. I was surprised by the almost girlish dress she had on, and the woolen shawl she wore over her shoulders.

But behind the grandmotherly façade was an energetic woman who was not ready to give me any more of her precious time than was necessary; she already had files prepared on Pierre Comte and Amelia.

"My colleagues, Professor Soler and Professor Muiños, have asked me to explain to you what happened to Pierre Comte and Amelia Garayoa when they arrived in Moscow in February 1938. Well, I don't know if you want to take notes..."

"I would prefer to record the conversation, as your Spanish is so excellent," I replied, trying to flatter her.

"Do what you want. I don't have much time. I'll give you the morning, but not a minute more," she warned me.

I nodded and started the MiniDisc recorder.

"As you will know, Comrade Stalin's perversity knew no limits. Nobody was safe, everyone was a suspect, and purges were taking place on a daily basis. Little by little he had removed the men who fought in the front lines of the revolution, lifelong Bolsheviks who were accused of treason. Nobody's head was safe on his shoulders. Stalin used men without scruples for his criminal policies, people who were prepared to commit the worst atrocities simply in order to serve him, thinking that this would be the way for them to keep their own lives, but many of whom ended badly as well, since Stalin felt gratitude toward no one and recognized nobody's service."

"By your age... Well... I thought that you were a revolutionary in your youth."

"I am a survivor. When you live under a reign of terror, the only thing you want to do is to survive one day further, and you put your head down: You hear nothing, see nothing, almost feel nothing, terrified that you are going to be noticed. Terror destroys human beings, and your worst instincts come to the fore. But this is not about me, it's about Comte and Garayoa."

"Yes, yes, I'm sorry for interrupting, I just thought that you were a Communist."

The professor shrugged and looked at me sourly, so I decided to shut up.

"My family fought in the October Revolution, but that didn't guarantee us anything; my father and some of my cousins and uncles all died in the gulags because they dared to say out loud what was obvious: The system wasn't working. It wasn't that they didn't think that Communism had the answers for building a better world, but they thought that the people running the country weren't doing it right. Stalin starved thousands of peasants... But this is history, a history that isn't the one you've come here to discover. I've told you that people adapt to circumstances in order to survive, and that my family put their heads down and shut up. Can we continue?"

"Yes, yes, sorry."

Amelia and Pierre stayed at the house of Pierre's Aunt Irina, his mother's sister. She was married to a civil servant in the Foreign Ministry, Georgi, a man with no important job and no responsibilities. They had a son, Mikhail, a journalist, younger than Pierre and married to Anushka, a real beauty who worked in the theater. The house had two bedrooms and a little salon, which became Pierre and Amelia's room.

The day after his arrival, Pierre went to the offices of the NKVD in Dzerzhinsky Square, the building sadly known as the Lubyanka...

Pierre was not received by anyone high up in the NKVD. A low-ranking functionary told him that he was now at the

NKVD's disposal and that they would assign him duties in due course. In the meantime he should write in detail about Krisov's network, the network he had been a part of, giving names and details about all the "blind" agents who had collaborated with the NKVD in Europe.

Pierre protested. If he was in Moscow, he said, it was to organize the congress of world intellectuals. The functionary didn't mince his words: Either Pierre fulfilled his orders or he would be considered a traitor.

Pierre did not dare argue further and grudgingly accepted the man's instructions.

"You will work in the Identification and Archive Department with Comrade Vasiliev."

Pierre remembered that Igor Krisov had told him about a friend who had been disgraced, Ivan Vasiliev, and he wondered if this might not be the same person.

Ivan Vasiliev was thirty-five years old at that time. He was tall, thin, and very strong, and had worked for the Foreign Department of the NKVD since its creation.

The Identification and Archive Department was in one of the basements of the Lubyanka, and it was accessible only via a set of stairs on which it was not unusual to meet prisoners descending with their heads bowed, aware that it was unusual for anyone to come out of that place alive.

Vasiliev pointed out to Pierre the desk where he was to work, lit by a powerful bulb. There was scarcely room to move because giant filing cabinets covered every inch of the wall.

"Were you a friend of Igor Krisov's?" Pierre asked as soon as he sat down.

Ivan Vasiliev looked sternly at him, reproaching him in silence for having uttered that name. Then he swallowed and seemed to be choosing his words with care.

"I know that you were one of Comrade Krisov's agents, and that he was a traitor of the worst kind."

Pierre started to hear this answer and was about to say something, but Vasiliev's eyes indicated that he should keep quiet.

Vasiliev dove into his papers, only emerging every now and then to go to other tables where men like him were working in silence. On one of these occasions he passed by Pierre's desk and slipped him a piece of paper. Pierre was surprised and unfolded it.

"Don't be stupid and don't ask questions that might betray us both. Tear up this note. When I can I will talk to you."

When Pierre got back to his Aunt Irina's house late that afternoon, Irina was waiting for him impatiently.

"What happened? Why didn't you call to say you were alright?" she reproached him in French, a language that she also used with Pierre's aunt and uncle.

Pierre told Amelia and his aunt and uncle every vivid detail of that day, sparing nothing of his sense of distress and disappointment. This was not the "homeland" for which he had been giving his all. Aunt Irina asked him to speak more quietly.

"Don't speak so loud and be more careful, or else we'll all end up in the Lubyanka!" she scolded him.

"But why? Can't we speak freely?" Amelia asked ingenuously.

"No, we can't," Uncle Georgi said.

Suddenly Pierre and Amelia came face to face with the fact that the myth they had sacrificed so much for was in fact a pitiless monster that could devour them without anyone being able to move a finger to stop it.

"So you've come here under false pretenses," Uncle Georgi said.

"It's clear from what you're saying," Aunt Irina said.

"Krisov warned you," Amelia said.

"Who is Krisov?" Aunt Irina wanted to know.

"A man I worked for... ," Pierre replied.

"His controller," Amelia said.

"This isn't the right time to say I told you so, but... well... Maybe it's not the best job, to be a spy." Aunt Irina did not want to hide her disgust for her nephew's work. "Dedicating yourself to snooping on other people and denouncing them..."

"I have never denounced anyone!" Pierre protested. "My only task has been to gather information that could be useful to the Soviet Union and to the revolution."

"Pierre's done nothing wrong," Amelia defended him.

"Spying is something naughty children do!" Aunt Irina insisted.

"Come on, woman, don't get upset, your nephew is one of the many innocents who believed in the revolution; we believed in it as well and gave the very best of ourselves," Uncle Georgi interrupted.

"Of course we did, but Stalin is..."

"Shut up! Now you're not being careful, you know that the walls have ears. Do you want us all to get arrested?" Uncle Georgi said.

Aunt Irina fell silent and knotted her fingers together to try to hide her tension. She would have liked not to have had to look after her nephew, but Olga was her only sister, and also her only hope for the future, in case one day she might escape from the enormous prison into which her homeland had been converted.

A little while later Mikhail arrived and joined the conversation. Pierre's comments upset the young man.

"You're exaggerating!" Mikhail protested, in Russian. "Of course there are problems! We're building a new regime, a Russia without serfs, where only free men live, and we have to learn to be responsible for ourselves. Of course mistakes are sometimes made, but the important thing is the path we have chosen and where it will lead us. Did we live better under the czars? No, and you know that for a fact."

"I lived better under the old czar," Irina affirmed, looking boldly at her son. "Look around you, and you only see hunger. People are dying of hunger, can't you see it? Not even you, who support the regime, not even you have more than the poorest people in this country. Yes, son, yes, I lived better under the old czar."

"But you're not an average Russian, you are a privileged bourgeois. Look around you, mother, and you'll see that we all have the same opportunities, we're all equal now."

"People are dying of hunger and sent to prison for protesting. Stalin is worse than the czar ever was," Irina replied.

"If you weren't my mother... !"

"You'd denounce me? Stalin has rotted the Russian soul so much that you wouldn't be the first son to denounce his parents. Even though Stalin is not the only guilty party, he alone is the favored disciple of Lenin, whom you hold up as a god. With him, human dignity stopped making sense, he turned it into worthless paper money."

"Enough, Irina! I don't want this argument to take place under my roof. And you, my son... you'll see one day that the reality is a little different from how you imagine it in your hopes and dreams. I was a Bolshevik, I fought for the revolution, but now I don't recognize it anymore. I don't say anything because I want to live and I don't want to put you in any danger, but I am a coward."

"Father!"

"Yes, my son, I am a coward. I fought for the revolution, I was almost killed and I was not scared. But now I tremble that they might take me to the Lubyanka to confess some nonexistent crime, just as they have done to some of my friends, or that they might send me to one of those work camps in Siberia from which nobody ever returns."

"I believe in the revolution," Mikhail replied.

"And I fought for the revolution, but this is not it. This is a nightmare unleashed by Stalin."

"Stalin watches out for the revolution, makes sure that no one goes against its aims!" Mikhail shouted.

They fell silent, exhausted, without looking at one another. Amelia and Pierre felt overwhelmed by what they had just heard.

Irina took Amelia's hand to try to cheer her up.

"Don't be afraid, these are family arguments, but Mikhail loves us and would never move a finger against us."

They stopped talking when they heard a key in the lock. Anushka was back from work, and even though she and Mikhail were married, neither Irina nor Georgi spoke freely in front of her.

"Uf! I can see you've just had another row," she said as she came in.

"My parents are too critical of the revolution," Mikhail said.

"They are old, and they don't understand that the revolution is only kept on track by freeing itself of its enemies."

Amelia said nothing, but she was not sure that Anushka was right.

That night, when everyone else was asleep, Amelia spoke to Pierre. They were sharing a mattress on the floor.

"We have to get out of here," she whispered.

"Out of my uncle's house?"

"Out of the Soviet Union. We're in danger."

"It's impossible. They won't let me leave, or you either."

"We'll think of something, but we have to go. I feel like I'm drowning. I'm scared."

Pierre held her hand, he was even more scared.

Aunt Irina started to give Amelia Russian lessons. They had been surprised to find that the young Spaniard had quite a good grasp of the language already.

"I don't have much to teach you, you speak very well," Aunt Irina said.

"Pierre has been a good teacher," the young woman replied.

She was a good student because of her skill with languages, but also because the lessons helped take her mind off the situation.

Pierre's aunt was a pleasant woman who looked after her family and who had looked after the house ever since a delicate heart operation six months before.

At the beginning of March, Uncle Georgi told Amelia that he had a job for her.

"We have a department at the ministry that receives newspapers and magazines from all over the world in order to assess how they discuss the Soviet Union. The relevant articles are read and classified, and the ones it is worth Molotov's while to read are translated into Russian."

"But I can't translate into Russian," Amelia protested.

"You don't have to translate anything, all you need to do is read the German, French, and Spanish papers, and if there's anything worth the effort, you give it to the head of the department and he'll send it off to be translated, although you could do that as well. It's a job just like any other; you can't stay at home, it wouldn't be good."

"But I'm a foreigner..."

"Yes, a Spaniard, and a member of the French Communist Party. An international revolutionary," Uncle Georgi replied ironically.

Amelia didn't dare refuse, and Pierre encouraged her to take the job.

"It's better if you work, if you don't do anything it's suspicious, they could accuse you of counterrevolutionary activity."

This was how Amelia started to go to the Ministry of Foreign Affairs every morning along with Uncle Georgi, and didn't get home until mid-afternoon. She had a bad time to begin with because, even though she spoke good Russian, her fellow workers looked at her without much confidence. The head of the department explained to her that she couldn't discuss the content of articles published in the foreign press with anyone, and if there was any criticism of the Soviet Union then she should take it to him personally.

On March 13, Uncle Georgi came home in extreme agitation.

"Hitler has annexed Austria!" he said.

"I know, I know," Mikhail replied. "That man is a danger and someone needs to stop him."

"Will it be us?" Anushka wanted to know.

"It might be," Uncle Georgi confirmed, "although for the time being our policy is to observe without interference."

That night, Pierre was able to whisper to Amelia that he had spoken to Ivan Vasiliev.

"It was on the way out of the office, he ran into me on purpose and we walked a while together."

"Why didn't you say anything at supper?"

"Because I don't trust Mikhail. He's my cousin, but even so I don't trust him, he's a fanatic and Anushka isn't much better. They're party members and tight with their bosses."

"And what did Ivan Vasiliev say to you?"

"He advised me to be cautious. Apparently they are observing me at the moment and want to give me some kind of test because they don't trust me, because I was one of Krisov's agents. Vasiliev thinks they'll have me in the department for a couple of months and then they'll decide what to do with me, the best thing, he says, is if they forget about me."

"And when do you think they'll let you go back to Buenos Aires?"

Pierre fell silent and gripped Amelia's hand before answering. "I don't know, he says maybe never."

"But your parents might need you!"

"They know I've got family here, Aunt Irina, Uncle Georgi... If my parents protest then they could take action against my aunt and uncle, so the powers-that-be are probably expecting them to say nothing."

"Pierre, you're a French citizen, let's go to the French Embassy."

"They won't even let us get close; according to Vasiliev, they're following me."

"But you haven't done anything wrong... What else did Vasiliev say to you?"

"That they might interrogate me and that I should be ready for it; there are people who don't survive interrogation."

"No, Pierre, they can't do anything to you, they can't torture a French citizen. As for me... I'm Spanish. They can't keep us here against our will. I want us to go. You've come as they asked you, if you'd done anything against the Soviet Union then we wouldn't be here, so they've got no cause to mistrust you. It's they who deceived you with this story about the congress of intellectuals in June."

"Don't talk so loudly, or Mikhail and Anushka will hear us," Pierre asked.

"You shouldn't be afraid of them."

"But I am afraid of them, and you should be afraid too. Don't think that Anushka is your friend, she's only trying to get information out of you."

Ivan Vasiliev was right. One afternoon, when Pierre was getting ready to leave work, two men came up to him.

"Come with us, Comrade," one of the two men ordered him.

"Where to?" Pierre asked, trembling.

"We'll ask the questions, you just obey."

Pierre was in the cells at the Lubyanka for three days and three nights without anyone telling him why he was there. Then, on the fourth day, two men took him up to an interrogation room where a short but tough-looking man, with sparse hair and an icy gaze, was waiting for him.

The man pointed him to a chair and went on reading some papers that were on the table in front of him. These few minutes of silence seemed eternal to Pierre.

"Comrade Comte, we can do this the easy way, or the hard way."

"I... I don't know what's going on."

"Ah, no? Well, you should. You worked for a traitor."

"I... I... I didn't know that Comrade Krisov was a traitor."

"You didn't know? That's strange, because he thought that you were one of his best agents, one of the people he trusted the most."

"Yes, alright, I did what Krisov asked me to do, he was my controller, nothing more. We were never friends."

"And he never told you that he was thinking of deserting?"

"Of course not! I'm telling you, we were never friends; when he deserted I wasn't working for him anymore, I was in Buenos Aires."

"Yes, I know, and Comrade Krisov went to see you there. Strange, isn't it?"

"I told my controller in Buenos Aires that Krisov had been to see me and what he said."

"I know, I know. It's one way of covering your tracks in case someone saw you with Krisov. You could have decided what you needed to say to your controller."

"Of course I didn't! Krisov turned up out of the blue and we had an argument, I even called him a traitor."

"We want to know where Comrade Krisov is now."

"I don't know, he didn't tell me."

"You think we'll believe that? Come on, an old agent like Krisov gets away and takes the trouble to travel to Argentina to see you and tell you that he's decided to run away. You think we're fools?"

"But that's what happened... He... well, he said that he felt responsible for his agents, for all of us who worked for him. And... well, he suggested that Latin America was the best place for someone to disappear."

"Krisov the traitor has lots of friends among the Trotskyites."

"I didn't know it, we never spoke about personal questions, I don't know who his friends are..."

"Comrade Comte, I want you to refresh your memory and tell me where the traitor Krisov is to be found. We know how to reward you for this information... And how to treat you if we don't get it..."

"But I don't know!"

"We will help you remember."

The man got up and left the room, leaving Pierre shuddering in his seat. A minute later two men came into the room and took him back to the cell where he had spent the previous three days. Pierre tried to complain, but a strong punch to the stomach stopped him from talking. And he cried on the cold floor of that Lubyanka cell.

The first night that Pierre did not return to his uncle's house, Amelia stayed up until dawn; when she could bear it no longer, she woke up Mikhail.

"Your cousin hasn't come home."

"Why are you waking me up? He'll be out getting drunk with some friend, or some girl, French people are like that," Mikhail replied grumpily.

"I know Pierre, and if he hasn't come back it's because something happened to him."

"Don't worry, try to get some sleep, you'll see how he comes home with a great story to tell you."

Amelia went back to the mattress where she slept and counted the minutes until she heard Uncle Georgi getting up.

"Uncle, Pierre hasn't come home, I'm worried."

"Irina and I haven't slept a wink. I'll try to find out what happened to him."

Amelia didn't want to go to work, she thought that she would go to the Lubyanka and ask for Pierre, but Irina disabused her of that idea.

"Don't be stupid, the best we can do is wait."

"But he should have come home!" Amelia sobbed.

"Yes, he should have, but in Russia nothing is normal. Wait for Georgi to tell us something, and... well, I'll ask Mikhail to try to find out what's happened as well."

In the afternoon when Amelia came home from work she prayed to find Pierre safe at his uncle's house. But Irina told her that they had had no news, so the two women waited in silence until Georgi came home, but he too said he had been unable to find out anything. He had telephoned a friend whose brother-in-law worked in the Lubyanka, and when he'd said what it was about the man hung up, threatening him and telling him never to call him again.

Mikhail and Anushka arrived a little later. He surprised Amelia by telling her that he had had lots of work to do and hadn't been able to worry about Pierre's absence.

"How can you be like this?" Amelia shouted at him. "Pierre is your cousin!"

"And why should I worry about him? He's old enough to look after himself. If he hasn't come back it's because he doesn't want to. And if he's done something then he should accept the consequences."

Amelia left the apartment, slamming the door behind her. She had decided to go to the Lubyanka and ask for Pierre at the door. Uncle Georgi left after her, trying to tell her to be careful, if she wasn't then the whole family could be in danger.

"There are families that have all suffered reprisals because one of their members is considered a counterrevolutionary. They send them all to labor camps, to the salt mines, to hospitals that only let them out once they're completely mad. Don't put us in danger, Amelia, I beg you."

But she did not listen to him and rushed out into the street, determined to go to the Lubyanka. She walked quickly, full of fear and anger, when she realized that a man was walking alongside her.

"Please, turn down the next street and follow me. I want to help you."

"Who are you?" Amelia asked in shock.

"Ivan Vasiliev. I've been hanging around the house all afternoon, I didn't dare come up."

Amelia followed the man, regretting having not thought earlier about going to see him. If anyone could tell her where Pierre was it would be Vasiliev.

She followed him a good distance, all the way to a dark apartment building, which the man entered and climbed the steps quickly to the second floor. He opened a door and went into the apartment, followed by Amelia.

"We can't be here long," Ivan Vasiliev warned.

"Isn't this your house?" Amelia asked in puzzlement.

"No, it belongs to a friend who's out of Moscow at the moment. We can talk freely here."

"Where's Pierre?"

"He's been arrested, he's in a cell in the Lubyanka."

"But why? He hasn't done anything. Pierre is a good Communist."

"I know, I know, you don't have to be a bad Communist to get arrested. They want Krisov and they are sure that Pierre knows where he is."

"But he doesn't know! Krisov didn't tell him!"

"Igor Krisov is one of my best friends, we fought together and... Well, we have a very special friendship."

Amelia looked at Ivan Vasiliev in astonishment. Krisov had confessed his homosexuality to Pierre, and Vasiliev's words seemed to suggest that he could be a homosexual as well. Vasiliev seemed to read her mind.

"Don't get me wrong. We were good comrades, just that, then he went to London. He had a perfect cover, one of his grandmothers was Irish. He had perfect English, and spoke French and German well, he was good at languages. Pierre told me that you are too. Well, in spite of our separation we have always remained the best of friends, even though they think we hate each other."

"They?"

"Yes, the bosses of the INO, the Foreign Department of the NKVD. Igor said that the best way for us to protect ourselves was to pretend to be irreconcilable enemies, and it was a farce that we kept up for years. It was I who told him that he'd lost the confidence of his bosses."

"I know, he told Pierre. Why is Krisov so important?"

"He was one of the main agents in Europe and knows a lot: names, codes, bank accounts, operating practices... They're scared he'll sell all this information to someone."

"Why?"

"Because they are assassins and scoundrels and it's the sort of thing they would do, so they think that others are as capable as they are of committing indecent acts."

"And who would buy this information?"

"Anyone, the Soviet Union has many enemies. England would be ready to pay a good price for the names of the agents who work there. The British government is worried about Communism being on the rise in its universities."

"But Krisov..."

"Igor was disgusted by what was happening here, just like anyone else who has a normal sense of decency. Overnight, anyone can become an 'enemy of the people,' it's enough if there's a report, a suspicion. They are killing people with no mercy."

"Who?"

"They do it in the name of the revolution, to protect it from its enemies. And it's not just the bourgeoisie to whom they show no mercy, no one is safe from being accused of counterrevolutionary activity, even the peasants are being persecuted. Do you know how many kulaks have been killed?"

"I don't even know what a kulak is..."

"I've told you, peasants, small landowners who are attached to their farms and who don't want to leave them and make way for stupid plans organized by party committees."

"What will they do with Pierre?"

"They will interrogate him until he confesses whatever it is they want him to confess. Or else he'll manage to convince them he knows nothing about Krisov. Nobody leaves the Lubyanka."

"Pierre is French!"

"And Russian, his mother is Russian."

"There are lots of people who know we are here, 'they' wouldn't want people to know that people disappear in Moscow."

"And who's going to believe that? How will they show that he's in the Lubyanka?"

"You..."

"No, my darling, no! I will deny having said anything to you, and if it's necessary I'll go as far as saying that I met you in this apartment for an amorous encounter."

Amelia looked at him in horror and read in Ivan Vasiliev's eyes that he was prepared above all things to survive; he didn't care what he had to do or whom he had to sacrifice.

"What can I do?" Amelia asked with a note of desperation in her voice.

"Nothing. You can't do anything. With luck they'll sent Pierre to a camp; if it's not for many years and if he manages to survive, it'll be a blessing."

They fell silent. Amelia wanted to cry and shout, but she held herself back.

"What will happen to me?"

"I don't know. Maybe Pierre will be enough for them. In their report it says that you are a devout Communist and a 'blind' agent, so it may be supposed that you don't know anything."

"I don't know what they want, but I know things about them they never would have wanted to be known."

"When you're young, you're arrogant enough to think you can change the world and... Look what we've done here, turned our country into the front hall of hell," Ivan Vasiliev tried to cheer up Amelia.

"They've betrayed the revolution," Amelia said prudishly.

"Do you really think so? No, Amelia, no. Lenin and all of us who followed him believed firmly that there was no way to create a revolution without blood, without terror. Our revolution sprang from a single premise, that human life is nothing extraordinary, and it is the job of religion to sanctify it; we have declared the death of God."

"Will they arrest me?"

"I don't know, I hope not. But follow my advice, when you speak with your work colleagues, make yourself out to be a fanatical Communist, certain that everything that doesn't follow Stalin down to the letter needs to be gotten rid of. Don't have any doubts, just be convinced that the party is always right."

"Will they let me leave?"

"I don't know, they might or they might not."

"You're not giving me an answer."

"I don't have an answer."

"What can I do for Pierre?"

"Nothing. No one can do anything for him."

They agreed to meet each other a week later in the same place. Ivan promised that he would try to bring some news of Pierre.

While she walked home, Amelia thought about what Pierre's uncle and aunt would say, what Mikhail and Anushka would say. The only thing she knew for certain was that she could not tell them she had spoken to Ivan Vasiliev.

When she got home, Aunt Irina was making dinner, and Uncle Georgi was arguing with his son Mikhail, while Anushka was painting her nails and pretending to be indifferent to it all.

"Where did you go?" Mikhail asked without hiding his anger.

"For a walk. I needed to get some air."

"Did you go to the Lubyanka?" he insisted.

"No, I didn't go. But I will go tomorrow, someone has to try to find something out about Pierre."

"Maybe he's not like you think he is," Mikhail said mysteriously.

"I don't know what you're trying to say... ," Amelia replied.

"Maybe my cousin is not a good Communist. Maybe he's betrayed the party."

"You're mad! You don't know Pierre, he'd sacrifice us all before he betrayed the party."

"Don't be so sure, Amelia," Mikhail insisted.

Aunt Irina was upset to hear her son talk like this.

"Mikhail, how dare you question your cousin? What do you know that you can talk like this about him?" the woman asked.

"Nothing, I don't know anything. It's just a hypothesis. The Soviet Union has many enemies, Mother, people who don't understand just how far our revolution reaches now. But we won't worry, maybe Pierre has had to go away on business and will be back in a few days."

"It's not possible, Mikhail. Pierre would never have left without telling me."

"You're a little naïve," Anushka snapped.

"Maybe I am, but, you know what, I think I might know something about the man for whom I abandoned my family and my son, and I can assure you that Pierre is not a drinker, nor is he someone who wouldn't come home if it weren't for a good reason."

"Maybe this 'good reason' really exists, but let's not worry, he'll turn up," Anushka insisted.

"And if he doesn't?" the young woman asked.

Mikhail shrugged and sat down next to his wife.

"Mikhail, where is Pierre?" Aunt Irina asked, planting herself firmly in front of her son.

He said nothing, wondering whether he should answer his mother, and then shrugged again.

"I don't know, Mother."

"But he went to work like he does every day, and went to the Lubyanka. We should ask about him there. If he has had to go away on business then they'll be able to tell us there."

Anushka looked at her nails, happy to have them painted. She seemed to be outside the conversation, except in those moments when she caught Mikhail's eye, and then you could see him urging her to maintain this distance.

"I will go to the Lubyanka tomorrow. I want them to tell me about Pierre, I want to see him," Amelia announced.

"It would be a useless errand, dear Amelia. Don't start doing these things that lead nowhere and might even be prejudicial to the family," Mikhail replied.

"Prejudicial? Why? To ask about Pierre? If I can hurt you by doing that then I'll leave this house. Tomorrow. I'll find a room to live and I won't prejudice you by my presence here any longer."

"Come on, Amelia, don't be melodramatic!" Anushka interrupted. "I'm the actress here, I'm the one with talent. Mikhail is right; if you turn up at the Lubyanka asking for Pierre then you could cause us problems, and he's already told you he knows nothing. What more do you want?"

"I want to know where Pierre is."

"Haven't you thought that there might be another woman?" Mikhail said, laughing.

Amelia was about to snap, shout, and let out all her disgust, but she managed to hold herself in. She couldn't tell them what Ivan Vasiliev had told her, so she clenched her fists until her nails cut into her palms. Any indiscretion could hurt Vasiliev as well as her and Pierre.

She knew that Mikhail would not hesitate to accuse her of anything at all, if he could turn her into a counterrevolutionary and an enemy of the people. She was surprised that he still had not denounced his parents; in those days it was normal for children to denounce the "ideological swerving" of their progenitors. It was not rare for the police to burst into a factory, a house, anywhere at all, to arrest someone who had been denounced by a family member, a friend, a husband, a wife, a lover.

And in Irina and Georgi's house, many things were spoken about with absolute freedom, and Amelia thought it was only a matter of time before Mikhail or Anushka denounced Irina and Georgi.

So Amelia swallowed and made light of things in order not to let slip the words she really felt like saying.

"Look, it's better for you to stay here, it's what Pierre would like. And don't worry about us, you don't cause any problems," Aunt Irina said.

"Thank you, and what with the circumstances and the fact that I am working, I should like to contribute to the household running costs," Amelia said.

"Don't worry about it," Uncle Georgi said.

"Amelia is right, she should help, that's why she's working. You know what, you're a bit more clever than you appear at first sight," Anushka said.

10

After Pierre's disappearance, the days were just endless. Amelia learned to hide her feelings, to pretend in front of Mikhail and Anushka. She never offered her opinion in any of the arguments that Irina and Georgi had with their son Mikhail. She kept her distance, as if she had no interest in what was going on around her. She also ignored the provocations thrown her way by Anushka, who seemed not to trust her.

A week later she met Ivan Vasiliev again. He seemed more worried than the previous time.

"I came because I was worried that you would try to be in touch with me, and I have to say that we can't see each other again, I think they're watching you, and me too."

"How do you know?"

"Have you forgotten that I work in the Lubyanka? I have friends, I hear things, I read documents... They asked for your file a few days ago, maybe Pierre has told them something about you."

"There's nothing he can say, I've never known what he does, I only found out by accident that he was an agent."

"People can confess anything in the Lubyanka."

"What do you know about Pierre?"

"Little more than what I told you last week. They interrogate him, they take him back to his cell, they interrogate him again... Like that until he tells them what they want to hear."

"He can't tell them what he doesn't know. Krisov didn't say where he was going to hide."

"Whatever the truth is, they'll keep on interrogating him until they are bored."

"What would happen if I went to the Lubyanka and asked for Pierre?"

"They could arrest you."

"Have you seen him?"

"No, and I haven't tried to see him. I know... well, I imagine that they will be torturing him and that he won't be in a good state. We should go now. You go first, and I'll stay here a while."

"When will I see you again?"

"Never."

"But..."

"I've already risked enough, I can't do anything else. If things change I know where to find you."

Pierre tried to protect his head with his hands in a vain attempt to escape the rubber truncheon that his interrogator was wielding with great accuracy.

How many blows had he been given that morning? The interrogator seemed particularly angry that morning. His breath smelled of vodka, mixed with the stench that came from his armpits every time the killer raised his arms for another blow.

"Speak, dog, speak!" he shouted.

But Pierre had nothing to say, and could only let out screams that sounded inhuman even to him.

When the interrogator grew tired of beating him with the rubber truncheon, he pushed him to the floor and put a long strip of cloth between his teeth; then, pulling this back over Pierre's shoulders, he tied the ends to Pierre's ankles.

This wasn't the first time that they'd submitted him to this torture, which turned him into a wheel, with his back bent round as they furiously kicked him in his exposed stomach.

If he had known where Krisov was he would have told them, he would have told them anything at all, but they did not want to know about anything at all apart from the whereabouts of Krisov.

This was a name that hammered at his temples, and he cursed the day he met him. He cursed himself, too, for having believed in the God that Communism had been for him.

He had been two days without drinking water, and his mouth was dry and his tongue was swollen. This was not the first time that they had punished him by refusing him water. His jailers liked to feed their victims salted anchovies from the Azov Sea and then refuse them water for days.

He didn't know if it was night or day, or what day it was, or how long he had lived in this hell, but he understood how infinite time could be now that he desired death. He prayed, yes, he prayed for one of his interrogator's blows to leave him unconscious, never to wake again.

In the beginning he thought of Amelia and regretted having made her take up a cause that had become a hellish nightmare. But he didn't care about Amelia anymore, he didn't care about his aunt and uncle, or his parents, or anyone. All he wanted was to die, to stop suffering.

Uncle Georgi kept Amelia up to date with developments of the war in Spain. He had first-hand information, for the Soviet Union was helping the Republican forces. And so, at the end of April, Amelia found out that Franco had launched a great offensive along the valley of the Ebro to the Mediterranean, and that he had divided the area under Republican control in two. Uncle Georgi also explained that unfortunately Franco had a great advantage, and great superiority, in his air and naval forces, over the Republicans.

Amelia wondered what would have become of her parents, her aunts and uncles, and above all her son. Javier was always in her nightmares, crushed by collapsing houses. From time to time she wrote long letters to her cousin Laura, and gave them to Uncle Georgi, hoping that he would know how to get them to besieged Madrid.

She hated Franco and all those who had rebelled against the Republic with all her strength, at the same time as experiencing a cold disgust toward Communism.

She, who had professed that faith with as much ardor as innocence, who had abandoned her son, her husband, and her family for Pierre, yes, but also for the conviction that she was destined to contribute to the flowering of a new society, she had discovered the brutality of those who called themselves Communists. And she was not like Krisov, she did not separate men from ideas, because she had met with the unimaginable brutality of these ideas via fanatics such as Mikhail or Anushka, or even some of her work colleagues. But worst of all, she had seen with her own two eyes that the promised paradise was in fact a nightmare.

She had decided to leave, even though the situation with Pierre weighed heavily on her. She couldn't do anything for him, but to leave Moscow seemed like an unpardonable betrayal with him still in the Lubyanka.

In June she was called to her supervisor's office. Amelia went worriedly, asking herself what kind of mistake she could have made.

The man did not invite her to sit down, but just gave her an order.

"Comrade Garayoa, as you know, a great congress of intellectuals was planned in Moscow, and we decided to delay the congress until September. Several dozen journalists, writers, and artists from all over the world will come to our country, and we want to give them a real picture of how the Soviet Union is. They will go to visit factories, they will speak with Soviet artists, they will travel all over the country with complete freedom, but guided by suitable people who can explain to them all the achievements of the revolution. Comrade Anna Nikolaevna Kornilova has spoken highly of you. As you know, Comrade Kornilova is part of the organizing committee for the congress and has asked that you join the group of comrades who should support the committee in everything it does: accompanying our guests, providing them with the information they require, showing them whatever they want to see... with the prior approval of the committee, of course. You speak French, Spanish, and German, and your level of Russian is acceptable, so you are suited for this new task. You will work directly with Comrade Kornilova. Go to her office at the Ministry of Culture tomorrow."

Amelia accepted what the man said, while hiding the terror that she felt in realizing that Anushka was an important figure in the Ministry of Culture. She had thought that Anushka was nothing more than an actress who was well connected in the party, but this showed that Anushka was an unknown quantity for her. Also, she would never have imagined that Anushka would speak out in her favor. Why would she have done this?

When she got back to the apartment she told Aunt Irina about the new job she had obtained via Anushka's mediation.

"She's a very special person. I don't know much about what she does either. I think she used to be an actress, but now she runs the theater or something like that. I think she works in a department that decides which plays can be put on. I am pleased that she has spoken up in your favor, if she's done that then it means that she has committed herself for you."

Amelia thought that perhaps Anushka was not as bad as she seemed, but she couldn't shake off her sense of mistrust.

That night Mikhail and Anushka seemed very excited, almost happy. Amelia thanked Anushka for speaking up for her, but the young woman seemed to laugh off her contribution.

"The congress is very important, we want the intellectuals to take the best picture of the Soviet Union away with them. We need people they can feel comfortable with, who speak their language. You'll do a good job. I'll give you the details tomorrow at work, I don't like to talk shop at home."

In the middle of September, Amelia found herself among a group of civil servants waiting at the airport for the planes to arrive that would take them to the congress. She was nervous, desperate to meet these unknown people who were an open door back into a world she had abandoned, but to which she was keen to return.

The congress began on September 20 with speeches by several ministers and various members of the Central Committee. The plan was for the Russian and European intellectuals to spend a fortnight debating questions of music, art, theater, et cetera.

The foreign guests would go to theater and ballet productions, and visit factories and model farms. It was rumored among the assistants that at some point Stalin himself would make an appearance.

Amelia was required to accompany a group of journalists to a meeting with their Russian colleagues to debate on the limits of freedom of speech.

While she went with them to the room where they were to hold their meeting, she heard someone calling her by name.

"But is it... Amelia? Amelia Garayoa?"

She turned round and found herself face to face with a man who at first she did not recognize. He spoke to her in French and looked at her in surprise.

"I'm Albert James, we met in Paris, at La Coupole. Jean Deuville introduced us, and you were with Pierre Comte. Do you remember?"

"Yes, I remember now, I'm sorry if I didn't recognize you right away, it's just that you are the last person I would have thought to meet here," Amelia explained.

"Well, I wouldn't have thought to meet you in Moscow, especially not working for the Soviets. Have you seen Jean Deuville?"

"No, I haven't, I didn't even know he was invited to the congress."

"Well, he's a poet and a Communist, so he couldn't well miss it, but tell me, what about Pierre? Is he here with you?"

Amelia grew pale. She didn't know what to say. She saw that some journalists were looking at her, but more importantly, so were some of the Soviet functionaries, highly attentive to her conversation with Albert James.

"Yes, he's here."

"Great, I'm sure we'll meet up. There are several friends of Pierre besides Jean who have been invited to the congress."

Albert James was particularly combative during the meeting between the Russian and European journalists. In the face of his Soviet colleagues, who defended the intervention of the state in the media as a guarantee of the general interest, Albert James defended freedom of speech, unlimited and with no controls. His position upset the Soviets and the debate grew tense at points.

When the session was finished, Albert James came to find Amelia, who had not taken her eyes off him for a moment.

"Whose side are you on, theirs or mine?" he asked her, knowing that this was an awkward question.

"I prefer absolute freedom," she replied, without ignoring the fact that the other functionaries were not missing a word of their exchange.

"Thank goodness. You're not lost yet."

"Come on, Mr. James, it's time for lunch," she said. "And then you have to carry on the discussion."

"Oh, it's all too much for me! I'd rather take a walk through Moscow. I've had too much discussion this morning. Why don't you come with me?"

"Because you're not scheduled to walk through the city today, you're meant to continue your discussion after lunch, so it's better if you stick with the program," Amelia replied.

"Don't be so rigid... You must understand that coming to Moscow is an opportunity I haven't been able to pass up, but this congress is boring, and it's already clear that it's not going to be of any use."

That night Amelia met Albert James again, in the theater during a performance of *Swan Lake*. He was with Jean Deuville and both men were looking for her.

Jean hugged her and kissed her on both cheeks. He was pleased to see her, but was particularly keen to know about his friend.

"Where's Pierre? I want to see him as soon as possible. When the performance is over we can go home with you, he'll have the surprise of his life," Jean suggested.

"No, it's not possible, you'll see him some other time," Amelia replied, uncomfortable.

"I want to surprise him," Jean insisted.

"Not today, maybe tomorrow."

All the Soviet functionaries stared openly at Amelia's familiarity toward these two men, she aroused so much interest that in the middle of the ballet Amelia felt a hand on her shoulder and turned around to see Anushka, who asked her to leave the box.

"Who are those men?" she asked.

"Albert James is a journalist and Jean Deuville is a poet, but you should know them, you invited them."

"How do you know them?"

"They are Pierre's friends and I met them in Paris. They insist on seeing him. But not just them, there are more people who know him at this congress and they're all asking for him."

Anushka regretted having chosen Amelia for this job, because her presence was now problematic.

"What have you told them?"

"They want to come home with me and surprise Pierre, but I've told them that it's impossible, that they'll see Pierre some other time."

As she said this, Amelia realized that it might be a problem for the Soviets if Pierre's friends insisted on seeing him but couldn't.

"Tell them that he's out of Moscow, that he's gone back to Buenos Aires," Anushka ordered.

"I'm sorry, I've told them he's here, and that they'll see him at some point, I couldn't think of anything else," Amelia said, trying to appear innocent.

When she got back to her box she stared at Albert James, trying to attract his attention. He saw her and smiled; he came to her box a little before the end of the performance. Anushka, who had not taken her eyes off them, came too. She didn't know why, but the relationship between these two people worried her.

"Have you changed your mind, are you going to show me Moscow by night?"

"Impossible, I have to start work early tomorrow."

"There's something odd about you, Amelia, and I don't know if..."

She tried to tell him everything just by looking at him, but Albert James did not grasp her meaning.

"Are you happy?" he asked suddenly.

"No, no I'm not."

He was surprised by her response and didn't know what to say. Anushka listened to them in a bad mood. She spoke French perfectly, as Amelia did, and had missed nothing of their conversation. She decided to interrupt.

"What strange things dear Amelia says! Of course she's happy, we all love her so."

Albert James turned to see who had interrupted them and came face to face with an attractive young blonde woman, tall and thin and with huge green eyes. He immediately realized that this must be one of the organizers of the congress.

"Ah, you are... !"

"Anna Nikolaevna Kornilova, Director of the Arts Division of the Ministry of Culture."

"And an actress and theater director," Amelia added.

"I've heard about you! I think that we'll see a production you directed tomorrow evening, am I right?" Albert James asked.

"That's right, it will be an honor for you to see my work."

"Chekhov, isn't it?"

"That's right. And now that the ballet is over we have work to do, we have to take you back to the hotel. Amelia, I think that your group should be going to their buses right about now."

"I'm in her group," Albert James said.

"Well, don't be late. I'll meet you in the hotel, Amelia, and we'll go home together. Mikhail will come with us. Is that alright?"

Amelia agreed and went to the lobby with Albert James and the rest of the journalists.

"An important woman, and very beautiful. I see you've got very good contacts here."

"She's married to Pierre's cousin. We all live together."

"Ah yes, Pierre's mother is Russian, is that right?"

"Yes, and her sister Irina is looking after us in Moscow."

"I'm sorry for insisting, but I thought it was strange for you to say that you weren't happy... I was surprised, to tell the truth."

"I'd like to leave the Soviet Union but I can't, maybe you can help me," Amelia muttered, looking to one side and hoping that no one overheard them.

"What are you scared of?" he asked.

"I'd have to explain so many things for you to understand… Pierre told me that you are not a Communist."

"I'm not. Don't worry, I'm not a Fascist either. I like my freedoms too much to allow other people to control my life. I believe in individuals above all else. But I must admit I was curious to see the Soviet Union."

"You won't be disappointed," Amelia announced.

"How can you be so sure?"

"You'll see exactly what they want. But you don't have a clue what's going on here."

They stopped talking to get on the bus. Amelia sat a long way from Albert James. She was afraid that if they saw her spending too much time with the journalist they would move her to another group, and she'd never be able to put into action the plan that was germinating in her mind.

On the way back to the apartment, flanked by Anushka and Mikhail, Amelia tried to control her nerves.

"Who is that journalist?" Anushka insisted.

"His name is Albert James, he's an American antifascist friend of Pierre's. They were inseparable in Paris," Amelia lied, "and he's insisting on seeing Pierre."

"That's going to be a problem," Mikhail said.

"I know, but neither he nor the other congress participants are happy with the excuses that Pierre doesn't want to see them because he's working, or because he's had to go on a trip. Things don't happen like that in Europe, you're going to have to do something."

Anushka said nothing, aware that the Pierre problem could end up ruining the carefully constructed image campaign that the Foreign Affairs and Culture ministries had set up. She had an appointment planned with her superiors first thing the next morning, but she knew that she was ultimately responsible, as Pierre was Mikhail's cousin, and she had recommended Amelia for this job.

The next morning, just as Amelia had feared, when she got to the congress she had been assigned to another group, of painters this time. She didn't protest and accepted her new task with apparent indifference, but she decided to look for Albert James as soon as she could. An opportunity presented itself at lunchtime, when the different groups met at the buffet table.

Amelia thought that if average Soviet citizens could have seen this meal they would have done anything at all to get hold of it, given how they dealt uncomplainingly with scarcity and hunger in their day-to-day lives; but at the congress it was as if the Soviet Union had an excess of food.

"You've run away from us," Albert James said when he saw her.

"They've assigned me to another group, they're worried that I might talk to you or to Jean Deuville. They might even stop me from doing this job, so I don't have much time for explanations. I know that you and Pierre didn't get on all that well, but I need you to save his life."

"What?" Albert James looked at her in shock.

"He's in the Lubyanka, and you only get out of there feet first or if you're sent to a labor camp."

"But what has he done?" Albert James's question was both nervous and incredulous.

"I swear to you he's done nothing, I beg you to believe me. They want some information Pierre doesn't have about... about a person he knew and who later turned out to be a spy who deserted. Pierre's been declared an enemy of the people."

"Good Lord, Amelia, how did he get caught up in this?"

"Please, talk lower! I don't think they'll let me speak to you again. Only if you and Jean and others start to insist on seeing Pierre will there be any chance of saving him. Insist on seeing him, please. As far as I'm concerned, if you could think of any way of convincing them to let me leave with you... I'm dying here."

"It's all so strange, what you're telling me..."

"I can't go into more detail, I'm just asking you to believe in me, I know you don't know me, but I'm not a bad person..."

A functionary came up to them with a cross expression on his face.

"Comrade Garayoa, you are neglecting your duties," he warned.

"I'm sorry, Comrade."

Amelia walked away, looking at the floor.

Albert James did not know what to do. Amelia's confession had left him confused. He did not understand what was going on, far less why Pierre was in prison. He didn't know why Pierre and Amelia had come to live in Moscow. His circle of Parisian friends thought that they were in Buenos Aires. In spite of so many unanswered questions he was affected by Amelia's anguish, which he saw her trying to control and turn into a cold sort of calm. He thought about telling Jean Deuville everything, but his poet friend was in love with the revolution and it would be a hard blow for him to know that Pierre was a prisoner and that the authorities considered him an "enemy of the people." His hands were sweaty and he looked for a chair where he could sit and think.

"Are you pleased with your work for the day?"

Anushka had stopped in front of him and was giving him a friendly smile. He thought that this blonde beauty was more like a storybook princess than a Communist Party functionary.

"I'd like to see Pierre," he replied, noticing how her smile immediately froze and she seemed upset.

"Pierre? That won't be possible, he's on a trip. Didn't Amelia tell you?"

"No, Amelia told us he was here. You must understand that it seems very odd that our friend hasn't come to see us. There are about twenty or thirty people here who know him."

"Ah? And you can't understand that for all his friendship he also has work to do? Unfortunately he's had to go on a business trip. If he comes back before the end of the congress then I'm sure he'll want to see you."

"But Amelia..."

"She must have been mistaken. Pierre's been out of the house for a few days because of his work."

"I don't know why, but I don't believe you..."

"Sorry?"

"I don't believe you, Comrade Kornilova. I don't believe you, nor do Pierre's friends."

"You're offending me, insulting us..."

"Yes? Why?"

"You doubt my word."

"I'm afraid that if we don't see Pierre then all your efforts to get us to praise the achievements of the revolution will have been in vain..."

Anushka turned away, furious. She decided that Amelia would pay dearly for not having obeyed her orders with respect to Pierre.

She found Amelia and took her to one side.

"What are you playing at?" Anushka shouted.

"Me? What do you mean?"

"I ordered you to say that Pierre had gone on a business trip."

"And I told you that I wasn't going to. No, Anushka, I'm not going to lie, not that I care too much about lying, but if I do lie, then I'm making Pierre's situation worse."

"You do not have the power to get him out of the Lubyanka."

Amelia shrugged and looked defiantly at Anushka.

"You could do something. All I want is to save his life and get out of here."

"With Pierre? You're mad! They'll never let him go. And as for you... You can go, I think it might be possible to arrange it."

"I'm not going to make a deal, Anushka, I'm not going to swap my freedom for Pierre's, I want us both to be released. You know what would happen if his friends don't see him? Imagine the headlines: 'Well-Known French Intellectual Disappears in Moscow.' And Paris and London and New York are nothing at all like Moscow, those are all places that have a free press. You're not going to like what they write about this congress, I assure you."

The next day, Maxim Litvinov, commissar of the Ministry of Foreign Affairs, received a document signed by twenty invitees of the congress asking to see Pierre Comte immediately. The document left no room for doubt: They knew that the Parisian bookseller was in Moscow, they had asked to see him several times, and the replies they had received had led them to think that something untoward had happened, so they asked the ministry for a coherent explanation, and to see Monsieur Comte.

Albert James had been working in the background to get his friends to sign this letter. He spoke to Jean Deuville, who said that Amelia was nothing but a charming madwoman, and denied the possibility that Pierre had been arrested, much less declared an "enemy of the people." James insisted so much, and even made the subtle threat of publishing articles about the "strange disappearance of Pierre Comte" in the American press, that he eventually convinced Jean Deuville to sign the letter and to talk some of his friends into doing so, too.

"I hope you know what you're doing, Albert, what Amelia said to you sounds very strange... I hope we're not being used to discredit the Soviet Union. You know that I'm a Communist and I have responsibilities in Paris."

"I know, Jean, but I also know that despite your unblemished faith you still have a certain capacity for free thought. If it is a trick I will take full responsibility."

"My comrades will never forgive me if I help the Fascists, even involuntarily."

Almost two hundred people had been invited to the congress, and it was a great success to get twenty of them to sign the letter.

The organizing committee had to find a solution, and asked Anushka to do so.

The torturer came into the cell and Pierre woke up and tried to roll into a ball, bursting into tears at the thought of another of those endless sessions in which his only desire was to die. They had just taken him to the cell and he had fallen deeply asleep after being seated in a chair for forty-eight hours, his hands and feet tied; various torturers had taken turns submitting him to more and more inventive punishments as they asked about Comrade Krisov.

He felt the torturer lifting him up and kicking him to make him walk.

He didn't want to walk, he couldn't, he only wanted to die and he started to beg for them to kill him. But they took him to a hospital wing where a robust nurse gave him an injection that sent him into a deep sleep.

When he woke up, he thought he could see a blurry face looking at him.

"Are you feeling better?" the face asked.

Pierre didn't answer, or even move his head. He thought he was dreaming, he had to be dreaming because no one was hitting him.

"I'll help you to get up now, you have to have a shower. Then we'll cut your hair and get you some clean clothes."

"Where am I?" he whispered.

"In the hospital. I'm the doctor in charge of making sure you get better. Don't worry, you will get better."

"In the hospital?"

"Yes, in the hospital. You had an accident, you lost your memory, but you're getting better. Your family will come to see you as soon as you're strong enough."

"My family?"

Pierre thought about his mother, Olga's smooth hands as she stroked his forehead when she gave him his goodnight kiss. His mother, hugging him, smiling, holding his hand to cross the road. Would his mother be here?

He felt more clearheaded in the afternoon, although there were still parts of his body he couldn't feel. The doctor explained that because of his "accident" he'd never be able to move one of his arms again. He had lost several fingers. As for his right eye, he's lost that as well, unfortunately. And Pierre remembered the night when one of those men had plunged a screwdriver into his eye and he'd fainted from the pain. What accident was the doctor talking about? He didn't ask, he didn't say anything, he felt tired and happy to be in clean sheets that smelled of disinfectant.

As for his testicles, the doctor said, the accident had been so bad that they'd been lost as well. Pierre saw his tormentor in his memory, taking that pair of pliers and crushing first one testicle, then the other. But the doctor said that it had been the "accident," and he agreed, comforted by the words of the man in the white coat.

Six days had gone by since Amelia had confronted Anushka. When they saw each other at home they barely talked. Mikhail also refused to hide his growing hostility, she had even heard him arguing with his mother, begging her to throw Amelia out, but Aunt Irina said that she would stay until Pierre turned up again.

One night Mikhail and Anushka arrived back home a little after Amelia. They had seen her at the congress, but Anushka had disappeared mysteriously in the early afternoon.

Mikhail cleared his throat and asked his parents and Amelia to sit down because Anushka had something to tell them.

Aunt Irina dried her hands on her apron, and Uncle Georgi put his newspaper down. Amelia tried to hide that she was trembling from her neck downwards. She feared the worst.

Anushka looked at all of them in silence, lowered her head, and then threw it back, shaking out her splendid blonde ponytail. All attention turned to her.

"Pierre is alive and well," she announced.

Aunt Irina and Amelia asked in unison where he was and when they could see him.

"Calm down, calm down. It's been very difficult for us to keep quiet about this, because," and here she took Mikhail's hand, "we thought he might not make it."

"But what happened?" Aunt Irina cried.

"Pierre had a very bad accident and almost lost his life. The worst of it is that he suffered amnesia until quite recently and was lost for a while; well, not lost, he was in a hospital but because he couldn't say who he was..."

"An accident? Where?" Amelia said, knowing that Anushka was lying.

"Amelia, what I am going to say will be particularly hard for you, but... well, I have to say it. Do not think that Mikhail and I did not try to find out where Pierre was, but what we found out isn't all that flattering to you. Pierre had another lover; they went out one night and were in her car driving to her dacha on the outskirts of Moscow. Pierre was going to call to say that he had lots of work and would be late, but they had an accident. There were roadworks and a crane fell on top of their car. She died at once and he... well, he suffered serious injuries and lost his memory. He has been in the hospital all this time, and it's a miracle that he's still alive, even though... well, you can imagine..."

"No, I can't imagine, and I want to see him." Amelia's voice was cold as ice. She would have liked to have called Anushka a liar to her face, as well as to have hit her, but she knew she had to keep control, to accept the role of humiliated lover.

"I'm telling you that he's in a very bad state, and won't even recognize you," Anushka insisted.

"I want to see him," the young Spaniard insisted.

"Alright, we will take you to the hospital tomorrow," Anushka said.

"Amelia, we have to apologize for not telling you about Pierre's lover, but we didn't want to offend you and make you suffer even more because of his disappearance," Mikhail said, looking at Amelia with sympathy.

"But I don't believe that Pierre could have had a lover!" Aunt Irina said. "It's impossible! I know how much he cares for Amelia. There has to be another explanation."

"No, Mother, there isn't. The worst of it is that the woman who was with him was... It's a disgrace to know that there are still prostitutes in the Soviet Union. Nobody claimed the woman's corpse, apparently she had no relatives and as Pierre didn't know who he was..."

"And how did you find him? How do you know it's him?" Aunt Irina insisted.

"Of course it's him. We'll all go to see him tomorrow. Don't worry about your work, Amelia, I've told them you'll be late, and they've been very understanding given the circumstances. They'll take our guests to look at some model factories."

Anushka and Mikhail replied unwillingly to Aunt Irina's innumerable questions. Uncle Georgi said not a word. He had realized that for some reason he did not understand they had decided to bring Pierre back, and he didn't dare ask where he had been or what they had done to him. They went to bed early. Anushka said she had a headache and Mikhail said he was tired. In fact neither of them could bear the incessant questions of Aunt Irina, who was implacable.

Amelia couldn't sleep a wink all night. She tossed and turned imagining the day that was to follow. *How could they have made up that story about Pierre having an accident!* she said to herself, at the same time feeling a great sense of relief that he was alive.

The doctor took them down a long corridor and stopped at the door to a room. He opened the door and invited them in. He had told them how to behave with the patient beforehand. No questions. Pierre was recovering his memory and his mental state was very confused.

At first they didn't recognize him. Amelia went up to the bed thinking that they were playing a trick on her, that they'd brought along a man who was not Pierre. But it was him, although he looked like an old man. He was nearly bald, and the little hair he had left was completely white. He was missing fingers and parts of his body seemed to be paralyzed. There was a bandage over the space that had once been his right eye.

Amelia burst into tears, and Aunt Irina couldn't contain herself either. Even Mikhail seemed affected by Pierre's appearance.

"It's a miracle he survived the accident," the doctor said. "Thank goodness he doesn't remember what happened to him."

"He doesn't remember anything?" Aunt Irina said.

"No, he doesn't. And we're treating him to try to help him avoid negative thoughts."

"Treating him? What are you doing to him?" Amelia asked in alarm.

"We're trying to alleviate his suffering, nothing more." The doctor seemed to think that Amelia's question was out of place.

She took one of Pierre's hands and stroked his cheek. He opened his eye and looked at her, but he seemed not to recognize her.

"Pierre, it's me, Amelia," she whispered in his ear, but he did not respond.

"He doesn't recognize you," the doctor said, trying to take Amelia away from the Frenchman's side.

But she felt the three fingers that remained on his hand gripping her own. She looked at him again, but his gaze was still absent.

"It doesn't matter if he doesn't recognize me, he likes to have me near."

"We mustn't tire him," the doctor said.

"Come on Amelia, we've seen him now, you can relax, he's being looked after," Anushka said, grabbing Amelia's arm.

"I want to be alone with Pierre." Amelia was not asking; she assumed that no one would stop her from being alone with him.

"It is impossible," the doctor said.

"No, it isn't. Pierre has suffered a great deal, I known he doesn't recognize me, but I am sure that it will help him to feel a friend's hand."

Anushka looked at the doctor. They both left the room and she came back alone a few minutes later.

"I've convinced him to let you stay for a while, but you have to understand that Pierre needs to rest. Promise me you won't force him to speak."

"I won't do anything that could harm him."

Aunt Irina gave Pierre a gentle kiss; it seemed that Uncle Georgi dared not touch him. As they were leaving, Anushka said she'd be back in a few minutes.

Amelia stroked Pierre's head and thought that she saw a slight smile trace itself on his lips. From time to time he opened his eye, but he didn't look for her, rather he seemed to lose himself in the white wall in front of him.

"It's been terrible without you, although now that I see you I know that my suffering is nothing compared to what you must have gone through... Good Lord, what have they done to you! I'll get you out of here, we'll go back to Paris, you'll get better, trust me," she said in a low voice, afraid that someone would hear her.

From time to time a nurse would come into the room and look mistrustfully at Amelia, as if Pierre's condition were somehow her fault.

Later, Anushka came into the room with the doctor.

"Amelia, dear, we have to go back to work. You'll be able to see Pierre again this evening."

She kissed his lips and they were cold as the lips of a corpse.

"Don't worry, I will return," she said, but he did not seem to hear her.

They went out into the corridor and Anushka said that the doctor wanted to talk to them. They went to his office. He asked them to sit down and then looked mistrustfully at Amelia.

"Comrade Garayoa, I am sorry to have to tell you that Comrade Comte is in a very bad way," the doctor said.

"That's obvious," Amelia said with a touch of irony.

"He's a strong man, but even so... He lost his testicles in the accident," he said, looking at her directly, as if trying to make her feel ashamed.

"Really? Well, as far as I know you can live without testicles."

"The blows he received... Well, you know a crane fell on him... He's had irreversible injuries."

"I am aware of his state, Comrade Doctor."

"His brain's been affected, his mental faculties... I don't think he'll ever be a normal person again. You have to be prepared for the worst, Comrade," the doctor said.

"The worst? There can be something worse than what he's gone through?"

"I assure you we've done everything we can," the doctor insisted, "but you have to bear in mind that... well, he wasn't looked after perfectly."

"I want to take him to Paris, to his parents," Amelia said defiantly.

"Impossible!" Anushka exclaimed.

"Why? It doesn't make sense for us to carry on here, not for either of us. Pierre needs expert care, he needs his family."

"We are his family, Amelia," Anushka said.

"His parents are in Paris, and that's where Pierre will want to be, where he needs to be."

"I don't know if it will be possible for him to be moved, given the state he's in…" The doctor looked worriedly at Anushka.

"I assure you that his condition will improve markedly as soon as we're out of here," Amelia replied, barely managing to control her anger.

"I thought that perhaps that journalist, Albert James, could come to see him, and the poet, Jean Deuville," Anushka said.

"That's very considerate of you. But I also ask you, Comrade Anna Nikolaevna Kornilova, to get hold of the necessary permissions for Pierre to be moved to Paris. I want to travel back with the intellectuals at the end of the conference, with Albert James and Jean Deuville."

Anushka gritted her teeth and her face hardened. She was annoyed by Amelia's attitude, but she knew that now was not the moment to argue with her.

For all that Amelia tried to stay by Pierre's side, the doctor was inflexible. She could not come back until the following day because some tests needed to be done. She could come back early the next morning with Pierre's friends.

That night Amelia went to the farewell dinner that the Central Committee had organized for the participants in the congress.

People were worried. On September 30 they had received confirmation of the agreement that France's Édouard Daladier and Great Britain's Neville Chamberlain had reached in Munich with Hitler and Mussolini. The two European powers had given way to Hitler's determination to take control of the Czech Sudetenland.

"It's a disgrace!" Albert James said. "France and England will pay dearly for their mistake. They are letting Hitler do whatever he wants, which is like feeding a mad dog."

The Soviet hosts listened to their guests' comments but prudently withheld their own opinions. They preferred to listen, to take the pulse of this group of people who represented European "intellectuality."

Amelia went up to the group with whom Albert James was sitting and took him aside.

"What's happening?" the journalist asked.

"I want to thank you for all you've done for Pierre. I saw him today and thank God he's alive, but he's in a critical state."

"Where was he? What's happened to him?"

"You'll see him tomorrow and... well, it'll be hard for you to recognize him. They've tortured him, but they'll say the same to you as they did to me, that he was in an accident and a crane fell on him."

She told him the story that the Soviets had invented to justify Pierre's condition, and asked him to come with them tomorrow to see Pierre in the hospital, along with Jean Deuville.

"Anushka and I will come to see you at eight on the dot. Now I want to ask you another favor."

"Right! What now?"

"I want you to tell Anushka that Pierre needs to come back to Paris, and that you and Jean Deuville will help me to look after him on the journey. But you have to insist that we travel with you."

"They could say no."

"Yes, but if you insist... They've been obliged to make him appear, and the Soviet authorities don't want any scandals connected with this congress, they want you to praise the system to the skies, which is why they invited you. It's worked so far, you got them to make Pierre appear."

"It's incredible that he'd been arrested for so long..."

"It is a common practice to torture and kill in the name of the people. If someone is declared an enemy of the revolution, from that moment on he deserves anything that happens to him. People are scared, hungry, censored, children denounce their parents, uncles denounce their nephews, friends look at each other with distrust. Stalin has instituted a regime of terror, although it's not his fault entirely, it was Lenin who planted the first seeds of barbarism."

"You've stopped being a committed Communist, then?"

"I've lived here long enough to want to run away from this thing they call Communism. But what I think isn't important, what we have to do now is save Pierre."

Jean Deuville could not contain an exclamation of horror when he went into Pierre's room. Albert James was also upset, but, to Anushka's relief, he said nothing. The doctor had explained the seriousness of Pierre's state, insisting that it was a miracle that he was still alive after the accident with the crane.

"Pierre, *mon ami*, what has happened to you?" Jean asked, making an effort to hold back tears.

Pierre's one eye was open but he seemed not to see them. Amelia thought that he was drowsier than the previous day, and she could see fear in his only healthy eye.

"We'll take him to Paris," Albert James said. "He'll come with us. The sooner he's with his family, the sooner he'll get better."

"I don't think... Well, his mental state might be permanently affected. Look, he's scarcely more than a vegetable," the doctor said.

"Even so, he's coming with us," Jean Deuville replied with determination. "His mother would never forgive me if we left him here."

"He will never get such good treatment as in a people's hospital," Anushka said.

"I disagree, Comrade Anna Nikolaevna Kornilova, there's nowhere in the world where he'll be better than at home," Jean said.

"Pierre's homeland is the Soviet Union, as it is the homeland of every worker. Also, you remember that the comrade has family here," Anushka insisted.

"Comrade Kornilova, as Pierre's friends and as the representatives of his parents, we insist on taking him to Paris. We don't understand why you are so keen to stop him from leaving... ," Albert James said.

"Comrade Comte is in no condition to travel," the doctor said. "I don't even dare to say if... well..."

"He will survive the journey," Jean Deuville insisted. "I know he will."

Albert James and Jean Deuville left Anushka and the doctor no choice, so the relevant forms were drawn up, but on the condition that if anything happened to Pierre it would be the responsibility of those accompanying him. Amelia had remained quiet the entire time, knowing that it was not for her to fight this battle.

Amelia was happy as she packed. Anushka had announced that she was free to travel with Albert James and Jean Deuville and for them to take Pierre with them.

Aunt Irina helped her to pack; she gave her advice about how to look after Pierre during the voyage.

"My sister Olga will never forgive me for what they have done to her son," she said. "I haven't done what I should have for him..."

"You and Uncle Georgi have both been very good to me and to Pierre, you have nothing to blame yourself for, it's this damn system..."

"I was never a revolutionary," Aunt Irina said, "but Georgi was, and, well, I ended up thinking that he might be right, that the people would live better, that they would build a freer society, but there is now more fear than under the czar. Mikhail gets upset if you say so, but it's the truth."

"Take care of yourself, Aunt Irina."

"Do you think my son would denounce me?"

"I haven't said that."

"No, but you think it, Amelia, I know you think it. No, he will never denounce us. I know that lots of children have denounced their parents, but my son will never denounce me. Mikhail has unshakeable faith in Communism, but he's a good boy really. Don't mistrust him."

Amelia didn't want to argue with the woman. At the moment, the only thing that was important for her was to close her suitcase and go to the Hotel Metropol, where Albert James and Jean Deuville were waiting for her. Anushka had promised that a car would take them to the hospital, where they would pick up Pierre and go to the airport.

Aunt Irina let fall a few tears at their parting.

"Look after Pierre and give my letter to Olga."

"I will, and you should take care of yourself."

Jean Deuville was nervous, and Albert James did not seem in a very good mood.

"If anyone had told me that I would go through all this I would have said that they were mad," Deuville said.

Anushka arrived at the appointed hour with a large cart so Pierre, as she said, would be more comfortable. She seemed uncomfortable and did not want to talk.

When they got to the hospital, Anushka told them to wait while she went to get the head of the hospital to sign Pierre's release papers.

Amelia agreed to this without enthusiasm. She knew that bureaucracy could be an interminable process in the Soviet Union.

Half an hour later Anushka appeared with Pierre's doctor.

"Come with me, please," the doctor said. "Comrade Comte's condition has worsened. He had a severe cardiac arrest this morning. We're doing all we can to save his life, and it's impossible for him to travel."

They followed him anxiously. Amelia felt her heart beating fit to burst, while Jean Deuville and Albert James looked at each other in surprise.

The doctor opened the door to Pierre's room, and they saw two nurses and two other doctors huddled around the bed.

"I'm sorry, comrades, the patient suffered heart seizure," one of the doctors said. "There was nothing we could do. He's gone."

Amelia went up to the bed and pushed the doctors aside. Pierre's face was drawn, as if his last moments had been terribly painful. She started to cry, at first silently, and then released an anguished howl. She held Pierre's inert body. The body of an old man. The body of a torture victim.

Albert James went to the bed and tried to get Amelia to let go of Pierre, but she did not want to do so, she wanted to feel this body pressed against her own and to murmur to it that she would never love anyone again the way she had loved Pierre.

With Jean Deuville's help, Albert James pulled Amelia to one side. The two men were moved by the scene.

"I'm sorry," the doctor said.

"You're sorry? I think you..."

Albert James did not let Amelia carry on speaking. He knew what she was going to say because he suspected it himself: They had killed Pierre.

"Please, Amelia! We have to leave. We can't do anything for Pierre," he said firmly.

"I want them to perform an autopsy! I want to take his corpse to Paris, and for them to do the autopsy there so I can see what killed him," Amelia shouted.

"Amelia, you're not well, maybe you should stay here to recover from losing Pierre," Anushka said coldly.

Her words sounded like a threat.

"Put yourself in her place, you can see why she's like this," Albert James said in a neutral voice.

"Come on, Amelia, there's nothing we can do here," Jean Deuville said as he put his arm around her shoulder.

"Remember that he suffered a terrible accident," the doctor said.

"We'll remember. The miracle is that he lived as long as he did," Albert James said ironically.

Amelia refused to say goodbye to Anushka, who promised Jean Deuville and Albert James that she would organize the funeral.

"Don't forget that Pierre did have family here," Anushka insisted, "and he will be buried as he deserves."

Amelia wondered for a second if she should perhaps stay for the burial, but Albert James insisted that it was time for her to go.

"Come with us, there's no point in your staying here. He wouldn't have wanted you to stay."

She refused to shake the hand of the doctor who had looked after Pierre. With Jean Deuville holding her she kept repeating the word "murderers" in Spanish, a language she thought none of them would understand.

They left the hospital and went directly to the airport. It was October 2, 1938...

Professor Kruvkoski fell silent and looked fixedly at Guillermo.

"That is all I can tell you."

"I feel burnt out."

"I beg your pardon?"

"I'm deeply affected. Stalin's crimes make your hair stand on end. It must have been a terrible time."

"It was, the system worked via terror, which was how it spread all over the country. Yes, it was terrible, millions of innocent people were killed, were assassinated by Stalin."

"Tell me, how can you be so sure about what happened? I'm asking because it can't be easy to know what went on in the Lubyanka."

"There are some archives and documents that have been opened to researchers."

"It's unbelievable to think that you didn't rebel against Stalin, and that there are still some people who miss him."

"Ask your parents why they didn't rebel against Franco," the professor said grumpily.

Silence fell again between them. Then Professor Kruvkoski sighed and seemed to relax.

"It's difficult for you to understand what happened. As far as missing Stalin is concerned... Don't be mistaken, the Russian people don't want him back, but what they can't stand is no longer being a superpower, no longer having the respect of other countries. The Soviet Union was a great power, feared by everyone, and this was a source of Russian pride. The fall of the Berlin Wall left us bewildered. We were poor, no longer a world power, everything was falling to pieces around our ears... The West thought that we were beaten and we Russians felt humiliated."

"But you must admit that democracy is better than dictatorship."

"Of course, young man, there's no doubt about that, but we Russians are proud and won't allow people to patronize us. The West has been mistaken about Russia."

"But you are part of Europe."

"That's the mistake you all make. We're a part of Europe but not entirely. Russia by itself is a continent, with its own peculiarities. That's why you don't understand how Putin can be so popular here; the answer is that he has given Russians back their pride. Anyway, I'm not going to give you a lesson in geopolitics or explain what Russians are like."

"Thank you for telling me about my great-grandmother."

"She was a notable woman, very brave."

"Yes, I suppose she was."

I had no excuse to stay in Moscow, although I was sad not to be able to spend a few more days there. I would have loved to go to Saint Petersburg as well, but I was well aware that my financiers were now the Garayoas, so I didn't feel happy abusing their trust. But I used the rest of the day to wander around Moscow. The next morning I had to go back to Spain early; I was keen to do so, because I wanted to know what my great-grandmother would have done when she got back to Paris. And I wondered whom Doña Laura would select now to guide my footsteps.

ALBERT

1

The row between my mother and me was more violent than usual, and she didn't soften when I told her that in the course of only two weeks I had been in Rome, Buenos Aires, and Moscow.

"Stop with all these stories from the past and get to work!"

"But I haven't stopped working!"

But for my mother any job that didn't have fixed hours and a salary was not a job. Also, she tried to bully me into giving up my investigation into my great-grandmother.

"Your Aunt Marta always goes over the top, and now she's put you in a tricky situation and doesn't want to know about it, which I suppose is for the best, but I don't like it that you're still burrowing around in this history."

She told me that it was my fault that she'd argued with her sister and that they hadn't spoken to each other for a week. Then she got back onto her old bandwagon and told me that I should settle down and look for a real job.

"Guillermo, dear, I don't know why there are people who are worse than you all over the place, appearing on television. Look at Luis, who was at university with you, who was always a bit slow, and who now does the news on the radio, or Esther... she's useless and now she's a "star" on the television... and Roberto... well, he's the stupidest of them all and they made him the director general."

"I'm sorry, but I've got a flaw: I don't shut up, and the bosses don't like that."

"And why don't your Socialist friends give you a hand? In the election campaign they said they wanted independent journalists."

"And you believed them? Come on, Mom, don't be naïve! Politicians hate people who are independent; anything that doesn't serve their interests gets pushed to one side. The right and the left are the same in this, and because I attack both sides, you see what happens."

Arguments with my mother always seem useless to me. She takes at face value everything the politicians say on television, and she can't believe that they'd say one thing and do another.

The best thing about my mother is the confidence she has in human nature.

I called Doña Laura to tell her that I was back in Madrid. She told me that she would call me to tell me what the next thing to do was, so I took these free hours to go see my girlfriend Ruth, to swing by the office of the newspaper, to have a drink with some friends, and to have another argument with my beloved mother. It was a week before Doña Laura called me.

"You need to call Professor Soler. He'll tell you what to do."

When I heard his voice on the other end of the line, I had the impression that I was talking to an old friend.

"Doña Laura has asked me to keep on showing you the way forward with your investigation. It won't be easy, but between what I know and some things you told me I think I can carry on telling you where to go, without you giving me any more information. You have to go to Paris. You should speak to an old friend, Victor Dupont; he knew Amelia when he was an adolescent a little older than I was."

"Who is he?"

"The son of an activist, a Communist. Our parents were friends, and we lived in his house in Paris for a while after the Civil War ended."

"You lived in Paris?"

"Yes, with my father."

"And your mother?"

"I don't know what became of her, maybe the Francoists shot her. She didn't want to go to France; she was prepared to carry on fighting even after Franco had won the war. My father fled to France with me."

"And what might Monsieur Dupont know about Amelia Garayoa?"

"More than you might imagine; he knew her and Albert James and Jean Deuville as well."

"You think he might remember what happened back then?"

"Of course. Also, Victor is a documentalist, his father was a journalist and when he died he left Victor all his papers. But I don't want to get ahead of myself. Go to Paris, Victor Dupont will see you whenever you get there."

It was raining in Paris, which didn't surprise me because it was not often that I had been to the French capital without getting caught in some downpour. But it smelled of spring and that cheered me up.

I had booked a hotel room on the Left Bank, near Victor Dupont's home.

I was surprised when I met him. He was very old, but he still emanated vigor and energy.

A documentalist and archivist by profession, Monsieur Dupont seemed like a wise old bird, not fading at all.

I could tell that he must have been handsome when he was younger; he was tall, with blue eyes, and now had the white hair and upright bearing of an aging gallant.

"So you're investigating your great-grandmother's history? You don't have any idea what you're caught up in!" Monsieur Dupont said as he poured out two glasses of Burgundy to accompany a plate of cheese.

"That's what my mother says, I'm in a tricky situation."

"There are things it's maybe better not to stir up, especially in a family. But it's your funeral. I'll help you as much as I can because my good friend Pablo asked me to. Where should we start?"

"Well, as far as I know, Amelia Garayoa came back to Paris at the beginning of October 1938, accompanied by Jean Deuville and Albert James. They were coming back from a congress of intellectuals in Moscow."

"Yes, a congress organized for the greater glory of Soviet propaganda, which was fairly effective in its moment."

I didn't dare ask if he was a Communist, given that his father had been and that he was a friend of Pablo Soler's father, who had also been one, but Dupont must have read my mind.

"I was a Communist, and you can't imagine how committed I was. The Communists have done terrible things, but they've also done a lot of good. They have numbered among their ranks people who have been modest and believing, as good as saints, dedicated uniquely to helping others. I stopped being a party member years ago, which has allowed me to analyze my own life with a sincerity and sense of perspective that would not have been possible had I continued as a Communist. But it's not me we're here to talk about. Did you know that your grandmother lived in my house?"

I was dumbfounded, although I should have realized by this stage that nothing ought to surprise me. Dupont carried on with his story...

Jean Deuville was a friend of André Dupont, my father. He called to ask if my father would rent a friend of his a room, because he knew that we had a spare room, as we lived in my grandmother's house, which was big. And besides, my grandmother had died a few months earlier.

My mother, Danielle, made the decision to accept Amelia, because it meant a little extra money each month. Until a few months earlier my mother had worked in a paper shop, but the owner died and his children closed the business, so a few francs for the rent would come in very handy for us.

We all benefited from the deal, because Amelia had been in a hotel since her arrival in Paris and she didn't want to waste what little money she had, so renting a room was more economical for her as well.

I was fifteen years old then, and I must admit that I fell in love with Amelia the moment I saw her. She seemed unreal, she was very thin and ethereal.

My mother wanted to know how long she'd be staying, but Amelia told her she still didn't know what she was going to do.

"Madame Dupont, I want to go back to Spain, but I don't know if that will be possible, and if it isn't then I will need to find a job."

"But you cannot go to Spain!" my mother exclaimed.

"The legitimate Republican government still holds Madrid, Catalonia, Valencia... but I don't think I can afford to be optimistic. General Rojo managed to break Franco's hold on the Ebro in July, but he hasn't been able to maintain that advantage. I don't think you can go to Spain," my father added.

Amelia shrugged. She appeared resigned to doing whatever was possible even if she couldn't defy fate.

Although she was very reserved and smiled very little, she was very patient with me and also helped my mother around the house. You know, washing dishes, and ironing, and sewing...

I listened to her conversations with my parents, and the ones she had with other comrades such as Jean Deuville.

Jean had told my parents what had happened in Moscow. It was such a shock for him that it destroyed his faith in Communism. He did not dare leave the party, but he had lost his ideological virginity in Moscow, as well as losing Pierre, his best friend.

It was not easy for Jean Deuville or Amelia to tell Pierre's parents that their son had died. The day after they arrived in Paris, Albert James, Jean, and Amelia went to Pierre's parents' house. As far as I know, the scene was something like this:

Olga, Pierre's mother, opened the door and when she saw that Amelia was alone she screamed and asked where her son was. Jean tried to hold Olga in his arms to offer sympathy and explain what had happened, but she pushed him away.

"Where is Pierre? What have you done to him?" she asked Amelia.

Albert James had to hold Amelia upright because she was trembling so much, and he thought that she could not deal with the situation. It was Albert James who controlled the situation, as both Amelia and Jean were too upset.

Pierre's father came out into the hall, summoned by his wife's cries.

"But what's going on here? What are you doing? And you, Amelia... ? Where's Pierre?"

"Amelia told them what had happened. She didn't hide anything. Not that Pierre had been a Soviet agent, not the details of their life in Buenos Aires, the order to travel to Moscow, the months they had spent in the Soviet capital, Pierre's disappearance, his stay in the Lubyanka, the torture they had inflicted on him and her conviction that he had been murdered. The only thing she didn't tell them, and which she had kept from Albert James and Jean Deuville as well, was that she had found out about Pierre's arrest from Ivan Vasiliev. She didn't want to put that man into danger; at least he had helped her to find out where Pierre was.

Olga cried uncontrollably as she listened to Amelia's story, and Pierre's father grew visibly older as he found out about the horrors his son had faced.

"It's your fault! You and you damned ideas about Communism that you put in our son's head! You wouldn't listen to me and now our son is dead. You killed him too!" Olga shouted at her husband.

"Madame Comte, calm down, please!" Albert James begged.

But there was no way to control Olga's anger and pain, or to find words to console Pierre's father. Jean Deuville was no help either, as he too could not hold back tears.

Olga threw them out of the house, cursing Amelia, whom she said she never wanted to see again.

Jean Deuville and Albert James took charge of Amelia. They seemed to feel responsible for her. Édouard Daladier was in charge of France at that time and foreigners, especially Spaniards, were starting to have trouble residing legally in the country. The flood of exiled Spaniards fleeing the war had overwhelmed the French administration, and Paris began to legislate against foreigners.

So it was that Jean Deuville and Albert James had to pull all the strings they could to get Amelia her residence papers. Nobody was surprised that Albert James would employ her as his secretary. He had not needed a secretary up to that point, but this was a way to help her without offending her. As for Jean, he turned into her shadow; he would go and pick her up from her house and force her to go for walks, to go to the theater, to go to concerts. Amelia allowed herself to be led around, and appeared to be an automaton, as if nothing that happened around her meant anything at all to her.

My parents wondered why a journalist like Albert James would look after Amelia as he did. Jean Deuville's case was different, he had been Pierre's best friend and they were Communist Party comrades, but this was not the case with Albert James, who did not know that much about Amelia either. But he helped her as much as he could.

Albert James worked with certain magazines and journals in America, as well as a few British newspapers. He was extremely independent for my parents' tastes. They thought that the era they lived in was one that demanded participation. James's objectivity irritated them, and they argued with him to his face. Albert James refused to be a "fellow traveler" of the party, an attitude that made him a difficult person to pigeonhole. They respected him, of course; he was extremely influential and his articles were taken into account by the French and British governments as well as the American.

His report on the Moscow congress of intellectuals was a disappointment to his Soviet hosts. James claimed that the farms and factories he had visited seemed designed to give foreigners a rosy idea of the Soviet Union, and that they had never been allowed to leave their programmed itinerary or to travel freely. In one of his articles he claimed that there was no freedom in the country. His criticisms were like a bath of cold water for the Soviet authorities, although they were of course balanced by more favorable ones provided by other European intellectuals.

Amelia went to James's office early every morning and dealt with his correspondence, sorted out his filing, prepared his schedule, wrote fair copies of his articles, and kept his accounts.

Perhaps the greatest joy they had in those days in Paris was the appearance of Carla Alessandrini. She was to spend a fortnight in the city singing in *La Traviata* at the Opera Garnier. Her arrival was a great event.

Jean Deuville arranged to take Amelia to the opera to hear Carla sing.

I still remember her on the night of the performance. Amelia was naturally elegant, and even though she did not have a large wardrobe at that time, she still looked like a princess in her plain black dress.

Carla Alessandrini was magnificent; she was given a standing ovation that lasted around twenty minutes. As far as Jean told us, Amelia cried with emotion and at the end of the performance she went to Carla Alessandrini's dressing-room, convinced that they would let her through to see the diva, but the Opera had put a guard at the door to make sure that no one not expressly invited by *la gran Carla* could go through to the dressing-room.

"Tell her that her friend Amelia Garayoa is here," she told the skeptical little man who stopped her from going through to the dressing-rooms.

He was surprised when the go-ahead was given and a few minutes later Vittorio Leonardi, the diva's husband, came out to meet Amelia.

Vittorio seized Amelia in his arms, scolded her for being so thin, grasped Jean's hand as if they were lifelong friends, and led the way to the dressing-room.

The two women fell into an interminable embrace. It was clear that Carla truly felt affection for Amelia, she thought of her as a daughter.

"Why didn't you tell me you were in Paris! You don't know how worried I've been. Gloria and Martin Hertz told me that you were going on a trip for a couple of months with Pierre, but that not only had you not come back, but they didn't know anything about where you were. Let me look at you... You're far too thin, and... I don't know... there's something different about you. Where is Pierre?"

"He's dead."

"Dead? I didn't know he was ill... ," Carla said.

"He wasn't. They killed him."

Carla and her husband Vittorio were upset by Amelia's announcement. The diva held onto her as if she were a mother embracing her daughter to protect her.

"You have to tell me everything!"

Amelia introduced them to Jean Deuville, who had remained silent, observing the scene. He was struck by the friendship between the two women. Carla Alessandrini was, however you looked at it, a world-famous figure, one of the most desired women of her time.

While Carla was in Paris, she saw Amelia every day. My parents and I went to the opera for the first time at *la Alessandrini*'s invitation, and it was a great event for us to be there, mixing with the rich and the bourgeois people who seemed to live with their backs to the real world, drinking champagne as if nothing that happened in the normal run of things could ever affect them.

Amelia would visit Carla in her hotel, or else Carla would invite her to the dinners and luncheons at which she was presented to distinguished people; one day Carla even came to have lunch at our house. I hid behind the door and spied on them, not because I cared what they talked about, but because I was truly fascinated by Carla, who had taken Amelia's place in my adolescent dreams.

"You have to decide what you are going to do, my girl, and I'd like you to think about maybe coming with us. I don't think that you have much of a future in France, things are getting so bad here for foreigners. I've spoken with Vittorio and he thinks that the best thing would be for you to come with us."

"I want to go back to Spain, I know that I can't at the moment because of the war, but the war will be over someday. I need to know about my family, I want to be with my son."

"I understand, but do you think your husband will allow it?"

"I don't know, but I need to ask for his forgiveness and I'll beg him to let me see Javier. He can't refuse me, it is my son we're talking about."

Carla said nothing. She thought that it would be difficult for a Spanish husband to pardon his wife after she had run away with her lover. But she didn't want to crush Amelia's hopes, and she knew that her friend must be feeling especially fragile after the nightmare of Moscow.

"I know that you want to go back to Spain, but as you say yourself it's not possible at the moment, so why not stay with us and we'll send you back to Madrid when the right moment presents itself."

"You and Vittorio are very generous, but I have a job here and I'm working to support myself, and I don't know what I would do if I went with you."

"Nothing, you don't have to do anything apart from the travel with us. You don't need to work, just accompany us."

But Amelia was proud, and not for anything would she accept being dependent on others, not earning her own keep. She tried to find a way to tell Carla this without offending her.

"I wouldn't feel comfortable, seeing you working and me not doing anything."

"Well, you could be Vittorio's secretary."

"But you don't need another secretary!"

They spoke for a while, and Carla made her promise that if she were ever in trouble then she would think of her.

When *la Alessandrini* left Paris, she left a great hole in all of our lives, not just in Amelia's soul.

One day Amelia came back home in tears. My mother tried to console her.

"I... I... had a great aunt who lived in Paris, Aunt Lily. I plucked up my courage to go and see her today to ask her for news of my family, but the porter told me she died a few months ago."

She wanted to find out about her family, and I told my mother to pray that they would forgive her.

She missed her parents, her son, her cousins, even her husband.

"I was so bad to him! Santiago did not deserve what I did to him," she said, regretfully.

On November 7, the secretary at the German Embassy in Paris, Ernst vom Rath, was attacked. When he died two days later, it provided the impetus for Germany's infamous Kristallnacht. More than 30,000 Jews were arrested, 191 synagogues were destroyed, more than 7,500 businesses were ransacked... Albert James always said that the worst was yet to come, and he was right. The European powers did not want to admit that they were face to face with a monster, and they allowed all this to happen and to keep on happening...

In the last days of 1938, it was as if everything were falling to pieces. In December, Franco started a large-scale military offensive against Catalonia, an action that all but decided the war in favor of the Fascists.

A little before Christmas, Albert James went to Ireland. Although he was American, his parents were from Ireland and regularly went back home to see their many relatives. James's parents had gone to Dublin and he wanted to spend the Christmas holidays with them there. I don't know if my dear friend Pablo Soler has told you this, but Albert James came from a well-off family and had famous soldiers among his ancestors. James's grandfather had served in Queen Victoria's court. At that time, some of the other members of his family had important positions in the British government, I think that a first cousin of his mother had a prominent position in the Foreign Office, and one of his father's uncles was in the Admiralty.

Albert James's departure made Amelia feel even more melancholy than usual, and on Christmas Day my parents, Danielle and André Dupont, invited Jean Deuville to have lunch with us to try to cheer her up a little.

They spoke, as was only natural, of Spain. Negrín still thought that it was possible to resist. But it was not; that was wishful thinking on his part. Also, England and France thought that the only important thing was for them to appease Hitler, and it was Hitler and Mussolini who were Franco's chief supporters outside of Spain.

On January 26, 1939, Barcelona fell into Franco's hands, but a massive exodus of refugees to France had begun a few days before. The French government tried to stop hundreds of thousands of Spanish refugees from crossing the border, but events overwhelmed them and they were forced to allow them entry.

The most reactionary parts of the right-wing press published truly xenophobic articles about the Spanish exiles; I'll let you see a few of them so that you can have an accurate idea of what was happening in France at that time.

Albert James decided to go to the border to report on the influx of exiles, and asked Amelia to come with him as his assistant.

"Four eyes see more than two, and you'll be able to help me with the language. I don't speak Spanish that well, and I can't understand it when they speak too fast."

Amelia accepted without hesitation. It was a chance to get close to Spain, and she even thought to herself that she might meet one of her relatives.

They arrived on January 28 and were met with a devastating spectacle. Women, children, the old, the sick, all were fleeing the Francoists. Desperate people, who were facing the abyss of exile without knowing if they would ever be able to return to their homeland.

The French authorities were overwhelmed and improvised refugee camps in the Pyrénées-Orientales department. The first of these was in Rieucros, near Mende (Lozère); then there were more, on the beaches of Argelès and Saint-Cyprien, in Arles-sur-Tech...

Albert James wrote one of the most heartfelt articles of his career; I still have some of the reports he published in the English press.

Those days, Amelia was his interpreter, and they interviewed dozens of refugees who told them clearly about the suffering they had been through and how the war was definitely lost.

On the night of February 5, just one day after Franco's troops took Gerona, the French government found itself once again in the position of having to allow a new wave of refugees to cross the border, this time troops who abandoned their arms as they entered France.

It was a miracle that in the middle of all this chaos Amelia was able to find Josep Soler and his son Pablo. She and Albert James were interviewing some refugees when she felt someone touch her on the shoulder. She turned round and saw Josep, holding Pablo's hand. It was a shock for Amelia to see them there.

"Good heavens, you're alive! I'm so happy! And Lola?"

"She didn't want to come, you know how she is. There wasn't any way to convince her to come," Josep explained.

"My mother says that she's not going to let the Fascists throw her out of Spain," Pablo said.

Amelia took them to one side. She was shocked by how thin Pablo had become, and how old Josep looked.

"The first thing we should do is eat something," she suggested.

"That will be difficult, the French are trying to stop us from splitting up," Josep said.

But Amelia was not prepared to leave Pablo and Josep to their fate. Money always works wonders, and there were class differences even among refugees. People who had money, or jewels, or valuable objects, or friends, had a chance to escape from the camps. Josep and Pablo had no money or valuable objects, but in Amelia they had found the best way of escaping from the chaos...

Victor Dupont served himself the last glass of wine.

"I think that's enough for today. Perhaps we should call our friend Pablo Soler to tell us what happened next, he was one of the protagonists of the story, after all."

"I'll do it as soon as I get back to Spain. It's been a big surprise for me to find out that Professor Soler saw Amelia once again."

"Yes, of course he did. He'll tell you about it. How about tomorrow?"

"Tomorrow?"

"Yes, he's getting into Paris quite early, so the three of us can meet up after lunch—if you have nothing better to do, that is."

Victor Dupont burst out laughing at my incredulous expression. He enjoyed having been able to surprise me.

"Pablo and Charlotte come to Paris every now and then, and they've had this trip arranged for a while."

"They didn't tell me anything..."

"I know, but they didn't have to, isn't that right?"

Whether it was right or not didn't matter, so I obediently accepted Victor Dupont's instructions and the next day met up with the pair of them at three in the afternoon. Well, the three of them, in fact, because Charlotte was there as well when I reached the Duponts' house.

"I won't get in your way, I'm going out shopping, so I'll leave you to it. I'll be back at seven, is that alright?" Charlotte said as she left.

"Alright, Guillermo, my friend Victor has got me up to speed about what he was telling you."

"I'm moving from surprise to surprise, professor," I said ironically.

"That's what research is all about," he replied, without giving any sign that he thought I was talking about him.

"So you saw my great-grandmother again..."

"I've told you already that I lived in Victor Dupont's house."

"That's right."

"And how do you think I got there?"

"I suppose that's what you're going to tell me."

"That's right," Professor Soler replied.

Amelia moved us into a room in the hotel where she was staying because she thought that she could convince the district officials that we were her relatives and that she could answer for us, but it was actually Albert James who found a way to overcome the French authorities' resistance. James was a very important journalist, and nobody wanted to be singled out for special treatment in any of his articles in the British or American press. Even so, we were not sure that we would be able to escape from the fate of being interned in one of the camps.

"I want you to tell me what's happening, if the war is really lost," Amelia asked Josep.

"Do you think I'd be here if it weren't? There is no point in fighting anymore, we've lost."

"But why?"

"They had more help."

"But we had the International Brigades, and Moscow," Amelia insisted.

"Don't be fooled, we were alone. Europe turned its back on us, France and Great Britain have looked at what was happening from a good safe distance, without wanting to get their hands dirty. And yes, people came from all over the world to support the Republic, they were brave and sacrificed themselves, but this was not enough. Franco had the help of Italy and Germany, but also the help provided by Europe's passivity. You can't imagine what it was like at the Ebro, that's where they really stuck the knife in. Thousands of us died, and thousands of them as well, but they won."

"He's a good strategist," Albert James said.

"Who? Franco?" Amelia seemed shocked by James's statement.

"You know what, Amelia? It is impossible to beat an enemy if you don't recognize his virtues."

"Virtues? How can you say that Franco has virtues? He's a traitor to the Republic, he has destroyed Spain," Amelia said angrily.

"But given the result of the war he's shown that he's a good military strategist. To admit that is not to stop him from being a Fascist and a disgrace to Spain. Will you calm down if I admit all that?"

"It's not about admitting it as if you were doing me a favor, it's about telling the truth."

"Well, let me tell you some more truths that you aren't going to like. Everything that Josep says is true, but there are other problems as well, in particular all the energy that the Republican side has wasted in infighting," Albert James said.

Josep bowed his head. It was as if he didn't want to hear what the journalist was saying.

"What do you mean?" Amelia said sharply.

"I mean that while the Fascist army had a single and clear enemy, the Republican side didn't. Am I wrong, Josep, if I say that the Communists wasted a lot of energy in fighting the POUM, and that the arguments between Socialists and Anarchists and Communists were continuous? Who killed Andreu Nin?"

"There have been problems, yes," Josep admitted.

"So, while Franco had a single, clear objective, to get rid of the Republic and establish a Fascist regime, the left-wingers were fighting him and fighting themselves at the same time. The worst aspects of people come out during a civil war, Amelia."

"You don't know my country. Franco is a traitor, as are all the rebels."

"Yes, Franco is a traitor, but that doesn't stop me from being right about what I've said," James replied.

"It wasn't just because of our differences of opinion that we lost the war," Josep insisted.

"Of course not, that would be a simplification as well as a lie. All I'm saying is that the people who defended the Republic wasted a lot of their energy, energy that was extremely necessary for them because they were faced with a foe who was fighting them alone, and which was also backed by Germany and Italy," Albert James replied.

"What's happening in Madrid?" Amelia asked worriedly.

"Madrid is resisting, and parts of La Mancha and Valencia are still in Republican hands, but I don't know for how much longer, I don't think they can resist much more," Josep replied.

"I know... I know it is unlikely for you to have any news, but have you heard anything about my family? Have you seen Edurne, or my cousin Laura?"

"No, Amelia, I don't know anything about them, we spent most of the war in Barcelona."

"And what are you thinking about doing now?" Albert James asked Josep.

"I don't know, just live for the time being. What do you think Franco will do with the Communists?"

Neither Albert James nor Amelia replied. Josep didn't need an answer; he knew better than anyone what fate awaited his comrades.

"I might join the Foreign Legion, they've told me that it's the only way to get out of one of those damned internment camps," Josep admitted.

"But what about Pablo? He's a child... he..." Amelia didn't take her eyes off me.

Josep shrugged.

"He should be with Lola, she's his mother, but things are how they are, we'll get by."

Amelia convinced Albert James to help me and Josep; she wanted to try to get the French to allow us to move to Paris and thereby avoid internment. It wasn't easy, because if there was one thing that the French officials wanted to avoid it was that the refugees would go to other parts of France, Paris in particular, but Amelia showed once again her talent for facing up to impossible situations. She had dealt with the Soviets in Moscow and had made them free Pierre, and now she wanted to rescue her friends.

The hotel where they were staying belonged to a married couple with two children, the oldest of whom worked delivering fruit and vegetables in a small truck. Amelia asked him to hide us among the boxes of vegetables and to take us to Paris. She would go with us in case there were any problem. Of course she offered him a considerable sum of money, everything she had managed to save. The young man hesitated for a bit, but eventually accepted the offer.

Albert James was unable to convince her that this was madness and that if we were stopped, even if her papers were in order, she would still be seen as a foreigner—a Spaniard, at that time the worst thing one could be in France—and might end up in a refugee camp.

But we were successful and got to Paris without problems. Amelia took us straight to the Duponts' house.

Danielle did not know what to do when she opened the door and found herself face to face with Amelia, holding a child by the hand and flanked by Albert James and a stranger. She invited the strange group into her house, even though she looked at them with a certain degree of apprehension.

When they arrived, the family was eating, and André Dupont and Victor's surprise was even greater, if such a thing were possible.

"Allow me to explain," Amelia said, trying to smooth the situation. "Josep is an old friend, a comrade, and this is his son,

Pablo. They've managed to escape from Spain. Franco won the war and I... I want to help them."

Albert James explained to André Dupont all the details of our journey from the south of France to Paris, and asked them to put us up until we could find somewhere to live. James himself promised to sort out our documentation that would allow us to stay in the French capital.

André Dupont said nothing. He didn't know what to reply, nor how to deal with the position in which Amelia and James had put him and his family. In the end he made up his mind.

"Alright, they can stay for a while, but it is not a good solution."

Amelia sighed with relief and Albert James, discreetly, made a sign to Danielle and gave her an envelope.

"It's to help look after Amelia's friends," he whispered.

"No... you needn't... ," she replied, a little upset.

"Of course I should, you can't take on something like this without any help," James said, considering the question settled.

Josep had to sleep on the sofa and Victor gave up a part of his room to that Spanish boy, an adolescent like himself, who had just burst in on the life of their family.

The days went by, and Josep carried on insisting that his only means of escape was to join the French Foreign Legion. The only problem he had was me, he didn't know what to do with me. On February 9, 1939, Franco passed the Law of Political Responsibilities, which was the first step in the long line of purges and persecutions to which the losers of the Civil War were subjected.

But a worse blow was the decision of the French and British governments to acknowledge the Franco government that had been installed in Burgos. At about this time, at the end of February, Albert James announced to Amelia that he had to travel to Mexico. He had been asking for an interview with Leon Trotsky for a while now, and the Russian politician had finally accepted. He was living in Mexico at that time, the last stop on a long journey of exile that had begun in Kazakhstan, and had passed through Turkey, France, and Norway before landing there.

I used to go with Amelia to James's office, and would sit in a corner quietly reading so as not to bother anyone. My father would go out early to look for work in order to keep us fed, and thanks to the help provided by some French comrades he got some odd jobs now and then. One day I was witness to an argument between Amelia and Albert James.

James was locked away in his office writing when he received the phone call that told him when Trotsky was willing to see him. It was in ten days' time, and he would have to reply immediately whether he was willing to go to Mexico. Of course, he didn't hesitate.

"Amelia, we're going to Mexico," he said as he came out of his office.

"To Mexico? And why should we go there?" Amelia asked.

"I've said that we're going, you and I. They've just called me and Trotsky has agreed to the interview. You have no idea the strings I had to pull to get this interview. We have to be there in ten days."

"But I can't go, and... well, I don't think I'll be very useful there."

"You're wrong, you'll be most useful of all in Mexico. You'll interpret for me, like you did when we went down to the Spanish border."

"But Trotsky can speak French..."

"Yes, but I don't speak Spanish, and in Mexico they speak Spanish. I'm not just going to speak with Trotsky; I'm also hoping to interview the people who have given him shelter as well as his enemies in the Communist Party."

They argued for a good long while. Amelia didn't want to leave Josep and me alone, but Albert James was inflexible and reminded her that travel was a part of the conditions of her job.

Amelia told Danielle that she would have to leave, and that she would be away for about a month. She knew that leaving us with the Duponts meant putting them into a difficult position, but she had no other option and she couldn't afford to lose her job with James. André Dupont didn't like the news at all, but in the end he accepted Amelia's proposal. When she returned, she said that she would find a solution for the problem, or rather, that she would take care of me, with all the consequences this implied, given that Josep was going to join the French Foreign Legion.

Professor Soler stopped talking suddenly, in a way that I must admit annoyed me a little.

"My dear Guillermo, you must go to Mexico, I don't know what happened there," he said, in the face of my surprise.

"But Professor, what does it matter? Tell me what happened when Amelia and James got back from Mexico. They must have just gone and done the interview and come back."

"Ah, but no! That's not what I'm going to do. The Garayoa sisters have employed you to carry out the investigation yourself, they want to know everything about Amelia's life in as much detail as possible, and I must say that historical research is not an easy task, sometimes it is unrewarding and hard."

"But..."

"No buts, Guillermo, you have to fill all the gaps. We don't really know what happened in Mexico, but trust me that the interview with Trotsky was important."

"Alright, I'll go, but why won't you tell me what happened when Amelia returned? Then, when I write it all out, I'll put things in the right order."

"No, no, you have to go step by step, listen to me. Doña Laura has asked me to guide you, and this is what I'm doing. In my opinion you have to go to Mexico."

I resigned myself to following his advice, although the journey seemed to me to be nothing but a waste of time. I didn't know how I could pick up Amelia's trail in the Aztec capital. But luck was on my side, because Pepe, the editor of my newspaper, called me to tell me he was sending me some books for immediate review.

"Hey, weren't you a Trotskyite?" I asked him.

"Yes, what's all this about?" he said in annoyance.

"Trotsky lived in Mexico, right?"

"Yes, that's where he got whacked."

"Do you think there are still Trotskyites in Mexico?"

"What's all this nonsense? Why do you care if there are still Trotskyites in Mexico?"

"I need you to get me in touch with a Mexican Trotskyite."

"You're crazy. I dropped all that nonsense twenty years ago."

"Yes, but you must be able to help me find someone who can help me. I'm looking for a Trotskyite in Mexico, not a Martian in the center of Madrid."

"Can you say why? I don't know what you're getting yourself into, but you're starting to annoy me..."

"I'm asking for your help, I didn't know it meant so much to you."

We argued for a while, but in the end I convinced him to give me a hand. While I was organizing my flight to Mexico City I waited impatiently for his call, which finally came.

"I've lost my whole afternoon looking for someone who knew someone in Mexico. I ended up talking to a friend of mine who worked for a while in the international relations department of the League office, and he gave me the number of a Mexican journalist who's as old as the hills. Call him, but don't get me caught up in your affairs anymore, I don't even know why I've bothered helping you."

"Because you may exploit the workers, but underneath it all you've got a heart of gold."

"Guillermo, don't tease me. I'm not in the mood!"

"It's because our dear leader exploits you, maybe a little bit less than he exploits me. At least he pays you better."

"Enough! Look, the sooner you send me the book reviews, the better."

I was lucky, because I rang the Mexican journalist and he said he would be more than happy to help me as soon as I got to his country.

He was hyperefficient, because when I rang him from the hotel to say that I'd arrived in Mexico he said that he had arranged a meeting for me.

"You can see Don Tomás tomorrow."

"Really? Great! Tell me... Who is Don Tomás?"

"A surprisingly interesting guy, he's very old, older even than me, he's going to be one hundred this year."

"A hundred?"

"Yes, one hundred, but don't worry, he's as sharp as a whip, still got all his marbles. He knew Trotsky, Diego Rivera, Frida..."

2

Tomás Jiménez was indeed a surprise. Although he was nearly one hundred years old, his eyes were still bright and he had an exceptional memory. He lived in Coyoacán with one of his sons and his daughter-in-law, who seemed to be almost as old as he was. He said that he had more than twenty grandchildren and a dozen great-grandchildren.

He had dedicated his life to painting, and had been friends with some of the group that had formed around Diego Rivera and Frida Kahlo, although he himself had never been part of the couple's intimate circle.

The house where Don Tomás lived was an old family home, large and with an interior patio that smelled of jasmine and enjoyed the shade of various fruit trees. I was extremely taken by Coyoacán, an oasis of beauty in the middle of the chaos of the Mexican capital.

Doña Raquel, Don Tomás's daughter-in-law, told me not to tire him out.

"My father-in-law is in good health, but he's not as active as he once was, so I'll leave it up to your good judgment," she warned me.

"So you're Doña Amelia Garayoa's great-grandson. A beautiful woman, yes indeed, a beautiful woman," Don Tomás said when he saw me.

"Did you know her?"

"Yes, we met by accident. She came to Mexico in March 1939 with a *gringo* journalist. I was a Trotskyite back then and tried to be up on everything that was happening around the leader."

"Did you work with Trotsky?"

"A little. He was scared. Stalin had tried to kill him several times and he trusted nobody. It was not difficult to get to see him, even though he had many supporters, myself included. You have to visit the Blue House."

"The Blue House?"

"Yes, that's where Trotsky and his wife Natalia lived. It was Frida Kahlo's house, and it's now a museum. When your great-grandmother and that journalist got to Mexico, things weren't going well between Trotsky and Diego Rivera and Frida. Diego was a genius with a genius's passionate temper. He acted on impulse and no sooner had he said that he was a committed Trotskyite was he arguing openly with Trotsky himself. They got cross with each other because Diego did not support Lázaro Cárdenas, for whom Trotsky had a lot to thank. Trotsky didn't trust Diego all that much, he admired him as an artist but didn't think much of his abilities as a politician. They got annoyed with each other and Trotsky and Natalia left the Blue House, but they stayed in Coyoacán, in a house which is now the Leon Trotsky Museum."

"How did you meet Amelia Garayoa?"

Don Tomás took his time in replying. He took out a cigar, lit it and breathed in the smoke, then continued with his narrative.

In March of 1939 some gallery owners invited me to participate in a collective exhibition. As you might imagine, this was a very important opportunity for me. Lots of my friends came to the opening, Trotskyite friends above all, and one of them was accompanied by Amelia Garayoa and the American journalist Albert James. Orlando, the guy who brought them, was a good friend of mine, a journalist and party activist; he was a member of Trotsky's inner circle and I think it was he who was the intermediary who helped James get his interview.

It was impossible not to notice your great-grandmother; she was gorgeous. She looked very fragile, almost ethereal; me and my buddies were immediately interested, even though us Mexicans don't really go for skinny women, but she was something special. I can also give you another reason why I haven't forgotten her, which was that she didn't hide her feeling that there was nothing special about my paintings. You can imagine that I was overwhelmed that day by congratulations and insincere flattery, but your great-grandmother had no hesitation at all in telling me the truth. My friend Orlando introduced us but neglected to say that I was the artist who had produced these paintings that everyone was praising so highly. Amelia seemed to frown and look at the paintings with indifference.

"Don't you like the paintings?" I asked.

"I think that the artist has good portrait technique, but he needs more soul; no, I don't think he's a genius."

We were all quiet and did not know what to say. Albert James looked at Amelia in annoyance, and good old Orlando was as lost for words as I was.

"Ah, women! Now they've got an opinion about everything. Look, kiddo, Tomás is one of the best, even if you don't know all that much about painting," my compadre said.

"I'm no expert, but you would agree that we're all capable of seeing when we're in front of a work of genius, a masterpiece. These pictures aren't bad, but they're also nothing special," Amelia said, without appearing to realize that she was talking to the artist.

I was annoyed by the Spaniard's comments, so I left the group and went to find people who would be more flattering. It was my day! And she had just ruined it.

I saw her three days later, at my friend Orlando's house; he had organized a dinner for us and said that Trotsky would be there. I wanted to be able to speak with Trotsky, but in the end he didn't come. I've said that he was obsessed with security, because Stalin had tried to kill him on several occasions, and of course, he finally succeeded.

Albert James was euphoric. He had managed to get his interview with Trotsky much sooner than he had hoped.

"I thought that they would keep me waiting for several days, but I arrived and got to do it straight away. He's a very interesting person, it's just a shame that he keeps on defending the excesses of the revolution," James said.

"Excesses? Do you think that it's possible to overthrow a regime without bloodshed? Tell me, how did the Americans free themselves from the British Crown? What did Lincoln have to do to get rid of slavery? My dear friend, history cannot move forward without blood being spilt," I said with conviction, cheered on by my friend Orlando. "There was no other option in Russia, no other way to get rid of the czars and their regime, or to get rid of the counterrevolutionaries, it would have been impossible for the workers to seize power."

"The problem is not the revolution, it's that Comrade Stalin doesn't want to share power with anyone. He's picking off all his old Bolshevik comrades from his side, one by one," Orlando added.

As well as being a foreigner, Amelia was the only one of us who knew anything about the Soviet Union, and, you know what? it wasn't until much later that I thought how reserved she'd been in her comments. For all that we asked her about what life had been like in Moscow, Amelia didn't offer any criticism or give us any clue about how things had really been. She described Moscow for us like a tourist guide, but told us little else.

I asked her what she thought of Trotsky, because she had been to the interview with Albert James.

"I think he is suffering a great deal. It can't be easy to be in exile and to know that at any moment someone might try to kill you. This makes him very cautious, unconfident; of course, he has reasons to be so. I was more impressed by his wife Natalia."

"Yes, well I didn't think that there was anything special about her," I replied, shocked that Trotsky's wife had drawn her attention.

"I suppose that at first sight Natalia doesn't seem a particularly special woman, but she is; she has followed her husband into exile, she looks after him, she comforts him, she protects him, she forgives him," Amelia said.

"Ah, so they've told you gossip about Trotsky!" Orlando exclaimed. "I don't think he's really a ladies' man, even though he's allowed to have a few adventures here and there, just like any other man."

"I think that living with a man like him in such circumstances is an act of heroism," Amelia said.

I know that they say that Trotsky and Frida Kahlo had an affair. It meant nothing for either of them because Frida was so deeply in love with Diego, and Trotsky needed Natalia. But women don't understand men and are very quick to judge them. Frida was a special woman, and Trotsky was under no obligation to resist a woman like that, don't you agree?

Amelia and Albert James stayed a few more days in Mexico. The journalist wanted to know more about Mexican politics, and even managed to interview Lázaro Cárdenas, the president, but he also made contact with groups of Spaniards who had arrived months earlier. I put them in touch with certain exiles, including my friend José María.

José María Olazaga was a Basque, and had escaped across the French border just before Franco's troops had beaten the Republicans and taken control of Asturias, Santander, and the Basque Country.

He arrived in Mexico with his wife and his son, as well as a young man who served as their secretary. They were Nationalists, from the PNV; they hadn't been important figures in the party, but they were significant.

I suggested to the American Albert James that they meet with José María, because he would be able to tell them how the Spanish exiles were organizing themselves in Mexico. James accepted immediately, and I went to the meeting with my friend who, like Trotsky, had moved into Coyoacán.

Today, Coyoacán is just one more suburb of the D.F., but back then it was a little village ten kilometers away from the center of the capital. My friend had set up a printing press and was doing well with it, it had become the place where all the exiles came to print their posters and propaganda.

José María was waiting for us expectantly; I had told him that the American journalist was traveling with a Spaniard. You can't imagine how shocked we were when Amelia, as soon as she entered my friend's house, let out a gigantic scream. It was a scream of surprise, of joy. José María was with his secretary, a kid named Aitor. Amelia and he knew each other; as they told us later, Aitor's sister had been Amelia's nurse.

"Good heavens! It's impossible!" Amelia cried.

They hugged each other and Amelia burst into tears, and even Aitor tried to hold his back.

"But what are you doing here? You were with your mother in the farm... ," Amelia said.

"I had to run away. I helped José María and his family cross the frontier. You remember that you made me show you the paths the shepherds used to cross the border into France? It was only thanks to a miracle that we escaped. Once we were in France I thought about going back, but..."

"But I told him not to," José María interrupted. "It was too dangerous. People knew that he worked with us and he was in danger. You know what was happening, the Falangists were going from village to village and there was always someone ready to denounce their neighbor. They were killing lots of people, don't think for a moment that all the casualties were at the front."

"And you, what are you doing in Mexico? Edurne told us that... Well, that you went to France... ," Aitor said, a little embarrassed.

"Yes, I suppose she told you everything."

Aitor lowered his head and murmured a "yes" that was almost inaudible. He seemed ashamed to know the things that he knew, and Amelia also seemed uncomfortable with knowing that he knew.

"My sister is still with your cousin Laura," Aitor explained. "I think that they're well, but I haven't heard from them for a long time."

"And your mother, and your grandparents?" Amelia asked.

"I know they're still on the farm. They were interrogated by the Guardia Civil, but then they were released. You know them, they never got mixed up in politics."

"And what was the last you heard about my family?"

"They're having a bad time of it. Your husband... well, your husband is with the Republicans, and as far as I know he was wounded and then got better and went back to the front; I don't know what's become of him now. Your father and your uncle also joined up and were mobilized, the women stayed in Madrid. My sister wanted to stay with your cousin Laura, so... You know that she was a Socialist, or a Communist..."

"Yes, I know. Do you know anything about my son?"

"The last thing that Edurne told me was that sometimes she takes Laura to see him when his nurse, I think she's called Águeda, takes him out for a walk. Your husband doesn't want to have any contact with your family, but this Águeda is a good woman and lets your parents and your uncle and aunt see Javier in secret. The child can talk now, and Águeda is scared that he'll say something to his father, so they've agreed that they will only see him from a distance, but they don't get any closer because they know that your husband would sack Águeda if he found out."

It was hard for Amelia to contain her tears. It was not hard to see that she felt humiliated. Her lower lip trembled and she wrung her hands.

"Are you going to go back to Spain?" Aitor asked.

"Going back? How? It's impossible, they might even have me on a list as a Communist, I don't know."

"Are you in the party?" José María asked.

"Well, I'm in the French Communist Party, they never issued me a card in Spain."

"In that case, you're not on anyone's list. They might let you back in," José María said.

I think that this was the moment when the possibility opened up in Amelia's mind.

"And you? Are you going to stay living in Mexico?"

Aitor said nothing, but José María spoke for him.

"I suppose we can trust you, so I'm going to speak openly. It's better that we stay here for the time being; also, from what we hear the French government isn't behaving well with Spanish nationals, and things aren't like that at all here. We think that we should try to help the people who are still there, even try to help people to leave who are stuck now that France has closed its borders. We were talking about this yesterday: Aitor knows the paths across the border, so even though he would be running a grave risk he might be the best person to be there. But we haven't yet decided anything. First we have to know what's going on, and if this damned war is finally over."

"The Fascists are winning," Amelia said.

We all looked at Albert James, waiting for him to corroborate what Amelia had said, and to tell us about the real situation.

"Amelia is right, the Republic has lost the war. It will be over in a matter of weeks," the journalist said.

"What do you think is going to happen?" José María asked.

"I don't know, but it's difficult to think that Franco will be generous toward those who fought for the Republic. The survivors on both sides will have to face up to a country that has been devastated, and will have to fight another battle, this time against hunger and poverty."

"And what about the European powers?" Aitor asked.

"They have never thought that the Spanish war was their problem. France and Great Britain have recognized the Burgos government; Germany and Italy are on Franco's side. No, don't deceive yourselves, Spain is alone, it has been alone all the way through the war and will continue to be alone now. Nobody thinks of Spain as a priority," James said.

"Maybe we should change our plans, and Aitor should go home as soon as possible. We have friends, we have our people on the other side of the border, in France. We won't have problems there, and maybe we'll be able to organize some kind of resistance, or help get people across the border... ," José María mused.

We were flabbergasted by the blunt report that Albert James had given us. José María and Aitor were no fools, but both had been unable to avoid maintaining a tiny modicum of hope that they could free Spain from Franco, and save themselves.

Over the next few days, Aitor and Amelia spent as much time together as they possibly could. José María was surprised to hear them talking in Basque. Nobody understood them, not even him. Back in those days Basque was a language that was spoken on farms, and not something that middle-class people spoke at all, in fact quite the opposite, which made it all the more strange that Amelia had learned it.

"I see you haven't forgotten it all," Aitor said.

"The truth is that I didn't know that I could still speak it, until I got the opportunity..."

"My mother said that you had a good ear for languages."

"Dear Amaya! Your mother was always so good and kind with me..."

Tomás Jiménez closed his eyes and I was worried, thinking that something might have happened to him. But soon he opened them again.

"Don't get worried, Guillermo, don't you worry, it's just that if I close my eyes then I remember things better and I can see Amelia and my friends once again. Aitor and José María gave Amelia lots of telephone numbers and addresses for members of the PNV who had been able to take refuge in France. Aitor told Amelia that if he went back then he would look for her. I suppose that he did because he left two months later. José María stayed in Mexico and never returned to Spain. Unfortunately he died before Franco."

Doña Raquel said goodbye and made me promise to come and see them again before I left Mexico.

I didn't keep my promise, I was so caught up in the life of my great-grandmother that all I could think of doing was writing her story and having someone tell me how it continued. I called Victor Dupont, to ask if Pablo Soler and Charlotte were still in the French capital. But he told me that they had gone back to Barcelona. It was clear that the next step in my story would come from the historian, so once again my destination was Spain.

"Why not come and have lunch with me tomorrow, and then we can talk all afternoon," Soler suggested when I called him.

I was on time for the meeting with the professor. I liked meeting with him, and he always gave me some surprising new revelation whenever I saw him. I told him about my trip to Mexico during the meal, and while we were waiting for dessert he told me what had happened when Albert James and Amelia had come back from Mexico...

We were pleased to have Amelia back with us. Danielle Dupont had grown accustomed to the "little Spaniard," and the house seemed empty without her. Monsieur Dupont said we had to celebrate as well. I think it was a relief for Josep to have her back, she was his guardian angel, his protector. Amelia wanted us to tell her everything that was happening in Spain.

"In Madrid, General Casado, with Julián Besteiro helping him, has taken control of the situation and has abolished Negrín's government. I think that Casado is negotiating with the government in Burgos to end the war, and that it'll all be over in a couple of days," Josep said in a faint little voice.

It wasn't even a couple of days. The very next day, March 28, 1939, the *nacionales* entered Madrid. For Josep and Amelia this was a hammerblow. Even though they expected the news, the truth is they weren't ready for it.

The worst was when Albert James came to the house on April 1 with a paper in his hand.

"I'm sorry, I've just got this, the last part of the war."

"Read it," Amelia asked.

"'Today, with the Red Army captive and disarmed, the National troops have attained their last military objectives. The war is over.' It's signed by General Francisco Franco."

Amelia burst into sobs and Josep could not hold back his tears either. Even Madame Dupont, Victor, and I were caught up. Only Albert James remained dry-eyed.

"I'm going to Spain," James said to Amelia. "I'm going to ask for the necessary permissions to travel to Madrid."

"I will go with you," Amelia said, drying her tears with the back of her hand.

"I don't think it would be very sensible, we don't know what might happen," Albert James said.

"If I don't go with you I will go alone, but I will go, I want to go to my house, and find out about my family. I have a son, I have parents, I have a husband... ," she said between sobs.

"I'll see what I can do."

Albert James left, promising to return later with more news, and my father left as well, to hunt down some of his comrades and share information.

We all ate supper at the Duponts' house that night, and we spoke until dawn was breaking.

Josep said he had no other option than to sign up to join the Foreign Legion; he did not want to go back to one of the refugee camps where thousands of Spaniards who had fled the war had ended up. He asked Amelia to take me to Spain so that I could try to find Lola.

"He'll be better off with his mother."

"But they might have arrested her, or maybe she's escaped too," Amelia argued.

"She would have found us. I know Lola, I know that she would have stayed to fight to the end. It's what she said to me. I've told you that I asked her to cross the frontier with us but that she refused. But the end is here and we have to do what's best for our son. Even if you don't find Lola, her mother can look after Pablo. She lives in Madrid, on the corner of the Plaza de la Paja. She's a good woman and she's never gotten mixed up in anything before, I don't think the Fascists will interfere with her. She'll look after Pablo." From his tone it was clear that Josep saw the decision as having already been made.

I said that I didn't want to leave my father and go to live with my grandmother, and Danielle, who was a kind woman, offered to look after me until the situation in Spain was clearer, but Josep was immoveable. He knew that there was no future for us at that point in France. The news that reached us about the internment camps was terrible, the French were overwhelmed by the avalanche of refugees. They put the old in the camp at Bram; the soldiers, especially the Catalans, went to Agde and Rivesaltes; Septfonds, Le Vernet, and Gurs were where the workers and intellectuals were held.

Albert James got permission to travel to Spain. It was dangerous because even though the war was over the Francoists were taking revenge on all who had fought on the Republican side. James was worried for Amelia, but she did not allow herself to be argued out of going. She told Danielle that if she was traveling with an American journalist then the Francoists wouldn't do anything, but even Albert James was not entirely safe.

Amelia, Albert James, and I traveled to the border by car. Albert drove what was a good car for the time, but the journey from Paris seemed eternal.

We arrived in Irún at eight o'clock in the morning on May 10. There were soldiers and policemen everywhere. Two members of the Guardia Civil's border patrol told us to get out of the car. Albert James could only mumble a few words of Spanish, so Amelia took control of the situation.

"Where are you going?" the officer asked.

"To Madrid."

"And what are you going to do there?" the officer asked while his colleague looked at our passports.

"Albert James is an American journalist, and he wants to write an article about Spain now that the war is over."

"Alright, that's him, but what about you?"

"I'm Señor James's assistant and interpreter. I've told you already that he's an American, you can see as much from his passport."

"And what about the kid? Why's he traveling with you?"

"Look, I'm a friend of his parents, and because I was living in Paris they sent him to stay with me so that he wouldn't be too affected by the war; now I'm taking him back to his family, who we hope are still alive."

"Are his parents on our side?" the officer wanted to know.

"They're excellent people, honorable and hard-working, and they've fought for Spain just like everyone else."

"And where's the paper that gives you custody over the child?" the officer asked.

"What, you think that during the war people were thinking about papers? It was enough for them to send him to Paris so that he wouldn't get shot."

The officers spoke among themselves for a good long while and in the end they must have reasoned that an American journalist, a young boy, and a woman couldn't be all that dangerous, for they let us pass.

Amelia, who had only recently taken up smoking, lit a cigarette as soon as we were back in the car.

"You're pretty good at evading direct questions," Albert James said.

"How do you know, if you don't speak Spanish?"

"Oh, I understand quite well enough, even though I don't speak so well. You've got quite some nerve! But I already saw that in Moscow."

It took us almost twelve hours to get to Madrid, not just because of the state of the roads, but because there were troops everywhere, moving from one place to another.

When we got to Madrid, Albert James took us to a hotel just off the Gran Vía, the Florida, which a friend had recommended. The Florida had been where the journalists who wrote about the war with the Republican forces had gathered. It had suffered during the war and was not in a very good state, so Albert James looked up another address, a pension where a friend of his, an American photographer, had lived out much of the conflict.

The owner was a short little woman, so thin that she appeared malnourished. I remember that she met us with gratitude.

"I don't have a single guest, so you can choose your room. I can't guarantee you that there'll be food, because there's nothing in the market, unless I go looking through unofficial channels. Oh, by the way, my name is Rosario."

The rooms were clean, and their balconies let onto the Gran Vía itself.

Once Albert James had explained that we had come on a recommendation from another American journalist, Doña Rosario seemed to look at us with more sympathy.

"You have to be careful who you let come into your house, and what you say, because you can end up in prison now just for saying nothing, the slightest thing."

Doña Rosario told us that her husband had been a civil servant in the Finance Ministry, and they had had all they needed right up until the war broke out.

"We lived well, you can see for yourselves how nice this apartment is, but my husband joined the ranks and they killed him at the front, on the Guadarrama sierra. And you should see for yourselves, I had to live somehow during the war, so I took in lodgers. One of my cousins told me about this, she was putting up foreign journalists in two of her rooms and she sent me some clients, and thanks to that I survived the war."

"Were you on the side of the Republic?" Amelia asked.

"Ah, who cares? We have to live with what we've got and there's no point saying anything. You know that Franco passed the Law of Political Responsibilities even before the war ended, and now he's putting lots of people in prison; they're taking everyone they even suspect was on the other side. No one gets away."

It was about ten o'clock when Amelia said that she was going to her parents' house.

"I can't wait for tomorrow, I won't be able to sleep."

"But you can't go out at this hour of the night," Albert advised. "We still don't know how things are; they could arrest you. It's better for us to wait."

It was hard to convince her, but he managed in the end. Amelia didn't sleep at all that night, and woke us at dawn.

Albert James said that the first thing they should do was to get him registered as a journalist with the Francoist authorities. James wanted to know the kind of ground he was treading on, although he had no intention at all of having his work censored by the Francoist authorities. He wanted to see things and hear them, and then write about Spain after the war.

He suggested that Amelia should come with him as he didn't speak very good Spanish, and that then he would go to her parents' house and then try to find Lola, but she resisted, was nervous and wanted to find out about her family as soon as possible. In the end he gave in and they agreed that I would go with her to her parents' house while he went to get himself organized so that he could start reporting.

I can still remember the impression that Madrid made on me back then. You could feel the misery and the desperation, as well as the euphoria of the victors.

We walked down Gran Vía toward Cibeles and then up to Salamanca, where Amelia's parents lived, as did her aunt and uncle.

I remember how she trembled as she rang the doorbell to her parents' apartment, but no one answered her impatient ringing.

We walked down the stairs to look for the doorman, whom we hadn't seen when we came in, but who was there in his little room.

"Señorita Amelia! Good heavens, what a surprise!" The man looked at her open-mouthed.

"Hello, Antonio, how are you? And your wife and children?"

"Well, well, all well. We've survived and that's good enough for us."

"Is there nobody in my house?"

The doorman was nervous and wrung his hands before he answered.

"Don't you know?"

"Know? Know what?"

"Well, some things happened to your family," the doorman replied uncomfortably.

Amelia blushed, humiliated to have to beg for news about her own family.

"Explain yourself, Antonio."

"Look, the best thing is to go to your uncle Don Armando's house, and they'll explain it all there."

"Where are my parents?" Amelia insisted.

"They've gone, Señorita Amelia, they've gone. Your father... well, I'm not entirely sure, and your mother... I'm sorry, but Doña Teresa died. They buried her a few months ago."

Amelia's shriek was heartrending. She bent double and I thought she was going to fall over. The doorman and I held her up. She hung there inert, trembling, and even though it wasn't cold at all, her teeth were chattering.

"Can't you see why I didn't want to tell you? It's better to hear about these things from the family... ," the doorman said, upset by Amelia's state.

"And my sister, where is she?"

"Señorita Antonietta went to be with her uncle and aunt, I suppose she must be with them. She wasn't well."

The man led us through to his room and offered Amelia a glass of water, although she seemed incapable of pulling herself together. She was so cold, so pale, she seemed so helpless...

We walked to her uncle and aunt's house, a few blocks away. Amelia, who was still crying, led me by the hand, and I can still remember how strong her grip was.

We hurried up the stairs. Amelia was desperate to know what had happened to her relatives. This time they opened the door at the first ring and we found ourselves face to face with Edurne, the daughter of Amaya, the woman who had looked after the Garayoa children from their earliest infancy. Edurne had been Amelia's maid, her confidante and friend, and because of Lola's influence had joined the Communist Party.

The meeting of the two women was a powerfully emotional one. Amelia hugged Edurne, and Edurne, seeing her old friend, burst into tears.

"Amelia! What joy! What joy! Thank goodness you're back!"

Amelia and Edurne's voices alerted Doña Elena, who came immediately into the hall. Amelia's aunt almost fainted to see her niece.

"Amelia! But... you're here! Good Lord! Good Lord! Laura, Antonietta, Jesús, come here!"

Doña Elena took Amelia by the hand and led her into the salon. I followed them in a state of shock, I felt like an intruder.

Antonietta came into the room followed by her cousins Laura and Jesús. Amelia tried to hug her sister but Antonietta did not let her.

"No, don't kiss me, I'm ill, I've had tuberculosis and I'm not yet better."

Amelia looked at her sister in horror, suddenly realizing the terrible state her sister was in.

She was extremely thin. Her face was incredibly pale, and her eyes stood out of it, huge and bright. But Amelia being Amelia, it would take more than tuberculosis to stop her from hugging her sister. There was no separating them for a long time, she kissed Antonietta and stroked her hair without ever stopping crying. Laura came to her cousins' side and hugged them both.

"How you've grown, Jesús! And you're still as serious as ever," Amelia said to her cousin, who was the same age as me, more or less, and who seemed very shy.

"He's also been very ill. He has anemia. We've been so hungry! And we still are," Doña Elena said.

"And Papa, where is Papa?" Amelia asked in a very low voice.

"They shot your father a week ago," Doña Elena murmured, "and your mother, my poor sister-in-law... I'm sorry, Amelia, but your mother died of tuberculosis before the war ended. Thanks be to God, Antonietta looks like she is getting better, even though she is still very weak."

Amelia had an attack of hysteria. She started to shout that all the Nationalists were bloody fascists and that Franco would be damned, and that she herself would take revenge for her father. Her cousin Laura and Antonietta begged her to calm down.

"For God's sake, if they hear you they'll shoot you too!" Doña Elena said in anguish, imploring that she lower her voice.

"But why? Why? My father was the best man in the whole world!"

"We lost the war," Antonietta said, in tears.

"We tried to do everything possible to get him a pardon," Laura explained, 'but it was useless. You can't know how many letters we wrote asking for mercy; we asked our Nationalist friends for help, but even they couldn't do anything."

Then Amelia collapsed, she threw herself to the floor and, sitting there, she held her knees up against her chest and cried even harder. This time it was Laura and Jesús who pulled her upright and helped her across to a sofa. Doña Elena dried her tears with a handkerchief and I held Edurne's hand, because I felt lost in this drama that seemed to have no end, now that Laura was explaining to her sister that grandmother Margot had also died.

"Grandmother had a weak heart, but I think she died of sorrow. Her maid Yvonne told us that she died in her sleep, that they found her dead in bed."

When Amelia seemed to be more in control of herself, Doña Elena explained to her what had happened.

"We had it very bad, with no food and hardly any medicine... Antonietta fell ill and your mother looked after her night and day and fell ill herself. Your mother suffered from anemia, she was very weak, and whenever there was food she gave it to Antonietta. She never complained, she stayed firm right to the end. She also had to cope with your father's imprisonment, which was the worst. She went to take him something every day but she wasn't always allowed to see him."

"But why did they put him in prison?" Amelia asked, her voice hoarse.

"Someone denounced him, we don't know who. Your father was at the front, just like your Uncle Armando, and they were both wounded and went back to Madrid," Doña Elena explained.

"My father is in prison," Laura added.

"In prison? Why?" Amelia seemed to be getting worked up once again.

"For the same as your father, because someone denounced him for being a red," Laura explained.

"My father was never a red, and neither was my uncle, they were with the Republican Left," Amelia said, knowing as she did so that this was an obvious point to everyone.

"It doesn't matter, it doesn't matter anymore, the only thing that counts for Franco is which side you were on," Laura said.

"They're murderers," Amelia said.

"Murderers? Yes, there are lots of murderers in this country, not just among the Nationalists, no, the other side killed lots of innocents as well," Doña Elena said as she looked around for another handkerchief.

Amelia said nothing, and waited without understanding what her aunt had just said.

"I am a monarchist, like my whole family, like your poor mother was. Do you want to know how my older brother died? I'll tell you: You know that Luis was lame and that they didn't call him up. One day a group of militia came to the village, asked where the Fascists were, and had my brother's house signaled out to them. Luis was never a Fascist; he was a right-winger and a monarchist, but never a Fascist. They didn't care, they went to his house and killed him in front of his wife and his son, they took him and shot him in a ditch. His son Amancio heard the shot and ran out of the house and found his father with a bullet in his head. You know what the leader of this group said to my nephew? That this was the fate that was waiting for all Nationalists, and that he should take care. Yes, they said that to a kid of twelve."

Doña Elena sighed and drank a sip of water from the glass that Edurne had brought.

"But I'll tell you more, Amelia, because I'm sure you remember my cousin Remedios, the nun. When you were young we took you to see her one day in the convent, near Toledo. Do you think that my cousin has ever hurt anyone? She had been in the convent from the age of eighteen... One night a group of militiamen, irregulars, came to the convent and raped the twelve nuns that were there and then killed them. Why did they do this? I'll tell you: because they were nuns, just for that."

"I can't believe it," Amelia said.

"It's true, what my mother says is true," Laura said.

"I can tell you more, people who were closer to you, your Aunt Montse for example, your mother's sister."

Amelia jerked upright and went tense. Aunt Montse was her mother's only sister, and Antonietta and she both loved her very much. She had never married and she regularly come to visit them in Madrid. Antonietta and Amelia liked her visits because she spoiled them and let them do more than their parents would.

"Montse went to Palamos, to take shelter in her friends' country house. She thought that at least she wouldn't be hungry in the country. You don't know this, Amelia, but we have been so hungry here, so needy. Your Catalan family suffered because they weren't Communists or Socialists or Anarchists or supporters of Companys... Oh, poor them, to be on the Right! Yes, right-wingers, but good people, hardworking and honest. But the people who shot them didn't care. You can guess what happened by now, militiamen turned up in the village and asked their 'comrades' if there were any Nationalists around. And someone pointed out to them the country house where your mother's cousins and Montse were living. They killed them all there, the old married couple, their three children and your Aunt Montse, who had gone there for safety. Tell me, Amelia, was that a murder?"

"Mother, don't speak like that!" Laura said, aghast at her mother's harsh tone.

"I just want you to know that lots of people have been killed here, that the Nationalists have killed the reds and the reds have killed the Nationalists, and not just at the front, but far away from any actual battle. Whom should I hate, Amelia? Tell me. The Nationalists have got my husband, my brother was killed by the reds, whom should I hate more? You know what? I hate them all," Doña Elena said.

"Where is Uncle Armando?" Amelia asked, affected by having heard so much.

"In Ocaña prison. He has been condemned to death just like your father was and we have asked for his sentence to be quashed, we've sent all kinds of begging letters to Franco. If it were necessary, I would go down on my knees and beg for my husband's life; if that's what they want then I'll do it."

"Mother, calm down!" Jesús said, grasping his mother's hand.

"I'm sorry, I'm sorry, I..."

"You went off and now you have no idea about what has happened here. I don't know if you've been happy or wretched, but I assure you that whatever you've lived through, it has been no worse than what we have lived through here."

Amelia bent her head, ashamed at her aunt's reproaches. It was not hard to guess that she felt guilty for having lived in the safety of Buenos Aires, where only echoes of the war reached them.

"And my son? Do you know anything about Javier?" she asked, looking at Laura because she could not bear her aunt's inquisitive stare.

"Javier is well. Águeda looks after him and loves him a great deal. Now he is living with his grandparents Don Manuel and Doña Blanca. They... well, you know that they were always more to the right, and now they're in no danger, but Santiago..."

It seemed that Laura dare not continue. She knew that her cousin was at the very limit of her resources, that she could not bear to carry on receiving bad news, and to tell her that Santiago was in prison as well would be another harsh blow for her.

"Santiago is a prisoner as well," Laura said, finally.

"You see, the country has gone mad. Santiago's political ideas, your husband's political ideas, were like your father's and my Armando's, he was never a radical, never a Communist, but that hasn't stopped them throwing him in prison," Aunt Elena added.

"Is he in Ocaña as well?" Amelia asked, having gone even paler.

"Yes, that's where he is," Laura replied.

"And his parents can't do anything for him? They've got friends... ," Amelia inquired.

"You think they're not moving heaven and earth for Santiago? Of course they are. They took Don Manuel to a secret police headquarters and it was only by some miracle that he got out alive. I think they tortured him. His wife, Doña Blanca, managed to get a message to Santiago to say that his father was taken prisoner. Santiago at that moment was at the front with the rank of major, much appreciated by his superiors, who pulled strings to get Don Manuel out of prison. Don't you think it was easy. But you see how things were: the son at the front fighting for the Republic and the father arrested at home by those who said they were defending it. We don't know anything directly, but Águeda has been telling us what happened," Aunt Elena explained.

"Your son is beautiful, and very friendly. We convinced Águeda to let us see him when she takes him out into the street; she used to take him round by your parents' house, so that they could pretend to bump into her and see the child. But now that he's older and can talk the hind leg off a donkey, we only see him from a distance. Águeda is scared that Javier will tell his grandparents that he sees other people. And we don't want to get her into trouble. Javier is very attached to her," Laura explained.

"I want to see him, can you help me?" Amelia begged.

"I'll send Edurne to wait near your in-laws' house, and when she sees Águeda coming out she can ask when you can see your son," Laura suggested.

It was lunchtime when Doña Elena said that the conversation should come to an end. I had been very quiet the whole time, sitting next to Edurne and not daring to make a sound. Even though I was only an adolescent I could see Amelia's immense suffering.

We ate potatoes with a tiny scrap of bacon. Amelia didn't try even a mouthful, and Elena had to force Antonietta to eat.

"Come on, you have to eat, you won't get better if you don't."

Amelia explained that she was working with an American journalist and that they had got across the border without many problems thanks to him. She also told them that she was looking for Lola to leave me with her.

"That woman was the source of all your problems," Aunt Elena said. 'If you had never met her you would never have got your head filled with all those revolutionary ideas and you would never have left."

"No, Aunt, it's not Lola's fault; I am the only person responsible for my actions. I know that I did bad, I was selfish, I did whatever I wanted without thinking about my family or the consequences of my actions. Lola didn't make me do what I did, it was me."

"That woman stirred up devils in your head, she's envious, bitter, she always hated you, or do you think that she felt any sympathy for you, who represented everything that she was fighting against?" Doña Elena insisted.

"I don't blame her for that," Amelia replied.

Laura looked at me and begged her mother to change the subject. Elena bridled, but obeyed.

"I haven't asked about cousin Melita, where is she?"

"Your cousin has gotten married. You weren't here, and that's why you don't know."

"Whom did she marry?"

"Rodrigo, do you remember him? He's a good kid, he ended up on the Nationalist side."

"When did they get married?"

"Just after the war started. They went to live in Burgos, which is where he comes from. He has some land and a chemist's shop. It'll all go well for them."

"And what did you say my cousin's husband was named?"

"Rodrigo Losada."

"Do they have children?"

"Yes, a daughter."

"They haven't named her Amelia, I suppose..."

"She's named Isabel, like her husband's mother. We haven't met her yet, she's a year old," Laura explained.

"Well, what are you going to do now?" Doña Elena asked.

"I don't know, it's so horrible, everything that's happened... I couldn't have thought that my parents might be dead, or that any of what you've told me might have happened."

"We've been through a war," Doña Elena said, tartly.

"I know, and I understand how you feel. Don't think that I don't feel guilty for not being here and going through all this suffering with you. I will never forgive myself for my mother being dead and for not having done anything to stop my father from being shot. I will look after Antonietta, we'll go and live in my house, I suppose it is still ours?"

"You think that you can take responsibility for your sister? Well, I don't. Antonietta needs help, full-time care that I don't think you will be able to give her." Doña Elena was hard as iron.

"I will work to help my sister, which is what my parents would have wanted."

"No, Amelia, your mother made me swear that I would look after Antonietta and that she would live here with us. I swore it to her the day she died. I asked her what we should do if you ever did come back, and she said that even if you did so then Antonietta should stay with us, to have a family that would look after her."

Amelia got up from the table in tears. She couldn't bear her aunt's judgments, which were like knives against her skin. Laura and Antonietta went with her, and I stayed behind, very quiet, without daring to lift my eyes off my plate. I was scared that at any moment Doña Elena would start on me. When they came back, Amelia was still crying.

"Aunt, I'm grateful for everything you've done for us. I can understand that my mother wouldn't have put all her trust in me, and would have been worried about Antonietta, so she should stay here until I can prove to you that I am capable of looking after my sister."

Doña Elena said nothing. She was thoughtful because she realized that she had hurt Amelia. She loved her niece, but the war had stripped her of that veil of sweetness that had previously covered her.

"Mama, Amelia needs your support, she's got a lot of trouble of her own at the moment," Laura said.

"I am sorry, I should have spoken to you differently. You've lost your parents and are upset, and I... I am very sorry, Amelia. You know that we love you and that you can rely on us for anything you need..."

"I know, I do know," Amelia replied through her tears.

"We'll go and visit your Uncle Armando tomorrow," Antonietta said, trying to change the subject.

"To the prison?" Amelia asked.

"Yes, to the prison, and I will go too. I haven't gone out yet at all because I haven't been well, but Aunt Elena says that she'll allow me to go out tomorrow. You could come too... ," Antonietta suggested.

"Of course I'll come!"

Doña Elena asked what Amelia's plans were. She wanted to know if she was going to stay in Madrid and if so, where, and then, generous as always, she offered her a bedroom. Amelia said that as she was working for an American journalist who didn't speak Spanish very well, he probably wouldn't be too happy to be left alone in the pension. Laura had the idea that Albert James should stay in the house as well.

"We can rent him a room. Instead of paying the pension he can pay us. We need the money, now that we need to do whatever we can to keep body and soul together," Laura suggested.

Doña Elena seemed to be mulling over her daughter's proposal. She was of course uncomfortable not to be able simply to invite the journalist to stay in her house, as she would have done before the war, but necessity and previous troubles had turned her into a practical woman.

"He could sleep in Melita's room, which we've had shut up since she got married... And the boy can sleep in the maid's room, we don't really have servants anymore, only Edurne. I would put him in with Jesús, but the boy is still ill and needs his rest. Yes, we've got more than enough space to fit you all in," Doña Elena accepted.

Amelia promised to suggest this to Albert James. It was a relief for her to be with her family, especially at such a time, when misery was feeding on them all.

Laura took us to Rosario's pension to help with our luggage. We met Albert James at the door and he was quite angry.

"I've been waiting for you since midday!" he said as soon as he saw us.

"I'm sorry... So much has happened in these few hours."

Amelia told him, through her tears, what had happened: her parents' deaths, her sister's illness, the misery that was feeding on them all. He seemed to be calmed by this news, but was not happy to hear about the move to Doña Elena's house.

"Look, it's normal that you want to be with your family, but I need to have a certain amount of independence, and I'll be fine here, or else I can go to a hotel. Given how bad the Florida is, I could go to the Ritz."

It was Laura who overcame the shame she felt to explain to James that it would be a great help for them to rent the room, and that he would not be disturbed and could feel himself just as independent as he did in Doña Rosario's house.

He hesitated, but in the end he allowed himself to be convinced by Laura's arguments. It was not difficult to see that even previously well-off families were now having difficulties in keeping themselves.

So we went with our suitcases in our hands once again to Amelia's aunt's house.

It was already late when we arrived there and unpacked, but Albert James suggested that he and Amelia should go to Lola's house in order to leave me with her.

I was keen to see my mother. Lola was a strong and determined woman, so I was sure that nothing could happen to me if I were with her. I wanted to stay in Spain, not to return to France where my father and I, despite everything, or rather with Amelia's help, had managed to survive with our dignity intact.

We walked to Lola's house, but once we got there no one could tell us anything. She had not returned there since the beginning of the war when we went to Barcelona, so Amelia suggested that we go to the address Josep had given us in the Plaza de la Paja, where my grandmother, Lola's mother lived. I started to shudder, I dared not say anything, but I preferred to live with Amelia rather than my grandmother. Dolores, which was my grandmother's name as well as my mother's, did not get on well with my mother and I remember that they always had political arguments whenever we went to visit her.

It wasn't hard to find my grandmother's house. We rang the bell but no one answered and it was the neighbor who eventually gave us news.

"They've taken Dolores to the hospital. She suffers from asthma and she had such a bad attack that she nearly choked. She's very ill, and so poor..."

Amelia asked if she knew anything about Lola, but the neighbor insisted that she hadn't seen her since before the war.

"Lola never cared very much about her mother, she cared more for the revolution, and all we know about Dolores's nephew, Pepe, is that he was killed by the Communists for being in the POUM," she said, looking from side to side in case someone was listening.

We went to the hospital, where a nun took us to the room where Dolores was staying. I hardly remembered her, and I was affected to see that this vague, white-haired old lady was my grandmother.

The poor woman didn't recognize me and she burst into tears when Amelia told her who I was.

"You're my Lola's young lady friend! And this is my grandson? How tall he is! Where's your mother? I haven't heard from her in months, I hope they haven't shot her; the Nationalists are shooting everybody. Of course, the revolutionaries are keeping their end up too. I said to Lola: I can't forgive them for killing my only nephew, Pepe, just for being in the POUM. And what's all this about, revolutionaries killing revolutionaries, who ever heard of such a thing? Lola hated the POUM, said they were traitors."

The dear old lady promised to look after me as soon as she left the hospital.

"I'm old and sick, but I'll do what I have to for my grandson."

Doña Elena seemed to be resigned to my staying with them until my grandmother left the hospital, especially when Albert James told her that he would pay for my upkeep while I was in their house.

The next morning, Albert James went with Doña Elena, Laura, Amelia, and Jesús to the prison to see Don Armando.

James wanted to see a Spanish prison up close, and hoped that the authorities wouldn't object too much.

He had to bribe a couple of officers to let all of us go into the long corridor where family members and prisoners were allowed to see each other for a few minutes at a time, separated by bars. Don Armando grew very emotional when he saw Amelia. Uncle and niece could not hold back their tears as they thought of the deaths of Amelia's father, Don Juan, and her mother, Doña Teresa.

"Oh, Uncle, it's so horrible! Father, mother, grandmother Margot, Aunt Lily... and so many family members we've lost. I don't know how I am going to bear it," Amelia said through her tears.

"We will come through, your father was strong right up until the last moment, and when they took him away he told me to kiss you all from him and to tell you all how much he loved Antonietta and you."

"Do you think he forgave me?"

"Of course he did, your father loved you a great deal and although he never understood why you acted as you did, he forgave you. He was saddest of all that you had left your child, this was always something that hurt him. He was so sad not to be able to see his only grandson..."

Don Armando told them about the confusion and uncertainty that all the prisoners felt.

"They take people away to shoot them every day... And sometimes you lose hope that your pardon will come. How many letters have you written asking for clemency?"

"Papa, we will never surrender," Laura replied.

"No, we will never surrender even when we are dead," Don Armando sighed.

"We will go see the Herreras tomorrow. Pedro Herrera is your friend, you were his lawyer and you won an important case for him, don't you remember? Now he's an influential man, close to Franco, he has a nephew who is colonel in the army and a brother-in-law who is high up in the Falange. And things are going well for him, too, he's already doing business with the new government. I went to his house and spoke to his wife, Marita, and she promised to talk to her husband. She has fulfilled her promise, because she has been in touch to tell me that we can go round to see them after eight o'clock tomorrow evening, which is when her husband comes home from work. We will get something out of this," Doña Elena said.

Upset when she left the prison, Amelia went with Albert James to the interviews he had arranged for his reports. They did not come back to Doña Elena's house until the evening. Edurne had granted me the protection I usually required from Amelia. Edurne cheered me up by telling me that my mother was a brave woman whom I should never forget. I also got on well with Jesús, we were more or less the same age, and although he was shy and tried not to be noticed, I soon found out that he had a good sense of humor.

Two days after moving into Doña Elena's house, Edurne came home very flustered.

"Águeda has told me that we should go to the main entrance to the Retiro at about five o'clock this afternoon, and that she will be walking there with Javier. She has also told me that they are going to release Santiago, that it's only a matter of days. She heard someone telling Don Manuel, who it seems has friends in high places, close to Franco."

Amelia cried to know that she was going to see her son. Doña Elena decided that Laura, Antonietta, Edurne, Jesús, and I should go with her. She was afraid of what Amelia would do when she saw the child.

At five o'clock on the dot we were at the Retiro. We waited impatiently until we saw Águeda coming along, holding Javier by the hand, about half an hour later.

Laura tried to hold Amelia back, but she broke free and ran to the child and burst into tears, hugging him and kissing him so much that he too started to cry.

"Please leave him!" Águeda begged, worried that someone she knew would see the scene, and especially worried that Javier would tell his grandparents about being kissed and hugged by a strange woman who made him cry.

But Amelia would not listen, she hugged Javier tight and covered him with kisses.

"My child! My child! How beautiful you are! Do you remember your mother? No, poor thing, how could you remember... But I love you so, my son..."

With Antonietta's help, Laura took Javier out of Amelia's arms and gave him back to Águeda.

"Ah, what will happen if Don Manuel and Doña Blanca find out!" Águeda fretted.

"But I'm his mother! They can't deny me my son," Amelia replied through her tears.

Javier was scared and wouldn't stop crying.

"It's best if you go. You'll see him another day, but now I need to take him for a walk to calm him down," Águeda added, frankly scared by now.

Laura and Antonietta managed between them to get Amelia away from Águeda and from the child, who set off running up the street in fear.

Amelia would not stop crying and did not listen to what her sister and her cousin had to say to her. Edurne, Jesús, and I said nothing, unsure about what we could do or say.

When we got back to Doña Elena's house, Antonietta made her sister take a strong cup of tilleul, but this didn't calm her down, she was in such a state. Albert James was the only one who could make her react. He treated her with a certain amount of distance, telling her that they were in Madrid to work and could not allow themselves to be affected by circumstances. I thought at the time that he was a hard and heartless man, but I realize now that his apparent rudeness awoke in Amelia the fear of ending up unemployed, and this was something she could not let happen, not for herself, nor for Antonietta, nor for the rest of her family.

One example of Albert James's businesslike treatment of Amelia was his insistence on attending the parade that Franco had organized for May 19, in spite of Amelia's protests.

"I am here to work, and so are you," he reminded her.

Amelia said nothing, aware of the importance that the money she earned as the journalist's secretary and interpreter had, for her and for us all.

We all went to the parade on May 19. Doña Elena decided that this would be the case, fearful that otherwise a neighbor might denounce her for not showing sufficient respect to the Caudillo, as Franco was by then called. We went, but grudgingly; even though I was only an adolescent I hated Franco with all my might for leaving me alone in the world, and so I protested, as did Amelia and Laura and Edurne, until Doña Elena, with Albert James's support, told us to shut up.

The Paseo de Recoletos, where the parade was due to pass, was not far from our house, so we were there early enough to get a space.

We could see Franco at a distance and Amelia muttered that he was a "dwarf," which made Doña Elena pinch her arm to get her to be quiet.

On that day Franco was presented with the Laureate Cross of San Fernando, the highest military honor, and the only one he had not yet received.

Albert James watched everything with interest and asked Amelia to translate the comments of the people around us. James was surprised by the enthusiasm of the spectators. Later he asked us how it was possible for there to be so much support for Franco from a city that had been one of the last to fall to his troops. Doña Elena explained.

"They're scared, of course they're scared, what do you want them to do? The war has been lost, although I don't really know if it's been lost or won. Nobody knows what it means, just imagine who might try to criticize Franco now. I don't know if they've explained all this to you, but the Law of Political Responsibilities is designed to punish everyone who has had anything to do with the reds, and you can imagine that there are lots of people whose families fall across the divide."

Amelia was deeply affected. She had been so moved to see her son that she didn't stop pestering Doña Elena until she got her to send Edurne to fix up another meeting with Águeda. Doña Elena agreed reluctantly, but sent Edurne out at the time that she knew Águeda would be going out to go shopping.

Edurne came back with good news. She had not had to wait long for Edurne to leave the house and had followed her at a discreet distance until they were far enough away to have little risk of being seen by anyone they knew. Águeda said that Santiago had been set free the day before and that he was thinner and had aged, but was safe and free. Javier would not leave his father, and had slept in his bed that night.

Santiago had decided to leave his parents' house and to go back to his own place. This was the good news, the bad news was that Águeda didn't dare organize another meeting with Amelia for fear that Javier would tell his father. It was not that Javier would be able to explain who this woman was who had seized and embraced him, but Santiago would be able to guess and Águeda was scared of his reaction. The most that she offered was that Amelia should see them from a distance, promising not to come too close.

These conditions seemed humiliating to Amelia, and she made a decision that scared us all.

"I will go see Santiago. I will ask for his forgiveness, even though I know that he'll never be able to forgive me, and I will ask if he will let me see my son."

Doña Elena tried to dissuade her: She was afraid of what Santiago's reaction might be. Albert James also advised her to think a little before acting, but Amelia had her mind made up and she agreed only to have someone accompany her to Santiago's house, although previously she had said she would go alone.

3

I think Amelia went to Santiago's house on the evening of May 22 or 23. Águeda trembled when she opened the door and saw the three Garayoa women.

"I would like to see Don Santiago," Amelia said in a faint little voice.

Águeda left them in the hall and ran off to find the master. Javier came in and stayed looking at the three women in surprise. Amelia tried to pick him up but he ran away, she followed after him and ran straight into Santiago.

"What are you doing here?" he said in a rage.

"I have come to see you, I need to talk with you... ," Amelia babbled.

"Out of my house! You and I have nothing to say to one another. How dare you come here? Is there nothing you respect? Get out and never come back!"

Amelia was shaking. She tried to keep back her tears, aware that Javier was watching her.

"I beg you to listen to me. I know that I don't deserve your forgiveness, but at least let me see my son."

"Your son? You have no son. Get out."

"Please, Santiago! I'm begging you! Let me see my child!"

Santiago took her arm and pushed her toward the hall, where Antonietta and Laura were waiting very nervously, having heard this conversation.

"Aha! So, you've brought company! Well, I don't care, you are not welcome in this house."

"Don't take my child away from me!" Amelia begged through her tears.

"Did you think about your son when you ran off to France with your lover? No, I don't suppose you did. So I don't know which son you are talking about. Get out!"

He threw them out of the house without showing the slightest compassion for Amelia. Santiago had loved her with all his heart and soul; his pain was as strong as his love had been and it stopped him from being able to forgive her.

After this traumatic reencounter, Amelia had a fit and spent three days in bed without eating anything. She showed a reaction only when Doña Elena came weeping into her room to tell her that the Herreras had not been able to find any way of getting a pardon for Don Armando. There was only one way out, they had been told as if it were a great secret, which was to go to a man who had very close links to the new regime and was known to provide certain pardons for a fee; he was not always successful, and he never returned the money.

Albert James, as the man of the house, agreed to speak to the authorities and to try to use his position as a foreign journalist as much as he could, but Doña Elena and Laura thought that they should go find this man and ask him to take charge of the situation.

Doña Elena, with her daughter and her niece, managed to get a meeting with Agapito Gutiérrez, which was the name of the dealer in favors.

He had fought on the Nationalist side, and had family members in good positions in the highest levels of the regime and in the Falange. He had been a panhandler with no job and no prospects before the war, but he was clever and unscrupulous and was prepared to do whatever it took to survive, so it was no problem for him to enter the army and go into administration, and do favors on the side for people during those years of poverty and scarcity.

Agapito Gutiérrez did not seem to lack anything. He had set himself up in an office on the Calle Velázquez, in an old nobleman's house. We would call it an "influence bureau" today, if it's true business had not been the lives of those who were in prison.

In a dress cut daringly low for those days, a dark-haired woman who said she was the secretary (although she looked more like a chorus girl) let us through into a waiting room where other impatient petitioners were waiting, most of them women.

They were there for more than three hours before it was their turn to see Agapito Gutiérrez.

He was a short, tubby man, dressed in a striped suit and a tie with a tiepin, in patent leather shoes and wearing a large gold ring on his right hand.

Agapito took a look at the group and his glance stopped at Amelia. Although she was thin she had an ethereal and brilliant beauty, of the kind that would be impossible for a man such as him to dream of in other circumstances.

He listened to us, bored, his eyes never leaving Amelia, until he seemed to be eating her with his gaze in such a way that upset both Doña Elena and Laura, as well as Amelia herself.

"Well, I'll see what I can do, although as far as I can tell this red husband of yours is in a bad way and miracles don't come round that often. My activities are expensive, so you'll need to tell me if you can pay or not."

"We'll pay whatever it takes," Laura said at once.

"It's fifty thousand pesetas, whatever the outcome. Everyone who comes to see me asks about people who are delinquents and have done a great deal of damage to our nation, and if I didn't have such a soft heart..."

Doña Elena went pale. She didn't have fifty thousand pesetas and she didn't know how to get it, but she said nothing.

"If you agree, then bring me the fifty thousand pesetas and come back three days later and I'll tell you what I can. It's better if you don't all come, there's no need, I'll wait for you, Señorita Garayoa," he said, looking at Amelia.

"For me?" she said in surprise.

"Yes, for you, you're the niece and you're not so directly implicated in this business, it's not the first time that people have made scenes in my office, and that's not good for my reputation."

Amelia blushed, and Doña Elena was just about to say that there was no way she would let her niece come by herself, but she held her tongue. Her husband's life was in danger.

Albert James was upset when they described this scene to him. He said he should go and show that scoundrel a thing or two, but the three women begged him not to. They couldn't waste their only chance. What Doña Elena did do, red with shame, was to ask James if he would help her to get the fifty thousand pesetas.

"I haven't got anything other than what's in the house, and some land in the village, it's all I can offer in exchange, but I promise you that when my husband is free and working we will give it back, down to the very last peseta."

Amelia said that she would give him her parents' house in exchange for those fifty thousand pesetas.

It was an excessive amount even for Albert James, but he promised he would help them. The next day, with Edurne's help, the women made contact with a black marketer who gave them a thousand pesetas for a pair of silver candelabra, the venetian crystal, some porcelain figures, and a pair of bronze lamps. Albert James said nothing, but he managed to get in contact with his parents and convince them to deposit a check for fifty thousand pesetas in a bank that he could cash in Spain. It was such a large amount that his father had first refused to lend it to him.

"I will give it back to you, but I can't do anything from here and I need this money urgently in order to save a man's life. Get in touch with a bank, with our embassy, with whoever you want, Dad, but get me that money or I will never forgive you," James threatened his father.

A few days later than had been arranged, Amelia turned up at Agapito Gutiérrez's office with the money. Albert James came with her to the door of the office, afraid that she might be robbed on the way, carrying so much money.

Agapito had a new secretary, a young woman with dyed red hair and an even more extravagantly cut dress.

The man himself was wearing the same suit, but a different tie, and a shirt with a pair of solid gold cufflinks.

"Well, I never thought you'd get the money together! Lots of people come here looking for charity, but I'm a man of business, and if you want something then you have to pay for it."

Agapito invited her to sit down next to him on a sofa, and as he spoke he put his hand on her knee. Amelia moved away, uncomfortable.

"You're not uptight, are you?"

"I don't know what you might mean."

"One of those prudes who want what's coming to them but who pretend they don't, who pretend to be fine ladies."

"I've come to bring you the money to get a pardon for my uncle, nothing more."

"Oh, so now you're being all standoffish! And what if I refuse to do anything for your uncle?"

"What are you doing!"

In spite of Amelia's resistance, who kicked and scratched, Agapito Gutiérrez came up close to her and kissed her.

"Oh, you cat! Don't pretend you don't like this as much as I do, you're on fire."

Amelia stood up and stared at him with anger and disgust, but she didn't dare to leave for fear that Agapito would refuse to get her uncle his pardon.

The villain stood up and looked her straight in the eyes as he seized her again.

"Let me go! How dare you! Have you no shame?"

"No more than you; I asked about you and they said that you were a slut who left your husband and your kid to run off with a Frenchie. So don't play with me anymore."

"Here's the money," Amelia said, handing him a thick brown paper envelope that contained the fifty thousand pesetas. 'Now, do what you promised."

"I haven't promised anything, we'll see if your uncle gets out, he doesn't deserve to, for the red that he is."

The man took the envelope and went through it, counting every note while Amelia tried not to cry. When he had finished he looked at her coldly and smiled.

"The price has gone up."

"But you said that it was fifty thousand pesetas! We don't have any more..."

"Oh, you can pay what I want. You have to do what I ask or

your uncle will never leave prison and they'll shoot him. I'll make sure they shoot him sooner."

Amelia was about to collapse, all she wanted to do was to run out of that little office that smelled of sweat and cheap cologne. But she didn't, because she knew that if she did then her Uncle Armando would end up in front of the firing squad.

He realized that he had won.

"Come here, we're going to do a couple of things together, you and me..."

"No, we're not going to do anything. I'll leave you the money, and if my uncle gets out of prison, then..."

"Now you really are a slut! How dare you give me conditions?"

"I'll come to see you the day my uncle gets out of prison."

"Of course you will! Don't think that you'll get away with not paying me."

Amelia left the office and walked across the waiting room, where the secretary was polishing her nails and talking on the telephone. The redhead winked conspiratorially at her.

"What's happened to you?" Albert James asked her, worried to see her coming out of the building with red cheeks and eyes filled with tears.

"Nothing, nothing, that man is a scoundrel, even the fifty thousand pesetas are not enough for him, and he hasn't given any guarantees about my uncle."

"I'm going to go upstairs and tell him a thing or two. Let's see if he's got the guts to tell me that he'll keep the fifty thousand pesetas for doing nothing."

But she wouldn't let him. Neither did she tell him what the ruffian's intentions were. She knew that the die was cast, and that only a miracle could keep her out of that man's hands.

The wait was agonizing. Amelia and Albert James would go out first thing in the morning to work, and sometimes they didn't come home until late afternoon, always with some small item of black market food: a box of cookies, a dozen eggs, a chicken, sugar... Doña Elena carried on running the household as best she could, and I tried to go unnoticed alongside Edurne, whom I followed everywhere. Edurne took me to the hospital a couple of times to visit my grandmother, but she was not getting better, so my stay in Doña Elena's house stretched on and on.

Edurne had spoken to Águeda and had convinced her that she should allow Amelia to see Javier from a distance. The woman accepted in spite of the fear that she felt for Santiago, and Amelia promised not to get close to the child. She watched him from a distance, overcoming the desire to run up to him and hug him.

One fine day, Doña Elena had a phone call from Agapito Gutiérrez. The man said that they were going to sign Armando's pardon that morning, and that he might be free as early as that afternoon, but that first she had to send Amelia to his office. Doña Elena asked why, but Agapito gave no reasons, all he said was that she should send her niece or the pardon might "get lost."

Doña Elena began to cry from happiness. The poor woman was exhausted by all the suffering and uncertainty. To celebrate, she allowed each of us a spoonful of sugar with our malt.

"I don't understand what this man can want... He insists that you go to his office alone, that he has something to talk to you about. I don't want to ask why, maybe he'll ask for more money..."

Albert James insisted on accompanying Amelia to the meeting with Agapito Gutiérrez, but she refused to let him come.

"You've got an interview with the British ambassador, and I don't want you to change it for me."

"I don't want you to be alone."

"Don't worry, the important thing is that my uncle leave prison."

Even though he was reluctant, Albert James had no other option than to accept. Amelia was more nervous than her aunt, and he did not want to upset the fragile mental balance that had been hers ever since their return to Spain. The loss of her parents, and of her son, as well as the discovery of a country sunk in poverty and, what was worse, in hatred, had gashed notches in her soul.

Early in the afternoon, Amelia said goodbye and headed off to Agapito Gutiérrez's office, and Doña Elena asked Edurne and me to go to the prison with Laura, Jesús, and Antonietta, as it was a visiting day and we might be able to return home with Don Armando if the pardon reached the prison director in time. Before leaving, she called Melita in Burgos to tell her that her father was going to be set free.

What happened that afternoon in Agapito Gutiérrez's office was something that Amelia told only her cousin Laura, but I had such good hearing and loved Amelia so much that I couldn't stop myself from listening through the door.

She didn't have to wait this time. When the secretary arrived, the same redhead as before, she winked at her and while she took her to her boss's office, whispered in her ear:

"Just shut your eyes and imagine it's someone else, although the worst bit is the smell, he smells of sweat so badly."

Agapito was sitting behind his huge mahogany desk and barely glanced up when she entered. He carried on reading some documents without asking her to sit down. After a few minutes he looked up and stared at her directly.

"You know why you're here. Either you pay or your uncle doesn't get out of prison."

"We've given you the fifty thousand pesetas."

"They're waiting for me to call to send the pardon across, so..." He shrugged his shoulders.

"Call them."

"No, pay first."

"I'll pay when you call, until I am certain that he's been pardoned..."

"You're in no position to make conditions!"

"I have nothing, so I have nothing to use; I know what you want and I will pay you, but only after you've called."

Agapito looked at her scornfully. He lifted the receiver and made a call. He spoke to someone who confirmed that the pardon had been signed and that it would be sent across to the prison.

When he hung up he remained looking at Amelia, up and down.

"Get undressed."

"It's not necessary... ," she muttered.

"Do what I tell you, you whore!"

He threw himself on her and hit her until she fell to the floor, then he picked her up and tore away her clothes and bent her over the mahogany table, where he raped her.

Amelia tried to resist the man's brutality, but he was like a madman who enjoyed causing her pain. When he had finished he threw her to the floor once again. Amelia curled into a ball, trying to hide her body from the heartless brute.

"I didn't like it, I didn't like those little groans. You're no good even as a whore, you're frigid."

Amelia got up and got dressed quickly, scared that he would hit her again. He tied his tie and insulted her the while.

"May I go?" Amelia said, trembling.

"Yes, get out. I don't know why I bothered getting your uncle out of prison; the best place for the reds is the graveyard."

When Amelia got home, we hadn't yet got back from the prison. When we did, Laura found Amelia crying in the bath. She told her cousin about what she had suffered, the disgust she felt at this monster's clammy breath, the blows that had excited him so much, the filthy words he had used; everything that she had suffered was laid open to her cousin, who had no idea how to comfort her.

Laura made Amelia go to bed. Doña Elena did not understand what had happened, or maybe she did not want to, as Amelia's face was covered with the marks of the blows she had received. She was nervous and didn't stop chattering about how tomorrow her husband would be out of prison, which was what they had told her that afternoon. She ordered Laura and Antonietta to help Edurne clean the house, so that everything would be as it was before the war for Don Armando.

Amelia did not want to come down to supper, and when Albert James appeared and insisted on seeing her, Laura asked him to let her rest until the next day. Doña Elena sent us all to bed to save electricity, and James went to Amelia's room and rapped softly at the door with his knuckles. I heard him and jumped out of bed, wanting to know if Amelia would tell all that had happened.

I heard Amelia's sobs and James's words of intended consolation. She told what she had done to try to save her uncle and he blamed himself for not going with her and not confronting the pig. He swore that the next day he would go to set things straight with him, but Amelia begged him not to because it would put her family in danger. I didn't want to hear more after that, I think that he hugged her to comfort her and that this hug was the prelude to their becoming lovers a few days later.

Don Armando left prison at first light on June 10. Doña Elena waited for him in excitement, and when she had him in front of her they fell into an embrace at the doors of the prison. She was crying, he was barely holding back his tears.

We were waiting for them at home. Laura was nervous and impatient, Antonietta was happy as always, although those days she seemed a little weaker.

Laura threw herself into her father's arms, and he hugged her emotionally. Then came Jesús, then Antonietta, then Amelia, then Albert James, whom he thanked for getting hold of the fifty thousand pesetas.

"I will be more than a friend to you, because I owe you my life. You didn't know me and yet you paid for my liberation, I will never know how to thank you. Of course I will pay you back; I will need time but I will pay you back. I hope I will be able to be a lawyer once again, and if not then I will work at whatever it takes to keep my family and pay off my debt."

The first days of freedom were euphoric ones. Melita, Doña Elena and Don Armando's oldest daughter, came from Burgos with her husband Rodrigo Losada and their daughter Isabel to celebrate their father's release. The family was happy, and little Isabel was the center of everyone's attention. Only Amelia could not shake herself out of the depression into which she had been sunk since her arrival in Spain.

Don Armando enjoyed every moment of his new freedom and was pleased to be able to eat once again "like a human being" as he addressed himself to a plate of potatoes cooked with lard, or a bowl of stewed lentils.

"We ate beans with worms in prison," he said, with a laugh. "They floated on top of the soup, and I won't tell you what they taste of, poor little things, it's better that you don't know."

Albert James had sent Edurne out with money to buy provisions to celebrate Don Armando's return to life. There wasn't much, what with the sky-high prices, but it was always possible to find something on the black market.

At the end of June 1939 Albert James announced that he was returning to Paris.

"My work here is finished, I have to go back and get writing. Amelia has decided to carry on working, so she's coming to Paris with me."

Doña Elena protested, saying that Madrid was the place for Amelia, with them, but Amelia explained why she was leaving.

"I can't do anything here. I work as Albert's secretary, I earn a good amount of money and I can help you and my sister with the money I get. I want Antonietta to have the medicine she needs to get well again, and I want you to be able to eat something more than just potatoes."

"But what about your son?" Doña Elena plucked up the courage to ask.

"Santiago will never let me get close to him. I deserve it. I will come to see you from time to time and try to get close to Javier, maybe I will be able to see him one day and ask his forgiveness."

Don Armando saw that his niece was right. What could Amelia do in Madrid? Laura, who had studied to be a teacher, could not get a job because she was the daughter of a red, and had to be content with a menial assistantship in a school run by nuns, the same school where she had been a pupil, and where the mother superior felt some affection for her and had allowed her to help out. She had to sweep the classrooms, clean them, look after the smallest children at playtime, and run errands, and for all this she only earned a handful of pesetas.

As for Don Armando, it was made clear to him by the authorities that he could not hope to practice his former profession, at least for now. It was better not to be noticed by the regime. Armando tried to earn money in a dignified way, but it was not easy, and to his humiliation he was forced to accept a job as an articled clerk in a Francoist lawyer's office, a man who was well set up with the regime and who needed someone whom he could trust and who knew the law and would work a lot for very little money.

Amelia signed a document granting her uncle the right to sell her parents' home, in order to pay off the debt to Albert James and for the family to have a little more money to get by on. At first Don Armando refused to accept this offer, saying that the apartment was Amelia and Antonietta's inheritance, but the two sisters insisted that he try to find a good buyer, sure that there would be people who were taking advantage of the situation and who would be able to buy an apartment right in the center of the Salamanca district.

When Albert James and Amelia left, we went to see them off at the North Station. We were all crying, especially Antonietta, whom we had to pull out of her sister's arms so that Amelia could board the train.

For those of us who remained, a new life was just beginning; and for Amelia as well.

Professor Soler finished his tale and got up to stretch his legs. Night had fallen a while back, and Charlotte, his wife, had put her head round the door several times to see if we were still talking.

"Professor, one question: Why don't you write Amelia Garayoa's story yourself?"

"Because I only know it in scraps and patches; you have to put the puzzle together."

I must admit that the more I knew about my great-grandmother the more surprised I became. My opinion had changed since when I had first found out about her and had thought her an uninteresting, badly-brought-up young girl. Amelia now seemed to me a tragic figure, destined to suffer, and to cause suffering.

"Well, now you have to carry on with your research," he said, as I had feared.

As had happened before, he had the next steps in my investigation worked out.

"They went to Paris from Madrid, but they weren't there for long. Albert James went to London and decided to take Amelia with him, so that's where you have to go. I've spoken with Doña Laura and she agrees, but you should speak to her as well. I'll arrange a contact for you in London: Major William Hurley, a retired soldier who is also an archivist."

"Do you know him?"

"Major Hurley? No, I don't know him. It was Victor Dupont who suggested Hurley to me; he met him at a conference of archivists. I think he can help you pick up Albert James's trail."

Before going to London I went through Madrid to see my mother. This time she was really cross; I could tell as soon as I walked through the door.

"Have you gone mad? Does this make any sense at all, what you're doing? I've told my sister it was her fault, a great idea she had! Who cares what your great-grandmother did? How's it going to change our life?"

"Aunt Marta has nothing to do with it anymore," I answered.

"But she was the one who poisoned you to start with. Look, Guillermo, as far as I'm concerned I don't want to know anything about my grandmother's life, I don't give a damn. But I'll say more: Either stop all this nonsense or don't count on me for anything more. I'm not ready to watch you throwing your life away. Instead of looking for a good job you're wasting your time trying to find out about Amelia Garayoa, who... who... who's still messing things up with this family even after her death."

I couldn't convince my mother that the investigation was worthwhile. She was not for turning, and she showed me how determined she was by saying that I shouldn't expect any more loans from her until I had given up on what she called "that madness."

Supper that night didn't sit well with me, and I left in a bad mood, but firmly decided to carry on with my investigations into Amelia Garayoa. Strangely enough, I didn't think that she had anything to do with me, that the interest she provoked in me had anything to do with her being my great-grandmother. Her life was just more interesting than those of so many other people whom I had known or written about as a journalist.

Doña Laura was extremely pleased with my progress and made no objection to my traveling to London.

4

I arrived in London on a day that was neither rainy, nor foggy, nor cold. It's not
that the sun was shining, but at least it was more pleasant than on
previous occasions. In fact, I had been to London only once before, when I was a teenager, and my mother had made me go on
an exchange to improve my English.

Major William Hurley seemed to be a grumpy old man, at
least judging by his telephone manner.

"Come tomorrow at eight on the dot and don't be late; you
Spaniards have the strange habit of arriving late to everything."

I was annoyed by the suggestion that Spaniards are unpunctual
and I told myself that I would ask him how many Spaniards he
knew, and if they all arrived late for their appointments.

At eight on the dot I rang the bell of a Victorian mansion in
Kensington. A perfectly dressed young maid opened the door.
She must have been from the Caribbean, because in spite of her
rigid posture she smiled at me warmly and said that she would
announce me straight away.

William Hurley was waiting for me by the fireplace in a huge
library. He seemed to be lost in thought as he watched a log burning, but he stood up and held out a hand to me; it must have been
made of steel, because he almost broke my fingers.

"I'm only seeing you because Monsieur Dupont asked a favor
of me," he said.

"And I thank you for it, Major Hurley."

"Monsieur Dupont tells me that you would like information about the Jameses, is that so?"

"Yes, I am interested in finding out whatever I can about Albert James, who had, as far as I have been able to discover, relatives in the Foreign Office and the Admiralty."

"Right, if that weren't the case then you wouldn't be here."

"I'm sorry?"

"Young man, I have devoted a good part of my life to the study of military archives, and yes, there was a James who worked in the Admiralty at about that time. Lord Paul James was an officer in the counterespionage division, and one of his grandsons married Lady Victoria, my wife's niece. Lady Victoria is a redoubtable woman, a great golf player and a historian. She has put all her family's archives in order, as well as those of her husband's family. Anyway," he concluded, "what are you looking for?"

I told him who I was and that it appeared that one of Albert James's lovers, Amelia Garayoa, was my great-grandmother, and that my only aim was to put her story together for the use of the family.

"A singular woman, your great-grandmother."

"Ah! So you know something about her?"

"I have no time to waste. Monsieur Dupont rang me and explained about your researches, so I have been looking in the Admiralty archives, the public ones, though there are of course classified ones filled with material that will never be released. There was a free agent, a Spaniard, Amelia Garayoa, who worked with the British Secret Service during the Second World War. Her protector was Albert James, Lord Paul James's nephew, who was also an agent, one of the best."

I was in shock. My great-grandmother never stopped throwing up surprises.

"A free agent? What's that?" I asked, trying to cover my surprise.

"She wasn't English, she didn't belong to any agency, but she, like so many other people all over Europe, helped the intelligence services in their attempt to topple Nazism. There were two fronts in the war; intelligence was as important as military activity."

Major Hurley gave me a master class on the secret services during the Second World War. He seemed to enjoy showing off his extensive knowledge, and I listened to him with great care and attention. As a journalist, one of the things I have learned is that no one can resist being listened to with attention. People need to hear their story told, and if you have the patience and the humility to listen without interrupting, then you will hear the most amazing things.

At ten on the dot, the Caribbean maid knocked gently at the door to tell the major that there was a car waiting for him.

"Ah, I've got an appointment with an old friend at my club. Well, young man, I think I'll ask Lady Victoria if she'll meet you, as she can give you information about the more... well, the more personal aspects of the relationship between Albert James and Amelia Garayoa. As for me, I will tell you all about her work as an agent. I'll call you at your hotel."

I was fired up when I left Major Hurley's house. Amelia Garayoa's story was taking on a new and unexpected perspective.

Lady Victoria met with me two days later. She was an attractive woman, although she must have been more or less my mother's age.

Tall and thin, with copper-colored hair, blue eyes, and white freckled skin, she had the typical elegance of upper-class women for whom nothing has ever been a struggle, even though she had been a good student at Oxford and had taken a history degree.

"What a worthwhile activity, to investigate your grandmother's past! We are nothing without our roots, they help us keep our feet firm on the ground. It must be terrible not to know who you are, and of course, we can know that only if we know who our ancestors were."

I had to struggle not to reply to her classist peroration, but I made the effort and said nothing; I needed her help.

"Young man, let me tell you that I have found a great deal of material about your great-grandmother in the archives. Letters, references in Albert James's mother's diary... I think I will be able to tell you things that will be useful for you. Of course, it's Uncle William who could tell you things more clearly. How exciting, to find out that your great-grandmother was a spy, risking her life against the Nazis! In spite of everything, you must be proud to have a woman like her in your family."

Just as before with Major William, I let the aristocrat take control of the conversation. The best thing was to listen; in any event, Lady Victoria had been brought up not to allow herself to be interrupted. She lit a cigarette and began to speak.

Albert James and your great-grandmother arrived in London in mid-July 1939. Exactly a month previously they had announced the creation of the Women's Land Army... but let's not get side-tracked. They moved into Albert's house in Kensington, a bachelor pad, roomy and comfortable. Albert's parents had a house very near their son, well, the house is still there, one of their grandchildren lives there now. Don't look so surprised. I'll tell you about the grandson, but it's not important now.

Albert's parents were in the family home in Ireland, in Howth, near Dublin, where they spent their summers, even though they spent most of the year in the United States. I don't know if you knew this, but the Jameses were an old landed family. Paul James was the oldest son, and it was he who inherited the big house; Albert's father, Ernest, decided to go to America to make his fortune, and boy! did he make it! He became a rich businessman, but never lost touch with his roots, and when he fell ill he returned to Ireland to die. Ernest would have liked his son to have been born in Ireland, but he was premature, so he had to put up with his son being a New Yorker. Well, it's not that bad to be born in New York, don't you think?

Albert wrote to his mother to tell her that he would go to Ireland with Amelia Garayoa; I found the letter in the papers of Lady Eugenie's, Albert's mother. They were not idle while they were in London. You can imagine the political situation of the time: Chamberlain doing everything possible to appease Hitler, convinced that this was the best thing to do, wrongly, of course.

Albert's uncle, Paul James, his father's brother, was working in the Admiralty.

Paul James invited his nephew and the beautiful Amelia to dine at his house, along with other friends, and everyone spoke about Hitler's intentions. There were people there who were convinced that Germany would provoke a European war, and others who naively thought that it was possible to stop one. But perhaps the most important event of this evening was that Amelia met an old friend, Max von Schumann, who was with his wife, Baroness Ludovica von Waldheim. Don't think that I'm relying on guesswork here, I'm related to the Jameses and I know for certain that my grandmother was at that dinner; she used to tell her grandchildren all about the war years.

Albert presented Amelia as his assistant, he didn't dare say more, given the fact that she was married, but it was clear to all present that the relationship between them was something more than simply professional.

Your great-grandmother was a very beautiful woman, I know this because there are some photos in the family archive, and apparently all the guests were conquered by her beauty and charm. She didn't seem Spanish; she was beautiful, intelligent, polyglot. Don't be offended, but women like your great-grandmother, especially Spanish women, were not very common at that time.

The last thing that either Amelia Garayoa or Max von Schumann expected was to meet each other at this discreet and exclusive dinner in Paul James's house.

"Amelia, what a pleasure! Allow me to present my wife, Ludovica, Baroness von Waldheim. Ludovica, this is Amelia, I have told you about her, we met in Buenos Aires at the Hertzes' house."

Ludovica held out a hand to Amelia and no one could fail to notice that the two women were eyeing each other up. Both of them were blonde, and thin, and elegant, with bright eyes; both of them extremely beautiful... They looked like a pair of Valkyries.

If it was a surprise for Albert that Amelia should know the German, it was a much greater one for Paul James.

Max von Schumann was in London on a secret mission: to try to convince the British government to clip Hitler's wings. Von Schumann was a member of an anti-Nazi group made up of intellectuals, Christian activists, and a few soldiers who had been trying for some time, although without success, to convince the Western powers that appeasement of Hitler was not something that would work, and that he represented a great threat to European peace. There were not many people in the group, but they were very active, and one of their last and most desperate attempts to get Great Britain's attention had been to send von Schumann to London.

Max von Schumann was a soldier and served in the Wehrmacht's medical corps, which added a great deal of weight to his presence.

Amelia presented Albert to Max and Ludovica his wife, and the four of them made small talk for a while. It was clear that von Schumann was looking for an opportunity to speak with Amelia alone, but Ludovica was not willing to give her husband such an opportunity.

It was here that Paul James weighed up Amelia's many qualities, and although he said nothing at the time, he thought that the Spaniard could be of great use in the future, if war were eventually declared, something he was convinced would happen.

"Albert, what are your plans?" Lord Paul James asked his nephew.

"For the moment, to write some articles about Spain, and then to go to Ireland to see my parents. I would like them to meet Amelia."

"May I ask if you are engaged?"

Albert cleared his throat uneasily, but decided that the best thing would be to tell his uncle the truth.

"Amelia is married, separated from her husband, and I am afraid that for the time being it is impossible for us to formalize our commitment to one another. But I am in love with her. She is a special woman: She is strong, intelligent, decisive... She has lived through such terrible situations, if you had seen what she was able to do in the Soviet Union to save a man's life... Her father was shot by the Francoists, and she has lost several members of her family in the war... Her life has not been easy."

"Your mother will be upset, you know she wanted to see you married... and, well, it's best that I tell you: She has invited Lady Mary and her parents to spend their holiday in Ireland. As far as I know, they are leaving for Ireland tomorrow."

Paul James could not have given his nephew a worse piece of news, even though at this time he really had more important things to worry about than Albert's love life. He was sure that war was coming, and he had plans in which he hoped Albert would play a large part.

"Are you intending to go anywhere else after the holidays?" he asked.

"Maybe to Germany, I want to see close up what Hitler is doing."

"Excellent, I'm happy you're going to Germany."

"Why, Uncle?"

"Because, however hard they try in the ministry not to see what's right under their noses, war is coming, and coming soon. Lord Halifax seems to have blind faith in the reports the ambassador in Berlin, Sir Neville Henderson, sends back, and I won't hide it from you that these are extremely soft on Herr Hitler. Chamberlain has dedicated too much time to trying to appease Hitler for him to think that war is in fact inevitable."

"And what does all this have to do with me?" Albert asked uncertainly.

"You were born in the United States, even though you are actually Irish, and it could be very useful to have an American passport these days..."

"I don't know what plan you're cooking up, but don't count on me. I am a journalist, and I'm not going to let myself get caught up in your spying."

"I have never asked you to get involved, and I wouldn't ask you now if these weren't exceptional circumstances. In a brief while we will all have to make a decision, it will not be possible to cross our arms and claim to be neutral. You won't be able to either, Albert, for all that you might want to. The United States will have to decide as well, it's only a matter of time."

"You're very pessimistic, Uncle Paul."

"In my job it's dangerous to try to fool yourself. We'll leave that to the politicians."

"In any case, don't count on me for anything that you might think up. I take my job as seriously as you take yours."

"I'm sure you do, dear Albert, but I'm afraid we will have to talk about these things again."

Later that evening, Max von Schumann found his opportunity to talk to Amelia. Paul James's wife, Lady Anne, had Ludovica caught up in a conversation with another woman, and the baroness found no way of escaping without calling attention to herself and what she was doing.

"You've changed, Amelia."

"Life doesn't just flow past you."

"Albert James is your... ?"

"My lover? Yes, yes he is."

"Sorry, I didn't want to upset you."

"You don't upset me, Max. How else should I describe my relation with Albert? I am a married woman, so if I am with another man he must be my lover."

"Please, forgive me, I only wanted to know how you were. I haven't stopped thinking about you since our conversations in Buenos Aires. I asked Martin and Gloria Hertz to tell me about you, but they only said that you went to this congress of intellectuals in Moscow and that you didn't come back. Gloria wrote to tell me that Pierre's father had gone to Buenos Aires to close the bookshop and deal with his son's possessions, and that he didn't want to say anything about you. I don't know if I should ask you about Pierre..."

"They killed him in Moscow."

Max didn't know what to say when he heard of Pierre's death. The woman who stood in front of him was nothing like the defenseless little girl he thought he had known in Argentina.

"I am sorry."

"Thank you."

It was as if they did not know what else to say to each other. Max was uncomfortable because he could feel his wife's curious glances, and as far as Amelia was concerned, one can imagine that she felt disappointed, perhaps wounded, to find that Max was married. It is not that she had expected him to remain faithful to her memory and to break off his engagement with Ludovica, but it was one thing to know this and another to see it with one's own eyes.

"Will you be in London long?" he wanted to know.

"I don't know, we've just got here. Albert will decide. As well as being his lover I work for him, I am his assistant, his secretary, I do a bit of everything for him. He saved me, he saved me in Moscow, in Paris, in Madrid; he has always been near when I have needed him and has offered me help without my having to ask anything of him."

"I envy him that."

"Do you really? You know what, Max? I missed you a lot when you left, and I dreamt that we'd meet each other again one day. Then I stopped dreaming forever when I was in Moscow. I learned not to think about anything more than the present minute."

"You've suffered a lot..."

Amelia shrugged, to show her indifference.

"I would like to see you again," he said.

"Why?"

"To speak, to... Don't make me feel like a little boy, is it so hard for you to see what you mean to me?"

"Goodness, what things you say!"

"You can scold me for lots of things, but whether or not you accept it, you still mean a great deal to me."

"If fate hadn't brought us together today we would never have seen each other again..."

"But fate decided differently, and here we are. May I invite you to take tea with me tomorrow in the Dorchester?"

"I don't know, I can't promise anything. It all depends on Albert."

"You need his permission?"

"I need him."

"I will be in the Dorchester at five o'clock tomorrow afternoon, I hope you can come."

Baroness Ludovica von Waldheim came up to them with a determined stride.

"Remembering old times?" she asked ironically.

"I was just inviting the young lady to take tea with me, and I hope that she will accept my invitation. Who knows when we'll see each other again?"

"Oh, destiny has her little whims! Don't you think so, my dear?" the baroness said, drilling Amelia with her gaze.

"I try not to think about destiny when I am making my plans," Amelia replied.

Albert James could not have cared too much about Baron von Schumann's invitation, because he escorted Amelia to the Dorchester himself.

"I'll come and pick you up in an hour," he said, kissing her on the cheek after greeting Max von Schumann.

"I am so pleased that you've come," Max said as soon as they were alone.

"Albert thought it was completely natural for us to have tea together, after I told him that we met each other in Buenos Aires and that we have mutual friends."

"Mr. James is very understanding."

"He's an extraordinary man, the best I've ever met," Amelia replied with a mild tang of irritation.

They spoke about the changes in their lives. He told her why he was in London and how his attempt to convince the British to stop Hitler had failed.

"I haven't even managed to get them to listen to me, but I will carry on trying. Another member of our group will arrive in a few days and arrange more interviews with important people in the British government."

"But the other night Sir Paul James said publicly that he was convinced that Hitler would provoke a war in Europe. How can you say that you've failed?"

"Sir Paul is an intelligent man, capable of seeing things clearly and of not insisting that things have to be as he would like them to be. But sadly, whether or not the British government takes our fears seriously doesn't depend on him."

"You know what? I'm surprised. I thought that you were a

patriot, incapable of doing anything to harm Germany, but here you are, a soldier coming to Great Britain to ask the English to stop Hitler."

"What I am doing is for Germany, and is precisely the reason why I am a patriot. Don't think for a moment that it was easy to get permission to travel at a time like this, but I suppose that old noble families still have certain privileges, for all that Hitler hates us. Also, I have an excuse: Ludovica has a cousin married to an English count, and we are officially here to attend the baptism of their firstborn son."

Then Max explained that he had made great efforts to find out what had happened to Herr Itzhak Wassermann, Amelia's father's partner, but that they had all been in vain. Helmut, Herr Itzhak's employee, had told him that he did not know where the family was.

"He was scared, he didn't trust me. Of course, nowadays, nobody trusts Germany. I wrote to you but I imagine you were no longer in Buenos Aires; you didn't reply to my letter."

An hour later, Albert James came to look for Amelia. Max invited him to take tea with them, he wanted to know what he thought about what was happening in Europe, and he was surprised when Albert said that he was thinking of going to Germany.

"Ludovica and I would be delighted to have you for dinner, and if we can be of any help..."

Amelia said nothing, it had been an even greater surprise for her to discover that Albert intended to go to Berlin, but she decided to say nothing.

Later, the journalist told her that when he finished writing up his articles on Spain, they would go to Ireland for a few days with his parents, and then would travel to Germany.

"There are lots of American papers that would like to know about Hitler and if he really has saved the country from the economic chaos it had fallen into. Will you come with me?"

"Of course, I wouldn't miss seeing Berlin for anything in the world. Who knows, maybe I will be able to get Herr Helmut, Herr Itzhak's employee, to tell me something. I miss Yla so much!"

It would be difficult to say that Albert and Amelia's stay in Ireland was a success. Lady Eugenie, Albert's mother, was a very stubborn woman, and although she greeted Amelia with a smile, it soon became clear that she did not consider her an adequate match for her son. Also, as Paul James had warned his nephew, the family had invited the Brians and their daughter Mary, who was, in Lady Eugenie's opinion, a person who united in herself all the necessary qualities to become Albert's wife.

There are certain passages in Lady Eugenie's diary that give a very clear indication of what happened over those days.

Amelia is charming, I cannot deny that, but she is married, so there's no other option for Albert than to break things off with her. As for Mary, I believe she is perfect for Albert. She is beautiful, well mannered, and comes from an excellent and well-connected family. Mary has been disappointed to see Albert so clearly infatuated with Amelia, and her parents are not comfortable with the situation either, which is why I have decided to make a move myself. I will speak with Albert tomorrow, and then with the Brians; they do not know that Amelia is married and I intend to tell them. As for Ernest, I do not know if he is to be relied upon, he has asked me not to play the matchmaker, and to respect our son's decision, for all that he does not approve of Albert's relationship with Amelia either. But Ernest is becoming very American, and he forgets that there are values and traditions that need to be maintained. A son must understand that whom he marries is not simply and exclusively his own decision, that he has to think of the family as well. But here it is not a question of making a decision between Mary and Amelia, because the Spanish girl is already married.

It was not easy to talk with Albert. I think that his education in the United States has made him rather unconventional. I told him that Amelia had my sympathy but that the relationship had no future.

"Will you agree not to have children?" I asked him.

Albert said nothing, I think that he had not thought about this before, or had not wanted to think about it.

"If you have children, you will make them bastards. Is that what you want?"

Then I reminded him of his obligations to the family, all the greater for his being an only child. Sadly I was unable to have more children and he now has to look after the family name and our property, for all that he says he is an American and he doesn't believe in classes. Like it or not, he is a James.

It was not easy to talk with the Brians, either. I told them that Albert's relationship with Amelia was nothing more than a childish infatuation. I think that they were calmer when they realized that, however much Albert might wish it, he cannot marry Amelia because she is married, and with Franco in power in Spain the chances of obtaining a divorce are nonexistent. They were very tactful and made no hurtful comments about Amelia. I asked Mary to be patient, telling her that men every now and then lose their heads for a woman, and that ladies like us need to accept these situations with good breeding. Better to pretend that nothing is happening than to make a scene or provoke a conversation which could lead to awkward truths being aired. Also, I am sure that hard as he may find it, and American as he may feel, Albert will do his duty by us.

Albert realized that he shouldn't spend much longer in Ireland so as to avoid a direct confrontation with his mother, and so he decided to return to Paris before heading for Berlin.

On August 22, 1939, Hitler, in a speech aimed at the German High Command, made clear his intentions of invading Poland. One day later, August 23, Albert and Amelia were dining in Jean Deuville's house. Amelia had remained friends with Pierre's best friend. She was grateful, as was Albert, for the disinterested help that he had given her in Moscow to try to save Pierre's life. Since Pierre's death, it had been difficult for Jean to get over the things he had seen in Moscow, as he had discovered a side to Communism that terrified him.

As if this weren't enough, Deuville had also heard that very day that Germany and the Soviet Union had signed a non-aggression treaty. Like so many other Communists he felt shaken, unable to find arguments to defend the Molotov-Ribbentrop pact.

Hitler was viciously attacking the German Communists, and it was impossible to understand how Stalin, against all his principles, was willing to give Hitler breathing space.

"How can you be so naïve?" Amelia said. "Don't you see that Stalin is gaining time?"

"Time? What he's doing is giving time to Hitler," Jean Deuville complained.

"They will end up fighting each other, wait and see, this is just a tactical decision," Amelia said.

"But what about his principles? I'm not one of those people who says that the end justifies the means."

"You always were a romantic," Albert interrupted, who had grown close to Jean after all they had been through in Moscow.

"Ideas cannot be tainted. How can I explain this pact to my friends, people whom I've convinced that Communism is the only idea that can build a new world? How can I ask them to carry on fighting against Fascism if Stalin makes a pact with Hitler?"

Jean Deuville was distraught and none of the arguments deployed by Amelia or Albert was able to calm him down. He was ideologically pure, so it was completely incomprehensible for him to imagine that Stalin, for whatever reason, had made a pact with Hitler.

When Amelia and Albert were preparing to leave the house after midnight, Jean hugged her for several minutes as if he wished he could keep her with him; then he shook Albert strongly by the hand and made him make a promise.

"Will you give me your word of honor that you will look after her?"

"That's what I intend to do, to look after Amelia for the rest of my life," Albert said solemnly.

"That's a reassurance."

Amelia was upset by Jean Deuville's distress and above all by his way of saying goodbye.

"We mustn't leave him alone," she said to Albert as soon as they left Deuville's apartment.

"Don't be a baby! Nothing will happen, it's just that he doesn't understand tactics or political strategies; he's an honest man. That's why he couldn't understand the Molotov-Ribbentrop pact. You were very generous, bearing in mind what you think of Stalin, to try to justify the pact."

"Jean's a good man and I didn't want to hurt him anymore."

They arrived in Berlin two days later and settled in at the Hotel Adlon. Amelia couldn't hide the emotion she felt in coming back to Berlin, a city she had first encountered when she was a girl and had visited Germany with her parents.

It was not hard for her to convince Albert to help her look for the Wassermanns. He trusted that someone would give her some clue as to the whereabouts of Herr Itzhak and his wife, Judith, or at least of their daughter Yla.

Amelia took him to the Oranienburgerstrasse, near the Neue Synagoge, the largest synagogue in Germany.

"It's so impressive!" Albert said, looking at the Moorish building.

"Yes it is, I still remember what Herr Itzhak told us about the synagogue... It was opened in 1866 and it was designed by Edouard Knoblauch, one of Karl Friedrich Schinkel's students."

"That's some memory you've got!"

"I've always been interested in art and history."

None of the people in the neighborhood could give them any information about Herr Itzhak and his family. Amelia insisted that they knock on all the doors of the building where the Wassermanns had lived, but all they could find out was that they had suddenly vanished one day.

Amelia felt that she was mistrusted by the few people who dared open their doors. This building, which had previously been inhabited by well-to-do bourgeois families, now seemed dark and run-down.

"I'm sure that the Wassermanns have left Germany. You told me yourself that your father insisted on it."

"Yes, but Herr Itzhak refused, he said that this was his homeland."

"Yes, but seeing how things have worked out, he might have had no other option than to leave. If I remember rightly, the Nazis closed the business and that ruined your father."

"Yes, but in spite of everything Herr Itzhak didn't want to leave Germany."

Amelia did not give up easily, so she insisted that they should try to find Helmut, Herr Wassermann's former accountant.

"He's a good man, and if we meet him he'll surely be able to tell us something about the Wassermanns."

"Don't you ever give up?" Albert replied, laughing.

Amelia didn't answer and took him to the Stadthaus, where they asked for Zur Letzten, the oldest restaurant in the city. A man explained that it was very close and told them how to get there.

"I know that Helmut lived round here, his house wasn't far from the oldest restaurant in Berlin. My father took us to Zur Letzten one evening and we went to see Helmut before dining."

After walking around a little they eventually found the building. The doorman, after looking them closely up and down, told them that Helmut was at home.

Albert had to run behind Amelia, who started to hurry up the stairs as if she were being blown along by some mighty wind.

They rang the bell and waited impatiently for an answer, which they got when an old and tired-looking man opened the door.

"What do you want?" he asked, looking at them mistrustfully.

"Herr Helmut, I'm Amelia Garayoa! Don't you recognize me?"

"Fräulein Amelia, good Lord, you're a real woman now!"

After his initial surprise, the German invited them into his house.

"Come in, come in, I'll make you some coffee, my wife is in bed with a fever, but I'll look after you."

"We don't want to bother you, I just wanted to know how you were and ask about the Wassermanns... ," Amelia said.

But Herr Helmut seemed not to hear her. He took them to the salon and asked them to sit while he made the coffee.

"He seems a good man," Albert James said.

"He is, of course he's a good man. My father trusted him a great deal."

The man came back with a tray and did not want to answer Amelia's questions until he had seen them taste the coffee he had made.

"Tell me about your father, it's a long time since I've heard any news of Don Juan. I knew that he was in the war against Franco... I wrote to him but didn't get any answer."

"My father is dead, he was shot just before the war ended."

"I'm so sorry. Your father was a good employer, just like Herr Itzhak, fair and considerate... Send my sincerest condolences to your mother and Antonietta, I still remember her and you when you were little girls..."

"My mother is dead as well, and my sister Antonietta is ill, although thank the Lord she is still alive," Amelia said, trying to fight back tears.

Herr Helmut was astonished to hear the sufferings of the Garayoa family. He didn't know what to say. Amelia asked him to tell them about the Wassermanns.

"I can't tell you very much, the same as I told your father, Don Juan. Anti-Jewish policies have been put into practice since Hitler's coming to power. You were too young to remember, but the first boycotts of Jewish businesses took place in 1933, and there were hundreds of picket lines manned by Nazis in front of businesses and shops owned by Jews. Then they were deprived of their legal and civil rights, and robbed of all they owned through a number of tricks and underhanded activities. They were expelled from public office, from the legal profession, from hospitals, from universities, from theaters, from newspapers... Some of them decided to leave the country, but most, like Herr Itzhak, resisted the pressure to leave. They were German, why should they leave their country? Then came the Nuremburg Laws... The National Socialist government preferred that Jews leave at the beginning, so that they could keep all their property, but you know what happened next, lots of countries were unwilling to accept them, and now we've got to the situation we're in at the moment: mass arrests, the destruction of the synagogues, expropriation of property, removal of passports... Your father and Herr Itzhak lost their business. I don't know if your father told you, but they inspected the company at the end of 1935 and said that there were irregularities in the accounts. This was untrue, I swear to you, I was the accountant, and I swear that everything added up. But there was no way to defend oneself against the accusations these people made, and so Herr Itzhak and your father lost their business. You know this was a great blow for them."

"Yes, I know all this, Herr Helmut, but what I want to know is what happened to the Wassermanns," Amelia insisted.

"Have you heard of Kristallnacht?"

"Of course."

"You can't imagine how many Jews have been arrested since then. They take them to labor camps and after that there's no way to find out what's become of them."

"Please, tell me where the Wassermanns are!"

"I don't know, I'm not sure. Herr Itzhak managed to send Yla out of Germany, I think to some relatives of Frau Judith in the United States. Yla didn't want to leave, but Herr Itzhak and Frau Judith were firm, they didn't want her to suffer all the humiliations that the German Jews were being subjected to. But they stayed here, thinking that the country would grow some backbone, that Hitler was only a bad dream, that the Jews would be considered good Germans once again... They got by with the little they had left, and I helped them when I could and then one day... well, Herr Itzhak disappeared; Frau Judith ran wild, nearly went crazy when we found out that he had been taken to a labor camp."

"And where is she?"

"They took her too."

Amelia burst into tears. Herr Helmut sat quiet looking at her, without knowing what to do.

"Please, Amelia, calm down! We can try to find out where they are and if there's anything we can do for them," Albert said, trying to console her.

"At least Fräulein Yla is alright. I know that she wrote to her parents when she reached New York."

The man assured them that he did not know Frau Judith's family's address in New York, but in the midst of such troubles it was a relief for Amelia to know that her childhood friend was safe.

"What happened to the factory and the business?" Amelia wanted to know.

"They confiscated them; they let me stay on the front desk of the factory for a while, then they said that they belonged to the state and were now in the hands of a member of the Nazi Party. But I was able to save some of the machines, that's why I wrote to your father. I didn't know what I should do with them."

"But are they still useful for anything?" Amelia asked in surprise.

"They were good machines, and I thought that if I couldn't sell them I could at least hire them out; I did that with one of the looms: I hired it to a small-scale shirt-maker. As for the sewing machines, I hired them out to a family that makes clothes for one of the stores. It's not much money, I know because I keep their accounts, but here it is, in case Herr Itzhak appears one day or... Well, your father is dead... but you are... well, you're his daughter, you have the right to some of this money."

"And what about you, what do you do now?" Albert asked.

"I do what I can. I am an accountant at the shirt factory and the dressmaker's; I don't earn a lot, just enough for me and my wife to live on. And I keep Don Juan and Herr Itzhak's machines running. My oldest son is married and went into the army years ago; he doesn't need anything from us.

Herr Keller insisted that Amelia should receive a part of the earnings he made from hiring out the machines.

She resisted, but in the end gave in.

"This is your father's money, so you should manage it as you see fit. I will give you the account books."

5

With her knowledge of German, Amelia was once again a great help to Albert.

"You're lucky you're so good at languages!"

"It's not that. If I speak French, it's because my father's mother, grandmother Margot, was from Biarritz; as far as German is concerned, I told you that I spent several summers here as a guest of the Wassermanns. Their daughter Yla is the same age as me. My father insisted that Antonietta and I learnt German and some English, which is the language I speak the worst, as you know very well."

"Not at all, you speak English very well, but you just need a bit more vocabulary. I know what we should do, instead of speaking French between us we should speak English, and practice that way."

And that's what they did. It was clear to Albert James that Germany was preparing for war, and that Hitler's threat against Poland was not just another one of his boasts.

Berlin was happy and excited, but with a hysterical excitement, something that could be seen at first glance.

In the face of Amelia's protests, Albert insisted on calling Max von Schumann. As a journalist, he was interested in finding out the baron's opinions as a soldier. Albert seemed not to suspect that there had been a connection between Amelia and Max in the past that circumstances had not permitted to flourish.

Max von Schumann invited the couple to dine at his house in the center of the city.

It was a two-story house with a burgeoning garden around it. A butler opened the door and led them to a library, where Max and Ludovica were waiting for them.

"I'm so glad you're here, although I don't think the circumstances suggest that this is the best time to visit Germany..."

"Come on, darling, let's not upset our guests!" Ludovica interrupted.

"The truth is that Berlin has surprised me a great deal," Albert admitted.

"It is impossible not to love the city," Ludovica said.

"Do you think Hitler will carry out his threat of invading Poland?" Albert asked.

Max cleared his throat uneasily and avoided the question, but Albert did not miss the glance that the baron shared with his wife.

And this passing glance was all the proof needed to know that Hitler's threat to invade Poland was about to become a reality.

Albert admitted having read some of Hitler's speeches and said that it was a mystery to him why the Germans allowed themselves to be carried away by the Führer.

"It's as if he were treating the German people like children."

"Oh, you have no idea what Germany was like before the Führer came to power! Germany was a nonentity, not to mention the lack of money, or work, or future... Hitler has given Germany back its dignity, we are respected in Europe and, as you can see, we are now a prosperous country. There is no unemployment in Germany. Go out, ask people in the street, Hitler is a blessing for the working classes, as he is for us, who were about to be ruined," Ludovica said.

"Who do you mean when you say 'us'?" Albert asked.

"I mean the families who have contributed for centuries to our country's prosperity. German industry was almost ruined, and I know what I'm talking about, as my family had factories in the Ruhr."

Max seemed to be uncomfortable with Ludovica's explanations. Amelia thought she saw an element of forced gaiety settling into his features while Ludovica talked and exalted the figure of Hitler, and she imagined that there must be deep-seated disagreements between the couple.

"There are lots of Germans who do not have the same ideas as Ludovica," Max said, finding it impossible to contain himself.

"But darling, those are the Communists, the Socialists, and all of that rabble who are incapable of admitting that it is thanks to Hitler that Germany is a great nation once again. But the good Germans have much to thank Hitler for."

"I am a good German, and I have nothing to thank him for," Max replied.

"We should thank him for putting the Jews back in their place. The Jews were parasites on the body of Germany."

"Ludovica, that's enough! You know I will not let you talk this way in my presence. Some of my best friends are German Jews."

"I'm sorry, darling, but even if you are my husband I cannot share these ideas you have of the Jews. They are not like us, they belong to an inferior race."

"Ludovica!"

"Come on, Max, let's try making some sense here. Aren't you in favor of freedom? Well, allow me to express myself freely. I hope I am not shocking our guests... I'm not, am I, Amelia?"

Amelia could scarcely repress a smile. She did not understand how Max could have married this woman. He had nothing in common with the baroness, apart from the fact that they both belonged to old families and had known each other since they were children. She felt sorry for him.

Four days later, September 1, 1939, Germany invaded Poland. Albert called Max to try to arrange another meeting, without Ludovica, alone.

"It's impossible for me to meet you today, you understand," Max apologized.

"I do understand, but what about in the next few days?"

"Of course, of course; I am going to stay in Berlin out of principle, and I will find a moment when I can see you."

Two days later, September 3, 1939, Great Britain, France, Australia, and New Zealand declared war on Germany. That was how the Second World War began. On September 5 the United States declared its neutrality, which helped Albert to stay in Berlin without any trouble, just as Amelia could because she was Spanish.

Max von Schumann did something more than meet with Albert James again, he also introduced him to certain of his friends who, like him, were opposed to Hitler.

The group was made up of professors, lawyers, a few small businessmen, and even another aristocrat, Max's cousin, as well as two Protestant pastors. Members of the enlightened bourgeoisie who hated what Hitler was doing to Germany.

Albert felt an immediate connection to Karl Schatzhauser, an old professor of medicine who had been one of Max's teachers when the baron was carrying out his studies.

Karl Schatzhauser lived in a building on the Leipzigerstrasse, dangerously close to the general headquarters of the Gestapo, something that did not seem to intimidate him when he invited his friends in the secret anti-Hitler group round to his house.

"Why don't you work together with the Socialists and the Communists?" Albert asked Professor Schatzhauser.

"We should, but there is so much that keeps us apart... I think that they wouldn't trust us and that some of us wouldn't trust them. No, now is not the time to work together. The Communists don't know what to do after the pact that Ribbentrop signed with the Russians. This is a tragedy for them: Hitler locks up and persecutes the Communists here in Germany, and then Stalin goes and signs a treaty with him. The German Communists want to turn our country into another Soviet Union, and what we want is to get back to some kind of normality."

"But that saps your strength when it comes to take on Hitler himself," Albert insisted.

"We want a Christian Germany, a democratic country where everyone is subject to the law rather than the crazy whims of whichever madman has installed himself as chancellor. And don't think for a second that the moderates are not also to blame for their part in Hitler's rise to power. People like him cannot be bargained with, it's a mistake that we have made here in Germany, and also that the other European powers have made. In order to be effective we need to be able to pass unnoticed, and that is why I tell my friends that we need to be like chameleons. For example, Max wanted to leave the army, but I convinced him not to because he is of more use to us inside, so we can know what the military leaders think, which ones might be sympathetic to our cause, what Hitler's plans are... We must all stay in our posts, we don't have to show any enthusiasm for the Führer at all, but we don't want to end up in the Gestapo's dungeons either. We wouldn't be any use to our country there."

Albert was impressed by the strength and clarity of Professor Schatzhauser's ideas, but Amelia thought that Max, the Professor and his friends were too weak to be effective against a monster like Hitler.

The Berliners seemed to live apart from the sufferings of the war, and Berlin, the *Stadt der Musik und des Theaters*, carried on as it had before.

"Albert, it says here that Carla Alessandrini will be premiering *Tristan und Isolde* in the Deutsches Opernhaus in a fortnight's time!"

"Your friend Carla is coming to Berlin? You told me that she was a committed anti-Fascist."

"And she is! But Carla, as well as being the greatest opera singer in the world, is an Italian, so it's not surprising that they should contract her in Berlin. And aren't we here, you and I? The Nazis think that because you're from the United States and your country has declared itself neutral that you are no danger, and I am Spanish, which means they must think that I'm a Francoist."

Albert said nothing, he knew how much Amelia loved Carla Alessandrini and that any critical commentary on his part would have led to an argument.

"But she's here!" Amelia exclaimed.

"What do you mean?"

"It says in the newspaper that Carla is staying in the Adlon. I'll ask for the switchboard to put me through to her."

A few minutes later Amelia heard the cheerful voice of Vittorio Leonardi, Carla's husband.

"Amelia, *cara! Come vai?*"

Amelia explained that she was staying in the hotel and was keen to see them, and Vittorio didn't need to be asked twice.

"Carla is rehearsing, I'll go to find her at the theatre, and when she comes back we can all go and eat together."

When they met in the hotel lobby, Carla hugged Amelia. Vittorio spoke with Albert as if he had known him all his life, even though they had barely known each other in Paris. But Vittorio was a man of the world, and understood straight away that Amelia's companion was more than just a good friend.

The four of them ate in the hotel restaurant, and Carla was extremely interested in the latest twists and turns of Amelia's life.

"*Cara*! It is as if tragedy followed you round the world! I don't understand how this can be, with you as beautiful as you are, but of course, life is like that, now the important thing is that you are well and that Albert is looking after you; and he should, because if he didn't then he would have me to reckon with," she said, pointing a menacing finger at Albert James.

The diva explained that even though she hated the Nazis, Vittorio had insisted that, with the Fascists in charge of Italy, it would be a step too far to reject an invitation to sing in Berlin. She was upset about her many Jewish friends, musicians, conductors, theater people, who had fled into exile.

"Don't let appearances fool you, this city is not what it once was, the best have been forced to flee. Don't imagine that I feel comfortable here..."

"But Carla, *amore*! You can't show your political beliefs so openly. In Milan she snubbed Il Duce when he wanted to see her after she had appeared in *La Traviata*. Carla locked herself away in her dressing-room after the performance and told me to tell him that she had a migraine and could not speak. Of course, Il Duce did not believe her, and we found out via some friends that he has set a watch on us. If we had refused to travel to Berlin, what do you think that Il Duce would have thought?

There was nothing we could have said to get us out of this engagement."

"I hate all Fascists, and the Nazis most of all!" Carla said, without caring that the guests at the neighboring tables were looking at her in stunned silence.

"Please, darling, don't shout!" Vittorio begged.

"I feel the same as you," Amelia said, taking hold of her friend's hand.

"We all feel the same, but Vittorio's right, we have to be cautious," Albert said.

"This is the problem, that prudence ends up turning into collaboration," Amelia said.

"No, that's not right. I think it is best for us to be able to come to Berlin and move around and talk to people and then tell the world just how dangerous Hitler is. If I get up now and start to take on the Nazis, then the only thing that will happen to me is that I'll get arrested, and then I won't be able to tell the papers just what is happening here," Albert said.

"And people say that men are impractical and uncalculating," Carla added.

Vittorio told them that in two days' time the leaders of the Deutsche Opernhaus were going to have a reception followed by a dinner in Carla's honor, and that he would ask for them to be invited.

"They had better invite you, or else I won't go to the reception myself," Carla said.

The German-Soviet pact reached further than people had imagined. Its secret agreements began to come to light as events moved on, and on September 17 Soviet troops entered Poland.

The next day, Albert and Amelia went to a meeting at Karl Schatzhauser's house. The doctor called for calm from the group.

"They have divided Poland between themselves," Max complained, "and the British Government has done nothing to save it."

"England does not seem to have a clear idea of the path it should follow," Albert said.

"The Poles are their allies, but they have let them fall into the hands of Hitler and Stalin!" Amelia replied.

A Protestant pastor was at the meeting and he attempted to halt the despair into which the group was in danger of falling by talking to them about faith.

"There are still things we can do, we are not going to give in. There are lots of people who are opposed to Hitler," the priest, whose name was Ludwig Schmidt, said.

The pastor said he knew of someone close to Admiral Canaris, the head of German counterespionage; according to his friend, the admiral did not share the ideals of the Nazi Party; what's more, he appeared to show his willingness to help anyone who wanted to oppose Hitler, provided his own involvement remained invisible.

Max von Schumann confirmed this information, and added that Colonel Hans Oster, the head of the Office of Counterespionage in the High Command of the Armed Forces, as well as other military leaders, was opposed to Hitler.

"They should join forces!" Albert insisted.

"We mustn't make any false moves, it's best that each group acts as it sees best, and then the time will come where we know who is who, and who is with whom," Karl Schatzhauser said.

"You are the leader of our group, and so you control our strategy, but I think that Albert James is right," Max said bluntly.

The pastor Ludwig Schmidt gave Albert James a brief analysis of the foundations of Nazism.

"There are three books that you need to read to find out what it is that holds this madness together: *Mein Kampf* by Hitler himself, *The Myth of the Twentieth Century* by Alfred Rosenberg, and Gottfried Feder's *Manifesto for Breaking the Chains of Gold*. But don't you imagine that Feder has managed to explain how to clean up the German economy. Rosenberg's book is stupid, all he wants to do is show how the Nordic races are superior. He attacks the fundamental bases of Christianity as well, because you must never forget that the Nazis hate and abominate God as well. But read, read *Mein Kampf*, and you will see pretty clearly what it is that Hitler proposes."

"The principle victims have so far been the Jews," Amelia said.

"You are right, but as well as getting rid of the Jews, the main aim of National Socialism is to remove Germany's Christian roots, to create a country without God and without religion," Pastor Schmidt said.

Amelia took advantage of a moment when Albert was talking with Professor Schatzhauser to insist that Max help her look for the Wassermanns.

"A friend of ours told us that they had been taken to a labor camp, there must be a register of names, of who has gone where..."

"It won't be easy to find out, but I will do what I can."

"You are an officer, they'll tell you."

"I am an officer, and one who will attract suspicion from the party if I show myself to be too interested in the Jews. Things aren't so easy, but I'll see if I can find anything out via a friend of mine who works in the counterespionage service."

At another moment in the meeting, Amelia asked Max about Ludovica.

"As you can imagine, she doesn't know anything about these meetings, there's no doubt that she'd denounce us if she did."

"Ludovica is a Nazi, isn't she?"

"You heard what she said, I have a wife who's a committed Nazi. She comes from a family of businessmen and Ruhr Valley industrialists who have all, like many others, offered their support to Hitler. They wanted strong government, a dictator. Many people who supported him now say that they thought they could control him, but that's just their excuse, and an excuse for people who are nationalists because it suits their own interests, and who don't care at all about Germany's moral degradation."

"I am sorry for what you're going through..."

"You can imagine how painful it is for me that Ludovica is a Nazi. Of course, I don't tell her everything, and our relationship has deteriorated, we only keep up appearances in public."

"Why don't you separate?"

"I cannot, I am a Catholic. In this majority-Protestant country there are still some Catholics, and Ludovica and I are among them. We are condemned to be together forever."

"But that's horrible!"

"We aren't the first couple to stay together and keep up appearances, and we won't be the last. Also, even if I wanted to separate, Ludovica wouldn't allow it, so we have both adapted to the situation. I have no hope of being happy, the only thing that obsesses me is the possibility of getting rid of Hitler."

Karl Schatzhauser, with Albert, came up to them.

"My dear Amelia, try to convince Albert to tell the British government that it is not Germany as a whole that has gone mad, that there are men and women who are prepared to fight against Hitler, but that we need help. We need help, but the British need to know that we would never betray our country, all we want to do is to get rid of Hitler and to stop this war from becoming a greater tragedy than the previous one."

Albert said that he would help them, and in this way he broke for the first time one of his hitherto unalterable principles, that of telling his readers what it was that he saw and heard, but without implicating himself politically.

At the end of September, Poland surrendered to Germany. The country was divided into zones: The western provinces were turned over to Germany, and the eastern ones stayed in the hands of the Soviet Union. Millions of Poles suffered the consequences of being under the jackboot of the Reich. The first victims were the Jews.

The premiere of *Tristan und Isolde* was a great success. The public was overwhelmed and made Carla Alessandrini take ten curtain calls. Joseph Goebbels and other members of the party hierarchy came to the performance. Some of them sent bouquets to the Italian diva or even asked her directly to have dinner with them. But Carla didn't even look at the flowers, and ordered her dresser to leave them outside the dressing-room.

"Even Nazi flowers smell bad," she said.

After the performance, Vittorio and Carla invited a group of friends, Albert and Amelia among them, to have dinner with them at the hotel. After the dinner, Carla excused herself, saying that she was tired, and asked Amelia to accompany her to her suite.

"We haven't had a chance to be alone for a minute, and I wanted to ask you if it is serious between you and Albert James."

Amelia thought about her response. She too was thinking about the importance of her relationship to the journalist.

"Albert has saved my life on more than one occasion. He is the most generous person I've ever met and he has never asked anything of me."

"I asked if you love him, nothing more."

"Yes, I suppose I love him."

"Well, that's a positive answer! So, you don't love him."

"Yes, yes, I love him! I just don't love him like I loved Pierre, but I suppose I will never love anyone again like I loved him. He hurt me so much!"

"Forget about Pierre! He's dead, and what's done is done, there's no way back. Don't become one of those people who moans about the past. You have to look toward the future and enjoy the present as much as possible. I'll give you my opinion: Albert is a good man, he loves you and is willing to do anything for you, and maybe that's why you don't value him as much as you should."

"But I know very well that he's an exceptional man!"

"A man who loves you and trusts you unconditionally. Vittorio is like that as well, and as you can see I couldn't live without him, but that is pure egotism on my part. He is my husband, yes, but he is also my support. I think that Albert is like Vittorio, and men like that deserve more than we can give them. It's a shame, but life is like that!"

"I don't like that you think I don't value Albert."

"Of course you value him! But you are not in love with him and you would leave him at any time. What about your German baron, Max von Schumann?"

"It's nothing, Albert and I have eaten in his house and we have seen him a few times."

"I seem to remember that you wrote to me to tell me how much he attracted you."

"It's true... but Max is married, I met his wife, the Baroness Ludovica. She is very beautiful but awful, she's a Nazi. Max is not happy with her."

"I spy conflict! You will end up falling into Max's arms."

"No, I don't want to, and he doesn't want it either. Max is a man of honor and he is married to Ludovica forever. They are Catholics."

"Don't talk nonsense! I'm a Catholic as well, and although I don't even dream of leaving Vittorio, what if some great love came along and swept me away? What would I be capable of doing? Up until now the men whom I've known and loved haven't been worth it to leave Vittorio for, and as the years go by it seems more and more unlikely that I will meet a prince on a white horse who will come and carry me away, but what if he does appear? The only thing we must not do is fool ourselves. I can see that you are still attracted to the baron, and, well, the only thing I wish is for you not to suffer too much. I don't want you to forget, ever, that if things go bad you can always count on me, all the more so now that you have lost your parents. Do you have any more news from your family?"

"My sister Antonietta is still weak."

"That girl needs to eat, why don't you bring her to Italy? You could take her to my house in Milan, or better, you could go to my villa in Capri and she could recover and breathe the pure sea air."

"You know that I can't, that I have to work, I don't want to take Albert's money except in exchange for my work. I can help my family with this money, my Uncle Armando earns barely enough to support them. And Pablo, Lola's son, is still in my uncle and aunt's house, his grandmother is not getting better and is still in the hospital. That is a lot of mouths to feed."

"And you are too proud to accept my help!"

"I am not proud, Carla, I am telling you that if I were not able to earn money for my family by my own efforts then I would of course ask you for your help before letting them lack necessary things, but I can send them enough money for the time being, and I spend hardly anything on myself."

"Yes, I have seen that. We're going shopping, you can't stop me from buying you a few little things, because, well, what do you want me to say, you always look like Cinderella."

A few days later, Professor Karl Schatzhauser called Albert and asked him to come immediately. He insisted that Amelia come too.

They reached his house as evening was falling and met Max and another man there. Karl Schatzhauser did not beat around the bush.

"Dear Amelia, they say that you are a friend of Carla Alessandrini."

"Yes," Amelia replied, a little confused.

"She might be able to help us to save a young woman's life."

"I don't understand..."

"Allow me to present Father Rudolf Müller."

Professor Schatzhauser indicated the man who had kept silence until that moment. The priest, who was no more than thirty years old, seemed nervous.

"Father Müller is a Catholic priest, and a member of our little group. Of course, he is with us in a personal capacity, rather than as a representative of the Catholic Church."

Amelia and Albert looked at the priest with interest, who in his turn looked at them with anxiety.

"I don't need to explain the situation that the German Jews find themselves in nowadays, nor the persecution to which they are submitted. Many of them disappear overnight to labor camps, without it being possible to find any information about them or what happens to them once they reach these places. A Jewish family, friends of Father Müller, has a problem and Max and I thought that you might be able to help. But it would be best if Father Müller explains the situation himself."

The priest cleared his throat before speaking and looked directly at Amelia as he explained what he needed from them.

"I am an orphan. My father died when I was a child and my mother brought me up, along with my older brother. My father had a bookbindery that allowed us to live on a modest scale, he even had an employee. When he died my mother took charge of the business, and my older brother helped her as much as he could, but I don't need to remind you of the economic crisis that Germany has been through, and along with my father's death, business began to fall off in the workshop as well. Right by the bindery, near the Chamissoplatz, lived some friends of my parents, the Weisses, who bought and sold books. Herr Weiss, as well as being a friend of my father's, was a client of his, he always used to bring old books for my father to bind. Herr Weiss is not a Jew, but his wife, Batsheva, is. They had a daughter, Rahel, the same age as me, we grew up together and you could say that she is like a sister to me. When my father died, Herr Weiss helped my mother as much as he could, and in spite of the difficulties he himself experienced he never stopped supporting us. A year ago, Herr Weiss died of a heart attack, and then two months later Batsheva was arrested by the Gestapo and accused of selling forbidden books. It was a false accusation, but they took her away and the only thing we have been able to find out is that she is in a labor camp. Luckily, Rahel wasn't there the day the Gestapo presented themselves at the bookshop, so she was not arrested. I will not rest until I know that she is out of the country, but it is not easy for the Jews to get travel documents. The government cancelled their passports a year ago... and, well, I'm sure you're up to date with what's going on. Some friends of mine, who know a civil servant, assure me that they will be able to get Rahel travel documents, but she needs a guarantor, someone who will support her application for the document, and who will take her away. Max tells me that Carla Alessandrini is very fond of you and I thought... Well, we thought that if Signora Alessandrini were to offer herself as Rahel's guarantor then it would be easier to get her permission to travel. If Signora Alessandrini says that she wants to have Rahel as her maid, or her assistant, or whatever is most convenient, then the authorities won't deny it to her. That's what I wanted to ask, for you to save Rahel, who is like a sister to me, and I would... I would... I would be eternally grateful."

"Let's imagine that Carla Alessandrini agrees to this and we get the necessary permission and we manage to get Rahel out of Germany. Then what?" Albert James asked.

"Save her. Get her to the United States, there is a Jewish community there that will provide her with support, maybe she'll be able to find some of her mother's relatives who moved to New York years ago."

"I can't promise anything, but I will ask Carla. She is anti-Fascist and hates the Nazis. And if she cannot do anything then I will try, I am Spanish and Franco is an ally of Hitler's. Even if Carla gets her out of Germany, I could still help Rahel to Spain and from Spain to Portugal," Amelia said.

When Father Müller had left, Max and Professor Schatzhauser apologized to Albert and Amelia.

"We know," Max said, "that we put you in a tricky situation there, and I must confess that it was my idea, and for that I ask your forgiveness. I have known Father Müller for some time and he is a good man and I would like to help him, even though I have put you in a difficult situation because of that. Especially you, Amelia, because Carla Alessandrini is your friend, after all."

On the way back to the hotel, Amelia and Albert had an argument. He was worried that Carla would feel that Amelia was using her, and that this might affect their friendship; he knew how important Carla was to Amelia.

But Albert did not know what kind of a woman *la Alessandrini* was, and as soon as Amelia had explained the situation to her she accepted in a flash, even though her husband Vittorio counseled prudence.

"Prudence? How can you ask me to be prudent when I have the chance to help a poor unfortunate? I will do it, of course I will do it, I will go to the police station and ask for Rahel to have her permission to travel, and I will say that I cannot do without her, that she is an amazing dresser. Even if I have to call Goebbels himself to get her this permission... we will get the girl out of here."

Amelia hugged her friend and thanked her, crying. She knew that the diva had a vast heart and had had no doubt that she could ask her such a dangerous favor.

Accompanied by Father Müller and Rahel herself, Carla went to the office that provided travel documents for Jews. The officer whose job it was to verify the paperwork had been bribed, by Max, in cash.

Carla filled out an endless number of forms, answered another endless series of stupid questions, and played the diva more than she had ever had in her life, knowing that this would impress these office workers. When one of the officials said that it would take time for permission to be granted, Carla, furious, made a scene.

"Time? How much time do you think I have to stay in Berlin? I will call Goebbels himself to sort out this problem, and then we'll see if he's happy with you blocking me like you are doing now. Let me tell you that if this is not sorted out now, then I will never sing in Berlin again!"

Rahel got her passport, stamped with the letter "J" for *Jude*.

Carla, Vittorio, Albert, and Amelia, along with Rahel, left Berlin on October 12. Before they left, Amelia insisted that Max help them look for the Wassermanns.

"I can't believe that you haven't been able to find out where they are," Amelia complained.

"You must understand that I can't ask about them directly, but I am doing everything in my power to find out what happened to them."

"When you find them you have to help them, swear to me that you will get them out of wherever it is they are!"

"I give you my word of honor that I will do whatever I can to help them."

"That's not enough! You have to get them out of the labor camp, or wherever they are!"

"I can't promise you that, Amelia; if I did I would be lying."

Getting Rahel out of Berlin was only the first part of the plan that they had worked out over the last few days. They would take the train to Paris, then Carla would return to Italy, while Albert and Amelia took Rahel over the border to Spain. Amelia had promised to cross Spain with her and get her as far as Portugal. Albert promised not only to help them, but also to get the necessary permissions from the British Embassy for Rahel to travel to New York. Albert thought that if he called his uncle, Paul James, then he could use the influence he derived from his important position in the Admiralty to push the British Embassy into providing Rahel Weiss with the necessary documents for traveling to America.

Carla's presence was a guarantee of safe conduct. The customs inspectors, the policemen, even the Gestapo all seemed to trust the diva, so in spite of Albert's worries, or Amelia's, or Vittorio's, or even Rahel's, the party was able to make it to the French capital without any trouble.

Rahel was a good-looking woman, with chestnut hair and eyes of the same color, shy and sweet and very well mannered; everyone was taken by her friendliness.

In Paris, Carla and Vittorio stayed in the Hotel Meurice, where the diva had decided to spend a few days before heading on to Rome. This was not a whim of hers, but rather a way to give Albert and Amelia time to make it to the Spanish border. Although they had not had any problems up to then, Carla thought it was better not to go too far, in case they were arrested because of Rahel.

France seemed sunk in depression. The country was officially at war with Germany, and Édouard Daladier, the prime minister, was starting to be overwhelmed by events.

Amelia's plan was to go to Biarritz and from there make her way down to the Spanish border, which she thought she would cross not at the official customs post but via the paths which Aitor had shown her so many years ago. She still remembered the time she had spent convalescing on her nurse Amaya's family farm, and the friendship that had grown up between her and Amaya's children Edurne and Aitor. Amelia wondered whether Aitor had come back from Mexico, and if so, whether he would be living in exile in the French Basque country. If that were the case, then surely Aitor would help them.

Albert drove to Biarritz without stopping, and when they arrived Amelia took them to her grandmother Margot's house. The old woman had died some time before, but Amelia trusted that Yvonne, her nurse, would have kept the keys or else would still be living in the house.

When they got close to the house, on a slope overlooking the sea, Amelia noticed that the shutters were open.

She asked Albert and Rahel to wait for her in the car, as she was not sure what she would find.

Yvonne opened the door and at first seemed not to recognize Amelia, but then she did so, and fell into her arms, crying.

"Mademoiselle Amelia, how marvelous to see you! Goodness, what a surprise!"

She invited her in and then told Amelia through tears what she already knew, that grandmother Margot had died.

"Madame did not suffer, but she was very anxious the last few days, it was as if she knew that she would die and she was sad that she could not say goodbye to her children or her grandchildren, especially to you and Mademoiselle Laura, who were her favorites."

Yvonne explained that grandmother Margot had given her permission to stay in the house, sure that her children, when they came to Biarritz, would carry on using it.

"Madame made her will a few months before she died; here is an envelope she gave me, it is still sealed, but Madame told me that it contains the name of the notary whom Don Juan and Don Armando should contact. Madame was very well prepared, and very worried about the war in Spain; she gave me some money so that I should lack for nothing in my old age and... well, here I am, waiting for one of the Garayoas to appear."

Amelia explained that she was on her way to Spain with some friends, and that it would be good if they could rest there and have some hot food.

It was also a relief for Albert and Rahel to find that this house was a safe haven. Yvonne didn't ask for any explanations, and didn't need any to know that this was something important and that Amelia was in a tight spot, and when Rahel went to bed that night and Albert collapsed out of pure exhaustion, Yvonne came to speak with Amelia.

"Mademoiselle, I think that you have problems, and if I can help you... Madame Margot trusted me and you know how much she loved your family, I met you just after you'd been born, the same as with Mademoiselle Antonietta. I came to this house because Madame Margot's mother, Madame Amélie brought me here, and you are named after her..."

"I know, Yvonne, I know... Of course I can trust you! Look, we are going to enter Spain, but not via the customs post; we're going to use the mountain passes. Do you remember Aitor, Amaya's son? He showed me secret paths that are normally only used by goats."

"Lots of Spaniards have come here running away from Franco, oh, if you could only see them, the poor things! I don't know about Aitor, but I do know of a Spanish refugee who came here and who was with the PNV. A good man, who worked a lot to feed his family. I think he had a business before the war broke out, but he lost everything when he went into exile. He was lucky enough to be married to a woman from here, and now he works in a hotel. If you would like... I don't know... Maybe he knows something about Aitor..."

"Thank you so much! Aitor could be a great help for us, I saw him a few months ago in Mexico and he was planning to return and help the refugees, I do so hope that he has!"

"I will go out early tomorrow to see if I can find this man, he'll be working at the reception of the hotel at seven."

Yvonne did as she had promised and told Amelia that the man from the PNV would come to see them that afternoon, as soon as he had finished his day's work. Albert decided to let Amelia plan this part of their mission, even though he had his doubts; he thought it was unwise to trust a stranger.

At half past six that evening, Patxi Olarra came to the house. Albert thought that he must be about fifty years old. He looked hale and hearty, but his hair was completely white.

Amelia asked him if he knew Aitor Garmendia, and told him a little bit about Aitor, where his family farm was and that the last time she had seen him was in Mexico, as secretary to one of the leaders of the PNV in exile.

Olarra listened in silence and took his time before replying.

"What do you want?" he asked straight out.

"Want? We don't want anything, I am a childhood friend of Aitor's..."

"Yes, but what do you want from him?" Olarra insisted.

"I've said that I would like to know if he's around here, and if he is, then I should like to see him. I suppose that the PNV exiles stay in touch, know about each other..."

"I will see what I can do for you."

Patxi Olarra got up and nodded his head and left the house without saying another word.

"What a strange man!" Albert said.

"Basques are men of few words, if they have to do something, they do it and that's that," Amelia replied.

"I don't know if he's an ally or if he's going to betray us," Albert said, worriedly.

"He doesn't know anything about us, he hasn't seen Rahel."

"Yes, but... I don't know... I'm worried."

"He's a good man, I promise you," Yvonne said.

They spent two days without hearing anything from Olarra, and Amelia decided not to wait any longer and instead to try to cross into Spain by themselves.

"But are you sure you remember the tracks that Aitor showed you?" Albert asked.

"Of course," Amelia replied with more certainty than she felt.

For her part, Rahel had put so much trust in Amelia that even though she was older she relied on Amelia like a child.

Amelia had everything organized for the next day, so she suggested that they go to bed early and rest.

"The mountain paths are not easy, so it's best if we rest now."

They had not yet gone to sleep when someone rang the doorbell. They tensed up, watchful. Yvonne sent Rahel upstairs and went down to open the door.

Outside someone asked for Amelia and she recognized the voice and cried out in happiness.

"Aitor! You've come!"

"Don't think it's that easy to get from one side to the other," Aitor said as he hugged his friend.

They spoke for a while. Aitor explained that his boss had decided to send him back to be a go-between between those who were trying to escape and those who had organized themselves in exile.

"We try to be discreet so as not to get the French authorities into trouble, because even though France is at war with Germany it hasn't yet broken with Spain, so we have to be careful. You can't imagine the hundreds of thousands of refugees that there are in the camps, nor the conditions they are living in... We are trying to help some of our own and to get people across the border, but it is difficult."

"We're trying to get into Spain via one of those mountain passes you told me about, we need to save someone..."

Amelia explained about Rahel and about how they were trying to get her to Lisbon.

"It won't be easy, especially not at this time of the year, it's almost winter and it's snowing. And there are soldiers and Franco's police everywhere."

"But you use the mountain passes; or if not, how do you get people out of Spain?"

Aitor said nothing. He didn't want to disappoint Amelia, but he also didn't want to put his organization in danger by trying to do something so complicated as bringing a Jew across Spanish territory all the way to Portugal. If they were stopped and tortured they would say where and how and with whom they had crossed the border and everything would be laid bare.

"I don't have the authority to make this decision, I need to talk to my superiors," Aitor said.

"You don't need to, if you don't want to help me, don't do it. We will be going tomorrow, and if you don't come then we'll try ourselves."

"Please, Amelia, don't do anything crazy! You'll probably get lost in the mountains, and that's all the more likely at this time of year. It's not a game, it's not a walk in the hills."

"We cannot stay here, Rahel is in greater danger with every day that passes. Her only chance is to get to Portugal."

"She could get a French residence permit... They are at war with Germany."

"Are you laughing at me? Do I need to remind you where the Spanish refugees have ended up? Do you want me to tell you about their Jewish policy? Get out, Aitor, I don't want to put you in a difficult situation, you're fighting your own war and Rahel is not a part of it, you don't need to help us."

"If anything goes wrong you're risking your lives," Aitor warned.

"I know, we all know, but we don't have any other option."

Aitor left in a bad mood. He hadn't been able to reason with Amelia, to convince her that the shepherd tracks in the mountains were dangerous.

Nor could Albert convince Amelia to try to find another solution.

"I am going tomorrow with Rahel, and I promise you that I will get to the other side," Amelia replied angrily to Albert's reasoning.

At three o'clock in the morning, when Albert, Amelia, and Rahel were saying goodbye to Yvonne, they heard some soft knocks at the door. The old maid went to open up and was surprised to see Aitor.

"You're as stubborn as a mule, so I've got no other option than to help you, or else you'll end up showing the police where the paths across the mountains are," he said.

Amelia hugged him in gratitude.

"Thank you! Thank you so much!"

"Are you well prepared? You need warm clothing or you'll die of cold."

"I think we've got everything we need," Albert said.

The first night they slept in the open air, and after that in shepherd's huts. Aitor led the way, his steps firm in spite of the darkness, and Albert brought up the rear. Amelia and Rahel walked in silence, without complaining about the hard ground or the fear provoked by the sounds they heard at night.

"There's not very far to go before we enter Spain, and it's better to do it while it's still dark," Aitor told them one dawn.

"How much further is there to go?" Albert asked.

"No more than fifteen kilometers. Then we will go to my grandparents' farm. They're waiting for us there."

Amelia spied Amaya in the doorway of the farmhouse and ran to her crying. She hugged her nurse and the woman covered her with kisses.

"But dear Amelia, how beautiful you are! How much you have changed! Good Lord, I thought I would never see you again!"

They went into the farmhouse, which held such memories for Amelia, and she was shocked to find out that Aitor's grandfather had died and that his grandmother lay sick in bed.

"She doesn't even talk anymore," Amaya said, pointing sadly to the old woman, who did not seem to recognize them.

Amaya made them some food, and cackled to see Albert's expression as he drank his bowl of milk.

"You don't like it? I suppose you've never had real milk before, fresh from the cow."

"What have you heard about my family?"

"Edurne writes from time to time, but she's very scared, you know that the police open letters and suspect everyone. Your sister Antonietta is getting better, Lola's son is still in your uncle and aunt's house because his grandmother is still in the hospital. Don Armando is working, and your cousin Laura is happy in her school. My Edurne looks after them well, don't you worry."

"I suppose she's told you nothing about my son Javier or Santiago..."

"They see your son at a distance and he's a beautiful boy who lacks for nothing. Águeda looks after him and keeps him wonderfully clean. Aren't you going to try to find a telephone and ring them?"

"Of course she isn't!" Aitor interrupted. "It's better to be discreet and the less notice we attract the better; the police monitor all calls."

"Yes, you're right," Amelia admitted.

"Now I will tell you how to get to Portugal. I have a friend who's in the scrap-metal business, and he goes all over the place with his little truck. He'll take you to Portugal, but you'll have to pay him. It's a long trip and they might stop you, so it won't be cheap, do you have any money?"

Albert said that he would pay whatever was needed, and Aitor looked at him, clearly thinking that this was no ordinary man. He wondered if Amelia might be in love with him and came to the conclusion that no, she probably wasn't, even though they made a good couple.

They didn't have to wait more than half an hour before Jose María Eguía, the scrap-metal merchant, came to the farmhouse. Aitor went out to see him as soon as he heard the truck's engine.

Eguía asked them to pay him in advance.

"If I get into trouble," he said, "then at least I'll have some pesetas, which I'll need. I've got a wife, three kids, and my mother-in-law living with us, and not a lot to throw in the pot. Also, if you do a job you've got to get paid for it, right?"

They didn't haggle at all, and said goodbye to Aitor and Amaya.

"Thank you, I'll never forget what you've done for me," Amelia said.

"Take care. I know your passport is in order, and Albert's too, but I'm not so sure about the Jewish kid... I don't know what they'd do to her if the police stopped her."

"We'll be careful, don't worry."

"You can trust Eguía. He's a good man, even if he is a bit rough. His grandparents have a farm near here, we used to play together when we were kids."

"Is he in the PNV?" Amelia asked.

"No, he's not interested in politics."

They barely fit in the truck. Albert sat next to Eguía and Amelia and Rahel got into the back, on top of a pile of scrap metal, but neither of the women complained.

"Do you think we'll make it to Portugal?" Rahel asked Amelia shyly.

"Of course we will. It's a long trip and it'll seem even longer on these roads, but we'll get there and Albert will help you get to the United States."

Rahel looked at her, grateful for these words of encouragement. It was not an easy journey and it soon became clear that the truck was in worse shape than it had at first appeared. They got a puncture in Santander and Eguía said, after taking the tire off, that it was no longer any use and that they would have to buy a new one.

"But don't you have a spare tire?" Albert asked, slightly alarmed.

"Bah! Where am I going to get a spare tire from? We don't have anything here."

In the end they found an old garage that sold them a used tire. Albert, naturally, paid for it.

"If I pay then the money doesn't add up," Eguía explained.

They bought bread and whatever they could find, and they ate and slept in the truck. Albert offered to drive, and although Eguía resisted at first he ended up accepting so that he could rest.

"What a trek! If I'd have known I'd have asked for more money," the scrap-metal dealer complained.

Later on, Albert James wrote some articles about postwar Spain in which he spoke of a country that lacked everything, and where fear had sealed people's throats.

He said that whenever they stopped to have a coffee in a bar, or to fill up with gas, or when they went into a little shop in a dead-end town to buy bread, they always met with a wall of silence in the face of any attempt to find out people's opinions about the political situation.

He was also surprised by the extremely patriotic speeches given by the new bosses, but above all, he was shocked by the hunger he saw. In one of his articles he wrote that the Spaniards of that time had hunger drawn on their faces.

No sooner had they reached Asturias than the truck stopped on a mountain pass. They had to get out and push the truck to the side of the road, and then Eguía tried to fix it.

"Oh, this is terrible!" he said when he took a look at the engine.

"But can you fix it?" Amelia asked.

"I don't know, maybe yes, maybe no."

They were lucky. A few army trucks were passing by and Eguía flagged them down.

The captain who was in charge of the convoy turned out to be friendly.

"I don't know much about this myself, but the sergeant is a whiz with engines and he'll sort things out straight away."

Amelia prayed that he wouldn't ask them for their papers. She was especially scared that they would ask Rahel questions, because she only spoke German, or even that they would speak to Albert, who spoke Spanish, but not very fluently. At first the captain was not particularly interested in the two women, but Albert did intrigue him.

"Where are you from, then?" he asked.

"I'm from the United States."

"Goodness! You wouldn't be one of those who came across to fight with the International Brigades?" he said, laughing.

"No, of course not."

"You can see it in your face, you can see that you're a rich fellow, one of those Americans with dollars to spare."

"There's never money to spare," Albert said, just to say something.

"And what about the girls?"

"My wife and her sister."

"You're a brave man to put up with the wife and the sister-in-law at the same time."

"They're good people," Albert said, who didn't understand all the captain's jokes.

"Don't you believe it, women are the same the whole world over."

"It's done, sir!" the sergeant interrupted. "It wasn't as bad a problem as it looked to begin with."

The captain mused to himself for a bit, thinking that it was a little odd to meet an American in Asturias, but then he remembered that Spain had nothing against the Americans, and so he decided to limit himself to wishing them a safe journey.

"Drive carefully!"

They reached Portugal three days later. Eguía told them to pass over the border through a little village where there were almost no controls.

"It's right on the border; they can see Portugal from their windows and cross the border trying to catch their chickens when they run away."

"Are you sure that there are no guards?" Amelia asked suspiciously.

"Sure I'm sure, and I've got a friend who'll help us too."

Eguía's friend was called Mouriño, they had met in the army and had got on so well that they had joined up in smuggling goods across the border, one of them bringing things from France, the other from Portugal. When the war was over they had gone back to this trade.

Mouriño invited them to bread and cheese and a glass of wine, while he and Eguía talked business. The Basque unloaded the scrap metal and Mouriño brought it to a shed where he took some packages out from under a tarpaulin and gave them to Eguía to take to San Sebastián.

"It's English tobacco," he explained. "The French love it."

Nobody asked anything and they went into Portugal without being seen by a single guard.

"This is incredible! I couldn't believe that we'd get over the border so easily," Albert said.

"Don't imagine that it's easy, it's just that this village is a ways away from the more widely used frontier posts and if you're lucky then you won't meet any guards and you can get across without any trouble. A lot of smuggling goes on here."

"I thought you sold scrap metal..."

"And other things."

They found a pension close to the port in Lisbon that Eguía had recommended.

"It's not much, but the sheets are clean and the most important thing is that they don't ask any questions."

That night, finally, they had a hot meal and slept in a real bed, even if it was much less clean than Eguía had intimated it would be.

The next morning, Albert called his Uncle Paul.

"Would you mind telling me where you are?"

"I'm in Lisbon now, but I've crossed half France and half of Spain to get here."

"Goodness, I didn't know you liked traveling so much," his uncle replied ironically.

"Neither did I. Look, Uncle Paul, I need your help."

"Right, I was wondering why you'd called. What's going on?"

"I have a friend, a very special person..."

"Amelia Garayoa?"

"No, not her, although she is with me. It's a person I met in Berlin, her name is Rahel Weiss and she's a Jew."

"Right. And what do you want?"

"I want our embassy here to get her some document or pass that will allow her to travel to the United States."

"You mean to England."

"No, I mean the United States, she has family there."

"Well, I can't do anything for you."

"Please, of course you can! I wouldn't ask if it weren't important. Do you know what's happening to the Jews in Germany?"

"I know that Hitler doesn't like the Jews, but we can't give refuge and shelter to everyone who is trying to run away from Germany."

"I'm not asking you to do anything impossible, all I ask is that you provide a document of safe passage to get her out of here."

"I can't make exceptions."

"Of course you can! All I want is for Rahel to get to the United States."

"And how do you know they'll let her in there?"

"If you'll give me the safe passage, then I will deal with the New York border control."

"I would like to help you, but I cannot."

"Do you know what this means? We have crossed half Europe to get here. I'm telling you that it was not easy, if Amelia and Carla Alessandrini hadn't helped us then we wouldn't have managed to do anything."

"Carla Alessandrini? The opera singer?"

"Yes, a very brave woman of decided opinions, Amelia's great friend."

"Well, well, well! Your Amelia is full of surprises."

"Will you help me or not?"

"I'll see if I can do something, but take care, there are Nazi agents swarming all over Lisbon."

"And British agents as well, I'm sure."

"I'm so charmed by your faith in us. Give me a number where I can get in touch with you."

Paul James called his nephew twenty-four hours later, after a tense argument with his superiors as he tried to get Rahel Weiss her document of safe passage. If he managed to convince them it was only because he told them that he would get a favor in return from his nephew.

Albert, along with Rahel and Amelia, went to the British Embassy. They asked for the man whose name Paul James had given them. It was clear to Albert that this must be an officer with British intelligence. He listened to Rahel's story patiently and showed more interest in their flight from Berlin, especially in the details about Amelia's contacts. Amelia started to feel uncomfortable in the face of this man's questioning: It was as if she were being interrogated.

"And if we can't get you the guarantee of safe passage, what will you do then?" the man asked, looking for Amelia to reply.

"Anything, rather than abandon Rahel. You are not our only option," she said defiantly.

The man took his leave, telling them they would have an answer in a few days, and also advising them not to call attention to themselves in Lisbon.

"You're a trio it's difficult not to notice."

They stayed almost entirely at the pension. Albert paid the owner to make them food and the most they dared do was to take a stroll by the sea.

Two days later, the man from the embassy called the pension and arranged to meet them in a nearby bar.

"Well, here are the necessary documents for Miss Weiss, it will be up to you to make sure they let her in once she gets to New York."

"Thank you...," Albert said, holding his hand out to the embassy official.

"Don't thank me; thank your all-powerful uncle. Oh, by the way, he asked me to ask you to call him as soon as possible, I think he wants to see you in London."

Albert bought a ticket for Rahel on a ship that left for New York the next day. It was a merchant vessel that took passengers, so Rahel would not be too uncomfortable and her arrival in the United States would pass more or less unnoticed.

He also paid the captain to take care of Rahel.

Amelia took a tearful leave of Rahel. She had become very fond of this shy and silent woman. Rahel took off one of her rings before getting on board the ship.

"This way you won't forget me... ," she said as she put the ring on Amelia's finger.

"Of course I won't forget you! Keep the ring, it's made of gold and with these stones... it must be very valuable, and you might need it if things go badly for you."

"No, I would never sell this ring, even if I were dying of hunger. It was from my grandmother, my father's mother. He gave it to me when I was eighteen. I want you to have it."

"But I cannot accept it!"

"If you do, then it will be as if we were still together. Please, don't reject it!"

They fell into each other's arms, and Albert had to separate them so that Rahel could board the ship.

"Don't worry, people will be waiting for you when you get to New York, you won't have any problem with the customs," Albert promised.

When they saw the boat sailing out of the harbor, Amelia felt a shiver of loneliness. Albert put an arm around her shoulders to comfort her. He was desperately in love with Amelia and there was nothing he would not do to please her.

"What shall we do now?" she asked him later, when they were back at the pension.

"Go to London. I have to speak to my father and ask him to speak to some friends of his to help Rahel get into the United States. My father is a friend of the governor of New York, so if he decides to help Rahel then there shouldn't be any problems. I also want to call a childhood friend of mine who works in the mayor's office. The man from the embassy told us that Uncle Paul wants to see us when we get to London, and after all he's done for us I can't say no."

"What will your uncle want?"

"Payment for the favor he's done us."

"What kind of payment?"

"I don't know, but I'm sure his price will be high."

"I... I'm sorry to have put you in this fix."

"It wasn't you, Amelia. It was a question of simple decency to save Rahel. It's terrible that we can't help everyone who needs our help. And it was Professor Schatzhauser and Max who asked us to help Rahel, and we could have done nothing without Carla."

"I would like to go to Madrid... We're so close..."

Albert hesitated, but in the end he held firm to his decision to go to London straight away.

"I'm sorry, Amelia, but after all he's done for us I can't just ignore my uncle."

"You're right, we'll go to Madrid in the future."

"I promise."

6

Amelia did not feel comfortable in London. She felt the hostility of the environment as a reflection of the hostility of Albert's friends and family, who had all found out that he was living with a married woman, something that was scandalous to puritanical British high society.

Albert found his parents about to return to New York, so he asked his father to talk to the state's governor and ask him to help Rahel. Ernest James adored his son and was incapable of denying him anything; he was also a fervent anti-Nazi, so he agreed to assist Rahel.

"Don't worry, we'll make sure that this woman gets into the country. Now that we're alone... well... I'd like to talk to you... Your mother is very worried, you know that she thought that you and Lady Mary... well..."

"I know, father, I know that you and mother would be very pleased for me to marry Mary Brian, and I am sorry not to be able to please you in this way."

"So your decision is final?"

"I introduced you to Amelia, and you know that I am in love with her."

"She is a very beautiful and intelligent young woman, but she is married, and you must know that your relationship has no future."

"It will have the future we both want it to have. You are Irish and much more concerned with tradition and custom than I am."

"You are Irish too, even if you were born in New York."

"I was brought up as an American, and I feel American. I respect your traditions, I try to obey your customs, but they are not sacred for me. I am in love with Amelia and I live with her, so it's best if mother stops trying to get me to marry Mary."

"You will not be able to have children."

"I hope that there will be a solution for our situation one day. But in the meantime I would like you to try to understand me, and if you cannot understand me, then at least try to respect my decision. I love Amelia, and I would like you to accept her into the family as if she were my wife."

"Your mother wants nothing to do with her!"

"Then she will have nothing to do with me either."

"Please, please think again!"

"Do you think I haven't thought at all about what it means to live with Amelia? Of course I have, and I will not allow anyone to embarrass her or do her down. Not even Mama."

Lord Paul James organized a farewell supper for his brother Ernest and his wife Eugenie, to which Albert and Amelia were invited. Albert's mother claimed that she was suffering from a severe migraine the night of the dinner, as well as saying that there was a great deal to organize before their departure to New York. For whatever reason, Eugenie was not there on the night of the dinner.

Albert and Amelia arrived at Albert's uncle's house at six on the dot, just as their invitation had asked them to. Paul James had invited a dozen friends, and all of them were surprised by the deferential way in which he spoke to Amelia, whose position in the eyes of the puritanical guests was nothing more or less than his nephew's lover. She also managed to cause a commotion by daring to say that Great Britain and all the European powers had washed their hands of Spain during the Civil War.

After all the guests had left, Paul James asked his nephew and Amelia to stay behind and take a glass of port with him in the library.

Albert whispered in Amelia's ear, "Now he's going to give us the bill for what he did for Rahel."

"I'm extremely impressed by the trouble you took to save that young Jewish woman, Rahel Weiss," he said as he poured them a glass of the rich purple Portuguese wine.

"Yes, it was complicated, but we were lucky," Albert replied.

"Lucky? I think that you were clever and good at improvisation. Congratulations."

Lord James cleared his throat before continuing, and looked at Amelia out of the corner of his eye. She seemed to be calm and sure of herself, her inner turmoil invisible.

"Right, we're at war, and people know how wars begin, but no one knows how or when they end. The enemy is strong, and it will be him or us. When I speak of 'us' I mean enlightened Europe, the Europe that holds within itself the values which we recognize and within which we were brought up. And there is no room in this war for neutrals. I feel sorry for you, Albert."

"I wanted to speak to you about some people we met in Berlin. I promised that I would try to help them prosecute their cause in England, so I am here before you to do so. Your friend Baron Max von Schumann belongs to a group of people opposed to Hitler."

"I know that already, what do you think he was doing here this summer? He asked us for help to get rid of Hitler, help which at that moment we were unable to give him."

"You were mistaken not to do so."

"Yes, there were those who were mistaken in thinking that the war would not break out, that Hitler would not dare invade Poland, would not dare to take the steps that he is now taking. I have always thought that he would take these steps, but my superiors thought the contrary. Even so, Baron von Schumann's group is... well, made up of people from here and there, disorganized, I am not sure that it is actually an effective opposition group, capable of doing anything more than getting together to complain that Hitler is now the ruler of Germany."

"Uncle, you're wrong. Look, apart from the Socialists and the Communists, I don't think that there are many organized opposition groups set up against Hitler. And the Communists, for all that they are persecuted in Germany, have now got to face the fact that their supreme leader, Stalin, has entered into a pact with

Hitler. The Socialists have no strength in themselves to topple the regime. What you have to do is convince all the opposition groups to work together. The leader of Max von Schumann's group is Professor Karl Schatzhauser, who is a well-known doctor and a respected university professor. I think that you should bear him in mind."

"Have you promised anything?"

"Only to pass on to you their plea for help and to give my opinion that they deserve it."

"Well, I will bear what you say in mind, even though all I can promise is that I will pass it on to my superiors. Now I want to talk about another matter... a delicate topic; let me say first of all that I trust I can count on your discretion."

Amelia and Albert both said that he could.

"Wars are not only won on the fronts, we need information, and we need people to gather it from behind enemy lines, brave men and women. My department in the Admiralty is preparing a group of select men and women to carry out this activity, all of them civilians and all of them with certain special qualities, qualities such as you yourself have, Amelia."

"Uncle Paul, what are you trying to do?" Albert interrupted.

"All I want to know is if you are ready to collaborate to help this war end as soon as possible."

"I am a journalist, and my only way of acting against the war is to tell people what is really happening."

"I have told you, Albert, you cannot be neutral in situations such as these. For all that Chamberlain's policy is one of appeasement, we find ourselves now staring war straight in the eye. Poland will not be enough for Hitler, especially now that the Soviets have decided to keep Finland. I am afraid that none of us know the eventual scale of the conflict, but my job is to bring my superiors enough information for them to make the correct decisions. We had to leave Germany after the declaration of war, but we need to have eyes and ears there."

"And if I am not mistaken, then you would like us to be a part of one of these groups that you are putting together."

"That is right. You are an American, and you can go everywhere without arousing suspicion, and Miss Garayoa is Spanish.

Your country is an ally of Hitler's, and you can travel all over Germany without provoking suspicion. You spoke to me of the Baron von Schumann: His role as an opposition figure does not interest me as much as the fact that he is a high-ranking soldier of good standing in the army. He has access to information which could be of vital importance to us."

"Max von Schumann will never betray Germany, he only wants to get rid of Hitler," Amelia said.

"But that is an omelette, my dear Miss Garayoa, which cannot be made without breaking at least a few eggs. I am afraid that we all will have to do things we do not like doing."

"I am sorry, Uncle Paul, but I cannot help you," Albert said.

Paul James looked at his nephew with distaste. He had hoped that the war would have opened his eyes, but Albert still had a romantic view of the journalist's role.

"Tell me, Lord James, if Great Britain wins the war against Germany, what effect will it have on the rest of Europe?" Amelia said.

"I'm afraid I don't understand..."

"I want to know if the defeat of Hitler will mean that the European powers will want to re-establish a European democracy. I want to know if you will carry on giving support to Franco and recognizing his legitimacy."

Lord James was surprised by Amelia's question. It was clear that she would help only if she thought she could be of some benefit to Spain, so he took a few seconds looking for the right words to use with Amelia.

"I cannot make any assurances. But Europe without Hitler would be different. The position of the Duce would not be the same in Italy, and as for Spain... it is clear that it would be very hard for Franco to lose German support. He would be seriously weakened."

"Well, if that is the case then I suppose I would be happy to collaborate against Hitler."

"Excellent! A very wise decision, Amelia."

"But Amelia, you cannot do it! Uncle, you mustn't lie to her..."

"Lie? Albert, I am not doing that at all. Amelia has done some calculating and the result is what I hoped it would be. I do not know what I can guarantee, but there will be immediate consequences in

European politics if we win this war, and these consequences will spread into Spain."

"It is enough for me that the possibility exists. What will I have to do?" Amelia asked.

"Oh, well, for the time being all you need to do is prepare yourself. You need to be trained and you need to practice your languages. What are they? Russian, French, German?"

"I speak French as well as I speak Spanish; I have few problems with German, people even say that my accent is quite good; as far as Russian is concerned I can get by, but little more. I have a good ear for languages."

"Perfect, perfect! You will work on your Russian, and polish up your German a bit more. You'll learn to send and receive and decipher coded messages as well as other important information techniques."

"Amelia, I beg you to reconsider what you're getting involved in. You don't have any idea. And you, Uncle Paul, you have no right to trick Amelia and put her in danger for a cause that is not her own. We both know that Spain is not a priority for British foreign policy, and that even Franco is less of an irritant for you while he's in power than the idea of a Communist government. I can't let you trick Amelia like this."

"Please, Albert! Do you really think I am tricking her? I wouldn't do this if it were just you we were talking about, but Germany has become a danger for everyone, and we need to win this war. I have not said that it will mean Franco's defeat if we win the war, all I have said is that things will be different with Hitler out of the picture. Amelia is intelligent, she knows how complex politics is."

"It's a bet, Albert, and in my case there is something to win and nothing to lose; I have already lost everything," Amelia interrupted.

"If you work for Uncle Paul you will live in an underworld from which there is no escape."

"I don't want to take this decision knowing that you are opposed to it. Help me, Albert, please understand why I said yes."

When they left, Lord James had another glass of port. He was content. He knew that Amelia Garayoa was a diamond in the rough. He had spent too long in Intelligence not to know who had potential to become a good agent, and he was sure of the qualities that this apparently fragile and delicate young woman possessed.

Lord James slept well that night, but Albert and Amelia stayed up till dawn, arguing.

At seven o'clock the next morning a car came from the Admiralty to pick up Amelia.

Lord James was in uniform and seemed pleased to see her.

"Come in, come in, Amelia. I'm happy that you haven't changed your mind."

"You think of England and I think of Spain, I hope that we can fit our interests together," she replied.

"Of course, my dear, that is my desire as well. I will now introduce you to your instructor, Major Murray. He will get you up to speed. You need to sign a document that commits you to absolute confidentiality. We need to work out your pay as well, because this is a job."

Major Murray was a cheerful forty-year-old who did not hide his surprise on seeing Amelia.

"How old are you, then?"

"Twenty-two."

"You're a girl! Does Lord James know how old you are? We can't win the war with kids!" he complained.

"I am not a child, I assure you."

"I have a daughter who is fifteen years old and a son who is twelve, you're almost the same age as they are," he said.

"Don't worry about me, major, I'm sure I will be able to do what you ask of me."

"The group you will be joining is made up of men and women in their thirties, I don't know what I'm going to do with you."

"Show me everything I have to learn."

Murray presented her to the rest of the group: four men and a woman, all of them British.

"You all have one thing in common, knowledge of languages," Murray said.

Dorothy, the other woman in the group, had been a teacher until her recruitment. She was dark-haired and not very tall, about forty years old; she had an open and friendly smile, and immediately got on with Amelia.

Of the other group members, Scott was the youngest, he was thirty, and Anthony and John were past forty.

Major Murray explained their training program.

"You will learn some things together, and others depending on your qualities. This is about getting the best out of each one of you."

Major Murray introduced them to their instructors and at lunchtime let them go, telling them to come back the next day at seven on the dot.

"Go and rest, you'll need it."

"Would you like to have some tea?" Dorothy asked Amelia.

Amelia accepted gladly. She wanted to go back home to talk with Albert, but she was afraid that they would have another argument.

Dorothy turned out to be a very nice person. She told Amelia that she was from Manchester, but that she had married a German, so she spoke the language very well.

"We lived in Stuttgart, but my husband died five years ago from a heart attack and I decided to come back to England. There was nothing to keep me in Germany, we didn't have children. You can't imagine how much I miss him, but life is like that. At least, I think I am doing something he would have liked, he couldn't stand Hitler."

She also told Amelia about the members of the group.

"Scott is a bachelor, the son of a diplomat, born in India, but British of course. He grew up in Berlin because his father was stationed there. He studied Semitic languages at Oxford, you know, Hebrew, Aramaic... He speaks German perfectly and also French, I think because of his family. He belongs to a very distinguished family. Anthony is a professor of German and is married to a Jewish woman. John was in the army and when he left he set up a business: a language school. I think he can speak almost any language, he's got a real gift. One of his uncles got married to a Russian exile and she taught him Russian, and he speaks Spanish because he was in the International Brigades during the Spanish war, and he learned some Hungarian while he was out there, as well as speaking quite good German. John isn't married, but I think he's been engaged for a while."

When Amelia got home Albert was not there. She waited for him impatiently. She needed him, she needed his approval more than anything. She depended on him more than she would have cared to admit, and even though she knew that their relationship had no future, she said to herself that she would be with him for as long as she could.

Albert came back later than usual, but in a better mood than the day before.

"I've managed it, I've got an interview with the Prime Minister tomorrow, I have to get it all prepared now. They're going to publish it in newspapers in the States, they're very interested in what the United Kingdom will do in the war. And how was your day?"

"Well, I suppose the really hard work will start tomorrow. I met the group I'll be working with, they seem pleasant."

"I will never forgive Uncle Paul for convincing you to work for him. This decision will change the rest of your life."

"I know, but I couldn't just stand by with my arms folded after what we saw in Germany."

"It is not your war, Amelia."

"No, it is not my war. I'm afraid it will be everyone's war."

Over the next three months, Major Murray trained Amelia to turn her into an agent. She had exhaustive classes in German and Russian, she learned how to make explosives, to decipher codes and use weapons. She started work along with the rest of the group at seven in the morning, and they did not get home until evening.

Albert was worried because he thought Amelia was exhausted, but he knew that nothing he could say to her would make her change her mind. Amelia had convinced herself that if Hitler were defeated then England would help Spain get rid of Franco.

Over those months, Amelia was regularly in touch with her family in Madrid. She sent money to her Uncle Armando to support her sister Antonietta.

Amelia still lived with Albert, but she paid her half of the bills, and this made her feel independent and almost happy.

In the meantime, after unexpected and heroic resistance by the Finnish soldiers, the Red Army finally got hold of Finland, which resulted in the Soviet Union being expelled from the League of Nations.

And even though England and France had officially been at war with Germany since the invasion of Poland, it was not until 1940 that the hostilities began in earnest.

"Right, I think you should speak to Major Hurley now," Lady Victoria said. "I still have some things to tell you, but the major can tell you about Amelia's work in the Intelligence Service in more detail than I can. Oh yes, I nearly forgot! I said that Amelia stayed in contact with her family, and I think that she visited them in February 1940. I'm not sure of it, but I found a letter of Albert's to his parents, where he says that Amelia is in Madrid."

I took my leave of Lady Victoria after extracting from her a promise that she would invite me to her house again to carry on our exploration of Amelia Garayoa's life.

I was stunned by what I had been told, so stunned that I nearly missed the e-mail that Pepe had sent me. He said that, given that I showed no signs of life and didn't reply to his e-mails, the director of the newspaper had decided to dispense with my services. In other words, I'd been fired. It really didn't matter to me, but I was annoyed about the scolding I'd be bound to get from my mother when she found out.

In spite of my insistence on seeing him as soon as possible, Major Hurley could only give me an appointment in a week's time.

I called my mother, and just as I had feared, she treated me like a wayward child. She was already aware that I had been fired because Pepe, since I hadn't replied to any of his e-mails, had called her to find out if I was still alive.

"I don't know what you're playing at, but you are sorely mistaken. Who cares about this woman's life?" she said.

"This woman was your grandmother, so you might have some interest in her life, I suppose," I said.

"What are you saying? Do you think I have even the slightest interest in what this Amelia did? She's not my grandmother!"

"What do you mean, she's not your grandmother? That's all I need to hear!"

"That woman abandoned her son, my father, and disappeared. We never heard anything else about her, and I couldn't care less why she did it. Will it change my life to find out why?"

"I'll tell you, your grandmother's life was pretty intense."

"Well, I'm happy for her, I hope that you have a good time with her."

"Come on, Mom, don't get upset!"

"Why shouldn't I get upset? Should I be happy that I've got an airhead kid who instead of taking himself seriously fannies around investigating some irrelevant piece of family history?"

"Look, I must insist that Amelia's story is not at all irrelevant. And it should matter to you, because she is your grandmother, whatever you say."

"Don't say another word about that woman! Look, either leave off your investigation or don't call me again if you get into trouble. You're old enough to look after yourself, and if you don't then it's because you don't want to, so consider yourself warned. From here on in, the only thing I'll do for you is give you a plate of food when you come to visit, but don't ask for any more loans to pay the mortgage on your apartment, I won't give you a penny."

My mother might have been right from her perspective, but from mine I had no option but to carry on. It wasn't just that I had promised Doña Laura and Doña Melita, but the investigation itself was like a poison that I was incapable of resisting.

7

I called Pablo Soler from my hotel to ask him to tell me, if he remembered, about Amelia's visit to Madrid in February 1940. Don Pablo didn't need to be asked twice and said I should come to Barcelona so that we could talk more calmly.

"Do you want me to tell you what I've found out?" I asked when I was sitting in front of him in his office.

"You shouldn't tell me. There are things that the ladies may not want to be known outside the family."

"Well, as far as I've been able to find out, you are practically family yourself!"

"No, don't you make any mistake about that, young man. I will be eternally grateful for what they did for me, but I have no right at all to know more than what they want me to know. You keep on putting the puzzle together, and when it is fully finished, then you can hand it over to them."

Don Pablo, who clearly had an exceptional memory, then told me about Amelia's visit. A visit that could without doubt be classified as "dramatic"...

Antonietta's tuberculosis worsened, and Don Armando and Doña Elena feared for her life, they had to take her to the hospital, and Don Armando asked Amelia to come to Madrid straight away.

Amelia had lost weight, but she seemed calmer, more sure of herself. As soon as she arrived she insisted that she wanted to go straight to the hospital, and her cousins Laura and Jesús went with her. I went as well, in fact wherever Jesús went, I went too.

Doña Elena and Edurne were looking after Antonietta, taking turns, and Don Armando and Laura came to the hospital as soon as they left work. Jesús was not allowed to go very often because he had suffered from tuberculosis as well, and Doña Elena was worried that he might have a relapse.

Amelia hugged her sister, rocking her as if she were a baby. Antonietta cried with the emotions she felt, she loved her sister very much and suffered when she was not there, although she never complained.

"How good it is that you've come! Now I will get better!"

"Of course you'll get better, or else I'll be extremely cross with you!"

"Don't say that, I love you so much!" Antonietta protested.

Amelia spoke to the doctor who was looking after her sister and told him to cure her.

"Whatever it takes, do what needs to be done, but if anything happens to my sister then I... I don't know what I'll do!"

"But how dare you threaten me," the doctor replied, obviously annoyed.

"I'm not threatening you, heaven forbid I should do such a thing, but... Antonietta is all that I've got left. I've lost my family, am I going to lose my sister as well?"

"No one is going to lose anyone, we do whatever we can to save lives, but I have to say that your sister is very weak and is responding badly to treatment."

"Tell me what I can do and I will do it, never you worry."

"We can't do more than we are doing, and your sister's life is not in our hands but in God's. If He decides to call her, then there's nothing we can do."

"I'm sorry?"

"Your sister's life, like all of our lives, depends on God."

"Well, that's not how I see it. Do you really think that God needs my sister's life? Why?"

"Please, Amelia, don't annoy the doctor!" Doña Elena begged, upset by the turn the conversation was taking.

"Aunt, I am not annoying anyone, I just want Antonietta to get the treatment she needs to get over her illness, and I cannot bear this resignation that says that people die because God wants them to."

"But the doctor is right, it is Our Lord who decides the hour of our death."

"No. I don't think that it was Our Lord who decided that my father should be shot, or that my mother... You know that she was ill when she died, without the strength to deal with her illness, because she was hungry and suffering, and poor. My father was killed by Fascist bullets, not by God."

"I will not have you talking about politics! We have suffered enough because of politics. Do you want me to remember all the people who have died? Do you know why I haven't gone mad? I'll tell you, it's because I believe in God and I accept that he has reasons which I do not understand."

"Well, I'm not going to resign myself to Antonietta dying. We'll move her to a different hospital, we'll look for other doctors who look after her and who don't wash their hands of the whole thing saying that they have nothing to do with my sister's life and that it's all up to God. Let's not get God involved in all this."

Doña Elena was scandalized by what Amelia had said. She looked at her as if she did not recognize her; maybe Amelia truly was a different person now. Even though she was physically fragile, she seemed a different person.

That night Amelia stayed to look after Antonietta, and Doña Elena and Edurne came back home with us. Doña Elena complained to Don Armando about their niece's behavior.

"If you had only heard what she said... I'm telling you, Armando, that Amelia is not the same as she used to be... I don't know, there's some sort of bitterness there..."

"Is that so odd? It's the same bitterness that has touched us too. We have lost a part of our family, we have been left with nothing, she is away abroad earning money to help us, did you think she'd be the same sweet little thing that we knew in the past?"

"But Armando, questioning God's will... That's too much."

"Do you want Amelia to accept that it might be God's will for Antonietta to die? No, you can't be serious. Do you think it was God's will for your cousin the nun to be tortured and murdered by a bunch of fanatics? Was it God's will for my brother to be murdered?"

"You're talking like her!"

"I'm talking sense. You know I'm a believer, but there are certain things... Amelia is right, let's leave God in peace and ask Him to give us strength to deal with everything that is surrounding us."

Amelia set out to find another hospital where they would look after her sister. She went to a couple of doctors and asked their advice, but they both said that the hospital itself didn't matter, that people were dying of tuberculosis every day, and that everything depended on how strong the patient was. But Amelia did not give in and searched without rest for someone who could give her hope.

We went to see Antonietta one afternoon, and she was worse.

I can still remember the scene... It was terrible... Amelia held her sister in her arms and screamed for someone to come and help her.

Jesús began to shake. He was a very sensitive child who loved his cousin Antonietta very much, and it was too much for him to see her in this state and he fainted. I think that his fainting was the cue for calm to return for a few seconds. His parents and Laura went to help him. One of the nuns who was looking after the patients in that room came running straight away. I don't know if she was a good nurse or not, and I don't remember her name, but she looked after Antonietta well and sat at Amelia's side.

"Your sister has a guardian angel who is looking after her," she whispered, "and God will help her, let us look after her now." The nun pushed Amelia gently to one side to try to make her let go of her sister.

Amelia did not respond, she only cried, she seemed not to hear, but maybe it was the nun's soft voice that calmed her. The doctor came with two other nuns and asked us to leave the room.

I stayed in the corridor with Amelia, waiting for the doctor to tell us how Antonietta was. He took a long time, I remember because there was enough time for Doña Elena and Don Armando to come back, with Jesús, very pale, holding Laura's hand.

"How are you feeling, Jesús?" Amelia said, nervously.

"I'm better now…"

"It was nothing," Don Armando said. "He was just affected by seeing Antonietta like that."

When the doctor came out, Amelia stood directly in front of him, trembling and scared of what he might say.

"Calm down, she had an attack, but she's better now. I gave her an injection to help with the pain and the sense of tightness in her chest. What she should do now is rest, it's better if we don't all go in now, too many people crowd her."

"But I want to stay with my sister."

"And so you can, but just don't upset her."

Don Armando thought that the best thing was for us all to go home and for Amelia to stay with Antonietta.

"But Edurne should come early tomorrow to take your place, or else you'll get sick again yourself."

The nun must have been right about Antonietta's guardian angel, because she started to get better until she was finally out of danger. The day she was given the all-clear and Amelia took her home, Doña Elena had organized a little party. Well, it wasn't a party, but she had found flour and shortening and pomegranates, and had made a cake.

Antonietta was very weak, but she was happy to be at home again with her family.

Doña Elena had told Jesús and me not to do anything that might upset Antonietta, and Edurne was given one task only, that of caring for the patient.

As soon as Amelia saw that her sister was better she said that she would be going back to England.

"I have to work, now more than ever, to buy Antonietta's medicines."

Amelia also took charge of my upkeep, given that my grandmother was still in the hospital and Lola showed no signs of life. Don Armando had done what he could to find out about her, but with no success. Some of her former comrades were in prison, and their families said all manner of things about Lola: that she had been shot in Barcelona, that she had died in the war, even that she had left the country. Amelia did not believe this last suggestion, because, as she said, if that had been the case then Lola would have come looking for me. As for my father, he was still in the French Foreign Legion, so we didn't know all that much about him either.

Don Armando and Doña Elena treated me as another member of the family; I suppose they had resigned themselves to having me with them. They were too good to have abandoned me, and Jesús and I were close friends.

Before going back to London, Amelia asked Edurne to go and ask Águeda if she would let her see her son. Doña Elena said that this was not a good idea, because if Santiago found out then Águeda would be in trouble, and might even be dismissed. Don Armando stepped in to support his niece.

"It's only natural that she should want to see her son, or at least should want to try, discreetly. Águeda is a good woman; I'm sure she'll do whatever she can to let Amelia see her son."

Even so, Doña Elena continued to insist that Amelia should not go see Javier, and she insisted so much that in the end Don Armando got annoyed with her and, to everyone's surprise, but particularly Doña Elena's, ordered Edurne to go to Santiago's house and try to convince Águeda to allow Amelia to see Javier.

Edurne spent two days wandering round Santiago's house before she saw Águeda, who to begin with refused to accept the idea that Amelia should see Javier. She was scared of Santiago's reaction, but in the end she gave in, after Edurne told her how sick Antonietta had been, and how they had feared for her life. We didn't know why at the time, but Edurne was nervous when she came back from her meeting with Águeda.

Águeda arranged to meet Amelia as before, at the entrance to the Retiro. Laura said that she would go with her. She was afraid of her cousin's reaction, and did not want her to go alone. Doña Elena said that Jesús and I should go with them as well.

I remember that it was cold that afternoon, but even though it was winter the sun was shining. When we got to the park entrance, Águeda was already there. Her overcoat was undone, it seemed too small for her, or else that she had gotten fat. She was holding Javier's hand. The child was trying to get free and run away, but Águeda would not let him do so.

Laura had to hold Amelia back to stop her from running to her child.

"Please, control yourself, and try to make it look like a casual meeting, or else Águeda won't let us come to meet Javier again."

The women greeted Águeda and Amelia asked the child if he wanted to give her a kiss. Javier thought for a moment before shaking his head.

"Come on, give the beautiful lady a kiss," Águeda said.

"I don't want to, Mommy," Javier replied.

Amelia looked like she was about to cry. It was a great pain for her to hear Javier calling Águeda "Mommy." But her cousin Laura whispered in her ear that she should control herself.

"Are you a good boy?" Amelia asked.

"Yes."

"And what do you like doing?"

"I like playing with Daddy and with Mommy, and I'm going to play with my little brother too."

"Your little brother?" Amelia was trembling.

"Yes, I'm going to have a little brother, isn't that right, Mommy?"

Águeda looked anxiously at Amelia, and could see in her what we could: despair and anger.

"Are you going to have a child, Águeda?"

"Yes, Madam."

"Are you married?"

"No... no, Madam."

"So, how are you going to have a child?"

Amelia's icy gaze made Águeda hang her head in shame. Javier looked at the two women without knowing what was happening, but, realizing that there was tension in the air, he started to screw up his face.

"Mama, I want to go home."

"I... I am sorry, Madam."

"Do you sleep in my bed?"

"For God's sake, Madam, don't ask me that! What do you want me to do? I... Don Santiago is very good to me, and I love the child very much, and you can see how the child loves me. These things happen, you know that very well... You left your husband."

"How dare you compare yourself with me! I didn't get into bed with any married man, and I haven't stolen a mother's love from any child."

Javier started to cry, scared of Amelia's tone of voice. She could scarcely control her rage.

"Please, Madam, don't talk like that in front of the child!"

"How dare you! You were recommended to my parents as a decent person, but we shouldn't have trusted you, you got yourself pregnant without being married."

"Please, Amelia, don't humiliate yourself like this," Laura said, trying to take her cousin away.

"You are not better than me, you are no one to judge me, if you have lost your child's love it's not my fault, you were the one who abandoned him."

Laura had to hold Amelia back to stop her from hitting Águeda. Jesús and I were frozen stiff by the violence of the scene.

"Come on, Amelia. And you, Águeda, you mustn't speak to Amelia like that, don't forget who you are, you have no right to judge her, and even less to speak of her son like that."

Águeda didn't know what to do, the poor thing, and seemed about to cry.

Laura took her cousin's arm and pulled her along, forcing Amelia to walk with her. Jesús and I followed without daring to speak. We could see Amelia trembling. When we reached home, we found Doña Elena extremely upset and arguing with Don Armando. They fell silent when they saw us.

"Uncle, you have no idea what's just happened!" Amelia said, falling into Don Armando's arms.

"I can guess, your aunt has just told me the secret she was keeping, why she didn't want you to see Águeda."

"But... you knew?" Amelia looked to Doña Elena for an answer.

"Yes, I knew that Águeda was pregnant by Santiago, that they are living together. I didn't tell you so as not to cause you pain, you've suffered enough already."

"But you should have told me," Amelia said.

"She didn't even tell me," Don Armando said.

"I didn't want anyone to feel hurt; if I was wrong then I am sorry, but my intentions were good," Doña Elena apologized.

"How did you find out about it?" Amelia asked, and it was clear that she was making a great effort not to lash out at her aunt.

"Because everyone's talking about it. I found out when I went to see Doña Piedad. You remember that Doña Piedad and her husband had those cake shops we liked before the war. They've lost it all: Doña Piedad is a widow now, and sick, and every now and then I go to see her. I found out about Santiago and Águeda there. Your husband has made her the lady of the house; he has not introduced her to his friends, but he does go out with her and with Javier. Your son thinks that Águeda is his mother and Santiago allows him to believe that."

"I suppose that's his way of punishing me. I know that I can't complain if Águeda takes my place in his bed, but it does hurt me a lot for her to take my son's love away from me."

"I'm sorry, Amelia," Don Armando murmured as he held his niece in his arms. "Maybe you should stay and fight for your son. We will go and see Santiago, I will speak to him and make him understand that he cannot take Javier away from his real mother. I don't think that Don Manuel and Doña Blanca agree with what their son is doing. We could talk to them..."

"No, Uncle, it's useless. I know Santiago well. He loved me so much that now his love is transformed into hate he will never forgive me. I deserve it; I will never forgive myself either. So how can I ask him to forgive me? I deserved to be punished and I'm being punished in spades. I only hope that Javier will listen to me when he is older, listen to me and forgive me."

Don Pablo fell silent after finishing his description of this scene.

I also said nothing, hoping that he would tell me more.

"Well, Guillermo, you need to go back to London now and carry on with your wanderings," Don Pablo said.

"Wow, that Amelia... I was surprised that she would treat Águeda as she did. My great-grandmother was a Communist, and very liberated for her time."

"Are you going to judge Amelia?"

"No, I don't want to judge her, but I was just surprised that she would treat poor Águeda like that: Whatever the truth of the matter, my mother thinks of her as her grandmother, and she is my great great-grandmother."

"Amelia was hurt, and was also being very hard on herself. But we are all products of our own time, and she was brought up as a scion of the enlightened bourgeoisie."

"Yes, that is how she was brought up, but she also broke all the social conventions of her time."

"Yes, but she never stopped possessing that background, you can't take her upbringing away from her. As for her being a Communist, I'd say that she wasn't, really. She fell in love with Pierre Comte, who truly was a Communist, but she was just a young idealist with her head filled with dreams, and she didn't have any guiding principles that could mark her out as being Communist."

I went back to London and called Lady Victoria and Major Hurley. Lady Victoria was on the Costa Azul at a golf tournament (traitor!), and Major Hurley could only see me three days later than he had said.

The major was up to speed with what his relative Lady Victoria had told me. He even showed me some notes that she had taken in case they could be of use when he was telling me his part of the story. So he cut to the chase and reminded me, with another warning gesture, that he had no time to lose; another way of putting it would be that he was wasting his time talking to me.

Major Hurley started his story.

In mid-March 1940, Amelia Garayoa joined Major Murray's unit. The United Kingdom was going through a very difficult time, made even worse by the war. Chamberlain and Halifax maintained their policy of appeasement with Hitler, something that was still showing no results; if they kept up this approach it was because they realized that a new war, even one in which they emerged the victors, would result in absolute financial and economic ruin. Some historians have been too harsh on Chamberlain and his attitude toward Hitler's Germany. But Churchill was right: A policy of appeasement would have been impossible to pursue in the long term, simply because Hitler was so keen on war.

Miss Garayoa joined her group and continued to receive training. She also continued her romantic relationship with Albert James. For a time, the articles that James wrote in the British press were among the harshest attacks on Hitler before the outbreak of war.

On April 9, without any prior warning, the German army invaded Denmark and Norway; this was Operation Weserübung. On May 5, France was attacked. On May 10, the same day that Churchill became Prime Minister, as well as Minister for War, Germany invaded Belgium, Luxembourg, and the Netherlands. This was the Blitzkrieg. On May 12 the Germans broke through the Maginot Line and on May 15 the Netherlands surrendered, and the Germans made it to the outskirts of Paris and began to shell the southern coast of England. Can you imagine what those days were like?

Lord Paul James asked Major Murray if his troops were ready to go into action, and he was told that they were. Before the end of 1940, Amelia would take part in two operations. In June, Major Murray brought the group together to tell them that they were going into action and to give them their orders.

"The time has come to act. I don't need to tell you what has happened: The Wehrmacht has taken a good chunk of France, Holland, and Belgium. The French prime minister has resigned and Marshal Pétain is now in charge in his place. Do any of you want to leave now?"

They all said no, and seemed to want to start work.

"Right, I will meet with each one of you alone. None of you will know what the others are going to do, from this moment on you can tell no one, not your family or your most intimate friends, what your mission will be."

Amelia was the last to receive her orders from Murray. He had deliberately left her till the end, because even though he was sure that she was capable of carrying out the mission he had in mind for her, he could not help but be worried about her youth.

"I want you to go back to Germany."

"To Germany?"

"Yes, you have important friends there."

"I have some friends, I don't know if they're important or not."

"Lord James has told me that you know an army officer, Max von Schumann, an aristocrat married to a fanatical Nazi. However, he is a member of an anti-Hitler group, am I right?"

"Yes."

"I think that you and Albert James, Lord James's nephew, brought a message from von Schumann's group back to Britain. I also know that you helped a young Jewish woman to escape from persecution in Germany."

"Yes, I didn't say anything because I didn't think it was necessary."

"Right, but it is my duty to know everything about all the agents we are to work with."

"I understand."

"Well, it's useful for us if you return to Germany and send us all the information that Max von Schumann can get his hands on regarding German troop movements. It is vital that we know whether or not they are preparing to invade the United Kingdom. After what the German army has done to France, after what happened at Dunkirk, the prime minister needs to make decisions, and this information is vital for him."

"Baron von Schumann will never betray his country; I don't think that he will give me any useful information."

"Von Schumann and you are old friends so he should trust you."

"But he will never give me information that could compromise Germany."

"But you don't need to ask him for that. Go to Berlin, look around, keep your ears open, and draw your own conclusions."

"Should I tell him that I am an agent?"

"For your own safety and for his, the best thing is if you tell him nothing. You said yourself that he will never work with us. We need to find an alibi that will justify your presence in Berlin."

"Perhaps... well, I don't know if it will help, but my father has business in Berlin, they confiscated his factory because his partner was Jewish, but the accountant saved several machines that he hires out, and a part of what he earns with them should go to my family..."

"Excellent! There's no better excuse to justify your presence in Berlin."

"How should I send you the information if I find out anything?"

"You will write letters to a Spanish friend, superficial letters that, naturally enough, will contain coded messages."

"A Spanish friend?"

"She doesn't exist. You will send the letters to the address of a woman who works for us. She will send them on to us and we will decode them. You should only write when you have information."

"How long should I stay in Berlin?"

"I don't know. Do you think you could get there in a couple of days, or do you need more time to arrange your personal affairs?"

"How should I go?"

"First go to Lisbon. From Lisbon to Switzerland, and then catch a train to Berlin."

It was just after five when she got back to the apartment and she was surprised to find Albert in the library drinking whisky and listening to music.

"What are you celebrating?" she asked, as Albert did not usually drink at this hour of the day.

"I have a very good piece of news. Come on, I'll pour you a drink, we have something to celebrate."

Amelia took the whisky he offered. She would need it to be able to give her the courage to tell him that she was going back to Berlin on her first mission for the British Secret Service.

"My father called me to tell me that Rahel got to New York safely and that thanks to his friends he was able to sort out the immigration process with no problems. So now, thank heavens, she is safe with her family. Is that or is that not a good piece of news?"

It was, and Amelia was happy, especially because she was afraid of what Albert's reaction would be when she told him she was leaving. She took a large gulp of whisky and after chatting about Rahel for a while, she told him that she had something to tell him.

"I hope it's some more good news, I don't want anything to spoil this happiness about Rahel."

"They're sending me to Berlin; I'm leaving in two days' time."

Albert kept looking at her without knowing what to say.

"It had to happen one day or another," he said, looking away from Amelia.

"I didn't think it would be so soon... I don't know what to say."

"Nothing, you don't have to say anything. It is difficult to love you, but I can't stop loving you. I knew that our relationship would not be easy, right from the start, and I have always been scared of losing you. I need you so much... I will never forgive Uncle Paul for having convinced you to join the Secret Service, and if anything happens to you..."

"Nothing's going to happen to me. They just want me to go to Berlin, and try to find out if Hitler is going to invade England."

"Just like that! They know that it's no mission for a girl. They should send experienced agents. How are you going to get that information?"

"They want me to make contact with Max and his group. Don't forget that Max is an officer in the army, so he must have access to certain information that could be useful for us."

"Come on, Amelia, don't be naïve! Do you think Max will tell you what the army's plans are? You really don't know him, do you?"

"I don't understand... Max is a member of the opposition and he hates Hitler," Amelia replied without much conviction.

"Yes, and he will do whatever it takes to get rid of him, because he will never betray Germany. That's what I think you haven't understood."

Amelia did not know what to say. She knew that Albert was right. When Major Murray was explaining the mission to her it had not seemed all that complicated, but Albert was making her face up to reality.

"I have to try."

"Yes, I suppose you have to try. And what about us?"

"I don't know what you mean..."

"Are you planning on being a spy while I wait here praying that nothing happens to you, desperate for you to come back from each mission?"

"I... I'm not planning anything, I'm not asking you to wait for me..."

"I think you haven't thought about me at all, and do you know why? Because you have never thought about me, I am just here for you, but if I weren't then you wouldn't mind too much one way or the other."

"Don't say that! It's not true! I... I love you, perhaps not how you want to be loved or how you deserve to be loved, but I love you, I love you in my way."

"That's the problem, the way you love me."

Amelia Garayoa reached Berlin on June 10, the same day that Italy declared war on France and on the United Kingdom. She gave a sigh of relief when she left the train station. The police seemed not to care about her. She was just one more woman with a suitcase and a bag. Amelia tried to walk with a firm and decided pace. Major Murray had told her that if the Germans suspected her, then they would shoot her for being a spy.

She went straight to the house of Helmut Keller, the accountant who had worked for her father and Herr Itzhak. She had worked out a clear plan over the last two days. She thought that she would ask Herr Helmut to rent her a room. She couldn't afford to stay at the Hotel Adlon anymore, and she would feel safer living in a house; In any case, if he took her in then it would help her alibi, she could always say that she was an old friend of the family and show off the ties that bound them, ties of family and business.

Herr Helmut was pleased to see her again. His wife, Greta, was still ill and he was looking after her, as well as dealing with all the household chores.

"It's a good thing that I can do most of my accounting work at home; if I had to go to an office I would not be able to look after Greta."

He was a little surprised at Amelia's proposal, but he accepted her as a guest readily enough.

"You don't have to pay me anything, I make enough with what I earn."

"You would be doing me a great favor taking me in, I would feel very lonely in a hotel. I can't pay you that much, but even a few marks would help you, I suppose, and of course I will contribute to the cost of my food, and help you look after your wife as much as I can."

Greta also made no objection to having Amelia as a guest. She felt sympathy for the young Spaniard, and also remembered her father, Don Juan, as a gentleman, as well as extremely generous. Also, she would have someone new to talk to, as she spent most of her time in bed. She had asthma, and got tired even after only walking a few yards.

Amelia's room was small; it had been a storeroom.

"I wish you could stay in my son Frank's room, but even though he doesn't come here very often because he's in the army, his mother wants to keep his room just as it was when he lived with us."

"I will be fine here, Herr Helmut, I don't need that much, just a bed and a table and chair, the wardrobe is big and really I don't need anything else."

Amelia explained that now that war had broken out between Germany and England, she was thinking of going back to Spain and looking for work, and because Germany was becoming the most powerful European nation, she had thought that she would perfect her German and try to get the old family business up and running again. Herr Helmut had saved some of the machines; maybe he could tell her how the business had worked before the war and what the chances were of setting it up again. She also hinted to them that she was trying to get over a personal crisis as well.

Helmut accepted what Amelia had to tell him, although later he said to his wife that he was sure that Amelia was running away from a breakup, perhaps with that rich American journalist who had been with her the last time she came.

The next afternoon, Amelia went to Professor Schatzhauser's house. She thought that the best thing would be to get in touch with the head of the opposition group rather than directly with Max.

Professor Schatzhauser did not seem too surprised to see her. He invited her through to his office and offered her a cup of tea.

"Do you have news from London? Are they going to take us seriously?" he asked her without beating around the bush.

"We told them everything you told us. Of course, the thing they are most worried about is whether Hitler has plans to invade England."

"Of course, the English are always most worried about things that might concern them. That's always the way of it."

"Well, it's difficult for them to help you if they can't help themselves, isn't it?"

"And what about your friend, Mr. James? Why isn't he here?"

"Albert is a journalist and limits himself to describing the things that he sees. His articles in the English and American press have had a significant impact. He talks about the danger posed by Hitler and has stirred up a real storm in the United States, because there are still people there who think that what happens in Europe does not concern them."

"So you are working for the British and Albert James is not. A shame! He seemed to me the sort of man you could trust. You are very young, and you're Spanish, how come you are working for the British?"

"Oh, I am not working for the British! I am just a messenger. And if I am doing this it is because I am Spanish, and hope that this war will help us to get rid of Franco!"

"Do you think that the war will move to Spain as well?"

"I want you to get rid of Hitler, and I think that with Hitler out of the way, then Franco will be left without his main ally after Il Duce."

"A very admirable goal, but allow me to say that I don't much trust that it will happen."

"I don't have absolute faith that it will happen either, but I can't just stand around with my arms folded."

"Well, tell me what your friends in London want and I'll tell you what we want from them."

Amelia was vague enough not to commit to anything nor to ask for things that she knew she would not receive. Her mission had very little to do with Karl Schatzhauser's opposition group. Major Murray had ordered her, via Max von Schumann, to find out as much as she could about the movements of the Wehrmacht. This was why she had to pay attention to Professor Schatzhauser's group.

Professor Schatzhauser asked her to come to dinner with him the next evening.

"We are meeting at a friend's house, Max and Father Müller will be there: He will always be grateful to you and Mr. James for what you did for Rahel. He is delighted that she is safe and sound in New York."

Amelia was surprised by the happiness and carefree nature that appeared to be a constant of Berlin life. The women still walked the streets with their children, unaware of any devastation else-where, the cabarets were still full to bursting and the shop windows were filled with enticing displays.

Even in London people were aware of the war, and the evacuation of the soldiers from Dunkirk had been received with anxiety and stress.

On the way back to Herr Helmut's house, Amelia went into a shop to buy tea and teacake as a treat for Frau Greta. Helmut's wife seemed to be well disposed toward her.

Amelia told herself that it had been the right thing to do to stay in that house. It let her pass more unobserved, even though in those days Berlin was a city of thousands of eyes, all of them looking into people's private spaces.

Greta was pleased with the tea and the teacake, and suggested to Amelia that they eat it together. Herr Helmut was not yet home, he was taking the books to a shop whose accounts he kept. He worked as much as he could to support his family, and in particular to pay for his wife's expensive medicine.

Professor Schatzhauser came to the Kellers' house to pick up Amelia. Herr Helmut opened the door and invited him in, but Amelia was ready, so she left straight away.

Amelia had explained to the Kellers that Professor Schatzhauser was an old friend of her father's, who had offered to help her with whatever she needed during her stay in Berlin.

Professor Schatzhauser drove an old black car and seemed not to be in a very talkative mood.

"Are you worried about anything?" Amelia asked.

"Max has told me that there will be two important guests, Admiral Canaris and Colonel Hans Oster, at the meal. They are important men because of their high position in the military hierarchy, and also because of their social position."

"What will you say about me?"

"Nothing that they shouldn't know, although of course they will try to find out by their own considerable means as much as they can about you."

"Is that dangerous?"

"I hope not, we hope not, they have even helped us on a few occasions in the past. In any case, my dear, there is nothing better than telling the truth, and given that you are in Berlin on a very honorable mission, that of recovering the family business, then we shouldn't worry at all, should we?"

Manfred Kasten's house was near Charlottenburg. It was a two-story neoclassical building, set in a garden filled with willows and fir trees.

Frau Kasten, their host's wife, met them at the door: She was past sixty, tall and thin with white hair.

"Professor Schatzhauser, what a pleasure to see you again! And you have a lovely companion... Come in, come in. You will find Manfred in the library with a friend of his, Baron von Schumann. I hope that you enjoy yourselves this evening and that you don't get caught up in political discussions. Can you promise me you'll behave yourselves?"

Helga Kasten smiled and offered them each a glass of champagne. And then she left them, to look after other guests.

The professor took Amelia's arm and headed to the library, but Ludovica von Waldheim met them en route.

"Goodness, Professor Schatzhauser and *la Señorita* Garayoa! I didn't know you were in Berlin..."

"I've just arrived."

"Have you left rich Mr. James? I wouldn't have done that if I were you, there aren't that many men like him in the world."

"Albert has some business to attend to, but he will come to join me as soon as he can."

"And how come he has allowed you to travel alone?"

"I was invited here by some old friends of my father's. My father had a business importing German machinery, and I am going to try to see if I can get the family business up and running again," Amelia said, a little disconcerted by the interrogation to which Ludovica was submitting her. "And how is your husband, the baron?"

"My husband is well, thank you very much. He's talking politics with his friends in the library at the moment. Are you interested in politics?"

"Only the bits I can't escape from, Baroness."

"I like that! Men get all wrapped up in it and can't enjoy life at all. You have to come to our house, we'll talk about the things that interest us, alright?"

"That sounds wonderful."

"You're staying at the Adlon, aren't you?"

"No, I said that some friends of my father invited me to stay with them."

"Well, tell me when it would be good for us to meet," Ludovica said as she walked away.

"Be careful with the baroness," Professor Schatzhauser said. "It's quite clear that she doesn't trust you."

"I don't trust her either."

"That's just as well, if she knew about what we do she would be sure to inform on us to the authorities."

"She wouldn't do that, she would have to denounce her husband as well."

"If the time came she might just do that. She's a committed Nazi. It was risky of Max to bring her to the party, but I suppose he had no option, she is his wife after all."

Admiral William Canaris was a charming man, who appeared to be reading Amelia's thoughts as he gazed into her eyes. He showed an advanced knowledge of the situation in Spain, and asked her several subtle questions aimed at discovering which side she was on.

Colonel Hans Oster also appeared to be interested in Amelia, whose presence at the dinner could not fail to draw people's attention.

Both men seemed to be very much connected with each other, and they shared glances over the heads of the other guests. If Amelia had expected to hear any criticism of the Nazi Party then she was to be disappointed, for nothing that either of the two men said gave any hint that they were anything other than entirely in agreement with the Führer.

Amelia was extremely happy to meet Father Müller again, the priest who had entrusted Rahel to their care, and she took the chance to speak with him away from the rest of the guests.

"I will never be able to thank you for all you have done. It is a real relief to know that Rahel is safe and sound."

"Tell me one thing, Father. Do you think that there are enough Germans who oppose Hitler?"

"What a question! I wish I could tell you that there are many thousands of us who see the danger that Hitler poses, but I fear that this is not the case. Germany only wants to be great again, to take the place that was taken away from them after the war."

"And what can you do?"

"I don't know, Amelia. In my case, I do what I can, but I am a priest, a Jesuit who only can represent himself. I think that the best we can do is to convince those who surround us of the inherent wrongness of Nazism."

"Father, in your opinion, how far do you think Hitler is willing to go?"

"He will not stop until he is the master of Europe."

Max came up to them, apparently idly; he had barely spoken to Amelia because he knew that Ludovica had her eyes on them the whole time. Although his wife had said nothing to him about the Spanish woman, he knew that she felt jealous of her.

"How long will you stay in Berlin?"

"I don't know, it depends what I can do here."

"Professor Schatzhauser told me that the British sent you... ," he said in a low voice.

"No, that's not true, I'm here in Berlin for other reasons, but they asked me to take a message to your group. They want to know what you think now that war seems to have gripped the whole of Europe."

"There isn't much that we can do. What do the British want?"

"They want to know how far Hitler intends to go. If he wants to invade Great Britain," Amelia said directly.

Max cleared his throat. The question appeared to make him uncomfortable and he looked around before answering.

"He might try, even though, as far as I know, he would prefer to strike a deal with the British, or at least that's what our host has just told me. Manfred Kasten is a retired diplomat, but he still has extremely good relations with the Foreign Ministry and usually knows very well what Ribbentrop's plans are."

"When can I see you?"

"Maybe in a day or so. They are going to give me my orders tomorrow. They might send me to Poland, or anywhere, even though I would prefer to stay in Berlin, at least for the time being. But that doesn't depend on me. I will get in touch with you via Professor Schatzhauser, and we can meet in his house. Where are you staying, by the way?"

"In Herr Helmut Keller's house."

Amelia told him Helmut's telephone number and address and Max memorized them. He knew that Ludovica had the habit of rummaging around in his jacket pockets.

On June 22 France signed an armistice with Germany, and two days later one with Italy. Hitler visited Paris on June 23 and was enchanted by the Opéra and Les Invalides, where Napoleon's remains are buried.

Amelia visited Professor Schatzhauser's house regularly, and he called regular meetings of the opposition group, which Amelia attended and paid very close attention to what was said. Lots of the attendees were important people, in important strategic positions within the administration, so they had access to information that, although not precisely relevant to the movements of the war, enabled Amelia to explain how the preparations for the next phase were taking place. In one of these meetings Amelia again met Manfred Kasten, the former diplomat who hated Hitler with all his might.

There were not many people there that night. Aside from Professor Schatzhauser there were two of his colleagues from the university, a Swiss diplomat, Father Müller, Pastor Ludwig Schmidt, an official from the Foreign Ministry and one from the Agriculture Ministry, as well as Max von Schumann and his adjutant, Captain Henke.

Manfred Kasten said that one of his friends, who had close links to the Nazi Party, had told him that they were working on a plan to have all the Jews removed to some territory outside of Europe.

"But why?" Professor Schatzhauser asked.

"My dear friend, Hitler and his followers say that the Jews are the worst enemies of the Reich and of the whole Aryan race. The Head Office for Reich Security, the one set up by Himmler and Heydrich, is keen on deporting many thousands of Jews out of Germany as a part of their plan to get rid of all of them, not just the German Jews, but the Polish ones as well, along with all the Jews in countries occupied by the Wehrmacht."

"Where are they planning on sending them?" Max asked, alarmed.

"They are thinking about sending them to some African country."

"But they're mad!" Father Müller said.

"They're worse than that; mad people aren't so dangerous," Pastor Ludwig Schmidt said.

"But can they do it?" Amelia asked.

"They are investigating how to do it. I will be going to a dinner at the Japanese ambassador's house in a few days' time, and one of my friends will be there and may be able to give me more details."

"I think we have one more thing to talk about, don't we, Max?" Professor Schatzhauser said.

"Yes, I need to tell you that I have been appointed to supervise the sanitary conditions of our army. So I am going to start traveling all over the field of battle, but wherever I may be I will be here for you, you know that you will be able to count on me whenever you need to," von Schumann announced.

"Will you be away for long?" Manfred Kasten wanted to know.

"For discrete periods of indeterminate length. I need to inspect the troops, check their medical provisions and write reports on whatever is lacking. I have the impression that my superiors want to keep me busy."

"Do you think they suspect anything?" Professor Schatzhauser asked in alarm.

"I hope not. I think they don't really approve of my lack of enthusiasm for what is going on. They tolerate me because of who I am and because I am a member of an old family of soldiers, and because they know that I would never betray the army nor Germany."

"Try to hide what you feel, you won't get anywhere telling people your true feelings, you might even put us all in danger," Pastor Schmidt said.

"Don't worry, I will. I know that I am walking on thin ice, even though there are moments when I find it difficult to hide the contempt I feel for some of the High Command, excellent soldiers who are like little frightened boys in front of the Führer."

"Don't be so hard on them. Who wouldn't think first of all about survival in days like these, when the power of the Gestapo has no limits and anyone can become a suspect?" Kasten said.

A few days later, Amelia had an invitation to tea from Professor Schatzhauser. When she arrived at his house, she found Manfred Kasten there already.

"I was just telling the professor that I went to the dinner at the Japanese ambassador's house that I was telling you about and I spoke to my friend who is working on the plan to export all the Jews out of Europe. Heinrich Himmler himself is supervising it."

"Where will they be taken?" Amelia asked.

"To Madagascar. This is what my friend tells me. They want to take all the European Jews there."

"Do they have a date for this exercise?"

"Not yet, they are just studying the logistics. It is not easy to move hundreds of thousands of people from Europe to the south of Africa."

"And what will the Jews do in Madagascar?" Professor Schatzhauser asked.

"Live in labor camps. They want to turn the island into a huge prison. My friend thinks that the plan is insane, but says that Hitler himself has given it his blessing and has told them to sort out all the logistical problems."

"But they would need hundreds of ships to carry so many Jews!" Amelia said, in a state of shock. "It won't be easy for them, Germany doesn't have a good navy."

"That is true, and what they are trying to do is to plan this forced emigration at minimum cost and risk. Will you tell London about this?"

Amelia was silent for a moment. Her orders from Major Murray had been clear. She was not to tell anyone about her mission to Berlin. She had told Professor Schatzhauser and Max several times that she had nothing to do with the British government, but she realized that the professor thought she was not telling the truth.

"I am sorry to disappoint you, Herr Kasten, but I don't work for the British government," she said with conviction.

"But Max has told us that your friend Albert James has contacts in the Admiralty," Professor Schatzhauser said.

"Yes, but that's a family contact, and I... well, I'll try to make sure that Albert finds out about what you've told me, and then he'll know what to do..."

Amelia used the night-time to write coded letters to her nonexistent Spanish friend. After dining with the Kellers she would listen to the radio with them, and hear all its propaganda, and then she would go to her room. She had been in Berlin for two months now, and although the Kellers were more than happy to have her as a guest, she thought that they were a little confused by her continued presence, so that one afternoon while she was alone with Greta she confessed to her that she had come back to Berlin to escape from her lover, Albert James. It was not difficult for her to explain that Albert's parents did not approve of the relationship, and that she was willing to sacrifice herself for him to be happy.

"He has no future with me, you know that I'm a married woman."

Greta Keller comforted her and told her that she was sure Albert would come looking for her.

In order to make her stay in Berlin more credible, Amelia had enrolled in a language school and went there every day to perfect her German. She spent the rest of her time at Professor Schatzhauser's house, as well as visiting Father Müller, with whom she had built up a close friendship.

Father Müller was not much older than her, and the fact that Amelia had helped with Rahel built up a special link between the two of them. Sometimes they discussed the Church's position with respect to Nazism. Amelia criticized the Pope for not setting himself directly against Hitler, but the priest tried to convince her that if Pius XII had decided to oppose himself directly to the Führer, then he would have put all the German Catholics in danger, as well as all those in the countries under German occupation.

"And you are trying to pretend to be above all of this, when you are really here for other reasons," he said, trying to provoke her.

"What other reasons? All I want to do is improve my German, now that it looks like Germany is going to control everything, and there is no other option than to have a good knowledge of the language," she joked.

Amelia would regularly go to church in the evenings when Father Müller was saying Mass. The priest was helping an old Jesuit who was sick but who refused to abandon his parishioners in such a moment of tribulation. The old priest was not as brave as Father Müller and seemed to know nothing about the younger priest's conspiratorial meetings, even though he approved of his attitude. He did not object either to the friendship that was growing up between Father Müller and Pastor Ludwig Schmidt; he blamed the pastor for the ever more intense political attitude of the young Catholic priest, even though he knew full well that it was the situation of the Jewish family to which he felt so close that had in fact confirmed Father Müller's opposition to Hitler. Rahel had been like a sister for him and for Hanna. Irene, Father Müller's mother, and Hanna had not hesitated in welcoming Rahel to hide in their house. One day Father Müller told Hanna that Rahel was safe; she had not asked how, nor had he offered any explanations. Now she saw that Father Müller spent ever more time with the young Spanish woman and she asked herself what the two of them were plotting, but she didn't ask them and preferred not to know. The old priest said that it was probably best not to know too much about his assistant's doings.

Amelia usually went to Father Müller's house to listen to the BBC. She was always made welcome by Irena and Hanna. The two women were fond of the Spaniard and were grateful to her for having saved Rahel.

On July 10, in Father Müller's house, Amelia first heard that Pétain's collaborationist government had decided to break off ties with England. The Vichy government had decreed full powers to the Marshal of France. This happened only a couple of days after the bombardment of Dover.

Amelia saw Admiral Canaris and Colonel Oster at another couple of receptions that she attended along with Professor Schatzhauser, the last of which was in mid-August at Max's house, a farewell dinner that Ludovica had organized for her husband before his departure for Poland.

Ludovica had invited Goering and Himmler, and all the important people who were still in Berlin, and she had accepted, through gritted teeth, all the guests her husband had proposed as well.

That night, Manfred Kasten came up to Amelia, all smiles.

"I have found out some more details about the Madagascar Plan, all that is needed is the Führer's final approval. Maybe you could come round to my house tomorrow to have tea with me and my wife."

Amelia accepted straight away. This was information that they could use in London, not so much because they cared about the fate of the Jews, but because a plan on such a scale would require the use of a great deal of resources, as well as control of the maritime routes of the Atlantic, which had been controlled by the British up until that moment. Winston Churchill was trying at that very moment to convince the Americans that if Great Britain were toppled, then control of the sea would pass into the hands of Germany. So information of this kind could help London establish just how far German sea power could extend.

Although they felt uncomfortable under Ludovica's inquisitive gaze, Max came to take his leave of Amelia.

"I would have liked to have seen you alone, but it has been impossible, because of my obligations, both to the army and to my family."

"I know, don't worry. I suppose I'll still be here when you get back. Do you know where you are being sent exactly?"

"I'm going to Warsaw first, but I need to visit all our troops wherever they are in the country, so I'll be going all over the place."

"And is Captain Henke going with you?"

"Yes, he'll be a help. Hans is a logistics officer, and he'll be responsible for relaying my orders for what we need at the front."

"At least you'll be with a friend."

"You can't imagine how hard it is to be able to trust someone. There are some other officers in the army who think as we do, but they don't dare take the next step. You know what the Nazis are capable of doing to those who oppose their plans; they're worried that they could end up like Walter von Frisch, the head of the army, whom Goering accused, via the Gestapo, of homosexuality. Or Marshal Blomberg, who was forced to step down as minister of war after pressure was put on him over his wife's past. And Ludwig Beck's opinions are no secret; he was chief of staff until a couple of years ago, and then he had to resign because of disagreements with the Führer. There are generals like Witzleben and Stülpnagel who have supported Beck in the past. There are confrontations brewing between some of the upper echelons of the army and the heads of the SS, whose influence is increasing. There were disagreements also between General Blaskowitz and the SS during the Poland campaign. Von Tresckow and von Schlabrendorff are worried by how German politics is developing."

"Why are you telling me all this?"

"Because I think I can trust you, and I care what you think; I don't want you to think that we're all Nazis here in Germany, there are people who are repulsed by everything that Nazism signifies, and who above all do not want another European war."

"Is it so difficult to get rid of Hitler?"

"It's not something that can be worked out on the hoof. Maybe after the war is over..."

"But that may be too late..."

"It will never be too late to make Germany a democracy again, to give it back its democratic institutions. We are opposed to Hitler, but we will never betray our country. Are you still in contact with Lord Paul James?"

"You know I've only seen him a few times with Albert, his nephew."

"I'm worried that people in London might see Germany as a unified bloc around Hitler, but it's not like that. There are many of us who are ready to give our lives to end this nightmare."

Ludovica came up to them, followed by a waiter bearing a tray of champagne.

"Darling, would you like to raise a toast with us to your safe return to Berlin?" Ludovica's voice was filled with irony and her eyes were filled with rage.

"An excellent idea," Max said. "Let us drink to being as happy again as we are today."

Max handed a glass to Amelia and they raised a toast along with Ludovica. Then Max decided to follow his wife's instructions and attend to his guests.

Amelia couldn't sleep that night. She should go back to London and try to speak to Lord Paul James personally, but would he want to see her? She knew that the person she should report to was her superior, Major Murray, but Max had asked expressly that she should speak with Lord James. There was only one way to get in touch with him, and that was via Albert. Yes, she would have to ask him to organize some kind of social occasion with his uncle before she had to go to the Admiralty and pass her findings on to Major Murray. It wouldn't be easy to convince Albert, but she hoped she could manage. Of course, she would first have to get Murray's permission to return to London, and she would have to convince him that the news she had was important enough for her to leave Berlin.

She got up early and found Herr Helmut preparing breakfast for Greta.

"I have to leave. Would you be so kind as to finish making this and to take it to my wife in her bed? I know that it is a lot to ask, but would you be able to help her get up and settled in the armchair by the window? I think she is a little better."

"Don't worry, Herr Helmut, I will look after Greta."

"Don't you have to go to class?"

"Yes, but I've got lots of time."

That afternoon Amelia went to Manfred Kasten's house. His wife, Helga, opened the door and led her to her husband's office. The former diplomat was waiting for her impatiently; he asked her to sit down and gave her a file of information about the Madagascar Plan. Amelia read it eagerly without saying a word, but her face displayed just how taken aback she was by the grandiose scale of the operation.

"Can I take these with me?"

"It would be dangerous. The Gestapo has eyes and ears everywhere and they may know more about our group than may appear. Trust no one. It's better if these documents never leave this room, for their own safety and for ours."

Amelia settled down to read these documents again, trying to memorize even the smallest details. The man who had put this plan together had calculated the number of ships that would be needed to take all the German Jews from Germany to Madagascar, as well as the support vessels that would be necessary. The documents also gave details of the German navy's current capacity. It could be vital information for the Admiralty, so Amelia reaffirmed in her mind her decision to go back to London at once.

"Thank you for trusting in me, Herr Kasten," she said after she had finished reading the papers.

"I am a Christian, Amelia, and I think I am a good German, and I hate what certain people are doing to my country. Deporting the Jews! Putting them on an island as if they were contagious!"

It was late when Amelia got back to the Kellers' house. Greta was asleep and her husband was in the kitchen, going through some account books.

Amelia said that she was thinking about going home.

"Has anything happened?" Helmut asked.

"No, but you know that my sister Antonietta is unwell and I don't want to be away from her for too long. But I will come back, Herr Helmut, and if you would be willing to carry on renting me the room then I would be very grateful. I think I could perhaps find work in Berlin, I have met some people who are in need of a fluent Spanish speaker. You know that our two countries are allies, ever since Hitler and Franco decided to work together..."

Helmut Keller agreed. He had never spoken of politics with Amelia; the two of them had avoided any mention of what had happened. He was surprised that Amelia did not mention Nazism, especially since the new regime had caused her father to lose his fortune, but he didn't dare speak openly in front of her about his hatred of the Führer, because he knew all too well that children don't inherit their parents' ideas. His son, Frank, seemed to be happy in the army; he said that Hitler was giving Germany back its greatness. They had argued about this at first, but then they had avoided the topic so as not to upset Greta, who did not like to see them argue.

Over the next few days, Amelia took her leave of Professor Karl Schatzhauser, Father Müller, and the rest of the opposition group. She told them she would be back soon. She also made a decision: She made her confession to Father Müller, and in it included the fact of her collaboration with the British.

"That's not a sin," he scolded her.

"I know, but I need to be sure that you won't share this information with anyone."

"I cannot, the confessional brings with it the obligation of complete confidentiality," he replied with annoyance. "Now tell me, why have you confessed this?"

"Because I need help, as well as to trust in someone."

The next day she went to the priest's house. She showed him how to encode relevant information and she asked him to send anything he found out in an apparently innocuous letter to the same Madrid address where she sent all her own letters.

"With this code, anyone who opens your letters will think that you are writing to an old friend."

"And shouldn't you tell someone else as well, in case anything happens to me?" Father Müller asked worriedly.

"Nothing is going to happen to you, and in any case, it's not a good idea for too many people to know this system. Don't forget that these letters will go to Madrid, where there are already lots of German spies. We could put the person who receives the letters in danger."

Father Müller took Amelia to the station and helped her to get settled in her compartment, which to their relief she was to share with a woman with three small children.

"When are you coming back?" the priest wanted to know.

"It doesn't depend on me... If it did, then I would be back very soon: I think I can be useful in Berlin."

Amelia was not going to Madrid, but to Lisbon, which was the most convenient point from which to travel to London. She knew that the English capital was undergoing bombardment by the Germans, and that this was causing a great deal of suffering and loss, both material and human, and she was keen to find Albert and see that he was alright.

She stayed in a little hotel near the port in Lisbon. It was no accident that she chose this place. Major Murray had given her the address and told her that if she needed help or wanted to get in touch with him, then the owner of the hotel would be able to contact the relevant people.

The Hotel Oriente was small and clean, and its owner was British, a man named John Brown, who was married to a Portuguese woman, Doña Mencia. Amelia thought that they both must work for the British Secret Service.

She told them that she wanted to travel to London, and asked them the best way to do so. She used the pass-phrase that Murray had given her: "I have business to attend to, but most of all I miss the fog."

John Brown nodded and said nothing, and a few hours later he sent his wife to her room to tell her that a fishing boat would take her to England. She left Portugal two days after Leon Trotsky had been assassinated in Mexico. She had heard the news on the BBC and had remembered the trip that she had made with Albert not so long ago. She remembered Trotsky well, his inquisitive gaze, his uncertain gestures, his fear of being assassinated.

And she was scared to think how far Moscow's reach must extend, and how she had managed to escape from that danger.

8

To Amelia's surprise, Albert was not in London. The apartment was freezing cold, and there was a layer of dust on everything. She found a note on Albert's desk, dated July 10.

> *Dear Amelia,*
> *I don't know when you will read this note, or even if you will read it. I have asked Uncle Paul how long he will be keeping you out of London, but he didn't want to answer me. In case you get back and find me gone, I want you to know that I have gone to New York. I have things to do there; I need to see the editors of the newspapers I write for, I need to see how my investments are doing, I need to talk to my father and argue with my mother... I think I will try to find Rahel as well, to see if she is alright. I don't know how long I will be in New York, but you know how to find me.*
> *The flat is at your disposal. Mrs. O'Hara will come to clean from time to time.*
> *And so it turns out, my darling, that I, who write so much for other people, don't know how to write to you.*
> *Yours,*
>
> ALBERT JAMES

Major Murray seemed pleased when Amelia came into his office.
"Good work," he said in greeting.
"You think so?"

"Of course."

"But I haven't sent you any substantive information, but I have the details of an operation that I think could be vitally important."

"I supposed you must have, because you made the decision to come back without my permission."

"I'm sorry, but I think that once I've explained about the Madagascar Plan then you'll agree that it is an important topic."

Murray asked his secretary to make them some tea. Then he sat down in front of Amelia, ready to hear her out.

"Well, what have you got to tell me?"

Amelia explained in detail what she had heard, from the day of her arrival in Berlin until her return to London. The contacts she had established, the opposition group she was working with, the Madagascar Plan, and everything that Max von Schumann had told her about the discontent brewing in various sections of the armed forces.

The major listened to her in silence and only interrupted her to ask for details every now and then. When she had finished, Murray got up and paced up and down in front of his desk for a while, ignoring Amelia's growing discomfort.

"So, you have found out that there is a little network in the heart of the Third Reich. We have a group of friends in Berlin who will give us information, and a place to go. I didn't expect so much of you, to tell the truth. As for the information that Baron von Schumann has given you, I won't say that it will help us win the war, but it will give us an idea of what is happening. His judgments on what Hitler is doing are more valuable than you can imagine... It is interesting to know that not all the Germans are behind Hitler."

"There aren't many of them," Amelia said.

"Yes, of course... It's very interesting. My dear, you have brought us some very valuable information. I want you to write down everything you have told me, and I want in within two hours. I have a meeting with Lord James. I think he will be very happy with the success of your mission, which is much greater than that of other agents who are working in Berlin at the moment."

Amelia started and looked defiantly at Major Murray.

"You sent other agents to Berlin?"

"Of course, you didn't think that we'd only send you, did you? The more networks we can set up, the better. You must understand that it is better for you not to have any contact with each other until it becomes truly necessary. And not just for security reasons."

"So there are other agents in Berlin at the moment... ," Amelia pressed.

"In Berlin, and in other parts of Germany. Don't try to tell me that you're surprised!"

She didn't say, but in fact she was surprised. This was the moment when she began to understand that in the world of intelligence nothing is what it seems, and that agents are only pawns in the hands of their controllers.

"Shall I return to Berlin?"

"Write the report over the next couple of hours. Then go home and rest. It's Friday today, take a couple of days off and come back at nine o'clock on Monday to get your orders."

Amelia followed Murray's instructions to the letter. She spent the weekend writing to Albert and putting the apartment in order. She didn't want to see anyone, and anyway, the people she knew in London were Albert's friends rather than hers.

On Monday at nine on the dot she arrived at Murray's office. He seemed to be in a bad mood.

"The Luftwaffe are getting ever more accurate in their attacks... ," Murray complained.

"I know, sir."

"We'll have to pay Berlin a return visit with our planes."

Amelia nodded, even though she couldn't suppress a shudder thinking of all the friends she had left in Berlin, all of them opposed to Hitler and ready to risk their lives to put the Third Reich to an end.

"Well, I have another mission for you. You have to go to Italy, straight away."

"Italy? But... well... I thought I was to go back to Berlin."

"You will be more useful for us in Italy. This is classified information that I am passing on to you now, but a few days ago an unidentified submarine destroyed the Greek cruiser *Elli*. We think that it was an Italian submarine."

"But why do I have to go to Italy? I insist that I am more useful in Berlin."

"You have to go to Italy because you are a friend of Carla Alessandrini's."

"Yes, I am a friend of Carla's, but..."

"No 'buts,'" Murray interrupted. "You know that Il Duce has declared war on us. We're not all that worried, but there is no such thing as a little enemy. *La signora* Alessandrini will help introduce you into Italian high society. The only thing I want you to do is to listen, to take note of everything that you hear, and to report back to us things that might appear interesting. It's the same work that you have been doing in Berlin. You are a pleasant, well-mannered, and personable young woman, and you will not be out of place in elegant company, nor in the company of powerful men."

"But I cannot use Carla!"

"I am not asking you to use her; she is your friend and she does not like Il Duce, and she is in contact with the Resistance already..."

"Carla! But that's impossible! She is an opera singer, and, yes, she doesn't like Fascism, but that doesn't mean that she's willing to get into trouble."

"And don't you think that she got into trouble when she helped that Jewish girl escape? Rahel, that was her name, wasn't it?"

"But that was a very special set of circumstances," Amelia protested.

"Go to Milan, or wherever it is that *la gran Alessandrini* is to be found at the moment, and tell us what they are saying in the Duce's 'court.' That is your mission. We need Signora Alessandrini to collaborate with us. She has free access to all the centers of power in the whole of Italy. Il Duce is her greatest admirer."

"And what shall I say to Carla?"

"Don't lie to her, but you don't have to tell her the whole truth either."

"And how do I do that?"

"Just carrying on as you have been until now will be fine."

"But what do you want to know?"

"I don't know, you will have to tell me."

"How can I get in touch with London?"

"I will give you another Madrid address to write to. You will send letters to another friend there. It will be a different code from the one you used in Berlin. We will teach you another one, I don't think it will take you that long to learn it. If you have to get in touch with us urgently, go to Madrid, you can always use the excuse of needing to see your family, and get in touch with Major Finley, Jim Finley. He works in the embassy as a minor official, but he is with us. I will tell you how to get in touch with him before you go. I want you in Italy in a week. I don't think that you need any particular cover if you are going as Carla Alessandrini's friend. I took the liberty of sending her a telegram in your name saying that you were going to see her, and she replied extremely happily, saying she'd be delighted."

"You used my name to get in touch with Carla!" Amelia protested.

"I've made a few things easier, that's all."

Amelia was not as surprised as she had made out to be that Carla should have connections with the Resistance. Her friend was a passionate woman, with very clear ideas about what Fascism signified and how much she hated it.

The major had arranged for her to travel to Rome via Lisbon, and he permitted her, through gritted teeth, to spend a couple of days en route in Madrid to see her family.

She arrived in Madrid on September 1. She left behind an England that had suffered stoically under the bloody attacks of the Luftwaffe, not only on London, but on a number of other cities: Liverpool, Manchester, Bristol, Worcester, Durham, Gloucester, and Portsmouth were all on the list of victims. The RAF tried to give an eye for an eye with their attacks, and Berlin suffered ever more severe bombardments.

Meanwhile, Churchill continued his secret diplomatic contacts with the United States, attempting to convince Franklin D.

Roosevelt that not only was England not being destroyed, but that it could even win the war, even if such a victory could be achieved only with the material help of the United States. Churchill sketched out for Roosevelt the dark future that might result if such help were not forthcoming, and Hitler took control of the whole of Europe and positioned himself for an attack on the United States. Churchill insisted to Roosevelt that it was vital for America that the United Kingdom should triumph.

The United Kingdom's financial situation was continually worsening, and the country had almost to go bankrupt before the Americans would accept that either they should help the United Kingdom, or else they should expect to find Hitler menacing their own coasts.

On September 2, 1940, the United States lent England fifty destroyers, in exchange for military bases at various points all over the world...

Major Hurley cleared his throat. Apparently, he had reached the end of his story. He looked at the clock without trying to hide that this was what he was doing. I asked myself if he was going to get rid of me without giving me any more information, or if he would send me back to Lady Victoria, but I decided not to ask anything.

I had listened to his story in silence, and I had not even asked a single question.

"Your great-grandmother also had a significant part to play in Italy. But, Guillermo, maybe you should find out what happened when she went back to Madrid. I cannot tell you about this, unfortunately. As far as Italy is concerned, I could give you some information about the work that Amelia carried out there, but it would not be very thorough, as I have not found very much in the archives. You told me that you yourself were in contact with a scholar who was an expert about Carla Alessandrini's life; maybe she will be able to help you with this part. Or maybe not... In any case, I need to go now and I will not be able to meet with you again for a few days.

I was about to protest. But I realized that Major William Hurley would care little about my protests. He had the information that I would like to have and he would control it as he saw fit. So I told him that I would be eternally grateful to him for the help he had already given me.

"I would not be able to carry out my research without you," I said, to flatter him.

"Of course you wouldn't, but as you will of course understand, I have other duties and responsibilities, so I will not be able to see you for several days, let us say not before Wednesday of next week. Call my secretary on the Tuesday to see if I am available."

I left the major's house in a bad mood. But then I thought that there's no cloud without a silver lining: I could call Francesca, and pretend to be upset with her that she had not told me a single thing about Carla Alessandrini's political activities, and I could use that as an excuse to go to Rome. I didn't want to abuse the funds that Doña Laura was placing at my disposal for the investigation into Amelia, but I managed to convince myself that the trip to Rome was more than justified. My luck was like my great-grandmother's: I kept on coming back to London, like it or not.

I called my mother, ready for the habitual scolding, and found her sarcastic and distant.

"Ah, Guillermo, so it's you. Glad to hear from you."

"Come on, Mom! You don't sound that happy to hear from me, to know I'm well."

"Well, I suppose you're well, and you're a big boy now, so if you're going to call me then it's enough for you to call me at Christmas and on my birthday, but if you're going to do that then you'd have to remember when they are, and as you're so snowed under with work, I imagine that might be difficult..."

There was the problem! I'd forgotten her birthday! My mother wasn't going to forgive me for this, it was one of the three immoveable feasts in her calendar: meals together for her birthday, for my birthday, and for Christmas. She didn't care about the rest of the year, but these were the sacred dates.

"I'm sorry, Mom, but you can't imagine how busy I've been investigating your grandmother."

"I've told you that I don't care what that woman did, and don't apologize, there's no need for you to apologize, you're free to call, or not call, whoever you want whenever you want."

"I'd thought about coming to Madrid and taking you out to dinner," I said, improvising.

"Really? How considerate!"

"Look, I'll be in Madrid tomorrow and I'll come get you at nine in the evening. Think about where would be nice for you to go."

9

When I got to my apartment it felt good to be home again. I thought about how comforting I found those four walls with their Ikea furniture. I had spent so much time going from one place to another in search of Amelia Garayoa that I had barely spent any time at all at home. It only took me one glance to see that the apartment needed an urgent cleaning, and I promised myself that one of the things I would have to do was convince my mother to send her cleaner along. With the understanding, of course, that I would pay.

I had a shower and then fell into my bed. How much I had missed it! I went to sleep straight away. My guardian angel decided to wake me up in time for me to go to find my mother, because if I had stood her up this time, then she would have been capable of refusing to talk to me for the rest of her life. I woke up with a start and looked at my watch. Eight thirty! I jumped up and rushed to the shower again. At nine on the dot, my hair still wet, I rang her doorbell.

"You look terrible," she said by way of greeting, without even giving me a kiss.

"Really? Well, I think you look lovely."

"Yes, well, you look terrible. Do you know what irons are for? I'm sure you do, because you're one of the clever ones."

I was annoyed at my mother's irony, and all the more so because she was right, and the shirt I was wearing was rumpled and my jeans needed a wash.

"I haven't had a chance to unpack, really. But I'm here, that's the important thing, you don't know how much I've missed you."

"Water! For the love of God, bring me some water!" my mother shouted.

"What? What's wrong?" I asked in alarm.

"I'm having palpitations. At the cheek of you."

"You really scared me!"

We went to the restaurant that she had chosen. The conversation took on the same tone throughout the whole evening. I regretted having invited her to dinner with me. What is more, my mother decided, just to give my fragile economic situation a further kicking, to have champagne with the meal, and ordered a bottle of Bollinger as if it were a bottle of Coke.

I called Doña Laura the next morning, to ask her if she would like me to come round and tell her about my investigations up to that point.

"I would prefer it if you delivered the manuscript when you have the whole thing ready and typed up."

"It was just so that you could see how I am getting on. Let me tell you that Amelia Garayoa's life is worthy of a novel."

"Well, well, when you know everything, write it all down and bring it to me. That's what we agreed, no?"

"Of course, Doña Laura, and that's what I'll do."

"Do you need anything else?"

"No, I think I'm alright for the time being. Professor Soler is being a great help. I offered to tell him everything I was finding out, but he told me that he didn't want to know anything apart from what was absolutely necessary for him to help me."

"And that's as it should be. Pablo is a good friend of the family, but he is not family, and there are things... Well, things that he doesn't need to know, that nobody needs to know."

"I need to call him now, because I need him to tell me if Amelia was in Madrid at the beginning of September 1940."

"If you want to, you can talk with Edurne, she can help you."

"And what about you, Doña Laura, don't you remember anything about that time?"

"Of course I do! But I don't want it to be my memory that tells you how to proceed, but the neutral memory of the people who were with us at the time."

"And Edurne, will she remember? It seems to take a lot out of the poor woman to have to remember these things."

"That's only natural, old people don't like it when we rummage in their memories. Edurne is very modest and loyal, and it isn't easy for her to tell things about the family to a stranger."

"I'm a part of the family, don't forget that Amelia was my great-grandmother. You are a kind of great-great-aunt to me."

"Don't talk nonsense! I think you should speak to Edurne. If you like, you could come round to the house tomorrow early in the morning, which is when her head is the clearest."

I don't know why Doña Laura insisted that Edurne speak with me. The poor woman couldn't hide her discomfort at having to tell a stranger intimate aspects of the life of the family to which she had dedicated her whole life.

When I reached the Garayoa house, the housekeeper told me that Edurne was waiting to speak to me, but that I should go to see the ladies first in the salon.

Doña Laura and Doña Melita were there. I thought that Doña Melita did not look that well, she seemed tired.

"Is it very hard for you to put the story together?" she asked me in a faint little voice.

"It's not easy, Doña Melita, but don't worry, I think that at the very least I will manage to get the most important details of my great-grandmother's life organized."

Doña Laura shifted uncomfortably on the sofa and told me not to waste any more time.

"Not just because of the expense, but because we are too old to wait much longer."

"Don't worry, I am as keen as you are to finish the investigation as soon as possible. I have left my job as a journalist and my mother is about to stop talking to me."

"Your mother is still alive?" Doña Melita asked, and this surprised me, as I had already explained what my family circumstances were.

"Yes, luckily enough my mother is still alive," I said, disconcerted.

"Right. Well, you are very lucky, I lost my mother when I was very young."

"Enough chatting," Doña Laura interrupted. "Guillermo is here to work, so he should go off to the library and talk to Edurne."

Edurne was sitting in an armchair and appeared to have dozed off. She jerked herself upright when she heard me enter.

"How are you feeling?"

"Fine, fine," she said in a dazed voice.

"I don't want to bother you, but maybe you remember about a visit Amelia made to Madrid in September 1940. I think that she was on her way to Rome, but that she came to see her family first."

"Amelia was always coming and going, and there were lots of times when she wouldn't say where she was coming from or where she was going."

"But do you remember what happened that time? It was September of 1940 and I think she came by herself, without the journalist, without Albert James. Her previous visit was when she discovered that Águeda was pregnant..."

"Oh now I remember! Poor Amelia, what a shock! Águeda had taken Javier to the entrance to the Retiro so that Amelia could see him, but she opened her overcoat and we could see that she was fat, fat and pregnant..."

"Yes, I know all that, but I want to know what happened the next time Amelia came to visit."

Edurne began to speak, her voice tired.

We weren't expecting her, she came without telling us. This was something that became a custom with her. We never knew when she was going to come. Antonietta was better, thanks to the money that Amelia sent, which let Don Armando buy medicine... well, medicine and food, because Antonietta needed to eat well. The money Amelia sent wasn't enough for luxuries, but it was enough to buy food. You could find good stuff on the black market back then, but it cost a fortune.

I think that Amelia came in the evening, yes, yes it was at night, because I was making the dinner in the kitchen and it was Jesús who opened the door.

"Mama, Mama, come quickly! It's cousin Amelia!"

We all rushed out into the hall and there she was, hugging Jesús.

"But how handsome you are! You've grown a lot and you're much less pale."

Jesús was getting better as well. He had always been a sickly child and he had gotten sick during the war. But over those months he had gotten better. The medicine, and the food above all, were working miracles.

Antonietta hugged her sister and there was no way to pry them apart.

Laura began to cry and it was hard for Don Armando to hold back his tears as well. We all wanted to hug her and kiss her. It was Doña Elena who showed her practical side and put all this hugging and tears in order, making us move into the salon. She sent Pablo to take Amelia's suitcase to Amelia's room, and asked me to go and finish making supper and to set one more place at the table.

Amelia was very affectionate with us all, she kissed me and Pablo.

Jesús and Pablo were good friends, and now that Jesús was better, Doña Elena had put Pablo's bed in his room, because she said that now he was growing it wasn't right for him to carry on sharing my room.

We ate rice with tomato and slices of fried streaky bacon that evening. I had bought the bacon that afternoon from a black marketer who had set his cap at me.

Rufino, for that was his name, had sent me word that they had fresh bacon, so Doña Elena sent me to buy some... Where was I? Yes... now I remember... Amelia said that she was not going to stay very long, just for two or three days because she had to go and work. She was Albert James's assistant, he was an American journalist who apparently was in New York but who had sent Amelia to Rome to prepare for a report he was doing, I don't know about what, but it was lucky that she had to go to Rome because it meant she could pass through Madrid on the way.

"How did you come here from London?" Don Armando asked.

"I came through Lisbon; it's the safest way."

"The English don't seem to worry too much about Franco," Don Armando said.

"The English can't fight against Hitler and against Franco, they need to topple Germany first and then everything will follow after."

"Are you sure? England is still issuing Franco the navicerts that allow him to import fuel and wheat; it's not much, but it is still something."

"You'll see how everything will change once we get rid of Hitler."

We told her all the family news. Antonietta said that she would like to work but that Doña Elena would not let her.

"She won't even let me help in the kitchen," Antonietta complained.

"Of course not! You're not better yet," Doña Elena said angrily.

"Aunt is right. The best help that you could give the family is to get completely better," Amelia said.

"The doctor told us that we need to take special care of her because she could still have a relapse," Don Armando added.

"And what about you, Laura, are you still at the school?"

"Yes, I'm going to start teaching French this term. The nuns are very kind to me. There's a new mother superior, it's not Sister Encarnación anymore, she died of pneumonia and has been replaced by Sister María de las Virtudes, who was our piano teacher, don't you remember?"

"Yes, yes! She was very kind to us, a good woman."

"They say that none of the nuns speak French as well as I do, so I will teach French this term, and when Antonietta is fully recovered, then I might be able to convince Sister María to let her give piano lessons... but she needs to recover fully before that can happen..."

"That would be wonderful! See, Antonietta, that you will be able to work? But you have to get better, I forbid you from doing anything until my aunt and uncle tell me that you are fully recovered."

Don Armando told them about his office, his new job as an articled clerk.

"I need to put up with a lot of things, but I don't complain, because what I earn is what allows us to stay on our feet. I have been marked down as a 'red,' so I am not allowed to defend cases in the courts, but I am at least working with what I know, preparing the cases that others will defend."

"They exploit him, he brings back work every day, and he doesn't even get Sundays or Saturdays off," Doña Elena complained.

"Yes, but I have a job, which is a lot, given that they were going to shoot me a few months ago. Amelia saved my life and I have a job, which is more than I could have dreamt of when I was in prison. We do well, with your help, Amelia."

"Do you know anything about Lola?" Amelia asked, looking at Pablo.

"No, we haven't heard a word. Pablo goes to see his grandmother in the hospital, but she gets worse every day. His father writes to him from time to time, but there's not a trace of Lola," Laura explained.

"The boys go to school," Don Armando added. "They're bright and get good marks. Jesús is very good at math and Pablo is good at Latin and history, so they help each other. They're like brothers, sometimes they even fight like brothers."

"But why would we ever fight?" Jesús protested.

"Alright, all I will say is that every now and then I hear shouts coming from your room," Don Armando continued.

"But that's not fighting! Don't worry, Amelia, I get on well with Pablo, I don't know what I'd do without him in a house that's so full of women, and bossy women at that... ," Jesús replied with a laugh.

"I... well... I'm very grateful that you let me stay here... , ," Pablo whispered.

"Oh, don't be silly! Don't thank us, you're another member of the family," Don Armando said.

Amelia spent two days with her family. She went to speak to Antonietta's doctor, and asked Laura to go with her to say hello to Sister María de las Virtudes, whom she gave a small donation for her to "buy flowers for Our Lady's chapel," and also, as we had all feared, she insisted on seeing Javier.

Doña Elena resisted sending me to go and roam around outside Santiago's house, but Amelia insisted so much that eventually she gave in.

"After what happened the last time, Águeda might refuse to let you see the child," Doña Elena said.

"He is my son and I need to see him. Can't you understand, Aunt? I can't be in Madrid and do nothing to see him. If only you knew how much I've regretted abandoning him..."

Amelia told Laura that she suffered from nightmares, and that on many nights she woke up crying because she had seen a woman running away with Javier in her arms.

One day I sat down at the corner of Don Santiago's house, waiting for Águeda to make an appearance, and this was how I spent the whole day. It was well dark by the time I got back home. All I had seen had been Don Santiago coming out early in the morning, and coming back home in the afternoon, but never a sign of Águeda or Javier.

Doña Elena grew nervous and said that the best thing was to leave it for some other time, but Amelia insisted; she could not spend much more time in Madrid, she had been there for three days already, but she would not leave without seeing her son. In the end, Doña Elena broke into tears.

"But Elena, what's going on?" Don Armando was alarmed by his wife's tears.

"Come on, don't cry, I didn't want to upset you," Amelia apologized.

Laura hugged her mother without knowing how to console her. When Doña Elena calmed down she sat for a while in silence.

"But you are so stubborn, Amelia! I didn't want to tell you anything because I didn't want you to suffer, but you insisted and insisted..."

"What, what's happened? Has anything happened to my son?" Amelia asked in alarm.

"No, Javier is well, he's with your in-laws."

"With Don Manuel and Doña Blanca? But why?"

"Because Águeda has had a daughter, a week ago, and it was a difficult birth and she's in the hospital. Santiago has taken Javier to be with his grandparents until Águeda is in a fit state to go back home with the child. I didn't want to tell you so as not to upset you."

Amelia did not cry. She trembled and made a great effort to control herself, swallowing her tears, and succeeded in not crying. When she could speak, in a tiny faint voice, she asked her aunt:

"How long have you known?"

"I've told you, for a week; I met a friend of mine and the first thing she said to me was that Águeda had had a daughter and that they were going to call her Paloma. She told me that it was a difficult birth and that Águeda was crying for nearly two days until the baby was born. Santiago never left her side. She also told me that ever since Águeda had got pregnant, Santiago had employed another maid to deal with the domestic chores, and that Águeda had become the lady of the house. She doesn't wear an apron anymore, and although Santiago still hasn't introduced her to his friends, there is no doubt that they are living together."

"I cannot blame him. I have no right," Amelia murmured.

"You're right, however hard it is, you cannot blame him. Santiago is a man... a young man, he can't wait for you," Don Armando said.

"He doesn't have to. It was I who abandoned him, and who went off with another man, leaving him with a baby only a couple of months old. I wish that I will be able to forgive myself one day!"

"If you want to, I can call Don Manuel and Doña Blanca and ask them to let you see Javier... ," Don Armando suggested.

"You don't need to humiliate yourself, Uncle. You know they won't let me see my son. I trusted that Águeda..."

"I'll come with you to your in-laws' house. We can wait until they take the child for a walk, and at the very least you'll be able to see him from a distance," Laura suggested.

"It's a good idea, at least I'll be able to see him from a distance. I'll delay traveling for one day more, I hope that... well, I hope that Albert isn't upset at the delay."

Doña Elena ordered me to go with the two cousins. She didn't want Amelia and Laura to go alone, she was afraid of what might happen. We turned up in the morning at Santiago's parents' house and did not have to wait long, because at round about eleven we saw Doña Blanca leaving the house, holding Javier by the hand. The child had grown a great deal and looked happy with his grandmother.

Laura was holding Amelia's hand, but could not stop her from pulling herself free and running toward her son.

"Javier! Javier! It's your mother!" Amelia cried out.

Doña Blanca stopped dead and blushed bright red, from anger I think.

"How dare you!" she shouted at Amelia. "How dare you show yourself here! Go away! Go away!"

But Amelia had grasped Javier in her arms and held him tight, covering him with kisses.

"My little boy! How beautiful you are! How much you've grown! I love you so much, Javier! Mother loves you so much!"

Javier was scared and started to cry. Doña Blanca wanted to take the child, but Amelia would not let him go. Laura and I did not know what to do.

"Please, Doña Blanca, have mercy!" Laura begged. "Put yourself in her position, she is the child's mother and she has a right to see him."

"She's a slut! If she had loved her child, then she would not have abandoned him and her husband to run off with another man. Let him go, you slut!" Doña Blanca shouted, and pulled Javier's arm.

"Doña Blanca, you are a mother, let Amelia at least kiss her son!" Laura insisted.

"If she doesn't let him go then I will shout even more loudly, I will call for a policeman and I will have you arrested. Didn't she run off with a Communist? You're all Communists and you should be in prison. All the reds are whores... Do you think I don't know how your father got out of Ocaña prison? That one there sleeps with anything in trousers," she shouted, pointing at Amelia.

Laura had turned as red as a tomato, and did something totally unexpected. She grabbed hold of Doña Blanca's arm and twisted it, separating her from Amelia and Javier. Then she pushed her against a wall and, paying no attention to Doña Blanca's cries of pain, stamped on her.

"Shut up, you witch! You're the slut. Don't insult my cousin again, don't do it or I'll... I swear that you'll regret it. My father is alive thanks to Amelia, because you Nationalists are a bunch of disgusting... You're scum... You and yours aren't worthy to crawl at our feet. As far as whores are concerned, the Nationalists have made whores out of many decent women, just go to Gran Vía and you'll see mothers forced to sell themselves just to get food for their children. Is this the prosperity Franco promised? Of course, you have everything you want, you won the war... and they were about to kill your son, because Santiago, thank the Lord, was not a Fascist."

Doña Blanca got free of Laura by giving her a good push. Amelia was trying to calm Javier, who was crying and scared because his grandmother was being treated in this way by two women who were strangers to him.

"Whether you want to accept it or not, Javier is my son and you can't lie to him and tell him he has a different mother. I may be the worst mother in the world and I may not deserve to have Javier, but he is my son and you will not snatch him away from me," Amelia said, staring her mother-in-law in the eyes.

"When Santiago finds out what you've done... All you reds are sluts, sluts! Leave us alone, you've done enough damage!"

Amelia put Javier down and gave him one last kiss.

"My son," she said, "I love you so much, and whatever they say you must never forget that I am your mother."

Once back in Doña Blanca's arms, the child began to calm down. Doña Blanca went back to her house, walking as fast as she could.

We walked home, worried about what might happen next. Knowing Santiago, it was clear that he would not just stand by and do nothing once he found out from his mother what had happened.

Don Armando tried to calm Amelia and Laura, he told them that he would not let Santiago do anything. But Doña Elena was not so sure, and so we spent the rest of the morning and a part of the afternoon waiting for something to happen. And it did. Of course it did. It was half past nine and we were having supper when the bell began to ring insistently.

Doña Elena sent me to open the door, and I did so trembling, because I was sure that it would be Santiago.

I opened the door and it was him. His face was twisted with anger and it was clear that he was making a great effort to control himself. His father was with him.

"Announce us," he said without any preamble.

I went into the dining room and, stammering, announced Don Santiago. Don Armando told us not to move from where we were; he would speak with Santiago. We were very quiet and said nothing, wondering what would happen.

"Good evening, Santiago, Don Manuel... How can I help you?"

"I want your niece to stay away from my family once and for all. She has no right to frighten my son. I want you to know that I will not tolerate my mother being treated as she was treated today by your daughter Laura." It was hard for Santiago to control his rage.

"If anyone lays a finger on my wife or my grandson, then he will go to prison. I will move heaven and earth to make sure that happens," Don Manuel said.

"I don't have any doubt at all that you could make it happen, but no one has attacked Doña Blanca. As far as I understand it, from what Laura said, she helped Amelia to be able to be free to hold her son in her arms. She was not disrespectful to Doña Blanca, but Doña Blanca was disrespectful to us, not just to Amelia and Laura, but to my entire family."

"My wife is a lady and always behaves in a ladylike fashion, something that cannot be said of your niece," Don Manuel said.

"Please, father, that's not necessary!" Santiago said, angry at his father's comment.

"If you are here to insult us, then it is better if you leave straight away. I will not have you say a word against Amelia. What has happened has happened. And you, Santiago, you have no right to stop her from seeing her son, and to confuse Javier by telling him that Águeda is his mother, that is cruel, you will have to tell him the truth some day, and do you think that Javier will forgive you for lying to him? That he will forgive you for denying his mother the right to see him?"

"I have not come here to discuss my decisions with you, but to inform you that I will not permit another scene like the one that took place today. My son is growing, he is happy, he has a family, and I am not the one who left him motherless."

"Don Armando," Don Manuel interrupted. "Let me warn you that I will do whatever it takes to ruin you. You will lose your job and they will re-examine your case and maybe send you back to prison. Everyone knows how you managed to be re-leased, there are rotten apples everywhere, and the one who managed to swap Amelia's favors for your pardon was just another unimportant rotten apple."

"How dare you insult her! Yes, I am free thanks to her, thanks to the money that she had to pay to that corrupt man who swaps lives for money, but that's the kind of people you Nationalists are. Don't you dare say a single word to insult Amelia!"

"Father, you shouldn't have said that!" Santiago said.

"Ah! Do you really not know? I can't believe you don't know, when the whole of Madrid knows! Ask your niece how she paid, what she gave as well as money, to get you released from Ocaña," Don Manuel insisted.

At this moment Amelia appeared on the threshold of the room and then put herself between Don Armando and Santiago and his father.

"You can insult me as much as you want. I won't deny you that right after all I've done, but it is you, Santiago, who should leave my family in peace. They have done nothing to you. As for Javier... he is my son, however much that upsets you, and that is not something you can change. I cannot turn back time, but I assure you that if I could then I would not have done what I did, that I am filled with remorse and will never forgive myself as long as I live, but I cannot change what I have done."

"Amelia, please, go inside, let me handle this. They have no right to insult you, I will not tolerate these insinuations."

"No, Uncle, it is me who has to tell them not to insult and threaten you. Don Manuel, I always took you for a gentleman, who would be incapable of the low act that you have just perpetrated by saying what you have just said. I am not an indecent person for saving my uncle from execution. It was not enough for your friends the Nationalists to win the war, they have to take their revenge on everyone on the Republican side who fought against them. Of course, Santiago, that was your side, although never that of your father. Will Franco be the stronger for shooting thousands of people who fought against him? No, no he won't; people will fear him and hate him, but it will not make him stronger."

"Stay away from my son," Santiago said, looking at her with fury.

"No, I will not stay away from Javier; I will try a thousand times, as often as necessary, to see him, to be with him, even if only for a few minutes, to remind him that I am his mother, to tell him that in spite of what I did I still love him with all my soul. And I will pray every day to ask forgiveness from God, and also that Javier will forgive me himself one day."

"I insist on what I said: I will not allow any member of this family to come close to my own. I want that to be clear, and also that there will be consequences if it does not happen," Don Manuel said.

Santiago took his father by the arm and ushered him out of the house without saying goodbye.

We all went out into the hall. Don Armando looked at Amelia with tears in his eyes.

"What did you do to get me out of Ocaña?" he asked, scared of what the answer might be.

"Nothing that dishonors me. I paid the price that Agapito, that bastard intermediary, demanded. And the fault is committed not by the person who pays the price, but by the one who asks it."

"Amelia, for God's sake, I want to know what you did!" Don Armando insisted.

"Uncle, please! I did what I was asked out of a sense of duty toward you, whom I love so much. I don't regret it, I would do anything to save a life. The price that is asked for a life is never too high, especially not for the life of someone you love."

Don Armando was in despair. Doña Elena embraced him, trying to make him feel all the love that she could.

"Amelia has been very good to us, don't shame her by insisting, by asking again and again," she begged her husband. "We will always have her to thank for the fact that you are still alive."

"But not at any price!"

"Don't say that! I don't know what Amelia did apart from give money to that scoundrel, but I swear that I would have done anything they asked to save you."

Amelia asked the family to gather in the salon.

"What Santiago's father suggested... It is true, nobody knew about it apart from Laura, or at least that is what I thought, but it is obvious that the bastard who served as intermediary, Agapito, has told everyone that I gave myself to him in exchange for your pardon. I would have preferred that neither you nor anyone else in the family had found out, and I swear to you, Uncle, that I have already forgotten all about it."

"My God, Amelia! My God! How your father would have suffered to have known about a thing like that! I... I don't deserve to live in exchange for such a sacrifice... I can never repay you..."

"For goodness' sake, Uncle, don't say such things! You don't owe me anything, nothing at all, there are no debts between people who love each other. And let me tell you again that I don't regret what I did, I have not had a bad conscience about this for even a single day, and if I feel anything for this Agapito it is hatred, and a desire that he catch syphilis and die. But I don't feel dirty myself, I don't regret anything. I know that you would have given your life to save mine, and all I did was give a couple of minutes of my life to some heartless brute."

None of us could sleep that night. I heard Amelia talking with Laura and Antonietta all through the night. Doña Elena got up to make a calming drink for Don Armando, and Jesús and Pablo spent the night murmuring in low voices. We were all upset.

Amelia left the next day and did not come back for a while.

Edurne fell silent and closed her eyes. It was clear that she was suffering. I was upset on her behalf that Doña Laura had made her remember this. I don't know why, but I took her hand and bent over her.

"Thank you, I don't know how I can thank you, I wouldn't be able to put my great-grandmother's life together without you."

"And why do you have to put it together? If you hadn't appeared in this house, then everything would have stayed the same and we would have died peacefully, without looking at the past."

"I'm sorry, Edurne, I truly am."

"Will I have to speak to you again?"

"I will try not to bother you again, I promise."

I wanted to say goodbye to the two old women, but the housekeeper said that they had gone out. I didn't believe her, but I accepted the excuse. Not only were they paying me, but I would never have taken even the slightest step toward Amelia without their help. They had the right not to see me.

I left the house with a strange sensation overwhelming me, a kind of unease. I didn't know why, I think that Edurne's story must have affected me. I didn't like Don Manuel at all; it was annoying to think that even though it was a distant relationship, we were still related: He was my great-great-grandfather; we were family.

I went to my apartment to write down what I had found out over the last few weeks. There was so much material that I decided to transcribe the tapes and get my notes in order before diving into them.

I worked for the rest of the day, and a good part of the night as well. I wanted to go to Rome as soon as possible to talk with Francesca Venezziani. Before I left I called Pepe to see how things were at the online newspaper. They had fired me, but maybe they would feel compassion and let me back in.

"No, Guillermo, no! The boss doesn't want to know about you. He says you're completely disorganized, and he's right. I am sick of sticking up for you, so you'd better go out and make your own way in the world."

I didn't want to get worried about this, but my mother was right: When my investigation into Amelia was finished, and once the story was written, maybe I wouldn't find another job. I said to myself that there was no going back and decided to make Julius Caesar's phrase from the *Gallic War* my motto: "We will talk about the bridge once we reach the river." Only later on would I worry about myself and my future.

10

I stayed once again at the Hotel d'Inghilterra, right next to the Spanish Steps, a
stone's throw from Francesca's loft.

I was sure that she would invite me to have dinner with her,
as indeed she did, so I bought a bottle of Chianti and arrived
punctually at her home.

"*Ciao, caro, come vai!*" she said in greeting.

"Well enough, now," I said with a smile.

I scolded her gently for not having told me that Carla Alessandrini had been politically active.

"I told you that Carla was a singular woman," she said as her
excuse.

"Singular isn't the half of it. She helped a Jewish girl to escape from Berlin and crossed half of Europe with her, and was
in touch with the partisans, so she did a lot more than just war-
ble her music."

"Yes, it's all true, Carla was an extraordinary woman."

"Yes, but you didn't tell me anything about her political activity."

"You didn't ask."

"Well, let me make it clear: I want to know everything, absolutely everything about Carla Alessandrini, and I don't care if
that's politics or gardening, everything means everything."

"I don't know if I can tell you everything straight away."

"No, why?" I asked, a little angrily.

"Because Professor Soler told me that you had to investigate
things step by step, that you had to find a thread to follow and

follow it, and find everything out in its order. I don't know what the order is, but every time Carla appears, please feel free to come to me."

"That's a good one! I'm a little sick of being sent here and there like a puppet."

Francesca shrugged, making it clear that this had nothing to do with her.

"What do you want to know?"

"I want to know what *la gran Carla* did in September 1940, when my great-grandmother came to see her in Rome, and I want you to tell me if you've already told anyone about this, because there's not a word about it in your book."

"And why should I have written about things that have nothing to do with her art?"

"You're her biographer."

"I'm something else as well, the guardian of her memory. I will tell you a secret: I am writing another book about Carla, but it will take me some time, I don't know much about what she did during the Second World War. Shall we start?"

Amelia reached Milan on September 5, 1940. Vittorio Leonardi, Carla's husband, came to meet her at the station.

"How good it is to see you here! Carla is longing to see you, you have to tell us about Rahel..."

A chauffeur with the latest model Fiat was waiting for them at the door of the station.

Carla was happy to have Amelia with her. Ever since she had gotten the telegram that said Amelia was coming, she had been redecorating her mansion with an eye to Amelia's tastes.

While the maid unpacked Amelia's bags, the two women did not stop talking.

Amelia explained that her relationship with Albert was going through a bad patch, and Carla said that if she did not love him then she should leave him.

"He's a good man, he doesn't deserve to suffer, not even because of you, *cara*. He is like Vittorio, but my husband is happy like this, and Albert wants to have all your love, and if you cannot give it to him, then at least give him the chance to find love with someone else."

"You are right, but even if you don't believe me, I do love him, in my fashion, but I do love him."

"I told you in Berlin: It's not whether or not you love him, you need him, he's a safe haven for you. But you do not need to take refuge in any man in order to feel safe, you have Vittorio and me, you know that we love you like our daughter. And now, tell me, why did you decide to come?"

Carla was too intelligent to believe that Amelia had come to Italy simply to see her. She was a passionate and open woman, and she could not bear ambiguity. Amelia was sincere with her.

"After we helped Rahel to escape from Berlin, Albert's uncle, who works in the Admiralty, suggested that I do some work for them. I accepted. I went back to Berlin and found out via Max that there are opposition groups scattered throughout Germany; some of them are Christians, some are Socialists, Anarchists, but they have no organization among themselves, each one works alone, something that takes energy from them. But it is a relief to know that there is an opposition, even if it is small and weak, and it is vital information for the British."

"Churchill is an extraordinary man. I spoke to him once: He was scathing about the policy of appeasement. He will get rid of Hitler, there's no doubt about it. If he is in charge of the war then he will win."

"It is a war for the future of the whole of Europe. I hope that if they get rid of Hitler, then the European powers will save us from Franco."

"Poor thing, how naïve you are! Come on, Amelia, Franco doesn't bother them, they prefer to have him rather than the Popular Front. They don't want the Russians in their back yard, they won't let Spain be a base for the Soviet Union."

"I don't want that either; I want Spain to be a democracy, like England."

"Good luck with that. I suppose that supporting Franco must be like us supporting Il Duce."

"The English say that you have contacts with the partisans..."

"They do, do they? Well, that's as may be. Why?"

"Because they think that you are an anti-Fascist and that you will help anyone who fights against Fascism in Italy and against Hitler in Europe."

"It's not that simple. I love my country, I wouldn't live anywhere else in the world, this is my home and whenever I travel I think about coming back here. I will never betray Italy, but as for Il Duce... I can't stand the man! He's a conceited oaf, a rabble-rouser. It makes me embarrassed to think that he represents us, that he's joined the war in such a shameful way. So I will help to get my country freed from him, and... I know that you will not like this, but I have some sympathy for the Communists, even if that would mean throwing stones against my own glass house; what would become of me if they won! But that is not what's important now, the important thing is to get rid of Il Duce and to get Italy out of the war."

"Can you tell me how you got in touch with the partisans?"

"People know me and trust me. They got in touch with me to ask for certain... favors. Nothing important, for the time being. I told you that my old singing teacher was a Communist. I owe him a great deal, all that I am. I will introduce you. His name is Mateo, Mateo Marchetti, and he is a legend among us opera singers. He asked me to hide a partisan a little while back, he was the one contact they had with people outside of the country and the police had him surrounded. I hid him in my house and managed to get him to Switzerland. I did something like I did with Rahel. And what exactly has Albert's uncle asked of you?"

"He wants to know what is happening with Il Duce, what his plans are and how far he intends to get involved in the war. He asked me to come; he knows that you move in the uppermost circles of high society, and he wants me to keep my eyes and ears open. I may hear something useful."

"So you're a little spy now," Carla said, laughing.

"Don't say it like that! I don't feel like a spy, the only thing I've done up until now is to listen to people and keep an eye on what's happening around me. I don't even know if what I'm doing is useful."

"Alright, I will organize a dinner and invite some of those bigwigs I hate so much. I hope that one of them says something that is worth the trouble, because I have to say that I hate the idea of having them in my house."

Carla organized a party that was attended by many of her friends and a good number of her enemies. No one could resist an invitation from Carla Alessandrini, especially when it was to dine at her own house.

The diva's house in Milan was a luxurious, three-story palazzo. It was lit only by candlelight that night, and Carla had made sure that the only drink available was champagne.

Vittorio Leonardi could not understand why his wife was being so extravagant, but he did not complain when Carla told him that she could not imagine giving a party if everything were not of the very best quality.

Dressed in a red gown of silk and lace, the diva greeted her guests at the palazzo door, flanked by Amelia and Vittorio.

"You have to be by my side, because then I can introduce you to all the guests."

Out of the more than two hundred invitees, Carla pointed out a couple to Amelia, indicating them with very little enthusiasm.

"They are friends of Galeazzo Ciano, the Duce's son-in-law. If you get on well with them then they will open the doors to Mussolini's inner circle."

Amelia deployed all her charm on Guido Gallotti and his wife Cecilia.

Guido was a diplomat and one of the advisers to Ciano, who was the Foreign Minister. He had passed forty, but his wife must have been around the same age as Amelia.

Cecilia was the daughter of a rich textile merchant, well connected, a fanatical follower of Il Duce, who had started to make good business moves once Mussolini was in power, in particular marrying his daughter to this high-ranking diplomat; it was a marriage that was convenient to both parties. Guido Gallotti brought social status, and Cecilia brought a clean bank account that allowed them to indulge their every whim.

"I know Spain, I was there before the Civil War. They are lucky to have a man like Franco. He's a great statesman, like our Duce." Guido said to Amelia.

Amelia jerked back a little. She could not bear to hear anyone showing admiration for Franco, but Carla pinched her arm and Amelia managed to force a smile.

"I want Guido to take me to Spain, he has promised me that. My husband is in love with your country," Cecilia added.

"I am so glad that you like it, and you should take your wife, I am sure that she will love it there as well," Amelia replied.

Carla went off to talk to her other guests, and Amelia tried to entertain the couple by telling them what Madrid was like after the war, trying to avoid making any political comments. Vittorio came up to them.

"We love this one very much," Vittorio said, winking at Amelia.

Cecilia seemed to be impressed by the friendship between Amelia and the Alessandrinis. There were not many people who were so close to the diva. Carla had a legion of admirers scattered all around the world, but she was very choosy when it came to her friends. Also, her opinion of the Mussolini regime was no secret, she didn't even mind her words when she spoke about Il Duce himself. So the Gallottis were a little surprised to have received an invitation from Carla, especially because some of the people at the party were absolutely committed Fascists.

"You have to visit us in Rome. You will be welcome to come to our home. Will you be in Milan for long?" Cecilia asked.

"I don't know, I won't leave before the premiere of *Tristan und Isolde*. I wouldn't miss Carla as Isolde at La Scala, not for anything."

"Marvelous! I am from Milan, my father has a factory near the city. We go there often to see my parents. We are going to go to the opera as well, we don't want to miss Carla either. Isn't that right, darling?"

Guido hid his surprise with a smile. Cecilia did not much like opera, she didn't understand it, but she was anxious to rub shoulders with people like Carla.

"It will be a pleasure to see you, and we would be pleased to put you up in Rome."

Later, Amelia told Carla and Vittorio that she had managed to get an invitation to stay with the Gallottis in the capital.

"And you accepted?"

"Well, I haven't promised anything yet."

"And you shouldn't. Let them insist. They know that I am not a great fan of Il Duce, and even though Cecilia is as dumb as a cow, Guido is sharp as a whip."

"Do you really have such a bad opinion of Cecilia?"

"She's a social climber. Well, both of them are, I suppose, but in complementary ways: Guido brings his social contacts, and she brings the money. They are made for each other."

"Don't you think that they are in love?"

"Yes, of course. Guido is madly in love with Cecilia's money, which allows him to spend freely with the group of friends surrounding Galeazzo Ciano, and she is in love with Guido's social standing. You have nothing to fear from Cecilia, but he is dangerous. Don't you forget it."

"What's more, he's an inveterate skirt-chaser," Vittorio said, "and I don't like how he was looking at you one bit. Neither Carla nor I want you to become another head on their trophy wall."

"A trophy! Don't exaggerate, Vittorio, I'm not anyone in particular," Amelia said, laughing.

"You're Carla's friend, so Cecilia can now claim to be connected to the great diva's inner circle of friends. As for him, I am sure that he would not mind adding you to the list of beautiful women he has sampled."

"I will be careful, I promise."

The premiere of *Tristan und Isolde* was set for the middle of October. Carla went to rehearsals every day, and also had two or three hours of training at home with her voice teacher, Mateo Marchetti.

For her part, Amelia, following the advice of Carla and Vittorio, accepted various invitations from the couple's friends. She was especially interested in Marchetti, because he seemed to be something more than just an old Communist.

He seemed distant and mistrustful to begin with, but Carla insisted that Amelia was trustworthy, and his resistance crumbled bit by bit.

Sometimes he stayed for dinner after his classes with the diva. They spoke about politics above all, and it was a rare occasion that Marchetti did not ask Carla for some favor or other for one of his comrades.

Amelia was usually quiet because she did not speak Italian very fluently, and she felt uncomfortable having a conversation on important topics; Carla and Vittorio insisted that she participate without fear.

One night, Carla surprised her teacher by speaking about the days that Amelia had spent in Moscow.

The professor was very interested in finding out the young woman's opinion about the revolution's achievements, and it was hard for him to control himself when he heard her talk about what life was like under Stalin.

"You don't understand anything," Marchetti told her, "you are very young and you obviously don't know what the revolution has meant. The world will never be the same again. So there are problems? How are there not going to be problems! So things still don't work as well as Stalin would like them to? I'm not surprised, there are still many counterrevolutionaries in Russia who are not willing to lose their privileges. You accuse Stalin of persecuting everyone who is opposed to the revolution. Of course he does! What else should he do? The Soviet Union is the beacon to which we all turn our gaze, knowing that it will illuminate a new world, a new mankind. The counterrevolutionaries must be liquidated, because of the danger they pose to the world we want to create."

Amelia tried to refute this harangue by offering little stories of daily life in Moscow, but Professor Marchetti was inflexible, and accused her of lacking the passion of a true revolutionary.

"Revolution is not democracy, then?" Amelia asked.

"What does revolution have to do with bourgeois democracy? Nothing, nothing at all! Stalin knows what he's doing, he needs to run a country that is almost a continent, he needs to convince millions of people that they are Communists, that their birthplace doesn't matter, that everyone is equal, that the party is the only arbiter."

"I have known lots of Communists, and it always surprises me that Communism with them is a dogma, and that the party is their church," Amelia said.

In spite of their arguments, the two of them got on well together, and, with Carla's encouragement, Marchetti began to speak confidently in front of Amelia, so that she began to find out how the Communist Party was organized in secret and what its relationship was with the Socialists and the other great opponents of Il Duce, and especially how orders were passed from Moscow to Switzerland.

The Tripartite Pact, signed on September 27, 1940, by Germany, Italy, and Japan, was just one more step on the path to total war.

The rehearsals had continued without interruption until the morning of October 2, when Carla woke up with a temperature and had to miss her classes with Professor Marchetti.

Carla was angry with herself for falling prey to what seemed at first to be nothing more than a simple cold, which caused her to lose her voice. The doctor ordered her to rest in order to speed up her recovery, but the diva was a rebellious patient, and in spite of Vittorio's protests, she spent most of the day walking around the house dressed only in a thin silk dressing-gown. On October 8 Carla had no voice at all. Her throat was terribly inflamed, which posed a real risk to the premiere of *Tristan und Isolde*, scheduled for October 20.

Marchetti advised Vittorio to call on Dr. Bianchi, an old retired throat specialist. The only problem was that he lived in Rome.

Vittorio got in touch with him and insisted that he travel to Milan to look after Carla, but his wife was inflexible.

"My husband is retired, he has arthritis, and I will not allow him to travel to look after anybody. The most I can offer is that he look at *la Signora* Alessandrini here, in our house."

Marchetti praised Bianchi's abilities so highly that he ended up convincing Carla to travel to Rome.

Carla could barely speak and still had a temperature, but she agreed to go to Rome, fearing that if she did not then the premiere of *Tristan und Isolde* would have to be delayed.

On the morning of October 10 they left for Rome by car. Amelia sat with Carla in the back seat, with Vittorio driving and Marchetti sitting next to him.

It was an exhausting journey for the patient, and her fever had gone up by the time they reached Rome.

Amelia was surprised to see Carla's marvelous top-floor apartment near the Piazza di Spagna. It was spacious, with the best views over the city.

Two maids were employed year round to make sure that everything was in order, and when they arrived, Carla and her entourage found everything ready to receive them.

Amelia and Marchetti moved into their respective guest bedrooms. The professor did not unpack, but called Dr. Bianchi immediately and told him to come and see the patient.

"But it is nine o'clock!" Bianchi's wife protested at the other end of the line.

"I don't care if it's four o'clock in the morning! Carla Alessandrini has come to be treated by your husband, and the journey has made her condition worse. She has a very high fever, and it will be on your head if anything should happen to her."

An hour later, Dr. Bianchi was examining the patient.

"She has a serious infection of the vocal cords. She needs medicine and absolute rest, she shouldn't even talk."

"Will she be able to sing on the twentieth?" Marchetti asked, afraid of what the reply might be.

"I doubt it, she is very ill."

"But we came here for you to cure her!" the singing instructor complained.

"And I will, but I cannot promise any miracles," Dr. Bianchi replied.

"You can work miracles, of course you can! I remember in 1920 how you cured Fabia Girolami in just three days."

"Yes, but what *la signora* Alessandrini has is not a cold that affects her voice; she has a major infection of the throat, the pharynx, the vocal cords... This will take time to clear up. I will give her a prescription for the medicine she should take, but I am worried by her temperature; if it has not gone down in a couple of hours it would be best to take her to a hospital. It was risky to bring her from Milan."

"But it is your fault that she came!" Marchetti shouted. "If you had come to Milan then she wouldn't have got worse."

Dr. Bianchi agreed to stay with the patient for a few more hours, but he was inflexible; if her fever didn't go down, then they would have to take her to the hospital.

At midnight, Carla seemed to fall into a delirium. Her fever rose and Vittorio had her transferred to a hospital, where they went with Dr. Bianchi.

He explained his diagnosis to the hospital clinicians, and, after assuring himself that Carla was in good hands, he took his leave and promised to return the next day.

Neither Vittorio nor Amelia nor Marchetti left Carla's bedside; she seemed to be struggling between life and death. It wasn't until the next morning that the doctors managed to lower her fever.

Dr. Bianchi fulfilled his promise of visiting Carla every day.

It was clear to Vittorio that Carla would need quite some time before she was in any state to sing, so he cancelled all her appearances for the next two months.

"And now we'll see what happens," he said sadly.

Professor Marchetti did not want to go back to Milan. He felt responsible for Carla, he was her father in all things musical, and he asked Vittorio to let him stay in Rome. Amelia, of course, did not doubt for a moment that her place was at her friend's side, and she did not leave the hospital.

News about Carla's health was published in all the newspapers. The diva could not inaugurate the season at La Scala, and had needed to cancel many other engagements as well, so the press was extremely interested in her illness. Vittorio told the journalists every day how she was progressing, and the hospital filled up with hundreds of bouquets sent by friends and well-wishers.

On October 18 Cecilia Gallotti turned up at the hospital and insisted on seeing Amelia. Carla was still in the hospital, but out of danger. When a frightened nurse came to the room to say that Cecilia Gallotti was threatening not to leave unless she could speak to Amelia, Carla first grew angry, but then seemed to think twice.

"Go on, my dear, go and see her, or she'll set up camp in the corridor," she said in the faintest of whispers.

"For goodness' sake, don't speak!" Amelia begged. "They've told you not to try to speak. You have no voice! I don't want to see Cecilia or anyone else; the only important thing is that you get better."

But Carla insisted. Every word was a torment to her, but she finally managed to convince Amelia to go.

"If you make me insist any more I'll have a relapse."

Amelia went down to the entrance hall in a bad mood, and met Cecilia there.

"Oh, my dear Amelia, I'm so happy to see you! I imagine that Carla got our flowers. Guido and I are so upset about what has happened. We were so looking forward to seeing her as Isolde! But she will get better, I'm sure she will get better. And you, my dear, have you managed to see anything of Rome? I came to invite you to have dinner with us. A group of our friends will be there, and I would so like to have you with us..."

Cecilia wouldn't stop talking, and she seemed excited by the idea of having Amelia as a guest.

"We would love Carla and her husband to come as well, but I imagine that must be impossible. Will she be ill much longer? I hope not and that she will get better soon. But will you come? Please, Amelia, say that you'll come!"

At this moment Vittorio arrived. He had just been speaking to the doctors, and came to greet the two women.

"Who is with Carla?" he asked worriedly.

"Professor Marchetti is in her room," Amelia replied, "and I'm just going up myself."

"Dear Vittorio," Cecilia interrupted, "I came to find out about your wife, you know how fond we are of her. We are so sad that it will not be she who starts the opera season... But Amelia tells me she is much better, and that is very good news. I came to ask Amelia to come to dinner at my house tomorrow. It will be a select dinner, with very special guests. Do you think you can do without her for a couple of hours? I will send a car to pick her up. Is that alright?"

Amelia tried to protest, but without any success, and Vittorio, tired of Cecilia's constant yapping, and wanting to get rid of her as soon as possible, decided to agree to everything she said.

"Yes, yes... Amelia will go to your house... It will be good for her... take her mind off things... I don't see any problem."

Carla was of the same opinion, when they told her why Cecilia had come.

"You have to go," she said, in the faintest of whispers. "Don't forget why you're here."

"I don't have anything more important to do than stay here by your side," Amelia said sincerely.

"I know, I know, but you should go."

At the arranged time, the Gallottis' car came to pick Amelia up and take her to their house in the Via Appia Antiqua, a luxurious residence hidden from prying eyes by a high wall.

There were fifteen people seated round the Gallottis' table. Amelia saw that it was the butler who seemed to be taking care of everything, and that Cecilia didn't seem to care too much about how things were organized.

As she was introduced to the other guests, Amelia started to realize that these were the most important of Il Duce's diplomats.

Cecilia presented Amelia as if she were a trophy.

"Allow me to present Amelia Garayoa, she is a very close friend of Carla Alessandrini, she's even staying in her house, isn't that so? Amelia can bring us good news about Carla's health."

Amelia gritted her teeth, because Cecilia's appropriation of Carla annoyed her, and it was an effort for her not to walk out and leave her hostess high and dry.

To begin with the conversation moved on trivial matters, and it was not until halfway through the meal that Guido, in response to questions from one of his friends, said something that made Amelia prick up her ears.

"Il Duce has told his son-in-law, our dear Galeazzo, that he is intending to teach Greece a lesson. But we must be discreet about this. Il Duce is going to give Hitler a surprise."

"But Hitler will be furious!" a gray-haired elderly man said.

"Yes, Count Filiberto, I suppose he will, but Il Duce knows what he is doing. He wants to make it clear to the Führer that we are his allies, but also that we have our own interests."

"And what does Galeazzo think about this?" the woman who was sitting next to Count Filiberto asked.

"What do you think! He supports the Duce's decision, of course. Galeazzo is sure that Greece will not find any strong supporters. It cannot rely on Turkey or Yugoslavia; and as far as Bulgaria is concerned, the king of Bulgaria supports the Axis," Guido Gallotti replied.

"But what about the English? Do you think that they'll just stand around with their arms folded?" asked one of the other guests, a middle-aged diplomat named Enrico.

"It will be too late when they find out, and anyway, they're having enough trouble with the Luftwaffe's attacks on London," Guido replied.

"But they do still have a powerful navy... ," Count Filiberto murmured.

"But Greece is a long way away. No, my friends, you don't need to worry about anything, Il Duce knows what he's doing." Guido was euphoric and unequivocal.

Amelia didn't dare say a word. She understood more Italian than her hosts and their guests imagined; she had let them think that she spoke barely a word, in order that they might talk among themselves more freely.

"And what does the Army High Command think about this?" asked one of the other guests, an older woman with bracelets on her wrists and her fingers heavy with rings.

"Romana, you are always so astute!" Enrico said.

"I am certain that the Duce can see a good way into the future," Romana said, with mild irony, "but it is the army that must decide if we are in a good enough state to face the Greeks; if you are going to fight a battle you need to be sure that you will win, and if not, it's better to stay at home."

"Well, well, well! I'll tell you how things are in Greece, but you will need to assure me of your complete confidentiality. We have agents in Greece who have bought good will toward Italy; a bit of money has ended up in the right hands and that will help people to be on Italy's side," Guido said with a smirk.

"Money can buy the goodwill of some people, but not of all of them. I know the Greeks, you know that we have spent our summers in Greece for very many years, and I don't think that we will be met with applause and cheers. The ones we have bribed will cheer, but not everyone. The Greeks are very patriotic," the woman said.

"If you tell me a secret I'll tell you a secret," came a voice from the other side of the table. It belonged to a man named Lorenzo, who had been prudently calm for most of the meal.

"Ah! And what do you know that you haven't yet told me?" an impressive-looking woman said, tossing her hair and staring fiercely at the man who had spoken, who was her husband.

"I didn't know... Well, I thought that Il Duce's decision was top secret... ," Lorenzo said to his wife.

"Well, tell us... ," his wife insisted.

"As far as I know, the Army Supreme Command has a few objections to the operation," Lorenzo said.

"Why?" Romana asked.

"Well, for one, our man in Athens is not as optimistic as our dear friend Galeazzo, and they think that they would need a very large invasion force," Lorenzo said.

"And when are they planning to attack?" Enrico wanted to know.

"In a matter of days," Guido said.

"What I don't understand is why Il Duce hasn't told Hitler," Count Filiberto insisted.

"He's tired, tired of Hitler presenting him with constant *faits accomplis*. We are his allies, but he never uses us when the time comes to act, we only find out about things after they happen. Il Duce is going to give him a taste of his own medicine. Hitler will have no option but to help us. Calm down, Count, Il Duce will write to Hitler to tell him of the attack, but we will already be in Greece by the time the letter reaches Berlin."

"Heaven help us!" Romana murmured.

Amelia arrived back at Carla's house after midnight. She was trembling and did not know what to do. She was aware of the importance of the information. But how could she leave Carla?

She went to the hospital early in the morning to see Carla. Vittorio rubbed his red eyes when he saw her.

"It's good you're here so early. If you take over from me now, I can go back home and get a bit of sleep and change my clothes," he said in greeting.

When Vittorio had left, Amelia went to Carla's bedside.

"I'm sorry, but I need to go to Madrid straight away."

Carla opened her eyes wide and stared at Amelia. She held out her hand and Amelia took it between hers and squeezed it.

"Will you come back?" the invalid asked in a faint little voice.

"Yes, or at least I will try to."

"What's happened?"

"I was in Guido and Cecilia's house last night, and I heard that Il Duce is going to invade Greece."

"He's a madman... ," Carla muttered.

"Will you forgive me?"

"What is there to forgive you for? The sooner you go, the sooner you will come back," Carla said, forcing herself to smile.

Amelia was lucky, because there was a plane to Madrid two days later. When she arrived, she went immediately to the address that Major Murray had given her, a house near the Paseo de la Castellana, the same address where she sent her letters.

Amelia asked herself who would live in this house. She was surprised when the door was opened by an older woman with a faint, unidentifiable accent.

"Señora Rodríguez?" Amelia asked the woman, who stayed looking at her in silence.

"That's me, and who are you?"

"Amelia Garayoa."

"Come in, come in, don't stand there in the doorway."

The woman asked her in and invited her to follow her through to a large salon whose windows gave onto the street. It was a plainly decorated room: a sofa, a pair of armchairs, a fireplace, and a few low tables with photographs in silver frames.

"Would you like a cup of tea?"

"I don't want to cause you any trouble."

"It's no trouble, it will only take a moment."

The woman left the room and came back a few minutes later with a tray of tea and plum cake.

"Try it, I make it myself."

"I think that you might be able to put me in touch with a friend... Mr. Finley," Amelia said, lowering her voice.

"Of course, when do you want to see him?"

"Today, if possible..."

"Is it really that urgent?"

"Yes."

"Well, I'll do what I can. You can wait for me here if you want."

"Here? I thought I might go home..."

"If it really is that urgent, then I am sure that Mr. Finley will come and find you straight away, and it's not really convenient for him to track all over the city. There are lots of eyes in Madrid, looking at things, seeing things we don't even imagine. I'll tell my maid to look after you while I am away, which will not be for too long. It's better like this."

The woman rang a little china bell, and soon afterwards a perfectly uniformed maid came into the room.

"Luisita, I am going out for a moment. Please look after the young lady, I will not be very long."

The maid bobbed and waited for Amelia to give her instructions, but she said that she needed nothing and would be happy to wait for the lady of the house to come back.

It seemed to take a long time. Señora Rodríguez was away for an hour, and found Amelia very worried when she returned.

"Don't be upset, Mr. Finley will come and find you."

"Here?"

"Yes, here. It's the most discreet way. There are no spying eyes in this house. Better this way. Would you like another tea, or something else?"

"No, no... maybe... well, no..."

"What do you want to ask?" It was as if the woman could read Amelia's thoughts.

"I'm just being curious, but are you from here?"

"Am I Spanish? No, no I'm not, although I've lived in Madrid for more than forty years. My husband was Spanish, but I am English. Sometimes people think they hear an accent when I talk."

"It's almost impossible to hear it, if you had said that you were from Madrid, I would have believed you."

"Well, it's as if I were. Forty years in a country make you feel as if you belong to it. I was only away during the war. My husband insisted that we leave, and then when we were back in London he sadly went and died."

"And you work with..."

"Yes, an old family friend asked me if I could help them, let my house to be used as an address for letters that I could then pass to Mr. Finley. I accepted without a second thought. I know that what's happening at the moment is far more important than we can imagine. And I am a great admirer of Churchill."

After a while, the maid announced Mr. Finley.

"Come in, come in, I want you to meet a friend of mine, Miss Garayoa."

"I'm Major Jim Finley, and frankly I'm a bit surprised to see you here."

"Well, I'll let you talk," the older woman said, leaving the salon.

"When they were alone, Amelia did not waste any time, and told Major Finley everything that she had heard in the Gallottis' house.

When she had finished, Jim Finley asked an endless series of questions in order to be sure that he had heard everything Amelia had to say.

"What should I do now?" she asked.

"You should go back to Rome. You've done a good job coming here. This is very important information, and it needs to be added to as quickly as possible," Finley replied.

"I'll try, but I don't know if I'll be lucky enough to hear another conversation like this one."

"You should make friends with Cecilia Gallotti, I am sure that she'll like boasting to you that she knows what is happening."

"I don't know if Guido will tell Cecilia all the details of his work."

"You have to try. But go and see your family now, it's the best possible alibi for justifying your trip to Madrid. The Italians aren't as neurotic as the Germans about security, but it's better to be careful. Of course, you mustn't stay longer than is necessary to justify your alibi. You should get back to Rome as soon as possible."

"What should I do the next time I have urgent information?"

"I have a telephone number for a friend in Rome, but you should only use it if it is absolutely impossible for you to come to Madrid and get in touch with me directly."

"Who is this friend?"

"An artist who loves Rome. He's a painter, a sculptor... He does a little bit of everything."

"Is he Italian?"

"Swiss."

"Swiss?"

"Yes, his brother is in the Swiss Guard. The family moved to Rome a few years ago. He's the family artist."

"And he works for the Admiralty?"

"He's an odd man, a man of principles... and we pay him well. But you should only get in touch with him if the situation absolutely demands it. Otherwise you should come to Spain."

Amelia followed his instructions to the letter and only stayed a week with her family, much to her regret. As he had said, they were her alibi.

When Amelia got back to Rome, Carla was still in the hospital, although she had gotten a little better in the past few days.

Vittorio was very pleased when he saw Amelia come into the room. Carla missed her friend's ministrations; it was good for her to have Amelia near.

Mateo Marchetti also seemed happy to see her return.

"I haven't argued with anyone for too long," he greeted her, smiling.

Carla asked the two men to leave and to let her spend some time alone with her friend. She wanted to know what had happened.

"They asked me to get to know the Gallottis better. The British think that the Italian invasion of Greece will only serve to lengthen the war."

"We have to stop it."

"Do you think that Cecilia will suspect anything if I call her?"

"No, I think she'll be over the moon that you're getting in touch with her. Tell her that you want to invite her to have lunch as a way of thanking her for the dinner she gave you. I'm sure she'll tell you whatever you want to hear."

"If she knows anything, of course."

"I'm sure she does, there's no older man who doesn't like to show off in front of a younger woman."

"But Cecilia is his wife," Amelia said with a laugh.

"Yes, and she cooks his meals, so I suppose he thinks it's a good idea to make himself look big in front of her."

Following Carla's advice, Amelia invited Cecilia Gallotti to have lunch with her. She accepted with alacrity.

Amelia chose a very popular restaurant in Aventino, Checchino dal 1887, through whose windows filtered the last rays of the autumn sun.

After asking about Carla Alessandrini's health, the two women chatted about unimportant topics. Amelia didn't know how to turn the conversation so that Cecilia would give her some political information, but in the end the Italian broached the topic herself.

"You have no idea how happy I am that you've invited me to eat with you, today of all days. Guido has been locked away in the ministry for two whole days, they're preparing... Well, I suppose I can tell you, Guido told you when you came to eat with us anyway. We're going to invade Greece. Anyway, it's not really a secret anymore, there are lots of people who are already in the know."

"And do you think Italy is ready for such an undertaking? It would mean entering the war fully and completely."

"Yes, but it's going to be easy. As far as I understand from what Guido said, they're going to attack via Epirus... Yes, I think he said Epirus. And we have enough forces to do it; you'd have thought that for something like that you would need at least twenty divisions, but the Greeks are so backward that we'll only need six."

"You know so much about strategy!"

"Don't you believe it, I don't know anything about war, and I'm not interested in knowing, either, but I hear so much about it that something's bound to stick. It was just the other day that Guido was talking to Count Filiberto about the divisions, and my husband said that the General Staff thinks that the six divisions that are already in Albania will be more than enough, especially with General Visconti Prasca in charge. They say he's a very good general."

"And what will Hitler say?"

"Il Duce is a genius. He has sent a letter to explain what his plans are, but because Hitler is in Paris, he won't get it until he gets back to Berlin. He cannot blame Mussolini for not keeping him informed, but Il Duce has made the best decision for Italy, without having to ask the Führer for permission. We'll have Greece in a week or so. I told Guido that as soon as the occupation is a reality, we should go there on holiday. I've always wanted to visit the Parthenon, haven't you?"

"I would love to."

"Let's do it! Let's go to Greece together! All of Guido's friends are so old… I really like having someone my own age around. But would you be able to leave Carla?"

"I hope that she'll keep getting better, they say that she's improved a lot over the last couple of days; if she carries on like this then the doctor will give her the all-clear in a day or so. I'm sure that's what will happen."

"And wouldn't she be able to come with us? It would be good for her to have a holiday after all she's been through, wouldn't it?

"It's a good idea, I'll ask her, although it all depends on what the doctors say, she's very weak still…"

When lunch was over, Amelia went to Carla's house. She wrote a coded message that explained everything that Cecilia had told her. Murray had to know as soon as possible that Il Duce was intending to invade Greece via Epirus. When she had finished writing the message, she went to the Trastevere; when she got there she looked for the Piazza di San Cosimato, which is where Jim Finley had told her that the artist lived whose brother was in the Swiss Guard.

Rudolf Webel's studio was on the ground floor of a building that looked as if it were about to fall down. The door was half open and Amelia pushed her way into the building. She found herself in the presence of a middle-aged man, tall and with blue eyes, his beard as blonde as his hair, looking at a woman covered by a purple cloth.

"Stay still, can't you, Renata? I can't work like this," the man grumbled.

"*Caro*, you have a visitor!" Renata said, pulling the cloth as close around her as she could.

"Well, tell him to go away, because I'm busy," the Swiss said without even looking at the intruder.

"I'm sorry, Herr Webel, may I speak with you please?" Amelia asked.

"No, no you can't. Go back where you came from. Can't you see I'm working?"

"I'm sorry, but I have to speak with you. I was sent by a friend of yours from Madrid."

"From Madrid? I don't have friends there. Well, I do, but the only thing I want you to do now is to go away. Come back another day."

"If you don't mind, I will wait until you have finished," Amelia said stubbornly.

Rudolf Webel turned round angrily to glare at her. He had never allowed himself to be contradicted in anything. He was surprised to find himself face to face with a young woman, who seemed clearly in no mood to be browbeaten.

"You're not welcome here, what do you want me to say?"

"I'm not asking you to welcome me, just to listen to me."

"Why don't you listen to her?" Renata shouted.

"Because I speak with who I want, when I want!"

"I don't believe you, Herr Webel, I think that sometimes you need to speak with people you don't want to talk to. And I must insist. I have something urgent to tell you. If it were only up to me I would never have chosen you as an interlocutor."

"You're ruining my inspiration!" he shouted.

Amelia shrugged and the model stood up and wrapped herself in the purple cloth.

"Talk with the *signorina* and let me rest for a bit. And I'm cold. Maybe you should do your nude sculptures in summer."

"You think that an artist should do what his model tells him to? If you're cold, you put up with it, it's what I pay you for!"

"Pay you? The pasta we ate today came from my mother. If it weren't for her then we'd both be dead of starvation."

Renata left the room and left them alone. Webel carried on ignoring Amelia, looking at the block of marble that he was turning into the pale body of his model.

"Are you going to listen to me or not?" Amelia insisted.

"What do you want?"

"Jim Finley told me to come to you if I had no other option, and sadly enough I don't."

"Finley's just a troublemaker."

"You tell him that, I'm only surprised that he trusts you."

"He doesn't, but let's just say that he doesn't have all that many options in this city, so he has to make the best he can with what he's got. Which is me. Now tell me what you need to say."

"You have to take a letter to Switzerland, today."

"I can't go today," he said obstinately.

"Herr Webel, I am not impressed at all by your attitude, so stop playing the artist and do what I'm telling you to do. This is not a game, and you know it."

Webel was surprised by Amelia's tone of voice. He stared at her, and saw a young woman whose face showed that she had lived through a lot.

"Alright, I'll take the letter to Bern. Do you have it here?"

Amelia gave him the letter, but Webel didn't even look at it. He put it in the pocket of his trousers.

"Where shall I go if there's a reply?"

"I'll come and find you. If it's alright with you, I'll come back here in a few days."

"I don't like you coming and snooping round my house."

"I don't want to snoop anywhere, especially not if it has anything to do with you. And let me say again that this is not a game, that the letter has to get to its destination as soon as possible."

Webel turned his back on her and started to rummage in the back of the room. Amelia left and shut the door behind her, wondering how Finley could trust someone like him.

On the morning of October 28, the Italian ambassador in Athens presented himself at President Metaxas's residence and submitted a formal request for him to authorize the presence of Italian troops on Greek soil. The president's response was unequivocal: No.

But General Metaxas did more than just say no to the Italian demands: He asked for help from Britain. Meanwhile, the Julia Division crossed the border between Greece and Albania. The General Staff's plan was to send part of its forces over the Pindus toward Thessaly, while sending other divisions toward Jannena in order to control Epirus from there; the remaining troops would start marching toward Macedonia.

Mussolini was euphoric. Finally he could present himself in front of the Führer after having taken the initiative in something.

What Il Duce had not counted on was the Greeks fighting heroically to defend their independence. The Greek chief of staff, General Alexander Papagos, had gathered the majority of his troops in Macedonia, and forced the Italian troops to retreat. The Italian forces advanced in Epirus, but Papagos managed to surround the famous Julia Division and decimate it.

At the beginning of November the British reinforcements arrived, destroying part of the Italian fleet at its base in Taranto.

The Royal Navy sent an aircraft carrier, the *Illustrious*, and used it to launch its Fairey Swordfish biplanes and destroy a large part of the Italian navy.

By the middle of November it was clear that Il Duce might lose his war against Greece.

Carla Alessandrini carried on getting better, having moved back to her house in Rome. Amelia stayed by her side, and carried on cultivating the friendship of the Gallotti family. Cecilia was now an inexhaustible source of information, and Guido was apparently happy with his wife's friendship with the Spaniard, whom he imagined to be a committed Francoist. He assumed this because Amelia always avoided talking about politics, making them believe that she didn't really care about it.

Without warning, Albert James turned up at Carla's house in Rome one morning. Amelia was extremely pleased to see him. Carla, with her habitual generosity, insisted on inviting him to stay with them. Albert resisted as much as he could, wanting to be alone with Amelia, but he soon realized that it was important for Carla to have Amelia nearby; she felt that Amelia was like a daughter to her.

When they could at last be alone for a few minutes, Albert confessed that he had come to take her back to London.

"I cannot go now," Amelia said. "Not just because of my mission, but because of Carla as well."

"I think Uncle Paul must have different plans for you. He wouldn't tell me what they were, but he sent me with a letter for you from Major Murray."

"And that's why you came?"

"No, I came to see you and to be with you, because I love you. Nothing else. But I must say that I am happy that they've ordered you back to London, even though, knowing Murray and Uncle Paul, they won't let you stay there for long."

Amelia introduced Albert to the Gallottis, who were pleased to meet the famous journalist, even though Guido had read some of his articles and knew of the criticisms he leveled at Hitler and Mussolini himself. Even so, the couple seemed pleased to be able to show themselves off with the American journalist. Guido even managed to arrange an interview with Mussolini's son-in-law, Foreign Minister Galeazzo Ciano.

Amelia could not ignore the orders in the letter from Major Murray. She had to go back to London, even if it meant leaving Carla.

"Why don't you drop it all and come and live with us?" Carla asked.

"Are you going to adopt me?" Amelia said, laughing.

"Oh, I wish we could! I wouldn't mind, neither would Vittorio. You are the daughter we would have liked to have. Think about it, you could do so much with me, and you could be as useful to your London friends from here in Rome. And as for Albert... I wouldn't tell you to stay if you were in love with him, but you're not. You love him, but you're not in love with him like you were in love with Pierre."

Amelia felt a stab of pain. Yes, she had loved Pierre, and she had loved him so much that she knew she would never love another man again in the same way, even though Pierre had destroyed her innocence, had trampled on the love that she'd offered, and had left a wound in her heart that was so deep it would hurt for the rest of her life.

"I'll do what I can to come back. It's like you say, I could be useful from Italy."

"I'm sure you already have been," Carla replied.

"End of the story."

Francesca yawned. She seemed tired. I had not interrupted her even once, and had allowed her to expand on her topics.

"Alright, Guillermo, now you need to carry on ploughing your own furrow."

"Is that it, then?"

"Looks like it, at least for now. As far as I can tell, you need to reconstruct Amelia Garayoa's story step by step, without jumping over anything. I've told you what happened to your great-grandmother up until the end of 1940 in Italy. I have no idea what happened next. Of course, I could tell you what Carla did, because that's what matters to me."

"Did Amelia ever go back to Rome?"

"She left in December 1940. If you carry on with your investigations I may see you again. But you can't jump around in time, not if you want it to make any sense."

"Professor Soler has taught you well," I protested.

"The only thing he has asked of me is that I help you as much as I can, but that I shouldn't tell you anything that allows you to jump around in time, because the important thing is to know, step by step, what Amelia Garayoa did with her life."

"It would be easier if you told me all you knew about her, and then I could put the puzzle together myself."

"Yes, but I'm not going to do that, so..."

So I said goodbye, even though we both knew that we would see each other again. I went back to London without going via Spain. I preferred to try to keep things moving. Also, Lady Victoria had called me to say that she was at my disposal to talk with me, and, knowing that her priority was golf, I couldn't afford to miss this opportunity.

11

Lady Victoria asked me to lunch at her house, because she said that this way we would have more time to talk.

When I saw her I thought once again that she was a truly impressive woman. Her interest in my research seemed sincere. I told her where Francesca had left me.

"So you are in 1940, December... ," she muttered as she looked through a notebook.

"Yes, I think that Amelia went back to London with Albert James."

"Yes, and then they went to the United States."

"To the United States? But why?" I asked in annoyance. I was getting tired of my great-grandmother's traipsing from one side of the world to the other. It was tiring for me track her journey over half the globe.

"Lord James had asked his nephew for a favor and he insisted that he would only do it if Amelia went with him. It's all here, in the notebook," Lady Victoria said, pointing at its cover.

"May I have a look?"

"It's part of Lady Eugenie's diary. It's thanks to her that we have the information we do about what happened. I don't know if I've said, but Lady Eugenie wrote in her diary every day; it was her way of letting off steam. Albert was a constant source of disappointment to her because of his refusal to break off with Amelia and marry Lady Mary Brian. Are you ready?"

I nodded. I knew that the best thing I could do would be to listen without interrupting until she got tired of talking.

Winston Churchill was trying to get the United States to join in the war. He knew that Great Britain could not hope to win the war without American help and he was trying to use all the tools in his power to convince President Roosevelt to give them his assistance. The United Kingdom was bankrupt and needed money as soon as possible to pay for the gigantic costs of the war.

Lord James had thought that, since his brother Ernest was a prosperous businessman in the United States, and his sister-in-law Eugenie was capable of gathering all of New York high society in her drawing room, and Albert was an influential journalist, maybe he could call upon his family to convince the leaders in Washington that American aid was vital if they were to defeat Hitler.

Ernest and Eugenie accepted this offer with alacrity to become extraordinary ambassadors for their country, and Albert also agreed to give a series of talks all across the United States to make clear the menace that Hitler posed, but he insisted that Amelia accompany him.

Here is what Eugenie wrote in her diary:

> *Albert arrives tomorrow. My brother-in-law has convinced him to come. All the better. Even Ernest, who is always so understanding with our son, was furious that he refused to get involved in everything that's happening. Of course, he's making us pay the price; he's bringing Amelia with him, who is a real nightmare. How will we be able to present her to our friends? We can't say that she is Albert's fiancée, because she's a married woman. We can't say she's a family friend. We don't know anything about her, and I think she's nothing more than an adventuress, for all that Paul has told Ernest that she's been very useful. I don't know what she could have done to have been useful, but I'm sure it was not as important as Paul has made Ernest believe. But anyway, whatever the girl has done, that doesn't make her somebody. Albert says that Amelia comes from a good family, but what sort of family lets a daughter run off and abandon her husband and her son?*

It will not be easy to put up with the gossip about Albert and his stupid insistence on having Amelia in his New York apartment with him, just as he did in London. My son living with that Spanish woman... What will people say?

If he weren't my son, I would never let him in my house again. He came here with Amelia even after his father had insisted that he had to speak to him alone. Albert is so stubborn. Lunch was impossible. The girl never stopped looking at me, and Albert was hanging on everything she said. The worst was that Albert went off to talk to his father alone and I had to spend almost an hour with this woman. I asked her if she had read Shakespeare, and she said she hadn't. I thought as much. She also doesn't have much musical taste, even though she can play some Mozart and Chopin and Liszt on the piano. I don't know what my son can see in this woman. It's enough to drive one crazy.

Ernest told me that Albert was a great success in Washington. Some of President Roosevelt's friends went to hear him speak, and also some of the president's advisers. I think that they were worried by what they heard him say. It's difficult to believe that the Americans find it hard to imagine that Hitler is a danger to them as well. If it weren't for Winston Churchill, Hitler would become the ruler of the world, that's what they don't want to understand here, even though Ernest tells me that President Roosevelt is open to some of the things that Churchill has been saying.

How disgraceful! Mrs Smith came to see me. The old witch just wanted to say what I already know, that Amelia's presence is a scandal and that Albert should respect people of good breeding and not take her everywhere he goes.

I told Mrs Smith that perhaps it would be better if she were to pay attention to her daughter Mary Jo, because she would not stop flirting with the oldest Miller boy at the Vanderbilt dinner.

I know she won't forgive me, but I couldn't think of anything else to say to stop her talking. I cannot allow her to come to my house and criticize my son.

If Ernest had not told me so himself I would never have believed it. Albert has asked that Amelia herself talk about what is happening in Europe. Apparently they have to turn people away when she speaks, but I'm sure they only come to gawp at her, to find out what kind of a woman it is who has turned Albert's head.

Ernest says that all of San Francisco high society has surrendered to Amelia and that she is invited everywhere. Amelia is giving talks in the women's clubs because Albert thinks that wives will be better placed to change the way their husbands think.

They will be back in New York in two days' time. Ernest wants me to organize a dinner for all our friends, and he wants Albert to give a speech.

The dinner was a success, even though I am exhausted. Everyone came; I think that anyone who is anyone in the White House, apart from Roosevelt himself, has come to see us.

Albert was wonderful. How good he is at explaining what kind of a man that Austrian corporal actually is! He scared the women and made the men think. Ernest says that Roosevelt needs a few little pushes to get him ready to help England. He has already started to help, in fact. For some of our friends, the war is a good opportunity to do business, because the help they give England will have to be paid for one way or another. Americans are very practical, but I am pleased that my son has given them arguments to help them understand what is happening in Europe.

Albert spoke to them as if he was one of them; this son of mine is more American than Irish, even though all of his blood is Irish. He even said that he understands Roosevelt because a ruler should avoid war unless it is absolutely impossible not to.

I didn't think he would ask Amelia to speak at this occasion, but he did, and she spoke to our guests without a trace of shame.

It wasn't a good idea of hers to tell the story of her friend, Yla, the daughter of her father's partner, who had to escape from Berlin, or else to tell us all about this woman Rahel. It was as if Amelia had only Jewish friends. It's not that I don't like Jews, some of our best friends are Jewish, but the way Amelia tells it you would have thought that the worst thing about Hitler was that he didn't like the Jews. She makes everything too simple.

I had to cut off a lot of people when they were making comments about Amelia and Albert, people were asking if they were more than good friends, as if it were anything but obvious that she is my son's lover. It is all so very disagreeable, and Albert won't hear a word said about Amelia.

How embarrassing: Albert had a fight with the oldest Miller boy, and in his house too. The Millers organized a farewell dinner for Albert, who will be going back to London in a few days. It was all going swimmingly until Bob, the oldest Miller boy, insisted on dancing with Amelia. He was a bit tipsy, but Amelia was like a shy little virgin, saying that she didn't want to dance. Bob wouldn't take no for an answer, he grabbed her by the arm and insisted that she dance with him. Amelia got hysterical and asked him to let her go, and Albert turned up to help her and socked Bob one. My son made a spectacle of himself, he was an embarrassment to us all. The evening couldn't have ended any worse. Mr. Miller and Ernest had to step in to end the fight, and we had to leave, with all the guests looking and murmuring. Amelia was pale, but I don't think she felt at all sorry for what had happened. They'll all criticize us now, and this will go all the way to London. Our friends are very generous and let Albert take Amelia to their houses, but I'm sure, after this, that they'll never invite us again.

I asked my son to come to see me, and he came by today to say goodbye. At least he had the good sense not to bring Amelia with him. Ernest asked me not to fight with Albert, but we weren't able to avoid it. I asked him to put an end to this situation once and for all, that he could not respect a woman who so

*clearly had no respect for herself. My son said that he would nev-
er forgive me for saying that about Amelia, whom he says is the
bravest and most honorable woman he knows.*

*I don't know what she's done to him to make him like that,
but he's changed utterly, he only cares about her.*

*My son said that if I would not accept the situation with
Amelia then he would stop coming to see us. The worst is that I
think he meant it. This woman will destroy us all. She is destroying Albert and now she wants to destroy our family.*

*Albert left without giving me a kiss, the first time he has done
that in his whole life. They are going back to London tomorrow.*

Albert and Amelia went back to London at the beginning of
March 1941. Their trip had been a success, or at least that is what
Lord Paul James thought. A lot of the ideas that Albert had laid
out seemed to have hit home among Washington's highest political and economic spheres.

They moved back into Albert's apartment, knowing that at
any moment Amelia could be sent out of England on another
mission. Albert asked his Uncle Paul to stop using Amelia, but
Paul thought that anything he owed Albert had been paid off by
his allowing Amelia to go with Albert to the United States.

Major Murray soon asked Amelia to go back to Germany.

"You told me that your friend Max von Schumann had been
sent to Poland," he said.

"Yes, that's right."

"Well, it wouldn't hurt us to know what's going on over
there. We have some information, but it would be useful to com-
plement it."

"Do you have people in Poland?" Amelia wanted to know.

"My dear, that is not for you to know. What you need to do
is to get in touch with von Schumann and try to go to see him,
wherever in Poland he is stationed."

"What will my excuse be?"

"That's up to you. We trained you to develop your own alibi
as a field agent, it's not something that's easy to do from an office
in London. Tell me what you need and we will try to get it for

you, but you will have to think about how best to get close to Max von Schumann. We understand that he is strongly attracted to you."

Amelia sat bolt upright in her chair. Major Murray's insinuation offended her.

"How dare you..." Amelia's tone was filled with indignation.

"I have no intention of offending you. I have the greatest respect and consideration for you, but you must not forget that you are an agent on a mission, and when we prepared you for this task we told you, along with the rest of your group, that you would have to lie, maybe even kill, that you would have to do things that under normal conditions you would find repulsive, but that are necessary in times of war. So don't get upset, this isn't a tearoom, this is the Admiralty. If you can't do this job, then tell me, but don't play the injured maiden. Of course you are a respectable woman, but you are also an agent, and so you may have to do things you never thought you would be obliged to do. In any case, I am not going to order you to do anything in particular, but I will just remind you of something that is self-evident: The baron is attracted to you and that could be a help with your work, but you have to decide how you are going to organize this operation."

They were silent for a moment, looking at each other. Major Murray was a gentleman, but he was also a dedicated soldier, an expert in espionage, where there are no norms or limits. He had not intended to offend Amelia, indeed he had felt a secret sympathy for her ever since the moment they met, but he treated her with the same severity as the rest of his men. They were at war and there was no room for social niceties.

"I will go to Berlin, and I will arrange things so that I meet Baron von Schumann in Poland," Amelia said, finally.

"You might have to stay close to him for some time, we are keen to have such a significant source of information in the army. As well as opposing Hitler, he is a soldier with a fairly high rank, which grants him access to other officers even higher up in the hierarchy."

"He hates Hitler, but he is a patriot. He will never say anything that puts the lives of German soldiers in danger."

"I am sure of it, but you should work with him and try to get information from him without his feeling that he is betraying his country. You can have some help on this occasion. Someone you know is in Berlin."

"Who is it?"

"A companion from boot camp. Do you remember Dorothy?"

"Yes, I was a friend of Dorothy's."

"Dorothy's husband was German, from Stuttgart, he died of a heart attack. She spoke German almost as well as Jan."

"Jan? I don't think I know him..."

"No, you don't know Jan. He's British, but his mother was German. He grew up with his maternal grandmother because he was orphaned at a very young age. He knows Berlin like the palm of his hand. He lived in the city until he was fourteen, when his father's family came and took him back to England to give him a better education."

"What is their cover in Berlin?"

"They're pretending to be a happily married couple. Jan is past sixty; he works for the Admiralty and even though he is near retirement age he has volunteered for this mission. We have created a false identity for him, officially, his parents were Germans who immigrated to the United States, and now he's the prodigal son who has been drawn back to Germany by Hitler's magnetism, and he has done so with his charming wife, a woman a few years younger than him. They are rich enough to live, but not to draw attention to themselves. Jan was an engineer and this has been very useful for us; we sent him with a special radio, very powerful, but he has to hide it from the Gestapo. From here on in, whenever you get any important information, you are to give it to them. And you will get my instructions from them as well. You will have to make sure that no one follows you when you go see them, and for the time being it's better not to tell anyone that they even exist, not even your friends, and certainly not Baron von Schumann."

Major Murray spent more than an hour telling Amelia what he was expecting from her.

Murray accepted her request to travel to Germany from Spain. He knew that the only thing he could not refuse her, if he wanted her to carry on helping them, was regular contact with her family. Also, it was only possible to travel to Germany from an allied country, such as Spain.

"I don't want you to go," Albert said when Amelia told him that she was going back to Germany.

"It's my job, Albert."

"Your job? Amelia, this is not a job. You have got yourself caught up in something you cannot control, you are a pawn being moved by other people. It will be too late when you realize that you want to take back control of your life, because your life will no longer belong to you. Leave it, I'm not asking for my sake but for yours, leave it before it destroys you."

"Do you think this is all for nothing, what I'm doing?" Amelia said angrily.

"No, I think that whatever is gathered by spying is of immense value, and will help win the war, but do you really think that you are ready to get involved in this simply because you have trained at the Admiralty for a while? They are using you, Amelia, they get you to work for them by saying that maybe when Hitler is gone then Franco will go too, but they won't do anything against him, they will prefer that Franco is in power rather than the Popular Front, don't you see?"

"No one has ever promised me anything, but I am sure that once Hitler is gone, Franco will start to totter. He will no longer have allies. I am sorry that you think I am so insignificant, so incapable of doing this work, but I will continue with my mission, I will give it my all to do it as best I can."

"Then we will need to think about our relationship."

Amelia felt a stab of pain in the pit of her stomach. She was not in love with Albert, but ever since Pierre's death he had been the pillar against which she had supported herself, the haven where she felt safe, and she was not prepared to lose him. Even so, when she replied it was her pride that answered first.

"If that is what you want..."

"What I want is for us to live together and to try to be happy. That is what I want."

"I want that to, but only when you respect what I do."

"I respect you, Amelia, of course I respect you, that is why I'm asking you to speak to Major Murray and tell him that you're giving up, that you're not going to carry on with this."

"I won't do that, Albert, I am going to carry out my promise to the Admiralty. My promise and my relationship with you are compatible, or at least they are for me..."

"I am sorry, Amelia, but if that is your last word on the matter then we cannot continue together."

They separated. Two days later, Amelia left Albert's house with a couple of suitcases containing all her belongings. An Admiralty car was waiting for her at the door. Major Murray had arranged her passage to Berlin via Spain.

"Well, my dear Guillermo," Lady Victoria concluded, "I know that Amelia spent several days in Madrid, I suppose she went to see her family. I have spoken with Major Hurley and we have a surprise for you. The major will come to dinner tomorrow at my house. He has said that he has some declassified documents about Amelia's journey to Germany, and that he will give us some more details over the meal.

"It's lucky that you and Major Hurley are related," I said with a certain degree of irony.

"Yes, you're lucky, and all the more because I am married to one of Lord Paul James's grandsons; if I weren't then it would be very difficult for you to find out what happened during those days."

I left Lady Victoria's house after promising that I would come for dinner the next day at six o'clock. When I got to the hotel I called Professor Soler. I asked him if he remembered whether Amelia had come through Madrid in mid-March of 1941, and he seemed unsure.

"I'll look at my notes and I'll give you a ring. Amelia came to Madrid a lot, sometimes for a day or so, sometimes longer. I don't remember anything in particular happening in March 1941."

"Did she never tell you anything about what she was doing?"

"No, never. Not even to her cousin Laura. Amelia appeared and disappeared without saying anything. Her Uncle Armando tried to find out how she earned her living, but Amelia told him to trust her, and that she earned her money honorably. We knew that she lived with Albert, and we thought that it was he who kept her."

"So not even you were aware of what Amelia did... ," I said doubtfully.

"Your great-grandmother was never the object of my historical investigations. Why should she have been?"

He called an hour later to tell me that he could find no note relevant to that time, so we agreed that Amelia must have come through Madrid and, apart from seeing her family, must have done nothing out of the ordinary.

There was nothing else I could do except wait to see what would turn up at the dinner with Major Hurley at Lady Victoria's house. I was a little aggrieved at such formality. I didn't see why Major Hurley and Lady Victoria didn't just tell me what they knew all at once, instead of measuring out their information drop by drop. But they had the whip hand, so I had no option but to do as they bid.

MAX

1

Lady Victoria's husband could not have been more different from Major Hurley. I had not met him until that night, and I warmed to him immediately. I arrived at five to six, and the maid invited me through to the library, where I met him, Lord Richard James, the grandson of Lord Paul James, who had signed Amelia up to work for the Admiralty.

Lord Richard James, a man of about sixty with salt-and-pepper hair and a ruddy face, greeted me with a smile and shook my hand.

"So you're writing about Amelia Garayoa, are you? She must have been quite something..."

"Did you know her?" I asked.

"No, but you must know that one of my relatives, my grandfather's nephew, Albert James, was deeply in love with her, which was a scandal at the time, and because he had broken with the norms of the family, everyone heard about it, even his descendants. So all of the Jameses have heard stories about Albert James's unhappy love affair with the beautiful Spaniard."

Richard James offered me a glass of sherry, which I did not refuse, even though it hit me like a shot to the gut. I have never understood why the English like sherry so much, because with me it goes straight to my head.

At six on the dot, Major Hurley and Lady Victoria arrived. They drank sherry as well. When Lord Richard offered us a second glass I thought that this was not likely to be an evening where much work got done, given that I was already feeling slightly giddy, and I worried about the effect that it would have on my sources of information for them to have a second glass. But I needn't have worried, Lady Victoria was as upright as always, and Major Hurley did not lose his dour expression for the whole meal.

I listened patiently as the conversation moved in directions that had nothing to do with the object of the evening. It was not until we were eating dessert that Lady Victoria asked Major Hurley to tell us about Amelia's journey to Germany. And then it was that he started his story...

Amelia arrived in Berlin on April 3, 1941. She had prepared her plan meticulously, and decided to go back to stay with Greta and Helmut Keller.

"I am so happy to have you back in our house, my wife missed you, even with Frank now back in our house. He's on leave. But women always want to have some feminine presence in their lives, I suppose there are things they only talk about with each other. Greta is no longer in bed any longer, she has been up for a few days, it looks like she's getting better, thank God."

"Thank you so much for letting me stay in your house..."

Greta Keller was extremely touched by the embroidered handkerchiefs that Amelia had brought as a present.

Frank, the Kellers' son, was a strapping young fellow with chestnut hair and blue eyes, who was very interested in Amelia.

"You've grown since I last saw you, I remember when you were a little girl, I saw you a couple of times with your sister Antonietta. I'm sorry about your parents... Don Juan was always very good to our family. Will you be in Berlin long?"

"I like Berlin. Your father will have told you that I'm doing what I can to save my father and Herr Itzhak's business... You can't imagine what Spain is like after the war... There are not many opportunities there. And what about you, will you be here long?"

"I have a few days' leave, and then I have to head back to Warsaw."

"And we are going to spend some time with my sister in the country. The doctor says that it will be good for me to get out of the city and breathe some fresh air," Greta said.

"I don't want to be a nuisance..."

"Oh, you won't be, we wouldn't have invited you if we'd thought that you would be," Herr Helmut added.

Berlin was still living in the euphoria of victory. The German army seemed to be attaining its aims without stretching itself too far, and the city seemed to be somehow isolated from the rest of the war.

Amelia went to Professor Karl Schatzhauser's house the day after her arrival in the city. He did not hide his surprise at seeing her.

"Well, well, well, I didn't think that you were going to come back. We haven't heard any news of you or your friend the journalist for some time, and nothing from your British friends either."

"I am sorry, I promise that I told them what you asked."

"It looks like they don't take us seriously. They didn't either when we told them not to carry on appeasing Hitler because it wouldn't lead anywhere. As you know, Max told Lord Paul James all of this before the war, but without any effect."

"Professor, you must know that my only connection with Lord Paul James is via his nephew Albert James. I am sorry I cannot be more useful, especially at this time."

"Why have you come back?" the professor asked.

"I have to tell you the truth, my relationship with Albert has come to an end. That's why I'm here... I... well, I didn't know where to go. Maybe it was not a good idea, but... well, I thought that at least here I could be useful. As I told you, my father's accountant saved some machines from the business and... Well, that brings me a little bit of money, which is vital for my family. But if I can help you as well... I don't know, in any way at all..."

"And what can you do? You are not a German and this is not your war. Germany and Spain are allies. Why don't you just go back to your country?"

"I cannot, I can't live there again, not for the moment. I cannot bear my parents' no longer being there."

"Max is in Warsaw, but he may be back in Berlin in a day or so. His wife, Baroness Ludovica, has told a few friends and is organizing a party to welcome him back," the professor said, looking at Amelia straight in the eyes.

"And what about Father Müller? And the Kastens?" Amelia asked.

"They are more active than ever, and working with Pastor Schmidt. Helga and Manfred are very brave and are helping us a great deal. Manfred is a man who is highly respected by his diplomatic colleagues, and they still ask his advice; also, his former position means that a lot of very important doors are open to him. He has a very busy social life, and you cannot imagine how much information he manages to gather at receptions and dinners."

"When can I see them?"

"We will be having a literary evening here in a few days' time, you know why we're really meeting. Come along, they'll be happy to see you too."

Amelia's next visit was to Dorothy and Jan, who were living in a modest apartment on Unter den Linden. Their neighbors were well-off supporters of the Third Reich, who did not seem at all surprised at this couple who had rented an apartment in the area.

Dorothy was pleased to see Amelia again. It had not been easy for her to pass as the wife of a man who had been a total stranger to her a few months ago. She and Jan had both been widowed and had reached that age where one learns how to control all one's emotions, but even so, they each felt uncomfortable when the time came to share an apartment, even though they had separate bedrooms.

Jan was a man of middle height, with light brown hair the same color as his eyes, methodical and cautious, to the extent that he asked Amelia several times if she were sure she had not been followed, and did not appear to be satisfied even when she said several times that she had not been.

Their code names were "Mother" and "Father," which was how they were referred to in London.

"He's a good man," Dorothy said of Jan, when he had stepped out of the sitting room for a moment.

"And very cautious."

"Imagine yourself in our situation, we have to be careful, any mistake could cost us our lives, and not just our lives, but yours and those of all the other field agents."

"Major Murray did not tell me who the 'others' were..."

"And I won't tell you either: The less we know about each other, the better; that way the possibility of danger is lessened. If the Gestapo arrest you and torture you then you'll only be able to tell them about Jan and me, and not the others."

"But if they arrest you then it will be worse, as you know the names of all the agents."

"If that happens, Amelia, then we won't live long enough to tell them anything. We have our... well, I suppose they've given you a cyanide pill as well. It's better to die than fall into the hands of the Gestapo."

"Don't say that!"

"When we accepted this mission we also accepted the possibility of dying. No one is making us do anything we haven't agreed to do. Our mission is to help win the war, and there are losses in every war, and not just on the front line."

Jan came into the room with a tray. On it were a teapot and three cups.

"It's not like our tea back home, but you'll like it," he said, looking at Amelia.

"Of course I will... and you shouldn't have gone to any trouble."

"It's no trouble, and visitors are always a good excuse for having a cup of tea. And now we need to think about protocols for your future visits. It is not a good idea for you to come to see us all that often, except if you have information that cannot wait. The Gestapo have eyes and ears everywhere, and we run an obvious risk every time we send a message."

"I know, I know, Major Murray gave me instructions about how we should work together."

"We should be even more careful than he suggested, and we shall need to think about a place where we can meet. I suggest the Prater, no one will notice us there."

"The Prater? I don't know where that is," Amelia replied.

"In Mitte, in the Kastanienallee; it's a very popular beer hall. In the summer it is overflowing with customers, it has excellent sandwiches and there's also a theater."

"Won't we call attention to ourselves?"

"There are so many people there that no one will notice us. Of course, we should be discreet, and wear unobtrusive clothing."

"I never wear obtrusive clothing," Amelia said, a little annoyed by Jan's warning.

"It's better like that."

Jan explained how they should prepare for their meetings, and what they should do if they thought they were being followed.

"If you carry a newspaper in your hand it means that no one is following you and we can meet; if you're not sure, then you should take a white handkerchief and blow your nose. That's the signal that we should abandon the meeting and get out of the area as soon as possible without attracting attention."

Amelia felt very happy that she had met Dorothy again, but even more happy for having got in touch with Professor Schatzhauser's opposition group. She told herself that she had been lucky so far. They had approved of her report on the Madagascar Plan in London, and had been even more impressed by her work in Italy and the information she had been able to give them about Mussolini's invasion of Greece. She trusted that her luck would hold, even though she was aware that the longer the war lasted the more danger she would be in.

Two days later, Amelia went to Professor Karl Schatzhauser's house once again. She found him in a nervous state, convinced that the Gestapo were monitoring him. He knew that some of his friends had disappeared without trace after the Gestapo had turned up at their houses. Friends who were not left-wing activists or Jews, but just normal people like him, teachers, lawyers, businessmen, who hated seeing Germany under Hitler's control.

Helga and Manfred Kasten greeted Amelia warmly, as did Pastor Ludwig Schmidt. Amelia was worried not to see Father Müller.

"Don't worry, he will come," Pastor Schmidt said. "We've called this meeting specifically so he can tell us what is happening in Hadamar."

"Hadamar? What is Hadamar?" Amelia asked.

"It's a lunatic asylum to the northeast of Frankfurt. A friend told us that horrible things were happening there. Father Müller volunteered to go over there and see if it was true what we were being told," Ludwig Schmidt explained.

"But what are the horrible things they have said are happening?" Amelia asked.

"It's so horrible that it can't be true, not even Hitler would sink so low. But Father Müller is young and passionate, and his intention, if what he has been told turns out to be right, is to inform the Vatican immediately."

Amelia insisted that the pastor tell her what was alleged to be happening there.

"They say that they are killing the mentally ill, to stop them being a burden on the state."

"How horrible!"

"Yes, it would be euthanizing poor innocents who cannot look after themselves. The person who told us about this has worked there, he said he fell ill because he couldn't bear to see mad and mentally ill people being put to death. I am still skeptical about what he said, he was a Socialist sympathizer and he might be exaggerating," Pastor Schmidt said.

While they were waiting for Father Müller to arrive, Manfred Kasten told them that Max von Schumann would be in Berlin in a week or so. That, at least, was what Baroness Ludovica had told him, and she had said that when Max was back in the city she would like to organize a little dinner to celebrate his return. Ludovica was sad that her husband had been sent to Poland.

Father Müller arrived at last, he was with a woman, his sister Hanna.

Amelia thought that he was changed, he was thinner and had a bitter twist to his mouth. He barely paid any attention to her, such was his need to tell everyone what he had seen in Hadamar, where he had spent the last two weeks.

"Everyone knows what's going on in the asylum, even the children. I saw a child in the middle of the street fighting with his brother, and saying 'I'm going to tell everyone you're mad and then they'll send you to Hadamar and cook you.'"

"Come on, tell us what you have seen, step by step," Pastor Schmidt said, trying to make Father Müller recover a bit of the calm that he seemed to have lost during his trip to Frankfurt.

"The man who gave us the information was telling us the truth. I went to the address he gave me, his brother's house; his brother is a gentleman called Heinrich who lives with his wife and their two children. Heinrich works in Hadamar as well, as a nurse. He corroborated what his brother had said in every detail. He said that he would leave too if he could, but that he had a family to maintain and so he was fighting against his scruples in order to stay working there. It was not easy, but he helped me get into the asylum. I turned up pretending to be a friend of his who needed work. The director of the asylum seemed not to trust me so much, but Heinrich told him that our families were good friends and that he had told me all about his work in the asylum. I had to play the most horrible role you can imagine, that of a committed member of the party, sure above all things of the superiority of the Aryan race and the need to get rid of every element that might affect or stain that race. I must have performed the part well, because the director seemed to trust me and said that what he was doing there he was doing for the good of Germany. I suppose that he must have thought it would be good for him to have a few more pairs of hands to help deal with the madmen. The villagers refuse to work there, and don't like to deal with those who do. When the day was over, Heinrich would go down to the local bar and have a couple of drinks before going home, he said that if he didn't then he would be unable to sleep. He needed to numb his conscience in order to look his children in the face. In the bar, the other clients avoided us as if we had the plague. Heinrich kept on drinking even so. What I saw in Hadamar... It was horrible!" Father Müller fell silent.

"Please, make an effort, it is important that you tell us what it is you saw there," Pastor Schmidt insisted.

"Do you want to know how many madmen have been through Hadamar? Heinrich thinks it must be about seven or eight thousand. There is not space there for so many people, they bring them from other psychiatric hospitals all over Germany. They come in cattle trucks, as if they were animals. The poor innocents don't know where it is they are going to end up. When they get there they are taken into the asylum without being given either food or water. If you could only see them... exhausted, nervous, disoriented. They are taken into the basements of the asylum. There are some empty rooms there, without even benches to sit down on. There are tubes that come in through the ceiling. The nurses make them get undressed and then lock them in. The screams are terrifying..."

Father Müller paused in his narrative. He covered his eyes with his hands as if he were trying to get rid of a horrible image that was floating before his eyes. No one there asked him to carry on speaking, not even Pastor Schmidt chivvied him along. It was Hanna, the priest's sister, who put her hand on her brother's shoulder and then stroked his hair and brought him back to himself. Father Müller's eyes were swimming in tears and he sighed and made a great effort and continued with his terrible tale.

"There is nothing in these rooms, just a grille in the ceiling. A thick smoke starts to come through the grille while the madmen shout in fear. It is the smoke that chokes them, the smoke that kills them. They have built gas chambers in the basement at Hadamar, and they take all the mentally ill of Germany there to get rid of them. Then they take their bodies to an oven and burn them."

"My God! How come nobody says anything, how can the villagers allow it?" Amelia exclaimed.

"Officially nobody knows anything, but it's no secret for the people who live in the village, the crematorium smoke rises over the roofs of their houses. Heinrich thinks that after they have gotten rid of the mentally ill they will turn their attention to the old and everyone they think of as being useless. He heard the director of the asylum say so."

"We have to do something!" Professor Schatzhauser exclaimed. "We can't let something like this be allowed to happen!"

"I have told the Archbishop of Limburg, whose diocese includes Hadamar, what I have seen. He had heard rumors, but I was able to confirm them. He has promised to speak to the authorities. He will say that he has heard several reports that have worried him, and he will ask for an official investigation," Father Müller continued.

"That may work," Helga Kasten said.

"I hope you're right!" her husband replied.

"And you... you... What did you do there?" Amelia's question had a devastating effect on Father Müller. He looked at her with his eyes wide.

"The director of the asylum didn't want me to help the other nurses transport the mentally ill people to those sinister rooms. The first week he gave me other things to do, but then he seemed to decide that he trusted me and... well, one day a consignment of the sick arrived, including women and children. Heinrich came to find me and told me that the director had ordered him to tell me that I should help take them to the gas chamber. I couldn't refuse, and I needed to keep on playing my part, but I couldn't do it; when we started to push them into the room I started to scream as loudly as they did, as if I were a madman myself. My screams made them even more nervous... Heinrich looked at me in fright and... I screamed that this was a crime, that we should let them leave... Someone hit me on the head with a truncheon and knocked me out. When I woke up, I was in the room where the patients were made to leave their clothes. Heinrich had dragged me there and he told me not to say a word. The director wanted to interrogate me; he had threatened Heinrich with the Gestapo, saying that he had brought an enemy of the Reich into the asylum. Heinrich swore that I was a good Nazi, but just too delicate for this work, and swore and swore again that I was no danger, but the director told him to bring me to his office. He didn't do it. He sent me out of the asylum through the coal bunker and told me that I couldn't even go to his house to pick up my belongings. 'Run away, and I will sort it out. If you are my brother's friend, then

I am sure that the two of you will be able to finish this together. I am not brave enough.' And I ran away. Yes, I ran away from that accursed place; I sought refuge, I went to see the archbishop, and I am here now thanks to him."

"And Heinrich? What happened to him?" Professor Schatzhauser asked in alarm.

Father Müller burst into tears. He gave way to the suffering that he had managed to control for so long.

"When he thought that I would be far enough away from the building, he went up to the director's office and threw himself out of the window."

"My God!" Professor Schatzhauser, Pastor Ludwig Schmidt, and the Kastens cried out, almost in unison.

"My brother has suffered much," Hanna whispered, putting her arms around her brother's shoulders again. "Perhaps we should go home. He needs to recover."

"Father Müller, you are a very brave man, and you have done God's work. By finding out about this we may be able to fight it," Pastor Schmidt said.

"Nazi ideology contains the idea of getting rid of the sick and the weak, it isn't the first we've heard about mental patients being killed. There was a similar plan mooted before the war broke out," Manfred Kasten remembered.

"The only way to stop these killings is to make sure that people know about them," Professor Schatzhauser murmured.

"The archbishop will denounce what is happening in Hadamar to the authorities," Father Müller said.

"But they won't pay any attention to him! What use is it to denounce the crime to the executioners themselves?" Amelia said, who was only just capable of controlling the horror that the priest's tale had awoken in her.

"But they will have to stop the killings in Hadamar, even if just for a moment. We have the duty to tell people what is going on there," Schmidt said.

"I am worried for your safety," Professor Schatzhauser said.

"So are we," Hanna, Father Müller's sister, said, "but the archbishop has decided to send Rudolf to Rome."

"So you are leaving... ," Pastor Schmidt said.

"It's for the best," Manfred Kasten conceded. "The Gestapo will work out who the worker was who disappeared from Hadamar. And if they find him... well, these people respect no one."

"When are you leaving?" Amelia asked.

"In a few weeks' time," the priest replied.

Father Müller was not the only one who could not sleep as a result of what had happened at Hadamar. None of the people who had been at the meeting in Professor Schatzhauser's house could stop thinking about what the priest had told them. Their impotence in the face of this criminal regime was painful.

Amelia went back to the Kellers' house with her mind firmly made up. Whatever happened, she would do what she could to bring down the Reich.

That night, alone in her room, she wrote a letter to London telling them about what was taking place in Hadamar.

Herr Keller insisted that she take a cup of tea with his wife Greta and their son Frank, but Amelia did not think that she would be able to pretend to be normal, so she claimed that she had a headache and retired early.

"She's a nice young girl, but a bit strange, don't you think?" Frank said to his parents.

"Well, she lost most of her family in the Spanish war. I think that it's difficult for her to stay in Spain surrounded by memories of her parents," Herr Keller explained to his son.

"She is a good companion to me," Greta added.

Amelia arrived at Dorothy and Jan's house so early that they were both worried.

"But what's going on?" Dorothy asked when she opened the door and found Amelia there.

Dorothy still had her dressing-gown on and her eyes looked sleepy.

"For God's sake, Amelia, it's seven o'clock in the morning! Tell me what's going on!"

"You have to send an urgent report to London, I have it here in code. It's not very long, but the sooner they have it the better."

Jan came and stood in the doorway. He was wearing a dressing-gown as well.

"I told you to come at a time when it wouldn't attract attention," he grumbled to Amelia.

"I know, but the information I have is extremely important, I wouldn't have come like this if it weren't."

She told them what Father Müller had told her, word for word, and although Dorothy and Jan both seemed affected, he continued to reproach her.

"All this could have been passed on in a couple of hours' time, or this evening. It is terrible what is happening in the Hadamar asylum, but you must not, I insist, you must not come to our house at this time."

"How can you say that! The Nazis are killing thousands of innocent people! Father Müller calculated that they must have already killed around eight thousand," Amelia said, with a note of hysteria in her voice.

"Of course it is horrible! But we have to be careful, we can't draw attention to ourselves. Do you think that if they find out about us we'll be able to help these people more? We will make the neighbors suspicious, someone will gossip about us to the Gestapo, and then... well, you know what that means."

Dorothy looked at Jan as if telling him not to be too hard on Amelia. Then she left the room to make coffee.

It was difficult for Amelia to recover her calm. Jan intimidated her, she felt like a schoolgirl in his presence. He reminded her of the precautions they had agreed to take.

"Right, you need to stay for a long time now. It may be that someone besides the doorman saw you come in. The best thing is if you now leave at a more reasonable time."

"When will you send this information to London?"

"As soon as I can."

"But when will that be?" Amelia insisted.

"You need to do your work and I need to do mine, each of us doing what he or she knows how to do best. Don't hurry me, I will decide when the right time is."

"Come on Jan, Amelia is upset, and it's not over just some trifle," Dorothy said.

"You think I'm not upset? What kind of person would I be if I weren't absolutely disgusted by what this priest has said about the Hadamar asylum? But we have to keep our heads, and not make and false moves. Of course I will send this information to London as soon as possible, but you know that we have to be careful in establishing contact. I will not do so before seeing someone else who has information to pass on to us. After meeting him I will send what he says along with Amelia's report, but I will not take the risk of getting in touch with London twice in the same day except in cases of extreme emergency."

"You are right," Dorothy admitted.

"Of course I am. Losing our nerve will not get us anywhere."

That day, Manfred Kasten and his wife had guests. Professor Schatzhauser had asked them to call a meeting to establish some facts about Amelia. He didn't know why, but he didn't trust her. It did not make sense to him that Amelia should have appeared out of the blue offering to help them.

"We might have been a little imprudent to accept her so quickly, we don't really know anything about her," the professor explained.

"Do you think that she could be a spy for Franco, and that the information she is gathering is ending up on Hitler's desk?" asked a gray-haired man, with an air of command.

"I don't know, General, I don't know... Max von Schumann seems to trust her, and she helped Father Müller a great deal in getting a young Jewish woman out of the country. But why has she come back? I don't believe her when she says that she is trying to recover her father's former business, or that she has broken things off with this American journalist, and has nowhere better to go," the professor replied.

"She might have a personal motive to be back here," Helga Kasten interrupted.

"What do you mean?" her husband said, looking at her with suspicion.

"We met her via Max, and as far as we know they met each other in Buenos Aires a few years ago. You don't have to be a psychic to know that she is important for him and he is important to her. If Amelia has broken off her relationship with Albert James, it's not entirely impossible that she has come to Germany looking for Max."

"The things you imagine!" her husband said.

"Helga may be right," the man they called general said. "But even so we cannot trust her fully."

"It is not a good idea for her to know just how many of the heads of the army are opposed to Hitler," a colonel suggested.

"Yes, it would be an incautious move," the general agreed.

"Yes, but perhaps she already knows more than is convenient for us," Professor Schatzhauser replied. "That is why I asked Manfred to call this meeting."

"Yes, I think that what we should now do is keep a certain distance from Fräulein Garayoa, without cutting her off completely; she might be useful to us, given her relationship with the British," Manfred said.

"I don't think that the British will listen to her now that she's broken things off with Albert James, her connection with the Admiralty was a personal one," the professor said.

The professor and his friends were right to be worried. It was a great risk for them to trust this Spanish woman about whom they knew so little. Even though the army had sworn loyalty to Hitler, there were some military officers in important positions who were plotting against the Führer and it was only natural that they should be suspicious.

Baroness Ludovica had decided to reclaim her husband. She wasn't going to accept Max's indifference simply because they could not agree about politics. Yes, she was a Nazi, and proud to be one. Was it not the case that the Führer was giving Germany back her former greatness? She was upset that Max refused to recognize Hitler as a man of destiny. When she heard him talk she was greatly moved, his speeches aroused in her a sense of pride at being a German. But Max was a romantic who made light of Hitler and who said that it was a disgrace for the German army to be under the orders of the Austrian corporal, as he referred to the Führer. She would make him see that they had to be practical; at the very least, he had to acknowledge that her family's factories in the Ruhr had been helped by Germany's economic recovery.

But Max's sense of honor came before any other consideration, so he would never accept the family's prosperity as a reason to accept the Third Reich. So Ludovica could only think of one way for Max not to end up abandoning her, and that was to get pregnant. It was not easy, because for some time now they had only lived together in the same house and had not shared a bed, but she was prepared to do anything to have a son, a son who would tie Max to her forever. He was the only male son of his family; his two sisters had sons, but it was only through him that the von Schumann name would be perpetuated.

And so Ludovica promised herself that she would not make any political comments when her husband came home, that she would even meekly accept anything he said against the Führer, and that she would pretend to find his irritating friends sympathetic.

Thinking about his return, Ludovica had prepared a dinner of her husband's favorite foods.

Max came back from Warsaw late in the afternoon on May 15, and his face showed tiredness but also some other emotion that Ludovica was not able to understand.

He kissed her briefly on the cheek and seemed not to notice her new haircut or her new dress, and he didn't seem to appreciate the glass of champagne that she gave him to welcome him home. Ludovica hid the annoyance that her husband's coolness had provoked in her, but she was not a woman to give in at the first hurdle.

"I am so glad you are back. Rest a little and then we will eat, I want you to tell me everything that has happened in Poland over these last few months. Everything is the same here, apart from the fact that the RAF are visiting us from time to time. We haven't suffered any setbacks because of that, though. Your sisters and your nephews are well, they want to see you. I told them I would tell you when you got back to Berlin."

"They're in the city?" Max asked.

"Yes, although your older sister told me that they would go to Mecklenburg when the weather got better."

Max nodded, and thought of the old family home in the lakes, not too far from Berlin. He had spent the happiest summers of his life there, riding his bicycle and fishing.

As soon as he had had a bath and a shave, Max went to find Ludovica. The months he had spent in Warsaw had made him think about his marriage, and he had decided to put an end to what was only a marriage of convenience.

"How have you been these last few months?" he asked politely as they ate.

"Bad, very bad," she said as he fixed his gaze on her.

"Why? What happened?"

"I've been thinking a lot about us, Max..."

"So have I, Ludovica."

"Well, in that case you will understand why it has been so bad. I love you, Max, and I have missed you, and I have realized that I don't know how to live without you. Don't say anything, listen to me... I know that my political comments have irritated you, and I am sure that none of this is so important as to drive a wedge between us. Remember the day we married? I was the happiest woman in the world... I didn't marry you because my parents wanted it, and I know that you also weren't simply motivated by your parents' desire to join our families."

"Ludovica, that's all in the past," Max protested.

"No, no it's not, at least it's not for me. I know I have not been a good wife, and I ask your pardon. You have always told me that I am too temperamental, and you are right, I put too much of myself into what I do and what I say. And what I want to say, Max, is that I won't let Hitler, and I won't let the Third Reich stand between us, I am a Catholic like you and our marriage is forever."

Max was taken aback by Ludovica's confession. How would he be able to tell her now that he was thinking about an amicable separation? He looked at his wife in surprise and he thought that he could see, behind her imploring smile, the same hardness as before in her eyes.

"We'll try to make it work, won't we, Max? she said, asking him for an answer.

"It may be too late..."

"No, it is not too late! How could it be too late? We made our vows before the altar, and I want to keep them. I am sorry for my behavior and for upsetting you with my defense of the Führer, but I assure you that it won't happen again."

Max looked directly at Ludovica once again. It was hard for him to recognize his wife in this apparently submissive woman, and he knew that this was all an act and that she would never accept the idea of a separation.

They finished their meal in silence, and then he excused himself, saying that he was tired from the journey. Ludovica told him to rest. Half an hour later, when Max was just about to fall asleep, he heard the door to his room open and saw Ludovica there, wrapped in a flimsy white nightdress. Before he could say anything, she had got into his bed.

2

The sirens broke the silence of the night. "The RAF might have decided to pay us a visit in return for the one the Luftwaffe carried out. I heard on the BBC that our planes have caused damage to the British Museum and Westminster Abbey," Helga Kasten said to her guests.

The Kastens were holding a dinner party in honor of Max von Schumann.

Amelia had spent the whole evening trying without success to talk to Max alone, but Ludovica would not leave her husband alone, and everyone could see that their relationship seemed to have improved. What is more, Ludovica did not make any of her usual comments in favor of the Third Reich that evening.

Amelia went up to Manfred Kasten.

"Do you think you could help me get to speak to Max for a moment?"

Manfred agreed. He thought that his wife might have been right and that Amelia had come back to Berlin in search of Max.

"I'll get Max to come to the library with me, go and wait for us there now. My wife will try to head Ludovica off, but you see how she hasn't left her husband alone all evening."

Amelia left the salon and went to the library. Max and Manfred Kasten did not take long to arrive.

"What is so important that you have to speak to me alone?" Max asked the diplomat.

"There is someone here who wants to speak to you."

Max stopped in the doorway when he saw Amelia's figure in the library; the rigidity of his posture showed how uncomfortable he felt.

"I want to talk to you," she said with a smile.

"What's going on?" he said, drily.

Manfred Kasten left the room to leave them alone.

"Have I done anything to upset you? If I asked Herr Kasten to bring you here it is because there are certain things I didn't want to talk about in front of Ludovica... ," Amelia said.

"Let's leave Ludovica out of it, and tell me what is so urgent that you need to talk to me."

"I would like to know what's going on in Poland..."

"So that's it, you need to tell your British friends all the news?"

"Max, please! What's got into you?"

"Why should I tell you what's happening in Poland? Will it help stop the war?"

"Will Hitler stop sending the Luftwaffe to attack London? What are you saying, Max? I don't understand you..."

"I am tired of it all, of everything I do, of seeing how useless my trust in Great Britain was, I thought that we could avoid going to war, and neither Halifax nor Chamberlain want to hear anything about it. And now what do you want me to do? Betray my country?"

"I will never ask you to do that!"

"Well, why do you want to know what's happening in Poland? Just for curiosity, or do you want to tell Albert James so he can write one of his little articles about it?"

"I thought you wanted to stop this war..."

"I do, but I never said I wanted Germany to lose the war. Do you think I don't care about the lives of my fellow Germans?"

"I don't understand you, Max."

"I see that... Let's leave it, Amelia, I'm tired and I got my orders today. Is there anything else I can help you with?"

"No, thank you, I am so sorry to have been a nuisance."

Amelia walked angrily out of the room and ran into Ludovica on her way back to the salon.

"I imagine you know where my husband is, my dear... ," Ludovica said.

"You'll find him in the library," Amelia said, without even pretending to be polite.

It was hard for her to get to sleep that night. She asked herself what could have happened to Max for him to treat her that way. The Kellers had gone to the country the day before and Amelia felt oppressed by the solitude in the apartment, even though she was happy that Greta felt well enough to take the trip to see her sister in Neuruppin.

A ring of the doorbell jolted her awake. She looked at the clock. Ten o'clock in the morning. She was scared for a moment, thinking it might be the Gestapo. Then she opened the door.

"Max! But what are you doing here?"

"I wanted to apologize for my behavior last night. I did not behave like a gentleman."

"Would you like a cup of tea?" she said to hide her nervousness.

"A cup of tea would be wonderful, but I don't want to be any trouble..."

"Oh, don't worry, it won't take a minute!"

While Amelia served the tea, Max started to talk.

"I want to be honest with you. You know what I feel for you and... it worries me, even in moments like this when Ludovica and I are trying to save our marriage."

Amelia was silent for a few seconds, and tried to smile when at last she did speak.

"I am pleased for you, I know that you and Ludovica had been having problems," she murmured, surprised by Max's unexpected confession.

"She thinks that we can still recover the feelings we had for one another in the past..."

"I am sure that it's worth trying. I wish you all the best."

"I am going back to Warsaw in a couple of days, and you asked me what was happening there..."

"Yes, but that was just an excuse to speak to you alone. I don't really want to know anything about Warsaw."

But Max seemed not to hear her and began to speak, staring into the middle distance.

"The poor Poles! You don't know what the Einsatzgruppen are doing out there..."

"The Einsatzgruppen?"

"Special units, 'action groups,' with the SS in their hearts and in their heads. You know what their task was? To clean Poland of anti-German elements. Can you imagine how they have gone about it? I didn't know this at the start, but the Einsatzgruppen went to Poland with a list of thirty thousand people considered dangerous for the Third Reich, people who have now been arrested and executed. Lawyers, doctors, members of the aristocracy, priests... Even priests!"

"And you... you... are participating in this?" Amelia asked.

"They are doing the work at the moment. They go around the villages, they group all the people together, they make them dig a pit and then they shoot them. Some people are luckier and only have their lands confiscated, or else get deported to other places. They are given a couple of minutes to get whatever they need together and leave their homes. The Jews get the worst of it, you know how Hitler hates them. I have heard about massacres in Poznan, in Błonie..."

"Is the army killing peasants?"

"No, we're not there yet. And anyway, I've told you that it's the SS and its Einsatzgruppen. Some of the Wehrmacht officers are still trying to preserve our honor."

"But why are so many innocent people being killed? Priests, lawyers, doctors..."

"They think that if they get rid of the country's 'intelligentsia,' the people who are best positioned to oppose them, then the ones who are left will not dare protest. And they are right about that. Warsaw is a living cemetery."

"And what are you doing in Poland, Max?"

"I'm looking after our soldiers, setting up field hospitals, trying to make sure that we have enough nurses and enough medicine... I visit the troops wherever they are deployed. You have to try to make sure that the men don't pick up venereal diseases... If you are asking me if I have blood on my hands, then the answer is no, but that doesn't make me feel any better."

"Will you be going back to Warsaw?"

"Yes, but not for long. The General Staff wants me to go and observe our units in Holland, Belgium, and France. Then they are going to send me to Greece. Our soldiers joined the Italian troops in Athens a few days ago."

"I have broken up with Albert," Amelia said suddenly.

Max was silent, looking at Amelia with pain in his face.

"I am sorry... I thought that you were happy together."

Amelia shrugged and lit a cigarette and took a swig of tea to hide her nervousness.

"He is a good man, a loyal man, and I love him a lot but I am not in love with him. We will always be friends, whatever happens, I know that I will be able to rely on him, but I am not in love with him."

"What are you going to do?"

"I came to Berlin to see you, to be with you," she said, looking at him directly.

Max did not know what to say. He had been attracted to her ever since they had met each other in Buenos Aires, and if he had not been engaged to Ludovica, he would surely have had a relationship with the young Spanish woman. But now he was not only married, but his wife had begged him to give their marriage another chance and he had promised that he would. He did not want to betray Ludovica, for all that he wanted to ask Amelia to come with him to Warsaw or wherever he was to be sent.

"I'm leaving in a few days..."

"I... I know, so..."

Max stood up and Amelia walked with him to the door, but she did not manage to open it. Max was embracing her with such strength... She gave herself up to him. That morning, in the Kellers' lonely house, she became his lover.

Father Müller could not escape the nightmares that had persecuted him ever since he had returned from the asylum at Hadamar. He had withdrawn into himself and the old priest whom he helped did not know what he could do to draw him out of this hell.

His mother and his sister were likewise unable to return to him the good humor that had always been such a feature of his character. For this reason they were delighted when Amelia came to visit them that Sunday, thinking that the young Spanish woman would help distract him. The next day, Monday, Father Müller was supposed to leave for Rome. The archbishop had organized the transfer, fearing that the Gestapo might seize the young priest at any moment.

Irene told her son to go out for a walk with Amelia.

"The fresh air will do you good, it's a beautiful day, and I am sure that Amelia would prefer to be outside, wouldn't you, my dear?"

"Of course, I think it would do us both good."

They walked to the zoological gardens, hardly exchanging a word as they did so. Once they were there they sat on a bench from which they could see the monkey house.

"I wanted to talk to you before you left," Amelia said.

"I'm afraid I'm not a good companion for anyone at the moment," Father Müller said.

"We're friends, so I was wondering if there was any way I could share your worries."

"No one can have any idea of the horror of what I saw," he said in despair.

"Rudolf, why don't you let your friends help you?"

Father Müller gave a start to hear his name. Nobody called him Rudolf apart from his mother and his sister, and here was this Spanish woman refusing to treat him as a priest, and instead using his real name.

"I know how impotent you must have felt not to be able to help those poor unfortunates, but you cannot indulge in your pain forever, the best thing we can do is to think about how to stop these murders. You have done something, the archbishop has protested to the authorities. We have to stop these murders. What we need to do now is to carry on fighting, now that we know the kind of people we are up against. I've thought about getting in touch with Albert; he's a journalist and he could be interested in what is happening in Hadamar, and not even Hitler will be able to carry on doing what he is doing if the British and North American press reveal that Germany is killing the mentally ill."

The priest looked at her, convinced. Her proposals had been extremely firm and coherent.

"What you cannot do is give up. You have seen evil with your own eyes, alright, but your duty as a priest and as a human being is to face up to these criminals."

"Do you think that you can get information about what is happening in Hadamar to your friend Albert James?"

"At the very least I will try. I have to find the right way because I cannot risk writing a letter that might fall into the hands of the Gestapo. But you could take a letter to Rome."

"To Rome?"

"To Carla Alessandrini. She will help us, she will know how to get my letter to Albert."

"You have solutions for everything!"

"No, I just thought of it while we were talking. And now I have something to tell you."

She confessed that her relation with Albert James had come to an end.

"I am sorry... and I am pleased," the priest said.

"Pleased?"

"Yes, because... well... you are married and... well... it's not good that you were living together."

"Do you think that matters?"

"Of course! You could never marry him, and if you had children, just think what their situation would be... Even if it hurts, it is still the best thing for you to do. And don't imagine that I don't feel any sympathy for Albert, he seems a good man and a courageous one, who deserves to find a good woman with whom he can share his life."

What Amelia had not told Father Müller was that she had become Max von Schumann's lover, and that the two of them, taking advantage of the Kellers' absence, were seeing each other every day. While Amelia and Father Müller were in the zoological gardens, Max was telling Ludovica that he was not willing to give their marriage another chance. He had tried, and tried sincerely, but this was before beginning his relationship with Amelia. All he wanted was to be with the young Spaniard and he was not willing for anyone to stand between them, not even Ludovica.

As evening fell, Father Müller and Amelia went to Professor Schatzhauser's house. The priest wanted to say goodbye to his friends before leaving for Rome.

When they got there, Manfred Kasten was telling everyone that something big was being planned. He said that there was a lot of activity in the General Staff, and that Hitler had seemed euphoric for the last few days.

"Who are we going to invade now?" Pastor Schmidt asked.

"I don't think that they would invade England... The RAF is holding the Luftwaffe back," Professor Schatzhauser said.

"You can't imagine what London is like now," Amelia said with regret.

"I suppose it is the same as Berlin, the same as Berlin... War is like that," Helga Kasten replied.

It was not the first time that Manfred Kasten had said that Hitler was preparing something important; but when Amelia asked Jan and Dorothy to convey these vague rumors, Jan protested:

"Can't you get any more information? To send a message saying that the General Staff are busy in the middle of a war is too obvious; the fact that the generals are busy is what you would expect, and if Hitler is happy, it doesn't seem relevant."

"Yes, but my sources think that something important is going to happen, and even if we don't know what it is, it's better to keep London informed."

It was not easy for Amelia to tell Jan and Dorothy that she and Max had become lovers and that he was going to take her to Poland with him, and so she would need new orders from Major Murray.

But neither of them seemed to be surprised, and Jan limited himself to saying that she should return in a couple of days, but that he had already been in touch with London.

Murray's orders were clear: Amelia was to travel with Baron von Schumann and get all the information from him that she could, especially relating to troop movements in the east. He also gave her a name, "Grazyna," an address in Warsaw where she could go to take the information she gathered, and a pass-phrase that would make welcome at that address: "After the storm, the sea is calm."

Jan gave Amelia a little camera.

"You may need it."

"It won't be easy for me to hide it."

"You will have to."

On June 2 Max and Amelia went to Warsaw. To all her friends, by this point, Amelia was Max's lover. She had told Professor Schatzhauser herself, saying that there was no longer any sense in hiding what there was between her and Max. It was hard for the professor to conceal his disapproval. He was not sympathetic to Baroness Ludovica, and he had suffered in silence the fact that Max was married to a Nazi, but in his eyes this did not justify Max taking this strange Spanish woman as his lover.

The news caused all kinds of gossip among Max's friends, but most of them did not approve. They were not the only ones: The Kellers were also taken aback. Amelia told them that she was going to Warsaw with the baron. She did not need to explain anything else. Herr Helmut said that she could rely on them and that their door would always be open to her. But Greta looked sullenly at her husband: She could not approve of Amelia's stealing someone else's husband and running away with him. No, that was not good.

3

Max and Amelia took the train to Warsaw, where Captain Hans Henke, Max's adjutant, was waiting for them. Then they headed south, to Krakow, where Hans Frank had his residence. Frank was the Bavarian whom Hitler had appointed governor-general of Poland.

"It is one of the most beautiful cities in the world," Max said, referring to Krakow.

She agreed with him when she saw it, but she was also affected by the sadness that she saw on the Poles' faces.

They did not spend much time in Krakow, Max had to have a meeting with Hans Frank and his military advisers about the medical needs of the German army, and then they went back to Warsaw.

Amelia felt an immediate antipathy toward Hans Frank, who had set himself up in Wawel Castle and was behaving like a little king.

He liked to organize dinners over which he presided like a monarch, his guests eating off expensive porcelain and drinking from Bohemian crystal glasses.

It was at one of these events that Amelia, flanked by Max and Captain Hans Henke, was presented to Hans Frank and his wife, as they were all going to sit and eat.

The table was overdecorated for Amelia's taste; Max sat opposite her and at her side was an SS officer. The man's blue eyes were as cold as ice. He was blond, and tall and athletic, but in spite of his physical charms Amelia found him repulsive.

"I am Major Jürgens," he said, holding out a hand.

"Amelia Garayoa," she replied.

Jürgens smiled politely and nodded. Of course he had not been unaware of the arrival in Krakow of Major von Schumann, that bigheaded aristocrat, along with a young Spanish woman whom everyone said was his lover. He thought that he would investigate the woman, whose beauty he was forced to admire. She did not seem Spanish, she was so blonde and so thin and so fragile; he had thought that Spanish women were all dark-haired and fleshy.

"Major Schumann, did you enjoy your stay in Berlin?" he asked Max.

"Of course," the baron replied uninterestedly.

"You've certainly come back with a charming companion... ," the major said, looking at Amelia.

"Amelia, allow me to introduce Major Ulrich Jürgens. Be careful with him."

Von Schumann's warning made Jürgens snort with laughter.

"Come on, Major, don't frighten the woman! The Wehrmacht aristocrats are always putting down those people who didn't happen to be born in a castle like they were. Apropos, how is your charming wife, Baroness Ludovica?"

Max tensed and Amelia paled. Major Ulrich Jürgens's words sounded like an insult.

An elderly woman seated at Max's side joined in the conversation.

"Oh, you young people are always so impulsive and indiscreet! Tell me, Major Jürgens, are you married?"

"No, Countess, I am not."

"Ah, well in that case you are not enjoying the advantages of matrimony. You should marry, you are of an age for it, don't you think? That will stop you from taking an interest in other people's marriages. And you, my dear, where are you from? You have an accent I can't quite place..."

"Spanish, I'm Spanish," Amelia replied, thankful for the woman's interruption.

"I am the Countess Lublin."

"And are you Polish?" Amelia asked out of curiosity.

"Yes, I am Polish, although I have lived most of my life in Paris. My husband was French, but I was widowed and decided to return to my country. I can see now that I got my timing a little wrong." A fine irony shone through the countess's words.

The countess led the conversation to more boring topics. She spoke to them of Paris, of a recent visit she had made to the United States where her oldest son lived, of the weather, of springtime in Krakow.

Major Jürgens seemed to be paying close attention to the meal, and made out that he wasn't paying them any attention, but Amelia could sense how he was scrutinizing her, and could see the glitter of anger in his eyes whenever he looked at Max.

They went back to Warsaw two days later and moved into the Hotel Europejski, where Captain Hans Henke, Max's efficient adjutant, had reserved for Amelia a room adjoining Max's.

"I am so pleased to have you here... But I'm scared that you will be bored and want to go back to Berlin," Max said.

"I only want to be with you; and it is always an adventure to get to know a city. I will meet people, don't you worry about me."

"But you must be careful, the city isn't safe. The Gestapo and the SS are everywhere."

"It can't be worse than Berlin."

"Trust no one here apart from Captain Henke."

"I know, I know..."

What Max could not imagine is that he couldn't even trust the woman with whom he was madly in love. Amelia had already started to photograph the documents he carried in his briefcase.

She took photographs of everything, trusting that the Admiralty would know how to select the most interesting documents.

Amelia only photographed the documents when Max was asleep, or in the shower. She shuddered to think of the terrible damage she would do him if he ever found out about it. Max was in love with her as he had never loved any woman before. Amelia was in love with him too, but not with such intensity, she told herself that she had given the best of her love to Pierre.

A few days after their arrival in Warsaw, Max had already established a work routine and Amelia was free to search for the address that Jan and Dorothy had given her on Major Murray's orders.

It was a building in the heart of Warsaw. A three-story house, one of whose corners abutted the Market Square. Amelia went up to the third floor and rang the bell and then waited impatiently.

A young woman answered the door and looked her up and down, and then asked:

"What do you want?"

"I'm sorry, I don't speak Polish," Amelia apologized in German.

"You only speak German?" the young woman said.

"And English and French and Spanish..."

"We will speak in German. What do you want?"

"After the storm, the sea is calm," Amelia said.

"Come in, please," the young woman said, and introduced herself as Grazyna.

The house was large and bright. The square and one of the side streets could be seen from its windows. It was a middle-class house, furnished with furniture and paintings of good quality.

Grazyna asked her to sit down.

"Who are you?"

"My name is Amelia Garayoa, and I think we have some friends in common..."

"Yes, it seems that way. What do you want?"

"They said that I could come here and leave some photos..."

"They said that you would come, but not when. What do you have?"

"I have been able to photograph some documents, they could be important."

"Give them to me, I'll make sure they get where they need to go."

"How do you get your material to London?"

"I can't tell you. We are running grave risks here, and if you get arrested then it's best if you don't know."

"Is the Resistance well-organized?"

"The Resistance?" Grazyna gave a bitter laugh. "You can't imagine what the Germans did when they invaded. They came with endless lists of people, of anyone who might be likely to put up the slightest resistance. The Einsatzgruppen have murdered thousands of people: doctors, artists, lawyers, civil servants... Yes, they killed anyone who could have tried to stand up to them, even if only in words rather than in deeds."

"I am sorry."

"No one did anything to stop them," Grazyna said sadly.

"Great Britain declared war on Germany because of Poland," Amelia protested.

"Too late. They were engaging with Hitler, and they refused to see what was happening, and the Poles were the first victims. If only Churchill is able to do something! At least he was never keen on appeasement. How could they have been so blind?"

While Grazyna spoke, Amelia looked at her. She calculated that she couldn't be more than twenty-five years old, although the lines around her mouth made her appear older. She was of medium height, with light brown hair and dark blue eyes, fleshy, not beautiful, but attractive. Amelia thought that Grazyna would pass unnoticed almost anywhere.

"Do you live alone?" she dared to ask.

"Yes, but my parents live near here. And what about you? What is your cover?"

"I am the lover of a Wehrmacht medical officer."

Grazyna gritted her teeth in order to avoid screwing up her face into a disgusted grimace.

"Where are you from?"

"Spain."

"You've come a long way... Why aren't you in your own country?"

"My father was shot after our Civil War; my mother died, and... well, let's just say that life has pushed me here. Oh yes, and even if you don't believe me, the officer I live with is a good person, not a Nazi.

"Right. He's only obeying orders, I suppose."

"Exactly. He was in the army before Hitler came along."

"But he doesn't know that you're a spy."

"No, he doesn't.

"And why are you doing this?"

"I hope that when Hitler is defeated it will help free my country from Franco."

Grazyna's guffaw irritated Amelia. She was sure that sooner or later Franco would be removed from power; she grasped hold of this dream because it gave her the strength to carry on living.

"It's not funny," she said dryly.

"I'm surprised that you're so naïve, but of course, I don't want to offend you. Give me the material."

Amelia took out a handkerchief in which the film was wrapped and gave it to Grazyna.

"I think that this house is still safe, but we shouldn't take any chances. There's a flowerpot in the window; if it is on the right-hand side then that means that you can come up without any problems, but if it's on the Left then either I'm not here or I am in danger, and then, whatever happens, you must not come up. Do you understand?"

"Of course."

"What do you think about Jews?"

The question confused Amelia and she didn't say anything, which Grazyna took the wrong way.

"So, you're one of those people whose principles soften when it comes to the Jews."

"What are you saying! My best friend was Jewish, my father's business partner was Jewish... It's just that I don't know what to say when you ask me what I think of them: Should I think anything in particular? That's the problem with people who think that you should think 'something' about the Jews."

"Don't get annoyed, it was only a question. My fiancé is Jewish. He's in the ghetto."

"I'm sorry, I know that they've been confined to certain streets and aren't allowed to move around freely."

"The conditions in the ghetto are getting worse every day."

"Can you see your fiancé?"

"You can't enter the ghetto or leave it without permission, but we can get past the guards, even though it isn't always possible."

"If there's anything I can do..."

"Maybe there is, given that you've got a Nazi for a lover..."

"Max is a soldier, a medical officer in the Wehrmacht, and I've already told you that he's not a Nazi."

"You'll have to tell him that we've met."

"Alright, I'll tell him that I bumped into you in the street, and that I was lost and you kindly showed me the way back to the hotel, and then I asked you to have a cup of tea with me to say thank you and then we got talking and became friends. Is that alright?"

"It's believable, I suppose. What hotel are you staying at?"

"The Europejski."

"We're more or less the same age, and you don't know anyone, so your lover will be glad to know that you've got someone to chat with while he's out killing Poles."

"I'm asking you please to stop talking about Max like this. You don't know him, so you shouldn't judge him. I can understand that for you all Germans are your enemies, but he is not."

"I suppose you have to believe that so as not to feel so bad while you do your work," Grazyna said.

"No, it's not that. I've known him for a while and I assure you that he's not a Nazi."

Grazyna shrugged. She wasn't going to make any more concessions about the Germans. She hated them too much to make any distinctions between them. Some of her best friends had been disappeared by the Einsatzgruppen, two of her uncles had been hanged, and her fiancé was in the ghetto. No, the Spaniard couldn't ask her to see beyond the pain and the hatred.

"I'll take you back to your hotel, so that you can tell your lover a believable story."

They left the house in silence. Amelia was wondering if she would ever form a connection with Grazyna. And Grazyna did not know what to think of Amelia. From what she had just said, it was clear that she was a British agent with a mission, and she needed this Wehrmacht officer in order to fulfill the mission, but even so, Grazyna didn't trust anyone who had amicable relations with the enemy.

Grazyna explained that she was a nurse and that she worked at the Saint Stanislaw hospital. Whenever she could she stole medicine to take to the ghetto.

It wasn't easy, but there was a nun who helped her, Sister Maria.

"She's an extraordinary woman, and extremely brave in spite of her age."

"How old is she?" Amelia asked.

"I think that she's past sixty; she's a bit fat and moans a lot, but she doesn't mind risking her life. She has access to the box where the keys to the dispensary are kept, and she helps me steal the medicine."

"A light-fingered nun... ," Amelia said, smiling.

"A nun who helps save lives," Grazyna said, angrily.

"Of course! Don't misunderstand me. I think that what sister Maria is doing is admirable, but I would be willing to wager that she never thought it was something she'd end up doing."

"And you, did you think you'd end up being the lover of a Nazi?"

"I am not the lover of a Nazi."

They didn't say anything else until they got back to the hotel. Amelia invited her in to have a cup of tea. Grazyna was right, it was important to give the illusion of truth to the lie that Amelia was going to tell Max.

Max did not get back to the hotel until late afternoon. He was tired and irritated, but his mood changed when he saw Amelia. She told him that she had met a young Polish nurse and that they had got on very well, and he encouraged her to cultivate the friendship.

"This way you won't be so alone; I know that I was selfish to bring you here, but I didn't want to leave you behind, not for anything in the world."

That night, and the nights that followed, Amelia took photographs of the documents in Max's briefcase. Every time she did so she felt extremely scared, and she wondered if he would forgive her if he ever caught her.

On the afternoon of the twentieth, Amelia went back to Grazyna's house. She had not seen her since their first meeting. She saw the flowerpot on the right-hand side of the window and went up without hesitating up to the third floor.

She rang the bell and Grazyna opened the door almost immediately.

"Oh, it's you!" she said, without hiding her surprise.

"Yes, I saw the flowerpot on the right and I came up... ," Amelia apologized.

"Come in, I'll introduce you to some friends."

There were two men and another young woman in the salon. They looked at her curiously.

"This is Piotr and Tomasz, and this is my cousin Ewa, the best pastry chef in Warsaw. You have to visit my uncle and aunt's cake shop one day, I promise you it'll be worth your while."

Piotr appeared to be closer to forty than to thirty; he was tall and strongly built, with dirty-blond hair and chestnut eyes that were almost green, and strong calloused hands; the exact opposite of Tomasz, who was some way shy of thirty, thin, of medium height, with hair so blond it was almost white, and intense blue eyes. Ewa was the youngest of the group. Amelia thought that she was probably around twenty: tall and slender with light brown hair and dark blue eyes like Grazyna.

"Have you got any more information?" Grazyna asked.

Amelia tensed up and didn't answer. She didn't know who Grazyna's guests were and was surprised that her contact could be so indiscreet.

"Oh, come on, don't worry! These are friends, I wouldn't have invited you in otherwise. Didn't you ask me about the Resistance? Well, here are three of them. We're planning a trip to the ghetto."

"And how are you going to do it?" Amelia asked with curiosity.

"Countess Lublin's house is in a street next to the wall around the ghetto. There's a service entrance round the back of the house; near to it there's a drain that Piotr found; it leads through to the other side of the wall. The drains are usually watched, but we are usually able to avoid the watchmen, isn't that right, Piotr?"

The man nodded. Grazyna was talking in German, a language which, Amelia noted with relief, her friends also seemed to understand.

"Piotr is the countess's chauffeur. She's a strange woman, she seems to be a friend to the Nazis, but Piotr thinks that this is only a façade," Grazyna explained.

"I met her in Krakow at a dinner given by the governor general, Hans Frank."

"That pig!" Grazyna spat.

"You cannot imagine how they are suffering in the ghetto," Ewa interrupted, "especially the children. We need medicine urgently, lots of them have typhoid fever."

"When are you going in?" Amelia asked.

"We hope to be able to do so in a few days," Ewa replied.

"Well, have you brought material or not?" Grazyna asked impatiently.

"Yes, here you are. I think it could be something important, they are sending large numbers of troops to the front."

Grazyna looked across at Tomasz and he nodded, as if answering a question that she had posed without saying anything.

"I'll send it at once, this evening," Grazyna promised.

"Yes, do it. Max is leaving tomorrow, he has said he'll be away for a few days, he's going north to where the major troop movements are. There are a lot of divisions in Poland..."

"Well, you'll get away from that man for a few days, at least," Grazyna said.

"Do you think I could come with you into the ghetto?"

"No!" they all replied, almost simultaneously.

"Well... I was just asking... I'd like to help..."

"You do your job and we'll do ours. Can you imagine what would happen if we were arrested? You don't want to run any more risks than necessary," Grazyna scolded her.

On June 22 Operation Barbarossa was put into action: The Wehrmacht invaded the Soviet Union. Great Britain was not taken by surprise by this development. British intelligence had gathered information on German troop movements via its agents. Amelia Garayoa's contribution helped confirm information that was already known in London. They had already managed to break the Enigma code, which the German army and navy used to encrypt their communications. This was good news for Churchill. He was certain that Hitler, even though he appeared invincible, would not be capable of fighting on two fronts at the same time.

Stalin, though he had received numerous warnings of what Hitler was planning, had never given them any credit. He had even had the bearers of such information shot.

The purges in the Red Army had been so harsh that Stalin's best generals had been shot. The German attack was brutal: 153 divisions, 6000,000 vehicles, 3,580 tanks, 2,740 airplanes, divided into three strike forces.

The chief of Soviet General Staff, Marshal Georgi Zhukov, called Stalin, who was at his dacha at Kuntsevo, twenty kilometers outside Moscow, to tell him that German troops had crossed the Soviet border with Poland. Stalin was stunned, and couldn't believe what Zhukov was saying. He had trusted Hitler to such an extent that he had left the Polish border very poorly defended.

Amelia began to visit Grazyna regularly. She had nothing better to do, given that Max was with the German troops, and was not in Warsaw. She managed little by little to lessen the antipathy that Grazyna appeared to feel for her.

Amelia went to look for her in the hospital one afternoon and met Sister Maria, who was in the infirmary looking over some papers.

"So you're the Spanish woman... Grazyna told me about you. Come on, I'll take you to find her, but I don't think she'll be long because her shift finishes at five o'clock."

Grazyna was in a room filled with women; she was taking the temperature of one old woman who appeared to be close to death. Amelia was surprised by the tenderness with which she treated the old woman. When she saw Amelia and sister Maria, she came toward them.

"Amelia, what are you doing here? What has happened?" Grazyna asked.

"Nothing, sorry if I frightened you, I was just passing and I came in to see you..."

"You gave me a fright! Now, meet my guardian angel," she said, smiling at Sister Maria.

"Don't try to flatter me, you know that it has no effect on me."

"She's my friend," Grazyna said to the room at large, raising her voice and calming the patients, who had been worried to hear the visitor talking in German.

While Grazyna was getting changed, Sister Maria invited Amelia to have a cup of tea with her in the infirmary. The two women got on immediately. The nun could see the worry in Amelia's eyes.

"Sister, we need medicine," Grazyna whispered in Maria's ear.

"I can't give you any more, we'll get found out," the nun said.

"There are children in a terrible state... It's difficult to control the outbreaks of typhoid in the ghetto," Grazyna replied.

"If we get found out it will be worse, because you won't be able to take any more medicine," Sister Maria replied.

"Yes, I know, but I need these medicines..."

"I'm going to take Amelia out to see the children's ward, we'll be gone for ten minutes."

"Thank you," Grazyna murmured gratefully.

When Amelia and Sister Maria left the infirmary, Grazyna opened the box where the nun kept the keys and took out the ones for the dispensary. When they returned, Sister Maria looked worriedly at the bulky bag in Grazyna's hand.

"But how much are you taking? We've got an inspection here tomorrow, and you know what they're like; they've got the inventory written down to the last sticking plaster. What am I going to tell them?"

"Say that the inventory must have been wrong."

"That's what I told them the last time... They transferred me for lack of diligence and for allowing medicines to leave the dispensary without being noted down."

"But the mother superior has never given you an official warning..."

"No, but she doesn't want to know anything about what I do, she says that the less she knows the better. Anyway, she doesn't know how to lie, the poor thing."

"Come to the ghetto one day and see how they need what we bring them! There are doctors there, but they have nothing to help them cure people with, and they are crying with impotence when they see people dying."

"Get out, get out before I change my mind. I need to think up a lie to justify the disappearance of all this medicine."

They went out into the street, which smelled of summer; the sun was shining in a cloudless sky.

"Let's go to my house; Piotr will come to find us when it gets dark. God willing, we'll be able to get into the ghetto tonight and bring them this," Grazyna said, indicating the bag.

"Let me go with you," Amelia asked.

"You're crazy! It's impossible. How many times do I have to tell you?"

"I could be useful, I could send information about the ghetto back to London, I think they're not aware of just how far the Nazis are taking their hatred of the Jews."

Grazyna was silent for a moment, thinking about what Amelia had said.

"I'll only take you if the others agree."

Piotr and Tomasz were doubtful, but Ewa and Grazyna managed to convince them.

"The British are not entirely clear about what the ghetto is like, it will help us if Amelia can tell them about it," Grazyna argued.

"At least they will have some first-hand information," Ewa said.

By the time night began to fall Piotr had been won over, and before the curfew was sounded they separated and made their own way to Countess Lublin's house. Grazyna took the medicine, and Tomasz and Ewa took bags that seemed to weigh more than Grazyna's.

Piotr let them in through a service door that gave onto a hall that ended in a swing door into the kitchen. There were three rooms for the staff at the other end of the hall. Piotr was lucky enough to have a room all to himself, as he was the only man in the house; the other two rooms were for the countess's cook and maid, and they shared them if necessary.

"I don't need to tell you that you shouldn't make any noise, and that you shouldn't leave my room under any circumstances. The servants probably hate the Nazis, but I don't want to take any risks," Piotr warned them.

Grazyna, Tomasz, and Ewa went to Piotr's room followed by Amelia. It was a small room, with barely enough space for a bed, a table and a wardrobe. They sat on the bed and waited for Piotr to come back.

Amelia was going to ask something, but Tomasz made a sign for her to keep quiet.

After they had waited in the room a good while, Piotr came back. He looked tired.

"The countess has guests, and there was nothing I could do apart from wait for them to leave. We need to wait a bit more and then go out, silently. You know what you have to do," he said, addressing his friends, "and you, Amelia, just follow us, but whatever you do, don't make any noise or say a word."

The night was sprinkled with stars. The sky over Warsaw seemed to have patches of light in it still, which did not bode well for them being able to move calmly, so they moved fast. Piotr lifted the drain cover and motioned for his friends to enter the city's underbelly. Tomasz was the first to go down the narrow iron stairs into the sewers. He was followed by Ewa and Grazyna, and Amelia brought up the rear.

Piotr put the cover back on the drain and went back to his room. He could not go with them that night. The countess was unpredictable and could call him at any moment. Ever since she had been widowed, she had used him to ease her nights, and he had accepted this duty, knowing that it gave him a privileged position among the other servants. She never told him in advance, but he knew from the way she looked at him when the summons would come.

But whatever happened that night, he would have to make sure that the drain cover was opened exactly four hours later, which was the length of time that his friends would stay in the ghetto.

Amelia had to stop herself from vomiting. The smell was unbearable. They walked over the rotting core of Warsaw, dodging rats, their feet sinking into the dirty water that filled the drainage system that went from one side of the city to the other.

Tomasz led the way, followed by Grazyna and Ewa, with Amelia at the back. A rat ran between her legs and she shrieked. Ewa turned back to her, saw the rodent and took Amelia's hand.

"It's better not to look at them," she said.

"And what if they bite us?" Amelia managed to say.

Ewa shrugged and pulled Amelia along by her hand. Tomasz had sped up, and so had Grazyna, and Ewa couldn't lose sight of them.

They didn't walk far; it only took them fifteen minutes, but to Amelia it seemed like an eternity. Then Tomasz stopped and pointed out some old iron stairs. He went up first. He knocked twice on the drain cover and someone opened it. A hand took Tomasz's and pulled him up. Then the rest had their turns.

"Hurry up, the soldiers will pass by soon," a man said, whose face was almost invisible in the night shadows.

He took them to a nearby building where another man was waiting impatiently in the doorway.

"You're late."

They went up to the fourth floor, the top floor of the building, where a man was waiting on a landing in front of a barely lit room.

"Thank God you're here!" a woman said, coming out to meet them. "And who is this?"

"She's a friend of ours who may be of some use. She speaks German, but she's Spanish," Grazyna explained.

"Have you brought medicine?" the woman asked.

"Yes, but not much, it was impossible for me to steal more."

The woman impatiently opened the bag that Grazyna gave her. Amelia looked at her. She must have been sixty or a little more, she was very thin, with her gaunt face covered in wrinkles, and white threatening to overtake the black in her hair, which she wore tied up with a bow; her eyes were very blue.

"It's not enough," the woman said, looking at what Grazyna had brought.

"I'm sorry, I'll try to bring more the next time," Grazyna apologized.

Amelia looked at Tomasz and Ewa, who were at the back of the room talking to the man who had led them there.

"Where is Szymon?" Grazyna asked impatiently.

"My son will be here any moment. He's in the hospital."

"Do you have a hospital here?" Amelia asked.

"It's not really a hospital, more a space where we put the people who are the most ill. My son is a doctor," the woman said in German.

"Sarah is Szymon's mother," Grazyna said by way of introduction.

"And now my son is madly in love with a guy," Sarah laughed as she took Grazyna's hand and led them to where Tomasz and Ewa were talking to the other men.

"This is Barak, Szymon's brother, and this is Rafal," Grazyna said, introducing the men to Amelia. "They make sure that our children still study, in spite of the war."

Ewa had opened her bag, which was filled with sweets and pastries.

"The children love the cakes you make," Rafal said.

"I'm sorry I didn't bring more, but it is difficult to carry a bag without calling the soldiers' attention to you."

"We should bring more bags," Tomasz said.

"They call too much attention to themselves; I prefer that you just bring what you can and avoid getting arrested." Sarah said.

Tomasz's bag was filled with teaching material: notebooks, pencils, pencil sharpeners, erasers... He was a teacher and some of the children in the ghetto had been pupils of his. Rafal had been a music teacher in the same school where Tomasz was still a teacher. They had been friends for too many years to let the German invasion break their friendship.

"I was just saying to Tomasz and Ewa that they've reduced the amount of food they allow into the ghetto, again. They say that 184 calories per person per day are enough. They are starving us to death. We have set up canteens where we distribute some soup that we make with whatever we can to the people who need it the most. But the worst thing of all is the lack of medicine, we have to get more." Rafal's tone was desperate.

"I will do it, but I'm afraid they will find me out. Sister Maria is very good and turns a blind eye to what we do, but one of these days she is going to be interrogated, and although I know that she won't give me up, they'll take the key to the pharmacy away from her," Grazyna replied.

"Szymon is desperate, he says that he can't bear to see the children dying without being able to do anything for them, just because of not having the necessary medicine," Rafal continued.

Some gentle knocks on the door put them all on the alert. Sarah went to open it and kissed the man who had just arrived.

"Mother, is Grazyna here?"

"Come in, son, she's at the other end of the room."

Szymon came in and went straight to where Grazyna was, and hugged her tight. They held each other close for a few seconds, then sat with the others. Grazyna introduced Amelia, and she was surprised to see how much the two brothers, Barak and Szymon, looked like their mother. Dark-haired, bony, thin, and with the same intense blue eyes.

"We have to do something, we can't carry on like this," Szymon complained.

"But what can we do? They watch the ghetto night and day, there's no way to get out except for those they take off to work," his brother Barak replied.

"The other day an SS officer had a party and took some of our best musicians," Rafal added.

"We need to get food and medicine. Maybe our brothers in Palestine will be able to help us. We need to get in touch with the delegation in Geneva or Constantinople. We might be able to bribe one of these Nazi pigs to help us get food and bring it into the ghetto," Szymon insisted.

"You're crazy! They'll report us and keep the money. But you're right that we should get in touch with the Jewish community in Palestine, or in America, and see if they will help us," Rafal said.

"Our organization will do what it can, Szymon, you know that," Barak said.

"I don't care about politics, my brother, all I want to do is save our people."

"For all that you claim the opposite, politics is everything, Szymon. The situation in the ghetto would be much worse if we did nothing," Barak said.

"The ghetto would be in a much worse situation if it weren't for the *Judenrat*, you have to admit it," Sarah said, looking straight at Szymon.

"I think that you're wasting your time, trying to make life in the ghetto normal instead of thinking of ways to face the Nazis," Szymon protested.

"Even behind the walls and behind the barbed wire we have to carry on being people, and people need more than bread to live," Sarah scolded him.

"We have to keep the children entertained," Rafal added.

"Poor things, it makes me sad to see them pretending to be normal in your schools." Szymon was still protesting.

"What should we tell them, then? That there's no hope?" Barak was annoyed with his brother.

Szymon was going to reply, but Grazyna spoke first.

"I understand your pessimism, but you're not right; life still goes on, even here in the ghetto, and our duty is to make sure that it continues, as if nothing were different in spite of the difficulties and the suffering. The *Judenrat* does what it can, and thanks to them everything works, more or less, and people feel protected."

"I saw five people die this afternoon, two of them children, and their mothers came to me crying: They asked me to do something to save them. You can imagine how I felt," Szymon whispered.

Grazyna held him tight and tried to contain her tears. Amelia didn't dare say anything, so affected was she by the scene that was taking place.

There were some more soft knocks on the door, which set them on edge again. Sarah got up and went to open the door. They heard a woman's voice, sobbing, asking for Szymon.

"What's happening?" Szymon asked the woman.

"You have to come, my husband is dying, you have to give him something, the cloths with cold water are doing nothing to lower his fever," the woman begged.

"I'll come with you, I'll see what can be done."

"Be careful, the curfew sounded a while ago and the soldiers shoot without asking any questions," Sarah said.

Szymon and Grazyna fell into each other's arms again. Then Szymon went with the woman, who told him to hurry.

"Complaints don't help anyone. Can you carry on bringing us what we need?" Barak asked Tomasz.

"You know that our organization is doing what it can, we'll try to come back in a couple of days with a few sacks of flour and some rice."

"A couple of days... Well, what can you do? We'll just have to wait. There's nothing left of what you brought the last time," Rafal replied.

"It's not easy to bring sacks of flour through the streets of Warsaw," Ewa interrupted.

"We know, and we're grateful for all that you are doing for us. What's happening here is so difficult for us to understand... We're trapped here as if we were filthy animals, and if this carries on for much longer then that's what we'll be," Rafal said, bitterly.

"Rafal, what a thing to say!" Sarah scolded him. "I don't want to hear you talk like that. We'll get out of here, the Nazis can't keep us locked away for ever; while we're waiting we need to organize ourselves as best we can."

"Mother, you were born in Palestine, and you lived there until you met our father. If one of us managed to escape and got over there, who could we turn to?" Barak asked.

"Escape... I wish we could escape and get to Palestine! But I think that the best thing to do would be to get news of our situation to the Jewish offices in Geneva... That's what we should do."

"We could get out of the ghetto through the sewers... ," Barak suggested.

"They'll catch you!" Grazyna exclaimed. "No, I don't think it's a good idea. I could go to Geneva, or Ewa..."

"What are they saying?" Amelia asked.

Grazyna told her of her friends' despair and their mad plan to go to Geneva and tell people what was happening in the Warsaw ghetto.

"I could go," Amelia said in a faint voice.

"You? Yes... maybe you could get to Geneva more easily than we could," Grazyna replied.

They discussed the question for a while. When only an hour was left before they had to leave the ghetto, Szymon came back. He was exhausted, with a grimace of pain on his lips.

"I couldn't do anything, the poor man died," he said. Then he took Grazyna's hand and looked at her tenderly. He loved her and admired her bravery. She was a woman who was happy to risk her life to help him, and not just him, but his people, the Jews of the ghetto.

Grazyna was the soul of this little group of resistance to the Nazis that was made up of other young people like her. She always played down the importance of what she did, but she was risking her life, especially because her group, as Szymon knew all too well, was passing information to the British.

"It's time," Ewa said, looking impatiently at the clock.

They stood up slowly. None of them liked saying goodbye.

"I'll expect you in a couple of days," Sarah reminded them.

"We will try," Tomasz said.

Barak was the one delegated to take them back to the drain through the shadows of the night. They had to wait for a patrol to pass, then they lifted the drain cover and descended quickly into the underground, praying that Piotr would be waiting for them at the other end.

Amelia was miserable, and walked without paying any attention to the rats that ran away when they heard the footsteps of intruders in the sewer. Not that she did not feel scared, but she was too affected by what she had seen and heard to care about her own fears.

The way back seemed shorter than the way out, although there was a moment in the darkness where Tomasz appeared to lose track of which path they should take; they arrived at the time agreed upon at the drain cover where they thought Piotr would be waiting for them.

Tomasz gave two light taps on the drain cover and it was immediately lifted up. Piotr was there, impatient.

"You're ten minutes late," he complained.

"I'm sorry," Tomasz said.

"I have to go back to the countess. I said that I was going to the bathroom and I don't think that she'll believe that I've been there all this time," he said, nervously. "Also, I don't know why, but it seems like there have been more patrols than ever tonight."

He took them back to the house and signed to them not to make any noise and not to leave his room. Piotr went back to the countess's bedroom, where he stayed until dawn, when she told him to leave and go back to his room. Until that time, Tomasz, Grazyna, Ewa, and Amelia sat on Piotr's bed, pressed together, without moving, trying to stay awake, even though none of them could avoid their head nodding every now and then.

Dawn had broken when Piotr came back into his room.

"You should wait a little longer before leaving. It's better if it's daytime, that way the patrols won't suspect you when they see you."

"I have to go as soon as possible, I need to be at the hospital by eight o'clock," Grazyna said.

"Alright, you can go first; Amelia can go with you. If they stop her she wouldn't be able to explain why she was out so early."

As if it were a ritual to which they were all accustomed, Tomasz, Grazyna, and Ewa sat down on the floor. Amelia imitated them. Piotr lay down on the narrow bed and fell asleep straight away. They sat in silence, lost in their own thoughts. The first noises of the day were soon heard, and Piotr woke up with a start. He calmed down when he saw his friends on the floor in the same postures they had been in when he had closed his eyes. He got up and went out into the corridor without saying a word. He didn't see anyone, so he came back into his room and made a sign to Grazyna, who came out quickly, with Amelia following her. A few minutes later, Tomasz and Ewa left too.

Although she was very tired, Amelia enjoyed the clean morning air. The sun seemed to be peeking through some high clouds that rolled over Warsaw. Grazyna seemed worried.

"I'm going to be late," she said. "Sister Maria will be annoyed."

"It's still only half past seven," Amelia said, trying to calm her.

"But it's a bit of a hike to the hospital. You should go to your hotel, do you know the way?"

"I'd prefer to come with you to the hospital, I can find my way back from there a little better."

"Will you tell your bosses in London what you've seen?" Grazyna wanted to know.

"I'll get a message prepared and I'll bring it to you later," Amelia promised.

"It's not that they don't know what's happening in the ghetto, but I think that the only aim of British policy is to win the war, and they think that the Jewish problem will be resolved as soon as that happens."

"Isn't that a logical position to take?"

"No, it isn't, the situation of the Jews is worse than the war itself. That's what I want you to explain to them."

"I will. Is there anything else I could do?"

"That will be enough. Well, I suppose you'll carry on spying on your Nazi."

"I have told you that he has been sent to the front. I don't know when he'll be back, so I don't have anyone to spy on."

"There are other officers in the hotel."

"I try to keep away from them. I prefer to be cautious, my situation here in Warsaw is not simple. I am the lover of a medical officer, it's probably better not to call attention to myself."

"Maybe you should take a few more risks. The officers all feel alone, far from home, I'm sure that any number of them would give in to a woman like you. You're attractive and well-educated, and Spanish, an ally. They won't mistrust you."

"I think that you've got the wrong idea about me. It isn't my job to be Max's lover, I told you that we met a long time ago and that I feel a great deal of affection for him. I am not a prostitute."

"I never said that you were, just that you should take advantage of your current situation. There are some men who talk only in bed."

Amelia thought that Grazyna didn't understand her. She admired the young Polish woman, but she was still being treated disdainfully; even so, she had to trust her.

They said goodbye at the entrance to the hospital and Amelia hurried back to the hotel. She felt the need to have a bath, her whole body reeked of the sewers.

She was at the hotel reception collecting her key when she felt a man's breath on her back. She turned round and found herself face to face with SS Major Ulrich Jürgens.

"Goodness! Max von Schumann's lovely mistress! You look terrible, have you slept badly? From the looks of things, you haven't even slept. It hasn't taken you long to forget von Schumann."

"How dare you!" Amelia wanted to slap this man in the face, this man who dared to look her up and down so impertinently and treat her as if she were a nobody.

"How dare I what? I don't know what you mean, have I said anything wrong? Maybe it was not very gentlemanly of me not to hide my surprise at the way you look. How would the baron have behaved in such a situation? Would von Schumann have pretended not to notice? I'm not an aristocrat, tell me, what would he have done in my place?" Jürgens's jocular tone was still rude.

"It's quite clear that you are not an aristocrat, and not even a gentleman," Amelia said, turning her back on him and heading for the elevator.

Ulrich Jürgens followed her, intent on offending her.

"Now that you're no longer keeping vigil for your lover, you shouldn't mind having dinner with me this evening. How about seven o'clock?"

Amelia got into the elevator without replying. When the doors shut she breathed a sigh of relief.

After a long bath she got into bed. She fell asleep thinking about how to avoid Major Jürgens.

It was already dusk when she woke up. She had promised Grazyna that she would take her a message to send to London, but she decided that it would be wiser to stay in her room until it was likely that Major Jürgens had stopped waiting for her in the lobby. She didn't want to give him the chance to cause a scene in public, especially not if she had a coded message in her pocket.

She took a book and tried to distract herself, but then there came some light knocks at the door.

"Who is it?" she asked through the door.

"Have you forgotten that I'm waiting for you?" It was Major Jürgens.

"Please stop bothering me," she said, trying to keep her voice from trembling.

"Don't play the innocent with me, I know your type. Your airs and graces don't fool me. You're nothing but an expensive whore."

Amelia had the urge to open the door and slap him, but she didn't. She was scared of this man.

"Leave now, or I will complain to your superiors!"

He laughed and carried on knocking at the door. Amelia kept silent and didn't reply to Jürgens's insults, and he grew bored after a while and decided to leave.

Amelia stayed by the door for a while, hardly daring to move a muscle, scared that the devil would return. Then she pushed an armchair in front of the door and sat down. Knowing that he might return made her unwilling to get into bed. But Jürgens did not come back.

The next day Amelia went to Grazyna's house. She went by an indirect route, scared that Major Jürgens might follow her, even though she had not seen him in the hotel.

Grazyna was tired; she had bags under her eyes and was in a terrible mood.

"Why didn't you come yesterday?" she said as soon as she saw Amelia.

"Because of an SS major with whom I don't get on all that well."

"Right, now she has friends in the SS too!"

"No, he's not a friend, he's a pig. He insults me every time he sees me, although I suppose that the person he really dislikes is Max. He met me on the way into the hotel and started to insult my appearance, as if he'd caught me coming back from an orgy. He invited me to have dinner and made horrible insinuations. He spent a long time knocking at my door. I didn't sleep at all last night, hoping that he wouldn't try to force his way into my room. It seemed to make sense not to leave the room."

Grazyna nodded, then she took the paper that Amelia took out of her bag.

"Is this what I have to send to London?"

"Yes."

"I'll try to make sure it goes this evening."

"I want to go back to the ghetto," Amelia said.

"Why?"

"Maybe I can be useful, maybe Sarah will be able to think of something."

"We mustn't run unnecessary risks."

"I know, Grazyna, I know, but I can help, even if it's only carrying a sack of rice."

4

Over the next couple of months Amelia went back to the ghetto on various occasions, helping to transport the meager aid that Grazyna's Resistance group had managed to gather.

The young Pole carried on stealing medicine from the hospital thanks to Sister Maria's goodwill. The nun protested but allowed Grazyna to continue.

Ewa hinted on several occasions that there were students in the group, as well as a couple of young lawyers and teachers, but Amelia never met them. Grazyna was very careful about the group's security, even though she knew that Amelia was working for the British.

On her visits to the ghetto, Amelia was witness to bitter arguments between Szymon and his brother Barak, even though their mother tried to insist on keeping the peace between her two children.

"How can you be so blind! The *Judenrat* are making you accept what is happening!" Szymon shouted at his brother.

"How dare you!" Barak seemed about to punch his brother.

"Because it's true! You think that it's alright just to administer the crumbs that we are being offered. I say we need to fight, we need to have weapons!"

"You don't know everything, Szymon! We need weapons, of course, but what are we going to do while we're getting ready? Or do you think we can face the German army as we are?" Barak replied, holding back the anger that his brother's reproaches provoked in him.

Sarah told them to be quiet, that they needed to be together in order to face adversity with a united front.

"But I hate seeing the *Judenrat* dealing with the Nazis just in order to get a few crumbs of bread!" Szymon protested.

"Of course, you could do better than them!" Barak said ironically.

Amelia listened in silence. She was studying Polish in her free time and was beginning to understand a little of what she heard. But it was Grazyna who kept Amelia up to speed with what the two brothers were arguing about, and she agreed more with Szymon. Later she asked Tomasz why they never tried to bring guns into the ghetto along with the food and books and medicine.

"It's not easy to find weapons. Where do you think we're going to find them? Even so, we try. Szymon is very fiery, but he is probably right. But I also agree with Barak and Rafal, that the important thing is to make the situation in the ghetto better. But do you think that the Jews here would have a chance if they had to face the German army? They'd be cut to ribbons in a heartbeat."

"But at least they would die trying to do something," Amelia replied.

"Death is useless. They kill you and that's that. It's not a good idea for people to allow themselves to be killed." Tomasz insisted.

"I'm not saying that they should let themselves be killed," Amelia protested.

"And what else could possibly happen? Do you think you can get rid of the German army with a couple of pistols? Come on, Amelia, try to be a little realistic! It would be suicide. Of course we must fight, but only when the moment is right. The younger leaders in the ghetto have not given up on fighting, but they need weapons and ammunition to be able to resist for any length of time."

Grazyna didn't take part in the arguments, and so Amelia was surprised when she came round to her house one afternoon to find her and Piotr taking their leave of a man she did not know.

"I didn't expect you," Grazyna said when she saw her.

"I'm sorry to come unannounced," Amelia apologized.

The man left without saying goodbye. Grazyna went back into her apartment, followed by Piotr and Amelia.

"You shouldn't turn up unannounced, I've got my own life too, don't you know?"

"I'm sorry, I'll come back another time," Amelia said, getting ready to leave.

"Well, now that you're here... Well, stay. We're waiting for Tomasz and Ewa to go to the ghetto."

"I'm telling you, there are too many patrols and the countess has sent for me tonight," Piotr said to Grazyna, ignoring Amelia entirely.

"I know, but do you want me to keep the weapons in my house? It would be crazy. The sooner we get them out of here the better."

"Yes, but not today. You know it will be difficult for me to help you. The countess is not a supporter of the Nazis, but she doesn't want to have any problems with them. And once she's got me in her room it's hard for me to escape. She's even given the maids the night off, and so we'll be alone."

"Well, you'll just have to think of something, Piotr, but we have to take the weapons in tonight."

"What weapons?" Amelia plucked up the courage to ask.

"We've got some pistols and some hunting rifles. It's not much, but at least it will stop the people in the ghetto from being so defenseless," Grazyna explained.

"Weapons? But how did you get them?" Amelia's surprise was displayed in her voice.

"We got the rifles from some friends of ours who are hunters, and as for the pistols... Well, it's better not to say. The less you know about some things, the safer you'll be," Grazyna replied, after exchanging warning glances with Piotr.

"I could help you take them to the ghetto," Amelia offered.

"Yes, now that you're here you might as well be useful."

It was barely dark when Ewa and Tomasz arrived at Grazyna's house. Ewa had a basket of sweets.

"We'll take the sweets another day," Grazyna said. "The weapons are heavy and we can't take everything."

"Oh, let's try it, the children will be so happy..."

Piotr led them through the night to the countess's house. He opened the back door that led to the kitchen and pushed them into his room when he heard a noise from upstairs.

"Piotr, are you there?"

It was the countess's voice.

"Yes, Madame, I'll be up directly."

"No, don't worry, I'll come down. It might be fun to change rooms."

Piotr tensed and started to hurry up the stairs. He had to stop the countess from finding his friends.

"Oh, but Madame, it's not a good idea if you come down here, my room is in no condition for you."

"Come, come, come, don't be so prudish. Imagine that I'm not the countess, but one of the maids, it will be fun."

"No, never," Piotr said, trying to stop the countess from coming further down the stairs.

Grazyna shut her eyes, fearing the worst. Ewa and Tomasz hardly dared breathe, and Amelia seemed to be saying her prayers under her breath.

They breathed with relief when they heard Piotr's footsteps, and those of the countess, moving away, and spent almost two hours without daring to move a muscle, speaking in whispers. At length Piotr came back. He was sweaty and half-naked.

"We've got five minutes. The countess is insisting on coming down to my room. Hurry up, if I don't go back soon then she'll come down and look for me."

They went out into the street and Piotr lifted the drain cover and helped them into the city sewers. He had managed to get the cover back on, and then turned back to the house, where he saw the figure of the countess standing in the doorway. She looked at him without saying a word, then turned away and headed back to her room. Piotr followed her upstairs, but she had locked the door and did not reply to his call.

At the pre-arranged time, four o'clock in the morning, Piotr went back into the alley to lift up the drain cover. Grazyna was the first out, and she immediately noticed that Piotr was worried.

"What happened?" she asked.

"I think she saw us."

"My God! And what did she say?" Grazyna asked.

"Nothing, she went into her room and locked the door. Maybe she will fire me, I don't know. We'll talk later, you should go now."

"We can't go now! The curfew is still in place," Tomasz said.

"And what will happen if she comes down to my room? What shall I say? That you're a group of friends who came through the sewers to visit me? I know that you're in danger, but you can't stay here."

"We are going to stay here," Grazyna said, surprising them all by her firmness.

"No... no, you can't... ," Piotr protested.

"Your countess may turn us in if she finds us here, but it's a certainty that if they find us breaking the curfew they'll hang us all. I prefer to risk the countess."

Piotr shrugged. He was too upset to stand up to Grazyna, and no one else said anything. It was clear that it was Grazyna who gave the orders.

At half past seven Grazyna left the house along with Amelia, and a couple of minutes later Tomasz and Ewa departed as well. As soon as they had gone, the countess came to Piotr's room.

"Have they gone?" she asked.

He did not reply, but he went up to her and hugged her as he guided her back to her own room. The maids would be back at eight o'clock, but if the countess wanted to be treated like a maid, then he would be only too happy to oblige.

Major Jürgens was still bothering Amelia with his shameful insinuations, and she did what she could to avoid him, but from time to time she ran into him at the hotel reception or in the dining room.

Every now and then she received a letter from Max at the front. They were formal letters, of the kind that one would write to a close friend, but nothing more. Amelia was not surprised that there were no words of love, as she knew that all the letters from the front had to go past the military censor.

She was not prepared for what happened in mid-November. One afternoon when she was coming back from Grazyna's house, she came into the hotel and bumped into the last person she would have expected, or wanted, to see.

The woman, of aristocratic bearing, was talking to Major Jürgens and two other SS officers, and she recognized Amelia when she turned round.

"Goodness, it's the little Spanish girl!" Jürgens said, raising his voice and calling the attention of the woman and the two officers with her.

Baroness Ludovica glared at Amelia and looked her up and down. Her eyes were filled with hate and contradicted the smile that played over her lips.

"Amelia, what a surprise! I didn't know you were in Warsaw. How lovely to see you!" the German said.

Ludovica came up to Amelia and pretended to kiss her cheek, enjoying her nervousness.

"Baroness... I didn't know you were coming to Warsaw."

"Of course you didn't! How could you? It's a surprise... I want to surprise my husband, and I'm sure that you don't know that he's coming back tomorrow on leave. We'll be able to enjoy some days together after a few months that have seemed like years to me... Also, I'm bringing him a present that I don't mind you knowing about before he does: We're going to have a son! You must admit that it's the best present you can give a man."

Amelia felt her legs shaking and her face burning. The baroness's mocking smile hurt her more than Major Jürgens's guffaws; he made no effort to hide how much he was enjoying the scene.

"Aren't you going to say anything, Amelia? Aren't you going to congratulate me?" the baroness said.

"Of course. Congratulations," Amelia managed to say.

"Join us, Amelia. The baroness is going to honor our table tonight with her presence," Major Jürgens said.

"I'm sorry... I am... I'm very tired... Some other time... ," Amelia excused herself.

"Of course, my dear, some other time! I am sure that Max will be happy for us to have dinner together to celebrate the news," the baroness said.

Amelia hurried toward the elevator, trying to control the shuddering that threatened to take over her entire body. Her room was just next to Max's, and although the door between them had been closed ever since he went to the front, she was scared of being so close to Ludovica, who had moved into Max's room without any qualms.

It was not her lucky day. An hour after getting to the hotel she was pacing up and down her room when there was a knock at the door. She was scared that it might be Major Jürgens, but was shocked when she heard Grazyna's voice.

"For God's sake, Amelia, open the door!"

Grazyna's appeared shaken, and it was difficult for her to talk.

"They've taken Sister... ," she managed to say.

"The sister? Who do you mean?"

"They've taken Sister Maria... Someone reported the missing medicine in the hospital pharmacy. They did an inventory without telling her and they've had a list of everything that was missing. The director called her to his office this afternoon; she said she didn't know anything about the disappearances, but they didn't believe her and took her away."

"Good Lord! And how do you know all this?"

"When I heard that the director had summoned her I went to see the mother superior. She was very nervous, and said that she hadn't said anything because she didn't want to know anything about the subject, but she was worried that they would make Sister Maria talk. I haven't gone home, that's the first place they would go and look for me."

"What are we going to do?" Amelia asked worriedly.

"I don't know... but if Sister Maria talks... they're going to arrest me, Amelia... I'm sure of it."

"And you came here! Are you mad? Most of the German officers and a good number of the SS officers are staying here."

"That's why I came, I thought it was the safest place, they won't look for me here. I have to stay here, you have to let me stay... ," There was both order and plea in Grazyna's tone.

"Of course, you can stay here, but I've got problems too. I met Max's wife in the lobby this afternoon, and she was with the SS major who hates me so. I don't know... It's not a coincidence that Ludovica should be here..."

"It's not important. You must go and tell Ewa, she will know how to send the alarm to the others. We were going to take more guns to the ghetto tonight..."

"Tonight? You didn't tell me," Amelia complained.

"No... we weren't going to," Grazyna said. "The person we got the weapons from was very nervous to see a stranger. It's a larger delivery this time and... well, other members of the group were going to help us carry them. They were going to take the weapons directly to Piotr's house. Ewa and I were going to take the other members of the group there. We have to stop them from being arrested."

"But Sister Maria doesn't know anything about your group, she can't give you away."

"But if they make her speak, then she'll say that it was me who took the medicine. Maybe she's already said so, and if that's the case, then they'll know where I live and they'll be looking for me. And it won't be too difficult to find out about my friends and arrest them."

"That's only what you suspect might happen," Amelia said, trying to calm her friend.

"Don't be so naïve! Do you think it'll be hard for the Gestapo to make a nun talk? We're in danger and we need to act fast, or else the group will fall. Go to Ewa's cake shop as if you were going to buy sweets. You have to learn a phrase, and remember it exactly, because it is important: 'I love sweet things, but sometimes they get stuck in my throat.' You'll remember it?"

"Of course. And you think that Ewa will know what it means?"

"Yes, and she'll tell the others. Go now, there's only half an hour until the cake shop closes."

"And if I don't find Ewa?"

"Then come back as soon as you can, it will mean that she's been arrested.

"But... well... what if they arrest me?"

"You? Well, it's possible, but I think they'd arrest us before you, you are the lover of a German officer."

Amelia followed Grazyna's instructions and went quickly to Ewa's cake shop, which was not far from the hotel. Grazyna waited for her in the hotel room.

Amelia reached the cake shop in ten minutes. The shop was sealed off, so she asked the doorman of the neighboring building what had happened.

"Oh, the police came a while back. Don't ask me why, I don't know and I don't want to know."

"But something must have happened... ," Amelia said, trying to make herself understood in her shaky Polish.

"Yes, I suppose so. Don't ask questions and leave me alone."

The doorman turned his back on her and Amelia felt completely lost. What could she do? She made a decision; she would go to tell Piotr, certain that he would know how to warn the rest of the group. It was a risky decision, but she had no other option: The only other members of the group she knew were Piotr and Tomasz, and she didn't know where to find Tomasz.

She took a bus to Countess Lublin's house. She walked quickly, looking to the left and to the right in case she saw anything suspicious, but nothing she saw seemed out of the ordinary. She walked to the back of the house and knocked gently on the service door, almost holding her breath.

One of the countess's maids opened the door and asked her sullenly what she wanted.

"I'm a friend of Piotr's and I need to see him urgently... It's... it's... a family matter," Amelia begged, hoping that she would be understood.

The maid looked her up and down before telling her to wait outside while she went to tell the countess's chauffeur he had a visitor.

Piotr arrived a few minutes later, accompanied by the maid. He drew himself up short when he saw Amelia, but he didn't say anything and only took her by the arm and led her into his room.

"Are you mad? How can you even think of coming here?"

"They've arrested Sister Maria, and Ewa. Grazyna is hidden in my room. You have to tell the group not to come tonight with the weapons, or else you'll all be arrested."

As soon as he realized the danger they were in, Piotr seemed to grow immediately old. It was difficult for him to think about what they should do.

"Ewa may have talked, they may all be under arrest already and may be coming for me now," he said, after pausing for a few seconds.

"I don't know, but you could still try to do something... If Ewa hasn't spoken, then you and your friends could still escape. I have to go back to Grazyna."

"No, don't go. It's easier for you to go all over town... I'll give you an address on Castle Square, where you can find one of our men, Grzegorz. It was he who had the weapons for tonight."

"And what will you do?"

"I'll try to run away."

"And what if they've already arrested Grzegorz?"

"Then it's only a matter of time before they arrest us all, including you," Piotr said, shrugging. "But you should go now."

Piotr opened the door and looked both ways down the alley, but didn't see anything that caught his attention. Each wished the other luck, and then Amelia left.

She took a bus to Castle Square. She kept looking impatiently at her watch, and prayed that she would be able to find Grzegorz.

She got out of the bus one stop before her destination and walked fast toward the address that Piotr had given her. She climbed the steps and rang the bell anxiously. The door opened and she saw a man silhouetted in the darkness.

"Grzegorz? You don't know me, I've come from Piotr to warn you..."

She couldn't finish the sentence: The man grabbed her by the arm and pulled her forcibly into the house, dragging her into a large salon, which was also half dark. When Amelia's eyes had grown accustomed to the absence of light, she was able to make out a man stretched out on the floor in a pool of blood. She hadn't time to scream before the man who was holding her arm threw her down on the floor.

From this new position she could see another man, seated comfortably on a sofa and surveying the scene.

"Who are you?" the seated man said.

Amelia was too scared to speak. The man kicked her in the face, and Amelia felt the metallic taste of blood on her lips.

"It's better if you talk, unless you want to end up like your friend."

She couldn't talk, she was too distraught.

"Boss," the man who had opened the door said, "it'll be better if we take her down to headquarters, they'll know how to make her talk there."

"Your name," the man on the sofa insisted.

"Amelia Garayoa."

"You're not Polish."

"I'm Spanish."

"Spanish?"

The two men appeared confused.

"What's a Spaniard doing fighting against the German people? Aren't our countries allies? Or are you a bloody Communist? Or a Jew?" the man insisted.

He kicked out at her again, but this time Amelia managed to cover her face. She felt them pulling her arm and making her stand upright. There was a sticky liquid on her hands and her legs, she realized it must be Grzegorz's blood.

"So you're a member of Grazyna's little group, like this bastard. Well, now you see how our enemies end up," the man said as he pushed her toward the door.

They put her in a car and drove her to Aleja Szucha where the central office of the Gestapo was to be found.

During the journey, Amelia realized that however hard the torment she was going to have to face, she would have to endure it. If she told them that Grazyna was in her hotel room then they would arrest her at once, and Amelia had only one thing in her mind: Ludovica had told her that Max would arrive the next day. If that were the case, then maybe Grazyna would be able to find a way to get close to Max and tell him what had happened. He was the only one who could save her. It was her only chance.

They took her to a damp basement and pushed her into a cell. She saw straight away that there were bloodstains on the walls and she began to shiver. Nobody had ever treated her badly before, and she did not know if she would be able to endure being beaten.

They kept her in the dark, without giving her anything to eat or to drink, until she lost all track of time. She thought about Pierre: The Lubyanka couldn't have been all that different from this Nazi cell. She went back over her life, deeply regretting the path she had taken that had led her to this cell. And then she told herself that it was entirely down to her. Then she started to pray, with the same faith she had had as a child. It wasn't that she no longer prayed, every now and then she would mutter a prayer when faced with some difficulty or other, but it was something she did almost automatically, remembering that her mother had always told her that God would be her best help whenever she needed Him. And now more than ever she needed her mother to have been right. She said all the prayers she remembered: the Our Father, the Hail Mary, the Apostles' Creed, and she felt sad that she didn't know any others.

When the door was finally opened, it was to admit a fearsome-looking woman who pushed her up to a higher floor, where they said that she was going to be interrogated.

Amelia felt dirty, hungry, and thirsty, and she prayed to God to give her strength to deal with what was coming.

The jailer told her to undress, and several men came into the room. One of them was an SS captain, the other two were dressed in workers' clothes, and they took off their jackets without even looking at her, hung them on hooks in the walls, and without saying anything tore off her clothes and started to hit her. She received the first blow in the stomach, the second in the ribs, and the third in the gut, and then at the fourth she fainted. When she came to, she felt that she was drowning. The two men were shoving her head into a bath filled with dirty water. They pushed her in and pulled her out without giving her a chance to breathe. When they got tired of this, they tied her hands together with a rope that rubbed against her skin and hung her from a hook on the ceiling. With her hands above her head, completely naked, and held up only by the rope around her wrists, Amelia felt that her bones were crunching and that every single muscle in her body was aching. She tasted her own salt tears as they rolled over her lips, and could hear, as if at a distance, her own cries of pain.

"Well, Fräulein Garayoa," she heard the SS officer say, who had been silent up until that moment, smoking cigarette after cigarette as he impassively watched what was being done to her. "I think that we can talk now. Alright? I want you to answer a few questions: If you do, then you won't have to suffer anymore, at least not until after you have been sentenced. And now, tell me, where is your friend Grazyna?"

"I don't know," Amelia managed to say.

One of the torturers punched her in the gut and Amelia howled with pain.

"Come on, come on... Let's start this again. Where is Grazyna Kaczynski? It's a very simple question. Answer me!" the officer shouted.

"I don't know, I haven't seen her for days."

"So you admit that you know her, that's good. And given that you're such good friends, you can now tell me where she is to be found."

"I don't know... I promise you. She... she works... We only see each other every now and then..."

"Especially on the nights when there's no moon, right?"

"I don't know what you're talking about... ," she said, while they hit her legs again, this time with a stick.

"I'm talking about weapons... Yes, who would have said that a young lady as delicate as you appear to be would help a band of dangerous delinquents to stockpile weapons to kill Germans. Because that's what those weapons were for, to kill Germans, right?"

"I... I don't know... I don't know anything about... any weapons."

"Of course you do! You and your friends are part of a criminal group that helps those dirty Jews, and prepares to attack our army. Scum!"

The captain made a sign to one of the workmen, who hit Amelia near the temple. She lost consciousness again, and regained it only when she felt a stream of cold water on her face. The jailer had a bucket in her hand, it was she who had thrown the water and she seemed to enjoy watching Amelia suffer. Amelia realized that she could barely see anything, everything she looked at was blurry and she burst out crying with whatever force she had left.

"I can send you back to your cell only if you tell me where your friend Grazyna Kaczynski is; if you want to suffer more, let me tell you that the worst is still to come," the SS captain said.

"Please, leave me alone!" Amelia begged.

"Where is your friend?"

"I don't know! I don't know!"

One of the men came up to her holding something in his hands. Amelia could barely see what it was, but then she screamed to feel two clamps grasping her nipples. Her own cries frightened her, but the men in the room looked at her in an indifferent silence. She did not know how long the clamps were on her nipples, because she fainted again. When she woke up, she was on the floor of her cell once more. She had no strength to move, and she did not want to, in case they decided to take her up to the torture chambers once again when they saw she was awake. She lay there curled into a ball and felt the cold floor through a pool of blood that came from her own wounds.

She was afraid to move, she didn't even want to cry in case the pain was unbearable. Her breasts ached and she wondered if she still had her nipples.

She lost all idea of time and trembled with fear when she heard the cell door opening again. Her eyes were shut, but she could feel the presence of the guard.

"She's destroyed, I don't think she'll last that long," the guard said to the man who was with her.

"It doesn't matter, the captain said we should do whatever it takes to make this bitch talk."

Amelia cried, thinking that if they tortured her again then she wouldn't have the strength to keep her mouth shut.

The captain was still in the torture chamber and looked at her tiredly, disgusted that she was making him lose his valuable time.

They tied the rope round her wrists again, and hung her from the ceiling. She felt the men's fists punching her in the ribs, in the stomach, in the chest, then they hit the soles of her shoes with a bar. Her mouth was so swollen that she could hardly shout, far less tell them to stop, that she was prepared to talk. She couldn't do it, they put her head in the tub of dirty water once again. Barely giving her time to breathe, until they finally gave her a break. They laughed as they made her eat her own vomit.

When they were tired of hitting her, the captain came up to her.

"We have arrested all your friends, we only need to find Grazyna Kaczynski, and I promise you we shall. Don't be stupid, and tell me where she is."

One of the men came up with the clamps in his hands, or at least that's what she thought, and then she cried with all the strength she had left. Scarcely had the clamps touched her nipples than Amelia fainted.

When she came to, she was sitting in a chair in the torture chamber. The captain was talking on the phone and seemed extremely excited.

"Hurry up, let's go to the Hotel Europejski! They've arrested a woman, it looks like it's Kaczynski."

Amelia looked at him through the fog that covered her eyes. She was sure she hadn't said anything, or had she?

"She's coming round," the guard said. "Maybe she'll say something."

"No, let's go to the hotel," the captain ordered. "We'll carry on with her later."

As he walked past Amelia, one of the torturers could not resist the temptation to punch her again.

5

For two days, Grazyna did not leave the room. She hid in the wardrobe every time she heard the key turn in the lock and the maid come in; the poor woman seemed surprised at Amelia's absence. She knew that the maid suspected that Grazyna was in the room. She had seen her the afternoon that Amelia left. She had said that she was a friend of Fräulein Garayoa's and that Amelia had asked her to stay until she got back. But Amelia hadn't come back for two days. She was scared by the maid, and also when, from her hiding place at the back of the wardrobe, she saw a German officer come several times into the empty room and look around, worried. He would leave almost immediately, and she thought that he could be Amelia's lover. Sometimes she heard him talking to a woman through the cracks in the door that joined the two rooms. He didn't seem very happy; she heard them arguing.

She had found Amelia's camera, the one she used to photograph her lover's documents, at the bottom of the wardrobe, hidden under some clothes.

As the hours went by, she became ever more certain that Amelia must have been arrested, or else she would have come back. She thought about how she might escape, and finally decided to leave when the entrance to the hotel was filled with people, so she might pass unnoticed. The worst of it was that she did not have anywhere to go, for if Amelia had been arrested, then she would not be able to warn the rest of the group. The only thing left to her was to try to get to Ciechanów, where her Aunt

Agnieszka lived; she had always been her favorite niece and was sure that her aunt would help her.

She had fallen asleep when the door opened, and she had not had time to hide in the wardrobe.

Several men came into the room, followed by the maid and a concierge. The maid pointed to Grazyna.

"This is the woman who has been here for three days in Fräulein Garayoa's room... I think she was waiting for her... I... I told the manager that it seemed very suspicious."

"Get out," one of the Gestapo agents said to the maid and the concierge. They both left, but unwillingly, wanting to see what might happen next.

Grazyna was frozen still. She knew that there was no escape. They grasped her arms and ordered her to tell them her name.

"My name is Grazyna Kaczynski," she murmured.

One of the men started to search the room. It did not take long for him to find Amelia's camera. She didn't know why she did so, but she started to scream at the top of her lungs, struggling against the Gestapo officers who were trying to drag her out of the room. Her screams were so loud that the guests came out of the neighboring rooms to see what was going on.

Grazyna could see the astonishment in the eyes of the officer who had looked into the room the day before.

Max von Schumann tried to use his authority as an army officer to get the Gestapo agents to tell him what was happening. Ludovica tried to get her husband to come back into the room.

"Mind your own business, Major," one of the Gestapo agents said dismissively.

"I order you to tell me what is going on here and why you are taking this woman..."

"You can't give us orders," the man replied.

A sardonic laugh drew Max's attention, and he turned round to see Major Ulrich Jürgens.

"Baroness." Jürgens made an exaggerated bow to Ludovica, who gave him a wide smile in return.

"What's happening, Jürgens?" Max asked the SS officer.

"As you can see, they are arresting this young woman. Am I

mistaken, or is this your good friend Amelia Garayoa's room? What a horrible coincidence, a criminal in your friend's room!"

Ludovica's face twisted and she stared daggers at Major Jürgens, who avoided looking at her.

Max shot a hate-filled glance at Jürgens but did not waste his time, knowing that this woman was the only person who could tell him where Amelia was.

"Who are you?" he asked Grazyna.

"You do not have the authority to question the detainee," Major Jürgens interrupted.

"You cannot give me orders! How dare you!"

"They've arrested her! They've arrested Amelia! I was waiting for her here! They've arrested her!" Grazyna shouted.

"But why? Who are you?"

"I work in the hospital... I knew Amelia... she... she..."

She couldn't say anything else. The Gestapo agents hit her and began to drag her down the stairs. When Max started to go after them, Ludovica grabbed him by the arm.

"Max, please, don't do anything foolish!"

"You are right as always, Baroness, your husband seems to need someone to counsel prudence, or else... Well, you know what might happen... You have some very dangerous friends, Baron von Schumann... friends who could be extremely inconvenient to you."

"Don't threaten me, Jürgens," Max von Schumann warned the Nazi.

"Threaten you? I wouldn't dare? Who would threaten a Wehrmacht officer, and an aristocrat to boot?" Jürgens laughed.

"Don't be impertinent!" Ludovica said.

"I'm sorry, Baroness, you know that nothing could have been further from my intentions than to be impertinent, friends do not stand in the way of their friends."

"You are not our friend, Jürgens," Max snapped.

"I am the baroness's devoted servant," Jürgens said, looking at Ludovica.

The baroness took hold of Max's arm and forced him to come back into the room. The guests from the neighboring rooms carried on observing the scene with curiosity, and she had a horror of becoming the subject of gossip among these people she so disdained.

"I'm going out, Ludovica," Max said as soon as the door had closed. "I need to find out what has happened to Amelia."

"I forgot to tell you that I saw her in reception a couple of days ago. It was a surprise to see her here, and with such a strapping young fellow, too," Ludovica lied. "I wouldn't worry about her if I were you."

"Didn't you hear what that woman said?"

"Good Lord, Max, we have no idea who that woman is! And if she's a criminal who was in Amelia's room, then it's not safe for us to go snooping around trying to find out. We don't know that much about the Spanish woman, either. She came to Berlin with that American journalist... A woman like that... well... I don't think we should get involved in her problems."

But Max did not seem to hear what Ludovica said. He walked round and round the room, resolved to try to find Amelia. Who was the girl who had been arrested? Maybe she was the new friend that Amelia had mentioned a couple of times... But what had she done? Why had she been arrested?

"Max, in my condition, surprises and annoyances are not a good idea." Ludovica had taken Max's hand and placed it on her stomach. "Can't you feel our son? You have a responsibility, Max, a responsibility to me, and to our son, and to your family name..."

Max suddenly realized that what had seemed entirely natural up to that point was in fact carefully planned: Ludovica had gotten pregnant before they sent him to Warsaw; she had tried to get pregnant because she was scared of losing him, and had come all this way to find him to make him behave like the man he was, a von Schumann, an aristocrat, an army officer who could not leave his marriage without dishonoring his family name.

But Ludovica must have known that Amelia was in Warsaw, that she had traveled with him.

He had come back from the front two days ago, and had dreamed of seeing Amelia again, but he had been surprised to run into Ludovica, and however much he asked about her in reception, no one seemed to be able to tell him anything about Amelia.

Ludovica had been very affectionate, and Max had been moved to think about the possibility of having a son; a son who would continue the family traditions, who would wear the von Schumann family name with pride. But he also felt remorse, because the fact of this child was a betrayal of Amelia.

He had no doubt at all that Amelia was in danger and that Major Ulrich Jürgens knew something about it. But did Ludovica know about it too? He had been surprised by the familiarity between his wife and the SS major.

"I am sorry, my dear, but I am going to look for Amelia, wherever she may be."

"Don't do it, Max, don't do it, you don't have the right to compromise me."

"What do you mean?"

"Do you think that it's a secret here in Warsaw that you have a lover? How long do you think it took for me to find out that this room was connected to one belonging to a young Spanish woman named Amelia Garayoa?" she said. Then she carried on, a little more calmly: "We are going to have a son, Max, and our obligation is that he can carry the family name with pride. Your name, Max, he will be a von Schumann, but my name as well, he will also be a von Waldheim. Our son will be the synthesis of all that is best about our race. Are you going to spoil his future by running off after that Spanish adventuress? How much humiliation do you think I can bear? I have kept quiet about things, even in the face of some fairly obvious proof, I didn't want to see what others saw only too clearly. And do you know why I have done it, Max? For us to be who we are, to fulfill that sacred vow that you and I made before the altar, that sacred vow which our parents made before us. We cannot run away from who we are, Max, we cannot."

"I am going to look for Amelia. I am sorry, Ludovica."

"Max!"

He left the room without knowing very well where he should go, fearing that Amelia would be in the hands of the Gestapo, like that girl who had been arrested. But why? What had Amelia done while he'd been away at the front?

Suddenly he remembered his lover's connection to the British, and wondered if that might be the cause of her arrest. But then he immediately told himself that he was being silly, that Amelia could not be an agent, that she had only been a messenger for the British because of her relationship with that American journalist, Albert James, nephew to Lord Paul James, of the Admiralty.

He went to the General Staff office without knowing very well whom to ask for help, someone who would have enough authority with the Einsatzgruppen, with the Gestapo, with the SS, with whomever it was who had Amelia.

He sought out his adjutant, the quartermaster captain Hans Henke, because he needed to speak with someone.

"You know General von Tresckow," Captain Henke reminded him.

"Do you think the general will be able to do anything?"

"Perhaps..."

"Get me in touch with his adjutant... I could try, at least."

"There's also Hans Oster, or even Canaris, maybe they can do more."

"Yes... yes... you're right, I've got a friend who works with Oster, the Abwehr has ears and eyes everywhere... I'll speak to him. I'll speak to Hitler himself if I have to."

They tortured Grazyna for several days, even more cruelly than they had tortured Amelia. They suspected that it was she who had run the Resistance group, and they needed to know what operations were under her control. Some of the group's members had also been arrested, including Grazyna's cousin Ewa and Tomasz: They had said that they were only trying to help some friends in the ghetto, but the Gestapo did not believe them.

The operation against this group had begun with a careless action on the part of the hospital director's secretary. She was the lover of a German soldier, and had once unwittingly let slip that her boss suspected that someone was stealing medicine from the hospital; but however much the director questioned Sister Maria, the nun in charge of the dispensary, they couldn't find out who was responsible for the thefts. Sister Maria told the director that she knew nothing, but it was clear that the nun was conniving with someone.

The hospital director had informed the police and they had set up a discreet and efficient watch over Sister Maria, who had not suspected that the new porter she had hired was in fact a police officer. He seemed a nice man, always ready to work more than his contracted number of hours.

It wasn't hard for him to hear conversations between Sister Maria and Grazyna, and he came to the conclusion that she must be taking the medicine with Sister Maria's tacit approval.

The police organized an operation to have Grazyna followed night and day, and with patience they uncovered most of the members of the network. They knew that the group was plotting something important, and decided to arrest Sister Maria, crediting her with greater involvement in the crimes than she in fact had. They arrested her on Saturday, after Grazyna had left the hospital so as not to make her suspicious, and tortured the nun cruelly, but she could tell them nothing because she knew nothing. When Grazyna came back to the hospital on Monday, they told her that Sister Maria was sick, and she believed this until a couple of days later a sympathetic nurse murmured to her that Sister Maria had in fact been arrested. Grazyna had decided to flee and tell the other members of the network, because that night they had planned to take weapons to the ghetto.

Max von Schumann found out about all this thanks to a contact given to him by his friend, who worked with Hans Oster, Canaris's adjutant. This contact, Karl Kleist by name, worked in the communications office and no one suspected that he was anything other than a good Nazi, even though he hated Hitler and all he stood for.

Thanks to his friends' efforts, Max managed to get Amelia out of the clutches of the Gestapo, but he could not have her freed, and she was transferred to Pawiak, a prison with both male and female detainees.

Max tried to see her, but unsuccessfully; SS Major Ulrich Jürgens had made sure that she was registered as a dangerous prisoner, and she was put in isolation, as was Grazyna.

In spite of this, Max kept on petitioning his friends in the High Command, continuously asking them about Amelia. What he did not know was that his wife Ludovica was using her connections to stop her husband from getting to her rival.

A few days after all this happened, Max received the order to return to the front. It came as a relief for Ludovica that he was leaving Warsaw.

"I will wait for you in Berlin, I have to prepare for the birth of our son. We haven't yet thought about what name we're going to give him, although I have some suggestions. Of course, I pray that he will be a son, I am sure of it, and I would then call him Friedrich, like your father; if it is a girl, I would call her Irene, like my mother."

Perhaps if Ludovica had not been pregnant, Max would have left her forever, but in spite of the aversion he felt toward her, he could not help but be pleased at the idea of having a son, a legitimate son to carry on his name.

Karl Kleist, the officer who worked with Colonel Oster, told Max that he would do whatever it took to get information about Amelia.

It was a relief for Amelia to be in prison. At least there she would not be systematically tortured, as she had been at the hands of the Gestapo.

The women's section was called "Serbia." She shared a damp and flea-ridden cell with several other women, some of them murderers. Women who looked forward to their final end with resignation. One had killed her husband with a kitchen knife, sick of being beaten. Another had been a prostitute and had killed a client to rob him. The youngest of them all said that she had never killed anyone, that she had been arrested by mistake. And then there were the political prisoners: ten women whose only crime was to have not been Nazis.

They were crammed into the cell, but that was the least of their problems. A few days after arriving in Serbia, Amelia started to feel stinging bites all over her body, and couldn't stop scratching her head. One of the prisoners said, indifferently:

"You've got lice, but you'll get used to them. I don't know which is worse, the lice or the fleas. What do you think?"

When Amelia arrived at the prison she was scarcely able to move. The torturers had left marks all over her body, and she was very weak and had been given hardly anything to eat or drink. It was weeks before she was able to talk to these women, who treated her with a mixture of curiosity and indifference.

One day, after she had fainted, they sent her to the prison infirmary. When she came to her senses she overheard a conversation between the nurse and the doctor who were looking after her. Her ears pricked up at the name Garayoa.

"Why did this Spanish girl get into so much trouble? At least she's still alive, I suppose, they hanged the other one, Grazyna, a few days ago," the doctor said.

"They'll kill this one too, the death sentence will be passed down any day now," the nurse replied.

"They say she was the lover of an officer and that he's moving heaven and earth to save her life, even though she's got pneumonia and probably won't survive anyway," the doctor replied.

Amelia felt happy to know that Max had not abandoned her, that he was fighting for her life.

Little by little she recovered and adjusted to prison life. There were times when the prisoners were allowed out to walk around the yard, but they spent most of their time locked in their cells. She heard nothing from Max, but knew that she was alive thanks to him. They took someone away to be executed nearly every day. The condemned women would divide their meager possessions among the remaining prisoners before being taken away to the courtyard to be hanged.

As Amelia had been very sick when she was brought to the prison, it took some time before she was allowed out of her cell, which meant that at first she did not encounter Ewa, Grazyna's cousin.

They saw each other the first time Amelia was able to walk by herself to the room that served as their dining hall. She didn't recognize Ewa at first: They had cut her beautiful chestnut hair, and her blue eyes had darkened, and she walked with a limp.

"Ewa!"

"Good God, Amelia, you're alive!"

They approached each other to embrace, but a guard hit them with a rubber truncheon.

"Stop it! None of that filth here!"

The two young women looked at each other fearfully, and held back from hugging each other, but at least no one stopped them from sitting next to each other at one of the tables where they were put to eat lumps of potato bobbing in a blackish liquid.

"What happened to Tomasz? And Piotr?" Amelia asked.

"They hanged Tomasz," Amelia replied with a grimace of pain.

"Grazyna... I heard that Grazyna... ," Amelia didn't dare repeat what she had heard the doctor and the nurse say.

"They hanged her too, yes," Ewa said.

"And Sister Maria?" Amelia asked.

"She couldn't cope with the torture and the mistreatment," Ewa said, lowering her voice because the guard had not taken her eyes off them.

"Poor thing... and you?"

"I don't know how I'm still alive. I fainted every time they hit me... They did so many things to me... Have you seen my leg? They broke it in one of the interrogation sessions and it didn't set properly... But I'm still alive. My parents spoke to some friends of theirs who are in well with the Germans, they sell them meat. I have been condemned to death and they went all the way to the Führer to ask for mercy, and I'm waiting for the answer from Berlin," Ewa said.

"I think that I'm alive thanks to Max," Amelia admitted.

"Your German lover?"

"Yes."

"I'm sure I will be saved," Ewa said.

"I hope so," Amelia replied.

It was not easy for them to be together, because the guards tried to separate them, but still they found moments when they could speak. The guards were too busy mistreating the political prisoners and attempting to impose a little order on the overcrowded area, so crammed that the women prisoners scarcely had room to stand up and walk a few paces.

"No plotting!" they said and hit them with rubber truncheons to make them sit far away from each other.

One morning Ewa and Amelia met in the yard. It was cold, it had rained all night, and the sky was a terrible color. The women shivered because they had very little clothing to cover themselves with, but they preferred to be cold rather than give up these moments of fresh air.

Ewa came up to Amelia. She seemed happy.

"Piotr is here," she whispered.

"Where?"

"Here, in Pawiak."

"How do you know?"

"They've just moved a woman to my cell. She's called Justyna. She's been in Section VIII, they took her there when they arrested her. Apparently some women are put in cells with men there. She saw Piotr, she told me that they went out for a while some years ago; she is a Communist, and Piotr was once as well, but he left the party, it seems."

"I didn't know that Piotr was a Communist..."

"Neither did I, I think Grazyna didn't either. This woman, Justyna, says that Piotr left the party because of a falling-out with one of the bosses, but that this was a while ago. Piotr asked her to look for me or Grazyna, and if she found us she was to tell us that he was alright, and that some of the group managed to get away, but he didn't say who. He has also been condemned to death. Apparently Countess Lublin has been to visit him a couple of times, and has brought clothes and food."

"How can we let him know that we're here?" Amelia asked.

"We can't, I can't think of a way..."

"Well, we'll see him the day they hang us together."

"Don't say that, Amelia! I know that it's difficult to get out of here, but I don't want to lose hope, I... I'm a believer, and I pray to God that he won't abandon me, that he won't let them hang me."

"I pray as well, Ewa, but I don't know if I believe in God."

"What things you say! Of course you believe in God! We need Him now more than ever!"

"We need Him, but does He need us?"

Ewa's faith helped her to put up with all the suffering that she was subjected to in Pawiak prison. Amelia, for her part, put her trust in Max von Schumann's ability to get her out of there.

To be close to each other was a help for Amelia and for Ewa. They had barely got to know each other during the time that they had secretly been going to the ghetto, because Grazyna had not encouraged personal relations. Amelia thought that Ewa was a wonderful person, full of good intentions, but that if she went to the ghetto, it was because she was following her cousin. She had not had the time to judge Ewa on her own merits, and it wasn't until they met in Pawiak prison that Amelia discovered the moral heights of this young cake-maker. Whenever it was possible they met and exchanged confidences and desires. Amelia did not let herself plan for the future, but Ewa did not stop dreaming about what she would do when she left Pawiak.

"We have to put the group back together and carry on Grazyna's fight. We cannot give in. I think about the children all the time, I'm sure that they're missing my sweets."

Months went by without Amelia hearing anything from Max. Not a single letter. Not a message. Nothing. She had been taken back to the infirmary on a couple of occasions. They gave her very little to eat. She suffered from anemia, and her cough was very bad, and she fainted regularly. At first her cellmates had called the guards to let them known that the Spanish girl had fainted again, but they soon stopped doing that. Before taking her to the infirmary, the guards would insult her and kick her.

"Get up, lazybones! Stop pretending to sleep! I'll give you something to wake you up! Here's a present for the fine lady!"

When she came to, her mouth tasted of blood. The guards liked very much kicking her in the face, it was as if they could not stand her beauty.

On more than one night, Amelia was woken by the shouts of the other prisoners.

"What's going on?" she would ask her cellmates.

"Apparently there have been some new death sentences passed down. Who knows, it might be our turn tomorrow."

Amelia sat up and pressed her head against the stone wall of the cell, murmuring a prayer that it would not be her door that would be opened. She heard footsteps coming and going, the screams of women being dragged to the courtyard, the cries of others, begging to be put in touch with their families, even as they knew it was impossible. Some women walked in silence, with their heads held high, trying to maintain their dignity in what they knew to be the last minutes of their life.

They executed dozens of prisoners every day in Smocza Street, alongside Pawiak. Men, women, adolescents... the Nazis didn't care. The orders came to the prison and were carried out immediately; this hubbub, these footsteps, screams and whispers... All of it affected the listener so much that eventually all they wanted was for this begging to end as soon as possible.

It was not until the end of May 1942 that Karl Kleist told Max von Schumann, who had become a colonel by that time, that all the efforts he was making on behalf of Amelia were about to bear fruit.

"I cannot guarantee you anything yet, but Oster's people are about to free Fräulein Garayoa. It might only be a matter of days."

"Thank God! I'll always be in your debt, and that of Hans Oster and Admiral Canaris," Max said.

"We are all in debt to Germany," Karl Kleist replied.

There were still a couple of months to go until Amelia was to be freed. In the meantime, Max got permission to go to Berlin on leave: Ludovica had given birth to a boy three months ago.

To hold his baby son in his arms moved Max more than he would be prepared to admit.

Ludovica was resting, as if it had been a magnificent feat to give birth. She allowed herself to be spoiled by her family and her husband's family, and could feel her influence in the family increasing after having managed to prolong the von Schumann lineage.

"Friedrich is beautiful, a pure Aryan," Ludovica said to Max.

The baroness was reclining on a chaise longue next to the window, and was observing her husband's emotions at handling the little pink-skinned baby with a touch of malice.

"Yes, he is beautiful," Max agreed.

"Your aunts say he looks like you, and they're right. I'm so happy you're here. We will baptize our child in the style he deserves. We will have a huge party and invite Hitler, and Goebbels, and all our good friends."

"We are at war, Amelia, and I don't think we should make unnecessary shows. People are suffering, they're losing their sons, their husbands, their brothers. We will baptize Friedrich, but we will only invite our closest family and friends."

"Well, that shouldn't stop us from inviting the Führer; I know he holds me in special affection, you can't imagine how he looks at me whenever we meet. We could even ask him to be Friedrich's godfather..."

"Never! No, I will not allow that. My son will not have that... that madman for a godfather."

"Max! How dare you!"

"That's enough, Ludovica! I am not going to argue about this. Forget about this... this insane idea. Don't make me forbid you. My older sister will be Friedrich's godmother, and the godfather can be one of your brothers."

"But Max, you can't prevent me from organizing a proper baptism for our son!"

"Friedrich will have the baptism he deserves, with his family and no one else."

Ludovica did not insist. She knew that Friedrich was the cause that had prevented Max from leaving her, but she knew him too well, and was aware that if she pressured him, then he would just leave again.

"Alright, my darling, we'll do as you wish. And now sit down next to me, I've got a lot of things to tell you."

Max took advantage of his stay in Berlin to meet up again with his friends who were part of the resistance to the regime. Professor Schatzhauser was more pessimistic than ever, and was surprised that Max should ask after Amelia.

"She's in Pawiak prison, in Warsaw. She was arrested by the Gestapo."

"Poor thing! We had heard rumors..."

"I'm doing everything I can to get her out of there."

"Yes, we'd heard about that as well. Be careful, Max, you have enemies."

"I know, Professor."

"Albert James, the American journalist, was in Berlin. He called me and came to see me; he asked after Amelia."

"Well, you know that Amelia and Albert... They had a close relationship."

"I told him the truth, that she had gone with you to Warsaw and that we hadn't heard anything else about her, but that I thought she was probably alright."

Max didn't say anything. He was upset that the professor should have mentioned Amelia's former lover. He didn't blame him for anything, it was just that, although he didn't care to admit it, he was jealous.

"Tell me about how things are here, if there's any news about our group."

"There aren't very many of us, Max, and we are badly organized," the doctor complained.

"Our problem," Manfred Kasten, the former diplomat, added, "is that those of us who are opposed to the Reich are not able to unite our forces. The Communists do their thing, the Socialists do theirs, us Christians don't agree on anything, and the army doesn't realize that there is this great body of people willing them to do something."

"I'm not so sure about that," Max said. "Also, it's not that easy, it's not even the case that those of us who are opposed to the regime can agree about what the best thing to do is."

"Everything would be easier if the head of the Reich were to be removed," Professor Schatzhauser insisted.

"The Führer insists that the army swear loyalty to him, and lots of soldiers feel bound by that oath," Max said.

"You too?" Manfred Kasten asked.

"The army should be loyal to Germany," Professor Schatzhauser said, without giving Max time to answer.

"Some of my friends have been arrested," Pastor Ludwig Schmidt said. "The Gestapo arrests people and they disappear forever."

"And you, Max, what do you think we should do?" Helga Kasten asked.

Max von Schumann had no answer to that question. All he could do was repeat that there were officers in the heart of the army who felt as he did, that something had to be done about Hitler and some of his brothers-in-arms had even said that the Third Reich would never fall if Hitler did not fall first, but had not said any more than that.

Four days before his return to the front, Max and Ludovica baptized Friedrich in a ceremony that was attended only by the immediate family. Ludovica had given in to her husband's insistence, but was planning another celebration for when her husband returned to the front. She had decided to gather together her friends in the Nazi High Command to celebrate Friedrich's birth and baptism.

Max had his own plans. He had arranged to pass through Warsaw before heading back to the Russian front. Karl Kleist, the officer who worked with Colonel Oster, had told him that Amelia was about to be set free and he wanted to be there when she was released, or at least he wanted to see her in Pawiak and explain what his plans were for when she would be set free.

What he did not know was that Amelia was ill. She coughed blood and was still suffering from anemia.

But the worst that Amelia had to face was not her fever, or the fleas that tormented her body, or the lice that made their homes in her shorn hair. The worst for Amelia was having to survive Ewa's execution.

"Did you know that my parents came to see me?" Ewa said one morning while they were in the yard, breathing whatever fresh air it was that managed to get into the prison.

"Have you seen them?" Amelia asked.

"No, they haven't let me see them, but I know that they were here because one of my cellmates told me; they use her to clean the commandant's office every now and then. She's a good woman and I trust her. You know, I think that they were bringing good news, I'm sure that I'm about to be pardoned. I've got a feeling."

Ewa smiled happily, convinced of her good luck, and only frowned when she thought that this would mean she would have to leave Amelia behind her, still immured in Pawiak.

"When I leave, I promise I will find Max wherever he may be and make him do whatever it takes to get you out. Trust me."

"If it had not been for you, then I don't know how I would have endured so long..."

"But you are so much stronger than I am! And you have a son to live for. I will go to Spain with you one day."

"Spain... my son... If I could only turn back time! I'm the only one to blame for what's happened to me, and sometimes I think that I'm here because I need to pay for all the bad things I've done to the people who love me: my son, my parents, my sister, my husband, my uncle and my aunt and my cousins, I've let them all down..."

"Don't blame yourself, Amelia, You'll get out of here and you'll be able to go back to Spain and sort things out."

"I can't bring my parents back to life."

"You're not guilty of their deaths. They were victims of your civil war."

"But I was not with them. I wasn't there when they shot my father, and I wasn't at my mother's bedside when she lay dying. I am not looking after my sick sister now. I have always left my responsibilities in the hands of others, and now I'm leaving my sister in the hands of my aunt and uncle and my cousin Laura. And my son... I can't feel sorry for myself for having become a stranger to my own little Javier. I abandoned him, and not a day goes past when I don't regret having done so."

"We will get out of here, you'll see, and it will be very soon, trust me. I feel that my freedom is getting very close."

That afternoon, like all afternoons, they were in their cells and heard the footsteps of the guards. They were going to read out the names of the condemned, who would be hanged at dawn.

Amelia had a temperature and could barely pay attention, so it took her a few seconds for her to realize what had happened, and to ask herself if it were really true.

"They're going to hang that friend of yours. They've just read out her name. Poor kid," one of her cellmates whispered in her ear.

Amelia's scream could be heard all along the damp corridor that led to the cells. But then it was lost among the weeping and wailing of all the people whose executions had been announced for the next day. It was the same noise as every day, but today Amelia found it unbearable.

One of the guards came into the cell and hit her with a stick to make her shut up.

"Shut your mouth, you foreign piece of shit! I hope that the order comes for you to get hanged soon, so we won't spend any more money on feeding you. Ungrateful bitch!"

Amelia felt so much pain inside that she hardly realized that one of the blows had broken her left wrist.

"I want to see her! I want to see her!" Amelia begged, grabbing onto the guard's skirt as the woman kept on beating her without pity.

"No, you won't see your bitch friend who's going to get what she deserves for being a traitor. She's a disgusting friend of the Jews, just like you. Pigs! You're all pigs!" the guard screamed as she carried on beating her.

It was dawn when the guards came to the cells to take away the condemned women. Some of them cried and begged, others kept silent and tried to focus on these few minutes of life remaining to them, minutes when they could only bid themselves farewell.

Helped by two other prisoners, Amelia managed to position herself in front of the little window that gave onto the corridor down which the condemned women were to walk. She saw Ewa hobbling along, with a serene look in her eyes, telling the beads of a rosary that she had made herself out of scraps of her petticoat. She was finding strength through prayer, and she smiled at Amelia as she came past her cell door.

"You'll get out of here, just you see, pray for me, I'll look after you when I'm in heaven."

The guard gave Ewa a violent push.

"Shut up, you hypocritical bitch, and walk! Your friend will be with you soon enough! They'll hang her too!"

Amelia tried to say something to Ewa, but she could not. Her eyes were flooded with tears and she could not find it in herself to say a single word.

Then she was overcome with despair and refused to eat the blackish bug-ridden soup that was all that kept them alive.

She hovered between life and death for several days. She had given up, and did not want to struggle anymore.

That was how Max found her when he went to look for her in Pawiak. He had arrived in Warsaw the same day, and was with his adjutant, Hans Henke, who had been promoted to the rank of major, and he also had Karl Kleist's guarantee that all the necessary papers had been signed for Amelia's release.

He went straight to Pawiak, where they did not seem all that impressed that a colonel in the army was so worried about this prisoner whom they had been ordered to release.

The prison commandant seemed slightly grumpy, and he told Max to stay in his office while they sent down to have the prisoner brought up from the cells.

"You can take her, but I'd be careful if I were you, she's got something wrong with her lungs and who knows what you might catch. I'd stay away from her if I were you."

Max could scarcely contain himself. He felt an instinctive dislike for this man, and was only keen to leave the prison as soon as possible, taking Amelia with him.

When he saw her he could not hold back a cry of pain.

"My God, what have they done to you!"

It was hard for him to recognize Amelia in that famished figure who could barely stand upright, with her hair cut so short that her scalp was visible, dressed in dirty rags, her gaze lost in the distance.

Max and Hans Henke took hold of Amelia, and once all the papers had been signed they led her out of Pawiak.

The two men were shocked and scarcely dared speak to the woman.

"Let's go to the hotel, I'll examine her there," Max said to his adjutant.

"I think we should take her to a hospital; I'm not a doctor like you, but I think that she's very ill."

"She is, she is, but I would prefer to take her to the hotel, and decide what to do once I've had a look at her myself: I don't want to put her into other people's hands."

Major Henke didn't insist. He knew his superior's stubbornness, and had seen him doing whatever was necessary over the course of the last year to ensure the young Spaniard's release. Henke wondered if the woman would one day regain at least a part of what had been her striking beauty.

When they reached the hotel, there was a certain amount of commotion at the sight of two Wehrmacht officers carrying between them what appeared to be a beaten-up tramp. The hotel manager, leaving the hotel with a group of officers, came up to them.

"Colonel von Schumann... this woman... well... I don't know how to say it, but I don't think that it is right for you to bring her into the hotel. If you want, I can tell you where to take her."

"Fräulein Garayoa will stay in my room," Max replied.

The manager quailed before the angry gaze of the aristocratic soldier who carried the beggar-woman in his arms.

"Of course, of course..."

"Send a maid up to the room," Max ordered.

When they reached his room, Max asked his assistant to run a bath.

"The first thing to do is to clean her and get rid of the parasites, then I will examine her. I think that one of her hands might have some broken bones, I'll need you to go the hospital and bring me everything you can to bandage it. But first of all, I would be grateful if you could go to the closest shop and buy some clothes for Amelia."

The maid arrived and seemed repulsed at first when Max asked her to help him bathe Amelia.

"I'll pay you a month's salary."

"Of course, sir," the woman accepted, managing to banish her scruples.

Amelia's eyes were closed. She hardly had the strength to speak or to move. She thought that she could hear Max's voice, but she told herself that it must be a dream, one of those dreams in which her loved ones visited her: her son Javier, her parents, her cousin Laura, her sister Antonietta... Yes, it had to be a dream. She didn't seem to realize that she was being put in a bath, or that they were rubbing her head so hard, her head hurt a lot, and she didn't even realize that Max and the maid were taking her out of the bath and wrapping her in a towel. Then they dressed her in one of Max's pajamas, which was so large on her that she lost herself in it.

"Thank you for your help," Max told the maid.

"At your service, sir," she replied, as she grasped the money the soldier had given her.

Max listened to Amelia's lungs and heart, took her temperature, and examined her whole body, looking at the traces of the torture she had suffered. He found it difficult to hold back his tears and his rage to see the woman he loved in such a state.

"She's got tuberculosis," he muttered to himself.

When Hans Henke came back with several shopping bags, he found Amelia asleep. Max had made her drink a cup of milk and take a sedative.

"I've bought some things, I hope they're suitable, it's the first time I've bought clothes for a woman. Truth be told, I've never even gone shopping with my wife.

"Thank you, Major, I'm very grateful."

"Come on, Colonel, you don't have to thank me! You know how highly I think of you and that I share your fears for Germany. As far as Fräulein Garayoa is concerned, I've always liked her and I am sorry to see what they've done to her."

"She has tuberculosis."

"In that case, she should go to a hospital straight away, where they can look after her properly."

"No, I don't want to leave her alone in a hospital, without any friends, without people to look after her. Who knows what might happen to her."

"But we have to get back to Russia..."

"Yes, but I think I can get a few more days' leave. You go back to the front, and I will follow you as soon as I can."

"And if they don't give you permission?"

"I'll think of something. Now, please go to the hospital and bring me everything that there is written on this list. I'll need it all to help her get well."

It took Amelia two days to awaken from the lethargy that had stolen over her, and when she did so she was surprised to see that Max was actually there.

"How are you feeling?" he asked her, holding her by the hand.

"So... it's true... It is you..."

"Who did you think it would be?" he said, laughing.

"I thought I was dreaming."

Max insisted that she rest, but Amelia paid him no attention because she needed to talk, to recover a part of what had been her life. They spoke for hours.

"You haven't asked me if I'm guilty," she said.

"Guilty? What would you be guilty of?"

"They arrested me, they accused me of conspiracy against the Reich, of helping the Jews..."

"Well, I hope that's all true," he replied, laughing.

"I didn't tell you so as not to implicate you, but Grazyna... well... She was helping the Jews, we went to the ghetto to take them food, and some other things."

"Don't blame yourself, Amelia, you did well."

"But... I have to tell you about it."

"Tell me everything when you are better, you need to rest now."

"I want to talk, I need to talk, you don't know how much I've missed you. I thought I would never see you again, I'd never see you, or... or my son, or my family. Pawiak is hell, Max, it's hell."

Three days later, Max told Amelia that he had obtained a safe-conduct pass for her to travel to Lisbon, and from there to Spain.

"You are still ill, but it's a risk we need to take. I have to go to the front, they won't let me spend more time in Warsaw and you are not safe here. Do you think you'd be able to look after yourself? I'll give you the medicine you need to take."

"So, once again, we go our separate ways," she said.

"It makes me very sad. But I am a soldier as well as a doctor, and I need to obey orders. My friends have managed to get me a few days in Warsaw, but they can't cover for me much longer."

"I know, and I shouldn't complain. You have done so much for me! Yes, I will go to Spain, I wouldn't want to go anywhere else. Maybe they will let me see my son. I haven't heard anything from my family in so long, they must think that I'm dead."

"Don't say that! Of course you will see your son and... Well, I have to tell you something that will upset you."

Amelia looked at Max in fear. She was afraid of what he might say.

"I've had a son. Ludovica has given me a son and heir."

"I know, Max, your wife told me that she was pregnant. I didn't know that you and Ludovica still... I thought that..."

"I didn't lie to you. Everything had been finished between Ludovica and me a long time before. You weren't there, Amelia, and I didn't know what was going to happen with us. You were with Albert James at the time, or at least that's what I thought. She asked me to give our marriage another chance and I... I didn't refuse. I have a son, his name is Friedrich, and I love him, Amelia, I love him like you love your own son. I cannot not love him. He is a part of me, the best part of me."

A tense silence fell, and Amelia felt her eyes filling with tears. She did not have any right to blame him for anything he had done, but she felt wounded.

"I cannot ask forgiveness for Friedrich," the baron said.

"It hurts, Max, of course it hurts, but I have no right to scold you. You have never betrayed me, I always knew that Ludovica was there and that your sense of honor would stop you from separating from her. I also knew, even though you never told me anything, that you were keen to have a son who would carry on your line, and I knew that this was something

I could never give you, as I am married. But it hurts, Max, of course it hurts."

He took her in his arms and saw how she was trembling and fighting back sobs. She felt more fragile than ever because of her extreme thinness, but he did not want to lie to her and tell her that he would have preferred Friedrich not to exist, because that was not true. He felt proud of that tiny child whom he longed to hold in his arms.

He loved Amelia, but he also loved Friedrich and did not want to give up either of them.

It was not easy for them to separate once again. Max took Amelia to the airport. She could barely stand upright. She was very weak.

They said goodbye without knowing when they would see each other again, but promising that they would not let anything separate them.

"If you cannot get in touch with me directly, try my adjutant, Major Henke."

"You've both been promoted, you're a colonel now and he's a major..."

"War is like that, Amelia. But listen to me, if you can't get in touch with Major Henke, then try Professor Schatzhauser, and he will know where I am."

It was hard for Amelia to keep from crying as she climbed on board the airplane, and she turned back several times to wave to Max, who was having a difficult time hiding his emotions as well.

Many hours later, after a long pause in Berlin, Amelia was looking out of the window trying to discern the contours of Lisbon.

She was keen to touch down on Portuguese soil, as that would be the prelude to her return home. She didn't intend to spend any longer in the city than was absolutely necessary. First she would go to the Hotel Oriente. That was where her contacts in British intelligence had sent her the last time she was in Lisbon. In London they must be asking what had happened to her after so many months of silence. Perhaps they had given her up for dead.

The Hotel Oriente seemed to be finding times hard. Its owner, the Englishman John Brown, recognized her as soon as he saw her.

"Goodness, it's Miss Garayoa! I wasn't expecting to see you here... You don't look very well. Shall I give you your usual room, would that be alright?"

Without giving her time to reply, he started to call for his wife, Doña Mencia.

"Mencia, Mencia! Where are you? We have a guest."

"I'm not going to stay, Mr. Brown, I just want to know if I can get in touch with some of your friends..."

"You want to speak to some of my compatriots."

"Can you arrange it?"

"Yes, of course, but in the meantime, why not go up to the room and rest, I'm sorry to insist, but you really don't look that well. Mencia will bring you something to eat."

"I want to go to Spain as soon as possible, on the first train."

"In that case you will have to wait until tomorrow morning. Don't worry, I'll get you a ticket."

Mencia knocked gently on the door to Amelia's room.

"How you've changed!" Mencia said when she recognized Amelia.

"I'm pleased to see you," Amelia said, taking no notice of Mencia's comment.

"My husband said that you looked like a ghost, and he was right. You're all skin and bone! Where have you been? You look terrible."

"These are hard times for us all."

"Yes, they are, and I'm scared that one day they'll come for my husband, there are too many eyes and ears watching everything that happens, and what with him being English... Of course, I'm Portuguese and that means I'm safe, or at least that's what I'd like to believe. What do you need? I think I'll bring you some food. Some salt cod? It's very good to help you get your strength up."

"No, Mencia, I'm not hungry."

"If you change your mind, call me. My husband has told me to tell you not to leave the room and to rest, and that someone will come to see you in a little while. I think I can guess who... but it's better not to say anything."

Amelia fell into bed and fell fast asleep. A little while later she was awakened by some knocks on the door. When she opened it, she saw John Brown accompanied by an arrogant-looking man who surveyed her sullenly.

"Miss Garayoa, here is a friend of mine. I'll leave you alone to talk together. If you need anything I'll send Mencia."

"Where have you come from?" the man asked without any preambles.

"Pawiak."

"Pawiak?"

"Yes, it's a prison in Warsaw. They arrested me."

"And why did they let you go?"

"It's a long story. I think that the best thing would be for me to tell you what happened and for you to tell London. I'm going home tomorrow, I'm going to Madrid."

Over the course of an hour, Amelia told the man everything that had happened, from the day of her arrest to the day of her release, including Max von Schumann's role in the latter. The agent listened without taking his eyes off her, scrutinizing her unashamedly.

When Amelia had finished her story, neither of them spoke for a while. It was the man who broke the silence.

"You should stay here until you receive orders from London."

"No, I'm not going to do that. I want to go home, I need to be with my family. I cannot continue, at least not for the moment."

"Are you telling me that you're leaving the service?"

"I'm telling you that I have just come back from hell, and that I need to rest."

"We are at war, there is no time to rest."

"If you are not giving me any alternative, then tell Lord James that I am leaving the service."

The man stood up. He did not seem at all surprised by anything that Amelia had told him, or if he was then he did not show it. She was surprised that he had not offered her a single word of sympathy for what she had gone through. Amelia did not know that this man had lost his wife and his three children in the Luftwaffe's bombardment of London, and that he had no tears or pity left for anyone else.

"Well, Guillermo, that's your lot," Major Hurley said.

I sat bolt upright in my chair. His last words had jerked me back to the present day. I did not know how much time had passed since the major had started to tell me about this latest episode in my great-grandmother's life. I looked at my watch and saw to my surprise that it was midnight.

Lady Victoria smiled with delight to see how surprised I was. She had added a few observations to Major Hurley's narrative. Her husband Lord Richard was sitting in his chair, his head nodding and a glass of port in one hand. I had gotten so caught up in the story that I had forgotten where I was and who I was with.

Major Hurley's narrative had transported me all the way to Warsaw. In my mind I had seen Amelia Garayoa walking through the city, and had shared with her the suffering of the months she had spent in Pawiak.

"I wasn't expecting anything like that," I said, just for the sake of saying something.

"What were you not expecting?" Lady Victoria asked with interest.

"I don't know... so much suffering."

"You see, your great-grandmother's life was not an easy one," Lady Victoria replied.

"Well, she didn't try that hard to escape it." And as soon as I had let this phrase slip I regretted it. Who was I to judge Amelia?

"It's very late, and we've imposed too much upon the hospitality of our hosts," Major Hurley said, getting up in order to take his leave.

"Of course... of course... ," I replied.

"You have to get up early tomorrow morning, don't you, old chap?" Lord Richard asked.

"I need to be at the Centre for Military Archives at seven on the dot," Major Hurley replied.

While Lady Victoria and Lord Richard saw us to the door, I realized that Major Hurley had not given me any idea about what Amelia had done next.

"I know that it's asking a lot, but do you know what Amelia did next? Did she go to Madrid? Did she carry on working for you?"

"I'm not going to talk about that now... ," Major Hurley complained.

"Oh, my dear, you have to carry on helping Guillermo! I'm afraid there's still a lot more to tell," Lady Victoria said, addressing the major.

Major William Hurley accepted in theory the idea that we would see each other again in a few days. I did not insist, for fear of annoying him.

"I have lots of work to do, I can't spend my whole time looking for references to your great-grandmother in the archives. I think she went back to Spain for quite a long time... ," he said as he left.

6

I decided to go back to Spain the next day. If Amelia had gone back to Spain in July 1942, then I would find my answers from Edurne, or from Professor Soler. I could also ask Doña Laura for her help.

My mother hung up on me when I called her from Barajas airport.

"You're a disaster area, Guillermo, and I'm going to wash my hands of you, call me when you decide to stop behaving like an idiot."

I knew that her anger would dissipate by the third phone call.

My apartment was knee-deep in dust and smelled musty.

Among the letters waiting for me, I found several from the bank, reminding me that I had a mortgage to pay. I was spending almost the whole of my income on traveling, which meant that I would have to sort things out with my mother as soon as possible, or else really make up to Ruth so that she would give me shelter if they evicted me.

The day after my arrival I called Doña Laura and asked her if I could speak with Edurne.

"She gets very tired when she talks to you. Is it really necessary?"

"Yes, Doña Laura, it is. Well, I'll talk to Professor Soler first, and see if he can help me not to have to resort to Edurne. If he can, then I won't trouble her."

"How is your research coming along?" she asked me.

"Very well, but your cousin's life is really a treasure trove. If you'd like me to tell you what I've found out..."

"I've already said that we want a full investigation, that when you know everything you should write it down and bring it to us, but that you don't have to tell me anything until then. But hurry up, we're very old and we don't have much time."

"I am trying to find things out as quickly as possible, but things are getting more and more difficult..."

"Look, Guillermo, call me if you need to speak to Edurne. And while we're at it, tell me, do you need any more money?"

I paused. I didn't dare admit that I did. I thought I could hear a chuckle on the other end of the line.

"Of course, you don't live off thin air, and it costs money to be going backwards and forwards all the time. Maybe we didn't send you enough last time. I'll tell my niece Amelia to send you money today."

"How is your niece? And Doña Melita?"

"Good, good, we're all well. Don't waste any more time, now, get back to work. Remember that we're all very old..."

Professor Soler asked me to visit him in Barcelona.

"I'm writing a book and I haven't got all that much time to spare, but come along and I'll see what I can tell you. I think I remember that Amelia turned up out of the blue that summer, in 1942."

So there I was at the airport once again, ready to spend the day with the professor and firmly of a mind to go to my mother's house that evening, when I got back from Barcelona. I knew her very well, and I was sure that however angry she was with me, she wouldn't shut the door in my face.

Charlotte, Professor Soler's wife, told me as soon as she saw me that I shouldn't take up too much of his time.

"He's finishing a very important book and his editor is nervous because he's already delayed."

"I promise I won't take up too much time, but I cannot carry on with my research without your husband's help."

The professor had a cold and seemed tired, but he was in a good mood.

"Doña Laura called me last night to ask me to carry on helping you. She's worried about relying too much on Edurne, who's in pretty ill health, poor thing."

"My investigation into my great-grandmother's life would be impossible without your help. Major William Hurley from the army's archives has been very useful as well. If you only knew what he's been telling me... And there's more, I'm going back to London in a few days, you can't imagine what he's telling me..."

"I don't want to know anything, I've told you before. On several occasions. It is not my business to know what Amelia Garayoa did or didn't do."

"You're a historian, and I'm shocked that you don't have any curiosity about Amelia's life."

"Oh, Guillermo, you're so stubborn! I've told you that even if I do feel curiosity I'm not allowing it to develop. I don't have any right to get involved in the life of a woman and a family to whom I owe so much. If they had wanted me to investigate Amelia's life, then I would have, but they haven't, they've asked you, Amelia's great-grandson."

I didn't insist. I was a little annoyed by the professor's firmness and sense of honor. In his position, I would not have accepted being ignorant.

"Can you tell me what happened when Amelia came here in the summer of 1942?"

"Turn on the recorder."

When he saw her arrive dragging a suitcase, the doorman in her house didn't recognize her.

"Where are you going?" he asked.

"To Don Armando Garayoa's house, don't you recognize me? I'm Amelia."

"Señorita Amelia! How you've changed! You look so ill! I'm sorry, I didn't recognize you. Give me the suitcase, I'll take it up for you."

With the doorman carrying her luggage, Amelia rang the door

to her uncle and aunt's home. It was Edurne who opened the door. She did recognize her mistress.

"Amelia!" she cried out and hugged her tight.

In Edurne's arms, Amelia felt that she was home at last, and she broke into tears.

Edurne didn't want the porter to see more than he should, and so she thanked him and shut the door. Doña Elena and Antonietta had come out into the hallway when they heard Edurne's cries. The two sisters hugged each other, crying. Amelia was even thinner than Antonietta, she looked as if she might break in half. Or at least that is what Jesús and I thought when we saw her.

After hugging Antonietta, Amelia did the same to her cousins Laura and Jesús, she even embraced me and her aunt, Doña Elena.

"And Uncle? Where is my uncle?" she asked impatiently.

"Papa will be back later from work," Jesús said. "But he won't be long."

Doña Elena complained about the state Amelia was in.

"But where have you been! We were so worried about you... You are ill, I can see that. Don't deny it. You're so thin, you look so sick with those bags under your eyes..."

"Come on, Mama, leave her alone!" Laura entreated. "You're upsetting her. Cousin Amelia is tired and needs to rest, and then we'll see her back to normal."

But Laura knew that Amelia was not simply tired, and that rest would not be enough to get her back to normal.

"Tell us, tell us where you've been... We didn't hear anything about you and we were worried. Laura called Albert James and he said that you were traveling," Antonietta said.

"Have you spoken to Albert?" Amelia asked Laura with a slight tremble in her voice.

"Yes, but months ago. It wasn't easy. If it's difficult to get through to Burgos to speak to Melita, imagine what it must be like reaching London... Albert was very kind, but he didn't want to say where you were traveling or why, but he said that you were well. He said that you had been in New York... ," Laura explained.

"Yes, I was," Amelia replied.

"Is Albert no longer with you?" Doña Laura asked, not beating around the bush.

"He is not," Amelia whispered.

"Well, that's a shame, he was such a nice young man," her aunt replied.

"Please, Mama, don't get involved in Amelia's affairs!" Laura complained.

"Don't worry, I don't mind," Amelia said. "I know that she's only worried about me."

For the rest of the afternoon Amelia showed herself eager for news, she asked for all the details of what had happened since her last visit, and could not stop commenting on how well Antonietta looked and how tall Jesús and I had grown.

"We still don't know anything about Lola, or his father. His poor grandmother died," Doña Elena said.

"I'm sorry that your grandmother died, Pablo," Amelia said to me.

"But he is not alone, Pablo is a member of the family, we wouldn't be able to cope without him; and Jesús and he are like brothers," Laura said.

"All the women here are very bossy, it's good to have someone like Pablo here," Jesús said, laughing.

Amelia grew sad when she asked after her son Javier, and Laura said that Águeda had carried on allowing them to see him.

"Every now and then Edurne goes and waits outside the door of Santiago's house for Águeda to come out with the children and asks her when we can come and see Javier. Your son is beautiful and looks a lot like you, with the same blond hair, and he's thin like you are as well."

"Is he happy?" Amelia asked.

"Of course he is! You don't need to worry about that. Your husband... well, Santiago loves the child, and Águeda is very good to him as well. The child loves her too... I know that it hurts you to hear this, but it's better for him to love her, it means that she treats him well." Laura tried to calm Amelia's roiling emotions.

"I want to go and see him, maybe I could go today..."

"No, no, not today, you need to rest. Edurne will go tomorrow and ask Águeda, and she'll tell us if we can see him and when, and we'll go with you," Laura said, worried that her cousin would try to go right at that moment.

"I cannot bear for that woman to decide when I can and cannot see my child!" Amelia exploded.

"Look, you have to put up with that. Santiago does not want to have anything to do with us, however much your uncle tries. He even spoke to Don Manuel, Santiago's father. But he's inflexible: He approves of his son's decision, he thinks it's the right thing to have done. They will never forgive you, Amelia," Doña Elena said, without thinking how much her words would hurt her niece.

"I will pay for the mistake I have made my whole life, and you know what? Sometimes I think that I haven't been punished enough, that everything bad that happens to me is well deserved. I was mad to abandon my son!"

"Amelia, don't worry, we'll sort this all out one day," Antonietta said, but was unable to prevent herself from sobbing.

It was late when Don Armando came home. He worked extra hours in the office in order to be able to support his family.

Amelia said nothing, but it was clear from her expression that she thought her uncle had grown old. And Don Armando was worried when he saw his niece's terrible physical state. He hugged her for a long time, fighting back his tears.

"You have to promise me that you will never go away again for so long without sending word, we were all very worried. Don't do this to us, think about how much we suffer for you. Your sister Antonietta suffers from anxiety attacks, hasn't she told you? And the doctor tells us that it's because she must be very worried about you. We should go and see Don Eusebio tomorrow so that he can have a look at you, I'm worried by how you look."

Amelia re-entered the family routine. Doña Elena was the one who controlled what got done in the family and we all obeyed her, even Don Armando. She had become a second mother to Antonietta and to me.

It also became a part of the routine for Amelia and Edurne to go and wander near to what had been her home as a married woman, and where her husband still lived with Águeda. Doña Elena kept on saying that she knew from her friends that Santiago maintained the distinction between his children, letting everyone know that Javier was his legitimate son and heir, and that the girl, whom they had called Paloma, was the daughter of his lover.

Águeda's reaction to Amelia was strange. Even though she had taken Amelia's place in Santiago's bed, she still seemed to think of Amelia as her mistress, even though she knew that Santiago didn't want to hear anyone mention Amelia's name. But Águeda's reaction to Amelia whenever they met was instinctively subordinate; she was worried what Santiago could do to her if he found out that she was letting Amelia see Javier.

They agreed, via Edurne, that Amelia would not try to approach the child, because Javier was now old enough to tell his father the details of the walks he took with Águeda and his little sister, Paloma.

It was wrenching for Amelia to see her son at a distance, to follow after him in the Retiro, to see him playing with other children, to see him happy, to see him laughing, to see him call Águeda "Mama." She was Javier's shadow for the whole of that summer, and her son never noticed. Every evening when the sun began to set, Águeda would take the children out to stroll in the Retiro. She stopped to talk to other women, almost all of them servants; she never dared talk to the mothers who took their own children out for walks.

Amelia would sit on a nearby bench and watch Javier playing, she suffered whenever the child fell over and scraped his knee, she looked at him lovingly, enjoying this kind of secret motherhood.

Don Armando would not allow Antonietta to go out to work. He also wouldn't hear of me doing so. I offered several times to go out to try to find work, but he insisted that I study, like Jesús. As for Laura, she carried on teaching at the school and took in sewing as well. The nuns had found her this second job. Lots of families needed a seamstress to turn overcoats, or let out trousers, or fix a dress to make it look different. Laura took these jobs and, with Doña Elena's help, performed them well. Doña Elena was happy to bring what she could to the family finances, even without counting all the work she did around the house. She divided the tasks with Edurne and they would not let Antonietta do anything, except give piano lessons to the children of some of their neighbors, who were moving up in the world. Their father, a Falangist, had been rewarded with a position in the Foreign Ministry, and he put on airs as if he were a nobleman. Before the war he had lived in an attic, with his wife working downstairs as the porter to the building. But now he had decided to turn his daughters into refined young ladies, as if they had grown up in the big house themselves. They lived three blocks away from Don Armando's house, and they came two days a week for Antonietta to give them piano lessons. Antonietta was pleased with the coins that her labors earned her.

As for Amelia, it was clear that her health was much affected, and Don Elena and Don Armando both forbade her from looking for work.

"You can look for work when you are better, but now you should do us all a favor and get well," her uncle said.

Amelia suffered to see her uncle reduced to being a clerk in a law firm. They abused him, because it was he who conscientiously prepared the most difficult cases, while the money and the reputation they earned went to other people.

"But Uncle, why don't you try to set up your own office?"

"And who will trust me? Don't forget that you saved me from being shot. I am grateful for being alive, and I don't dare ask for anything more than to be able to support this family."

"But you're doing all their work! They're taking advantage of you!"

"Nobody will employ a Republican lawyer who was condemned to death. I don't have any influence, and everyone mistrusts me. Let's leave things as they are."

"You have to accept that your uncle lost the war," Doña Elena said.

"We all lost," Amelia replied.

"We are all facing the consequences, but it was the reds and the Republicans who lost. Franco isn't doing too badly, and they seem to respect him abroad," Doña Elena insisted.

"Who respects him? Hitler? Mussolini? They're as bad as he is! The other European countries don't respect him, and you'll see what happens when England wins the war," Amelia replied.

"I don't expect any help from anyone, after they abandoned the Republic during the war," Don Armando complained.

"And things aren't too bad here. Yes, there are things that are lacking, but at least there is order and one day things will get better, you'll see." Doña Elena was getting accustomed to the new situation.

"And freedom? What about freedom?"

"What freedom? Look, Amelia, if you don't talk about politics here, nothing will happen to you, so it's best just to keep your mouth shut. We've had enough politics in this family, and I just want us to live in peace. The whole of Europe is at war, and we don't know how it will end, and at least Franco's been clever enough to keep us out of it."

"For God's sake!"

"Yes, Amelia, everyone knows it's true, that Hitler came to ask for help in the war, and Franco managed to get rid of him without saying yes and without saying no, just like a true Galician..."

"And what help were we going to give? Who were we going to send? The country is in ruins! The men don't have the strength to carry on fighting! It's not that he didn't want to help Hitler, but he didn't have any way of helping, anything to offer. And even so, he's sent the División Azul to Russia."

"Amelia, please, stop talking about politics. We've suffered too much because of politics, and you've paid a high price for your Communist ideas... Leave it, Amelia, we'll be able to forge ahead with work and effort. And what I say to my children, I'll say to you as well: I don't want anyone else in this house getting involved in politics. It's enough for people to know that we were on the Republican side. We shouldn't draw people's attention. Things aren't going too badly," Doña Elena insisted.

Don Armando spoke with his niece about politics when his wife was not present. He didn't want to upset her. He also knew that Doña Elena was worried that their neighbors would hear them criticizing Franco.

"Your aunt is a good woman," Don Armando said on her behalf.

"I know, I know. And I love her very much and I'm extremely grateful for what she is doing for us and for Pablo, but I'm surprised that she's accepting the new situation with such good grace."

"It is she who makes this house possible, and she has her feet firmly on the ground, unlike us. She doesn't daydream that someone is going to come and save us, so she has decided to adapt herself to the new regime, she knows there's no other option."

"And you, what about you? What do you think?" Amelia asked.

"What do you think I'm going to think! Franco is a damned monster, but he won the war and there's not a lot we can do about it. What can we use to fight with? We don't have any weapons, or any money, or any hope. No one will help us, Amelia; France and England have abandoned us, and we will carry on alone. I'm sorry, but I don't think that if Churchill wins the war then he will have strength to help us afterwards."

"Of course he'll help us! Trust me, I know what I'm talking about," Amelia insisted.

Amelia's physical deterioration was a mystery to all of us. For all that Doña Elena tried to find out what had caused it, Amelia kept quiet about the reasons she had lost her health.

Laura was still her cousin's confidante, and her best friend, but even so Amelia was not entirely sincere with her. One Sunday, a few weeks after her arrival, at siesta time, the two of them were in the sitting room while the rest of the family were sleeping. You know that August in Madrid is like an oven, so there's nothing better to do than spend the first half of the afternoon asleep. I got up to go and get myself a glass of water, and heard their voices as I passed by the door to the sitting room. I was more curious then that I am now, so I stayed to listen.

"Have you really left Albert forever?" Laura asked.

"Yes, it's better for him, I never loved him enough. Well, I did love him, but without being in love with him, or at least not enough."

"He's such a good person... Why don't you like good people?"

"You think I only like bad men?" Amelia asked, surprised at her cousin's question.

"No, it's not that, but... I suppose that you'd recognize that Santiago is a good person, and Albert as well, but you left them both."

"Although it hurts to admit it, I suppose that yes, Santiago is a good man, but I was not ready for marriage, and I doubt that he was, either."

"And what was it about Albert that you didn't like?"

"There wasn't anything about him that I didn't like, it's just that... how to explain... I love him, yes, but I didn't feel anything when I was with him."

"I know why."

"Really? Do tell."

"Because you like challenges, you like to conquer impossible odds, and both Santiago and Albert loved you and gave you everything, and so you didn't feel any interest in them because of that. Tell me about this German."

"Max? There's not much to say. He's brave, and intelligent, and handsome."

"And married."

"Yes, Laura, yes, he's married."

"Have you been with him all this time? Why don't you tell me where you have been and what you have been doing?"

Amelia stood up and nervously began walking round the room without answering her cousin.

"Come on, don't get upset, I just wanted to know what happened to you. You used to trust me."

"And you still are the person I trust most in the world, but I prefer not to get you mixed up in this. It's better this way. I've told you that I've left Albert for Max, and nobody knows that apart from you."

"Mama would have a stroke if she knew that you had a lover who was married."

"And your father wouldn't deal too well with the fact of his being German."

"My father loves you a lot, Amelia, and he would never judge you."

"But he would not understand, and that would cause him a great deal of pain. That's why I prefer them not to know anything. And I don't want to bother my poor sister with my affairs either."

"When will you see Max again?"

"I don't know, Laura, perhaps never. He is a soldier and we are at war."

"You don't know where he is?"

"No, I don't."

We anxiously followed the progress of the war. The radio told us that Hitler was going from victory to victory, as was Mussolini, and the enthusiastic commentators told us that Franco was as "great" as the Führer or Il Duce.

"The Allies are going to win," Amelia said stubbornly.

"I hope to God that's true!" Don Armando said, although he was more skeptical than she was about the eventual outcome of the war.

"And what do we care which side wins?" Doña Elena said, worrying that the greed of the Germans or the desire of the British to re-establish the Republic would lead to another war in Spain.

She had suffered so much that the only thing Doña Elena wanted was to survive, and she dreamed of a return to how things had been in the past, when she had been a wealthy member of the bourgeoisie, and the house had shone with silver plate and fine crystal.

In the middle of September, Jesús and I started the new school year. We were studying with a scholarship at a Salesian school. Laura went back to work with the monks, and Antonietta started to teach the Falangist children again. Amelia was the only one who was not working, and this frustrated her greatly. One day she went to her aunt and insisted that she help her find a job.

"You're still not well, you're still very thin and the doctor says you need to rest."

"But I can't stand being a burden on you."

"The best help you can be is to get better, and I don't want to hear you say ever again that you're a burden. You are another daughter to us, like Antonietta, another daughter. Be patient and wait until you are better, and then you can work."

But Amelia didn't listen to her, and started looking for a job in secret, without telling anyone at home. One day she surprised us all by saying that she had found one, not very far from the house, as a shop assistant in a haberdasher's.

"But good heavens, you can't work there!" Doña Elena said.

"Why not, it's a good honest job."

"But we've shopped there all our lives and... No... I don't want you to work there, they'll talk about us behind our backs."

"And why should we care what other people say? You spend all your time telling us to adapt ourselves to the new situation. Well, we don't have money and we're going to have to work. I don't see any problem in working at the haberdasher's."

"The owner is a real witch. She never liked me. Everyone knows that she used to be on the stage, but she was very bad at it as well, poor thing; well, she was good enough to capture her manager. She got pregnant by him and because he was married he had no option but to look after the pair of them, her and the child. So they came to the agreement that he would set her up in the shop if she wouldn't cause a fuss."

"We've always bought from that shop," Laura said, in support of Amelia.

"They always have good stock, the best lace and ribbons... But that woman is what she is," Doña Elena insisted.

"Well, I'm grateful that she has given me a job. Her daughter is married to a lieutenant who is stationed in Ceuta, they have four children, so she can't help her mother with anything, and she's old and needs help. It will only be a few hours in the morning, but at least I'll earn some money," Amelia argued.

"But what will they say about us in the neighborhood?" Doña Elena whimpered.

"Are they feeding us? If not, why should we worry what the neighbors say?" Amelia replied.

She would not allow them to change her mind, and in spite of Doña Elena's entreaties and Don Armando's worries, Amelia started to go to the haberdasher's every morning.

"Doña Rosa is very nice," Amelia said.

"Doña Rosa? When did we start calling her Doña Rosa? We've always known her as Rosita," Doña Elena complained.

"Yes, but it's not nice to speak disrespectfully to a woman who is old enough to be my grandmother. I have decide to be polite to her, and she's pleased that I do so."

"I'm not surprised! A well-brought-up-lady like you showing respect to a showgirl, as if she were a fine lady. I don't approve, it upsets me."

"Don't be so hard on her, Aunt. What do we know about her life? I think she's a pleasant enough woman who has done what she has needed to do in order to make a life for her daughter."

"Thanks to the shop where her lover set her up," Doña Elena insisted.

"Well, that only goes to show that she's clever," Laura said. "Us women normally get taken for a ride, used and then thrown away like old shoes."

"The things you say! If your father heard you talking like that, he'd be shocked, I tell you. How can you justify that woman going with that man and... and... well, having a child with him being married? Is that decent? Is that what I've taught you?"

"What do we know about her circumstances? Nothing. I'm with Amelia, we shouldn't judge her," Laura insisted.

"What do you think they say about me?" Amelia asked.

"About you? Why should they talk about you? You're a young woman from a good family and you can hold your head high because of it."

"Yes, but I got married and then I left my husband and my child to run away with another man. Do you think I'm better than Doña Rosa?"

"Don't compare yourself to that woman!" Doña Elena said, offended.

"You know that your friends, whenever they see me, murmur to themselves and treat me condescendingly. It's offensive. They think I'm a fallen woman."

"Don't say that! I won't let anyone refuse to show you the proper amount of respect."

"Come on, don't get upset, just accept that I'm working in the shop. Doña Rosa has promised to pay me thirty pesetas a month."

The money was a great help to the family finances. Don Armando earned four hundred pesetas working fourteen hours a day, and Antonietta's piano lessons, and Laura's lessons and sewing meant that the family barely made six hundred pesetas per month. We were lucky, I suppose, and weren't at the level of some families, whose food consisted of stewed chestnuts or carob gruel. But I have never eaten as much rice or potatoes as I did then. Doña Elena made rice with garlic and laurel and put paprika, and the same old laurel, on the potatoes to give them a little more flavor.

Doña Elena accepted that Amelia should work in Doña Rosa's shop, but she was reluctant about it, and never went there again herself.

One night while we were listening to the radio we heard news of violent combat taking place around Stalingrad. In spite of the reporter's boasts that Germany would not leave a single Bolshevik alive, that was not what was happening on the Russian front.

Amelia seemed very worried. I never knew why. Jesús said that it was because she had run off with a Communist and therefore felt sympathy for the Russians, and was worried that the Germans might win.

One day Laura came home and said that they were going to raise her wages at the school.

"The mother superior said that she was very happy with my work."

Doña Elena decided to celebrate by making a potato pie with a little bit of the butter that she kept as if it were a treasure. Melita had brought it from Burgos. Melita didn't come to see us often, but she had wanted to see her cousin Amelia and introduce her to her husband and her little daughter Isabel.

The two cousins had not seen each other for many years, and Amelia was surprised at the change that had taken place in Melita; she had become domesticated, subordinate in all things to her husband. It's not that Rodrigo Losada was not a good man: He was, and he loved his wife, but he had very clear ideas about the role that wives, especially his own, should fill. Melita did everything he said, and his opinions were her own. For his part, Rodrigo seemed doubtful about Amelia, the black sheep of the family, who had run away and abandoned her husband and her son, and who appeared and disappeared without telling anyone where she was going, just as if she were a man.

Rodrigo Losada was friendly and polite with Amelia, but he could not hide his mistrust of her. Some of the few arguments he had with his wife arose when she supported her cousin, saying that she had always been special, and that she was a good woman. But he would not admit the rightness of what she said, which made her sad.

I must admit that Jesús and I looked forward to the visits of Melita and Rodrigo, not just because we liked them, but because they always brought a lot of food.

Whenever we went to pick them up at the station, we would bet how many baskets they would bring. Rodrigo's parents were well-off before the civil war and, without being millionaires, they lived much better than we did; Rodrigo's mother was from Cantabria and owned a farm with some land and animals, so they were never hungry.

Melita used to bring chorizo in oil, butter, ribs, and marinated pork loin. She also brought chickpeas and jars of honey and plum jam, and sweets that her mother had made. This was a feast for postwar Madrid.

Melita was pregnant again, and Rodrigo said that this time he was sure that it would be a boy. As for little Isabella, she was a plump and calm little girl whom Doña Elena and Don Armando spoiled whenever they could, given how little they saw their granddaughter.

Doña Elena, like all the mothers of that time, worried about the future for her children. She was happy with Melita's marriage, but she was on the lookout for husbands for her daughter Laura and her niece Antonietta; she would take care of Jesús and me later, because we were still too young.

The good woman, unaware of her husband's suffering, tried to get to know the wives of several important figures in the regime who were our neighbors. From time to time she would invite them to come and take tea with her, and would insist that Laura and Antonietta were there so that they could be seen and so that the women would take them into account when choosing partners for their offspring.

These occasions put Laura in a bad mood and she would argue with her mother.

"But what's wrong with you! Do you think I'm some kind of fairground attraction? I refuse to let your friends examine me whenever they come to our house. I hate them! You would never have invited them before the war."

"Do you want to stay single the whole of your life? These women are well-positioned and have children your age; if you carry on like this, then you and Antonietta will miss the boat."

"But I don't want to get married!" Laura replied.

"What are you saying? Of course you'll get married! Do you want to become an old maid? I won't allow it."

Antonietta appeared to be more docile, more accepting of her aunt's wishes. I saw her at these tea parties, and she was suffering, but she never said anything, and tried to behave well, as she had been brought up to do.

Doña Elena showed her friends Antonietta's cross-stitch, and assured them that the cake they were eating had been made by Laura herself.

One night, she announced at dinnertime that we were to go, that Saturday, to a tea-dance organized by one of these neighbors.

"The husband of Señora de García de Vigo is the right-hand man of the undersecretary for agriculture, and she had assured me that lots of interesting young men will be there, some of them well-connected in the Falange, others from good families, I think that there is one who is the son of a count or a marquis or something. The De García de Vigo family has a daughter, Maruchi, who is a little long in the tooth; she's twenty-seven, and she's going through the same torments as you, she hasn't yet found a husband."

"I wouldn't dream of going," Laura said.

"Of course you will go! You and Antonietta and Amelia, we will all go. Your father will go with us, it's a good opportunity for him to meet Señor de García de Vigo."

"What do you expect me to do at this dance? I am married, after all," Amelia said, trying to get out of this annoying social engagement.

"You will be with me, I have told Señora de García de Vigo that I will be with her to keep an eye on the festivities. You will accompany us."

"I don't think that this is a good idea, You know what these women think of me, they see me as a fallen woman, I don't think that my presence there would help Antonietta or Laura," Amelia argued.

"What are you saying! You are my niece and no one will say a word out of place, they are very polite to you when they come here."

"But that's in your house, where they wouldn't dare to be rude. No, I won't go," Amelia replied.

"Amelia is right," Don Armando added, "these women are capable of saying anything, and it's not that I care about you feeling obliged to leave early, but I am worried that Amelia would have a bad time of it. Look, the best thing to do is for her and me to take Jesús and Pablo out for a walk."

Patiently, diplomatically, Don Armando nearly got away with it, but Doña Elena had a brainwave: Jesús and I should go to the party as well.

"You aren't old enough to dance, but you can very well have tea, so let's not waste the opportunity. It's always a good idea to have little brothers near older sisters, as chaperones. It's decided, I'll tell Señora de García de Vigo."

Jesús and I protested, but unsuccessfully. Amelia had escaped from the dance, in exchange for us.

On Saturday at six on the dot we turned up at the de García de Vigo house on Calle Serrano. Doña Paquita, for that was Señora de García de Vigo's name, received us with a warm smile and invited us into a large room that she had arranged for dancing.

"Come in, come in, you're the first," Doña Paquita said.

"I told you I would come in time to help you." Doña Elena replied.

"I've invited thirty young people, you'll have a wonderful time. And you," she said, referring to Jesús and to me, "you should be careful that nobody oversteps the bounds of propriety with the young ladies, tell us if you see anything odd. We will be on the lookout as well, but if by any chance we get distracted, then you will be there keeping your eyes open. You should also take charge of putting on the music, we have some very lively pasodobles."

Jesús and I had agreed to attend on our own terms, which was to eat as much as possible. We had not the slightest intention of keeping an eye on the girls, unless one of the young men should cross the line with Laura or Antonietta. About the others, we couldn't have cared less.

The first guests soon arrived. They all looked alike to Jesús and to me: the men in suits and ties, with very carefully styled hair, and the women in starched skirts.

Doña Paquita had put out a soup tureen filled with punch; to its side were plates covered with croquettes, tortillas, and sliced sausage, all neatly displayed.

After the first glass of punch, the young people started dancing. And, as could have been predicted, as soon as Doña Paquita and Doña Elena were distracted, the boys' hands were distracted as well, and started to move down the girls' backs. Sometimes they were pushed away indignantly, sometimes the girl in question, with a wicked smile, would pretend to reject them but not too severely.

We did not lose sight of Laura and Antonietta, and if any of the boys tried to go too far, we would approach them and make it clear that it was better for them not to try anything. Laura had, for her part, discovered the way to repel unwanted attention: Whenever anyone came closer to her than he should have, she stamped heavily on his foot.

We were having fun. I am sure that I ate all the cod croquettes that, according to Doña Paquita, had been made by Maruchi herself. As for Maruchi, she pretended not to notice when any young man came closer to her than he should have.

Meanwhile, Doña Paquita told Doña Elena about the guests.

"Look," she said. "That one with the gray jacket and the moustache is the son of the undersecretary, and the one standing next to him has a great future ahead of him; he's in the Falange and has an excellent position in food wholesaling. The dirty blond one is called Pedro Molina; keep an eye on him because he's a good boy, even though his father's dead: The poor man was killed in the war at Paracuellos. His mother is the cousin of a soldier who's very close to the Caudillo. I think that Franco holds him in very high esteem, and he's one of the few men permitted to be on familiar terms with him. Her mother has been issued the license to run a government store, and he has been put into a good position in the Tax Office. Look, look how he's looking at Laura... Oh, what luck! If your daughter catches him, you can think yourselves very fortunate. What a wedding that would be!"

Antonietta came to sit with us. She was a bit tired, and these young men, with their jokes and essential liveliness, rather tired her out.

"Aren't you enjoying yourself?" Doña Paquita and Doña Elena asked in unison.

"Yes, yes, a lot, I'm just a little tired," she apologized.

"Rest for a while, but not for too long, or some other girl will take your admirers away," Doña Paquita warned, without realizing that being ignored would be a relief for Antonietta.

At ten o'clock on the dot, Doña Paquita announced that the tea-dance was over. We went home, fired up by Doña Elena's enthusiastic stream of commentary on the party. For her it had been a success. The nephew of this soldier who was on good terms with Franco, who they said was named Pedro, had come up to pay his respects and to ask if he could visit Laura. Doña Elena had ignored her daughter's look of horror and had replied to the young man that they would be delighted to expect him next Thursday afternoon.

Laura complained to her mother.

"You shouldn't have invited him, he's repulsive."

"He's a good boy, they killed his father at Paracuellos, and well, you see... he's studying business and his mother has a government shop. It's not a match we can afford to let slip."

"Well, I don't like him, so don't talk him up because I have no intention of going out with him. He's a Fascist."

"Mind what you say! I don't want you to say that word ever again, never, do you hear me? There are no parties in Spain anymore, we are all Spaniards and that's that."

"Yes, Fascist Spaniards, because everyone else has either been killed or sent into exile."

"What have I done to deserve this? Don't you realize what our situation is like? Even your father has realized that there is no other way than to get accustomed to Franco; anyway, say whatever you want to say, he's doing well, at least we have peace here now."

"Peace? What peace? Is it peace when everyone opposed to the regime is killed?" Laura protested.

"You'll get us all sent to prison, just you see... ," Doña Elena groaned.

In spite of Laura's protests, Pedro Molina started to come regularly to the house. Doña Elena was kind to him, but Laura did not hide her antipathy. The young man appeared not to notice Laura's disdain, and the worse she treated him, the more interested he seemed to be.

"He's so affected! I hate him."

"He's a gentleman and a good match. Do you want to be an old maid?"

"I'd prefer it. I promise you, mother, I'd prefer it, anything would be better than to be at the side of that stuck-up prig."

Doña Elena ignored Laura's protests, and one day when Pedro Molina was having tea with us, she let slip that she would like to meet his mother.

"One day you will have to bring your mother to have tea with us, it would be a great honor to meet her."

"Of course, Doña Elena! But we should invite you. You can't know how much my mother would like to meet Laura."

"You only need to ask, next Thursday we've got some friends coming round for the evening, and your mother is more than welcome to come. You can talk with Laura, and we'll entertain her. The poor woman, the things she has had to put up with!"

"If it weren't for her cousin, I don't know what would have become of us... But Mama's cousin is a soldier who is very close to the Caudillo, and he has made sure that we lack for nothing. You know that I have a good job where they appreciate me."

"Of course, of course! Well, you're an upright young man, you'll go far."

"I only want to be worthy of Laura," Pedro Molina sighed.

Pedro's mother's visit turned the house upside down. Doña Elena asked Don Armando to try to come back early from work to meet the widow.

"But my dear, how am I going to be allowed to leave work early?"

"It's a good match for Laura, so we should do what we can to give the engagement as much encouragement as possible."

"What engagement? Laura doesn't want anything to do with this Pedro Molina. You're playing matchmaker and this will only end badly. The boy is getting his hopes up, not because of anything Laura says, but because of you."

"Armando, you should help me, instead of making problems."

"No, Elena, I have no intention of trying to force a marriage that our daughter hates the very idea of. Leave her alone, she'll find her own husband, and if she doesn't, it will be because she doesn't want to."

"So you don't mind if Laura ends up an old maid? What can a single woman hope for in this life? No, I will not allow it, even if you are not on my side."

Pedro Molina's mother was a flabby woman, not at all prepared to have her son marry someone who had not been chosen by her. Laura did what she could to make her dislike her, but even if she had been charm itself, the good lady would not have liked her either.

She was quite clearly extremely jealous, which is to say that until she had been given the government shop she had not had a penny to spend, and she was upset by Doña Elena, whose bearing and elegant manners were signs of an upbringing that she herself had never had.

Doña Elena was extremely charming, and introduced her to her friends, trying to make her feel comfortable, but did not succeed. The widow Molina sat very tense at the edge of her chair and did not praise the cakes that Laura had "made" (they had been baked by Antonietta), or the milk chocolate that it had been so difficult to get hold of (a present from Doña Rosa the haberdasher). As for the milk itself, Doña Elena had gotten it on the black market. Edurne had even starched her uniform. But not even this seemed to move the old lady. An hour after she had arrived, she said that she should be leaving, and not even Pedro's silent but supplicating glance could move her. She said that they were going, and they went. After this, much to Laura's relief, Pedro Molina started to visit the house less. It was clear that his mother did not approve.

A few days before Christmas, an unknown woman turned up at the door of the house asking for Amelia Garayoa. I opened the door.

"Amelia Garayoa?"

"Yes, she's here," I said, looking surprised at this thin and resolute-looking woman, with her blonde hair that was turning gray. Her coat was of fine material, and her pearl necklace shone as much as the leather boots she was wearing. She seemed to have a slight foreign accent, but that might have just been my impression.

"Will you tell her that I am here? My name is Señora Rodríguez."

I went to tell Amelia. She seemed surprised to hear the name.

"Who is she?" Doña Elena wanted to know.

"A woman I met through Albert, I think she's a friend of his parents," Amelia replied.

Amelia took her through to the salon and offered her a cup of malt "coffee," which she refused, and then they spent a long time talking in low voices. When Señora Rodríguez left, Amelia seemed worried. But she didn't say anything, and fended her aunt's questions off with vague replies; she didn't say anything more to her uncle.

I remember that Christmas as being special because Melita came to spend it with us, along with her husband and her daughter Isabel. Melita was now heavily pregnant and had told her husband that it was her wish to spend Christmas in Madrid. He had resisted, not wanting to spend too much time away from his family in Burgos, but whether Melita's annoyance with him made her ill, or perhaps because of his fear that something might happen to the baby, the result was that they arrived in Madrid on the morning of December 24, bringing with them a basket containing two plucked chickens, two dozen eggs, the much beloved butter, and a chunk of marinated pork loin, as well as peppers, onions, and parsley. They even brought two bottles of wine.

We had not had such a happy Christmas for a long time. Doña Elena and Don Armando were happy to have their children with them, as well as their nephew and niece; as for me, I was another member of the family. My mother Lola was showing no signs of life, neither was my father. I was still hoping that they would turn up one day, that they would come for me, but in the meantime my only family was this one, which had welcomed me so generously.

We got up late on Christmas Day and ate in the kitchen in pajamas, in spite of Doña Elena's protests; she always used to insist that we could not sit at the table unless we were all washed and dressed, but Don Armando said that relaxing the rule for one day wouldn't hurt anyone. We hadn't finished breakfast before Melita started to feel unwell.

Don Armando and Rodrigo took her back to bed, and Doña Elena called the doctor.

"You must have indigestion, perhaps you ate too much," Rodrigo said.

We didn't think that it could be anything other than indigestion, because there were still a couple of months to go before the child was due. But Melita said that she felt her contractions.

"I'm telling you, I'm having a baby, I remember very well how it was when Isabel was born."

"No, it's impossible, calm yourself, woman," her husband said.

Don Eusebio, the doctor, soon arrived, looking sleepy. He told us all to get out of the room, apart from Doña Elena.

When Don Eusebio came out of the room, he made it very clear:

"Melita is going to have her child, it's impossible to take her to a hospital, we wouldn't get there in time. So Laura, you put some water on to heat up, and you, Amelia, bring some towels and some sheets."

Rodrigo turned pale, worried that something might happen to Melita.

"Doctor, are you sure that we wouldn't get to the hospital in time? I don't want there to be complications..."

"There will be complications, it's a seven-month pregnancy, so start praying, that's the best you can do. Oh, and call this number, which is a midwife I know, a good woman who may be willing to come and help me."

Rodrigo called the midwife immediately and promised her a generous tip if she would come straight away to help with the birth.

Antonietta told us that we should all help Melita, and the best thing that Jesús and I could do was to be quiet and not get into trouble.

The midwife took almost an hour to arrive, and Melita did not stop screaming in all that time. When she came, the doctor told Laura and Amelia to get out of the room.

I remember Rodrigo crying silently. He was in the sitting room, smoking cigar after cigar, with tears rolling down his face.

"He really loves her," Jesús said in surprise. He had never seen a man cry before.

"How can he not love her? She's his wife," I replied.

"Poor thing!" Rodrigo muttered, regretting his decision to allow Melita to come to Madrid when she was seven months' pregnant.

The baby was not born until well into the afternoon, and, thank the Lord, both he and his mother survived the complications of the birth.

"She has lost a lot of blood and she's very weak, but she's a strong woman and she'll recover. Her son is very small, of course, but hopefully he'll make it as well," Don Eusebio said to Rodrigo, who didn't know how to show his gratitude to the doctor for having saved his wife and son.

"I will always be in your debt. Tell me what I owe you, no matter how much, after what you've done..."

"Young man, there are things one doesn't do for money. Do you know how long I've known Melita? Since she was about the age of her daughter Isabel. I'm not here for money, but for my friendship with the family, only that."

Even so, both he and the midwife accepted the generous sum that Rodrigo offered them.

"She will have to rest for a long time. As for the child, he will need a lot of looking after, given that he is premature and still in a lot of danger," Don Eusebio warned.

"We'll take them to the hospital at once," Rodrigo said.

"No, no, don't even think about taking them out of the house. The best thing is for them to stay here. Listen to me. I'll come back this evening, but if you need me at any time, call me."

"I will get a nurse. Can you recommend me one?"

"Yes, Doña Elena. Who better than her mother to look after Melita?"

Doña Elena allowed Rodrigo to come into the room for a minute or so, telling him not to tire out Melita.

"And don't scold her. The poor thing thinks that you will be cross with her for having given in to her whims and traveled to Madrid."

"How could I be cross with her! I thank the Lord that she's alive."

Melita asked Rodrigo to allow her to call the child Juan.

"I want him to be named after my uncle."

He accepted without complaint. He was too scared to do anything else.

Rodrigo had to go back to Burgos in the middle of January, leaving Melita, who was still in bed. Don Eusebio would not let her travel, far less the baby, whom we all called Juanito.

Doña Elena was happy to have Melita and her two grand-children with her. She didn't want to let them leave until her daughter and her grandson were both perfectly well again. Don Eusebio jokingly said that it would be Doña Elena who decided when they could be given the all-clear, although he recommended that they stay in Madrid at least until the summer.

Rodrigo accepted what he was told without argument. He felt happy that Melita and his children were alive, so he decided to come to see them in Madrid every week. He took the earliest train on Saturdays and went home on Sunday evening. He could only spend a couple of hours with his wife and his children, but that was better than nothing.

Melita didn't seem to mind staying under the wings of her family. It's not that she was unhappy in Burgos, where she had a lovely house and her husband's family were sincerely fond of her, but Melita missed her parents and her little brother Jesús, who had always been her favorite, even though she also loved her sister Laura. But Laura had always got on better with her cousin Amelia, and Melita respected the relationship between them.

As for Don Armando, he spoiled his two grandchildren as much as he could. Isabel was a very kind child, always ready to smile at her grandfather. As for little Juanito, we all prayed that he would recover as soon as possible, but it was hard for him to put on weight, and he had frequent attacks of diarrhea, which worried Don Eusebio.

7

In May 1943 Javier broke his leg. He was seven years old and very handsome. Blond and slim, with green eyes, he was a rascal who ran Águeda ragged. She was incapable of stopping him from climbing the trees in the Retiro, even though they were too large and too tall for him. But Javier was like a squirrel, twisting his way through the branches in the face of Águeda's horrified entreaties for him to come down, or else she would tell his father. But Javier had inherited Amelia's rebellious temperament and he would not let himself be swayed by a threat that he knew kindhearted Águeda would not carry out, so he climbed up as high as he could.

One Saturday morning we went with Amelia to the Retiro so that she could see Javier, as she had done before. The day before, Amelia had sent Edurne to wait outside Santiago's house for Águeda to come out, to ask when she could see her child. They had agreed to meet at ten o'clock the next morning.

Jesús and I used to go with Amelia, because Doña Elena did not like to think of Amelia out walking alone and maybe meeting Santiago, which would cause trouble. We would take advantage of this to bring a ball and play soccer, whereas Antonietta would normally bring a book, although ever since Melita began living with us she had liked taking care of Isabel, who enjoyed running around the park.

We sat down on a bench not too far from Águeda, Javier, and Paloma.

Amelia watched Javier without losing sight of him. He was particularly rebellious that day and refused to obey Águeda. He had chosen a leafy tree with many branches for his climbing exploits, and started to climb it, without paying attention to Águeda's entreaties.

"His hands must be torn to shreds from so much climbing, maybe he should wear gloves, I don't know why Águeda doesn't think of it," Amelia said.

Jesús and I started to play soccer without paying attention to Javier, while Antonietta kept Isabel entertained with a rag doll that Doña Elena had made.

Suddenly Amelia screamed and ran away. We were scared and followed her.

Javier had fallen out of the tree and was groaning with pain while Águeda screamed and didn't know what to do.

Amelia pushed Águeda out of the way and took Javier in her arms.

"Where does it hurt? Tell me, my son, where does it hurt?" she asked, her eyes filling with tears.

"My leg... my leg hurts a lot, I can't move it... and my arm, but my leg hurts the most..."

Javier cried and his knee began quickly to swell. Amelia wasn't listening to anything Águeda was saying, and took the boy in her arms and headed for a hospital.

I don't know where she got the strength, she was a thin as a whisper, but she ran so fast that it was hard for us to keep up with her. Águeda took Paloma in her arms and ran after them, and Antonietta took Isabel, but eventually had to hand him over to Jesús.

We got to a hospital near to the Retiro and they took charge of Javier.

"What happened?" the doctor asked.

"He fell out of a tree, he's a very unruly child and there's no way to stop him doing what he wants to do," Amelia said.

"You are his mother, aren't you? I don't need to ask, he looks so much like you."

"Yes, he is my son," Amelia said as she pressed Javier's hand.

"No, no... my mother is this lady... ," Javier said, pointing to Águeda, who had just come in, sweating, with Paloma in her arms.

684

"This lady?" the doctor looked incredulously at Águeda.

"Yes, she's my mama..."

Amelia and Águeda looked at each other without knowing what to say, which surprised the doctor.

"Well, which one of you is the boy's mother?" he asked angrily.

"I, I am his mother, she is... well, she is like a mother to him; she's looked after him ever since he was a little baby," Amelia said, pointing to Águeda.

"No, you're not my mother!" Javier shouted.

"And his father? Where is he?"

"At work," Águeda replied.

"Call him," the doctor said, and started to put a cast on Javier's leg and a bandage on his arm, which fortunately was not broken.

"Well, young man, you're not going to be climbing trees for a while, and I hope that this is a lesson to you to obey your mother when she tells you to take care and not climb up so high."

"Yes, sir," Javier said, hanging his head.

We were just about to leave when Santiago arrived, after Águeda had called him on the doctor's advice.

As soon as he saw Amelia his face grew tense and he snatched the child from his mother's arms. The doctor looked at him in surprise.

"The child is well, I have told your wife that he needs to rest and to wear the cast for forty days. But don't worry, the bone should set well."

"Thank you very much, Doctor, I'm very grateful to you," Santiago replied drily.

Águeda knotted her hands together nervously and Amelia was so pale that she looked like she were made out of wax. Antonietta said she felt sick, and Isabel was crying in Jesus's arms, and I was shuffling from one foot to the other without knowing what to do.

"Águeda, tell me what happened," Santiago ordered.

"The boy was climbing a tree and suddenly he fell... I... I'm sorry... I couldn't stop... stop it," Águeda stammered in reply.

Amelia looked at him, her expression a plea for help. Santiago's eyes seemed to soften for a moment, but then he turned his face, ignoring her.

"Santiago, I want to speak to you," Amelia begged.

"This lady told the doctor that she's my mama," Javier said suddenly.

Santiago held Javier tight and turned to Amelia.

"I do not want you to come close to Javier. Do not do it, or you will regret it."

"For God's sake, Santiago, we're in the street, can't we talk? You can't stop me from seeing my son, you can't lie to him telling him he has another mother, you don't have the right to do this to either of us."

I think that Santiago would have hit her if he had not been holding Javier, such was the fury in his eyes. I stood next to Amelia, intent on protecting her, even though I too was trembling at Santiago's rage.

"You have no son. You have nothing."

"Javier is my son, and someone will have to tell him so one day. He has my name, and that is something you cannot change. You will have to tell him who his mother is, and even if you tell him that I'm the worst woman who ever lived, you will never be able to tell him that I don't love him, because I love him with my heart and soul and will do whatever I can for him."

"Papa..."

"Be quiet. And you... How can you be so shameless? Let me tell you again: Stay away from Javier, or you will regret it."

"Papa..."

"Shut up!"

"Don't shout at him! He hasn't done anything."

"You dare to tell me what I can or cannot do?"

"Yes, I dare to tell you not to shout at the child and I dare to beg you to talk to me, for us to reach some kind of agreement, so that the child can know who I am, and how much I love him."

"Go away, Amelia, and don't come near us ever again or you will pay."

"What more can you do to me? You have no right to lie to Javier, telling him I'm not his real mother, telling him that Águeda is someone she is not."

"How dare you tell me what I can or cannot do! Who was with Javier when he was sick? Who put cloths soaked in vinegar on his forehead to lower the fever? Who changed his diapers, has dressed him, bathed him, fed him? Who was at his bedside when he woke up during the night? I'll tell you who: this woman, yes, because *you* were with your lover, in whatever bed you happened to find yourself at the time. And you dare to come here as if nothing has happened and claim that you are his mother. What sort of woman would abandon her son to run off with a scoundrel?"

I saw that Amelia was about to burst into tears, and that she had been deeply wounded, feeling cruelly embarrassed for what Santiago had said to her in front of her son.

"You need to destroy me so that my son doesn't love me, you need me to be abhorred, you need him to think the very worst of me. Do you think that is good for him? You hate me and I understand that, but your hatred stops you from thinking that Javier has a right to his mother, even if she is a mother as... as imperfect as I am."

"But you are not my mother," Javier said, upset at Amelia's continued presence.

"Yes, I am your mother, of course I am your mother, and I love you more than anyone else in the world."

"Why aren't you with me, then? No, you're not my mother, this is my mother," Javier said, pointing at Águeda, who was very quiet and still and did not dare to move a muscle or say a word.

"Motherhood is not just giving birth to a child. You gave birth to Javier, but that moment did not make you his mother."

Santiago turned and began walking quickly away, without even waiting for Águeda, who followed him tearfully with her daughter in her arms, scared of the storm that would fall on her when they got home.

Amelia stood very still, she was so pale that she could have been dead. Antonietta spoke to her, but she did not reply, she didn't seem to hear Jesús or me either. Antonietta shook her by the arm, trying to bring her back to herself.

"Come on, Amelia, let's go home."

We went home in silence, most of us shocked and stunned by what had happened, and Amelia feeling the deep pain of Santiago's words.

When Antonietta told Doña Elena what had happened, she got very upset.

"I don't believe it! Santiago has forgotten that he is a gentleman and that he owes you a certain amount of respect as the mother of his child."

"A moment... He said that Javier was only a moment of my life... that moment did not make me his mother... ," Amelia sobbed.

"Well, you are Javier's mother, whether he likes it or not," Laura said, deeply affected by her cousin's sorrow.

Melita took Amelia's hand and pressed it close, trying to comfort her.

Don Armando came home at lunchtime and found all the women in the family sunk in a sea of tears.

"We have to sort this out. Santiago cannot carry on denying you access to Javier."

"What if we took him to court?" Doña Elena said.

"No, not in court, we'd definitely lose. Don Manuel is a powerful man and we... well, we wouldn't be able to justify some things..." Don Armando explained.

"I know, Uncle, I know, it would be impossible to justify the reasons why I left my husband and my son to go off with another man, and a Communist to boot," Amelia said.

"Don't say such things. Let me think, let me think... We will find a solution."

"No, Uncle, there's no solution. Santiago hates me and will never forgive me. His revenge is to deny me my son."

Two days later, Edurne met Águeda near our house.

"Tell Amelia not to worry about anything, that Javier is well, although upset about what happened."

"I will tell him."

"I... I'm sorry, I'm so sorry for what Amelia is suffering. Tell her that Don Santiago loves the child with all his heart, that he doesn't want for anything, and that I... I love Javier very much, it is as if... as if he were my son. The boy's been asking his father why the woman from the park took him to the hospital and said she was his mother, and he has asked me if I am his mother. I didn't know what to say."

"What did you say?"

"I said he is the son of my soul, and he asked me what that meant. Don Santiago asked him to forget about the woman, that he has no other mother but me, but Javier isn't happy. Even though he is very small, he is intelligent and he's going round all these things in his head. Edurne, do you think that Amelia will ever forgive me? I wasn't able to resist, well... You know what men are like, and what with it being Don Santiago and all, I didn't know how to refuse when he..."

"Do you love him, Águeda?"

"How could I not love him! He's a gentleman, and such a good person... Women like us cannot reject gentlemen. I have a daughter with Don Santiago, Paloma, and he loves her in his way. I know that she will never be what Javier is to him, but he loves her and won't let her lack for anything. He doesn't refuse to acknowledge her as his daughter, and he's said that we'll send her to a good school, one run by nuns, and that she'll have a good dowry when she gets married, and he will be proud to take her up the aisle himself."

"Well, there's a long time to go before that happens, your daughter is still a little girl. Do you trust Don Santiago so much?"

"He's a man of his word, he would prefer to die than break a promise. I know that he won't abandon me or Paloma. Edurne, tell Amelia that she should forgive me and that I will do whatever I can to make sure that she sees Javier again, even if it is better for her not to try again for a while."

"I will tell her, don't worry, I will tell her."

We were all of us moved by Águeda's gesture, all of us apart from Amelia, that is. She still thought of the woman as an intruder in her own house, someone who was stealing her son's affection from her.

"It's not her fault what happened." Laura tried to calm her cousin.

"She's a good woman, Javier is better off with her than with anyone else," Doña Elena said.

"And Santiago still loves you," Antonietta said, to general disbelief.

"What are you saying? How could you say a thing like that? He hates me, he hates me from the bottom of his soul."

"Well, I think he loves you, but he cannot forgive you because his pride won't allow him. If you could conquer his pride then you could be happy again."

"Happy? You know what, Antonietta? We were never happy."

A month later, Señora Rodríguez, the woman who had turned up so unexpectedly at Christmastime, came round again to ask for Amelia, but she was not at home, so the woman left a card and told us to give it to Amelia as soon as she returned.

We could see over the next few days that Amelia was upset. Doña Elena thought that it must be the heat, it was June in Madrid and very hot; it was hard to sleep at night, so we blamed anything that happened on the effects of the heat. But I realized that Amelia's worry must have something to do with the visit of Señora Rodríguez.

One afternoon Amelia came back from work later than usual, and said that she had been to see Señora Rodríguez.

"Did she tell you anything about Albert James?" Doña Elena asked Amelia, remembering that Amelia had told us that Señora Rodríguez was a friend of the American journalist.

"Yes, she told me that Albert was well," Amelia replied drily.

"Where is he now? In London or New York?" Laura wanted to know: She seemed particularly interested in the journalist.

"In London, he's still in London... Or at least that's what Señora Rodríguez told me."

The family still paid a good deal of attention to the radio. Every evening after supper we sat in the living room to listen to the news. We followed news of Mussolini's overthrow, and his eventual liberation by a German commando squad, and the proclamation of the Italian Social Republic, a phantasmagorical political entity created by Il Duce in northern Italy around a few ardent Fascists.

Autumn of 1943 came round without it seeming possible that the routine of our lives would change at all.

One afternoon at the end of October an unexpected visitor came to the house. I was at home because I had caught a chill.

Amelia, Laura, and Antonietta had accompanied Doña Elena on a visit to a friend's house, and Jesús had gone to see his father at the office where he worked, in order to walk home with him. So, apart from Edurne and me, there was no one else in the house.

I was dozing in my room and Edurne was sewing in the kitchen when we heard the bell.

Edurne opened the door and let out a cry that woke me. I left my room at once and was rendered speechless to find a uniformed German officer in the hall: tall, blond, blue-eyed, handsome. He had a scar shaped like a sickle moon that crossed his face from his right brow down to his nose.

"I should like to see Señorita Garayoa."

"Which one?" Edurne asked in a faint voice.

"Señorita Amelia Garayoa, I... I am an old friend of hers."

"I am sorry, but she is not at home at the moment. Would you like to leave your card?"

"I would prefer to wait. Do you think that she will be long?"

"I don't know," Edurne replied drily, beginning to find the strength to speak with this man in his intimidating uniform.

"She may be quite some time," I said, scared by the thought that this man might intend to do Amelia some harm.

The German turned to me and looked at me with sympathy.

"Are you her cousin Jesús, or are you Pablo? You have to be one or the other."

I was terrified. This officer knew who we were. Suddenly I thought that he was going to arrest us all. I didn't know what to say, I was struck dumb, when suddenly I heard the key turn in the lock and Doña Elena's voice. When she came in, with Laura, Antonietta, and Amelia close behind her, Doña Elena gave a little cry to see the German soldier.

"But who are you?" Doña Elena asked.

"I am sorry to bother you, but I am looking for Señorita Amelia Garayoa..."

He did not say any more, because at this point he saw Amelia: They looked into each other's eyes and then embraced without saying another word. Doña Elena nearly had a stroke, and had to be supported by Antonietta and Laura, who led her into the sitting room.

I stayed behind to watch Amelia and the officer, fascinated by the scene. Amelia was crying, and he was holding back his tears only by a great effort of will. Suddenly Amelia seemed to pull herself together.

"Come, I'll introduce you to my family."

"Perhaps it was not a good idea for me to come without announcing myself in advance... I think I've scared them all."

Amelia took him by the hand and led him to the living room, where Doña Elena was drinking a glass of water.

"Aunt, I would like to introduce you to the Baron von Schumann, an old and very dear friend."

The officer clicked his heels in front of Doña Elena and bowed to kiss her hand, something that dispelled some of the fears that had affected the woman, who was incapable of resisting such a display of good manners.

Laura and Amelia shared a glance that did not go unobserved by any of us present.

Doña Elena invited the officer to sit while she waited for Amelia to explain in a little more detail who this officer was. Everyone in our house hated the Germans, we wanted them to lose the war, Amelia more than anyone, saying that when this happened then France and England and the Allied powers would band together to free us from Franco. So it was difficult for us all to accept a German official with good grace: For us, he represented the dark side of the conflict. He was the enemy, and here he was sitting in our living room.

But Amelia did not seem keen to tell us anything more about this man. She said that he was an old friend whom she had known years ago. We all asked ourselves where this might have been, but no one said anything. We spoke about generalities and nobody mentioned the war. He explained that this was the third time he had visited Madrid, that he had traveled all over Spain with his father when he was younger, and had been in Barcelona, Bilbao, and Seville. Doña Elena said that the autumn was proving very cold and rainy, but that the sun came out even in winter in Madrid. A little while later he asked if there were still bullfights at this time of year, and we told him no, and Doña Elena took the opportunity to say that she was opposed to the national sport.

"I can't bear to see blood being spilled unnecessarily."

This made Laura come out in favor of the activity, telling her mother that she obviously just couldn't see the grandeur inherent in the struggle between bull and toreador. And so, interchanging banalities, about half an hour went by, and then Don Armando came back with Jesús.

Don Armando's face showed shock and worry in roughly equal proportions.

Amelia introduced him without saying anything more about her relationship to Baron von Schumann, and then surprised us all by saying that she would go out with him to take a walk.

"It's a little late, isn't it?" Don Armando said, very seriously.

"I won't be too long, Uncle, it's just that the baron doesn't know Madrid very well, and I'll see him back to his hotel, he's staying at the Ritz, so I should be back soon."

"Maybe it would be better for him to go with Jesús and Pablo."

"No, and anyway we need to speak, we haven't seen each other for a long time."

Don Armando knew that Amelia was going to go out with the German with or without his permission, so he preferred not to confront his niece at this moment.

"Alright, but don't be long."

We said goodbye to the German officer, whom we never saw again.

Amelia came back two hours later, and the whole family was waiting for her in the living room.

"Well, tell us, who is that man?" Don Armando asked.

"I met him a long time ago when I still was living with Pierre. Then I met him in Berlin when I was working as Albert James's assistant. We went to Berlin to gather material for articles and I met him there by chance."

"And you haven't seen him since?" Dona Elena wanted to know.

"Yes, we have met on a couple of other occasions."

"He's a Nazi," Don Armando said, making no effort to hide his disgust.

"No, he isn't. He's a German who has been caught up in the war, like so many other men who have been caught up on one side or the other."

"He's a Nazi," Don Armando repeated.

"No, Uncle, he is not. I tell you, he's a great man, and I owe him a lot."

"What do you owe him, Amelia."

"Please, Uncle, don't insist that I tell you. There are things I don't want to talk about. I am sorry. I cannot."

"The Nazis bankrupted your father, have you forgotten? And you told me yourself that when you were in Berlin it was impossible for you to find out what happened to Herr Itzhak and his family."

"How can you say that!" Amelia was about to burst into tears.

"Because I can't understand how you can be a friend to a man who wears that uniform and that you can forget what the Nazis did to your father! And do you think that the way they're behaving in the war is nothing to worry about? No, Amelia, I cannot accept a Nazi officer in my house. I will not tolerate it. For the memory of my brother and for our own dignity."

I had never seen Don Armando so serious, so strict. We were all silent, not knowing what to say, and Amelia covered her face with her hands.

"Think about what I've just said to you, and be very clear about one thing: I will not allow this man to set foot in this house again."

Amelia looked at her uncle straight in the eye before replying.

"But you are completely happy with Franco, because you don't do anything against the regime."

"Amelia!" Laura bounded up from her chair and stood in front of her cousin, trying to control her anger.

"It's true, we've all submitted to Franco, we don't do anything. Do you think he's better than Mussolini or Hitler? I don't think so, and here we are, not moving a finger to stop him."

"We have lost the war, Amelia, but not our dignity," Don Armando said in a faint voice.

"What do you want us to do, Amelia, haven't we paid for everything in spades?" Laura said.

"Why are you judging Max if you know nothing about him?" Amelia said.

"Because he was able to choose which side he was on and he chose Hitler," Laura said grimly.

"He's a soldier, he cannot choose."

"Yes, Amelia, he can choose, that's what a lot of our soldiers did even if we were then on the losing side," Don Armando said.

"You don't understand... you don't know... I'm sorry, but you cannot see what's going on here."

"Yes, we can, you need to fool yourself because of what this man means to you," Laura said without pity.

The two cousins looked at each other, both of them about to break into tears. It was the first time in their life that they had argued, that they had confronted one another.

We were all silent. Doña Elena broke the tension by sending us to bed.

"We have to get up early tomorrow, leave whatever's disagreeable to talk about in the daylight, it's always better than talking about it at night. At night there is only darkness."

We went to bed, but I got up soon enough; I was sure that Amelia and Laura were talking to each other. And they were. They were in the salon, and were whispering rather than talking. I stood still at the door and listened.

"The things you said to me, Laura! You, in particular..."

"But Amelia, why won't you tell anyone, why won't you even tell me what it is that connects you to this man?"

"For your sake, Laura, I don't tell you anything for your sake. It is better if you do not know certain things, at least not for the time being, I will tell you them one day, I promise, but you will have to trust me for now."

"I was terrified when I came into the house and saw a Nazi. For a moment I thought he was going to arrest us all."

"Poor Max!"

"Who is he to you?"

"I've told you, he is a very important person, so important that it was he who drove me and Albert James apart. If I had not met Max then I would surely still be with Albert."

"I can't believe that you're in love with a Nazi!"

"He's not a Nazi, Laura, I promise you that he is not. He has no option other that to fight with the army; he's an officer, an aristocrat, he cannot desert."

"It's better to be a deserter than to fight for Hitler."

"He does not fight for Hitler."

"Yes, of course he does, you're just fooling yourself, Amelia. Tell me, what did he want, why has he come?"

"He is here on official business and decided to come to see me."

"Don't lie to me, Amelia, I know when you're not telling me the truth."

"In that case don't ask me questions, Laura, don't ask me until I can tell you the whole truth."

I heard them moving and hurried back to my room. If Amelia was not telling Laura the whole truth, then it was clear that she would never tell it to us, so I told myself that we would never know who that man was. And so it was, we never found out, or at least I never found out. Doña Laura may know, I don't know, I never asked her.

Amelia and the German officer carried on seeing each other. He came to find her in Doña Rosa's haberdashery, and would take her out for lunch, and then she would show him her favorite corners of Madrid. One Sunday they even went to the Escorial. But he never came to our house again, and Amelia never again mentioned his name. Don Armando preferred to ignore Amelia's comings and goings, and it was only Doña Elena who was brave enough one day to ask about him.

"Let me tell you something, my dear: Don't fall in love with this man, he can only bring you trouble; you had enough worries with Albert James, who was a good man, and I don't know why you're not still with him. He was a gentleman. It's a shame that you could not get married, but even so. . . If you have to be with a man, you should be with someone who's worth the trouble."

A few days later, one evening at dinner, Amelia told us that she was leaving.

"But where are you going?" Don Armando asked, worried.

"To Rome, I've decided to accept my friend Carla Alessandrini's invitation. I've told you about her, and we write to each other regularly, as you know very well. She has been insisting in her letters that I go to see her, and now I have the chance."

"The chance? But now, so suddenly... and what about your work?" Doña Elena wanted to know.

"I have spoken to Doña Rosa and she says that there's no problem, that I can take a little holiday; I won't be gone for more than a month."

"Are you going with that man, Amelia?" Don Armando asked directly.

"Uncle..."

"You are not completely well yet; yes, you have gotten a little better, but you are so thin... You should not go, Amelia. You said that you never would, that you were going to stay with your family forever."

"I am not going to leave, Uncle, it's just a trip that will not last a long time, I promise. Carla insists so much in her letters that I should go, she says that she needs me, and you can't imagine how kind and generous she has been to me."

"Amelia, I do not think it is a good idea for you to go with that man, who is a Nazi officer," Don Armando interrupted.

"For God's sake, please don't talk like that! Max is a very dear friend of mine, who also knows Carla, and we have been speaking

about her a lot these days. He has to go to Rome, so he has offered to accompany me on the journey. I will go with him to
Rome, yes, but I will stay in Carla Alessandrini's house, I promise. You don't need to worry."

"Italy is at war, it's not the best place for a holiday."

"Nothing will happen, I'm traveling with Max and Carla will
be there to look after me."

"I'm not convinced, Amelia, I'm not convinced. All I know
is that you haven't seemed the same ever since this officer
turned up. I don't understand how you can think about going
to Italy. I want to trust you, Amelia, I owe you a lot, but this is
worrying."

"Trust me, I am not going to do anything bad, I promise. I
will only be gone for a few days, by the next time you think about
me I'll be home for Christmas. I wouldn't want to be away from
home over the holiday for anything in the world."

Edurne, as she helped Amelia pack her suitcases, also complained about the journey she was making.

"How can you leave Antonietta again? Can't you see how
much your sister suffers whenever you go? It's not good for sisters to be apart."

"How long has it been since you've seen Aitor?" Amelia replied.

"A long time, years."

"And he's your brother and you love him, right?"

"Yes, and it hurts me not to see him. He has three children
now. You see, I have nephews and nieces I haven't even met. My
mother suffers on his behalf," Edurne replied.

"Dear Amaya... I miss her so much... ," Amelia replied.

"It was politics that ruined my brother, and you too. A good
thing that he married that woman in Biarritz. It's a disgrace that
he has to live there because of politics. Damn politics!"

"Goodness, I thought you were a good Communist!"

"That was before the war... After what happened and all the
disgrace and shame we've been made to live through, do you
think I still am interested in politics? I just want to live in peace,
I'm like your aunt in that respect."

"So you're not a Communist anymore?" Amelia joked.

"How could I be? You and I didn't know what one was, we were very young and got carried away... Lola, Pierre, Josep Soler, all of those people who seemed to know what was happening. Who were so passionate, they all made us get carried away... They were going to change the world... Well, look how that turned out!"

"What happened is that the Fascists won the war, but that doesn't make them right."

"It doesn't make us right either. No, I'm not a Communist anymore, and I don't think that you are one either."

The day of Amelia's departure was a sad one. Doña Elena fainted and had to be given lemon balm water, Antonietta could not stop hiccupping, Laura cried without stopping, and Jesús and I were affected by so much emotion and ended up crying ourselves. It was only Don Armando who was able to keep his composure.

"Amelia, write to us, please, give us your word that you will."

"I give you my word; I will write and I will come home soon."

Amelia refused to allow us to go with her to the door. She said that people would come to pick her up, but we knew that she meant the German officer. We went out onto one of the balconies and saw him arrive in a black car and then get out of it to help Amelia with her luggage. Before getting into the car she looked up at us and waved her hand with a smile. She was happy, and that is what confused us the most. We did not see her again for a long time..."

"Well," Professor Soler concluded, "that's all, or at least all I can tell you of what happened between the spring of 1942 and the autumn of 1943, a long year that Amelia was with us."

The professor rubbed his eyes with the back of his hand. He seemed tired. I was impressed by his prodigious memory and his ability to recount events in a way that made them not only alive once more, but also so vivid that they seemed to be my own memories. I tried to get him to tell me if Amelia had come back and if so, when, but he did not want to say anything else.

"Come on, Guillermo, you know I'm not going to tell you anything else. At least, not now. You have to fill in the blanks. We agreed not to jump in time. In order for your research to make sense you need to go step by step; if you run ahead of yourself, then you might get confused and might even think that it is not worth coming back, and that is not what the Garayoa ladies want."

"Yes, but where should I look now?" I asked, worriedly.

"I don't know, what about Rome? Amelia told us that she was going to Rome. You could go to see Francesca Venezziani. If Amelia was with Carla Alessandrini, as she told us she would be, then Francesca should know about it, don't you think?"

"What I think is that sometimes you know more about Amelia than you want to let on, but for some reason or other you don't want to say anything about it."

Professor Soler's laughter disconcerted me, but confirmed my intuition.

"Don't be so mistrustful, aren't I helping you as much as I can?"

"And I am very grateful; I wouldn't have been able to take a single step without you."

"Of course you would have, but it would have been more difficult. Don't put yourself down; I have the very highest opinion of you."

"Pah! That's some responsibility to have to shoulder."

"And what about your work? Are you still writing for that online newspaper that you interviewed me for?"

"They fired me. My only job at the moment is this investigation; it's a good thing that the Garayoas are generous enough with what they pay me, or I would have been evicted by now. My mother barely speaks to me, she thinks that I'm wasting my time."

"And she's right."

"What! Do you think I'm wasting my time?"

"You are earning time for the Garayoa sisters, and in that sense your work is very valuable, but as far as you are concerned this is not helping your professional career, in fact it's getting you sidetracked from it."

"I'm surprised you're so calm about that, Professor."

"If you were my son, I might be as upset as your mother appears to be. I won't tell you to hurry up with your job because it is impossible for you to know how much longer it will take, but I would start thinking about what to do when you do finish."

"I have a very serious problem as far as working in my profession is concerned."

"What problem is that?" Professor Soler asked.

"Well, I believe that journalism is a public service whose most important duty is to truth, not to the interests of the politicians, the bankers, the businessmen, the unions, or whoever it is who pays my wages."

"Well, you've got a problem, then."

"You can't imagine how big it is."

After I had said goodbye to Professor Soler I walked along thinking of Francesca Venezziani. I was happy with the idea of seeing her again, it was pleasant when she'd invited me to dinner at her loft. My mother would be angry, of course, when I said I was going away again. Maybe I would have to sit her down and tell her something about her grandmother, maybe that way she would forgive me. But no sooner had the thought crossed my mind than I regretted it. It was not ethical to give out information that didn't belong to me. But I had to tell my mother something to make her trust me, and I couldn't imagine what that might be.

I was lucky, because as soon as I arrived at Prat airport I found a flight for Madrid just ready to leave. When I got back to Madrid I went straight to my mother's house.

"Surprise!" I said when she opened the door.

"Haven't I told you not to call on me unannounced?" she said, as her way of greeting me.

"Yes, but I didn't know I wasn't allowed to come and give you a kiss whenever I felt like it," I said as I hugged her, trying to overcome her ill humor.

My mother gave in and invited me in for dinner, and to my surprise we argued less than we normally did, I don't know if it was because I was tired or simply because she thought that it better to give up on me as an impossible case.

The next day I decided before leaving for Rome to call William Hurley, the important military archivist. I wanted him to clear something up that Professor Soler had mentioned: those two mysterious visits of Señora Rodríguez. I knew something that I thought Professor Soler probably did not, that this woman was in fact an agent of British intelligence. I needed to know if she had visited Amelia for questions of "work."

Major Hurley was not at all pleased that I should call him so soon after our last meeting. He had thought that after telling me about Amelia's adventures in Warsaw he would be free of me for a good long while, but here I was, just a week later, ringing at his door, or rather, his telephone.

He tried to give me excuses: He said that he was very busy with a bowls tournament that the veterans of his former unit were organizing, and that he had no time to tell me why Señora Rodríguez had visited Amelia in Madrid.

"Are you so impatient you can't wait even a week?"

"You don't know how sorry I am to interrupt your planning for the bowls tournament, but I cannot continue without you."

"Young man, you are the one investigating your great-grandmother's past, not me."

"Yes, but I think that the past I am looking for is in your archives, so I have no option other than to bother you, Major. But I promise it will not take long."

"I have to admit that I was expecting this call, though not so soon, but I must insist that I cannot help you now, I am going to Bath tomorrow afternoon and neither you nor I nor any force on God's green earth will stop me from attending the bowls tournament."

"Nothing was further from my intention…"

"Well, the only thing I can tell you is that your great-grandmother was persuaded to return to her collaboration with the British Secret Service."

"So it was Señora Rodríguez who convinced her to return to action."

"In fact, it was not down to Señora Rodríguez's powers of persuasion, but the cause espoused by Carla Alessandrini."

"So now you are leaving me with more questions than answers. Couldn't you tell me something else? I am going to Rome soon and I don't know where to start."

"Call me in the morning," he ordered me, ill-humoredly, and hung up.

I called him the next day, with British punctuality.

"You are right, at the end of 1942 and later in 1943, the British Secret Service got in touch with your great-grandmother in Madrid. It wasn't the first time that they did so, but it appeared that she didn't want to hear anything else about the war or spying, and so they sent Señora Rodríguez. After her life had been saved in Poland, Amelia had sent a long report to Lord Paul James in which she told everything that had happened to her and at the end said that they shouldn't rely on her for any more help. Lord James was not one to turn away from problems, or allow flaws in his plans, so he did not give up: It was only a question of waiting for an auspicious time to bring Amelia back to spying. And such an occasion arose in Rome, where she and Colonel von Schumann were going to have a nasty surprise."

"Yes? What happened?"

"Señora Rodríguez got in touch with Amelia Garayoa to tell her that her friend Carla Alessandrini was collaborating with the Allied secret services, and that she had run into some problems. No, I'm not going to tell you anything else. I've told you that I'm heading off this afternoon and I have a lot to do. Call me in a week and I will see you with pleasure."

There was no point insisting. Major Hurley was implacable. We agreed that we would see each other in a few days, and so I could spend the time in between investigating with Francesca in Rome. The plan seemed perfect.

8

I went to Rome without telling Francesca in advance, taking it for granted that she would be pleased to see me. I called her as soon as I arrived at my hotel.

"*Cara*, I'm in Rome! Can I invite you to dinner this evening?"

"What are you doing here?"

"I came to see you... Well, I came for you to help me with my investigation into my great-grandmother. I'll tell you tonight. Apparently Amelia Garayoa came to Rome in the autumn of 1943 to meet your diva, Carla Alessandrini. I'm sure you can help me. But we can discuss the details over dinner. How about Il Bolognese?"

"I'm sorry, Guillermo, but I cannot have dinner with you this evening, I am otherwise engaged."

"Oh, what bad luck! How about lunch tomorrow?"

"No... I can't do tomorrow either. Maybe it's better for you to tell me what you're looking for and then if I find it I can call you, how about that? Where are you staying?"

"Close to your house, at the Hotel d'Inghilterra. I want to know if Amelia was here with Carla in Rome in the winter of 1943."

"I'll call you," she said, and hung up.

I was very disappointed. I hadn't thought that Francesca would be so indifferent to me. I was sure that we had hit it off, and that we'd had a good time together the last two times we'd seen each other; and now here she was, evasive, even unfriendly. It was upsetting.

I walked around Rome for two days, my mind made up not to call her. I wanted her to realize that I had no intention of following her around like a lapdog. But I got nervous and decided that I couldn't waste my time anymore, and on the third day I called her.

"Francesca, *cara*, have you forgotten about me?" I said in my best tone of voice.

"Oh, it's you! I was going to call you to ask if you would like to have dinner with me this evening at my house."

"Wonderful! You can't imagine how much I want to see you. I'll bring the wine, is that alright?"

"Yes, bring what you want. Come at nine."

What a weight off my shoulders! It's not so much that Francesca had been friendly with me, but at least she had invited me to dinner in her wonderful loft, so I couldn't complain. I was sure that she must be going through a bad time professionally, and that this had meant that she wasn't in as good a mood as she had been the last couple of times. Nothing better than a good meal and a good bottle of wine to sort things out.

I went out at once, to find a shop where I could get a bottle of excellent Barolo. I was so excited that I decided to buy a cake for dessert as well.

Francesca seemed a little distant when I arrived at her house. She opened the door and scarcely allowed me to brush her cheek with my lips.

"You don't know how much I have wanted to see you," I said in my most seductive tone of voice.

"Come and sit down, so I can explain some things to you before we eat."

"Alright, we're in no hurry."

"It depends for what."

"If you want, we could eat first and talk later," I suggested.

"No, we have to wait for Paolo, we can't eat until he gets here."

"Paolo? Who is Paolo?"

"Didn't I say?"

"No," I said, slightly annoyed.

"Goodness, how strange! I'm sure I told you that Paolo was coming."

"Well, who is Paolo?" I insisted.

"Paolo Plattini is an expert in the history of the Second World War in Italy. There isn't anything he doesn't know. He has spent years working with archives and classified documents. You can't imagine how much he is helping me. And you. Because if it weren't for him, it would be difficult for me to tell you what you're going to be told about Amelia's stay in Rome at the end of 1943."

The bell rang and Paolo came straight in to Francesca's apartment.

"Hello everyone!" he said, and went over to Francesca and gave her a kiss straight on the lips. Then he held out his hand to me and smiled broadly.

I had no sooner seen him than I thought that it must be a man I had seen that morning, looking at the Piazza di Spagna.

Sadly for me, Paolo Plattini was charm personified. He was an extroverted Roman with a great capacity for communication, which made him the center of attention. He was too clever and attractive to compete with, and he was at that mature age that makes sensible women lose their heads. I immediately said goodbye to Francesca in my mind.

"I don't know if you know, but there's a book of memoirs written by a partisan a few years after the war ended that mentions your great-grandmother. This is the most trustworthy and direct source of information on Amelia's travels and adventures in Italy, because it's by a person who knew her and who had a close relationship with her. He was called Mateo Marchetti, and he was Carla Alessandrini's singing teacher, an old Communist whom the diva worshipped."

"I had no idea that the book existed," I said, interested.

"That's not surprising, it has only ever been published in a very limited edition, only two thousand copies. It was a favor from the editor of a small publishing house, another Communist, to Marchetti. The book didn't make much of a splash, but it has a certain historical value. I remembered it when Francesca told me that she was finding it hard to get information about what Carla Alessandrini had done in the war. Can you read Italian?" he said, and held out to me an old paperback book.

"I can try."

"Well, I think that it will be of use to you. In any event, if you want to take notes or record what I'm going to say, then I think I can reconstruct pretty well certain details of your aunt's stay in Rome in the winter of 1943."

Paolo began talking, and I must confess that I said nothing until he was finished.

Amelia came to Rome accompanied by a colonel in the German army, Baron von Schumann, whom Carla had met years ago in Berlin. According to Marchetti, von Schumann was no fan of Hitler's, but, like a good Prussian, he obeyed orders without complaint.

Colonel von Schumann was staying at the Excelsior, a very elegant hotel, and accompanied Amelia to Carla Alessandrini's house. The diva would not have forgiven Amelia if she had stayed anywhere else. Carla had asked her on numerous occasions to come and visit, you know that she loved her like a daughter. But Amelia and von Schumann were surprised when they arrived at Carla's house and found, not her, but her distraught husband, Vittorio Leonardi.

"Amelia, how happy I am to see you!" he said, embracing her tightly.

Then he greeted Colonel von Schumann politely, but coolly, which surprised Amelia. Vittorio had met Colonel von Schumann in Berlin and they had spent several evenings together, and this new coolness was at odds with their former relation. Amelia saw Vittorio's nervousness without understanding his hostility toward Max von Schumann. He didn't even invite him into the house. Von Schumann took his leave. He had to go and report to his superiors. As soon as Vittorio and Amelia were alone, she asked him straight out.

"Vittorio, what's happened? Where is Carla?"

"She's been arrested."

"Arrested? But why?" Amelia said in alarm.

"For collaborating with the partisans. Really, it's my fault."

"My God, tell me what happened!"

"The SS have her."

"Why?"

"I've told you, Carla has been working with the Resistance and I think that... well, I think that she's also been in touch secretly with the Allies."

"And you?"

"This is my fault for having allowed such things to happen. We even fought about it, but you know the influence that her singing teacher Mateo Marchetti has over her. Carla has always helped Marchetti's friends, she's been opposed to Mussolini ever since he became leader of Italy, and she has never been shy about showing it. But she is *la gran* Carla Alessandrini, and so everyone was nice to her, as if her opposition were merely an eccentricity. But actually, Carla's collaboration with the partisans has grown ever closer. Our house in Milan became a refuge for fugitives, as did our place in Rome. Then she started to help take people over the border, people who were about to be arrested by the police or the SS. People whom Marchetti asked Carla to save. And not just him, but also that German priest who's a friend of yours, Father Müller. You can't know how many times he's come here asking us to help some Jewish family or other to escape."

"Father Müller is still here?" Amelia asked in surprise.

"Yes, he lives in the Vatican, and he is with them."

"With whom?"

"With the partisans, he collaborates with the partisans. Carla put him in touch with Mateo Marchetti. Father Müller is a minor official in the Foreign Office, and every now and then, don't ask me how he does it, he steals Vatican passports to help certain people escape."

"You still haven't told me why they arrested Carla."

"I wasn't here. We had fought for the first time in our life together. I was scared of what might happen because every day, without thinking of the consequences, she was getting more and more daring. She took lots of risks. I tried to reason with her, to make her understand that she shouldn't be so open about what she believed, but she wouldn't listen to me. And she didn't practice much anymore, because she had lost all interest in singing, in what had been her reason for living, what she had sacrificed her whole life for. She lived only to meet with Mateo Marchetti, to cross the border, to conspire with your friend Father Müller. It was clear that they were beginning to suspect her, but she didn't want to notice or listen to reason. I told her, I kept on telling her: Colonel Jürgens suspects you, I said, but she didn't want to listen to me, she thought that he was on his knees before her, like all men had been up to that point."

"Colonel Jürgens?" Amelia asked in alarm.

"Yes, Colonel Ulrich Jürgens. Apparently he's been promoted recently because he was wounded on the Eastern Front. Everyone in Rome is afraid of him."

"Tell me what sort of a man he is."

"He's tall, and blond and handsome, but he hasn't got any class. He's successful with women. I think he was on the Russian front and then in Poland. He's very popular here, there's no party to which he isn't invited."

Amelia felt as if she could no longer breathe, and she started to shake. Her path had crossed once again with that of Ulrich Jürgens, the man who had broken Grazyna Kaczynski's network in Warsaw, who had ordered Grazyna to be tortured, along with all her friends and Amelia herself. The man who had condemned her to a year of living hell in Pawiak, the prison where they had tortured her and had murdered her friend Ewa. She relived everything she had suffered in Poland, and cried for Grazyna and for that group of young people who had traveled through the sewers, mocking the Nazis and plunging into the heart of the Warsaw ghetto to bring a little bit of help to their Jewish friends. Faces swam into her memory, the faces of Grazyna, of Ewa, of Piotr, of Tomasz, of Szymon, Grazyna's lover, his brother Barak, their mother Sarah, Sister Maria, the Countess Lublin... She remembered her time in Warsaw so clearly that she felt once again the blows of the SS torturers, the laughter of Major Ulrich Jürgens, as he had been at the time. The cold floor of her cell in Pawiak, the lice that ran through her hair and bit into her head until they made it bleed... And now Vittorio was telling her that the devil was back, that Ulrich Jürgens was here, in Rome.

"Amelia... Amelia... what's wrong?" Vittorio grasped her shoulder, to try to bring her back to reality.

"How did you meet Colonel Jürgens?"

"At a party. Immediately he was extremely interested in Carla, and said that he remembered her performances in Berlin. He praised her voice and her beauty. He flattered her ridiculously. But Carla ignored him, or rather, she didn't even bother to hide how much she disdained him. We started to run into him everywhere. I told Carla that this man had an unhealthy interest in her, but she thought that I was jealous, can you imagine that! She didn't want to see something that was so evident, that this man wanted to possess her, yes, but also to destroy her. One day he asked after you. Carla was surprised that he should know about you and he laughed and said, 'Oh, you'd be surprised just how much I know about her!' But she didn't believe him, and said in a very undiplomatic way that it was impossible for a woman like you to pay any attention at all to a man like him."

"I know him, Vittorio, I know him," Amelia said. "He... he ordered me to be arrested in Warsaw and... Well, I'm not going to say what happened, it's not important now, the important thing is Carla. Tell me, how long has she been detained?"

"She was arrested five days ago. I wasn't here. I told you that I had argued with her; I went to Switzerland. I wanted to try to make her give up all this political activity, or at least not to get so involved in it. I was waiting to see her in Switzerland, because Marchetti had asked her to cross the border with a man whom the Resistance had managed to infiltrate close to Mussolini. He was one of Il Duce's stewards and he knew the family very well. He had passed as a Fascist for years, but he thought that they were starting to be suspicious of him. I think he had smuggled out important documents in Il Duce's possession that spoke about the German plans for Italy and other places in Europe. His comrades decided that the moment had come to get him out of Italy. As you can imagine, he was a man with important information and the Allied secret services were anxious to get in touch with him. Marchetti asked Carla to help him, and she met with Father Müller and asked him for one of his Vatican passports. Father Müller promised to get hold of one, but he took longer than he had promised and Carla grew impatient. She decided that it would be she who took this man to Switzerland. She worked out the plan herself: They would go alone and he would pretend to be her chauffeur. If they asked, they would say that Carla was planning to go to Zurich to meet me. It wasn't a bad idea, but they decided not to go through the mountains because the man was already past sixty and was not in very good health, and there were German troops all along the Swiss border. The night before they left, Carla went to dinner at a friend's house and met Colonel Jürgens. He was particularly ironic that night, and even said in public that they would soon be spending more time together than she could possibly imagine. He even hinted to Carla that he would get to know every inch of her body. Carla laughed at him, and was more sarcastic and disdainful than usual. She even said that she wouldn't let men like him even take off her shoes. Jürgens said that very soon he would do more than that to her. The next night, Carla and the Duce's steward headed off toward Switzerland. She drove, because although the man was supposed to pretend to be her chauffeur, he was unable to drive. In case they were stopped, he was to pretend to be suffering from muscle spasms that prevented him from driving. Carla drove almost all through the night and they reached the border. They stopped at the border post and were asked for their documentation. Everything seemed to be going well, until Colonel Jürgens came out of the shadows. He ordered them out of the car and laughed at the Duce's steward's passport.

"'So you're this lady's chauffeur, are you?' Jürgens said, looking straight at the old man.

"'Yes... yes... ,' the man babbled.

"'Well, it's just that Il Duce is missing one of his stewards, a loyal man who has served him for many years. Mussolini is very worried; as an Italian, you must be aware of how much Il Duce worries about his household staff and the people who surround him: They're like his family. So, do you know where Il Duce's steward could be? You don't know? And what about *la gran* Alessandrini?'

"'Why should I know?' Carla said, defiantly.

"'You are so clever. You are unique! Come on, I think I'm going to have to refresh your memory.'

"They were surrounded by some policemen and put into a car. They were driven to Rome and are now in the hands of the SS."

"My God! What are we going to do, Vittorio?" Amelia said in alarm.

"As you might imagine, I've asked all our friends to do what they can, but no one has any influence with the SS, not even any of the people in Il Duce's entourage. I am desperate."

Vittorio rubbed his eyes with the back of his hand, trying to wipe away the tears that he had not been able to hold back.

"We will do what it takes, we won't leave Carla in the hands of that murderer... We'll ask Max to see what he can do for her, maybe there's something..."

"The baron?"

"Yes, at least he will be able to find out how Carla is and what they intend to do with her. One more thing, can you arrange a meeting for me with Marchetti?"

"With that man? Don't get mixed up with him, Amelia, look at where Carla is because of him... No, I don't want to hear anything about Marchetti. He came to see me but I didn't meet him, he has brought enough trouble on us as it is. It was his fault that all these political ideas got into Carla's head in the first place."

"But he might be able to help us."

"Help us? How will he help us? He was the one who asked Carla for help, who bent her to his will and made her risk herself too much. No, I don't want to see this man in my life ever again."

"You don't need to see him, just tell me where I can find him."

"I don't know, he never sleeps two nights running in the same place, and he's in Rome as much as he is in Milan, he moves all over the place. Maybe your friend the German priest will know how to find him."

"Father Müller?"

"Yes, and him I know how to find. He takes confession two days a week in San Clemente, do you know where that is?"

"No."

"In Laterano, in the Via San Giovanni. On Tuesdays and Thursdays he is there from five to seven. You can call him at the Foreign Office as well. But be careful, Amelia, the priest will only bring you problems, like Marchetti will."

"What about that diplomat friend of yours who worked cheek by jowl with Il Duce's son-in-law, can't he do anything?"

"You mean Guido Gallotti? No, he hasn't been able to do all that much. It is difficult for him to stick his neck out for Carla because she was helping one of Il Duce's employees to escape. But even so he stood up for her in front of Colonel Jürgens, but that man said that if he was a true Italian patriot then he should be happy that the SS had arrested a traitor."

"Vittorio, I know this might be difficult, but you need to trust Max."

"But he is a German! A Nazi!"

"No, he's not a Nazi. You knew him in Buenos Aires before the war, then you saw him in Berlin, you know how he is and how he thinks. Please believe me when I say we can trust him!"

Vittorio was silent for a moment, looking straight at Amelia. What he saw was a young woman in love with this German, who might possibly be in love with her in return, but to tell a Nazi that his wife had worked with the partisans? No, he would never do that.

"No, Amelia, I am not going to put Carla's life in the hands of any Nazi."

"Her life is in the hands of the SS."

"I know that you trust him... but I... I cannot."

Amelia nodded thoughtfully. She understood Vittorio. Her uncle had felt the same mistrust toward the German, and nothing she had said to him had been able to make him change his mind.

"I wouldn't hesitate to put my life in Max's hands. He saved me from Pawiak in Warsaw, where... Well, I'll tell you one day what they did to me there, it is why I would do anything to save Carla from the SS. Colonel Jürgens had me arrested, so I know quite well what he is capable of. If it had not been for Max, I don't know what would have become of me."

"The baron and you... Well, I know that he has feelings for you, but why would he do anything for Carla?"

"Because he's not a Nazi, and he hates the SS just as much as any normal decent person.

"Amelia, you're such an innocent! I'm sure that Baron von Schumann is a decent man, and that he feels distaste for these SS brutes: Given his aristocratic background, he could hardly feel anything else, but he fights alongside them, cheek by jowl, for the same ends, and he has sworn loyalty to Hitler. Conscience sometimes goes one way, and necessity the other."

"You're wrong about Max, but I know I won't be able to convince you. At least let me ask him to look into Carla's case, I won't say a word about her work with the partisans."

"If you just say that she's been arrested and ask what he can do, then... all right."

Vittorio asked her to dinner in a restaurant near the Piazza di Popolo. He was keen to hear about her stay in Madrid and wanted to know how Franco was governing, and she spoke at length about how much it hurt her not to be able to see her little son.

Max came to visit her two days later. It was Sunday, and in spite of its being winter, he suggested that they go for a walk under the tepid sun. The soldier seemed happy to be in Rome, and they walked all the way to the Piazza Venezia.

"Look, it was from this window that Il Duce fired up his followers," Amelia said to Max. "If you want, we could carry on until we get to the Forum."

"What's worrying you, Amelia?" Max asked.

"They've arrested Carla."

"And you've only told me now? We've been walking around for an hour talking about nothing."

"I didn't know how to tell you."

"It's very simple, why can't you talk to me anymore?"

"I'm sorry, Max, it's just that... Vittorio... well... he didn't want me to say anything to you. He doesn't trust any Germans."

"You can't blame him for that, but he knows me."

"Even so... he's scared. Colonel Ulrich Jürgens has Carla."

"I found out yesterday that Jürgens is here... I wouldn't have insisted that you come if I had known, and now you tell me that he's arrested Carla..."

Max fell silent. He feared for Amelia, all the more now because he had found out that Carla had been arrested.

"Why did they arrest her?"

"She was going to Switzerland and they stopped her near the border. She was driving with her chauffeur, who's an elderly man and who hasn't been with her very long. She gave him the job via some friends. Apparently, the man had been in the service of Il Duce. But he was scared when Mussolini was arrested, and even though he came back when the Republic of Salò was proclaimed, he preferred to retire and have a quieter life. He was afraid that if things went badly for Il Duce in Italy, then he could be accused of being a Fascist simply for having worked for Mussolini; so he decided that, having saved a bit of money, he would go to Switzerland and start a new life. And Carla was just a useful way of getting there."

"You want to make me believe that Carla would willingly and knowingly help a Fascist? Why are you lying to me, Amelia? Don't I deserve your trust? I prefer to be silent than for you to lie to me."

She lowered her head in embarrassment. She trusted Max and knew that he was incapable of unworthy behavior.

"Vittorio doesn't trust you."

"You've already said that, but do you?"

"I don't know much more than what Vittorio told me. This man was not as big a supporter of Il Duce as he claimed to be, and he was going to Switzerland because he had certain information."

"And that's why Carla helped him. Was it so hard to tell me the truth?"

"I'm sorry, Max."

"I'm sorry, sorry that you don't trust me," he said with a bitter smile on his lips.

"I wasn't trying to lie to you," she insisted.

"Don't apologize, Amelia, I know that you have a conflict of loyalties."

"For God's sake, Max, I trust you! I owe you my life!"

"But your family and your friends don't believe that I am a decent person, and you have no way of convincing them otherwise."

Amelia started to cry. She felt terrible for not having told the truth.

"Come, come, don't cry!"

"I'm just ashamed not to have told you the truth. You are right to scold me for my behavior."

He dried her tears with his handkerchief, then looked straight at her before speaking.

"I want you to promise me one thing, Amelia, and I want you to think about it before you do."

"Yes... yes... Whatever you want..."

"No, think about it, because I can't stand duplicity. If you promise to do what I am going to ask you to do, I want it to be whatever the circumstances."

"Whatever you want. Tell me what you want and I will promise."

"That you will never lie to me again, that you will prefer to remain silent than to lie to me, that you will look at me and tell me by your look that you cannot say more, but that you will never lie to me again."

"I give you my word, Max."

"That's good, I believe you. And now tell me as much as you can about what happened to Carla."

Keeping hidden that Carla openly worked with the partisans and that her music teacher was a committed Communist, Amelia told Max a good part of what Vittorio had explained to her, and asked him to do what he could to find out about her friend.

"It won't be easy, you know how much Ulrich Jürgens hates me. And I'm afraid for you: I regret having brought you to Rome. You should go back to Spain before Jürgens decides to do something to you."

"More than what he did to me in Warsaw?"

"That was a defeat for him, he hasn't forgiven me for being able to get you out of Pawiak. He didn't want them to hang you, he was happy to think of you suffering in that prison. He will do anything he can to hurt us."

"Do you know why Jürgens hates you so much?"

"He knows that I dislike the SS, that I don't agree with what Hitler is doing," Max replied.

"No, he doesn't hate you for that. He hates you because you are everything that he is not. A gentleman, and an aristocrat, and a member of a powerful family, who has studied at the best schools of Europe and who has trained to become an important doctor."

"And he hates me because I have you, Amelia, that is what he really envies, that he will never be able to have you. That's why you have to go back to Spain; he will do whatever it takes to destroy us."

"I can't do it, Max, not before doing something for Carla."

"It will be easier for me to act if you are not here."

"Carla has been like a second mother to me and I cannot abandon her. Also, Vittorio is distraught and he needs me."

"If you stay, Jürgens will try to do something to you... For God's sake, Amelia, don't put yourself in danger!"

"I have to stay, Max, I can't leave Carla. She wouldn't abandon me."

Max promised to look discreetly into Carla Alessandrini's whereabouts.

"But things might get worse for her if Colonel Jürgens finds out that I'm investigating her."

"Does he know you're here?"

"I'm sure he does, but what I'm really worried about is that he knows you are here as well."

Amelia waited until Tuesday to go to San Clemente. Vittorio told her how to get there, and she decided to walk.

There were several women praying inside the church. They didn't look at the new arrival, and she paid them no attention either. She looked for the confessionals; nobody was in them, so she sat to wait and tried to pray. But she could not; she was too nervous and too eager to see Father Müller.

She had to wait another half an hour before she saw him appear, talking to another priest, and they both went to the confessionals.

She was just getting up when a women cut in front of her and knelt down in front of the confessional where Father Müller was.

Amelia waited impatiently until the woman had finished her confession.

"Hail Mary most pure."

"Conceived without sin."

"Rudolf, it's Amelia."

"Amelia! Heavens, what are you doing here?"

She told him what her life had been since the last time they had seen each other, as well as the motive for her journey to Rome. He told her about Carla's situation.

"She's an extraordinary woman, extremely brave, you can't imagine how many people she's helped escape from Rome, Jews above all."

"What can we do? We have to help her."

"We can't do anything, the SS have taken her prisoner. The only thing I know is that she's alive. The SS don't let priests visit the prisoners, except if they are going to be hanged. A friend was in prison last week helping various prisoners through their last moments. I found out via him that Carla is still alive, although she is in a very bad state, she's been brutally tortured."

"We have to get her out of there."

"Impossible! I've told you that the SS have her."

"Do you know Marchetti?"

"Carla's singing teacher?" Yes, I know him, Carla introduced us. We have helped each other. I got him some passports and he has helped get small groups of Jews out of Rome."

"Do you know where I could find him?"

"We always used to get in touch via Carla, although occasionally, if he was very busy, he would come straight here, to San Clemente. Once he gave me the address of a Jewish family he was hiding until he could get them out of Italy. But I don't know if that's still a safe house. There was a woman who lived there whom I never even spoke to. She opened the door, let the fugitives in, and then almost pushed me back out. But what about Vittorio? Carla's husband should know how to find Marchetti."

"No, he doesn't. Marchetti has not gone back to his house, and no one answers the telephone at his singing school in Milan. He's gone into hiding."

"In that case, we should try looking at the address I've told you about, even though I don't believe that Marchetti can do anything for Carla. I don't think anyone can."

"Don't say that, Rudolf!"

"You think I don't know what might happen just as well as you do? I love her too."

They agreed to go together to the address where they might be able to get some information about Carla's whereabouts.

"But go now, go and come back at seven."

The house was in the Via dei Coronari, just off the Piazza Navona. They hurried up the stairs, scared of running into someone who might ask them where they were headed.

Father Müller knocked gently on the door with his knuckles, just as he had been told to do when he had come here previously with the Jewish family. They waited impatiently without hearing a single noise from inside the house, and they were just about to leave when the door opened a crack. A woman's face appeared in the shadows.

"What are you doing here?" she asked Father Müller.

"Let us in."

"You shouldn't be here."

"I know, but... Please, let us in and we'll explain."

The woman seemed to hesitate, then took off the chain that served as a bolt and let them pass.

They followed her down a dark corridor that led onto a salon crammed with furniture. An upright lamp scarcely lit the room and it took Amelia some time to make out the woman's face. She must have been around fifty years old. She was dark and of medium height, with her hair drawn back into a bun. She was dressed in a black skirt and a gray sweater and wore no jewelry.

"You have put me in danger by coming here," she said accusingly to the priest.

"I am sorry, but I have to find Marchetti and I didn't know how."

"And you want me to tell you how to find him?" she said ironically.

"If you won't tell us how to, then you could at least get in touch with him and tell him that we need to see him urgently."

"Right, you've given me your message, now leave."

"We need him to help us to..."

The woman raised her hand so that Father Müller would stop talking.

"I don't want to know. The less we know about each other and our operations, the less danger we are in. You have already broken the rules by coming here. You didn't know if this house were still safe or if it had been discovered by the SS. You have run unnecessary risks."

"I had no other option."

"In any case, don't come back here. I will try to get him your message, but I won't tell you how or when I will, or if he will reply. So if you don't hear anything don't get impatient, and above all don't come back, do you understand me?"

"Yes, of course."

They hurried out of the house and didn't speak to each other until they were in the street.

"She didn't even look at me," Amelia said.

"She prefers not to see or hear what she has not been told to see or hear. It is not easy to live in hiding, Amelia."

"Tell me, Rudolf, how many people are there in your organization?"

"My organization? I wish I had an organization! You have misunderstood me. I came to Rome on the recommendation of my bishop to work in the Foreign Office. The fact that I speak German and English and French and a little Polish and Russian helped me to get a low-ranking job. I am a secretary, an office worker. I have no responsibilities. There are no secrets that pass through my hands, no important documents. Shortly after I arrived they sent me to San Clemente to hear confessions two days a week. Two priests take charge of this, sometimes I finish early, sometimes he does. One day I was taking confession until after eight o'clock, and when I had finished and went to the sacristy I found a man hiding there, along with a woman and two small children. The man told me that he was Dr. Ferratti, a surgeon, and he told me that he had kept the woman and the children in his house. Her husband had long since been deported to Germany.

"He said that there had been a raid on their district that afternoon and asked for my help. And I helped them. I didn't know where I could hide them, so I thought I'd open the door that led to the cellars. They're from the first century and in a pretty poor state, but what could I do? The parish priest at San Clemente had told me that I shouldn't even think of going into the catacombs, because who knew what I might find. Apparently, this used to be a temple dedicated to the Persian God Mithras. And it wasn't until the last century that an Irish priest, Father Mullooly, discovered that there was another church under this one and started to excavate it. I took the woman and the two children there. They were trembling from fear and cold. We heard the sound of water as we walked, because there is a spring in the catacombs. I set them up as best I could; luckily Dr. Ferratti had a bag with food and a couple of blankets in it, and I brought some candles.

"'Stay here until I can find a way of getting you out of Rome and taking you to Lisbon, and we can try to get you from there to America. It won't be easy, but we'll manage it somehow,' I said. The children started to cry and their mother didn't know what to do to calm them down.

"Dr. Ferratti explained that he lived very close to San Clemente, on the corner of the Piazza di San Giovanni in Laterano, and that he felt an obligation to help his fellow men. There were some Jews who were his neighbors; some of them had been arrested by the SS and sent to Germany; others were hidden in the houses of good Christians who were not willing to work with the Nazis.

"Ferratti and two other doctors had banded together to help and assist the Jews who were still hidden. They moved them from house to house so as not to compromise the people they were staying with, and had even managed to get a few of them away to Switzerland. As you can imagine, I immediately offered to help them however I could. Carla helped us whenever she was able to, hiding families in her house and getting some of them sent to Switzerland."

"But it was so risky to drive them over the frontier!" Amelia exclaimed.

"She didn't take them in her car, that would have been very dangerous. Carla's relationship with the partisans meant that we could get some of them out over the mountains. Of course, only in spring and summer, because it would have been impossible in autumn. Even so, this was always the most dangerous option, because we were dealing with families, women, and young children. The truth is that most of the families we were helping are still in Rome: As I said, we have moved them from house to house and sometimes have even used the basements and forgotten underground shelters such as the ones under San Clemente. And we have used the catacombs, which have been sheltering Christians for twenty centuries."

"The catacombs? They can't be very safe, everyone knows where they are."

"Don't you believe it. I have a good friend in the Vatican, Domenico, a Jesuit who works in the archives; he's an archaeologist and knows the underground areas of the city very well. Rome still has many secrets. I'll introduce you, I'm sure that you'll like him."

"Can't the Vatican do anything for Carla?"

"The relations between the Vatican and Germany are not what you might call good. You don't know what the Pope has to deal with."

"So your group is three doctors and two priests. That's not a lot," Amelia said, regretfully.

"You can't imagine how active and brave some of the nuns are. Dr. Ferratti also has some friends who help us out now and then, but we can't ask people to be heroes, because if the SS arrest them... I don't need to tell you what will happen to them."

"We have to save Carla," Amelia insisted again.

Vittorio was worried about Amelia. She had been out all afternoon, and when she got home, accompanied by Father Müller, it was already dinnertime.

"Tell me when you're going to be late, I thought something might have happened to you."

In fact, it was Amelia who grew more worried about Vittorio every day. Carla's husband scarcely ate anything, he suffered from insomnia and never stopped running around the city, ringing the doorbells of influential people who in the past had been his friends, whom he begged to do something for Carla. But nobody wanted to commit himself, and people even started to avoid him. It was rumored that Carla Alessandrini was to be tried for high treason.

If it had not been for her worries about Carla, Amelia might have been happy in Rome. Max spent all his free time with her, and both of them felt as much in love as they had felt on their previous times together in Warsaw and Berlin.

The baron asked his superiors about Carla Alessandrini, and they told him to forget about the diva, as she was now in the hands of the SS. Even so, he managed to discover that she was still alive.

One night when Rome's military governor held a reception for all the members of German High Command, the diplomatic corps and everyone who was anyone in occupied Rome, Max insisted that Amelia accompany him. She was unsure, she felt disgusted by the idea of shaking the hands of those men who sowed misery, death, and destruction in their wake, but she thought that maybe she would get the chance to hear something about Carla.

That December night was cold and rainy. On her way to the party, Amelia thought that it would soon be Christmas and that she had promised her family to be back in Spain for the festivities, but she knew now that she would be unable to keep her word, not until she had done something for Carla.

She was happy to see Major Hans Henke, Max's adjutant.

"Colonel, I don't think it was a good idea to bring Fräulein Garayoa here," Henke said as soon as he saw her.

"Well, I think it was a great idea," said Max, happy to have Amelia by his side.

"Look who's over there," Hans Henke said, pointing discreetly to a group of SS officers at the back of the room.

Even though they had their backs to her, Amelia could recognize Ulrich Jürgens at once, and felt a wave of disgust wash over her. She reddened.

"I'm sorry, Amelia, I didn't think we'd run into him, if I had then I wouldn't have come. They told me that Jürgens was in Milan."

"He came back this evening," Major Henke said.

"We should leave discreetly. Hans is right, it would be a risk if Jürgens were to see you."

They were just leaving the room when Colonel Ulrich Jürgens headed toward them. A moment before, another SS officer had alerted him to the presence of Max von Schumann and Amelia Garayoa.

Jürgens cut them off, holding a glass of champagne in either hand.

"Well, well, well, if it isn't my old friend Amelia Garayoa! Surely you wouldn't leave without raising a toast to our happy meeting?" he said, holding out a glass to Amelia and ignoring von Schumann.

"Get out of the way, Jürgens," Max said, taking hold of Amelia's arm.

"But my dear baron, you've only just arrived at the party! A gentleman like you, surely you're not going to disappoint the hosts by leaving before dinner is served?"

"Leave us alone, Jürgens," Max insisted.

Suddenly he realized that they were surrounded by a group of SS officers.

"Baron, aren't you going to introduce us to this beautiful lady?" one of the soldiers asked with an ironic smile.

"You can't keep her all to yourself, allow us at least one dance," another one said.

"We've heard so much about Fräulein Garayoa, isn't she an old friend of Colonel Jürgens's?" a third said.

Amelia felt her body becoming rigid and her voice freezing in her throat. She had not thought that fate would place her once again face to face with a man who had personally tortured her. She could still hear in her ears Colonel Jürgens's shouts of laughter as she twisted with pain and shame when he ripped her clothes off to examine her naked body before torturing her.

Max pushed one of the officers out of his way and pulled Amelia toward the exit, but luck was not on his side that evening, because at that very moment the commander of his division came over to the group with two other generals and asked Max to come and talk to them for a moment.

"We won't be a moment, we just need to discuss one point, Colonel. Let's leave these gentlemen to look after the lady."

"I am sorry, general, but we were just leaving, the lady doesn't feel very well," Max replied.

"Come on, it will only be a moment! Colonel, look after this young lady while we talk to Baron von Schumann."

Amelia was face to face with her torturer, and when Jürgens held his hand out to her, she pulled back brusquely.

"Don't you dare touch me!"

"But my dear, I did rather more than touch you in the past! Where does this sudden prudishness come from?"

His SS companions laughed at Jürgens's riposte and at a signal from him they withdrew, leaving him alone with Amelia.

"You shouldn't be so fierce with me, you know that hell hath no fury like a gentleman scorned," he said, sarcastically.

"What do you want, Jürgens?"

"Oh, you know what I want! Do you want me to say out loud that I want what Baron von Schumann has? Why aren't you as kind to me as you are to him? I assure you that I will be far more generous to you than Baron von Schumann is. He's only offering you love, but I can offer you the whole world, I can offer you the chance to share the glory of the Reich."

"If you only knew how much you disgust me!"

"Your resistance only makes you all the more attractive."

"Never, Jürgens! You will never have me, even if you torture me again!"

"If you had been more reasonable, then I could have over-looked your little peccadillo: helping those poor wretches. I'll never understand why you joined up with those pigheaded Poles just to save a few Jews!"

"No, of course you'll never understand it; it's beyond your capacity to understand it."

"You know what? I don't know why, but I feel attracted to you... I never usually like women who are so thin. Your friend

Carla Alessandrini is far more attractive, at least she has curves like a real woman, and you look so fragile..."

"You are disgusting! What have you done to Carla?"

"Ah, well! Your friend is a traitor! You should be careful not to deal with traitors, you know what happens when Reich justice catches up with them."

Colonel Ulrich Jürgens gave her a hard look. Then he grabbed her hand and squeezed it so hard that he hurt her.

"If you resist me, you know what the consequences will be. Why not try to avoid problems? You know I will not be as kind as I was in Warsaw."

Amelia could not constrain herself, and kicked him in the shin in an attempt to get away. But she didn't manage. Jürgens grabbed her forcefully and twisted her arm.

"If you want to declare war on me, then so be it!" he said, his eyes filled with fury and a wicked smile on his lips.

She broke free, finally, and ran off looking for Max.

"What happened?" the baron asked.

Amelia told him what had happened, and what Jürgens had threatened.

"He's a scoundrel, a bastard!"

On the way back home, Amelia did not stop shaking. She was afraid of the threats that sadist had made.

"Calm down. It's been decided, you'll go back to Spain. I don't want you to stay in Rome while Jürgens is here. I will find you a plane ticket for Madrid tomorrow. Try not to leave Vittorio's house unless I come looking for you, it would be better if you didn't even see Father Müller."

"I don't want to go; I can't leave Vittorio."

"Amelia, I will not allow you to stay in Rome, I have to leave in two days to survey our troops; I will be in the north and I cannot begin to think what Jürgens is capable of."

But Amelia knew what Jürgens was capable of, even though she said nothing. She did not want to remember the months she had spent in Pawiak, even though they came back to her every night in her nightmares.

Vittorio agreed with Baron von Schumann and asked Amelia to go back to Spain.

"My dear, you can't do anything here apart from be at my side. You have a family which is waiting for you, and it will be Christmas in a few days' time."

But there was no way of convincing her, and so Max von Schumann went to Milan, worried about what might happen in his absence.

9

Two days before Christmas, Father Müller turned up unexpectedly at Vittorio's house and asked for Amelia.

"Marchetti has sent word that he's prepared to see you," he said in a low voice.

"When?" she asked nervously.

"On Christmas Eve, during the Midnight Mass, in San Clemente. He will try to get lost in the congregation. He's in a lot of danger because they've put a price on his head."

That night, Amelia didn't sleep, thinking about what she was going to say to Mateo Marchetti, who had seemed such an inoffensive singing teacher when she had first met him, but who had turned out to be one of the leaders of the Resistance.

December 24 dawned cold and foggy, just like her mood. She thought about her family, and imagined them making the Christmas Eve dinner. Perhaps Melita's husband had brought a good basket of food, which would help the family's difficult situation.

She decided to write them a letter: She had not finished it when the door opened and Vittorio came into the room, pale and trembling.

"What happened? What's going on?" Amelia stood up and put her arms round Vittorio, who seemed about to fall.

"The radio... They've just said it on the radio..." The man began to cry, holding tight to Amelia.

"Vittorio, calm down! What have you heard on the radio?"

But he could not calm down, and his sobs turned into howls of grief.

"Tell me what's happened! Please, tell me!" Amelia begged, scarcely able to keep Vittorio's weakened body upright, as he still held tightly to her.

"They've killed her," he managed to say.

Amelia wanted to scream, but nothing came out of her mouth but a broken moan. She felt the salt taste of her tears in the corner of the mouth, and held Vittorio tight with all the strength she could manage.

"They've killed her! They've killed her!" Vittorio cried out.

She managed to get him to a chair and call for a maid to bring her a glass of water. The whole house had discovered what had happened. Everybody had heard it on the radio. There was no doubt in the report: "This morning, at the woman's prison, guilty of the crime of high treason, the bel canto diva Carla Alessandrini was hanged."

The servants muttered nervously among themselves while Amelia tried to take control of the situation.

She couldn't stay sitting and weeping until she had no more tears, she could not allow the pain and grief to carry her away. She had to take charge of Vittorio, and she had to decide what to do next.

Would the SS come to her house? Should she go with Vittorio to recover Carla's body? She didn't know what to do. But Father Müller's arrival was a small relief.

"I am so sorry," the priest said as he embraced Vittorio, who had not stopped crying and who was starting to shake.

"What should we do?" she asked him in a whisper.

"I don't know, I'll ask. The family has the right to the body. But they didn't even tell you that they judged her and condemned her to death."

"Judged her? There is no justice here, the SS don't know what justice is, they only murder. They murdered Carla."

"I don't know how they could do it on Christmas Eve!" Father Müller said.

"Do you think that Christmas Eve means anything to them? Don't be naïve, Rudolf, the Nazis don't believe in anything, you know that. They have no mercy, no compassion. They are not human."

"Don't say that, Amelia!"

"Do you think they are?" she said, grimly.

Very few of Carla's friends rang to offer their condolences, and far fewer dared to turn up to Vittorio's house to offer him comfort. They were all afraid of marking themselves out as friends of a woman who had been hanged for high treason.

All those who months before would have begged for the diva just to look at them now stayed at home, trembling and hoping that the SS would not connect them to her. If they had dared to hang the most beloved woman in all of Italy, what else would they be capable of!

Vittorio was ruined, incapable of making decisions, so Amelia and Father Müller needed to call Carla's lawyer to find out what they should do. The man was not keen to give any advice, but Amelia insisted.

"You should have told Don Vittorio that there had been a trial, and what... what was going to happen."

"I promise you that I did not know. Don Vittorio Leonardi knows that I have done my duty as his lawyer, I did not stop trying to find out about Carla Alessandrini's situation. But do you think that the SS follow legal procedure? They didn't let me see her the whole time that she was in prison. They refused to tell me the charges on which she was being detained. I... I found out what had happened from the radio, and I am in shock."

"Well, go to the prison and take charge of getting Carla's body so that we can give it a Christian burial."

"Me? I... I don't think that's a good idea. It should be her husband, Don Vittorio Leonardi, who goes to pick up the body."

"You are being paid a sizeable retainer to deal with family affairs."

The lawyer said nothing. He wanted to get away from Carla and from Vittorio, and from anything that might connect him to them. He forgot that he had been a recently credentialed lawyer when he had met Carla in the office of a much more important lawyer where he worked as a clerk, and that she had thought him amusing and had employed him then and there to handle all of her business affairs. In a second he thrust away from his heart all those years shared with the diva and her husband, all those parties where he had rubbed shoulders with Italian high society, all those arrogant *principesas*, some of whom had become his clients, all the business opportunities that would not have come his way had it not been for the diva.

Yes, he had grown rich thanks to Carla Alessandrini, she had taken him from nothing and turned him into an important lawyer; but now she was dead, they had hanged her for high treason, and he thought that his loyalties now lay with himself and his family. What would it help anyone if they hanged him too?

"We will wait for you, don't be long," Amelia ordered him, trying to put a firmness into her voice that she did not in fact feel.

"I will come by the house one of these days to give Vittorio my condolences; as for the will, well, he knows what to do."

"He won't come," Amelia told Father Müller.

"I will go," the priest offered.

"You? In what capacity?"

"As Carla's confessor, as a family representative, as a priest who wants to give her a Christian burial."

"Be careful, Rudolf."

He shrugged. It is not that he was not scared; he was, but he felt that his office obliged him to face up to evil, and Nazism seemed to him to be the personification of evil; so he decided to follow his conscience even though it might cost him his life.

Vittorio insisted that the family chauffeur drive him, and he accepted.

Father Müller came back at midday with Carla's body. He did not explain how much he had needed to humiliate himself in order to get it, and he brought it up to the house in his own arms.

Vittorio fainted when he saw the bulky object wrapped in coarse hessian cloth, knowing that it was his wife's corpse.

Amelia did not allow him to see it, and with the help of Pasqualina, Carla's dresser, who was one of the very few people who had come to show her grief, she prepared her friend's body for Christian burial.

They dressed her in one of her best dresses, and wrapped her in the mink stole that she had loved so much. When they put her into the coffin, they would not let anyone see her. They did not want people to remember a hanged woman's face, but the face of the Carla they had known in her lifetime. They wouldn't even let Vittorio see it.

They would have to wait until December 26 to bury her, for it was not possible on Christmas Day.

As evening fell, Father Müller went back to the Vatican.

"I don't think you should go to San Clemente this evening. Marchetti will have heard the news and he will not come."

"Of course he will come, and I need to talk to him."

"Why? We can't do anything for Carla now."

"Yes, I can."

The priest looked at Amelia with a worried expression, wondering what she might be planning.

"She's dead, we can only pray for her."

"You pray, I will not."

"You haven't cried yet."

"Do you really think so? You haven't seen my tears, but I have not stopped crying."

"Amelia, we will stand vigil for Carla, we will pray for her, and we will give her a decent burial. It's the only thing we can do, the only thing that Vittorio wants us to do, Then, you should go home, you are not safe here. Max is right, Colonel Jürgens is capable of anything."

"You know something? I think he ordered her to be hanged just to hurt me, to show me how powerful he is. I will live with this guilt for the rest of my life."

"What are you saying! Carla was arrested a long time before you came to Rome. We all know what the SS do to their prisoners. They wanted to teach people a lesson, they wanted the Italians to know that no one is immune, not even their most beloved symbols. Her murder has nothing to do with you."

"Well, I think it does, it's Colonel Jürgens's way of hurting me."

"He would have killed her even if you did not exist. Carla was a legend, and the SS wanted to teach the Italians a lesson."

But Amelia was convinced that Carla's murder was directly connected to the ignoble desires that Jürgens felt for her. Because of this she decided, as they washed Carla's body, on a plan that she would carry out to its bitter end.

Dr. Ferratti, Father Müller's friend, came to the house at Amelia's insistence to give Vittorio something that would help him sleep.

"I want to sit up with her all night, I don't want her to be alone," Vittorio said between sobs.

"She will not be alone, I will be there with her," Amelia assured her, "but you have to sleep, you need to sleep."

Amelia convinced him to stay up with his wife until around midnight, and then she would relieve him until dawn.

"I want to go to Mass, Vittorio; I need to pray; when I come back from Midnight Mass then you will go to bed, promise me."

Dr. Ferratti gave Amelia a sleeping pill for Vittorio.

"I will come and see you tomorrow," the doctor promised, upset by the tragedy that had struck this house.

The few friends who had come left the house. It was Christmas Eve and in spite of the pain they felt for the loss of Carla, they had families, children whom they had to look after and make feel happy on a night like this.

Vittorio and Amelia stayed behind, with Carla's dresser as their only companion. She was a widow with only one daughter, who had married a teacher in Florence a long time ago; she had all the time in the world to mourn the diva, with whom she had forged a sincere friendship.

They had put the coffin in the middle of the large room where Carla had in days gone by organized her finest parties.

At eleven o'clock, Amelia said goodbye to Vittorio and Pasqualina, the dresser.

"Look after Don Vittorio, I'll come back once the Mass is over. And if you want, Pasqualina, you can stay here to sleep, it's late for you to go home."

"I would like to sit up with the mistress."

"Of course, please stay."

When she walked out of the door she felt a chill. She walked slowly, trying not to draw the attention of the few people whose paths she crossed, and who, like her, carried missals in their hands and were on the way to some church or other to celebrate Midnight Mass.

She reached San Clemente at the stroke of midnight, when the bells were just falling silent, having summoned the faithful.

She sat in the back row of the church, her body tense, trying to spy Mateo Marchetti. Father Müller had told her nothing more than that the singing teacher would be in the church. She waited for him to approach her, or for someone to give some kind of a sign. She followed the progress of the Mass like a robot. She prayed without paying attention to what she said, looking all over the church for Marchetti.

She looked at the congregation, trying to imagine which of them could be with the partisan, but they all seemed to be peaceful families, celebrating Christmas Eve together. The Mass ended and the faithful began to file out of the church. She was wondering what she should do when she felt someone nudge her arm. A woman had stood next to her and, without saying a word, indicated that Amelia should follow her. They walked out of the church, side by side, as if they knew each other, and Amelia followed her a long way without daring to say anything. Then the woman stopped outside a door, which she opened quickly. They went up to the first floor in absolute silence.

Mateo Marchetti looked much older, but his eyes still shone with the same intensity that they had in Carla's house. He was seated in the shadows, with three men who appeared to be on guard standing around him.

"Why did you want to see me?" he asked directly.

"I wanted you to help me save Carla."

"That was impossible. She was condemned from the very first day she was arrested."

"Was it you who put her in harm's way?"

"You knew her, do you think that she was capable of standing on the sidelines while all this happened? She wanted to have a role to play and she was given one, the most difficult and dangerous role of her life. She was very brave and saved the lives of a lot of people. Her last mission was difficult. It was not very likely that it would succeed. She knew what might happen."

"It was insane to send her to Switzerland with that man, Il Duce's employee."

"She wasn't really taking that man, she was serving as bait."

"What are you trying to say?" Amelia felt all her muscles tense.

"The Allies needed the information that this man could give her, so we set up a decoy operation. She knew that the SS was watching her, especially Colonel Jürgens, who seemed to be obsessed with her. We organized it so that Carla traveled with a man who looked a lot like Il Duce's steward, while we got the real man out of the country by another route."

"You sent her right into the lions' den!"

"Carla agreed to do it. She laughed at the shock that Jürgens would get to discover that the man she was bringing with her was nothing but a poor shoemaker. A Communist, yes, but not the man they were looking for. Jürgens was enraged when he found out he'd been tricked, and well... you know the rest."

"Everyone thought that Carla was traveling with Il Duce's steward."

"Yes, the SS spread that story, and as you can imagine, we weren't going to deny it."

"You used her," Amelia said.

"No, don't think that. Carla never did anything she didn't want to do. She helped us, yes, like she helped that priest, Father Müller, and worked in collaboration with him and with us. In short, there's nothing we can do about it."

"Yes, there is something that can be done." Amelia's voice piqued Marchetti's curiosity.

"Tell me."

"I am going to kill Colonel Jürgens and I want you to help me."

The singing teacher said nothing, and looked straight at Amelia. He could never have imagined that he would hear such words from this thin and fragile-looking girl.

"And how are you going to kill him?"

"He... he wants... he wants to..."

". . . he wants to sleep with you," Marchetti said, having arrived at this conclusion from Amelia's blushes.

"Yes."

"And you don't think that he will mistrust you, especially now that he's just hanged your friend? Jürgens might want you very badly, but he is a cold-blooded and intelligent man. He will suspect something is wrong if you suddenly fall into his arms."

"But he won't say no. He will mistrust me, he will think that I'm planning something, even that I'm planning to kill him, but he won't say no. I need a pistol, that's all that I need from you."

"A pistol? The first thing he'll do will be to look in your bag."

"I want a pistol that I can hide in my underclothes."

"He will kill you. It's impossible that he will not realize what's happening."

"Yes, it's likely, but I might be lucky and kill him first."

"What does it matter if he dies?"

"He deserves to die, he's a murderer."

"Do you know how many murderers there are like him out there?"

"If it doesn't work, it will be my fault; if it does work then the Resistance will be able to say that this is what happens to people who kill innocents."

"Even if you manage to do it, they will arrest you. You will not be able to escape."

"I have a plan."

"Tell me what it is."

"I prefer not to. All I ask is a pistol, nothing else."

"This will not turn out well."

Amelia shrugged. She had decided to risk her life to end Jürgens's. It was an account that she needed to settle; she owed it to

Grazyna, to Justyna, to Tomasz, to Ewa, to Piotr, to all her Polish friends, to Carla... and she owed it to herself.

"Go to confession in San Clemente in three days' time. And now leave. Forget about this house and forget that you have seen me."

Marchetti made a sign to one of the men who was watching the street from the window.

"There's no one out there, boss."

Trembling with fear, Amelia faced up to the darkness of the night and, walking pressed to the wall and stopping every time she heard a noise, she made it to Vittorio's house.

"I was worried about you! It's two o'clock in the morning. I thought you had been arrested."

"I got lost. I stayed behind after the mass to pray."

"Don't lie to me, Amelia! I know that they lock the church after the Midnight Mass."

"I'm not lying to you, Vittorio, trust me. And now let me take over. I'll sit up with Carla."

"No, I can't leave you here alone."

"I won't be alone. You need to rest, tomorrow will be a long day."

"It's Christmas Day."

Amelia sent Pasqualina to get some water, and insisted that Vittorio take the pill that Dr. Ferratti had given her.

"It will help you rest."

"I don't want Carla to be alone," he insisted.

"I will be with her, I promise."

Then she sent Pasqualina away and remained in the salon alone. And that is when she started to cry.

They buried Carla on the afternoon of December 26. Barely twenty people came to the burial. If Carla had died of natural causes, before the war had broken out, the whole of Italy would have come out into the streets to cry. But she had been hanged for high treason.

"She would have preferred to have been buried in Milan. We have a mausoleum there."

"One day, when this war is over, you will take her there. For the time being, let her rest in peace here," Father Müller said.

Meanwhile, Max was still in Milan. He called Amelia and asked her to return to Spain.

"I am sorry about Carla and I know what she meant to you; but please, don't stay in Rome. We know what we can expect from that damned Jürgens."

"I will wait for you, Max."

"It's just that... I'm sorry, Amelia, but once I've finished inspecting the troops here, I have to go to Greece, they told me this morning."

"To Greece?"

"Yes."

"Can I go with you?"

"Do you really want to come with me?"

"I don't feel like going to Spain."

"You could go to see your family and then come to see me in Athens."

"No, I want to come with you."

"You are in danger, Amelia. I have spoken with some friends, and they all say that Jürgens is obsessed with you."

"I won't do anything that will put me in danger."

"Promise me."

"I promise."

Of course she did not intend to keep her promise. She had not told Max that she had been invited to a New Year's ball. The invitation had arrived on the same day that they hanged Carla, and Amelia had not even glanced at it. It was from Guido and Cecilia Gallotti, Vittorio's friends who had been so close to Il Duce's son-in-law, and who had been so nice to her when Carla invited her to Rome for the first time. They had even been an excellent source of information; she could still remember the reports that she had been able to send to London thanks to the couple's lack of discretion.

To Amelia's and Vittorio's surprise, Cecilia had even come to Carla's funeral.

On December 28, Amelia went to San Clemente and headed to the confessional where Father Müller usually sat. There was another priest there, whose face she could not see.

"Hail Mary most pure."

"Conceived without sin. Are you still going to go ahead with this?"

The priest's phrase shocked her. It was not Marchetti's voice. Was this a trap?

"Yes," she said, fearfully.

"On the floor, to your right, is a package. Pick it up. Wait, don't go yet, it will look like a confession that's far too short. The pistol is small, like you asked, and there are bullets as well. Be careful they don't arrest you on the way back home. It will fit in the pocket of your coat. Now go."

Amelia called Cecilia Gallotti to say that she would be going to the party.

"Oh, my darling, how happy I am to hear it! The truth is, I didn't think that you would come. We sent the invitation a few days before Carla... We thought that it would take Vittorio's mind off... but now..."

"No, he will not come, but I will."

"Of course, of course, you have to take your mind off things. What happened with Carla was so terrible!"

Amelia thought about how Cecilia spoke about Carla's murder with the euphemism "what happened with Carla." She knew that Cecilia would be surprised to hear that she was going to the party, and that she would tell all her friends. She hoped that it would reach the ear of Colonel Jürgens and that he would be there or else would get Guido Gallotti and his wife to invite him.

Vittorio did not get annoyed when Amelia said that she would be going to the New Year's party.

"Go and try to relax, it doesn't make sense for you to stay here."

"When... well... You'll soon understand why I went."

"Please, Amelia, don't do anything that puts you in danger!" he replied, put on the alert by the young woman's words.

"I don't want you to think that I'm just a frivolous woman, capable of going out to parties with Carla's body scarcely in its grave."

"If there is anything at all that ties you to me, promise me that you will not do anything that puts you in harm's way. I couldn't bear it, I couldn't stop Carla from doing what she did, but I couldn't bear to have more guilt on my head."

Pasqualina helped her adjust one of Carla's cocktail dresses. She was thinner than the diva had been, and not as tall. The dresser managed to fit her fairly easily into a black dress. She was going to remain in mourning for her friend.

Vittorio's chauffeur took her to the Gallottis' house. Cecilia whispered that the announcement that she would attend the party had raised a great deal of interest, and that some officers had asked to be invited to the party. Amelia pretended that this meant nothing to her.

Guido and Cecilia introduced her to some of their friends, although Guido was quite clearly uncomfortable with Amelia's presence. Some of his guests asked who the young Spaniard was and he had to try to avoid telling them that it was Carla who had introduced them.

"You've been very careless," he whispered to his wife, "and I'm surprised that she would have come anyway, being in mourning for her friend as she is. She's not to be trusted, as Carla was not to be trusted."

"Don't be ridiculous, she's Spanish, a Fascist like us, and she's as surprised by Carla's betrayal as we are. If she has come, it's to show us all which side she's on, if there's one thing about you that's certain, it's that you don't know women," Cecilia defended herself.

After midnight, Ulrich Jürgens arrived with various SS officers. His arrival was noticeable, not just because he came late, but because of the rowdiness of his companions. They had been drinking, and they seemed euphoric.

He lost no time in paying compliments to the hosts, and headed immediately over to where Amelia was standing.

"I thought you'd be crying."

She looked at him and turned away, but he grasped her by the arm and pulled her back.

"Come on, out with the old, in with the new. And don't kick me like you kicked me last time. Tell me, why are you here?"

"I don't need to tell you why I do what I do."

"So little mourning for your good friend Carla Alessandrini? I see you don't waste any time."

"Leave me alone." This time she managed to break free and turned her back on him.

"Why do you insist in going against my will? You would do better if you didn't. I could have saved your friend if you had played nice," he said, grabbing her again and stopping her from walking away.

"Can you play nice with a hyena?" Amelia replied, angrily.

"That's how you see me? A hyena? I would have preferred another comparison."

"Well, look in the mirror."

He looked at her harshly without letting her go, but keeping her at arm's length. She could see from his eyes that he had a surprise for her.

"Your friend the baron should be careful of his friends."

She stood up straight, she didn't understand what he had just said, but it sounded like a threat.

"I didn't know that you controlled the friendships of the Wehrmacht as well!" Amelia said, trying to keep the disgust she felt out of her voice.

"There are lots of traitors around at the moment, even in the heart of Germany. People who can't understand the Führer's dream. Lots of the baron's friends have been arrested by the Gestapo, didn't you know? Hasn't he told you? I thought he trusted you more than that."

No, Max had not told her anything, so as not to frighten her, she assumed, but who did Jürgens mean? Father Müller hadn't said anything either. Did he not know, or did he not want to worry her either?

"Stop your insinuations and let me go! You disgust me," she said, knowing that the more disdain she showed toward him, the more eager he would be to take her.

"It must be hard for your friends to be traitors. First of all those Poles, what was your friend's name? Grazyna? That's it, and then there was Ewa, do you remember them? And now Carla Alessandrini. Careful, there are too many traitors hanging around you!"

"How can you slander these people!"

"You could have saved your friend Carla Alessandrini, but you missed your chance and now... Well, I suppose I could distract the people who suspect the baron. Don't go running to warn him, by the way!"

"What do you want?"

"You know what I want. Do I have to spell it out? If you care so much about the baron, you shouldn't care about sacrificing yourself for him. Or will you leave him to his fate, just as you did with Carla?"

"You disgust me," she said, but her tone of voice suggested that she had given in.

"I will help you get over your repugnance."

"Will you leave Baron von Schumann in peace?"

"You have my word."

"Your word? That means nothing. I want a document that removes the baron from all suspicion."

He laughed at her and twisted her arm even more.

"You will have to accept my word or else get ready to mourn the baron. Now stop making me beg, and come with me."

Amelia looked down and seemed to be thinking. Then she lifted her chin high and looked defiantly at Jürgens.

"It will not be tonight. It will be tomorrow," she replied.

"Alright, tomorrow. We will go out to dinner first."

"No, no preliminaries, nothing like that. These are not necessary between us. Tell me where to go and I will go."

"A woman like you is worthy of the Excelsior, don't you think?"

"The Excelsior?"

"It's where the baron stayed, you should know it well enough," he said, laughing.

"Alright. When?"

"At nine o'clock. We'll toast our business deal with champagne."

"Send word of where I am to go, which room. In fact, I'd prefer for you to send me the key to the room so that I can go up there directly. I don't want people to see me with you in the hotel."

He let her go with a cruel laugh and she hurried away to find Cecilia Gallotti and say goodbye. She had achieved her objective, or at least the one she had set herself for that night. The most difficult part was the one she would have to play tomorrow evening.

"But the party is going well, you can't just go!" Cecilia exclaimed, trying to get her friend to stay a little longer.

"I don't feel well, I shouldn't have come, I thought that I would enjoy myself but in the end I find I can't stop thinking of Carla, I'm sorry, and thank you very much for your hospitality."

When she got home, Vittorio was still awake.

"I couldn't sleep, I was worried about you."

"You shouldn't worry, I'm alright."

"Did they treat you well?"

"Guido was put on edge to see me there, but Cecilia was charming."

"I was surprised that she came to Carla's funeral. I always thought she was an idiot," Vittorio said.

"I was surprised as well. Perhaps we've misjudged her and she's not such a bad person at bottom."

"Now I want you to tell me the truth. Why did you go to that party? I know how much you loved Carla and that you didn't feel like having fun."

"No, I didn't, but I need to do something that I cannot tell you about yet. Trust me."

Alone in her room she wept for a while. Colonel Jürgens's threat against Max had been clear, there was no room for doubt: The SS suspected the baron. She also knew that whatever she did, Jürgens would not keep his word. If Max was in danger, then he should be told about it as soon as possible.

She barely slept, going over again and again in her mind the plan to kill Jürgens. She got up very early to call Max before he went off to see the field hospitals. She knew that their communications were being intercepted, but she preferred to warn him.

"Max, I was at Guido and Cecilia Gallotti's house last night, and someone told me that some of your friends might have had some problems in Germany."

"You shouldn't worry, I'll tell you about it when I come back to Rome."

"Be careful," she warned.

"I'll see you in a few days," he replied.

She spent the day with Vittorio, trying to cheer him up and counting the hours until night fell. At eight o'clock she said that she was tired and went off to sleep.

Amelia had got into her nightdress and was yawning while the maid pulled back the bed covers for her.

"You must be tired. I'm not surprised, these are hard days for us all, what happened to the mistress was terrible."

"Yes, I'm tired. I wish I could just go to sleep!"

She drank the glass of milk that the woman had left on her bedside table and watched her go out. Then, when the door was shut, she took her nightshirt off and started to get dressed. She had chosen a diaphanous white blouse and a black skirt. Once she was dressed, she hid the little pistol in her garter belt. It was uncomfortable, and she had to make sure that she didn't walk like a duck, but it was the only place that no one would suspect if they stopped her in the street or at the hotel.

Early in the afternoon Ulrich Jürgens had sent her a note, which had come with a key that seemed to be a copy of one from the Excelsior. He must have threatened the manager to get this copy made for him; he said in the note that he would be waiting for her in Room 307.

When she had finished getting dressed and was sure that the pistol was securely fastened, she sat down and tied her hair back in a bun. Then she put on one of Carla's theatrical wigs. It was black, with mahogany highlights. It was too big for her, and she had spent two days trying to make it fit, but even though it was difficult, she had managed. She didn't look like herself. The dark hair made her look different, older, and if it had not been for the mahogany highlights then she could have passed almost unnoticed. But Carla had never wanted to pass unnoticed, so Amelia had to make do with the least imposing of her friend's wigs. The smooth bangs fell down on either side of her face, and the fringe covered her forehead. Even so, she covered her head with a scarf that she knotted at her neck. The she put on a black overcoat that she had found in a wardrobe in the guest bedroom. It was a little wide, and unfashionable.

She did not say goodbye to Vittorio, and instead left, avoiding the servants. It was nearly nine o'clock, and the doorman was not on duty that night, because it was the first night of 1944, and a holiday in spite of the war. No one saw her leave. She mingled in the streets with the people and was relieved that no one seemed to be looking at her. She walked slowly so as not to call attention to herself.

The reception at the Excelsior was full of Wehrmacht and SS officers. She walked quickly to the elevator, but a captain cut off her path.

"And where are you going, *bella signorita*? Do you have a partner for the night?"

Amelia did not reply, and got into the elevator, worried that he would follow her. She pushed the button for the fourth floor in case anyone was watching her. Once she was on the fourth floor she went down the stairs, worried about perhaps running into a guest, or the workers on the night shift. But luck appeared to be on her side. She opened the door to Room 307 and was shocked to find it dark. She felt her heart start to beat ever faster when a hand fell on her shoulder and turned her brusquely round.

"So you have come," Colonel Jürgens said in a lascivious voice.

He had been drinking. Amelia could tell from the thickened edge to his voice, and because he smelled of alcohol. She turned toward him, trying to overcome the repugnance that she felt at his presence and his smell. She could not avoid his embrace, nor stop him from kissing her. He held her tight, and after the kiss he bit her lips until she could taste blood.

"You must love the baron a lot to have come here tonight."

"We have an agreement," she replied.

He let her go and laughed.

"Your problem, my dear, is that you are accustomed to deal with men like the baron. But I promise you that you will not find your experience here tonight disagreeable. Take off your jacket."

She obeyed. Her eyes started to grow accustomed to the dark and she could see his face. It seemed more brutal than usual as he manhandled her.

"You didn't want me to treat you like a lady, didn't want me to invite you to dinner, so I will treat you like what you are. What is that?"

Jürgens pushed her against the wall when he found out that Amelia's hair was not the same as normal.

"I got dressed up for you, to be at the level you expect from me," she replied.

He went to turn on the light, but she pressed herself against him and kissed him. While Jürgens carried on trying to remove her blouse, she put one of her hands between his legs and stroked him, which seemed to arouse him like a dog in heat. With her free hand she reached between her own legs for the pistol that was hidden there.

"Do you want me to take you now? Are you getting yourself ready for me?" he laughed when he saw that she had one hand underneath her skirt. Amelia smiled and asked him to kiss her. He was going to, but she did not give him time. It took him a second to feel the cold barrel of the pistol against his stomach and the awful pain tearing up his guts. He fell to the floor, dragging Amelia with him, pressing against her body as if he wanted to take her down with him.

Amelia managed to pull herself free and looked for a light switch. When she turned it on, she saw Jürgens stretched out on the floor with a grimace of surprise on his features. He was holding onto his stomach where his guts were spilling out, but he had not yet died.

"I will kill you," he managed to say in a thin little voice.

She was scared, thinking that he might still be able to carry out his promise, and looked for something she could use to finish him off, because she was scared of firing another shot. The dry sound of the first shot could be mistaken for a bottle of champagne being opened, but she could not justify another one in case someone from the hotel staff came to see what was going on. She went to the bed and took hold of the pillow, then knelt down next to him, watching the life running out of him, and covered his face, holding the pillow down with all her strength. For a few minutes, which seemed interminable, he struggled in vain, trying to get her to remove the weight that was suffocating him. Then suddenly all his struggles ceased. When Amelia was sure that he was dead, she took the pillow off his face and looked at Jürgens's face. She put a hand close to his mouth to see if he was still breathing. But he was dead. Then she heard some knocks on the door. She stood up and went to ask who it was, but without opening. It was a member of the hotel staff.

"Is everything alright?" she asked. "A guest called saying that he had heard a loud noise."

Amelia forced herself to laugh.

"He obviously doesn't drink much champagne, does he, darling?" she said, addressing Jürgens's corpse over her shoulder.

"I'm sorry, Madam, I didn't mean to disturb you."

"Well, you did, you did, and there are some situations that shouldn't be interrupted." And she laughed again.

She heard the maid's footsteps retreating away from the door. Then she went through the room, top to bottom. She recovered a couple of the clips she had used to hold the wig in place, then put on some gloves and cleaned everything she had touched with a clean handkerchief. Then she took the cover off the pillow and put it in her bag. She went over the room once again, until she was sure that there was nothing there that could give her away. She put the wig back on and returned the pistol to her garter belt.

She waited for an hour before deciding to leave. She spent the whole time looking at Ulrich Jürgens's body, repeating over and over again in a low voice how much she had hated him, and how happy she was that justice was finally done. She was surprised to feel no regret, she didn't know if she would be attacked by emotions later, but at that moment the only thing she felt was a deep satisfaction.

When she left the room an officer and a blonde woman were going into the next room alone. She didn't look at them, and they seemed not to pay her any attention. They were drunk and seemed happy.

She waited impatiently for the elevator to come, and didn't breathe again until she was out in the street.

She walked along calmly, telling herself that nothing could connect her to the murder. She reached Vittorio's house at one o'clock and entered very slowly, trying not to wake up Vittorio or the servants.

She got into bed and fell fast asleep until late the next morning. It was Vittorio himself who woke her up; he seemed extremely agitated.

"There was a murder at the Excelsior. An SS officer."

"Why do we care about that?" she said boldly.

"They are stopping people all over Rome. I don't know how many people have been arrested. Cecilia called for you a moment or so ago to talk about it."

"I'll call her as soon as I am dressed. We had arranged to meet and have lunch at her house."

"It would be better if you were to stay here."

"Don't worry about me. Cecilia said she would send her own car."

"Amelia, they are stopping people in the streets, and arresting lots of them. It is not a good idea for you to go out."

But Amelia insisted that this had nothing to do with them, and called Cecilia to confirm that she would go to her house for lunch.

When Amelia arrived, Guido was just leaving.

"It's not a good idea for you to go out," he said. "They're looking for a dark-haired woman, they think it was she who killed Colonel Ulrich Jürgens."

"Jürgens?" Amelia said, surprised.

"Yes, the SS officer who has turned up dead. The police think that it was a prostitute, but apparently nothing was taken, so why should she kill him? A couple saw a dark-haired woman leaving Jürgens's room around midnight."

"But who would dare kill an SS officer?" Amelia said as if she were not only scared but surprised.

"Well, it might not have been a prostitute. Apparently, one of Jürgens's friends gave them another clue, that Jürgens had a meeting with a woman, someone who didn't like him very much but who was still prepared to go to his hotel room."

"Who could that be?" Cecilia asked with interest.

"I don't know, I don't think Colonel Jürgens had many friends," Amelia said.

"Well, you knew him, apparently you were seen having a discussion at the New Year's party. I'll tell you, I thought that the colonel had quite a liking for you."

"How silly! We were just talking about how the war was progressing, nothing else."

Guido left them talking about who the mysterious woman could have been, even though he was inclined to believe the version the police favored: that Jürgens had been murdered by a prostitute. Perhaps he had been violent with her: He was a fearsome man, who made even Guido nervous.

When Amelia got back to Vittorio's house, she found Father Müller waiting for her.

"I didn't expect you, Rudolf," she said with a smile.

"Do you know what happened?"

"I suppose you're going to tell me what everyone already knows, that someone killed Colonel Jürgens."

"Yes... Amelia, forgive me for asking, but..."

She let out a shout of laughter that sounded false to Father Müller, given how well he knew her.

"Rudolf, I'm not going to deny that I'm happy he's dead."

"I came because Marchetti sent word that he wants to see you."

"Me? Why?"

"You know what you talked about the last time you met."

"I asked him if I could work with the Resistance, if I could take the place of Carla," she lied.

"Well, he may have decided to accept your offer. He wants to see you tomorrow, in San Clemente. Come a little bit before they lock the church."

"I'll be there. But you needn't worry about me."

"How can I not worry! I've lost too many friends."

"I wanted to ask you about that..."

"Amelia, I didn't want to say anything so as not to worry you. Max asked me not to. The Gestapo arrested Professor Schatzhauser a few months ago. He was at the university, and they burst into one of his lectures and took him. We haven't heard anything more about him. They also arrested Pastor Schmidt."

"And the Kastens?"

"No, they're still in Berlin, but the Gestapo must be keeping an eye on them. Everyone knows that they were Dr. Schatzhauser's friends. And if I went back... well, maybe they'd arrest me too."

"You should have told me."

"Understand me when I say that... Max doesn't want you to suffer."

The police came to Vittorio's house four days later, the same time that Max von Schumann arrived in Rome.

They made Amelia come with them to a police lineup. An SS officer who was a friend of Colonel Jürgens's insisted that Jürgens had been going to meet the baron's lover.

Amelia shouted and even cried, and appeared scared; but even though Vittorio told them to leave her in peace, they took her down to the station.

There she found herself face to face with the couple who had been going into the room next to Jürgens's. They looked her up and down, but said straight away that she was not the woman whom they had seen leaving Jürgens's room on the night of the murder.

"No, it's not her," the officer said. "She was dark-haired."

"With mahogany highlights in her hair and dark eyes, and this woman has light eyes," the woman added.

"She was taller," the officer said, "and fatter."

They gave her a routine interrogation about where she had been that night. She said that she had been in Vittorio's house all night and that the servants could confirm that. She didn't deny that she knew Colonel Jürgens, or even that she didn't like him very much. She knew that they knew everything that had happened in Warsaw, so that it was better to tell the truth, or at least most of the truth.

They interrogated her for two days and two nights without her falling into any contradiction in her story. On the third day, Max came to find her at the police station. He had asked his general to do whatever he could to stop her from falling back into the hands of the SS. The general only made one condition: The police report had to absolve her of any possibility of being the murderer.

The police had the description given to them by the couple who had stayed in the neighboring room, so they concluded that it was extremely unlikely that Amelia could have been the murderer. They let her go. Max was waiting for her.

"We're going to Athens," Max said as they walked back to Vittorio's house.

Amelia gave a sigh of relief.

"Well, that's it."

Paolo Plattini gave a satisfied smile, aware that Francesca and I had listened to him with such interest that we hadn't opened our mouths the entire time.

"What a story!" Francesca exclaimed in shock.

"My great-grandmother is a real Russian doll: the more I find out about her, the more shocked I get," I said.

"I have something for you." Paolo gave me some folders.

"What are they?"

"Photocopies of newspaper reports about the murder of Colonel Jürgens. As you can see, for the first few days the newspapers spoke about the murder having been carried out by a prostitute, but then they started to blame the partisans. Look here," he said, pointing to one of the photocopies. "It says that several districts of Rome were papered with posters that said that the partisans claimed the assassination of Colonel Jürgens to be revenge for the hanging of Carla Alessandrini."

There was nothing I could do but thank Paolo Plattini for the information that he had provided, for all that I felt annoyed to leave him standing in the doorway, his arm around Francesca's waist. I'm sure that they would finish the bottle of Barolo together and wake up in the morning to look at the iridescent reflections on the rooftops of Rome.

In spite of the hour, I decided to walk around the city a little. I needed to think of everything I had heard that night. My great-grandmother was turning out to be a strong and unpredictable woman. Nothing that she did seemed to have anything to do with her true nature. Was she a romantic bourgeois woman who let herself get carried away by events, or did she really have a much more complex personality? I was surprised that she had been capable of killing a man in cold blood, even though he had been a disgusting Nazi. I decided to go back to the hotel. When I was in the room, I opened my suitcase and took out the copy of the photograph of Amelia Garayoa that Aunt Marta had given me. I looked at it from time to time to try to understand how this young blonde woman, with her apparently ethereal and aloof personality, had been able to live so dangerously and with such intensity.

That night I found it hard to get to sleep, not just because I was annoyed that Paolo and Francesca were a couple, but because I was upset to think of my great-grandmother as being a murderer.

Paolo had lent me the book written by the partisan, and so I decided to have a look at it, and fell asleep with it in my hand.

The next day I called Francesca to thank her for the dinner and the revelations that Paolo had provided. She was friendly and affectionate, as if a weight had been lifted off her shoulders by making it clear that she and I would never again watch the dawn from the windows of her loft.

"What are you going to do now?"

"I've booked a flight to London."

"Are you going to meet with Major William Hurley?"

"I hope so. I've told you that the major is very British and that you have to book things a long way in advance with him. But I will try."

"Paolo has told me to tell you that he'll carry on looking, that if he finds out anything else about your great-grandmother he'll call you."

"Tell him that I'm very grateful, that he has been *molto gentile*, as you Italians say."

"Yes, he is. Well, call me if you think that we can help you with anything else. *Ciao, caro!*"

The next thing I did was to call Major William Hurley, and to my surprise he did not seem as distant and tense as he had on previous occasions.

"Ah, Guillermo, it's you! I was wondering why you didn't call. Lady Victoria has been asking about you."

"I wanted to know if you could meet with me."

"How was Rome?"

"Very useful. I'll tell you what I've found out."

He made an appointment for two days' time, which for him was as if he'd agreed to see me that very afternoon.

10

It was raining when I arrived in London. At least it was not too cold. I booked into the hotel that I normally used and called my mother.

"Where are you?"

"In London."

"But you said you were going to Rome!"

"I was in Rome, but I had to go back to London."

"Guillermo, I'm sick and tired of telling you to give up on this ridiculous activity, that this investigation will not take you anywhere. If I don't care what this woman did or didn't do, and I'm her granddaughter, you should care even less. It's only Marta who could have made such a mess out of our grandmother!"

"And I'm sick and tired of your lectures. I don't care what your grandmother did, or my great-grandmother: This has nothing to do with family history. It is a job I am doing, which they have paid me to do, and which I will carry on doing, and I'm happy that Aunt Marta doesn't have any control over it anymore."

"You're getting obsessed."

"No I'm not, it's just a job."

I didn't dare tell my mother that her grandmother had been capable of rubbing out a man without blinking. It would have upset her, or maybe not: Knowing my mother, she would have been capable of saying that Colonel Ulrich Jürgens had it coming to him.

Two days later, at the agreed-upon time, eight o'clock in the morning, Major Hurley received me in his office at the military archives. He was in a better mood than I was, given the hour. This was a man who started to fade at nine o'clock at night, whereas at eight o'clock in the morning I was barely capable of keeping my eyes open.

"Well, I lost track of my great-grandmother in Greece."

"In Greece? Ah yes, of course! After her time in Rome Amelia went to Greece with Baron von Schumann, and started to work for us again. As you will know by now, the loss of her great friend, the diva Carla Alessandrini, marked her so deeply that your grandmother was never the same again."

I was about to get annoyed with the major: He had known about my grandmother's movements in Rome and had not wanted to help me. I mentioned this.

"In fact, I don't know much of what happened in Rome. Colonel Jürgens's death was not something we planned ourselves. We knew about it via the Resistance: They organized it."

I took my revenge by giving him a lecture about what had actually happened in Rome, and made it clear that it was not an operation carried out by the Resistance, but by my great-grandmother.

"Our archives record that the free agent Amelia Garayoa, working on the orders of the Resistance, executed one of the bloodiest officers of the SS, Colonel Ulrich Jürgens."

"Well, if you want to be true to what actually happened, then listen to me: My great-grandmother killed Jürgens on her own account and at her own risk. The only thing the Resistance did was give her a pistol."

It was clear that however much I argued with him, Major Hurley was not going to change what was recorded in the archives.

"Amelia Garayoa left Rome at the beginning of 1944. The trial was taking place in Verona of those who had tried to overthrow Mussolini. They were all condemned to death, including Il Duce's own son-in-law, Count Ciano. Only Tullio Cianetti survived. On January 17 came the battle of Monte Cassino. Have you ever heard about this battle? On January 22, the Allies landed at Anzio, near Rome. Let's see… let's see… yes, here we go, your great-grandmother arrived in Athens on January 16, just one day before Monte Cassino. We knew via the Resistance that Jürgens had been executed and so we supposed that Amelia Garayoa might be willing to go back to work. So when we knew she was in Athens we got in touch with her."

"Just like that."

"Who said anything about it being easy?" Major Hurley said grumpily. "Young man, you need to listen and not be so impatient, because I haven't got any time to lose."

I shut up, worried that I might have spoiled the Major's good mood, and let him begin his story.

Major Murray received a report that said that Amelia Garayoa, working with the Italian Resistance, had killed an SS Colonel in Rome. Murray was surprised at Amelia's action because, even though he had trained her to kill if such a thing should become necessary, he had doubted that she would be capable of it. Her fragile appearance was deceptive.

Murray decided to try to get the young Spaniard to collaborate with them again. She could be very useful in Athens, working with the Resistance and providing reports about the disposition of German troops on the Greek islands.

Baron von Schumann took two neighboring rooms in the Hotel Great Britain. It was no secret that Amelia Garayoa was his lover, but Baron von Schumann was too much of a gentleman to crudely display their relationship. The Hotel Great Britain is right in the center of Athens, close to the Acropolis.

Amelia enjoyed visiting the archaeological ruins and regretted, silently, to herself, that the Nazi banner should fly over the Acropolis.

Max von Schumann went to visit the various German battalions and to assess their wounded and see which medical supplies were required. Then he wrote long reports to Berlin, which he sent to them knowing that very few of his demands would be fulfilled.

What neither Amelia nor any of the German officers staying at the Great Britain were aware of was the fact that one of the waiters who served them so politely at the bar was in fact a British agent.

His codename was "Dion." His real name is still classified.

Dion spoke German and English perfectly. His father was Greek and worked for the British Embassy. He had met a young woman there, the personal maid of the ambassador's wife. They fell in love, they married and had a son. When the British ambassador went on to his next posting, the young maid stayed with her husband and son in Athens. She was an excellent maid, so she found work in the house of a German historian who spent large periods in Athens. He must have been a good man, because he allowed her to bring Dion to the house with him, and spent his free time teaching him German. This was how Dion managed to gain his knowledge of languages, which was so useful for his profession. He listened to conversations among the guests without giving any sign of being able to understand them. And they spoke with the confidence that came from assuming that no one could understand what it was they said.

A little after Max and Amelia arrived at the hotel, Dion sent a report of one of the conversations he had heard.

"The war isn't going well," Max said to Amelia.

"Will the Allies win?" she asked, without hiding her hope that this would be so.

"Don't you see what that would mean?"

"Yes, the end of the Third Reich."

"The British should start to worry about the Russians. We are their natural allies against Stalin. We have to work out a way to work together."

"What are you saying? You know what I think of Stalin, but in this war... Well, he made the right decision to face up to the Germans."

"He wants Communism to spread all over Europe: Is that what you want?"

"What I don't want is the Third Reich, that's what I don't want."

"You have to think about tomorrow. Hitler is just a circumstance, an event, but we will get rid of him."

"When, Max, when? Neither you nor your friends can decide to do anything about him."

"That's not true! You know it's not true. But we can't take the decisive step without being able to count on the support of certain generals or else we will just provoke an even worse disaster."

"And some of these generals are scared of committing themselves, and others are fanatical Nazis, and you worry about what Stalin might do in the future. You know what I say? However much I hate Stalin, at the moment he's a blessing."

"Don't say that, Amelia! Don't say that, please."

One afternoon, while she was waiting for Baron von Schumann to arrive at the bar, Dion came over to Amelia and spoke to her.

"A friend of yours from London would like you to visit the cathedral."

Amelia grew nervous, but managed to control herself almost immediately.

"What are you talking about? I don't know what you mean."

"Trust me. I'm bringing news from Major Murray."

When she heard his name, Amelia calmed down.

"When should I go?" she asked the waiter.

"Tomorrow, around eleven."

"You..."

"We've spoken enough."

The next day she went to visit the Metropolitan Cathedral in Athens. She walked slowly, looking around all the while. The Greeks were very sullen with the occupiers, and wherever she looked she saw only hostile faces.

Lots of officers had been billeted in the homes of Athenians, who had been forced to turn into hosts for their occupiers.

She was looking at the icons when she felt a man's breath behind her.

"Good morning. Are you interested in our icons?" someone said in English.

She turned round and found herself face to face with a priest, a tall man with a black beard and bright eyes, and his hair tied back in a ponytail.

"Good morning. Yes, I like them and I find them surprising, they're very different from Catholic religious paintings."

"This is Saint Nicholas," he said, pointing to one of the images. "You'll find him in all our churches. And this is an icon of Saint George; look at this one, the Virgin and Child, a gem."

There was almost nobody in the cathedral, apart from a few women who crossed themselves and lit candles and put them on the tables under the icons.

"As well as art, are you interested in Justice and Truth?" the priest asked in a husky voice.

Amelia tried to hide the surprise that she felt on hearing this question.

"Of course," she replied.

"Well, we may have common friends."

"I don't know," she murmured.

"Come with me and we will talk."

She followed him out of the cathedral. It was cold, but the priest seemed not to feel the temperature. Amelia was shivering.

"We work with friends of yours in London, and your friends ask me if you might be interested in coming back to work with us here. Major Murray congratulates you for Rome."

"Rome?" Amelia was shocked.

"That's the message I was to give you, I don't know any more."

"Who are you?"

"Call me Yorgos. We don't like having the Germans here. The Greeks have always fought against invaders. Ask Xerxes, or Darius."

"Who?"

The priest laughed at having surprised her.

"We defeated the Persians when they were a great empire. Do you know what happened at Thermopylae? A small army led by a Spartan king, Leonidas, faced an immense Persian army. The king of Persia sent a messenger to Leonidas asking him to surrender, but the Spartans refused, and withstood the Persian onslaught, fighting so strongly that the Greeks were later able to defeat the Persians at Salamis. Not a single Spartan survived. If we hadn't won at Marathon or made the sacrifice we made at Thermopylae, then you'd be wearing a veil today and praying to Mecca."

"I can see that you're proud to be a Greek."

"The Western world owes its existence to Greece."

"I hadn't thought of that."

"Maybe you didn't know. And now tell me, are you ready to work with your friends again, and to work with us?"

"Yes."

Amelia surprised herself by the determination with which she gave her answer. She knew that after she had killed Colonel Jürgens she had perhaps taken a step into the unknown. She still asked herself why she felt no remorse, why she was not tormented by visions of Jürgens's face, why she felt like laughing when she remembered killing him.

"We may never see each other again, or we may yet. Go to Monastiraki tomorrow; look for the Café Acropolis; they're waiting for you there.

"Who?

"A man called Agamemnon. He'll give you instructions. Now we need to separate; I'll point as if I were telling you the way to get somewhere. If you need to see me, come to the cathedral, I come there on some mornings, but not always, and don't even think about asking for me."

"But... are you a real priest?"

"A man who dedicates his life to God needs to fight the Devil. Now go away."

She felt a secret pleasure that Major Murray wasn't upset with her for having left the service after Poland. She had told Señora Rodríguez, Murray's agent in Madrid, that she would never go back to spying. But killing Colonel Jürgens had given her the strength to carry on fighting in the shadows. She told herself that she couldn't abandon it now, not with all the evil that she saw around her. She remembered what had happened in Poland, and Carla's murder, and that aroused a potent rage within her, and a desire to kill all those who were spreading this evil.

That afternoon Baron von Schumann thought that she was distracted, as if nothing that he was telling her really interested her.

Amelia tried to avoid looking at Dion, but she couldn't stop herself from looking at him out of the corner of her eye. It was clear that he worked for Commander Murray. And she laughed to herself when she realized that Commander Murray had never had any intention of letting her go: Not only had he sent Señora Rodríguez to Madrid to find out how she was, but he also knew perfectly well the steps he was taking.

"I'm going to go and walk in the Plaka tomorrow," she told the baron.

"I'm sorry not to be able to spend more time with you, but I have to go to Thessaloniki tomorrow, I'll be away for three or four days, can you look after yourself?"

"Of course I can!"

"Please, Amelia, be discreet; after what happened in Rome I am sure that they are keeping an eye on you."

"But I had nothing to do with Jürgens, the police report absolved me of any crime."

"But this friend of Jürgens insists that you had a meeting arranged with him."

"Do you think that I would have arranged to meet that man?"

"No, I don't, but..."

"This time you have to trust me."

"I have something else to say... I hope you don't get angry."

"Is it about Ludovica?"

"Yes... how did you know?"

Amelia said nothing. She was not jealous of Ludovica, she knew that Max loved only her.

"As soon as she knew that I was in Greece she said she was going to come to see me. I asked her not to, not to subject the baby to a journey in wartime, but she didn't pay me any attention."

"As it's Ludovica, I suppose that means we should expect her to appear at any moment."

"I promised her that if she did not come I would go to Berlin to see her and Friedrich."

"You miss your son, don't you? Friedrich is now almost a year old, isn't he?"

"Nearly two, and I haven't seen him much since he was born, but I love him with all my soul, as you love yours."

"Yes, not a day goes by when I don't think about Javier."

"Let's not be downcast; I just wanted you to be on your guard in case Ludovica arrives."

"The last time I saw her was with Ulrich Jürgens in the reception of the hotel in Warsaw. They were getting along like a house on fire."

"Let's not think about Ludovica. Shall we eat away from the hotel tonight?"

Amelia smiled so as not to upset him, but speaking about their children, and remembering Javier, had made her sad.

She didn't dare ask Dion where to find the café that the priest had told her to visit. She knew that she shouldn't show any sign of familiarity with this man so as not to put them both in danger, so she left the hotel with sufficient time to walk to the Plaka and stare at the Parthenon, which stood out majestically on the top of the Acropolis. The swastika was flying high there, in spite of the continued and suicidal attempts of Greek patriots to climb the rock and replace it with the Greek flag. Only one had succeeded, paying for his exploit with his life.

Amelia was surprised that the Greeks should be patriotic, and envied them for a moment. She remembered, with a surge of anger, how Franco had classed all the people who fought for the Republic as unpatriotic, and said to herself that she would prefer to be unpatriotic rather than patriotic in the way that Franco understood the word. With these thoughts she made it to Monastiraki and, strolling through the streets without asking anyone, found the old café.

There was a man behind the bar, engaged in serving a thick

coffee to one of his customers. He looked at her incuriously, and she waited for him to finish.

"Is this Agamemnon's café?" she asked, when he turned to her and asked what she wanted.

"Yes."

"A friend of mine, a priest, asked me to come here."

The man made her a sign to follow him and she walked behind the counter to where a black curtain separated the bar from the tiny room where boxes and bottles were stored. They scarcely fit there.

"Your friends in London," the man said, in English, "want you to send them all the documents you can get hold of: plans, troop movements, anything that might be of interest."

"That's it?"

"That's what they want for now. Here, they gave you this. It's a microcamera. The keys for enciphering messages are in this envelope. Be careful."

"Where should I deliver the messages?"

"You should come here if you can't give them to Dion. You could go to the cathedral as well, the priest goes there every now and then."

"What else do they want in London?"

"They want you to work with us. Given your relationship with that German, you could be useful."

"Alright."

"We may need you very shortly for an operation."

"Turn around," she said.

He obeyed and she hid the camera in her brassiere. Then they took their leave of each other.

When she got back to the hotel, she went into Max's room. It connected with hers, so this was not difficult. She looked through his wardrobe without finding anything apart from his clothes; there was nothing interesting in the desk either. She would have to wait for him to come back in order to photograph the documents that he would have with him in his briefcase. She had already done it in Warsaw, but because she was keen to start working, she wrote a summary of all the conversations she had had with Max about the progress of the war, with some strategic details that might be useful for London. She wanted to feel useful.

Max called her from Thessaloniki and said that he was going to Berlin for two days.

"I'm sorry, but they've ordered me back to the General Staff. Apparently they don't like my reports, they say I'm too pessimistic. I suppose I'll have to sweeten reality so that I don't make them feel uncomfortable. Be careful."

It was starting to be annoying, that Max would tell her so often to be careful. But she couldn't blame him. He always believed her, he never mistrusted her, in spite of the evidence to the contrary.

Waiting until the baron returned, Amelia dedicated her time to familiarizing herself with the city. She walked everywhere, without stopping, acquainting herself with the intricate layout of Athens.

One afternoon, coming back from one of her walks, the concierge told her that Max von Schumann was in the hotel bar with two other officers.

Amelia went there immediately, she had missed him. Max was talking animatedly with his adjutant Major Henke and another officer she did not know. He was wearing the uniform of a naval officer.

"Ah, darling, you're here at last!" Max could not hide his satisfaction at seeing her. "You know our dear friend Major Henke, but allow me to present you to Captain Karl Kleist."

The naval officer clicked his heels and kissed her hand. Amelia noticed that he was an extremely attractive man.

"I have wanted so much to meet you, Fräulein Garayoa."

"Captain Kleist helped us a great deal in Warsaw. He did great things to... well, to get you out of Pawiak," Max said, slightly uneasily.

"No more disagreeable talk! We are in Athens! Let's enjoy the privilege of looking at the Parthenon," Captain Kleist interrupted him. "And please, call me Karl, I hope we are going to be friends."

"Thank you," Amelia replied with a smile.

The three men took up the conversation that they had been having before Amelia's arrival. From what she could gather, the sailor went to South America frequently. At one point he referred to a recent journey to Spain, to Bilbao, and she could not avoid showing her interest.

"Do you know Spain?"

"Yes, I know your country and I like it very much. Your surname is Basque, is that right?"

"Yes, my father is Basque."

"We have good friends there."

Amelia didn't ask any more. She knew that the best way of finding out information was to listen, to let the men expound and forget her presence. But Kleist was a professional and much too experienced to commit simple errors and trust a stranger; added to which, she was in his debt for the help he had given Baron von Schumann in getting her released from Pawiak.

She had to wait until she was alone with Max, in the intimacy of the night, to get a clearer idea of Captain Kleist's activities.

"He's a good soldier. He doesn't approve of what is happening, he... Well, he's always been loyal to Admiral Canaris and Captain Oster."

"But he obeys orders just like the rest of you, is that it?"

"We've spoken about this before," Max said with a tired gesture.

Amelia apologized. The last thing she needed now was to have a fight with Max. What she needed was information.

"You're right, I'm sorry. What is it that Captain Kleist does, then?"

"Come on, Amelia! I can't believe you couldn't work it out!"

"He works for the secret service?"

"He has to get raw materials from South America, without which Germany would not be able to continue fighting: platinum, zinc, copper, wood, mica..."

"I didn't know that Germany needed anything from South America, I always thought that those countries were very poor."

"No, they're not poor, but they have the misfortune to be run by corrupt governments. I don't think that abandoning their colonial status has really helped them advance."

"Well, they might have lots of raw materials like you say, but they were a great financial burden for Spain," Amelia said, just to say something.

"Well, they are rich, Amelia, very rich. They have copper, oil, precious stones, wood, zinc, quinine, antimony, platinum, mica, quartz, even liver."

"Liver? I don't understand..."

"I was asking Kleist to do what he could to get more liver. Haven't I ever told you? We make a tonic out of liver extract which is extremely invigorating, and which we give to shock troops and submariners. Maybe I should bring you a bottle."

"How horrid! I should hate to drink liver tonic."

"Well, it does provide a great charge of energy, I wish we had enough to give some to every soldier! It's very good against tiredness, and it is an invigorator."

"And what about platinum? Why do you want platinum? I can't imagine that you need to keep the jewelers supplied during wartime. Who has money to buy jewelry nowadays?"

"Platinum is for something more than rings and necklaces," Max said, laughing. "It's used to make nitric acid, in heating elements, in manufacturing fibres, optical lenses... I won't bore you with a chemistry lesson about the properties of platinum. Karl Kleist told us something very funny about platinum smuggling. Some of our sailors in the Spanish merchant marine make cornerpieces, little reinforcing triangles that go on the corners of trunks or boxes. Instead of metal they use platinum, which they then paint black to hide it, so that when the boat goes through British customs at Trinidad nobody realizes that these little cornerpieces are in fact made of platinum."

"How clever my countrymen are!"

"Yes, yes they are."

"And Captain Kleist organizes this smuggling."

"Yes, but Kleist is also a lucky businessman. He has set up companies in South America to guarantee the export of these raw materials. He's a very important man, many lives depend upon him."

Max suddenly fell silent and stood in front of Amelia, looking at her with a certain degree of worry.

"What's wrong, Max? Why are you looking at me like that?"

"I want you... I want you not to lie to me..."

"Lie to you? Why would I lie to you? I don't know what you're trying to say..."

"Are you still in contact with... with... the British?"

"For God's sake, Max! My contact with the British only came from my relationship with Albert James, and the only thing I did was to pass onto them the worries that your group had before the war. And if you want to know, I haven't seen Albert James since."

"You had a good relationship with Lord Paul, and he's in an important position in the Admiralty."

"You surprise me, Max. An intelligent man like you should know that Lord Paul's trust in me was based on my relationship with Albert. In any case, I'm a little offended by your lack of confidence in me."

Amelia turned round, hoping that she had proved convincing. It was difficult for her to lie to Max von Schumann because she was in love with him, and if she acted behind his back it was out of a conviction that Max desired what she did, the end of the war, the destruction of the Third Reich and a new Europe in which the Allies would depose Franco and Spain would be a republic once again. She said to herself that she was deceiving him for his own good, as if Max were a child. Max held to his code of honor rigidly, and for all his contempt for Hitler, he would never do anything that could damage Germany. She didn't think like he did: She would betray Franco's Spain a thousand times if it meant she could get rid of the dictator. This was her manner of understanding the notion of loyalty to her country, and the ideas that had brought her father in front of the firing squad.

"I'm sorry, Amelia, I didn't want to upset you."

"I have never worked for the British, Max, never. I was a messenger, using my relationship with Albert James to help you and your friends in the run-up to the war. You went to England yourself to meet with Lord Paul. You have nothing to blame me for."

He hugged her and asked her to forgive him. He was so much in love with her that he could not see the lie in Amelia's eyes.

Over the next few days, Amelia found out more and more information from conversations that she had with Max and Major Hans Henke, who seemed to admire Captain Karl Kleist greatly. Kleist himself had left Greece to go to Spain, and had a large number of helpers in the Spanish merchant marine.

"And the Spanish work openly with... German spies?" Amelia asked ingenuously.

"Lots of them do it for money; others for ideological affinities, and money. Don't think that it's easy; there are also lots of merchant seamen who are Basque and who work for their *lehendaraki* Aguirre, who is in exile in New York."

"And what do they do, all these seamen who work for Aguirre?"

"The same as the others: They spy, they pass information to the Allies about the contents of the boats, and point out the members of the crew whom they think are working for us; anything that could be useful to the Allied cause."

"So the Spanish merchant seamen are a nest of spies," Amelia summed up.

"More or less."

"And the Basques work for their *lehendaraki* Aguirre."

"Not all of them, some of them work for us. Your *lehendaraki* has put all the information services of the PNV at the service of the Allies in the hope that, if they win the war, then they will recognize Basque independence."

Amelia sent several messages to London via Dion. It wasn't easy, because the Hotel Great Britain housed all of the German High Command. Dion once missed his work for three days because of the flu, and Amelia had no other option than to go to the cathedral to look for the priest named Yorgos. The first day she had no luck, but on the second she was able to hand over a report, as well as photographs of documents about the position of troops in Crete that Max had in his possession.

But she was not ready for the new task given to her by Major Murray.

Dion told her that she should meet Agamemnon immediately: London had sent her some very particular instructions.

She had not gone back to the Café Acropolis; Agamemnon himself had recommended that she did not do so unless it was absolutely necessary, but it seemed as if that time had now come.

It was cold and raining, so she wrapped herself in her overcoat and put a scarf on her head.

"Are you going out, Madam?" the porter asked. "In weather like this?"

"I can't stand the rain against my window. A walk will do me good."

"You'll get soaked... ," the porter insisted.

"Don't worry, nothing will happen."

She did not go straight to Monastiraki, but wandered through Athens for a while in case anyone was following her. When she was sure that no one was, she headed toward Plaka and then down the little streets into Monastiraki. It was raining heavily, so that no one was surprised to see her turn for refuge into the small café.

Agamemnon was behind the bar and looked at her without giving any sign that he knew her. A couple of men were playing backgammon at one of the tables, and another was leaning against the bar, apparently absorbed in a glass of ouzo.

"What would you like?" Agamemnon asked.

"A coffee would be wonderful; it's raining a lot outside and I got soaked."

"There are days when it's better not to go out, and today is one of them," Agamemnon replied.

Amelia drank the coffee and waited until the café owner gave some sign of wanting to talk to her. But he seemed caught up in organizing glasses and cups behind the bar and paid her no attention.

"It looks like the rain's stopping," Amelia said as she paid for her coffee.

"Yes, but you'd do well to go home, it will rain again soon," the man replied.

She left the café without asking for any explanation. If Agamemnon had made no sign of knowing her then it must have been for a good reason. She went back to the hotel and found Max in a bad mood.

"I have to go to Crete."

"When?" Amelia asked, with a sullen face. "Can I come?" she added.

"I don't know, but it's not a good idea for you to come with me. The Greek Resistance is winning the battle there. There are lots of casualties. They are getting help from the English, who send them weapons and whatever else they might need. Things aren't going well."

"I should like so much to go to Crete..." Amelia put on her brightest smile and tried to look affectionate.

"I would like you to come with me, but I don't know if I will get permission, we'll see. Perhaps, but Captain Kleist will definitely go with me."

"Kleist? Didn't you say he was in Spain?"

"But he might come back to Athens in a few days. He's an expert in naval information and the High Command needs him in Crete. It seems impossible, but the British submarines are approaching the coast of Crete with impunity."

Amelia listened to him without stopping to wonder why Agamemnon had made no sign of recognizing her. It was not until the next day that Dion, whispering between his teeth, gave her an explanation.

"One of the men in the bar was a German."

"Do they suspect Agamemnon?"

"It may be that they suspect you. We have to be careful. You have to go to the cathedral tomorrow, there's an important religious festival; lots of people will be there and you are to meet the priest, he will give you the orders from London."

"Why can't you give them to me?"

"Everyone has his part to play. You play yours."

Max thought it was odd when Amelia said that she was going to the cathedral again.

"Again? Are you thinking about converting?"

"Converting?"

"Yes, stopping being a Catholic and becoming an Orthodox."

"Of course not! But I must say that I love their ceremonies, the incense, the icons... I don't know, I feel happy in their churches."

"Be careful, Amelia, there is someone in Athens who does not wish you well."

Internally, Amelia gave a start, but she tried not to show anything on her face.

"Who does not wish me well? Why? I don't know who it could be..."

"It is Colonel Winkler, an SS officer, a friend of Ulrich Jürgens. He is still convinced that you had something to do with the murder of Jürgens."

"But you told me yourself that the Italian partisans claimed that it was they who carried it out, and as you well know, I didn't rub shoulders with the partisans in Rome," Amelia said, trying to make a joke out of it.

"Winkler thinks that it was you who killed Jürgens and no one is going to convince him otherwise."

"How long has he been in Athens?"

"For a few days already, but I didn't find out until yesterday."

"Why didn't you tell me?"

"I didn't want to worry you, but in fact we should both be worried. I've had a few run-ins with the SS because they refuse to collaborate with some elements of logistics, the supplies of medicine for our troops. They confiscate them for themselves. They won't let us give medicine to prisoners. We should try to go unobserved, please, for the good of you and of me."

"I don't think that it will compromise us to go to the cathedral. Where's the harm in that?"

"Be careful, Amelia, anything will be excuse enough for Winkler to get you arrested."

She left, worried and scared by what she had just heard. Was it Winkler who had been in the café? Had he ordered her to be followed?

When she reached the cathedral she found it so full of people that it was difficult to enter. She asked herself if Winkler might have sent men after her. She hid behind a column and hoped that Yorgos would find her himself. A group of women came to stand near where she was, and this made her feel much more secure. Deeply focused, they prayed with a great devotion. Was one of them a traitor? She rejected the idea immediately when she remembered what the priest had told her the day they met: Greeks always vanquish invaders, no matter how strong and powerful they are.

The ceremony went by without anyone paying her any attention. She felt woozy with the smell of the incense. She didn't know how he had got there, but suddenly she realized that the priest was by her side.

"We don't have much time, even though those good souls are keeping us covered," he said, indicating the women who were a closed circle around them.

"What's going on?"

"London wants Captain Kleist."

"What do you mean they want him? I don't understand."

"They want to get their hands on him and they want you to help."

"But how?"

"He knows you and trusts you. You can be the hook that brings him to the surface, and then our British friends can grab him. He's an intelligent and mistrustful person, and he knows too much, so that it's not just him looking after his own safety, but the whole Abwehr as well. You'll have to go to Spain."

"To Spain? But what excuse will I give?"

"Your family is there, isn't it? Well, there's your excuse. It will be easier to do it there than here. But you have to be fast; the captain is going to go back to Greece, they want him to go to Crete. The Germans are suffering heavy losses on the island and they cannot cope with the boats and submarines that bring weapons to the Resistance."

"When would I have to go?"

"Tomorrow if possible. Ask the baron, he can arrange it."

She waited until the ceremony was over, although the priest had already disappeared from her side as stealthily as he had approached her.

She walked home, thinking about how she could ask Max to send her to Madrid. She realized that a man was following her, but she got back to the hotel without any complications.

"I've been thinking about what you said about Colonel Winkler and I got scared," she said to Max as soon as she arrived.

"Scared? I thought you couldn't feel fear," he said, joking.

"Max, I think I'll go to Spain. Let me go for a couple of weeks, I'll see my family and maybe this Winkler will forget about me. I may have been wrong, but I think I was followed to the cathedral; on the way back, a man was behind me all the way to the hotel steps."

Max could not help showing that he was worried. He was scared of Winkler. It had not been easy to save Amelia from him in Rome, and he would want to get his revenge.

"It is hard for me to think about separating myself from you, Amelia. You are all that I have."

"If you want me to stay?"

"No, you're right, it might be better if you left for a while. But promise me you'll return soon."

"I won't be in Madrid for more than a few days, I don't want to be away from you."

"Alright."

She was surprised at the speed with which Baron von Schumann had accepted her request, and at his faith in her.

He sorted everything out and three days later Amelia left Athens to go back to Madrid in a plane that made stops in Rome and Barcelona.

From the report that she herself sent to London at the end of the operation, we know that she went home. It was her alibi to justify her stay in Madrid. But on the day of her arrival she got in touch with Señora Rodríguez, who had orders for her about how to run the operation.

Amparito, Señora Rodríguez's maid, was surprised to see her when she opened the door.

"Madam is not receiving visitors today, she's resting," she said, like a good guard dog.

"I am sorry to have turned up without warning, but I am sure that Señora Rodríguez will receive me. I am coming through Madrid and I didn't want not to come by and see her."

The maid hesitated for a few seconds then let her pass, and led her to the salon.

"Wait here," she ordered.

Señora Rodríguez came out straight away.

"What a pleasure to see you, Amelia!"

They spoke about generalities until Amparito had left and come back with tea and pastries.

"Have they told you what the mission consists in?"

"Just that London wants Captain Kleist."

"I know that this man made great efforts to have you removed from Pawiak. Is that a problem?"

"No, although I wouldn't like him to be hurt."

"We think that he is 'Albatross,' the best spy the Germans have in South America. We have been on his trail for two years. We didn't know who he was. He uses a lot of names. He is a very good spy."

"What will they do to him?"

"Interrogate him, get what information we can from him and nothing else."

"Nothing else?"

"He is in Madrid. Of course, he always goes accompanied; he watches his back and he has his back watched for him: He always travels with two other men."

"I thought that the Germans were more relaxed here in Spain."

"Spain is officially neutral, but no one misses the fact that it is a country allied to Hitler, and a large part of the success of Kleist's activities comes down to the fact that the Spanish and the Germans are collaborating."

"What does Kleist do, exactly?"

"You know what he does, he has an intelligence network in South America. He has men everywhere: Venezuela, Argentina, Peru, Mexico... But it's not just that, he has also set up various import-export companies to provide Germany with vital materials. And he has spies on all the Spanish and Portuguese merchant vessels; sailors who are happy to collaborate with the Third Reich: Some of them because they are convinced Francoists, and others simply for the money. We do the same, of course. We rely on the help of sailors, the majority of them Basque, who bring us information about what the merchant ships are transporting, and if there is some special passenger or other. You have appeared in their reports yourself."

"They spy on each other, and both sides know that they do," Amelia concluded.

"Yes, it's like a game in which both teams are trying to score as many goals as possible. Lots of these ships are carrying important materials that are then picked up by German submarines on the high seas. Captain Kleist has personally recruited all his men. He has a great deal of information: names, codes, bank details..."

"And why haven't you tried to kidnap him earlier? That's what the aim of this mission is, right?"

"It is not easy to get close to him, he's a professional, he doesn't trust anyone."

"But what can I do?"

"Bump into him."

"Won't he think it's odd?"

"Why? You're Spanish, your family lives in Madrid, you've come to see them, there's nothing strange about that."

"But what do I need to do?" Amelia asked.

"Get him to trust you, offer to be his guide to the city, teach him everything he doesn't know about Madrid, flirt with him, he's a very attractive man and you are an attractive woman."

"He is Max von Schumann's friend, and I have a serious relationship with Max von Schumann," Amelia said uncomfortably.

"I've only said that you should flirt with him, nothing more. And now let's talk about the details of the operation."

Señora Rodríguez spent two hours telling Amelia the steps she should take until she had memorized all the details. Then they said goodbye.

"When the mission is over, you will go back to Athens." It sounded more like an order than a suggestion.

"I hope so," Amelia said with a sigh.

"So it's best if we say goodbye now, as we won't see each other again for a long time. Take care of yourself."

Amelia's family had been made extremely happy by her return to Madrid in March 1944, but they were now no longer surprised by her sudden appearances and disappearances.

The day after her meeting with Señora Rodríguez, Amelia went out for a walk with her cousin Laura and her sister Antonietta. They had convinced her to go out for tea and stroll around the city, which seemed to be waking up for spring.

The three young women chatted together animatedly and seemed not to be paying any attention to things external to themselves. They didn't even notice that a swastika flag a few meters ahead of them proclaimed the presence of the German Embassy. Amelia looked absentmindedly at her watch before replying to a comment her sister had made.

Some men came out of the German Embassy and one of them looked at her curiously. They didn't seem to notice. Suddenly, one of the men came up to where the young women were standing.

"Amelia!"

She looked at him surprised, she seemed not to recognize this man in his suit and gray overcoat and with his hair covered by an equally gray hat. He came up to her quickly, accompanied by two of the other men.

"How happy I am to see you! But what are you doing here? I thought you were in Athens."

She seemed confused, as if she were trying to remember who this man was who was talking to her with such familiarity, and he, taking off his hat, began to laugh.

"Don't you recognize me?"

"Kleist! I'm sorry, Captain, I didn't recognize you," she said shyly.

"Of course, in civilian clothes... I suppose it must be difficult to recognize me. But what are you doing here?"

"I'm with my family, allow me to introduce my cousin Laura and my sister Antonietta."

"I didn't know you were coming to Spain."

"Well, I come when I can."

They stood in silence for a few seconds without knowing what to do. Then he took the initiative.

"May I invite you to come out for a walk and to have tea with me some afternoon when you are free?"

She seemed to think about this, then she smiled.

"It's better if you come to visit us; I'll introduce you to the rest of the family."

"Wonderful, when can I come?"

"Tomorrow? If you are free, we'll expect you at six."

"I'll be there."

They said goodbye, and when they were walking away he could hear Amelia's cousin begin talking.

"It wasn't a good idea to invite him, you know that Papa can't stand the Nazis."

At six o'clock in the evening on the next day, Edurne, the family servant, opened the door and found herself face to face with a tall and very attractive young man who asked for Señorita Amelia Garayoa.

"Come in, they're waiting for you."

"No, I'd prefer to wait here, tell the señorita."

Amelia came out with her aunt, Doña Elena, her cousin Laura, and her sister Antonietta.

"Karl, please come in, we're waiting for you. Allow me to introduce my aunt."

The man kissed her hand gallantly and gave her a package wrapped in the recognizable paper of a famous pastry shop.

"Oh, you shouldn't have gone to so much trouble!" Doña Elena said.

"It's no trouble, it's an honor to make your acquaintance. But I don't want to bother you, I would like, with your permission, to take Amelia for a walk. I won't be too long. Shall we say eight o'clock?"

Doña Elena insisted politely that he take a cup of tea with them, but he declined.

When they were out in the street, Amelia asked him why he, had rejected her aunt's hospitality.

"I'm sorry, but I couldn't help overhearing your cousin's comment. You don't like Germans in your house."

"I'm sorry, I didn't know that you had heard Laura."

"I think she said what she said with the intention of being heard," Kleist replied with apparent anger.

"My father was shot by the Fascists. My Uncle Armando was in prison and was only saved by a miracle."

"There's no need to explain, I understand. I don't know what I would think if they had shot my father."

"My family was never Fascist, we are Republicans. That is how I was brought up."

"It's difficult to understand your relationship with Max, then... He's a German officer."

"Why is it difficult? We met in Buenos Aires, then we met again in London, and then in Berlin... and... I... I trust Max, I know who he is and how he thinks."

"But even so, he's an officer and his loyalty is to Germany."

"As is yours."

"That's right."

"I have never lied to Max about what I think, he knows my family, he knows what we have been through."

"I'm not judging you, Amelia, I'm not judging you. There are many people in Germany who don't share the ideals of Nazism."

"Many? In that case why have they let..." She fell silent, scared of upsetting him. Max had told her that Kleist was not a supporter of Nazism, and that he obeyed simply as an officer, but was that true?

"Don't be scared, I have no intention of hurting you. I helped you in the past without knowing you. You did something very risky helping those Poles get into the ghetto."

"My best friend when I was younger was a Jew, her father was a partner of my father's. They disappeared."

"You won't shock me by telling me you have Jewish friends. I have nothing against the Jews."

"In that case, why have you allowed them to have everything they own be taken from them, to be sent to labor camps, to have to walk around with stars sewn to their clothes? Why have they suddenly stopped being Germans and why do they have no rights?"

Karl Kleist was impressed that Amelia was brave enough to speak to him, a German officer, in this way. Either she was naïve, or else Max had managed to convince her that she should trust him. In either case, her attitude seemed imprudent.

"You shouldn't speak to strangers like that; you don't know who could be listening, or the consequences of your words."

She looked at him in fear and he was moved by her helpless gaze and turned the conversation to other, less controversial topics.

He invited her to have a cup of hot chocolate with him, and it was at this point that Amelia noticed the presence of two men, who were the same two men who had been with Kleist when he had left the embassy.

"These men... ," she said, pointing to them.

"They're good friends."

"Don't be scared of the Spanish! Franco is proud of the fact that with him in charge, the country is safe. In fact no one dares do anything for fear of the consequences. I don't think that any-one will try to rob you, even if you are a foreigner."

"Better safe than sorry."

She didn't insist in order not to upset him. Kleist left her in front of the door to her house just before eight o'clock.

"It was very nice to see you."

"Yes, it was."

Karl Kleist thought for a moment. Then with a smile, he asked her to have lunch with him in two days' time.

11

They started to see each other fairly regularly. Amelia had decided not to follow Señora Rodríguez's recommendation that she flirt with him. She was sure that if she did it would drive him away. Kleist had a code of honor that would have led him to reject the advances of a friend's lover. This did not mean that he was not attracted to her, and with every day that passed he longed more to be with her. He liked Amelia, and this tormented him; but if she had hinted as to her availability then he would have found excuses to distance himself from her.

A few days after their first meeting, Kleist announced that he had to go to Bilbao and suggested that she accompany him.

"No, thank you, I don't think it would be correct," Amelia said.

"Don't misunderstand me, it would be a short journey, and as you are half Basque I thought you would like to see your father's homeland."

"Yes, I would, but that doesn't mean that I should go with you. I am sorry."

Kleist was disappointed, but at the same time his interest in Amelia grew more intense. He was debating between his loyalty to Max von Schumann and his attraction to Amelia. If she allowed herself to be seduced, then he would be able to disdain her, but her sincere refusals awoke his interest.

When he returned from Bilbao he went to see her.

"Tell me about the city."

Kleist explained at length what he had seen. Amelia listened to him with so much attention that it was as if nothing could have been more important than what he was saying.

That day she dared to complain about the presence of the two men who were always following him, although they did it so well that most of the time they were invisible, she didn't even know they were there.

"Don't you trust me?" she said suddenly when she caught sight of one of the men.

"Why do you say that?" he asked in surprise.

"We're always being followed by these two men, as if I were going to do something to you."

"Do they annoy you?"

Amelia shrugged, and he understood that she felt inhibited by the presence of these two men, that if they weren't there then maybe...

"I'll tell them to go."

"No, don't do it, it was silly of me to say anything."

They carried on talking about banalities, and she enthused about the arrival of spring, and remembered her childhood.

"When the weather was good, my father and my Uncle Armando organized a trip for the whole family; we went to the mountains at El Pardo, a wonderful place, where you see deer and rabbits running about. We took baskets full of food and spent the whole day there. We could run, and jump and shout... Well, I was the one who ran and jumped and shouted, my sister Antonietta stayed with my mother and I played with Laura and Melita, my cousins. Jesús was still little and my aunt wouldn't let him leave her."

"How long has it been since you've been there?"

"Since before the war, our war. I'd like to go, but I don't have a car. My father and my uncle had a car, but now..."

"I will take you."

"I wish we could go! But I'm going back to Athens next Monday, Max is waiting for me, I've only got a few more days left in Madrid."

"We can go this Sunday. Make one of those baskets, or better still, I'll make it. We'll go alone, without my guardian angels.'"

That's what Amelia called his bodyguards.

"No, no, don't do that," she protested. "I'm used to them, I don't mind."

"Even so, we'll go alone."

That night Amelia asked Edurne to take a note to Señora Rodríguez's house.

"I'm going back to Athens soon and I would like to say goodbye."

That night Albatross, which was Karl Kleist's codename, also received a note, but longer than that which Amelia had sent Señora Rodríguez. It was an extensive report on Amelia and her family. One of his "guardian angels" gave it to him and told him to take care.

"She left her husband and her infant son to run away with another man. Then she had a relationship with an American journalist, the nephew of Paul James, one of the chiefs of the Admiralty. Now she is sharing her life with Baron Max von Schumann. She is a woman who..."

The bodyguard was not allowed to continue the phrase. Kleist cut the man off and gave an order to leave him alone so that he could read the report in peace.

He knew part of the information contained in the report via Max, and Amelia herself had spoken about her former life, saying how much she suffered from not being able to see her son.

His "guardian angel" had been right, though; the report showed that there were gaps in Amelia Garayoa's career, like the Rome incident, in which she had been connected to the murder of an SS officer, but he rejected all possible doubts, he prided himself on knowing people well, and she had been sincere with him and had said that she was not a Fascist and that she hated Nazism. She had said that she was a Republican and a liberal, and even that she thought that if the Allies won the war it would mean the end of Franco, as he would lose his main ally, Hitler, given that Mussolini was no longer a powerful force.

On Sunday Kleist came to pick her up at eleven on the dot. He had a basket with enough food in it for a couple of days, as well as wine and cakes. Amelia seemed radiant.

As he had promised, they were not followed by the "guardian angels."

She took him to the place that her family used to visit and ran up and down the mountainside, with him following her, enjoying her enthusiasm.

After eating they lay down on the grass a prudent distance from each other. Amelia subtly marked out how large this distance should be and he, in thrall to her, accepted. Not much time had passed before Amelia said that she was feeling unwell.

"I don't know, something is making me feel queasy, perhaps I'm not used to drinking wine."

"But you only took a sip. Maybe it was the pâté."

"I don't know, but my stomach hurts a lot."

They had intended to return to Madrid late in the afternoon, but like a gentleman Kleist immediately offered to take her back home.

When they got there, he parked the car and offered to walk her up to her apartment, but she would only allow him to take her as far as the elevator. She said goodbye to him there in the presence of the doorman, who had come out to say hello.

"Your aunt and uncle are at home, but I think that Laura and Antonietta have gone out and are not home yet," the doorman told her.

She got into the elevator and warmly squeezed his hand before closing the door.

"Have a safe journey, and give my regards to Max."

"Take care of yourself," she said.

Amelia went up to her aunt and uncle's apartment and went straight to her room, barely pausing to greet Doña Elena and Don Armando, who were listening to the radio in the salon. She ran to the window and saw Karl Kleist's car pulling away from the side of the road. Someone had gotten into it and was stretched out in the back seat, waiting for the German to return. When he was about to start the car he saw a man's face appear in the rear-view mirror, and felt the cold barrel of a pistol at his neck. Another man opened the car door and sat at his side. He also had a weapon. He only said one word.

"Drive."

Albatross was now in the power of agents of the British Secret Service. The British government accepted Franco's fiction about neutrality, but they had agents in Spain, who spent most of their time gathering information. At sea, the British Secret Service had no compunction: No ship headed for Spain was allowed to proceed without stopping at Trinidad to have her cargo and passenger list checked. But until this moment, no action this risky had taken place on Spanish soil.

Amelia went to Athens next day to be with Max. A few days later he told her about Karl Kleist's disappearance.

"Amelia, something terrible has happened. Karl has disappeared."

"Karl?" she said, surprised, as if she didn't understand what he was talking about.

"Yes, our embassy in Madrid hasn't heard anything from him for several days. They've looked for him everywhere but there is no sign of him. They are investigating. The last person he was seen with was you." Max could not stop a flash of pain from showing itself in his face.

"But Karl often goes to South America, maybe he's headed there."

"Yes, there's a chance of that, but he would have left a message. But you were the last person who was with Karl," Max insisted.

"I don't know... I told you that I was with him on the Sunday before heading back to Athens. We went to the country. Has no one really heard about him since then?"

"He did not go back to the embassy that day. His men thought that he... well, that he was with you. He had insisted on going on the trip to the country alone. They didn't start to worry until late Monday morning. They went to your uncle and aunt's house..."

"Good Lord, that must have given them a real shock!"

"The doorman said that Karl went with you to the elevator and that you said goodbye there, and he saw him going back to his car. He also said that he didn't see you again until the next morning, when you left with your uncle, carrying a suitcase."

"I can't understand what happened," she said, apparently stupefied. "He was very discreet and didn't say anything about his work, so he didn't tell me if he was thinking of going anywhere. Do you think something might have happened to him?" Amelia tried to seem innocent.

"I don't know, but no one just disappears. The police are looking for him. I've told you that they've interrogated your family, and the doorman."

"But my family has nothing to do with Karl!" she cried out in anguish.

"Amelia, the Gestapo want to interrogate you here. Colonel Winkler wants the investigation into Jürgens's murder to be re-opened. He doesn't think it's a coincidence."

"Coincidence? What do you mean, coincidence?" she asked, without hiding her fear.

"Colonel Winkler insists that his friend, Colonel Jürgens, had arranged to meet you the evening of his murder, and Kleist disappeared just after spending a day with you in the country. This, for him, is irrefutable evidence that you are behind both events. He thinks that you're a spy."

"He's mad! I'm not a spy! Max, please, stop this man!"

"I'm trying to, Amelia."

She was really scared. She cursed Major Murray in her mind. Operation Albatross had been a success for the British Secret Service, but she asked herself if Major Murray had perhaps thought that she would be a suitable price to pay to get hold of Captain Kleist. She felt like an insignificant piece in the secret game of the war.

She started to cry. She had been holding her tears back for days and had barely been able to sleep. She had handed Kleist over to the British, and he would now be in London, being interrogated by Major Murray, and even though she had no doubt about where her political loyalties lay, her conscience tormented her.

Karl Kleist had helped her when she was in a Warsaw prison, he had helped Max to get her out of that prison, he had been a gentleman, quite charming, over the last few days in Madrid, but she had betrayed him and handed him over to the British, and he was now in London where, in the best of cases, he would be in prison until the war was over. She had been able to do this to a man who had been nothing but kind to her, and she felt miserable, thinking about the ease with which she hurt the people who were good to her. Santiago came first, whom she abandoned for Pierre; then she had betrayed Max in order to spy for the British, and now she had handed Kleist over to them as well.

She despised herself, even more so when Max put his arms around her and tried to calm her.

"Please, don't cry, you know that I would give my life for you, that I will do whatever I can to make sure that you don't fall into Winkler's hands, but you have to tell me the truth, you have to trust me, that's the only way I can help you. And don't worry about your family, they won't suffer anything at all, it's clear that they don't know about Kleist's disappearance."

"But what do you want me to say!" Amelia shouted. "I've told you everything: We went to the country, then I felt ill after our picnic and he took me home; I said goodbye to him at the door to the elevator and I don't know anything else. The next day I came here. I don't know what happened, I don't know."

"You're unlucky enough to be always in the wrong place."

"Colonel Winkler wants to blame me for Jürgens's death because he saw how I pushed him away at the New Year's party, and Jürgens swore that he would make me pay for that. It's his chance to get revenge on me, now that Jürgens himself can't."

"It's alright, I'll do what I can to save you from Winkler, trust me."

But Max could not prevent Amelia from being "invited" to visit the Gestapo headquarters in Athens. It was very close to the Hotel Great Britain, in what had once been the house of Heinrich Schliemann, the discoverer of Troy and the tombs of Mycenae.

Max came with her and together they withstood the humiliation of waiting two long hours until a man, who told them his name was Hoth, invited them to follow him to an office on the second floor. They were surprised to see Colonel Winkler sitting on the other side of the desk. There were no other chairs, so Hoth kept them standing.

"I hope that you are not upset by the presence of Colonel Winkler, he came to see me and I think he knows you, Fräulein Garayoa."

She nodded.

"And you are accompanied by Colonel von Schumann! What an honor!" the SS officer said sarcastically.

"I am a great friend of Fräulein Garayoa's."

"Yes, I know, and the General Staff knows it as well. Your friendship is not a secret for anyone, not even your lovely wife, Baroness Ludovica," Hoth replied with a sardonic smile.

Max did not reply to the provocation. His only objective was to get out of the building with Amelia, and he knew that to face up to Hoth with Winkler present could only make things worse.

"Fräulein Garayoa, we have a report from Madrid which assures us that you were the last person who was seen with Captain Kleist. You spent a day together in the country, you had a picnic, and then the captain disappeared."

"Captain Kleist is a close friend of ours whom I spent a day with in the country, and who then took me to my house, where we said goodbye. I have not seen him since, and I am extremely upset by his disappearance."

"Which, naturally, you had nothing to do with." Hoth was playing cat and mouse.

"Of course not. I repeat that Kleist is a fried of Baron von Schumann, who introduced us, and I feel strongly positive feelings toward him."

"The captain didn't tell you where he intended to spend the rest of the afternoon?"

"No, he didn't. I was feeling ill and the captain and I didn't talk that much on the journey home."

"And the captain didn't come back to ask after your health?"

"No, he didn't. I spent the rest of the afternoon with my uncle and aunt, and I went to bed early, given that I had to travel to Athens the next day. I think that the doorman has already told the police that Captain Kleist and I said goodbye at the door to the elevator and that I didn't leave the house again that day."

"Yes, but even doormen nod off, my dear! He left his post at ten o'clock, so if you went out again later, or if the captain came back to see you, then that's not something he would know about."

"My family can confirm what I've just told you."

"And why wouldn't they? The testimony of one's family is not conclusive, Fräulein."

"I assure you that I do not know where Captain Kleist is."

"And you weren't with Colonel Jürgens the night he was murdered in Rome."

"There are two witnesses who have vouched that it was not I who was in Colonel Jürgens's room the night that he was murdered," Amelia replied, holding back her indignation.

"Yes, two drunk witnesses who saw a woman for a couple of seconds in the corridor of the hotel; I don't think their testimony should be taken into account either."

Amelia said nothing, but she felt the sullen gaze of Colonel Winkler upon her. He had said nothing all this while. She could sense Max's tension, and how upset he was not to be able to defend her.

"You will have to stay here for a couple of days. I need to carry on with the interrogation, but now I have other things to do."

"Fräulein Garayoa can come whenever you have the time; as you know, she is staying at the Hotel Great Britain. She does not need to stay here." But Max's statement did not affect Hoth at all.

"I am sorry, Colonel, but it is I who decides where suspects should be kept."

"Suspects? What is Fräulein Garayoa accused of? Of having a picnic with Captain Kleist? Kleist is my friend, is our friend, a person we are both very fond of. There is no accusation you can level against Fräulein Garayoa. If you need to clear up any point, then please call her again and she will come with pleasure."

Amelia was pale, and didn't dare say anything. She knew that whatever Max said, Hoth would not let her leave.

"I am sorry, Colonel, but I have to do my job. Fräulein Garayoa will stay here."

Max felt impotent when two of Hoth's subordinates came into the room and took Amelia away with them.

"You are responsible for Fräulein Garayoa's safety and continued good health," he said to Hoth.

"Responsible? This woman is a suspect in the case of Kleist's disappearance and my obligation is to make her talk. If you get in my way, it will be me who makes you responsible for obstructing the course of justice and stopping the Gestapo from convicting a criminal."

"Fräulein Garayoa is not a criminal, and you know that very well."

"I don't know it, and when I do know it I will tell you. And now, if you will excuse me, I have a lot of work to do. Sadly, I need to fight against the enemies of the Reich."

Amelia was taken down to the basement of the mansion, where she was locked in a windowless cell. Apparently this had once been a storeroom.

One of Hoth's subordinates manacled her hands and feet and pushed her into a corner of the room.

"Alright, keep calm, you won't have time to get bored," he said, showing a mouth filled with gold teeth.

She didn't even protest. She knew what awaited her, the horror of Warsaw was ever present in her mind.

There, locked away, she lost all notion of time; she didn't know if it was night or if dawn had broken, there was no way to tell. She also didn't hear any sounds. Her hands and her ankles hurt because of the manacles. She felt her fingers swelling up and wanted to scream. She decided not to, knowing that this was nothing compared to what was awaiting her.

She didn't know how much time had passed before they opened the door and the same man who had put her in there removed the manacles from her feet and told her to follow him.

She could scarcely walk. The pain in her feet had spread up her legs. She felt a sharp pain, but told herself that the worst was still to come.

They took her back up to the second floor, to Hoth's office. He was alone, and ordered her to sit in the chair that Colonel Winkler had occupied.

"Have you thought things through?" he said in a neutral voice, as if he didn't care what her answer would be.

"I told you everything I know yesterday," she replied.

"So you are not going to collaborate..."

"I cannot tell you what I do not know."

He shrugged and pressed a bell under his desk. Hoth's adjutant came in, followed by Max. Amelia felt extremely relieved.

"Take her away," Hoth said to Max von Schumann. You are responsible for Fräulein Garayoa not leaving Athens without the permission of the Gestapo."

Max agreed, and bore Hoth's hyena-like gaze unflinchingly.

"We will see you again, the investigation is not over."

With Max's help, Amelia tried to move her legs. One step, two steps, three... Each step caused her pain in her swollen feet.

As they were leaving they found themselves face to face with Colonel Winkler, who stopped in front of them and obliged them to pause.

"You have not won the game, Baron. It was clever of you to ask for help from Reichsführer Himmler's personal physician. But not even the Reichsführer can stop this woman from paying for her crimes."

"Get away from me, Winkler! And don't even think about threatening me again."

Amelia could not stop herself from crying once they were out in the street again.

"Can you walk to the hotel? We only need to cross the street."

"Yes, I think I can."

When they at last reached Amelia's room, Max helped her to her bed, where she collapsed, and then he examined her hands and ankles with care.

"Did they chain you up?"

"Yes, they put some manacles on my hands and feet. I couldn't move the whole time I was there, I don't know how long it was..."

"An afternoon and a night, Amelia, an eternity."

"I am so grateful to you; I was scared that I would have to go through what I went through in Warsaw again; I would have ended up admitting that I was guilty of anything that they wanted to accuse me of."

"In fact it was Kleist who saved you, indirectly."

"Kleist? Has he turned up?" Amelia said in surprise.

"No, not exactly. My adjutant Hans remembered that when you were in Warsaw, Kleist spoke about taking your case to Felix Kersten."

"Who is Felix Kersten? The doctor Hoth spoke about?"

"No, he's not a doctor, although they treat him like one. He... he's a strange man, he was born in Estonia and he has a great reputation for being good at manual therapy."

"I don't understand."

"Massages, nothing more than massages. Kersten is a pleasant man who gets on well with his patients, and he had important clients all over Europe before the war. Apparently Himmler has very bad stomach pains, and only Kersten can help him with them. He has a great deal of influence over him. The Reichsführer's head of information, Brigadeführer Walter Schellenberg, is the other person who can influence Himmler."

"And you spoke to the pair of them?"

"I have friends who are good friends of theirs."

"Thank you, Max, thank you."

While he was rubbing an ointment on Amelia's feet, Max warned her:

"I don't think that they will help us again, Amelia, so... Please, be careful!"

"But I didn't do anything, Max..."

"Colonel Winkler will not stop until he has managed to avenge the death of his friend Colonel Jürgens, and he has decided that you will pay for his death. The SS are taking charge of espionage cases and... well, Winkler is convinced that you are an Allied spy."

"And do you believe him, Max?"

"When I was in Berlin I saw Ludovica and Friedrich, my son. I love my son with all my heart, I would give up my life for him, but even so... I would abandon any chance I had of ever seeing him again if it meant I would not have to leave you. I said so to Ludovica."

Amelia burst into tears again. She was ashamed of having betrayed him, of not being entirely loyal to him, of not telling him about her collaboration with the British. Max hated the war, but not so much that he would betray his country. That's why she couldn't tell him what she was doing.

"Don't cry, Amelia, you're not responsible."

"I am, Max, I am; I shouldn't let my love for you carry me away, I know better than anyone what it means to renounce a son."

"Ludovica can't stop me from seeing him and from being involved in his upbringing. But that will be when the war ends."

"And what about your family, Max? And your sisters? You have never told me what they think about your being with me."

"They don't approve of it and they will never accept you. But that should not worry us for now. Our problem is named Winkler."

"And Hoth."

"He's just a policeman who wants to get a pat on the back from the SS by showing that he can be as much of a brute as they are."

Amelia did not leave the hotel room for a few days. She could barely walk, and Max made her stay seated. Then he helped her take her first few paces in the hotel entrance hall. Amelia wanted to talk to Dion, but did not get the chance. Max did not leave her side. Her chance came one afternoon, when Max's adjutant, Major Hans Henke, came into the bar to tell him that he was urgently required in the General Staff office.

"I'll take you up to the room."

"Max, please, let me stay here just a little while! It's still early, just let me stay and finish my tea... ," she asked him with a smile.

"I don't want to leave you alone..."

"I won't be here long, just a couple of minutes more. I spend so much time in the room!"

"Alright, but promise me that you'll go straight to your room."

"I promise."

Dion came up to her as soon as the baron had left.

"Would you like anything else to drink?"

"No, I don't want anything, but I've got something for you," she said in a low voice as he bent forward to take the tea-tray and, as he did so, she pressed a roll of film into his hand.

"Alright, Madam, I'll bring you a jar of water."

He came back and bent over to pour the water.

"The priest wants to see you. It's urgent."

"Urgent? But you see how I am... the baron won't let me go out..."

"You'll have to do it somehow. The day after tomorrow, in the cathedral. They've carried out a roundup and Agamemnon and many other patriots have been arrested."

Amelia went back to her room, wondering what she should do. She had to convince Max to let her go. She felt better now, the swelling in her legs and feet had gone down, she could walk. Yes, she had to convince him to let things return to normal.

When Max came back that evening, Amelia started to butter him up from the moment he came through the door.

"Come on, tell me what you want!" Max said, laughing.

"I want to go out, I need to go out, I am suffocating in this room. Let me go for a walk, go to the cathedral, you know I like to go there to relax, go back to looking at the archaeological sites, anything apart from staying here."

He resisted for a while, but in the end he gave in.

"You have to promise me that you will not talk to any strangers, and that you will tell me where you are going."

"I promise," she said, wrapping her arms around his neck.

She didn't see the priest when she went into the cathedral. Women were lighting candles, and others were seated and seemed to be sunk in their prayers. She looked for a dark and private corner to sit down. Without realizing it, she began to pray. She thanked God for having saved her from the Gestapo, for having Max's love to support her, for being alive. The deep voice of the priest brought her back to reality.

"Orders have come through for you from London. They congratulate you for Madrid, whatever it was you did there, but they need to know about the deployment of German troops on the border with Yugoslavia."

"I'll do what I can," Amelia promised.

"We need your help as well, are you prepared to give it? They have arrested Agamemnon and some of our friends, but they will resist, they won't talk even if they are put to death."

"What can I do?"

"Can you drive?"

"Yes, but not very well, I haven't had time to practice."

"It's enough. We need to collect some weapons your British friends have sent us. A fishing boat will bring them across; they collected them from a submarine off the coast of Crete a few days ago. The boat gets here tomorrow. We need these weapons for the Resistance. A German convoy with tanks and heavy artillery will head for the north in a few days, to bring their reinforcements to the Italian-Yugoslav border. We want to stop them from reaching their destination. That's why the British shipment is important, they have sent us a good load of explosives and detonators, and we will use them to attack the convoy. It will be a blow to the Germans, and our response to the arrest of the patriots."

"Where is the fishing boat going to arrive?"

"To the north of Athens, we will go out to sea to collect the weapons."

"Do they know in London that you are asking me to help with this mission?"

"No, London has nothing to do with it, I am asking you myself."

"It will be very dangerous."

"Everything is very dangerous. Will you do it?"

"Yes, but you still haven't told me what it is I need to do."

"Join our group. We need people, we need another driver."

"Alright, but... I don't know if I'll be able to get away at night. It is difficult to get out of the hotel."

"You will not need to get away at night. We will unload the weapons and hide them in a safe place near the beach. The weapons will be distributed among little groups. You will need to drive two friends there and then drive them back to Athens. Nothing else. They will show you the way to go."

"And neither of these two men knows how to drive?"

"No, they don't. Not everyone can drive. I've told you that there have been arrests, we've had losses."

"Very good. What else?"

"I'll get word to you of the day and the place where you need to go to help us."

Amelia went out to walk around the Acropolis, as the priest had told her to do. She didn't know who would get in touch with her, all she knew was that she had to walk.

A car stopped next to her and she saw a woman's face and heard a voice asking her to get in. She did so instinctively.

"Get down on the floor," the woman sat next to the driver said.

"Where are we going?" Amelia asked.

"To find your car."

She couldn't see where they were going, all she felt was her stomach turning over from the twists and turns the car was making. They stopped after half an hour. She was surprised to see that they were in a garage.

"Get out, we're here," the woman said.

A man came hobbling toward them. He had a pistol in his belt.

"You're late," he said to them in Greek.

"We had to get past the patrols," the driver said, and then he, pointing to Amelia, added in English, "She'll take you."

"Can you drive?" the limping man asked her, looking at her for the first time.

"Yes, fairly well."

"You'll have to do better than that," the man said grumpily.

"Does it hurt?" the woman asked, looking at the man's bandaged leg.

"That's not important. The important thing is that I can't drive."

They showed Amelia an old black car parked nearby, and she was worried that she would not be able to handle it. Albert James had taught her in London and she had passed her driving test, but she had never really driven at all.

"Let's go," the lame man said.

The couple got back into the car and drove out first. Amelia suffered the humiliation of stalling the engine before she could even get the car started.

"Can you drive or can't you?" the man said, annoyed.

"I've told you, I can, a little."

"Well, come on, let's go."

He showed her the way to go. He seemed preoccupied and made no effort to be friendly.

"What's your name?" Amelia asked him.

"What do you care? The less you know, the better."

She fell silent, but she blushed with annoyance. The man seemed to regret having been so brusque.

"It's for your own safety, you can't tell anyone what you don't know if they arrest you. But you're right, you have the right to have a name you can use to get in touch with me. How about Costas?"

"I don't care," she said in annoyance to the tall dark man, who wore a bushy moustache.

"You are a British agent, you must be very good at it to live with a Nazi and not have anyone suspect you."

She was going to defend Max, to say, again, that he was not a Nazi, just a soldier doing his job. But she knew that Costas wouldn't understand, wouldn't want to understand. For him all the Germans were the same, and Max wore the uniform.

"Are we going to pick up all the material?" she asked.

"Not all of it, a part. Other members of the group have already taken the rest. Last night. They've left us the explosives and the detonators. We're going to blow up a convoy of tanks. You will be my driver, you're not that bad at it."

When they reached the warehouse where the weapons had been stored, the other couple was already there. The man was carrying boxes to his car, while the woman stood watch with a pistol.

"You will keep watch too. Get up there on that rock and tell me if you see anything strange. Take this," he said, holding out a pistol.

"I don't need it," Amelia said, without daring to take it.

"Take it! What will you do if they discover us? Cry at them?" Costas shouted.

Amelia took the gun and climbed up on the rock without saying another word.

She waited impatiently for the two men to finish camouflaging the weapons in their cars, which took them around an hour. When they had finished, they made a sign to the two women.

On the way back to Athens, Amelia drove in silence; it was Costas who started to speak.

"The operation will take place in three days. We'll put the charges in tomorrow morning. Then we'll wait for them to pass and... Boom!"

"Good," Amelia replied without too much enthusiasm.

"Are you scared?"

"It would be stupid for me not to be. You should be scared as well."

"No, I'm not scared. Whenever I kill Germans I feel something in my gut, as if I were... bah! You're a woman."

"A woman who's driving your car and is going to help you blow up a convoy." Amelia couldn't bear the lack of respect that Costas was showing her.

"Yes, women are brave as well, our female comrades in the Resistance don't complain, they know how to obey orders and they don't quake when they have to pull a trigger. We'll see what you can do."

"Why don't you use your female comrades?" she asked in annoyance.

"The last roundup decimated our forces. My leg is a reminder, I had to jump over a wall with a bullet in my knee. Lots of us are in the hands of the Gestapo. They won't get away alive."

"And what if they speak?"

"They will never speak! We are Greeks."

"I suppose that you are human beings as well."

"So you would speak, then," he said mistrustfully.

"How many times have you been arrested? How many times have you been interrogated by the Gestapo?" Amelia asked.

"No, they've never been able to catch me."

"So don't say what you would or wouldn't do."

"And what about you? How many times have you been arrested?" he replied in a mocking tone of voice that offended her.

She was about to stop the car and roll up her sleeves to show him the marks of the handcuffs on her wrists, or else roll down her stockings to show him her legs, but she did not, she realized that he was just like this, and did not speak to upset her.

"In three days' time," he reminded her when they said goodbye.

Max was in the bath when she got to the hotel.

"Where have you been?" he asked from the bathroom.

"Out for a walk. I went to the cathedral," Amelia said, tensing up.

She let him carry on enjoying his bath and left the room to take advantage of the few minutes she had and photograph some of the documents he had spread out over the desk.

She didn't even look at what she was taking photographs of. She had no time. She would give them to Dion as soon as she could.

The night before the Resistance operation, Max said he had to go away for a few days to a village where several German soldiers had fallen ill.

"I don't know what it is, but I need to go and have a look."

"When are you leaving?"

"Very early tomorrow morning. My adjutant will come to pick me up before dawn."

"You look worried..."

"I am, I'm worried about how the war is going. In Berlin they refuse to see what is happening."

"And what is happening, Max?"

"We might lose. It was a mistake to attack the Russians and we are now paying for it."

Amelia gave a sigh of relief. She fervently hoped that Germany would lose the war, even though her main worry at the moment was how to leave the room without Max noticing. They hadn't slept together since last night, because she had said that she was not feeling well. He had accepted her sleeping in the neighboring room, but was not happy about it and insisted that they kept the doors between their rooms open.

There was no problem now. Max would go at dawn, and she would go soon after. She had to go to Costas's house, and from there they would go to the point the convoy would pass by in order to place the explosives. She calmed herself down by saying that she only had to drive.

Max came to her bedside to say goodbye, and kissed her on the forehead, thinking that she was still asleep. When he had left the room she got out of bed in a single bound. She was ready in fifteen minutes. Dion had given her a plan of the hotel with the service exits marked, so she could get out without being noticed. He had also given her a maid's outfit. She had put it on, wrapped her hair in a scarf, and put on a pair of glasses that disguised her face.

She went out of the room and went to the service staircase. She was lucky, she only passed a grumpy waiter who was cross at having to serve breakfast so early. He didn't even reply to her greeting.

She left the hotel and walked quickly until she reached Omonia Square, where the couple were waiting for her.

"You're late," the woman said.

"I came as soon as I could."

They took her to Costas's house. The man was waiting for them impatiently in the garage.

"Our friends will be asking where we are. We have the explosives," he fumed.

Amelia didn't know where they were going, she only followed Costas's instructions. After a while they left the city and she was pleased to see the green shoots of spring on both sides of the road.

"This way... Look, you can see some houses over there, the rich people live there... It's not so hot in the summer."

Then he pointed out a sloping dirt road; Amelia was afraid that the car wouldn't be able to climb up it. But they managed, and after driving for a while they came to a building that looked like a place where agricultural implements were stored. Costas told her to stop, and without warning five armed men appeared.

The lame man greeted them effusively and introduced them to Amelia. The men helped him to unload the explosives and the weapons they had carried in the couple's car.

"It's not bad," said one of the men, who appeared to be the leader of this little group.

"What do you mean, it's not bad!" Costas grumbled. "The English have done what they said they'd do, Dmitri; Churchill isn't one of us, but he wants the same things."

Costas gave Amelia a pistol and told her and the other woman to take some bicycles, which were leaning up against one of the walls of the building. They obeyed without question, they took the bicycles and walked with them into the pine trees until they reached the edge of the next road.

No one was coming by this spot, but Costas sent three men into strategic spots to keep watch, and told Amelia and the other woman to ride up and down the road on their bicycles, each one in a different direction, and if they saw anything they should say so at once.

They obeyed at once; as she was getting onto her bicycle Amelia saw them placing the explosives on either side of the road.

She thought she could hear the noise of truck engines, and left the road so that she could spy, in the distance, the military convoy slowly approaching. She pedaled as fast as she could back to where Costas and his men were working.

"They're coming!"

"Hurry up! We have to finish, the bastards are nearly here!"

They went to hide in the trees and Costas made a sign to Amelia.

"We've put explosives in several places, and each of us will have a detonator. That way it's safer; if one charge fails to go off then the others won't. Come with me, I'll show you which one is yours."

"Mine? I don't know anything about explosives..."

"All you have to do is push this switch when you hear my whistle. Just that. You can do it. It's easier than driving. Then you know what you need to do. Run back to where we left the car; if I'm not there, then wait for me, and if I take longer than five minutes then go."

"Without you?"

"I can't run, not with my leg how it is. I'll get along as best I can."

"You shouldn't be here," Dmitri said, "but you have to be involved in everything, we couldn't have done it without you."

"Shut up, and help me get to the car when the time comes."

"The doctor said that you could lose your leg if you keep on walking on it."

"What do doctors know!" Costas said disdainfully.

The noise of the trucks and the cars was ever louder. Amelia took up her position. She was tense and tried not to think about what she was about to do. She knew that lots of men would die.

Costas had organized the explosives so that the convoy would be trapped by several explosions along the road.

Amelia saw trucks and cars drive past, followed by an official vehicle containing members of the Wehrmacht. When it came past she would have to set off her explosives. She held the mechanism tight, and looked down at the detonator, waiting for Costas's whistle. When she heard it, she pushed the switch. The road became an inferno. Several vehicles were thrown up into the air, others set on fire, a tank blew up when its ammunition exploded. The fragments of various bodies were thrown dozens of meters away from the roadside. The flames devoured the remaining trucks, and the heartrending screams of the wounded mingled with the orders an officer was giving from the turret of a tank. She heard the whistle of bullets cutting through the pure morning air mix with the desperate cries of the wounded. She knew that now was the moment to run back to the place where the car was, but she was paralyzed when she looked toward the car where the officers had been traveling. A terrifying scream came from her throat.

"Max! Max!" she cried out wildly, running into the inferno. She didn't think, she just knew that she had to get to the side of the road where Max was lying, covered in blood and flames. Amelia tried to put out the fire with her bare hands.

Costas saw Amelia running toward the road. "She's mad," he thought, "they'll catch her and she'll talk and then we'll all be caught." He aimed his pistol at her and saw her fall to the ground near one of the officers. Then he fled up the hill, supported by one of his comrades.

Amelia fell to the ground a few meters from where Max was lying. She was shouting: "What have I done! My God, what have I done!"

Caught up in his pain, Max thought he heard Amelia shouting, and thought that he must be dying, as he could hear her voice.

It was not a good day for the Germans: June 6, 1944, and a few hours earlier, on the beaches of Normandy, the Allies had begun their invasion.

When Amelia started to regain consciousness, she was in a hospital, and the first face that she could see was SS Colonel Winkler's. She wanted to scream, but her voice was stuck in her throat.

"Wake her up, I need to interrogate her," Winkler said to the doctor who was at her side, along with a nurse.

"You can't interrogate her; she's been in a coma for more than a month."

"The safety of Germany is more important than whatever might happen to this one woman! She is a terrorist, a spy!"

"Whatever she is, she has been in a coma, I informed you just as you ordered, because it looks like her situation has been improving over the last few hours. But we will need to wait until we know if her brain has been damaged. Let me do my job, Colonel," the doctor asked.

"It is a matter of the highest importance that I interrogate this woman."

"In order to do it successfully, you will have to let me do my job; as soon as she can talk I will tell you."

In spite of her state, Amelia could see the look of hatred in Colonel Winkler's eyes, and so she closed hers.

"Now you will have to go, Colonel, or the patient may go back into her coma."

The words seemed to reach her from a long way away. There were several men talking around her, but she did not want to open her eyes, afraid that one of them might be Winkler.

Several more weeks went by until Amelia was fully conscious once again. Every moment of consciousness was a pain to her, as she remembered Max and her soul burned within her. She couldn't bear to think that she had killed him. She had pressed the detonator when the officers' car had come past. Max's bloody body as he fought against the flames came always to her mind's eye, and she wanted to slip away into an eternal sleep.

But in spite of her desire to die, she kept on getting better, and while she did so she thought of the moment that would come when Colonel Winkler would return to interrogate her. She said to herself that they were bringing her back from death in order to send her back to death again, for that was all she could expect at the colonel's hands, but she didn't care. She said to herself that she deserved to die.

She had to make an effort to think, but her instinct told her that it was better to keep silent, that they would think that she could not speak because of the trauma she had suffered; better still, that they would think she had lost her memory.

The doctor saw her every day and consulted with his colleagues over which might be the best treatment to remove her from this vegetative state in which she appeared to be sunk. He suspected that she could hear him, that she understood him when he spoke, but that she did not want to answer him, although he could not prove that or be sure of it.

Amelia tried to look lost, as if she were sunk in her own world.

"Any news, Nurse Lenk?"

"None, Dr. Groener. She spends the whole day looking straight ahead. It doesn't seem to matter if she's in the bed or if we're walking her around; she doesn't seem to understand anything."

"Anyway... Leave me with her for a moment, Dr. Bach needs help in his ward, go and give them a hand."

Dr. Groener sat in a chair next to Amelia's bed and looked closely at her. He saw her eyes moving, almost imperceptibly, as she kept her gaze unfocused and lost.

"I know you are in there, Amelia, that you are not confused and unconscious, even if you seem not to understand us. Colonel Winkler will come here soon to take you away and interrogate you. I have to let you go because I can't do anything else for you. I would recommend that you be sent to some institution, although your future does not depend on me, but on the colonel."

Amelia spent the rest of the day praying to herself that she would be able to find strength to withstand Winkler. She knew that the colonel would take her to the limits of pain to make her talk, and, whether or not he succeeded, he would kill her.

When she completely recovered consciousness, she was given therapy to try to make her talk. Dr. Groener decided to tell her how her bloodied body has been discovered on the road where a German army convoy had been attacked by a small group of terrorists.

They had taken her to a hospital along with the rest of the wounded soldiers, and it was there that they had operated on her. A bullet had gone through one of her lungs. They thought she would not survive, but she survived. It was Colonel Winkler who asked the doctors to do what they could to save her, because it was of vital importance that they interrogate her. So they pulled her from the far side of the river of death back to the land of the living.

That afternoon, Colonel Winkler arrived at the hospital, and Dr. Groener took him to Amelia's room and advised him not to put her under too much pressure because she was still convalescing.

"You do your job, Doctor, and I'll do mine. This woman is a murderer, a terrorist, a spy."

Dr. Groener did not say another word.

Two of Winkler's men took her to the hospital basement, to a room guarded by two more uniformed men. On a table by the wall, torture instruments were lined up in perfect order.

They sat Amelia in the center of the room and Colonel Winkler shut the door. He sat behind a desk and the room fell into darkness, apart from a powerful cone of light shining onto the prisoner's face.

First they stripped her, then they asked her for the names of members of the Resistance, the ones who had helped her, then for the names of her contacts in London, and they even tried to make her denounce Max as a traitor. Every question came with a blow, and they hit her so often that she regularly lost consciousness.

Amelia wanted them to hit her hard so that she would fall into darkness and not be able to speak. But she could not resist the pain and she screamed, screamed with every blow, and screamed even more when one of the torturers, using a scalpel, started to peel the skin from the back of her neck as if she were an animal to be skinned. They took up patches of skin and then poured salt and vinegar into the open wounds, while she carried on screaming. But she did not speak, she merely screamed and screamed until she was hoarse and had no voice left.

She lost all sense of time, she didn't know if it was night or day, didn't know if they had spent a long time torturing her or if they were taking a rest. The pain was so great that she could not bear it; she wanted only to die, and prayed for that moment to come.

The only word Winkler got out of Amelia was when she shouted "Mama!"

When they sent her back to Dr. Groener, he seemed not at all surprised to see her once again closer to death than to life.

"I told you that she had suffered a concussion and that it would be some time before she got better and would be able to speak. If you believe that what she has to tell you is truly important, then you need to give her this time."

"She's not going to stay here."

"Where are you going to send her? Germany?"

"Yes."

"To a camp?"

"She'll be with people of her kind, criminals like her, until she is able to speak."

"And what if she never speaks?"

"Then we will hang her for being a spy and a terrorist. Tell me how long it will take for her to be able to speak again."

"I don't know, with the proper treatment... perhaps a few months, perhaps never."

"In that case, the murderer doesn't have much time left to live."

The next day they put her in a cattle wagon. Winkler had personally made sure that they would send her to Ravensbrück, ninety kilometers north of Berlin. The instructions sent to the camp doctor were very specific: If, after six months, he could not send word that Amelia was ready to talk, then she was to be hanged.

Major William Hurley paused in his narrative to light his pipe.

"Please, carry on," I begged.

"Our archives show that Amelia was taken to that place and stayed there to the end of the war."

"So she survived," I said with relief.

"Yes, she survived."

"When exactly did she reach the camp?"

"At the end of August 1944."

"Can you get me information about Ravensbrück?"

"Not in sufficient detail, for that you will need to go to Jerusalem."

"Jerusalem? Why Jerusalem?"

"Because the Holocaust Museum is there, and that is where they have the best information about what happened in Germany during those horrible years. They have a database about the survivors, who they were and which camp they were sent to; they have been able to use this to reconstruct the hell that was in each of the camps."

"My great-grandmother wasn't Jewish."

"That's got nothing to do with it: The Holocaust Museum has information about all the camps and who was in them."

"What happened when the war was over?"

My question upset Major Hurley, who cleared his throat.

"There is still a great deal of classified information to which I do not have access."

"You could give me some kind of clue, some idea at least about where my great-grandmother went."

"I will try to help you as much as I can. But I need to get in touch with my superiors and ask them if such information as has been declassified can be handed over to individuals such as yourself, especially with your being a journalist as well."

"You know that I have no journalistic interest in this story, I only want to find out about my great-grandmother."

"In any case, I need to consult with my superiors. Call me in a few days."

I accepted without complaint. I was shaken by Major Hurley's story. I tried to imagine what it must have felt for my great-grandmother to believe herself responsible for the death of the man she had loved.

I went back to the hotel and called Doña Laura.

"I'm sorry to bother you, but I think that the investigation is getting more and more complicated, whenever I think I'm coming to an end I find something that forces me to carry on."

"So carry on."

"Carry on?"

"Yes. Do you have a problem with doing so? Do you need more money? I'll send word to the bank today for them to make another transfer."

"No, it's not just that, but... I don't know, I feel that the more I know about Amelia Garayoa, the less I move forward."

"Do your job, Guillermo, although... well, we're very old and maybe don't have that much time."

"I'll do what I can, I promise."

Then I called Professor Soler, but he was not at home. His wife said that her husband was at a conference in Salamanca.

"Call his mobile, he won't mind, but do it in the evening, he doesn't like people to disturb him while he's working."

When I finally managed to get through to Professor Soler, I told him about my worries.

"I don't think I'm ever going to finish, Amelia's life is a continual tragedy. You always think you're near the end, and then something else happens. I have to go to Jerusalem. Do you know anyone at the Holocaust Museum?"

I think that Professor Soler was curious about what it was that took me to Jerusalem, but he forbore to ask me. He didn't know anyone at the Holocaust Museum, but he gave me the telephone number of a friend, a professor at Jerusalem University.

"Avi Meir is a Pole, he survived Auschwitz. He has retired, he's an emeritus professor, he can help you find what you're looking for."

"Amelia, I am looking for Amelia," I replied, resignedly.

"In Jerusalem?"

"No, but I think that they can give me some news of her there."

Pablo Soler didn't ask anything else. He had given himself the stricture of not knowing more than the Garayoas wanted him to know. He owed them a great deal, he owed them everything that he was.

I decided not to call my mother to tell her that I was going to Jerusalem. Instead I would call her from there. I wasn't in the mood for another maternal scolding. But I thought I would calm her down by sending her some flowers. I ordered them at the hotel reception. She couldn't complain now that I was forgetting about her.

12

My arrival in Tel Aviv did not get off on the right foot. I was irritated by the interrogation they put me through at customs.

"Why have you come to Israel?"

"Tourism."

"Do you know anyone here?"

"Nope."

"Have you been given any present for anyone in Israel or the Territories?"

"No, no one has given me anything and I'm not bringing any presents."

Then I had to say where I was going to stay and what my intended itinerary was.

Already in a bad mood, I rented a car, thinking all the while that as far as security was concerned the Israelis were a little paranoid, even more so than the Americans.

The Jerusalem Sheraton, in the center of the city, was not that far from the historic King David, although it was quite a walk if I wanted to see the old town. Although I told myself that I was not there to be a tourist, I said that I would go to the Holy Sites after my business here was done, to get some souvenirs for my mother. I thought about how contradictory she was, so modern about some things, so Catholic and traditional about others.

Professor Avi Meir was a charming old man who was ready to see me straight away.

"Professor Soler called me yesterday to tell me that you were coming. If you don't have any other appointments, then I'll expect you for dinner at eight."

I accepted gratefully. Apart from three cups of coffee, I hadn't had anything all day, and I was starving. After having a shower, I asked the concierge to tell me how to get to the address Professor Meir had given me.

The professor lived on the second floor of a three-story house. He opened the door himself and gave me a handshake that surprised me by its strength, given that the owner of the hand was a man of advanced age. I thought that he must be around ninety, but he moved as if he were much younger.

His house was simple, with bookcases on all the walls, and books piled on the floor. There was a table in the middle of the living room, perfectly laid for dinner.

"Sit down, you must be hungry after your journey. I don't know about you, but I never eat on airplanes."

We set to with gusto. There was a baked fish, and the professor had laid out several salads, hummus, and a basket of flatbreads.

"You'll like the fish, it's called *Tilapia galilaea*, but I think you call it St. Peter's fish; it's from the Sea of Galilee, a friend brought it over today."

We gave a good account of ourselves with the meal, while I told him that I needed to find out information about Ravensbrück concentration camp, and especially to find out if my great-grandmother had been a prisoner there.

"We are not Jews, but my great-grandmother was very involved in the war, working for the Allies. If you could arrange a meeting for me with someone from the Holocaust Museum, it would be extremely welcome. Almost as welcome as this magnificent dinner," I joked.

The professor sat in silence, looking straight at me, as if he were trying to read my most intimate thoughts. Then he smiled before replying.

"I'll do something better, I'll introduce you to someone who actually was in Ravensbrück."

"It's not possible! Are there still survivors?"

"We grow fewer every day, but we are not all dead yet. You know what? Sometimes I think that when the last one of us dies, there will no longer be any testimony of what it was like, because the world tends to forget, does not want to remember."

"But there are books, documentaries, the Holocaust Museum... The memory of what happened will never be lost," I said, trying to cheer him up.

"Bah! All these testimonies are nothing but a drop in an immense ocean. Men need to forget their crimes... Anyway, going back to what interests us, I will introduce you tomorrow to someone who can help you, someone who survived Ravensbrück just as I survived Auschwitz."

"Thank you, Professor, it's much more than I could have hoped for."

"I will come to find you at twelve at your hotel, but I would like you to do something first. Go to the Holocaust Museum, first thing tomorrow morning. Then it will be easier to understand."

When I was back at the hotel, I felt that I needed to talk to someone to explain that I had just met an exceptional man. The long conversation I had had with Avi Meir had impressed me. He had barely mentioned his time in Auschwitz, but he had explained what Europe had been like before the war, and we then got into a discussion about the existence of Israel; I felt so comfortable that evening that I even allowed myself to criticize the policies Israel enacted toward the Palestinians.

Avi Meir didn't accept any of my criticism and we argued with the confidence that only comes between people who are going to be good friends. I felt at home.

The next morning I got up early. I wanted to make the most of the day, so I took a map of Jerusalem and, thanks once again to the receptionist, found the Holocaust Museum fairly easily.

When I arrived, I found myself behind a group of American Jews and a school party. There was a Spanish tour group as well, waiting for their guide. I stayed close to them to hear the tour.

I was overwhelmed when I left the museum, my stomach turning over and a sensation of nausea gripping me. How was it possible that a whole nation had gone mad enough to kill millions of people simply because they belonged to another race, another religion? Why hadn't they rebelled against their leaders? I remembered Max von Schumann and his friends; they were not in favor of Hitler, but their opposition was entirely intellectual. How many Germans had really risked their lives fighting against Hitler?

I got back to the hotel at the same time as Professor Meir arrived. Surprisingly, he still drove, an old truck.

"Get in. Are you coming from the Museum? The place we're going is not that far away, about twelve kilometers, you'll see."

We left the city without the professor telling me anything about where he was taking me, and I didn't ask him either. I thought that we were heading out into the desert, until suddenly I saw a green oasis in the distance. It looked like a village, a little village with a wall around it and armed men and women patrolling the perimeter. They weren't soldiers, they looked like normal people, civilians, wearing comfortable clothes, without any military insignia.

"This is Kiryat Anavim, a kibbutz, there are mostly Russian Jews here. It was founded by Jews who came from Russia in 1919. There are ever fewer kibbutzim in Israel; it is very difficult to live here, pure Communism."

"Communism?"

"Private property does not exist, everything is held in common, and the community provides for everyone's needs; the children are educated communally, and they share the work, everyone doing everything: You can be an engineer or a doctor, but you have to cook and plough as well. The only difference from Soviet Communism is that there is freedom here: If someone wants to go, then they're free to go; everything is voluntary. It is very hard to live in a kibbutz, especially for the newer generations, young people today are very spoiled and can't cope with a Spartan life."

"I'm not surprised," I said, with a sudden attack of sincerity.

"I lived in a kibbutz for a few years when I first came to Israel, I met my wife there and spent the happiest years of my life."

"Your wife?"

"My wife died years ago. It was cancer that took her. She was Russian, a Russian Jew. She came here with her parents as a child. They were the first pioneers and they came here, to Kiryat Anavim."

"Do you have children?"

"Yes, four. Two of them are dead. Daniel, the oldest, was killed in the '67 war, and Esther in a terrorist attack on the kibbutz where she lived in the north of the country, near the border with Lebanon. I have two left: Gideon lives in Tel Aviv and is about to retire, he's a television producer, he's got three children and two grandchildren, so I'm a great-grandfather; Ariel, the youngest, lives in New York. He married a New Yorker and left. I've got two New York grandchildren who did their duty and did military service here. Good kids, they got married and have children as well."

He stopped the truck at the door of a modest little house. All the houses were the same, made of stone, built in a line with very little to tell them apart.

The door to the house was open and Avi Meir walked in as if it were his own house.

"Sofia! Sofia! I'm here!"

An elderly woman appeared, smiling, and she held out her hand to us.

"Avi! Come in, come in! I was so happy when you called me this morning. You haven't come for too long. And what about your children? Have you heard from Ariel? I'll never understand why children want to run off to America so much nowadays. And this young man is... ?"

"Guillermo, the young Spaniard I told you about. He's a journalist, but he's here to write a book about his great-grandmother."

"When you called me to ask if I knew a Spaniard called Amelia Garayoa in Ravensbrück, my heart skipped a beat. Amelia, poor thing!"

Sofia asked us to sit down and brought me a jug of lemonade with mint, then she looked me up and down as if trying to find some trace of Amelia in my face, but seemed to be disappointed.

"Tell us all you know, I'd like to hear it as well," Professor Meir asked.

Sofia didn't need to be asked twice and started to tell her story.

I was eighteen when they took me to Ravensbrück, in May of 1944. My mother was a political commissar and I was desperate to become one as well. I was a Young Communist as well, one who adored Father Stalin and who had been a star of the Young Communist League, helped by my father, who was a political commissar like my mother.

I'm not going to tell you what the Germans did when they invaded Russia, just that my mother and I were lucky, we had better luck than many other women, such as those who as well as being raped were then gutted in front of their husbands and their children, or those who had to watch their children being cut into pieces in front of their eyes.

We were in a village, organizing the villagers, when the Nazis suddenly arrived... They were furious because they were losing the war. They killed the old men and women and the children, and took prisoner anyone who was wearing a uniform; in my case I was wearing the Young Communist League scarf and shirt. I still feel scared when I think today how they herded us into trucks, hitting us with the butts of their rifles. When they found out that my mother and I were Jewish, they separated us from the rest. We were the worst of the worst: Jews, Russians, and Communists. They sent us to Ravensbrück, a prison camp near Berlin.

We slept in barracks, all of us piled up on each other on hard mattresses, with scarcely space to breathe, and enough to do with the constant battle against the bedbugs and the lice that ran all over the beds and our clothes.

One of the camp bosses was an SS commander called Schaefer; he was a brute: short, fat, swarthy, the opposite of the Aryan ideal. But he read us sermons about the superiority of his race as he tortured us. Schaefer took a personal interest in the interrogations and liked to put all his macabre ideas into practice with the help of Dr. Kiefner.

Dr. Kiefner was a sadist who, like Schaefer, raped many of the prisoners.

He liked to perform what he called his "experiments," aimed at establishing how much pain an individual could endure without dying.

Most women in the camp were mutilated. "Can one live without nipples?" Dr. Kiefner would ask himself as he cut the nipples off a prisoner. He did it with a scalpel and no kind of anesthetic to lessen his victims' pain.

He was a sadist and enjoyed mutilating the genitals of the women of Ravensbrück. He disemboweled others because he said it gave him a better idea of how the human body was put together.

"Come on, dear, it's for the sake of science. I studied with corpses, but it's not the same as being able to look at how human organs behave as they gradually stop working," he would say to the woman he had chosen as his next victim.

If any of us were sent to the hospital we would be terrified, as we knew full well that even if we came back alive, we would never be the same again. They cut off my breasts... I spent several days hovering between life and death. I was saved by the fact that one of the nurses who worked in the hospital was also a prisoner. She was not a Jew, and they made the poor woman participate in this butchery. I think she was Czech, I'm not sure, she spoke very little and she had been a nurse ever since being sent to Ravensbrück as a prisoner. I don't know why she was there, but Dr. Kiefner never used her for his experiments. She helped us as much as she could, which wasn't much, but she sometimes managed to steal small quantities of antiseptics and painkillers which she gave to the prisoners who had passed through Dr. Kiefner's "operating table."

I suppose I survived because I was young and I wanted to live; I also had my mother, and I wouldn't have lived without her.

But I'm telling you what happened to me, which is not what you are here to hear about; you want me to talk about the Spanish woman. She arrived at the beginning of September 1944, she was sick and they sent her to our barracks. I remember her well. She could scarcely walk, it was clear that she had been tortured not long before. It was hard for her to open her right eye, and her face was bruised with the blows she had received. She was extremely thin and her neck and her back were scarred by the marks of the torture instruments.

I remember the first day I saw her as if it were yesterday...

"Find yourself a space, bitch!" The guard on duty pushed her into our barracks.

Amelia took a couple of steps and sat down on the floor without looking anywhere, as if she didn't see us or else didn't know we were there. My mother went up to her and spoke to her, but she got no answer.

"We don't know where she's from, she doesn't look Russian," a woman said.

I don't know why my mother was moved by the Spanish woman, but she dragged her over to our side and put her on a corner of the mattress. Amelia let her do this without showing any emotion.

"The clothes she is wearing are very dirty, but they are good quality," one of the prisoners said.

From that night on Amelia slept with us. My mother had adopted her, apparently.

We thought that she didn't speak to us because she didn't speak Russian, but two days after she had arrived my mother whispered to me that she had caught Amelia looking at her when she spoke to another woman, as if she understood them.

Several days went by before Schaefer called her into his office.

As she could barely stand up unaided, my mother decided to help her to Schaefer's office.

My mother came back, but we didn't see the Spanish woman until two days later, when the door was opened and one of the guards threw into the center of the barracks what seemed to be a bundle of old clothes.

They had raped her. This was normal when a new prisoner arrived. If she was young, Schaefer was the first to rape her, or else sometimes Dr. Kiefner himself. But even the oldest endured this humiliation, as Kiefner enjoyed putting all kinds of objects into their vaginas.

"None of you can complain, you all get your 'treatment' to calm your feminine urges," he would say, laughing.

When they brought her she was in a very bad state, but she didn't say anything, she just cried to herself in silence. Her tears fell and she held her jaw as if she wanted to hold back the screams that were choking her throat.

My mother cleaned her wounds as best she could, and discovered as she did so that there were spots where they had pulled her skin away.

They came for her on other occasions to interrogate her again. Soon we found out that a colonel in the SS had ordered Schaefer to make her talk using any means he desired. Dr. Kiefner's nurse whispered to another patient that she had heard them say to the doctor that Amelia was a murderer, a terrorist. Apparently, she was accused of the murder of an SS officer, and of taking part in kidnappings and bombings.

It seemed impossible that this fragile-seeming woman could have done anything like that. She was a sack of bones, and I think that even if she had been in a better state she would never have been what you might call fleshy. My mother called her "the broken doll."

But in spite of her state she survived. It was a miracle. And one day the SS colonel who had unfinished business with her turned up in the camp. I can still remember his name: Winkler; Schaefer grew very nervous when his visit was announced. We all thought that if Schaefer trembled before Winkler, it must mean that Winkler was even worse than he was, and so we felt all the more scared.

Winkler left and we thought that the Spanish woman must have died. The nurse said that Winkler had locked himself in a room with her and that her screams had not seemed like noises a human might make.

When we saw her again, she was a mass of bloody flesh and it was difficult to tell if she still had a face. She hovered between life and death for several days, and my mother thought that she would not survive. Her legs and her arms were broken, her feet had been crushed, and there was not a single inch of skin on her body that was not covered with cigarette burns. In the darkness the nurse came to our barracks. She cleaned the wounds with care and put an unguent on all the burns. Then, with my mother's help, she tried to set the broken bones. She also brought a bottle that contained a strong painkiller.

"I couldn't bring any more," she said, "but it is very powerful, you have to give it to her bit by bit. And she mustn't move, it's the only way that her bones will knit properly."

We found out from the nurse that Colonel Winkler had left without achieving his objective.

"This woman has her mind on the next world, she's not here, and so even if the torturer kills her she will never speak."

We heard her voice for the first time that night. My mother thought that she heard a noise and put her ear to Amelia's mouth.

"She's saying 'Mama,' she's calling for her mother."

I sank into my mother's arms, it made me stronger to have her there with me. Otherwise I could not have put up with the tortures and other humiliations that they subjected me to.

The number of prisoners who died on Dr. Kiefner's "operating table" grew by the day. His latest vile activity was, with the youngest prisoners, to sew up part of their vaginas, as he had read they did in some African tribes to prevent women from taking any pleasure at all in sexual relations.

"No, you haven't come here to enjoy yourselves, but to pay for your crimes, so I'll stop you from feeling pleasure," he said, as he prepared the material with which he would sew us up.

He mutilated all of us, Amelia included, and some of us died when the wounds got infected.

Then, whenever he or one of the guards raped us, the pain would be unbearable. I don't know how we survived it.

Before spring, I'm talking about February 1945, the news came that the Russians were near. We heard our guards talking about it, and the Czech nurse confirmed it to us. We were expectant, hoping that the rumor would prove to be true.

The Germans were scared of the Russians. Yes, they were scared of us because we would respond with the same brutality that the Germans had shown when they invaded us.

There wasn't a single Russian soldier who hadn't lost a brother or a father, who didn't have a friend whose mother or sister had been raped by the Germans. So for every foot of ground that the Red Army regained, they took their revenge on the Germans without any worry or remorse.

I think it was at the beginning of March that the man arrived in the camp, a mutilated German in an officer's uniform. We were in the yard when they made us stand aside to let a black car drive to Schaefer's hut.

My mother said that the commandant was nervous, I don't remember too well.

We saw Schaefer open the door to the car and try to appear like a real soldier in front of the man whom another officer helped out of the car. He had previously unpacked a wheelchair, and took the officer out of the car and put him into the chair while Schaefer clicked his heels and attempted a salute.

He was a Wehrmacht officer who had a large iron cross and other decorations on his jacket. His aristocratic bearing was impressive, in spite of the wheelchair. The stumps that had once been his legs were covered by a blanket. He was little more than a trunk.

They took him to Schaefer's office and all of us asked ourselves what could possibly have been the cause of this mutilated general's visit.

We were shut into our barracks. After an hour, a guard came looking for Amelia and told her to gather her belongings together. How ironic! We had nothing, no belongings. My mother started to cry, afraid that they would take her to another camp, or else to Colonel Winkler, who seemed to hate Amelia so much. We followed her out of the barracks, and saw the guard leading her to the terrace of Schaefer's hut. Schaefer was there, as well as the general in his wheelchair. Amelia walked along indifferently, her eyes unfocused, as if nothing of what was happening around her were important, just as she had been since the day of her arrival at Ravensbrück. Suddenly she seemed to stand alert, there was something about the general that seemed to attract her attention. I remember seeing her run toward him, shouting "Max, Max, Max!" and then falling to the ground. The general's adjutant ran over to her and helped her lift herself up.

We all looked at the scene in shock, we didn't understand anything. The Spaniard had not said a word since her arrival at Ravensbrück. When they tortured her during the night we heard her calling in the silence of the night for her mother, "Mama" was the only word she said the whole time she was there, and suddenly she was shouting this name again and again: "Max, Max, Max!"

The adjutant took her to where the officer was seated and she threw herself on her knees, begging him for forgiveness.

"Forgive me, Max, forgive me! I didn't know... Forgive me!"

The officer made a sign to his adjutant and he picked the woman up and put her in the car. We saw Schaefer clicking his heels once again in front of the general. His adjutant came back for the officer, and with the help of the driver they put him into the car. Then they left, and we never saw them again.

As you might imagine, there was no other topic of conversation in the camp for several days afterwards. We couldn't work out who this mutilated general had been, nor why the Spaniard had thrown herself on the ground in front of him and begged his pardon. Neither did we know where they had taken her.

Not even the nurse could give us any idea about what had happened, just that the general had a written order for the prisoner to be set free, and that Schaefer had no option other than to release her. We learned from the nurse that when the general had gone, Schaefer called Colonel Winkler to tell him what had happened, but did not manage to speak with him.

I suppose you can guess what happened next. A short while before the fall of Berlin, my compatriots liberated us. The war came to its end. We never knew anything more about the Spanish woman, your great-grandmother. I hope that she survived, but in those days...

Sofia fell silent and let her thoughts wander through the past, forgetting that we were there. Avi cleared his throat to bring her back to the present.

"Thank you, Sofia," he said, and he took her hand and squeezed it affectionately.

"Thank you so much, Señora, you don't know how much, and... Well, it hurts to hear everything you went through," I said, just to say something. I was still in shock from the story she had told.

"Señora? Why call me 'Señora'? Call me Sofia, everyone else does. You know what? I never thought I would ever hear anything else about the Spanish woman, and now Avi calls me to tell me that there's a young Spaniard looking for information about Ravensbrück, that he's the great-grandson of a woman who was a prisoner there... I never thought anything like that would happen. Has it been useful, what I told you?" Sofia's voice had grown firm again.

"It has been a great help; without your story, my research couldn't carry on. You also told me that Max was alive, when I thought that he'd been killed."

"Who was Max?" she asked with interest.

"He was an officer who had been opposed to Hitler before the war, a Prussian aristocrat who hated Nazism," I explained, trying to give a good account of Max.

"He can't have hated it enough, as he wore the German uniform and killed people in defense of those horrible ideals."

"He was a doctor, so I don't think he killed anyone," I went on, but Sofia had known Dr. Kiefner, so it didn't make any difference to her that the German officer had been a doctor. Her mutilated body was the proof of what some German doctors had been capable.

"And what happened next?" she asked, so as not to argue with me.

"I don't know, that's what I need to find out now, what happened next. My great-grandmother's story is like a Russian doll, just when you think you've found the last layer, then there is something else to discover. I don't know what happened, or if they survived. I just don't know."

"He was a general; look in the archives, maybe they put him on trial at Nuremberg," Sofia suggested.

"I will."

"Or maybe he died peacefully in his sleep, like so many other German soldiers," Avi Meir said.

Sofia insisted that we have lunch with her, although in fact we ate with all the other members of the kibbutz, in a communal eating area. The food was simple but tasty, and everyone was pleasant toward me. Avi was right, he had said that it was like a synthesis of the Communist ideal, a Communist utopia. If Communism had truly come into existence anywhere in the world, it was in the kibbutzim. I thought that my friends would be surprised if they found out about a place like this, and I wondered to myself how many of them, myself included, would be capable of living here, sharing everything, taking part in all the tasks of the community, without having anything that the community had not decided was necessary, based on how much money there was in the cash box and the idea that money had to be divided equally. Here no one had more than anyone else.

But to live like this? I would not be capable of it, it was easier to talk about equality on a rhetorical level.

Sofia whispered in my ear that if my grandmother had survived, then there would be a record of her passage through Ravensbrück.

"They had to operate on me after the camp was liberated. The Red Cross took charge of all of us, trying to remedy some of the barbarous actions that Kiefner had committed. You know, I was never a normal woman again... The effects of not having breasts, or of having your vagina sewn up... You can't imagine what that does to you. And your poor great-grandmother went through the same torture... I don't know if she was as lucky as I was. Of course, the operations meant that I was hospitalized for a long time. My mother recovered before I did, and before she went back to Russia she asked an American doctor to help me get sent to Israel. She was convinced that it would be best for me. I was surprised; I was sure that we were happy in the Soviet Union, that we had to fight for the revolution, and that my mother believed all that as well, so I never understood why she would insist that I be sent here. 'Sofia,' she said, 'I want one of us at least to see Jerusalem.' I replied that we had no God, and no other homeland than Russia, but she insisted. She made me promise. I managed to come here... and I never saw her again."

It was after four o'clock when we got back to the hotel. Avi was as friendly and communicative as he had been the night before.

"Do you know where to carry on looking?" he asked.

"No, not really; perhaps Major Hurley will be able to reveal what he has in his archives about Amelia."

I told him who Major Hurley was and how he had helped me up to the present moment.

"In my opinion, if your great-grandmother worked for the British during the war, then they might have given her more work... if she survived, of course. I have a friend, an American although he's of German origin. He's a historian, and he knows everything about what happened after the war. He wanted to fight, but they wouldn't let him enlist because he was not old enough, and when he was old enough, then the war had finished, but even so he managed to get them to send him to Berlin. He felt indignant that Hitler and his filth had tarnished the name of Germany. He used to say: 'Avi, it's Hitler's fault that everyone now thinks of Germans as being the same as him; it's like original sin for Germans.' He was born in New York but his parents were German, and he was brought up along German lines. He was a Catholic, and a devout one; so much so that he became a priest. He was already a priest when I met him in Jerusalem, where he lived for a while and got a doctorate in Biblical theology from the university there. We became close friends, and he used to tell me lots of things about Berlin that he found out when he arrived there in 1946. If you want me to, I could call him, he might be able to help you; but he lives in New York and I don't know if..."

"I'd be very grateful. Avi, I need whatever help I can get, someone to tell me what to do; so, if you talk to him and tell him who I am... Maybe I could use his advice."

We said goodbye at the hotel and he promised that he'd call me when he'd spoken to his friend, the American priest.

I booked a ticket to return to London the next day, and took advantage of the time I had left to look around Jerusalem. Avi had recommended that I enter the old town through the Gate of Damascus, and that is what I did. I walked around, guiding myself with the plan I had brought with me; I bought an olive-wood rosary for my mother, and a Bible with covers of the same material. Then I bought several *kufiyyat*, Palestinian scarfs, to give out to my friends, and I don't know why, but I let an old trader haggle with me for a burnished copper teapot. I didn't like it very much, but I couldn't resist the entreaties of the old man. I went back to the hotel satisfied with my purchases.

I think that Major William Hurley would have liked for me to have spent more time in Jerusalem, because when I called him and told him I was in London, he did not seem very happy.

"You do everything far too fast, Guillermo," he reproached me.

"I was just very lucky and met with the right people, which stopped me from wasting my time," I defended myself, thinking that if Major Hurley weren't so rigid and had decided to let me know once and for all everything that he knew about Amelia Garayoa, then I could finish my work and he wouldn't have to put up with me anymore. But he was British and well-off, so it was only natural that he should have such a phlegmatic nature.

"Well, what have you found out?" he asked me, as if whether he agreed to see me depended on this.

When I had finished telling him there was silence on the end of the line for a while, but then he told me to wait until he got back in touch with me.

"And when will that be, Major?"

"In a day or so," he replied, and then hung up.

As he was a mature gentleman, he waited until the absolute limit, that is to say, he called me fully two days later, when I was already thinking about going to New York to see Avi's friend, more than anything else because it was eating away at me not to have anything to do. Before he rung off this time, he said:

"Lady Victoria has been kind enough to invite us to luncheon at her house tomorrow. At midday."

I celebrated this piece of news by treating myself to a meal in a restaurant. I liked Lady Victoria; just like the major, she was genuinely British. The fact that she was married to one of Lord Paul James's grandsons, and that Lord Paul James was Albert James's uncle, converted her into an expert on everything related to Amelia Garayoa.

I bought a bottle of the best port in a Bond Street off-license. The salesman looked as if he wondered if he should serve me or call security, because I didn't look very like one of his usual distinguished clients. I didn't understand why he had stared at me so mistrustfully until I got back to the hotel and realized that I was wearing a Palestinian scarf round my neck. At the very least, he must have thought that I was bin Laden's cousin.

I was tempted to buy a tie in one of the exclusive Bond Street shops, as I owned only one tie and it was the one I always wore to see Lady Victoria, but the prices made me abandon my good intention; there was no tie that cost less than three hundred euros, so I decided that the money was better spent on Scotch whisky.

It was twelve on the dot when I arrived. It seemed to me that Lady Victoria had more freckles than usual, and her alabaster-white skin was reddened, as if she had caught the sun.

"Ah, dear Guillermo! How pleasant to see you again!" Her warm welcome seemed sincere.

"You can't know how grateful I am for your invitation," I replied, trying to reach her level.

"Your research is exciting, truly exciting. My husband thinks the same as I do, don't you, dear?"

Lord Richard agreed and held out his hand. His nose was red, I don't know if it was because he, like his wife, had caught the sun, or if it was a consequence of his liking for sherry.

I regretted my wicked thoughts. Lady Victoria and Lord Richard had spent a few days on holiday in Barbados, at a friend's house, and that explained the reddened skin.

I knew that before Lady Victoria and Major Hurley decided to get to the point, we would have to talk about generalities, and that it wouldn't be until we got to dessert that they would get to work, so I decided, possessing my soul in patience, to enjoy lunch.

"My dear Guillermo, we have had a stroke of luck; I was horrified when Major Hurley told me what you had discovered in

Jerusalem... I thought of the suffering of all those poor women... But we have had a stroke of luck. Look, I've found one of Albert James's notebooks in the archives, personal reflections that he wrote at the end of the war, about the surrender, the division of Berlin and also his meeting with Amelia. Imagine the moment! I remember having skimmed these notebooks, but there is still so much to catalogue! So I set myself to looking for them; I remembered that Albert had made reference to Amelia, although I didn't know why. I think that with these notebooks, and with what Major Hurley can tell us, we can have some idea of what happened to your great-grandmother after the war."

"You may still need other sources," Major Hurley said.

"You are both helping me a great deal and I am very grateful," I said, with my best smile.

Lady Victoria and Major Hurley exchanged a quick glance and he let our hostess start to tell the story.

You need to know that Albert James began to work for the American secret service. Lord Paul could not get his nephew to work with the British intelligence services, but a good friend of Lord Paul's, William Donovan, an important lawyer and a veteran of the First World War, managed where Lord Paul had failed. Donovan had been charged by President Roosevelt with organizing a network of spies for the course of the war that would work closely with British intelligence.

Donovan convinced the best of the best to join American intelligence, and Albert was one of them, although he didn't join until well into 1943. His romantic idea of what a journalist should do prevented him from taking the necessary step until he realized that in this war it was impossible to be neutral, that one had to choose sides.

Because of his knowledge of French, he was assigned to France and Belgium. He had lived for many years as a correspondent in Paris, and he had good contacts. He also worked in Holland.

When the war came to an end, Donovan sent him to Berlin. He knew that this city was where a "new war" was going to start, a silent and never openly declared war with their old allies the Soviet Union. So Albert was set up in Berlin under cover of being a journalist. This was where he met Amelia a little later; in his notebooks it says that he met her in November 1945, a few months after the end of the war.

Amelia was walking with a child holding her hand. It was difficult for him to recognize her at first. She had always been thin, but now she was painfully so.

"Amelia!"

She turned to hear her name, and seemed not to recognize him immediately. Then she stood still waiting for him to come up to her.

"Albert... I'm pleased to see you," she said, holding out a hand.

"So am I. What are you doing here?"

"I live here," she replied.

"Here in Berlin? Since when?"

"Always asking questions..." Amelia smiled.

"I'm sorry, I didn't want to bother you. I asked after you on several occasions in London, my uncle Lord Paul didn't want to be very clear, so I couldn't find out what had happened to you since... well, since we separated."

"I survived, which is much more than a lot of others can say. But tell me, where have you been? I suppose that you've been telling your American readers about the war, or am I wrong?"

"No, you're not wrong, I'm still in the same business, you know me. And this child?" he asked, pointing at the little boy who was the silent witness to this encounter.

"Friedrich, say hello to my friend. He's Max's son."

They were silent without knowing what to say. As well as the war, it was Max von Schumann who stood between them.

"So he survived as well. I'm pleased for the pair of you," he said without much conviction.

"Yes, he survived. Do you want to see him? He'd like to talk to someone who can remember the good times."

Albert felt very little urge to talk to Baron Max von Schumann, but he didn't dare say no.

"Come with us, we live nearby, a couple of streets further down, in the Soviet sector."

"Not the best spot."

"It's the only building that Max owns which is still standing. It belonged to his family, they rented it out as apartments; now we live in one of them, there are other tenants in the rest, although at the moment no one pays any rent."

They walked up to the third floor. Amelia opened the door and Friedrich let go of her hand and ran into the apartment.

"Papa, Papa! We've brought a friend of yours!" the boy shouted.

They went into a room lined with bookcases groaning with books. The former tenant must have been a great reader, or else a professor.

Max was in the shadows, sitting in a chair and covered with a thin blanket.

Amelia went over to him, kissed him and stroked his head.

"Max, I've found an old friend of ours, Albert James, I've got him here."

Albert did not understand why Max didn't get up to greet him, and when his eyes got used to the dark he had to make a great effort for his expression not to give him away. The formerly proud and attractive Baron von Schumann's face was ruined by scars of burns and shrapnel.

"Come closer," Amelia said to Albert.

"Albert, my dear friend, I'm glad you're here." Max reached out his hand without standing up, and Albert saw that he must not be able to see too well, as one of his eyes was half shut and he had a huge scar that stretched across his forehead to his eyelid. "I'm sorry not to get up, please don't think me rude."

"Of course not, I am pleased to see you, Max. Your son's quite a little man now," he said, to make conversation.

"Yes, Friedrich is a dream."

Amelia, who had left the room, came back with a tray on which were balanced three cups and a teapot.

"It's not the best tea in the world, but it's all I could get on the black market."

They spoke of the Berlin they had known, the evenings they had spent at the Adlon and Professor Schatzhauser's house, the wicked and cheerful city that it had been in the past. Max made him promise that he would come back again to chat, and Amelia saw him to the door.

"I'm sorry to see him like this. Where did it happen? On the Russian front?"

"I did it to him," Amelia replied.

Albert looked at her in shock. Amelia was a stranger to him, he couldn't find any trace in her of the woman he had known. She must have been twenty-seven or twenty-eight at that time, but her eyes showed that she had been through hell. He did not know how to reply to Amelia's assertion.

"I know that it might be presumptuous, but is there any way I can help?"

She thought for a moment before answering.

"Get them to leave him in peace. The Soviets are arresting people, looking for Nazis everywhere. I don't know how many committees have examined Max's file: He has been interrogated, they've called for witnesses... They haven't found anyone who is willing to say that Max is a criminal, not yet. You know that he was not a Nazi, that he went to your uncle to see if there was any way to set aside the policy of appeasement that did nothing apart from support Hitler. If you could get them to leave him in peace..."

"I will try. Give me the summonses that you've received, the papers, whatever you've got; I can't promise anything, this is the Russian sector and they don't let people stick their noses in their affairs."

"Tell me, where do you want me to bring them?"

He gave her the address of a little hotel in the American sector.

"I'll bring them to you tomorrow morning, early."

"Excellent. We could have a coffee, how about it?"

The next morning he saw her walking toward the hotel, her back straight, sunk in her own thoughts. She smiled to see him waiting for her at the hotel door.

"Are you leaving?"

"No, I was waiting for you. Come in, the manager makes a good cup of coffee."

"Is it authentic?"

"Yes, I provide it for her," he said with a laugh.

She gave him the papers and he asked her to tell him what she had done in the war.

"I worked for your uncle."

"All the time?"

"All the time apart from when I was in Pawiak and Ravensbrück."

"Pawiak? You were arrested in Warsaw?"

"Yes, that was the first time. I worked with a group of Poles who helped people in the ghetto. We were all arrested. I was lucky, Max saved me from being hanged. I thought that my time in Pawiak had taught me what hell was like, but I was mistaken. The true hell was Ravensbrück, but I didn't care what they did to me there, I just wanted to die."

"Yesterday you told me that what happened to Max was your fault..."

"Didn't your uncle tell you?"

"No, he's never told me anything about any intelligence operation."

"I helped a group in the Greek Resistance. We had to blow up an arms convoy that was heading from Athens up to the Yugoslav border. Max was going that day to inspect a battalion near Athens. He decided to travel with the convoy because the man leading it was a friend of his. I didn't know. I pressed the detonator just as the car with the officers came past, and I saw him being blown out of his seat and covered in flames. He lost his legs, and you can see how his face ended up, but the rest of his body is worse. In spite of what I did, Max forgave me, he got me out of Ravensbrück after a few months there. He has saved my life on two occasions, and I... I took his life away from him. He spent several months fighting for his life, but he survived. When he saw himself, he said that he would have preferred to have died. He says that to me every day."

"He's a soldier, Amelia, and a doctor. He knew what was happening every day, and what could happen to any one of us."

"Are you sure? Do you think that any one of us could have been left in that state by the woman he loved?"

"And you don't work for Lord Paul anymore?"

"No, I don't want to know anything else about the war, about dead people, about the intelligence service. And I couldn't work for anyone anyway, my whole time is spent with Max, for Max. I owe him, and he needs me."

"And the child?"

"Friedrich is the only person who keeps Max alive. He loves him."

"And Baroness Ludovica?"

"She died in one of the British bombing raids over Berlin. Friedrich survived by a miracle. They only have each other."

"They have you."

"Oh, I just try to make things easier for them. They have lost everything."

"And you feel guilty and have decided to sacrifice the rest of your life to them? What about your family? What about your son?"

"I have lost Javier for ever. My husband won't let me come close to the child. My family misses me, I'm sure, but they don't need me like Max and Friedrich need me."

"Do they know that you are here and what you went through?"

"No, they don't know, I don't want them to know, it's better this way, I'd only make them suffer."

"Don't you think that not knowing anything about you is what might really make them suffer?"

"Maybe, but I can't do anything apart from what I'm doing, not for the moment, at least."

"Are the Soviets harassing you?"

"I've got good credentials, I was a prisoner of the Nazis twice, in Pawiak in Warsaw, and then in Ravensbrück, what more can they ask for?"

"You can always show them your membership card for the French Communist Party," he said with a smile, trying to lighten the tension.

"Do you think that if I showed it to Walter Ulbricht they'd give me a good job? Or maybe I should try to get an appointment with Wilhelm Pieck? They're the ones in charge here, as well as the Soviets," Amelia said, picking up on Albert James's joke.

"Well, Ulbricht was the head of the German Communists in exile, and Pieck is a man they think a lot of in Moscow, so it's only natural that they should be the men of the moment. But tell me, how do you manage to get by? Do you have enough to live on, what with Max as he is..."

"We do what we can. There are no family estates anymore, they are all rubble. As for our money and our stocks, they are worthless. We've sold some things, and if a tenant gives us anything, well, then it's a feast day. Sometimes they pay us in kind: a loaf of bread, a few teabags, a chunk of meat of dubious origin... whatever they have."

"Have you spoken with the British?"

"Only to put my papers in order, and I don't think they showed themselves very keen to help me. They don't understand why I want to stay here. But tell me about yourself, did you ever get married?"

"No, I haven't had the time, a war is not the best moment to do so."

Albert made it his job to look after Amelia, Max, and the little boy. He visited them regularly, sorted out the paperwork so that they didn't bother the baron anymore, and tried to bring them food whenever he could.

It affected him to see Amelia so submissive with respect to Max. She seemed to revere him and she spoiled Friedrich as much as she could. But she had changed, she was not the lively young woman he had known, the beautiful idealist. This woman had very little to do with the one he had fallen in love with, but she was the same Amelia.

Albert spoke to his uncle and told him that Amelia was in Berlin. But Lord Paul explained that the woman was not willing to come back to work for them. Not only had she rejected the possibility, but the men who had contacted her wrote in their reports that she did not seem quite in control of herself.

"And what would you be like if you had been tortured for months?" Albert asked his uncle angrily. "You have no idea what they did to her in Ravensbrück."

She never told him what they had done to her, but Albert had read reports from some other survivors of the camp, and he was tormented to think that what had happened to them could also have happened to her. They had all been mutilated, they had all been raped, and he imagined that Amelia had not been an exception to this sad rule; she, however, did not talk at all about what had happened, as if she had deserved her suffering, as if it were a part of the payment she had to give for what had happened to Max.

Her remorse for that operation in Athens was so great that Albert suggested that she go to see a priest.

"You need someone to pardon you; that's the only way you will gain peace."

"Max has pardoned me, he is an exceptional man."

"His pardon is not enough, you need God to pardon you."

He never thought that she would listen to his advice, and he didn't insist, either. Meanwhile, the tension began to mount in Berlin between the victors of the war. The relationship of the Western powers with Russia became ever more tense. They had fought together, but now they were no longer side by side in the trenches.

American intelligence asked Albert to hunt down a Nazi scientist who had fled just before the end of the war. Lots of Hitler's scientists had happily accepted posts with the Americans or the Russians as long as they were guaranteed immunity. But this was not the case with Fritz Winkler.

Albert had not told Amelia that he was working for American intelligence; he pretended that he was still just a journalist looking for stories, and so he decided to try his luck with Max, who might perhaps have heard of Fritz Winkler. Max's family had been very well connected, after all, and had known everyone who was anyone in Germany. Maybe Max would be able to give him a lead.

"I have been commissioned to write a report on scientists who worked for Hitler. Some of them escaped and we don't know where they are."

"They say that some went your way and the others went to the Russians," Amelia said.

"Yes, that's true, but not all of them. Apparently Dr. Winkler managed to get out of Germany with the aid of his son, who was a colonel in the SS and organized his flight; what we don't know is where he escaped to."

"Winkler?" Max grew tense.

"Are you sure that they said 'Winkler'?" Amelia asked.

"Yes, apparently he was a scientist who had been condemned by the Geneva Convention, but who still carried out a secret weapons project using poison gas. His son was a very well-connected SS colonel. We haven't found him either. The pair of them have disappeared."

Albert deduced from the oppressive silence in the room that both Amelia and Max must have known at least one of the Winklers, or maybe both of them. Max had turned his face away, but Amelia was pale and silent, as if she had suddenly died.

"What happened?" he said to the air, without addressing either of them directly.

Max broke the silence.

"Colonel Winkler sent Amelia to Ravensbrück. He hated her because he thought that she had killed an SS friend of his in Rome."

Albert didn't know what to say, but he praised himself for his intuition.

"Where could he be now?" he asked, ignoring the tension in the room.

"Who knows! Lots of Nazis, lots of members of the regime, managed to escape, they even had escape routes planned in case Germany lost the war," Max replied.

"Did you know Fritz Winkler, Max? They say that he was very well connected and was invited to the houses of many of the great German families; some of them even financed his experiments before the war."

"No, I didn't know him. I was unlucky enough to know his son, Colonel Winkler, in Rome. I told you, he wanted to have

Amelia hanged. I'm sorry, I can't help you, I wouldn't know how to."

Albert was about to ask him if he would help if he ever found out where Fritz Winkler was, but he did not. Max was tormented by his transformation into an invalid, but in spite of what he had suffered, he was still unshakably loyal to his compatriots, in spite of the barbarous acts some of them had committed.

He thought about how contradictory a character Max was, about his efforts to make Great Britain put a halt to Hitler before the war started, about the repugnance and disdain he felt for the Nazis, but even with that in place he had fought alongside them because they represented Germany at that time and he would never have betrayed his country, as if Nazism itself were not the worst possible betrayal. But Albert said nothing: He didn't want to argue with Max, and even less with Amelia. He saw them as lost souls, with no future and no hope, tied to one another as if it were a punishment. It was only Friedrich, little Friedrich who could laugh in that silent and sad house. Albert took note of the fact that if Max and Amelia both knew Colonel Winkler it might be useful; he didn't yet know how, but he would think of something.

He left the house and decided to take a walk before returning to the American sector of divided Berlin.

Later, Albert arranged a meeting with Charles Turner, a member of the British intelligence services who was, like him, stationed in the former German capital. They had met each other during the hardest days of the war, and they had got on so well together that they had ended up carrying out certain joint operations.

"I need you to let me have a look at Amelia Garayoa's file."

"And who is Amelia Garayoa?"

"Come on, Charles, I'm sure you know who Amelia Garayoa is!"

"I don't, but it sounds like you do," Charles Turner replied ironically.

"She's worked for you, she was recruited by my own uncle, Lord James, so let's not waste our time with this dialectical cut-and-thrust."

"And might you mind telling me why you want to see Amelia Garayoa's file? First of all, I don't have direct access to the agents' files, which are all of course under lock and key in London. Second, Garayoa doesn't work for us anymore. One of our men found her in Berlin a little while after the war ended, and in her opinion she was not quite right in the head, which is not that surprising, given that she'd been a prisoner in Ravensbrück. No woman who went through that place is going to be quite the same again."

"Goodness, I see that your brain's starting to work, and that you do know something about Amelia Garayoa."

"I can't give you her file, but I might perhaps be able to help you if you tell me what you want to know about her that you don't know at the moment."

"I need to know what happened in Rome; apparently they accused her of having murdered an SS officer, but there was no way to prove the case against her. I want to know if she did it or not."

"I'll see what I can do."

Charles Turner called him the next day to invite him out for a drink.

"Your friend took care of Colonel Ulrich Jürgens of the SS; apparently, she did so with the help of partisans from the Italian Communist Party. Jürgens had ordered a friend of Garayoa's, the diva Carla Alessandrini, to be hanged. Alessandrini had worked with the partisans and a German priest in the Vatican Foreign Office, who helped them to get Jewish families out of Rome. As far as I have been able to establish, your friend was a very effective agent. A shame that she's not all there now. As you know, she's living with a former German officer, the man who was her alibi during the war."

"Mentally she's perfectly fine, she just doesn't want to have anything more to do with wars or violence. It's not that strange, she's suffered a lot."

Turner nodded, apparently indifferent, but really he was keen to discover why his American colleague was so interested in what had happened in Rome so many years ago.

"Charles, you know that you and I, and the Russians as well, are interested in the German scientists who worked on secret weapons projects. Some of them have escaped, among them Dr. Fritz Winkler, a fanatical Nazi whose son, a colonel in the SS, was the main accuser of Amelia in Rome. This Jürgens whom Amelia shot was a friend of Winkler's, and he swore vengeance on her; years later he managed to get her sent to Ravensbrück."

"And you're looking for Fritz Winkler."

"Yes, but it's as if the ground had swallowed him up, him and his son the colonel. They're not on any official lists of SS officers who have been arrested, or on any list of the dead. He and his father have disappeared, just like so many other high-ranking Nazis. I thought that I would ask Baron von Schumann if he knew them, and he and Amelia went pale."

"If they knew where he was they would tell you, or at least Amelia Garayoa would, she has no reason to feel anything other than hate for him if he was the cause of her internment in Ravensbrück."

"Yes, Amelia would tell me, but she doesn't know. I've bought some information, but you must know that nowadays they try to sell us anything, and try to trick us most of the time, but my informant tells me that the Winklers left on the very day that Hitler killed himself. My informant tells me that they escaped to Egypt, where some of Winkler's friends are also hiding."

"So you're going off to Cairo."

"I need to know more about the Winklers first; I haven't found any photographs of them, except one of Fritz Winkler saluting the Führer. As for his son, the colonel, he tried to destroy his records in the SS archive."

"Lots of people ran away just before the end of the war: to Syria, Egypt, Iraq, South America... Your man could be anywhere."

They spoke for a while, and when they were taking their leave of each other Turner seemed to be wondering if he should give Albert James a piece of advice.

"I think there is a way to catch Winkler."

"Yes? Do tell," Albert said ironically.

"Put out some bait for him, a piece of bait he won't be able to resist."

"Bait?" Albert was starting to see what Turner might be suggesting, and he didn't want to hear it.

"If Colonel Winkler has escaped with his father, as seems to be the case, and if he hates Amelia Garayoa as much as you say he does, which also seems to be the case, then he will only show himself if he has the chance to put an end to her. There are lots of Germans living in Cairo, some of them under their own names, some of them with false names. Nobody would be surprised for Baron von Schumann to go and live the expatriate life there. Once Winkler found out that Garayoa was there he would be sure to try to kill her; he wouldn't improvise, he would put a plan together, and to do that he would have to make himself visible; this would be the moment to get on his trail and, through him, get to his father, this Fritz Winkler you are looking for."

"It's a crazy plan!" Albert exclaimed.

"No, it's not, it's a good plan and you could have thought of it yourself if you weren't sentimentally implicated in all this. In our line of work there is only one way to survive and do a good job, and that is, as you are well aware, by getting rid of any personal attachments. The advice is free, but you should pay for the drink. American intelligence is richer than British intelligence."

Albert knew that Charles Turner was right. It was the only viable plan that might catch Fritz Winkler, but he would have to have Amelia's consent to put it into action; she would not separate herself from Max for anything in the world, and he was not willing to let her go; both he and Friedrich depended implicitly on the tormented Spanish woman.

In spite of his doubts, Albert laid out Turner's plan to his bosses and asked them to give him a free hand to convince Amelia by any means necessary.

Then he decided that the best thing to do was to talk to her alone, so he went out one morning and walked up and down outside Max's house until she came out.

"What are you doing here?" she said, surprised to see him.

"I'm going to invite you to breakfast, I need to speak to you."

They went to a café, and in spite of Amelia's protests, he ordered an elaborate breakfast. He made her eat. There were shortages of everything in Berlin, especially for those people who had barely nothing to begin with, as was the case of the family made up of Max, Friedrich, and Amelia.

Albert told her that he worked for American intelligence, that journalism was now his cover, and that he was on a mission to find Fritz Winkler. She listened to him in silence and only furrowed her brow a little when he confessed that he was an agent, but she said nothing. Albert told her of Turner's plan and waited to hear her reaction.

"So in the end... Well, I understand why I became a spy, but why did you?"

"My country entered the war and I couldn't be a simple observer anymore."

"You did well, I'm glad you took the step."

"Will you help me?"

"No, I won't. I'm finished with all of this, and 'all of this' was quite enough, don't you think?"

"Just tell me if there is anything that will make you do it."

"There is nothing in the world that would make me abandon Max, not even my own son. Is that good enough for you?"

"So you would only do it for Max."

Amelia was going to reply but she said nothing. Albert was right, she would do anything for Max, but looking for a Nazi scientist had nothing to do with the two of them.

"Amelia, things aren't going well for you and Max. He has lost everything and you have nothing. Friedrich lacks the most necessary things. He has lost his mother, his father is an invalid, and there are days when he goes to bed with only tea in his stomach."

"It's the same as happens to thousands of other German children," she said grumpily.

"We will pay you well, well enough for you to be able to live without worrying for some time at least. I'm not asking you to do this in the name of any ideal, or to save the world, but I'm offering you a job that will help you help Max and Friedrich, that's all."

"So, you're offering me money... well, well, well! I've never done anything for money before!"

"I know, but you've lived long enough to know that money can be necessary. You need money now. What will you do when you finish selling everything that used to belong to Max? You have very little left to sell, what, a lamp? Your mattresses? The clothes you wear? Show me what you're taking to sell on the black market today."

Amelia took half a dozen silver-plated napkin rings out of her bag.

"They're not silver," he said.

"No, they're not, but they're pretty, and I guess someone will give me something for them."

"And what will you do when there's nothing left? You can't even..." He fell silent, afraid of what he had been about to say.

"I can't even prostitute myself because I have been mutilated, and who would pay for a mutilated woman? Is that what you were going to say, Albert?"

"I'm sorry, Amelia, I didn't want to offend you."

"And you haven't offended me. There are lots of women in Berlin who are prostitutes in order to provide for their families. Why should I be the exception. I just don't have a body I can offer, because Winkler ensured that they destroyed it."

"So tell me: How will you get food for Max and Friedrich?"

"You think I don't ask myself the same question? You think I don't go to sleep asking myself this? I don't know what to say to Friedrich when he's in bed and he says to me in a little voice before going to sleep that he's hungry."

"Well, think about my offer. Come to Cairo with me, let yourself be seen; if Winkler is there, then he will want to kill you and will come out of his hidey-hole. We will take care of him, then we'll get his father, and that's an end to it."

"Just like that."

"Just like that."

"Max and Friedrich can't stay here alone."

Albert tried to hold back his smile. He could see that Amelia was not so obdurately opposed to his offer as she had been at the beginning of the conversation.

"We could look for someone who would come and take care of them who could cook and clean, who could look after Friedrich and Max."

"No, Max would never allow it. He won't let anyone else touch him. He only allows me to help him. It's impossible, Albert; as much as the money tempts me, it's impossible. Anyway, I swore that I would never lie to him again, that I would never work for any intelligence agency under any circumstances."

"In that case, let me speak to him, let me make the offer, let's see what he says."

"No, please, please don't do it, he'll think that we're conspiring behind his back. Things are not so easy between us... We love each other, but I don't know if he will ever be able to forgive me for what I have done to him."

"You can't forgive yourself; he has already forgiven you. Do you think he would have taken you out of Ravensbrück if he hadn't forgiven you?"

"I wish you were right."

"Go and sell your napkin rings, I'll go to see Max, I won't tell him that we've talked."

"Yes, tell him, I don't want to lie to him ever again."

"I'll go and see him right now."

Max listened to Albert without interrupting him, but Albert could feel the anger that was building up in that mutilated body.

"Do you think that Amelia's contribution to winning the war was so little? Do you still want more? What are you trying to do, Albert? Get her back for yourself?" Max could not hide his fury.

"No, I don't want to get Amelia back. You know that she never loved me enough and that she didn't hesitate to leave me for you. I won't deny that it was hard for me to get over her, that I suffered from her absence for weeks and months, but I managed to get over it, and now the love that I felt for her is only a distant memory, not even embers."

They sat in silence and measured each other up. Albert felt the baron's anger dying away and he waited until his breathing had calmed down.

"Let's talk about you, Max. Do you really love her? Are you making her pay for what she did, perhaps? You are a soldier, and soldiers know that they could die or that what happened to you could happen to them. It's not the fault of the person who pulled the trigger or planted the bomb, the fault is the people who provoked the damn war in the first place, people who don't go to the front but send people to be killed. Don't make Amelia pay for the war, you know that Hitler was the guilty party, Hitler and Hitler alone, although the rest of the world could have clipped his wings a little earlier than they did, just like you and your friends in the opposition wanted to happen. No, Max, you're not in a wheelchair because Amelia was a British agent who worked with the Greek Resistance; the person responsible for your state is your Führer, Adolf Hitler, whom I hope God will not pardon for the crimes he committed."

Silence fell again. Max thought over Albert's words, and Albert sensed the German's pain.

"I will go with her, that is the condition I put. Friedrich and I will go with her to Cairo."

Albert did not know what to say. Max had suddenly agreed to allow Amelia to serve as bait to catch Fritz Winkler through his son, but he had put a condition that it would be difficult for Albert's superiors to accept, although Albert didn't dare to contradict Max.

"I will ask my superiors; if they accept your condition I'll tell you."

"If they don't accept it, then there's no deal. I will go with Amelia wherever she goes. And if we go to Cairo you will give us a house while we are there, and will arrange for Friedrich to go to school. As for money, talk it over with Amelia."

At that moment Amelia came back to the house, annoyed because she had sold the napkin rings for so little that she had been able to buy only half a loaf of bread.

She looked at the two men, hoping that they would say something to her, and sensing the tension between them.

"Max will explain things. I'm going now, I may come back later, or if not, then tomorrow. Is that all you got?" he said, pointing to the half loaf.

"Yes, that's it," she said, trying to control her anger.

When Albert left, Max asked Amelia to sit down next to him. They spoke for a long time and she cried in acknowledging that they were desperately short of money, that Friedrich was always asking to be given something to eat, but that he only did so when he was sure that his father would not hear him, so as not to make him sad.

"If they accept my conditions, then we will go to Cairo; I know I will not be very much help, but at least I will be calm if I am by your side. Winkler is a murderer, and he will kill you if he can."

"We will only go if that's what you want; I will never ever do anything behind your back again, and I will never leave you."

He stroked her hair; he felt comforted by her presence. They were two losers with no more future than to spend their lives next to each other.

Max was very grateful to Amelia for how she looked after Friedrich.

The little boy never spoke of his mother, as if to mention her by name would be an unbearable sorrow for him, and he sought in Amelia the maternal affection he needed. For her part, she looked after the child as she had been unable to look after her own son, and it was Friedrich with whom she stayed up when he was sick, whom she taught to read and write, whom she bathed and dressed, and for whom she reserved what little food they had.

Amelia and the child loved one another, and their affection had little to do with Max: It was love that came from necessity, from the absence of Ludovica, the lost mother, and of Javier, the abandoned son.

Albert explained the plan to American intelligence's head of operations in Berlin, and they decided to accept it, given that it was the only viable and available option to get hold of Fritz Winkler.

"But talk to the Brits as well, the girl was their agent, after all, I don't want the Americans to have to deal with the Admiralty accusing them of having stolen their agents."

"Amelia doesn't work for the British anymore, she's doing this because she's desperately in need of money. And don't worry about them, anyway, it was Charles Turner's idea in the first place."

"In that case, tell him that we'll carry out his plan and tell London. Now I need to call New York and convince them to turn over the money that you've promised Amelia Garayoa. A good thing that everything's cheaper in Cairo, I'll have to call our men to try to find a place for Amelia and this man and the kid to live."

Three days later, when Albert went back to Max's house, everything was ready for them in Cairo.

13

Friedrich seemed happy to be leaving Berlin, and even Max was a little more excited than usual. Only Amelia appeared indifferent.

Albert traveled with them to Cairo and helped them to move into an apartment on the banks of the Nile. Large and sunny, the apartment was in a three-story house. The neighbors had been checked out by American intelligence, and seemed to be harmless: The second floor was occupied by an old married couple and their widowed daughter and three grandchildren; the third floor was taken by a teacher who had a wife and five children. Amelia and Max took the first-floor apartment.

"You'll be fine here, take a couple of days to rest and settle in and then we'll get to work. Our office here tells us that there is a colony of Germans in the city; some of them arrived just after the war was over, others have come more recently, lots of them don't even talk to their fellow countrymen. This is a safe haven for lots of the former SS officers who managed to get away, as well as for businessmen who were enthusiastic collaborators with Hitler in their day. Our plan is simple: You have to be seen, people have to know that you've arrived. It won't be difficult; they won't mistrust Max and all the doors of the city will open for him. It's only a question of time: If Winkler is here, then he will show his face."

"And if he's not here?" Amelia asked.

"You asked me that back in Berlin. We'll wait some time; if he doesn't appear, or if we don't find any trail that leads to him, then you'll go back to Germany. By the way, our office here has recommended a school for Friedrich. A private school where lots of German children go, he'll like it."

"I'd prefer it for Friedrich to stay here, he's very small," Amelia replied.

"It'd be good for him to be with other children."

"I will not let you use him as bait," Amelia said, looking him straight in the eyes.

"The thought never crossed my mind."

"In any case, we will be the people who decide what is good for Friedrich," she said.

Suddenly they heard a few soft knocks on the door, and Albert, smiling, went to open it. He came back into the room with a young woman following him, a small suitcase in her hand.

"This is Fatima, she'll look after you. She can cook, and clean and iron, and she speaks a little bit of German, so she'll be able to help you until you can get by in the language. I don't think it will be that hard for Friedrich, and you two are polyglots, so it shouldn't be that much of an effort for you either."

Fatima must have been about thirty years old. She was widowed, she had no children, and her husband's family had abandoned her.

She had worked in the house of a German couple and could get by in the language, but one fine day her employers had vanished into thin air, without even saying goodbye.

Amelia installed Fatima in a room next to the kitchen, and she seemed happy.

Amelia allowed the good spirits of Friedrich and Max to affect her as well. For the first time in a long while they had food. They had money to buy food, which was a great relief. Friedrich ate so much that Amelia worried about him, scared that he might make himself sick, he was so unaccustomed to it.

For a few days, Amelia let Fatima take her everywhere, and the woman showed her the city on the way to the market.

She enjoyed shopping in Khan el-Khalili, with its narrow and mysterious streets, where the traders offered all kinds of goods: a lamb or some precious stones or a cooking pot or some item stolen from a tomb.

One morning, still accompanied by Fatima, she took Max for a walk through the city.

Their neighbors were pleasant and helpful, and the teacher from the third floor offered to give them Arabic lessons very cheaply. He even suggested that he might take Friedrich to study at the school where he taught.

"If he's with Egyptian children then he'll learn the language sooner. It will be difficult to begin with, but I'll be there to look after him."

Albert told them that there was one café, the Café Saladin, where Germans tended to meet up.

"You should go there tomorrow afternoon. The three of you are a family that has run away from Berlin, scared of the reprisals taking place there, and desperate to forget about the horrors of the war. You will of course go back once things are better. This is what you have to say."

The Café Saladin was run by a German who was delighted to see them and who found a place where Max could comfortably put his wheelchair; then he submitted Max and Amelia to an interrogation that appeared inoffensive.

"So, here you are, to swell the numbers of our little colony."

Max played his role well: In fact, he was himself, a Prussian officer and aristocrat, taking refuge in Cairo after the war. He was polite, but he kept his distance from the owner of the café, who was after all someone he did not know.

They greeted the other Germans who sat down at tables nearby, but they didn't enter into conversation with any of them.

They made it their custom to go to the Café Saladin every day. Max was the one who spoke, Amelia stayed discreetly in the background; so much so that she attracted the attention of the more expansive German women who visited the café.

One afternoon, now that they were regulars at the café, an elderly man who was smoking a cigar at a neighboring table addressed himself to Max.

"If the lady is bothered by the smoke from my cigar, I will be happy to smoke it later."

"Are you being bothered, darling?" Max asked Amelia.

"No, not at all, don't worry about me."

"Thank you very much; my wife doesn't let me smoke in the house, so I normally come here."

"It's a pleasant place," Max replied.

"Have you been in Cairo long?"

"Not long," he replied.

"My wife and I came here just before the war ended. I was already retired, so I thought that it would be a good place to stay and see how the situation developed. Did you know that next week in Nuremberg they are starting the trials of everyone who collaborated with Hitler's government? It will be a difficult task, they can't judge the whole German people, and who was not on the Führer's side?"

"Yes, it will be a difficult task," Max said, while Amelia sat silently at his side, watching Friedrich, who was playing with some other children in the café doorway.

"Forgive my indiscretion, but are you that way because of the war?" the man asked with open curiosity.

"I am Baron von Schumann, I was an officer in the Wehrmacht," Max said, holding out his hand.

"An honor, Baron, at your service. I am Ernst Schneider, I own a currency exchange here in Cairo. It would be an honor if I could invite you and your wife and son to have dinner at my house."

"Well..." Max thought about it. "Maybe at some point in the future."

"I understand, it's a little hasty to accept a stranger's invitation. And rightly so, when one is away from one's homeland, sometimes one is apt to forget the social conventions."

"I had no intention of offending you," Max apologized.

"No offense taken, none at all! I behaved incorrectly. I will tell my wife to come with me one of these afternoons so she can meet your charming wife as well, would that be a good idea? We lost both our sons in the war, and our grandsons. We are alone, and so we come here to the Café Saladin, where it seems that the heart of Germany still somehow manages to beat."

The next afternoon, Herr Schneider came to the café with his wife, who was a pleasant motherly woman who spoke without stopping. Amelia realized that Frau Schneider could be an inexhaustible source of information. She seemed to know all of the Germans who lived in Cairo, and even though she didn't have dealings with them all, she had an exhaustive knowledge of their lives and activities.

"Look, my dear, that man who has just come in through the door with that rather... striking woman used to be an important government official in Bavaria. He fled before the war was over. A clever man. And she, well, it's clear that she's not his wife, she used to sing in a Munich cabaret. He didn't see any problem in abandoning his wife and their three children to run away with her. As you may imagine, they are not really welcome in some people's houses, in others... Well, you know what it means to be an expatriate, and here sometimes people's sense of social categories weakens somewhat and one treats a shopkeeper the same way one would treat a businessman."

Amelia listened to her and memorized the names and jobs of everyone the woman pointed out to her.

Two weeks after spending a couple of afternoons with the Schneiders in the Café Saladin, Max and Amelia accepted an invitation from them to have dinner the next Saturday at their house.

"It will be a dinner among friends, it will be just like being back in Berlin, you'll see."

That very day, Albert told them that he could not stay in Cairo any longer and would have to go back to Berlin.

"I'll be back in the future, but if you need to get in touch with our people, then call this number and ask to speak to Bob Robinson, he's a good man and he'll be dealing with this case. Everything's running very smoothly at the moment, people are getting to know who you are, but you're not calling too much attention to yourself, and that's good. The report that Bob sent me about the Schneiders tells me that they were fanatical Nazis. He was an accountant for a company that served as a cover for the SS's shady deals. Their two sons were mobilized and sent to the front, where they were killed. One of them, the oldest, was an officer in the SS.

As for the owner of the Café Saladin, Martin Wulff, you need to be on your guard, he came here a little more than a year ago and bought the café and fixed it up. He has good contacts with the Egyptian authorities. He was badly wounded in the war, so they demobilized him and he decided to come over here. He was a sergeant in the SS. If he had been really badly wounded then there might have been some later consequences, but he seems sound as a bell. It's surprising that an SS sergeant would come here with enough money to set up a business... Be careful and don't trust him. Our office thinks that Wulff belongs to an organization that helps former SS members who managed to flee Germany to get new identities. It's a secret organization that some members of the SS set up when they realized that the war was not going their way. They knew that if the Allies won the war then they would all be put on trial, so they decided to find an escape route that would let them have a safer future. Maybe he will lead us to Winkler."

Albert's instructions were clear: They had to have social interactions with the German community in Cairo, until Winkler realized they were there and felt confident enough to turn up and try to kill Amelia.

The Schneiders had invited four couples, so they were ten at the table, including Martin Wulff, the owner of the Café Saladin, who came to the meal with a middle-aged Egyptian woman.

The Schneiders' house was almost a mansion. It was in a quiet suburb of the city, Heliopolis, where many of the most important Egyptians lived. They had several servants.

Amelia was surprised that they lived in such a large house, as there were only two of them.

"Don't you feel alone in such a big house?" Amelia asked Frau Schneider.

"When we bought it we thought that we would have our children here with us, but the war has destroyed our hopes."

Frau Schneider insisted that Amelia call her by her first name, Agnete, and in order to mark them out from the other guests, she sat Max on her right-hand side, and Amelia between Herr Schneider and Martin Wulff.

"So you've decided to come down here and mingle with the rest of us," Martin Wulff said.

"I'm so sorry?" she said in surprise.

"I imagine that the fact of your being aristocrats must make you think that we're no great shakes, but we are the people who fought to make Germany great. Our Führer is dead, but we are his legacy, and one day we will make his dream come true. No, we have not been beaten yet, Frau von Schumann, or should I call you Baroness?"

"The war is over, Herr Wulff, and we're beginning a new era, and the sooner we accept it the better," Amelia said drily, trying to overcome the repugnance she felt toward this SS sergeant.

"You are right, we live in different times, if they had not changed then an aristocrat and his wife would never sit down at the same table as people like us. But here we are, all of us equal, living as expatriates while the Allies destroy our country. They dare to judge us, but who are they to judge anyone? Haven't they killed the same number of people as we did? The Nuremberg trials are a new humiliation for the German people."

Amelia controlled her urge to give him a sharp answer. She was there to get Winkler out of his hidey-hole, and to do that he would have to know that she was there. She deflected the conversation by asking Wulff about his "feats" during the war, then asked him about the success of the Café Saladin.

"I don't think there's a single German in Cairo who doesn't visit your café."

He didn't reply to this, but instead enjoyed rubbing shoulders with fellow countrymen who wouldn't even have looked at him before the war.

"It's a shame that the best German scientists have seen their research frustrated and that some of them have felt the need to go to America or Russia in order to save their lives," Amelia said, to see the effect that this would have on Wulff. And it had an effect, because he did not reply, but merely turned to look at her and then deliberately turned away to talk to the woman on his other side.

When they got home, Max seemed exhausted.

"So much vulgarity!" he exclaimed.

"I'm sorry, it comes with the job."

"I know, I know, and I think that we'll have earned whatever money they end up giving us. I had to listen all evening to the plans that Herr Schneider has made for the future. He told me that Nazism was not dead, that it is like a reed that grows on the banks of the Nile, which bends with the wind and is covered by water but is never uprooted, and never dies."

"They haven't disbanded, Max, they're still here."

"I don't understand..."

"They've lost the war, but they're ready to fight for a future Fourth Reich. They've tucked their heads in for the time being, but they will come out again when they find an opportune moment. They will return, Max, they will return. What we have to find out is if they are organized, if they are something more than they seem to be. That's the case with Wulff, at least. Albert told me."

"I am not a spy," Max said, uncomfortably. "The only thing we are doing here is getting Winkler to leave his hidey-hole, if indeed he is here."

"I know, but we can't ignore the information we do get here, it could be useful. I want you to tell me in detail everything you heard tonight, and then I'll write a report for Bob Robinson."

"Is that what you did when you were spying on me?"

Amelia lowered her head in shame. Sometimes Max made her feel that she was a wicked person. It was not that he blamed her for anything that had happened in Athens, but some of his comments, such as the one he had just made, reminded her that he would never forget how much she had betrayed him.

"I'll smoke a pipe while I tell you all the stupidities I have heard, and you can note them down for your report, alright?"

One afternoon, their neighbor from the third floor, Dr. Ram, suggested that they go to the Valley of the Kings.

"I am going to take my family, I want my children to know the history of our country. I speak and speak about this history in school every day, but the children will understand it better if it is something they can touch. I thought that maybe you would like to come with us. We will stay in Luxor, at the house of some friends of mine; they would be happy to put you up."

Amelia was pleased with the invitation, but Max did not want to go.

"Do you think I'm in any state to go on archaeological expeditions? What am I going to do? Sit next to Fatima while you and Friedrich run from one side of the dig to the other? No, I won't go, but I think it would be good if you and the boy went with Dr. Ram. I will stay here with Fatima. She'll look after me."

Friedrich said that he would not go anywhere without his father. The child had not yet gotten over the horror he had lived through, trapped with his dead mother under the rubble of their house. When they rescued him, they took him to an institution with other orphans, until they found his father. His uncles and aunts had also been killed. He had no one in the world apart from his father, and would not allow himself to be separated from him.

In the end, Max gave in for Friedrich's sake.

At that time, he did not seem to have too many problems with Arabic, and started to be able to chat with the boys in the street, as well as go happily to Dr. Ram's school.

Max, on the other hand, did not try very hard to learn the language, in spite of Dr. Ram's patience: He came every afternoon to give Max and Amelia lessons. Amelia applied herself with interest to the task of learning the language, whereas Max seemed distracted and indifferent.

Amelia and Friedrich were deeply affected by their visit to Luxor, and Ram and his family did everything possible to make Max comfortable.

Dr. Ram's brother's house was a safe distance from the Nile, a sensible precaution in the face of the annual floods. Ram's family made a living from agriculture, and they also helped with the archaeological expeditions that had been common in that part of Egypt before the war. The French, the English, and the Germans all competed to sift through the sands of the desert and discover its secrets and hidden treasures.

Dr. Ram's brother put the visitors up in a cool room with a view of the Nile. Fatima had a nook in the corridor.

It was impossible that Max's wheelchair would not get stuck in the sand, but Dr. Ram would not be defeated, and improvised a stretcher to be borne by his donkey. The baron refused to contemplate such a mode of transport at first, fearing to appear ridiculous, but Friedrich insisted so much that in the end he decided to give it a chance. And that was how he was able to get onto the road that led down to the Valley of the Kings. Dr. Ram's nephews helped him to go down into some tombs, carrying the stretcher themselves.

After four days, they came back happy from the trip.

"Friedrich is enjoying himself here," Max admitted.

"He eats, he plays, he studies, he interacts with other children, and he has you. Also, this sun makes him more cheerful; it's probably snowing in Berlin at the moment."

Amelia was upset by the lack of news about Winkler. As much as they went to have dinner at the houses of the expatriate Germans they met, no one ever mentioned any scientist who had sought refuge in Cairo. Either Winkler was not there, or else he valued his life and his father's life too much to expose himself to risk by trying to kill Amelia.

"I think I'm wasting your money," Amelia admitted one day to Bob Robinson.

"Don't you believe it, Amelia, your reports are extremely helpful."

"But they're irrelevant!" Amelia protested.

One month later Albert came back for a few days to Cairo. He explained to Max what was happening in Europe, and Max listened attentively.

"Tito has created a Federal Republic in Yugoslavia, made up of Serbia, Croatia, Slovenia, Bosnia-Herzegovina, Montenegro, and Macedonia. The Italian monarchy may be living on borrowed time: There's an unstoppable movement to establish a republic."

It was not until mid-April that Frau Schneider confessed a secret to Amelia.

"I trust you, my dear, and the baron, of course. You've suffered so much in this terrible war. But my husband tells me that there are things I can't tell you."

"I trust you too, Agnete. Max always asks me to be careful as well: He says that us women talk too much. But we know who we can trust and who we cannot. I knew that you would be my friend as soon as I met you. In fact, you're my best friend here."

"You don't know how happy I am to hear that! You are a great lady, and it cost Ernst a great deal to finish his studies, he worked all the time to earn money to pay the university. We were engaged at that time, and I must say that I felt envious of the carefree young men who went to class with Ernst."

That afternoon, Amelia used all her tricks as an agent to make Frau Schneider "confess" something to her.

To begin with, she said that she and Max would both like to help contribute to the regaining of Germany's former grandeur.

"Max has paid a high price for defending the fatherland, and now he wishes he could return to doing so. But there's very little we can do here, of course it's better to be here than in Berlin, exposed to the persecution that the good Germans are faced with. You can't imagine how often they've interrogated Max for having been a Wehrmacht officer. They don't even respect his physical state... ," Amelia complained.

Frau Schneider listened with interest, and Amelia could see in her eyes the struggle that she was undergoing internally to decide whether to tell her secret.

"Oh, I'm so sorry! I'm doing everything I can to make sure... that... that our little group can count on the baron."

"Really? What can Max and I do?"

"Well, first of all you need to let me convince Ernst, and he'll take care of the rest."

Amelia did not insist. She had managed to make Frau Schneider speak about her little "group." That was enough for one afternoon.

"Agnete, maybe you and Ernst would like to come have dinner with Max and me. I'd love the four of us to be able to speak calmly, in confidence. What do you think?"

"At your house?" Frau Schneider seemed enthusiastic.

"Maybe next Friday, if you don't have any other engagements."

"Black tie, of course, a dinner with the baron...," Frau Schneider stated more than asked.

Amelia managed with some difficulty to conceal her laughter, and assented.

Max got cross when Amelia told him that she had invited the Schneiders to dinner.

"Here, in our house? I don't think that's a good idea. And I don't know why we have to wear dinner jackets. It's ridiculous for us to wear black tie to a dinner with these people."

Amelia took his hand and sat down next to him, then looked into his eyes, where she could see all his rage held with difficulty at bay.

"We had nothing to eat in Berlin. Friedrich cried at night because his stomach hurt because it was empty. We had nothing left that we could sell. Now we lack for nothing: We have a good house, abundant food, even a nursemaid. Friedrich is happy: Didn't you see his smile when he came back from bathing in the Nile with Dr. Ram's sons? But we have to pay for all of this, and the price we have to pay is that we need to deal with people whom you would not even have looked at in the past, as well as making ourselves visible so that Winkler can find out that I am here. I think that Frau Schneider is about to reveal to us the fact that there is a secret Nazi organization here in Egypt. I don't know if they are just a band of nostalgic fools who gather to talk about times gone by and dream about the future, or if they are really doing anything more than that. The only way to find this out is to be part of this group, and for that I need you to help me. They like you, they are interested in you. They are astounded that Baron von Schumann might be on their side."

"This was not what I agreed to with Albert James."

"Yes, Max, it was a part of the bargain as well. There are no impassable barriers in the world of spying, they can all be crossed, nothing is sacred; you can't wait for the information to get to you, you have to go out yourself and find it. We may find the Winklers via this group."

"Or we may not, and then we will have gotten caught up in a group of fanatics."

"You were already caught up in a group of fanatics, they ran your country and drove it to war," Amelia said coldly.

"So I have to pay my part in earning our food, is that what you're saying?"

"Yes," she replied, and returned his gaze without blinking.

Amelia organized the dinner as if they were going to receive the Queen of England. She asked Bob Robinson to lend them some porcelain and some Venetian or Bohemian crystal glasses, as well as a fine tablecloth and silver cutlery.

She made Fatima put on a bonnet, and bought a dinner jacket for Max, and she and Fatima between them made one for Friedrich. She bought a black silk dinner dress and asked Bob Robinson to lend her some jewels with which to dazzle the Schneiders.

Bob arrived early that afternoon with what Amelia had asked for.

"The tablecloth belongs to the embassy, and the jewels are from the wife of a diplomat friend of mine; as for the crockery, they lent it to me as well. Don't break a single glass or I'll lose my job! I hope these people tell you something worth the effort."

"I'm sure they will," Amelia said.

"I'll come and pick everything up tomorrow. Ah, and thank you, Baron, for taking part; Amelia was right, you are the one they are really interested in."

On the night of the dinner, Frau Schneider wore a mauve dress and a fur stole. Amelia felt sorry to see her wearing fur when the temperature was round about twenty-five degrees Centigrade, as it was in Cairo in those days. Herr Schneider's dinner jacket was straining at the seams, it must have been one he had grown out of, or else he had borrowed it.

The dining room was lit with candles, and the noise of a record, playing Wagner, wafted across it.

Agnete seemed happy to have been invited into the baron's house, a house that was indeed more modest than the one she lived in, but which was decorated with a taste which made her feel inferior.

It was not until they were eating dessert that Herr Schneider suggested to Max that he join their group.

"Lots of us expatriates think that we can still be of use to Germany, that our commitment to the Führer has not lapsed, and that we need to fight to make the Fourth Reich a reality. We need a new Führer, a man who is as exceptional as Adolf Hitler was, and we will find him, we will choose the best man from among us all. If we could count on you for your help... it would be an honor, Baron."

"Ernst, your invitation does me honor, but what exactly is it that your group does? How can a man like me be of any use?"

"As you know, I own a currency exchange, and that is not the result of chance or improvisation. The SS planned for what might happen if the Allies won the war and we were toppled. A group of officials planned an escape route for that eventuality, if it should ever happen. You know that the SS had storerooms where they kept works of art confiscated from the Jews and the enemies of the Reich, as well as gold and precious stones, and other objects of value. Each group of officers took one escape route: Some fled to South America, some to Syria, to Iraq, Spain, Portugal, even to Switzerland. The treasure was divided into several parts and sent out of Germany under conditions of absolute secrecy. Each group took care of one of these parts. My group decided to come to Cairo, and that is why I came here a few months before the end of the war, in order to set everything up."

"That's impressive," Max said with complete sincerity.

"Many of the men you have met in the Café Saladin are former officers or people whose work, like mine, depended on the

SS. They are all unsullied patriots, men and women who are prepared to die for the fatherland. We will look after our treasure and use it for the best possible goal, to recover the Fatherland."

"And how will you do this?" Max asked.

"There's not much we can do at the moment, we have to wait for the Allies to get tired of putting Germans on trial, for them to lose interest in us. Then we will help those comrades who are huddled down and waiting for the wind to change. In the meantime, we are helping all of us who were forced to flee. We give them a new identity, and protect the ones who are particularly valuable, deleting all trace of them from the records so that no one knows where they are."

"That's impressive," Max repeated. "And how can I help?"

"For the time being, it will be enough to have your advice. You are a man of the world, with good contacts, and there is no open case against you in Germany, which could be very useful for us."

"Did many patriots manage to escape?" Max asked.

"Lots of them left Germany days before the final collapse. Each one took his own route, as had been decided previously."

"And how did you manage to get in touch with each other?"

"You know what? Bankers don't look at the color of your money. They didn't mind having Jewish property in their coffers before, and now they don't ask us where our money comes from. Some of the members of our organization have settled in Switzerland, and they serve as the link between our various groups. And that's how things will be until we are able to return."

"When do you think that will be? I would love to return to my fatherland," Max said, with such conviction that Amelia thought that he was being sincere.

"We mustn't be too hasty, but who knows? Maybe in two or three years' time. Lots of us have had to leave Germany, but there are lots of us back there who are still resisting. Can we count on you, Baron?"

"Of course, I have said that it is an honor for me. And now let me propose a toast: to the future of Germany!"

"And the Führer," Frau Schneider added.

When Bob Robinson came to Max and Amelia's house to pick up the material he had lent them, it was hard for him to imagine just how successful the dinner party had been.

"It's what we suspected, but now we have proof! We have to keep on pulling the line until we catch a really big fish."

"And isn't the big fish Professor Fritz Winkler?" Max asked.

"Of course, but we may be able to fish more. I'm going to send a message to Albert James, I think that this merits his coming to Cairo. You must do whatever it is they ask, keep on gaining their trust, and get the real names of the people who are part of the group, the banks they use, the contacts they have in the higher echelons of Egyptian government... Well, we really need to know everything."

"You shouldn't come here," Max said. "They've welcomed us into the group, but I suppose they'll be watching us until they are sure of our loyalty. So it will be difficult to explain an American visiting our house."

"You're right, but sometimes doing things in a simple way is how you end up complicating them. My cover in Egypt is that I am a traveling salesman for American manufactured products. This means that I can have contacts at the highest levels, and I have met a number of businessmen. You could say that you met me at a dinner with one of them."

"What, and we suddenly became friends?" Max said.

"No, it's not a good idea, Bob. Maybe... I don't know... It might work," Amelia said.

"What?" the two men asked in unison.

"You could justify your presence in the building by coming to have lessons with Dr. Ram. He's a teacher, and he makes money on the side by teaching Arabic to foreigners like us. You could arrange to come and have lessons with him a couple of times a week."

"But I speak the language quite well," Bob complained.

"But you want to perfect your knowledge, tell him that you don't write it too well, and you need to know how to write to do your business. Maybe one day a week will be enough."

Throughout 1946, Amelia and Max ingratiated themselves step by step into Ernst Schneider's group. They didn't share much information with them to begin with, but they invited the couple to patriotic displays that took place in the basement of the Schneiders' enormous house. Agnete talked Amelia into helping her embroider a large swastika flag.

Albert James came to see them on three occasions and told them that the information they were gathering was of immense use to American intelligence.

"Now we know the modus operandi of the groups that fled Germany. It is difficult to get bank information in Switzerland, but we've been able to follow certain operations made from here. Their organization is much more complicated than they have told you."

On one of these visits, Max asked Albert how long they would have to stay in Cairo.

"Fritz Winkler has not yet shown his face, but if he is here, then he will. It's just a question of time. In any case, the information that you have given us ever since you infiltrated the organization has been of great use to us."

"I would like to go back to Germany. Friedrich is now happier speaking Arabic than German. He's growing up like the boys do here, without any reference to the German system of values, to German culture, apart from what Amelia and I are able to offer him. I think that he would prefer to be here than to be in Germany."

"You are here voluntarily; if you want to return, I will arrange things so that you can," Albert said, without hiding the fact that he was strongly opposed to Max's suggestion.

"No, we won't go, not yet," Amelia interrupted. "What do you want to do in Berlin? Do you want us to die of hunger? Nobody there needs us, and here they do. They pay us well for it, too. I am saving money, I'm doing it for when we have no option but to return, and then we will be able to buy food. But we don't have enough yet, and I don't want to go back to Berlin in order to become a beggar. I'm asking you to hold on a little longer, Max."

"I feel disgusted with myself, having to see these people, listen to their stupid speeches, hear them assert that the Fourth Reich will come into being, even suggest that I might make a good Führer, having suffered so much for the fatherland. They see me on a podium, me, a cripple, calling for Germans to rebel. They are mad! But I hate deceit, I am not like you are. I feel disdain for these people, but I feel disgust at deceiving them."

"Think about it. I am going back to Berlin the day after tomorrow. If you want to go back I will organize everything," Albert replied.

Amelia went with him to the door.

"He's depressed, you can't imagine what all these meetings are like, with the swastika banners and everything."

"It would be a setback if you decided to return, but it would be worse if you stayed and Max couldn't deal with it and got nervous. He has learnt the trade much later than you, Amelia, but you have to have nerves of steel for this business."

"It's a business that has changed you, Albert," Amelia said.

"When I first met you, what I loved most was my job, and then I fell in love with you, and then the war came and I had no choice."

"You have a choice, Albert, you can leave all this and go back to work."

"No, I can't, I can't now. Once you have dedicated yourself to this line of work, there's no way back."

Albert came back the next day and Max told him that he had made a decision.

"One more year, Albert, one more year. If Winkler doesn't turn up in that amount of time, then he's not here. We will go back to Berlin in a year."

"Alright, a year."

14

But the wait went on for longer than a year. At the end of 1947, Ernst Schneider received a letter that provoked in him happiness and anxiety in equal measure.

By then Max had become Schneider's right-hand man when it came to investing the group's property in the international market.

Schneider seemed to trust Baron von Schumann unreservedly, but even so he did not give him details of the contents of the letter that had affected him so much. He only said that they would shortly receive a visit from a war hero and from his father, a pre-eminent figure; both of them had been in hiding so that the Allies would not take them.

Max told Amelia this immediately.

"I don't know who it could be, but we need to tell Bob Robinson at once."

"It could be Winkler," she said.

"I don't know, but they are very important people. Schneider told me that they will be staying in his house, and that he had to speak with Wulff in order to get a guarantee of safety for the two who will be coming."

"Where are they coming from?"

"He didn't say."

Frau Schneider was more explicit than her husband, and when she met with Amelia two days later in the Café Saladin, she couldn't resist offering confidences.

"The baron will have told you that we are expecting guests. You can't imagine who they are, my dear, the Allies were looking desperately for one of them, he's a very important man. They left Berlin the same day Hitler killed himself, and they've been in Spain almost all this time. Franco has good relations with the British and the Americans, so even though he does protect our people they will be safer here. Our group will protect them. Sergeant Martin Wulff—and here she looked at the owner of the café out of the corner of her eye—served with one of them. We still can't tell you who they are, but I assure you that you will know them. They will be staying in our house, and I've asked permission from my husband to organize a dinner in their honor."

Neither Max nor Amelia got any more information out of the Schneiders. All they could do was wait, to Max's despair, because he had organized their return to Berlin for the beginning of 1948. Now they had no option but to wait and find out who these mysterious strangers would be.

Herr Schneider told Max that he wouldn't see them for a few days.

"Our guests are coming and I have to make sure that everything goes well. I'll keep you informed."

As 1947 came to an end, they received an invitation from the Schneiders to see the old year out at their house along with other fellow-countrymen.

The day came, and as Amelia helped Max to dress for dinner, she couldn't but be aware of how worried he was.

"Don't worry, it will all be alright," she said, to cheer him up.

"It could be Winkler and his father, it could be others, but whoever they are they must be very important. I can't help but be worried; if it is Winkler, he'll recognize us, and then what will we say?"

"You are an officer and a hero, and so you are free of any suspicion."

"Please, Amelia! Winkler knows where and why I lost my legs. And he knows you. He'll tell the others who we really are."

"We've never hidden who we are. And even though Winkler has always suspected me, he's never been able to prove anything."

"Except that you had in your hands one of the detonators with which the Greek Resistance blew up a German convoy. I have to tell you that I thought Winkler was never going to show up."

"It may not be him," Amelia said.

"I have a foreboding."

"Don't worry, Bob or his men will be close. The taxi driver who is taking us to the Schneider's house is with American intelligence."

Amelia didn't say anything, but she had in her bag the little pistol that Albert James had given her when she had arrived in Cairo.

Max knew that the weapon existed, but he never thought that Amelia or he would have cause to use it.

Frau Schneider had pushed the boat out to create a Christmas-like atmosphere for the end-of-year party. There was a fir tree in the garden decorated with lights and crystal balls. Amelia wondered how she could have gotten a Christmas tree in Egypt. The hall and the salon were also decorated with ribbons and candles.

They said hello to the Schneiders' guests. They knew them all, they were the most important members of that group of exiled Nazis. But they did not see any new faces. Agnete whispered to Amelia that the two special guests were about to come down from their rooms.

Suddenly Herr Schneider rang a bell to get his guests' attention.

"Ladies and gentlemen, we have two great patriots with us tonight, two men who have sacrificed themselves for Germany, and who were able to escape in time, so as not to fall into the hands of our enemies. They have been in hiding for a long time, but we finally have them with us. Their journey here has not been easy, and they only got here a couple of hours ago. Like many of you, they now have new identities, and we will address them by their new names. Ladies and gentlemen, please give a round of applause for Günter and Hans Fischer."

Two men came into the salon. One of them was an old man who walked with a stoop and bore a tired look in his eyes; he was leaning on the arm of the other man, who walked upright and looked like a soldier. When they came in, everyone applauded enthusiastically.

Schneider introduced the two men to the rest of the guests, and as he did so, Amelia tried to keep a hold on her emotions, while she squeezed Max's hand.

She had seen those eyes before, years ago, those blue eyes, cold as snow. She had seen them filled with hatred and anger. There was no doubt in her mind that Günter Fischer was Colonel Winkler, and Horst Fischer must be his father.

They waited their turn to be introduced. Herr Schneider pointed proudly to Max.

"I would like to introduce you to an exceptional man, a hero, Baron von Schumann and his charming wife Amelia."

A tremor crossed Günter Fischer's face while he looked first at Max and then at Amelia, but he made no sign of having recognized them. He shook Max's hand and kissed Amelia's.

"So, even heroes have been forced into exile," he said sarcastically, to Herr Schneider's amazement.

Frau Schneider asked them to go through to the dining room, so there was no time for more comments. The dinner took place amid a welter of toasts to Germany, the Führer, and the Third Reich, but also to the future, to the Fourth Reich, which the men gathered here today would shortly help to rise victorious over its enemies.

Dr. Winkler, under the name of Horst Fischer, was the center of attention of all the guests. They listened with devout attention as he spoke of Germany's technical superiority, assuring them that German scientists were a long way ahead of both the Americans and the Russians, not just in arms development, but also in medical science.

"I would prefer to die rather than to fall into the hands of the Allies. I know that a lot of my colleagues have turned traitor rather than go to trial, they carry on their research and tell all our secrets to the new masters of the world. I will not do that. I swear loyalty to the Führer, and above all I swear loyalty to Germany, and I will never betray either of them."

His son heard this in silence, looking first at Max and then at Amelia.

It was not until the end of the dinner, after moving to another salon, that Günter Fischer went over to Herr Schneider and whispered something in his ear that appeared to alarm his host. Immediately Schneider, Fischer, and certain other guests left the room and headed to Schneider's office.

Amelia, who had seen what was going on, took the opportunity to leave the salon and get to Herr Schneider's office before the others, where she hid behind the thick curtains. She prayed that they would not discover her: If they did, then they would surely kill her then and there.

"Do you know who you have in your house?" Günter Fischer said, talking angrily to Herr Schneider.

"I hope that none of my guests has upset you. They are all people in whom I have the greatest trust."

"Trust! We have a spy among us."

"A spy! What are you saying!" Schneider's tone of voice was almost hysterical.

"Amelia Garayoa is a spy," Fischer insisted.

"What are you saying? Explain yourself," his father ordered.

"Herr Fischer, I assure you that..."

But Fischer didn't let Schneider continue.

"Stop talking nonsense and use my real name now that we're alone."

"It's better if we get used to the new ones, or else we might give ourselves away in public," Wulff said.

"Alright, then I'll carry on being Herr Fischer. But now listen to me. This woman is a spy. She killed an SS officer in Rome. She was involved in the disappearance of one of the Reich's best agents. There was nothing that could be proven against her until she was arrested in Greece along with a group of partisans after they had destroyed a convoy, killing dozens of Wehrmacht soldiers and blowing up a large quantity of military supplies."

"But she is Baron von Schumann's wife! You must be mistaken!" Schneider dared protest.

"The baron was in the convoy; she left him a cripple. I've told you that she is a dangerous woman, a murderer. And she is not his wife. His wife died in Berlin, in an RAF bombardment."

"I know, I know, and when he was widowed, he married Amelia."

"No, no, they never got married. She is married, she has a husband in Spain, although they have been separated for years. She has a son."

"But the baron... ," Schneider insisted.

"You're an idiot! What don't you understand? You're a real idiot! She left him a cripple, he lost his legs because of her, and instead of killing her, he forgave her, he even got her out of Ravensbrück. He's one of those decadent aristocrats who have no place in the new Germany. His code of honor is only a front for his weakness. He should have killed her personally; but here they are, holding each other's hands."

"Son, if that is the case, then we have to act. Do you think she recognized you?" the false Herr Fischer asked his false son.

"I think so, I think so. The baron didn't recognize me, but she did... I realized how she was looking at me. Of course we have to act."

"I'll take care of both of them," Wulff said.

Schneider seemed distraught, and the other three guests who had come with them supported the Fischers.

"We have been in hiding for two years, with the Allies and their spies on our trail, we've managed to escape from Spain, we've been through things you couldn't even begin to imagine and we will not fall into the hands of the British, or whoever it is this damn woman works for," the false Günter Fischer said.

"Of course, they have to disappear, we're running a great risk. The Baron has been collaborating with our friend Schneider on the financial side of things, and if he talks... It could have very disagreeable consequences for all of us," one of the others said.

"I can't believe what you're saying, if it were the case, then they would have turned us in a long time ago, and they have not," Schneider said, trying to defend himself.

"The baron is a puppet in the hands of this woman, maybe he doesn't even know what she is doing, but she... I'm telling you, I know her well. She is a spy and a murderer."

Günter Fischer touched his face as if it were a mask.

"My father and I have had to have plastic surgery in order to get our new identities. You should know that I still feel the pain of the two operations I had to undergo. No, I am not willing for my father to run any risk. We cannot recover Germany without men like him. We have to get rid of this woman, and of the baron, and as soon as possible. Tonight."

The men looked at him in silence, and one by one they nodded. They agreed that they needed to finish with Amelia and the baron. Martin Wulff took a pistol out of a shoulder holster and got up, heading toward the door.

"What are you going to do?" Schneider cried. "You can't kill them here. They'll hear the shots. Do you want them to arrest us all?"

"Schneider is right," one of the other men said. "We should do it when they leave here, before they get home. It has to look like an opportunistic crime, as if someone wanted to rob them and then threw their bodies into the Nile."

"You are right, Herr Benz," Günter Fischer said, looking at the man who had just spoken, "and now we should go back to the salon or else the witch will realize that we're plotting something."

"But are you sure she recognized you? It's impossible, your face has changed, I don't think she could connect it with your true identity, Colonel Winkler," Herr Schneider insisted.

"I want them dead, Herr Schneider, or else I will make you responsible for whatever the consequences are."

Schneider could not support Colonel Winkler's cold gaze.

Amelia stayed still where she was for several minutes more until she was sure that the men had left the office. She had to get Max out of there, and she asked herself if Bob Robinson really was nearby and on the lookout, as they had arranged he would be.

Bob had given her a small lantern, and told her that if Fischer was Winkler, then she should go to a window and make a signal. Something simple, just turning it on and off. Now was the time to do it.

When she came back to the salon, Herr Schneider was talking to Max, and Frau Schneider came toward her anxiously.

"But where have you been? I looked everywhere for you: I was worried."

"I went out into the garden for a moment, I felt a little woozy, I didn't want to say anything so as not to upset you or the baron."

"My husband wanted to know where you were..."

"Well, here I am, no one gets lost in a house," she said, forcing a smile.

Günter Fischer came up to them, and Amelia, in spite of the fact that the face she looked into was not the one she had known Colonel Winkler to have, was sure that it was him.

"So you are Spanish... well, well, well... You speak German perfectly."

"It's a language that I love as much as my mother tongue."

"Do you like living in Cairo?"

"Sadly, we won't be here very much longer. We are going back to Germany. We can't deal with the homesickness."

"Yes, our dear baron and Amelia will be leaving us in a few days' time, they're going back to Berlin. We'll miss them," Frau Schneider said, ignoring the tension in the air.

"So you're leaving... And why did you decide to come to Cairo?"

"After the war we thought that it was probably best to leave the country for a while until everything calmed down."

"And you don't think that you'll be in any danger in Germany?"

"I hope not, Herr... Fischer."

He didn't say anything else, merely nodded politely and left the two women.

"Poor thing, he must have suffered much. He used to be a very handsome man, but those operations..."

"Was he wounded?" Amelia asked.

"Oh no, it's just so that no one recognizes him, neither him nor his father. You've realized, haven't you, that old Herr Fischer is a scientist, one of the best ones Germany has to offer. The Allies would have given anything to have arrested him and forced him to work for them. But Fritz Winkler would have killed himself rather than work for the Russians or the Americans." Frau Schneider had mentioned Winkler's real name without realizing it.

870

"Yes, they definitely deserve our admiration," Amelia replied.

"Of course, my dear, our admiration and our thanks. It can't have been easy for them to live all this time in Spain, and it was very hard for them to get here. They should have come here more than two years ago, but old Herr Winkler nearly died after the first operation on his face, he got infected. Luckily he got over it, but he has been very ill, and his son, Colonel Winkler, didn't want to take any risks. You were surprised that we lived in such a large house, weren't you, my dear? Well, it was meant for them; Herr Winkler needs space to set up his laboratory, his office. I will look after them, and make sure that they're not missing anything."

They went up to where Max was seated, talking to Herr Schneider.

"Darling, I think it's time that we left," Amelia said.

"I'll tell Wulff to go with you," Schneider suggested.

"Oh, there's no need! We arranged it that the taxi driver would come and pick us up now to take us home, I'm sure that he's already waiting for us."

"Wulff doesn't mind, and I'd be happier knowing that you weren't alone at this time of night."

"Don't worry, Herr Schneider, we know the driver, he's like our chauffeur in Cairo."

Wulff came up to them. To Amelia, the owner of the Café Saladin seemed even more sinister than usual.

"I'll take you home," he said so bluntly that it seemed impossible to refuse.

"Thank you, Herr Wulff, but we've already told our hosts that we have a taxi waiting for us. But we're very grateful for the offer, aren't we, Max?"

Amelia started to push Max's wheelchair toward the exit. When Frau Schneider opened the door, the taxi was there waiting for them. The driver got out and was very solicitous toward Amelia and the baron.

"I'll help the gentleman while you fold the seat and put it in the front seat."

Neither Wulff nor the Schneiders could stop Amelia and Max from leaving in the taxi.

Two streets further on, they turned a corner, and the taxi stopped. Bob Robinson got out of a car that was parked a few feet away.

"What happened?" he asked straight out.

"It's Winkler and his father, and they gave the order to kill us."

"I'll send to get Friedrich from your house, and I'll get you to a safe place."

"If you do that, they'll know we've found them out and they'll disappear. We have to take the risk that they will try to kill us."

"I'll have a couple of men watch your house," Bob Robinson said, accepting Amelia's assessment of the situation.

"Alright? Can you get Winkler?"

"Our aim is to get Fritz Winkler, and we hope to do so."

"Tonight?"

"No, I don't think so, they'll be on the alert. We can't just burst into the Schneiders' house, we'll have to wait for them to come out."

That night, neither Max nor Amelia slept peacefully, even though they knew that Bob Robinson's men were watching the house.

"We have to go as soon as possible, we can't wait two weeks to leave," Max said.

Nothing happened the next day. Bob came to see them and reassure them, and also to listen to all the details of the dinner and what Amelia had found out.

"We have the Schneiders' house under close watch, and I think that with the description you've given us of the Winklers they won't escape. We've also increased the watch on this house, no one can come in or go out without us seeing them, and if we see anything suspicious we'll act at once."

"They'll try to act soon, they can't allow us to stay alive knowing what we know," Max said.

"The strange thing is that they haven't tried yet," Amelia said.

"They lost their best chance last night, Wulff only had to take you somewhere out of the way and kill you, then steal whatever you had on you to make it look like a robbery and throw you into the river, just as you heard one of the men suggest. But now they need to think up a new plan. And they need to be careful, the Egyptians know who they are and leave them alone, some civil servants get hearty bribes, but it's all on the condition that they are discreet. They can't go around killing people in broad daylight," Bob Robinson insisted.

"I want you to protect my son," Max said.

"We will. Two of my men are following him whenever he leaves the house, they'll go everywhere with him, they'll wait for him at the school door, but he won't realize a thing, don't worry."

"Yes, I will worry. We should never have agreed to do this...," Max complained.

"But you did, and you are being paid for it, so you shouldn't complain." Bob Robinson didn't beat around the bush and wasn't prepared for the baron to ruin everything at this late stage.

"You have to kill Colonel Winkler or he will kill me. He doesn't care about Max or Friedrich, it is me whom Winkler wants to see dead. And this time he'll try not to fail," Amelia said.

"My orders are to take Fritz Winkler, if possible without making too much noise about it. We don't want problems with the Egyptians either. But if Colonel Winkler comes for you, then we will protect you, I've told you that already," Bob Robinson insisted.

On January 2, 1948, Amelia received a note from Frau Schneider asking her to go shopping with her in Khan el-Khalili. Herr Schneider called Max to ask him to meet up with him and some other friends at the Café Saladin.

"Don't go," Max ordered her.

"I have to go, and you know it."

"Do you want them to kill you? What do you think will happen if you go to Khan el-Khalili? You'll disappear and then you'll be found dead in an alleyway."

"I'm going, Max. If I don't, then they'll suspect and hide the Winklers. They want to know if we suspect anything, if we recognized their guests. We committed ourselves to doing a job, and they have paid us for it, we have to keep our side of the bargain, and then we'll go back to Berlin. I promise you, Max."

They sent word to Bob Robinson and he ordered them to keep their appointments.

"If you don't go then they'll suspect you, and it'll blow the whole operation out of the water. I am sorry for the risk that you are going to face. The most I could possibly permit would be for you, Max, to say that you weren't feeling well, but Amelia, you can't give any excuses, you have to go. They think that they know you, Max, so they think that if you suspected anything then you wouldn't let Amelia go to the meeting with Frau Schneider."

"Apparently they don't know that when a man sells himself he stops being the same," Max said, trying to control the anger he felt.

"Call me any names you want, but if I were you I wouldn't worry. The work is like this, and the pay is good. There's nothing more to talk about. But the people who do this job also believe in things," Bob Robinson replied.

Max decided to go to the meeting at the Café Saladin, but before he went he made Bob Robinson swear that if anything happened to him or Amelia, then American intelligence would make arrangements for Friedrich's care, and would ensure that he was educated in Germany.

"No one is going to kill you this afternoon, Max, they just want to check what you know. If you don't leave the script we've prepared then they won't suspect anything, but everything depends on you."

Frau Schneider came to pick up Amelia. She was nervous and, normally so talkative, she scarcely spoke a word. As for Max, the taxi driver who worked for Bob took him to the Café Saladin with instructions to wait until his meeting was over and then take him straight home.

"Are you feeling better?" Frau Schneider asked Amelia.

"Of course, why do you ask?"

"The other night you said that you were feeling unwell..."

"Oh, it was hot and... Well, you know, things happen to women..."

They walked toward the old town and Amelia was surprised that Frau Schneider was walking so fast, as if she were keen to get somewhere.

"What are you going to buy?" she asked.

"Oh, nothing important, but I don't like going to Khan el-Khalili alone, I sometimes think that it's so easy to get lost in those little streets. I want to buy a present for my husband, and he told me about a jeweler's that has lovely pieces at a very good price, I'd like to find him some cufflinks, I don't know... maybe rubies or aquamarines. What do you think?"

They walked into the old town and Frau Schneider slowed her pace, looking to the left and to the right as if waiting for someone to tell her where to go. Amelia didn't take too long to see that they were following a shortish man, dressed in traditional clothes, who always walked a few paces ahead of them. They went on moving into ever more twisty and narrow alleyways.

"Are you sure we know where we're going?" she asked Frau Schneider, who seemed more and more nervous.

"Don't worry, my dear, I'm very good at orienting myself, I don't think we're lost."

The man who seemed to be Frau Schneider's guide stopped in front of a dark doorway, then carried on walking. Frau Schneider stopped in the doorway and indicated to Amelia that she should follow her.

"It's here, yes, this is the address."

They climbed up some narrow stairs that ended in front of a door, which Frau Schneider pushed open to let Amelia go in first.

She could see nothing for a few seconds, but then her eyes began to grow accustomed to the dark, and she suddenly heard the door shut behind her. She turned around, looking for Frau Schneider, but she had vanished.

"Come in, Amelia," came a voice that she recognized immediately. It was Colonel Winkler.

"Ah, Herr Fischer! I didn't know we were going to meet you

here," Amelia said in an innocent voice, while taking a quick look around the room to see that she was alone with Winkler.

"You didn't know?"

"No, of course not. Where is the jeweler's? It's a slightly strange place, don't you think?" Amelia could now see that Fischer was seated in a chair, the only chair in the room, and that he seemed to be hiding something in his lap.

"Enough! You know who I am, don't you?"

"Of course, Herr Fischer, how could I not know you?"

Colonel Winkler stood up and could only take one step forward. He didn't have time to realize how, but he felt something hit him in the face. The darkness had made him unaware that Amelia was taking her hand out of her jacket pocket, and that in her hand she held a pistol. He died realizing that Amelia was shooting him.

She did not stop shooting until she had emptied the magazine. She shot him in the face, the gut, and the heart. She couldn't stop shooting him because she was afraid that he was still alive. Then, when she saw him on the floor, motionless, in the middle of a pool of blood, she calmed down a little. She heard no noise, as if the shots hadn't alerted anyone. She turned around and ran back the way she had come until she reached the doorway, then slowed down so as not to draw attention to herself. She wore a handkerchief over her head, but even so it would not be difficult for someone to remember her features and describe them when they found the body of Colonel Winkler and were looking for suspects.

Suddenly a man came up to her and she recognized him: He worked for Bob Robinson.

"What happened? I saw Frau Schneider coming scared out of this house you've just left. Who was waiting for you?"

"It was a trap. Colonel Winkler wanted to kill me, but I killed him."

"You... but... what! You weren't meant to kill him, no one ordered him to be killed. Bob's not going to like this, and Albert James even less," the man said as he grabbed her firmly by the arm.

"Let me go! The colonel wanted to kill me himself and he wasn't going to wait to see if I had recognized him or not. He knew I had, so he needed to kill me as soon as possible. If I hadn't killed him, then you would have found me dead. Now he's dead. What's happening with Max?"

The man did not reply. He made a sign to two other agents whom Amelia had not seen.

"Colonel Winkler is dead," he told them.

He grabbed hold of Amelia's arm again and pulled her out of Khan el-Khalili.

"I have to go and look for Max."

"No, you're not going anywhere. You haven't fulfilled your part of the plan. I'll take you home and we'll wait there for Bob and Albert James, and I swear that I will not let you move an inch away from where I am."

"Albert is in Cairo?"

"He arrived this morning."

Max came back two hours later. His face was tense.

"What happened?" Amelia hugged him as soon as she saw him come back into the house, helped by the taxi driver who worked for Bob.

"I don't know. Schneider made me answer all kind of questions: about you, about what we were going to do in Berlin, about Friedrich... but neither of the Fischers was there, neither the father nor the son. Herr Schneider seemed to want to keep me busy, I don't know, it was all very strange. Wulff was very nervous and didn't do anything apart from look at his watch. He told his assistant that he was going out for a while and left the café without saying goodbye. And what about you, how was your shopping trip with Frau Schneider?"

"It all went well, don't worry."

Bob Robinson came to the house an hour later, along with Albert James, and they seemed to be feeling a mixture of anger and euphoria.

"Albert, I didn't know you were here!" Amelia said, happy to see him.

"Bob told me, and I came along in time to help you with the operation. But you..."

"You put us in a tricky situation. You shouldn't have killed Colonel Winkler," Bob interrupted.

"What!" Max exclaimed in shock.

"I didn't have any choice, if I hadn't killed him then he would have killed me."

"You don't know that," Bob protested.

"He was carrying a pistol. Do you think they'd arrange for me to go to an abandoned house in Khan el-Khalili in order to drink tea? It was him or me."

"And you shot him, even though I ordered you not to. My men were close behind you."

"But they couldn't have stopped him from killing me, how could they have managed to do that? He would have shot me and would have left the house peacefully, just as I did. Your men would have found me dead."

"Did you need to empty the whole magazine? You fairly shot him to pieces..." Bob seemed affected by what his agents had told him of the scene in the abandoned house.

"I started to shoot him and... I wanted to be sure that he was dead."

"He is dead, you can be sure of that, and now I have a body to get rid of."

"Enough, Bob! This can't be undone, and we'll sort it out," Albert James interrupted.

"And Winkler's father?"

"He's well, very well. We made an unexpected visit to the Schneiders' house. There were several armed men protecting him, but we managed to get him out of there without a shot being fired," Albert said.

"How did you manage that?" Amelia asked.

"They didn't feel the need to be suspicious of a well-dressed Egyptian who said that he was the secretary of an important politician who has been on the payroll of the Schneider group for some time. He came to pay his respects to Herr Fischer, and said that he was at his disposition to provide him with whatever it was he might need. They went to Schneider's office to talk more peacefully. A man who works for us has been on the Schneiders' household staff for years, he works as a gardener, so false Herr Fischer's bodyguards didn't mistrust him. He went into the office, pointed his pistol at Herr Fischer to get him to be quiet, and then, with the help of the supposed secretary, chloroformed him and got him out through the basement in a large rubbish bin, one of the ones they use for garden waste. The false secretary left the house unmolested. Everything went smoothly apart from the small detail of your killing Colonel Winkler. But we can't change that now," Albert concluded.

"It was him or me," Amelia repeated.

"You know what?" Bob said. "You've put me in a tight spot. Now, if you don't mind, let's sort out your alibi. If you don't mind, I'll hit you on the head, and in a bit you should go to a pharmacy, and say that you were out with Frau Schneider shopping in Khan el-Khalili, and you went to a jeweler's, you can't remember where, and that a little while before you got there you were hit on the head and left unconscious on the ground by a robber. You are very worried about Frau Schneider, you don't know what happened to her. This is the version that you'll stick to in front of everyone, even Frau Schneider herself. Then you can carry on preparing for your journey and you can leave as planned." Bob explained the plan in a tone that left no room for debate.

"And what shall I do till then?" Amelia asked.

"You'll have to carry on pretending to be innocent German expatriates. They won't tell you anything about the Winklers' disappearance, and you will ask about the Fischers, but without showing too much curiosity," Bob said.

When Albert and Bob had left, Amelia had to face Max's shock and fear.

"How could you kill Winkler?"

"I told you, it was him or me," Amelia said, upset.

"You left the house with a pistol, which I did not know, and your intention was to kill him if you came across him."

"Yes, that's true, I'm not going to lie to you. I wanted to kill him."

"Sometimes... sometimes... I don't recognize you."

"I am sorry, Max, I am sorry that this upsets you. But believe me that if I hadn't killed Winkler then I would now be dead. I was lucky and was able to shoot first, which is why I'm here now."

Frau Schneider couldn't meet Amelia to say goodbye because she was feeling indisposed. Herr Schneider did meet Max to see him off, as well as some of the other members of the group. Wulff seemed to be extremely angry, but said nothing.

Schneider kept up the front that his guests had needed to go off on an unexpected journey, but that they would be back soon.

They wished him luck in his return to Germany, and Max saw that Herr Schneider was rather confused, as if he couldn't believe that Fritz Winkler had disappeared and that the corpse of his son, the colonel, had turned up floating in the Nile, and that Max and Amelia had had absolutely nothing to do with these two occurrences.

When he looked at Max, all he saw was an invalid, a war hero. Winkler must have made a mistake, it wasn't possible that the baron was a cripple as a result of Amelia's actions. No one would pardon anyone who had left him blind in one eye and without any legs. No, it was impossible, but even so, Herr Schneider thought it was better not to trust in Max any longer.

Amelia sighed in relief when she saw, through the plane window, the figure of the Sphinx below her.

"I don't want to go to Berlin," Friedrich whispered in her ear. "I want to stay here."

She squeezed his hand and looked at Max. She could see his worry in spite of the joy he felt to be going home. Albert James sat two rows in front of them, without giving any signs of knowing them at all, just as he had arranged with them beforehand.

When they landed in Berlin, it was snowing heavily. Friedrich complained about how cold he was, and said again that he wanted to go back to Cairo. Amelia told him to shut up.

"Well, that's it," Lady Victoria and Major Hurley said, almost simultaneously.

"What do you mean, 'that's it'? What happened when they got back to Berlin?" I asked them.

"As for me, I can't tell you anything else. This is everything that my superiors have allowed me to tell you. The operation in Egypt was not run by us, although we were kept up to speed about everything that happened. But there's no record in our archives of who was involved in the operation. As you can see, without Albert James's notebooks, the ones Lady Victoria possesses, it would have been impossible to be sure that your great-grandmother had anything to do with this operation."

"Right, but what did they do next? Did they carry on working for American intelligence, or for British intelligence? There must be something written down somewhere, right?"

"I'm sorry, Guillermo, I've told you that I can't help you anymore. Everything that has anything to do with operations that took place after the war is classified."

"But why?" I insisted, trying to overcome Major William Hurley's resistance.

"You have to understand," Lady Victoria interrupted. "The major can't tell you if your great-grandmother carried on working as an agent. If she did, then it's a secret, and if she didn't then he simply doesn't know."

"But we're talking about what happened after the war," I protested.

"Exactly, we're talking about what happened in the Cold War."

"But the Cold War's over."

"Ah, is it?" Lady Victoria's voice was filled with irony. "I don't want our dear friends the Russians to find out the details of operations that took place behind the Iron Curtain. I suppose that some of the agents involved are still alive. No, Guillermo, there is information that we will never know, that won't be put into the hands of historians for a century, or perhaps even more. And by then we won't be here."

"What happened to Albert James?" I insisted.

"Oh, well, I can't tell you much more about him, either, he carried on living in Europe... here and there."

"Did he get married?"

"Yes, he got married."

"Can you tell me who to?"

"Yes, Lady Mary Brian. That's why he stayed in Europe, although sadly Lady Mary died in a car accident."

"Did they have children?"

"No."

"So they can't give me any more information."

"You'll have to carry on investigating on your own account," Major Hurley said.

"If you could give me a clue..."

"You might be able to find something in Germany, don't you think?" Lady Victoria interrupted. "After all, it's where your great-grandmother ended up."

"And do you have any suggestions?" I said, slightly annoyed.

"If I were you, I'd try to find out what happened to Friedrich. He might still be alive."

This time, Lady Victoria had spoken without irony.

"I'd thought of that," I lied, because in fact I hadn't had time to think about what I might do next.

"Well, in that case you know what to do now," Lady Victoria smiled in a way that was open and charming.

I went back to my hotel on foot because I needed to think. It was clear that if Major Hurley didn't want to give me any more information, then it was because Amelia must have carried on being involved in espionage work. As for Albert James's notebooks, surely Major Hurley would have suggested that Lady Victoria didn't tell me anything that could still have been classified information. And if there is one thing that unites the British, whatever their ideology might be, it is that they are extremely patriotic.

It was a good idea to go to Berlin. Perhaps I would be lucky and meet Friedrich von Schumann, or someone who had known his aristocratic family in the past.

I called Doña Laura to tell her I was going to Berlin, and I sent flowers to my mother again, with a card saying how much I loved her, so that she wouldn't give me another telling-off when I called her from Berlin.

I also called Professor Soler to see if he had any contacts in the German capital. He seemed to know people everywhere.

"So, you're going to Berlin, my dear Guillermo, well, well, well... You're a right little globetrotter," Professor Soler said, with a certain degree of irony.

"So it seems, but I don't have any other options."

"I may be able to help you. I struck up a friendship at a conference with a professor from the University of Berlin, but he must be pretty old, because he was just about to retire, and this was six or seven years ago. But I'll look for his card and if I find it I'll call you, is that alright?"

Professor Soler called me an hour later. He had found the card and had spoken to his friend.

"He's named Manfred Benz, and he lives out by Potsdam. He said that he would be pleased to see you. I hope it's a useful trip."

"So do I, and thank you very much, Professor."

FRIEDRICH

1

Berlin surprised me. It seemed one of the most interesting cities I had ever visited. Full of life, avant-garde, transgressive, beautiful. I fell in love with it almost immediately, in the three hours after my plane landed, after getting a taxi driver to give me a tour of the sights.

I don't know why, but I decided to try to find a member of the von Schumann family by myself, if indeed any one of them was left. I said to myself that if I failed in the attempt, then I would give Professor Manfred Benz a call.

The hotel receptionist gave me a phone book, and I found, to my surprise, various people named von Schumann. I called the first one on the list.

I crossed my fingers, hoping that they would speak English. A voice that sounded like a teenager's answered the phone, and I asked for Herr Friedrich von Schumann.

"Ah, you want to speak to my grandfather! You have made a mistake, he does not live here. Would you like to talk to my mother?"

The kid spoke English, but with a very strong German accent. Of course, I spoke English with a Spanish accent: We understood each other perfectly. I was tempted to say yes, that I would talk with his mother, but my instinct told me not to.

"Don't worry, I suppose I must have picked the wrong number from the phone book."

"If you are looking in the phone book, he's under F. von Schumann. That's granddad's phone number."

I found the number and dialed it. My pulse started to beat

faster as I realized that Friedrich von Schumann might be alive; of course, it was another matter whether he might want to talk to me.

A deep voice reached me over the line.

"Good afternoon, I would like to speak to Friedrich von Schumann."

"Who is it?" the voice asked.

"He doesn't know me, but I think he knew a relative of mine, my great-grandmother."

There was a silence over the line, as if the deep-voiced man were weighing what I had just told him.

"Who are you?" he asked.

"I am Guillermo Albi, and I am the great-grandson of Amelia Garayoa."

"Amelia..." The voice sunk into a whisper.

"Yes, Amelia Garayoa, she... Well, it was she who knew Friedrich von Schumann."

"What do you want?" It really was an impressive voice.

"If Herr von Schumann could spare me a few minutes, I could explain it to him face to face."

"I am Friedrich von Schumann; come to my house this afternoon at three o'clock, if that is convenient. I'll give you the address."

When I hung up the phone, I couldn't believe my luck. I celebrated by taking a walk around Berlin with the map that the receptionist had given me. I did what any tourist would do: I took a photo with the Brandenburg Gate in the background, I looked for Checkpoint Charlie, I tried to see where the Wall had been...

The address was in what had been East Berlin. The house was in a clean and well-kept district, with some art galleries on the same street. It could have been a bourgeois suburb in any European city.

When I rang the doorbell of the second-floor apartment, I realized that my heart was starting to beat more quickly once more. A man opened the door; his hair was completely white and he had intense blue eyes. He was wearing black trousers and a black polo-neck sweater. I thought that he was probably about seventy years old.

He looked at me with curiosity for a moment before holding out his hand.

"I am Friedrich von Schumann."

"I am Guillermo Albi, and I am extremely grateful that you agreed to see me."

"I was curious. Come in."

He led me to an office whose walls were covered in books. A set of open sliding doors led onto a library.

"Sit down," he said, pointing to a chair on the other side of the desk. "So you are Amelia's great-grandson. Your grandfather would have been Javier, then?"

"Yes, my maternal grandfather was Javier."

"Well, tell me what you want."

I explained to him that I had spent a long time engaged in investigating Amelia Garayoa's life, and told him who had helped me, the countries I had needed to visit, and the final clue that led me to Berlin.

"And you must be the son of Max von Schumann, my great-grandmother's lover."

"Yes, but please, don't speak about the relationship between Max and Amelia as that of lovers: They were much more than that. Also, Amelia was the only mother I ever really knew. And now you appear and tell me that her cousins Laura and Melita have asked you to write the story of her life... She loved them a great deal, especially Laura. I never met them, but Amelia showed me photographs of them and of her sister Antonietta."

I asked him to help me, because I would find it difficult to continue without his help. Before he gave me an answer, he got up and asked me what I would like to drink. Then he left, and when he came back, he was followed by a woman about his age.

"Ilse, this is Amelia's great-grandson."

The woman held out her hand to me and smiled. She looked friendly, just as one hopes grandmothers will look. She was tall, and in spite of her age, stood upright. Her hair was as white as Friedrich's.

"My wife couldn't resist taking this opportunity to meet you. She knew Amelia and she feels very close to her."

"Oh, she was such a brave woman! I learned so much from her."

"Yes, she must have been brave," I said, anxious to know more.

Ilse left the room and came back with a tray, a bottle of whisky, and an ice-bucket.

"Call me if you need me, and... well, maybe you'd like to have dinner with us..."

"I don't want to be any trouble..."

"You are Amelia's great-grandson, it's as if you were a part of the family, and... I owe Amelia my life," Ilse replied.

I felt euphoric. Not only had I found Friedrich, but he seemed happy to cooperate, and his friendly wife had told me that Amelia had saved her life. So I waited for them to dazzle me.

Friedrich listened carefully as I told him all I had found out about their travels in Egypt.

"I think that was the happiest part of my childhood, and maybe even the happiest part of my life. If it had been down to me, I would have stayed in Cairo and we wouldn't have returned to Germany," he said, as an introduction.

"How old were you?"

"When we came back, I think I was about six."

"So you remember well what happened during that time."

"More or less, although my later memories are much more concrete. My wife Ilse can also tell you about her. She loved her very much. I met Ilse via Amelia, even though we both studied at the university. I was a medical student, I'd always wanted to be a doctor like my father, and Ilse studied physics. But before I tell you anything, I want to have your word that you will use this information carefully. You have told me that you're a journalist and... well, I don't trust journalists all that much, I don't have much confidence in them."

"I'm not surprised, I don't trust them either."

Friedrich von Schumann looked at me in astonishment for a moment and then burst out laughing.

"Right, well at least we have something in common apart from Amelia. Well," and here he turned serious, "although the Wall fell twenty years ago, those of us who grew up with it still feel it here, in our heads. What I'm going to tell you has to do not just with Amelia, but also others, who wouldn't like people to know what they did in the past. And they have the right to their privacy. So I won't tell you their real names, and I don't want any of this to travel outside the family. Don't give in to the temptation of publishing a book about your great-grandmother's life. If you don't promise that in writing, then I won't tell you anything."

I accepted his conditions, and wrote a document whose words he dictated, which I then signed.

"For me, when a man gives his word, it should be guarantee enough, but life has sadly taught me that the code of conduct into which my father brought me up is no longer current."

When I looked at him I imagined him as Max von Schumann. Friedrich had the manners, the bearing, and the elegance that one would expect from an aristocrat. And he was an aristocrat, on both sides of his family, because his mother, Countess Ludovica von Waldheim, had also left her trace on him.

"Of course, you inherited your father's title, you are a baron, is that right?" I asked him out of interest.

"Yes, that's right, I inherited my mother's and my father's titles. I think that I'm the only survivor of both families. But titles mean nothing to me, absolutely nothing, remember that I grew up in a Communist country. It's strange that anyone could call me 'Baron.' No, the title means nothing to me, nothing to me and nothing to my children."

It was almost four o'clock when Friedrich started to tell me what he remembered.

I can still remember the cold when we landed in Berlin. But more than anything else, I remember the controls at the airport. The relations between the Russians and the rest of the Allies were very tense at that time, and even though the Wall was not yet built, there was a psychological wall in place. There were differences between the Berlin that the Soviets controlled and the sections controlled by the other powers. Our house was on the Soviet side, unfortunately, but close to the American zone. In fact, there was an invisible border there. We could see the American sector from our windows; we could almost touch it.

It wasn't the family's best house, but a house that they had owned and had rented out before the war. When we got to our house and tried to open the door the key would not turn in the lock, someone had changed it. Amelia looked for the caretaker to get an explanation, but a neighbor told us that the woman didn't live there anymore, that she had gone to live with her daughter in West Berlin, and that our house had been handed over to another family. The woman told us that the Soviets were taking stock of the apartments and of their owners, and that when they couldn't find the owners they confiscated the apartments and handed them over to the people. You can imagine that in 1948 in Berlin there were many people who had nothing at all, who had lost everything in the bombardments. The Soviet authorities rehoused people whom they judged to be acceptable, members of what would become the Communist Party, in the best possible accommodations. Our apartment was occupied by a man who collaborated with the Soviets in local administration for this part of the city. He lived with his wife and children, who were not at home at that moment. All of our furniture, the neighbor said, not without a certain scorn, had been deposited in the basement, in a small room used by the inhabitants of the building for storage. Before the war, the doorman had kept his tools there, as well as the rubbish bins, the children kept their bicycles there, and it was where people stored old furniture that they had no immediate use for but did not want to throw away. You got down to the basement via some little stairs that were next to a landing that opened the door from the caretaker's apartment, which was not immediately visible to anyone who came in through the door. The caretaker's room was next to the elevator, and was a tiny little cubbyhole, which barely had room for two chairs and a table.

I'm telling you all this because the neighbor told us that she had been informed that if we came back then we were to be allocated the caretaker's apartment. She had the key.

My father said nothing, he never showed any emotion in front of the neighbors, and Amelia acted as if this were the most natural thing in the world as well, as if my father were not the owner of the whole building. We took the key from our neighbor and went into the caretaker's apartment without knowing what we might find.

The apartment was empty, without a single stick of furniture, and no sign of its former occupants. Dust and dirt had built up on the floor and on the windows, which gave onto a little garden that led into the building itself.

My father's face showed his indignation.

"We can't stay here," Max said.

"We have to," Amelia said.

"No, we don't have to. We'll go to the Soviet authorities right now to get them to return to me what is mine. This building belongs to me, it is the only thing still standing that belongs to my family. I own it, I have the title deeds, they can't throw me out of my own property."

"You don't know what the Soviets are like, Max. They won't give it back to you."

"We'll go right now," he insisted, though we were all tired from the journey.

"Maybe we should speak to Albert James, perhaps the Americans can bring some pressure to bear."

"It is my house, Amelia, and they cannot take it away from me. If you won't go with me, then maybe Friedrich will: He's old enough to push a wheelchair."

I looked sadly at Amelia. I didn't like it when they argued, I suffered, and I was scared that they would have a fight, but that didn't happen. Amelia shrugged her shoulders and agreed to go to the Soviet General Staff office.

Nobody appeared to know anything, just that houses that were still standing and contained empty apartments were to be placed at the disposition of all those who could prove that their houses had been destroyed, and who had no place to live. If we had left the apartment unoccupied for more than two years, it was because we did not need to live there, and so there was nothing that we could reclaim. And if we had another apartment in the same building, what was there to complain about? Was it that it didn't seem worthy of us to live in the caretaker's apartment? Did we think that we were better than the caretaker?

My father said that he would file a written complaint, and that he wanted to speak to whoever had the authority to resolve this situation, but his protests were in vain.

Amelia took control of the situation with a degree of resignation that shocked me. When we got home, she sent me to a nearby shop to buy cleaning products. While I went out on this errand, she headed down to the basement to see if our furniture really was there.

The house was small, a single room, a kitchen, a tiny bathroom, and two bedrooms, so she got it cleaned up very quickly. What worried her most was how we were going to get the furniture up from the basement, but she soon had an idea.

"Come out with me into the street, Friedrich, I've seen that there are some children who don't have anything to do hanging around out there. If we give them some coins they'll help us."

We couldn't get everything up from the basement because some of the furniture was very heavy and others wouldn't have fit, so we had to make do with only what was truly necessary. Night had fallen by the time Amelia had finished bringing all the furniture up. My father barely spoke, he was so upset.

"At least we have money to stay here a while," Amelia said.

"We're not staying here," my father said listlessly.

"We'll stay while they sort things out, it won't be too bad. Look, with the house clean and with our furniture in place, then it's like a completely different place. I think we should paint it. I'll do it with Friedrich's help."

"We're going to paint our own house?" I asked, shocked.

"Why not? It will be fun."

My father protested. He said that we would have to keep the windows open and that it would be too cold. But she was not to be swayed. We would feel better with clean walls, painted in bright colors.

I went with her to a warehouse, where we ended up buying wallpaper instead. The man who sold it to us assured us that we wouldn't be able to put it up ourselves, but said that for a small fee he would be able to help us. Amelia accepted, but haggled with him over the price until she had beaten him down.

Three days later the house looked entirely different, even my father had to acknowledge it.

"You see? It was a good idea to paper it instead of painting it, it doesn't smell of paint this way," Amelia said.

And this house became our home, the place where I lived until I married Ilse. I think that the house in some ways was our destiny, because lots of the things that happened to us would not have been possible if we had not lived there.

The Soviets ran Berlin like they ran the rest of Germany that belonged to them, and the breach with the other zones of the city, the ones run by the Americans, the French, or the British, widened day by day. I don't need to remind you about the crisis of 1948. The Americans and the British had created the Bizone in western and southern Germany, putting their occupied territories together, and France joined them, creating the so-called Trizone, to be governed by a constitutional assembly and a federal government. But this did not cause the crisis, rather it was the currency reform, which caused the Soviets great problems and led them to respond by enacting their own currency reform, and in turn led to the Berlin Blockade, which took place between June 1948 and May 1949. The Americans broke through the blockade by running an air bridge. The partition of Germany had begun long before this, at the Yalta Conference, and maybe even before that, at the Tehran Conference, when the Americans, the British, and the Soviets had decided to divide Germany into occupation zones. They had redrawn the map, changed the border with Poland, and all that had previously been central Germany became a part of the Soviet empire, and Berlin was like an island with four administrators, in a sea of territory entirely controlled by the Soviets.

In the same way that the policy of appeasement with Hitler had been a disaster, the Western powers started to do the same with Stalin, allowing him to avoid fulfilling all the promises he had made at Yalta: for example, allowing free peoples to decide how they wished to be governed. Stalin did not allow any such choice. It was a promise he had no intention of keeping.

Some newspapers argued that we had to understand that Stalin wanted "secure" borders, and that this obsession with security was what led him to enact particular policies.

But I don't want to distract you with political discussions. In our small house, it was difficult to avoid hearing long conversations, even some arguments, between Amelia and my father.

Before they cut off communications between our Berlin and the Berlin of the Allies, Albert James used to visit us regularly.

For me, Albert James was like an uncle, who appeared with bags of sweets and English and American toys that made me the envy of my friends.

He would play chess with my father, they would talk about politics and discuss the future.

On one of his visits, Albert said that he had a proposal for us. In fact the proposal was for Amelia.

"We need to have eyes in this part of Berlin."

"Eyes? What for?" Amelia asked.

"We would not have won the war without the help of the Soviets, but we mustn't ignore the fact that we have different interests. Churchill has said that the Soviets are pulling shut an Iron Curtain across the zones of their influence, and he is right. We need to know what's going on."

"So now the Russians are going to be your enemies." My father's voice was full of irony.

"We have opposing interests. They could be a danger for us all... but we've talked about this before."

"What do you want, Albert?" Max asked directly.

"I want you to work for American intelligence, the group we have here, I want you to join us."

"No, all that's over," he said bluntly.

"I'd like you to think it over, at least."

"No, there's nothing to think about," Max said.

"What would we have to do?" Amelia said, without looking at Max.

"I'll tell you that if you accept my proposal, and our British friends will not mind if you work for us, Amelia."

"I don't belong to the British," Amelia said, angrily.

"I know, but they think that you are still their agent, even though you worked for us in Cairo. In any case, we have very good relations, we're all in the same boat."

When Albert had left, Amelia and my father had an argument.

"You like danger, don't you? You can't live like a normal person, you just have to walk along the edge of the abyss. In Cairo you told me that you were done with this kind of work."

"We have to be realists, Max. What are we going to live on when the money from Cairo runs out?"

Max spent several days barely talking to Amelia. He only spoke to her in my presence and I suffered to see them suffer.

I think that it was in May, before the Soviets cut off communications with occupied German territories entirely, that Albert James came back to visit us.

Max greeted him coldly and claimed to have a headache in order to get out of the game of chess, but Amelia had made a decision.

"I will work for you, but only under a number of conditions. I will not be an American agent; I will not be anyone's agent. I will collaborate as much as I can, but I won't feel obliged to do so if what you ask me is beyond my capacities or puts Max or Friedrich in danger. Also, a part of my salary will be sent to my family in Madrid. They don't need to know where I am, or what I'm doing, but every now and then someone should go to my uncle and aunt's house and give them an envelope with some money."

"Why don't you want them to know where you are?" Albert James wanted to know.

"Because I would only cause them pain and worry. No, I want to help them without causing them any more suffering. There is a third condition: If, for whatever cause, I decide to abandon this work, you have to allow me to do so without reproaches or problems."

Albert accepted Amelia's conditions. Max said nothing: Once again, he felt like he had been defeated.

A few days later, Amelia started to work as the assistant to a local functionary. Garin spoke Russian and had been able to show that he had been opposed to Hitler, and that he had been in the Socialist Party before the war, as well as having been a prisoner in a camp. This made him acceptable to the Soviets, who mistrusted all Germans, and not without good reason. The fact that Amelia could get by in Russian made it easier for Garin to convince his superiors that he needed someone who could help him. Amelia also introduced us to a new friend of hers, Iris, who worked as a typist in the municipal office.

Garin had studied Russian literature before the war; he was dark-haired and tall, with dark eyes and a large moustache, and above all he was very friendly, he liked to laugh and eat and drink. Iris was blonde, with blue eyes, of a medium height and very thin.

As opposed to Garin, she was always serious and preoccupied. She had been in a relationship with a young exiled Russian who had disappeared at the beginning of the war without saying goodbye. She was ironic about this, and said that at least the relationship had allowed her to learn a language.

At this time, neither of the two of them was in any key position, but they were a part of the army of "eyes" that Albert had established in East Berlin.

Amelia was happy with her new job, or at least this is what I thought. Apparently, Garin was in charge of a department that dealt with cultural activities in Berlin. In fact, there was neither money nor time available for such activities; Garin's anti-fascist past meant that they trusted him.

It was hard for Max to accept the new reality, but he ended up surrendering to the evidence he was offered, and I remember that I was impressed by a conversation I had heard one night when they thought I was asleep.

"My life is already destroyed, but I will not allow you to put my son in danger. If anything happens to Friedrich because of you... I swear that I will kill you myself."

I cried to myself in silence. I adored my father, but I adored Amelia as well.

Albert carried on visiting us, but not as often as before. Officially, he was a journalist who worked for an American press agency, and this was his justification for his comings and goings in Berlin.

In October 1949, the German Democratic Republic came into being. We had our official government, but we belonged to the Soviets. A few days after the new government came into being, Amelia came back home in a highly excited state. They were going to transfer Garin to the Ministry of Culture. Iris was going to work in the Foreign Ministry, for a civil servant who worked for a department linked to the Soviet Foreign Ministry.

In fact, the GDR was governed from the Soviet Embassy in Berlin.

To begin with, my father refused to allow Grin and Iris to come to our house, he didn't want to know them, but Amelia insisted so much that he eventually gave in.

One day Garin came with flowers for Amelia and a book for my father, and Iris brought a cake that she had made herself.

My father got on well with Garin; it was impossible for anyone not to do so, because he radiated vitality and was a very positive person, as people say nowadays. Iris was more discreet, less talkative, but she seemed to get on with Amelia.

"Is it worth it for you to risk your lives?" my father asked them.

"I think it is, we can't just sit on the fence and watch what they're doing to our country. The Soviets treat us like we belong to them."

"The people responsible for this are the Allies, they handed us over to the Russians, and now... now they want us to defend their interests against the Russians," Max complained.

"Yes, you're right, politicians are capable of these things, but we can't let the Russians turn our country into their backyard, Max. Don't you see that we're their servants now? We don't have any autonomy, we don't do anything that Moscow doesn't order us to do. No, we didn't want to get rid of the Third Reich for this," Garin replied.

"And you, Iris, why do you do it? Why do you work for the Americans?"

Garin made a sign to my father to stop talking, but it was too late. Iris grew very tense. She turned pale and then her face grew red, a sign of the rage she was trying to hold back.

"My father was a conservative, he never liked Hitler, but then again he never stood up to him. But who did? We lived well until the war began. My parents died in a bombardment, and they killed my brother in Stalingrad. He didn't want to go to war, he didn't want to fight for the Reich, but they took him. It was only my little sister and I who survived. I remember that my father said that if we ever got rid of Hitler then we would have to deal with the Russians, and he regretted that the British didn't realize that the true enemies were the Soviets. But that is not why I work for the Americans. I had a fiancé, he was Russian, his parents were exiles in Germany after the October Revolution. He grew up in Berlin. In spite of his parents' opinions, he gravitated toward the Communists during his years at the university; he sympathized with them and said that we would go to visit Mother Russia one day. A little while before the war broke out he disappeared. I went crazy looking for him, no one knew where he was, not his parents, not his friends... nobody. I suspected that he had decided to go back to Russia, and had told no one, neither me nor his parents, because he didn't want them to try to stop him. When my parents died I took charge of my sister, we had only each other. She was so terrified every time we heard the bombs over Berlin that she had convulsions. When the Russians entered the city... some people received them as liberators, but they were our torturers. The day they arrived there was a great deal of confusion, no one knew what to do, whether they should hide or not. We were in the street looking for food when we saw the first tanks and groups of Russian soldiers approaching. We ran to hide in the rubble of a bombed-out building. Some soldiers saw us and ran after us, laughing. One of them grabbed hold of my sister and threw her to the floor. He raped her right there, and then came another one, and another. I... well, the same thing happened to me, I don't know if it was two or three soldiers who raped me, because I shut my eyes, I didn't want to see what was happening to me, I didn't want to see my little sister thrashing around and begging for mercy. They laughed the entire time. Suddenly an officer arrived. He told them to stop and called them beasts, monsters. He tried to help my sister to stand up, but she was so scared that she started to shout, and then he came to me and I could see the shame in his eyes that his men had done this, but he didn't ask for forgiveness, he just turned away and left. The soldiers said that they were just doing to us what the Germans had done to their mothers and their sisters, and that we were lucky they had let us live. My sister was stretched out in a pool of blood, her own blood. She was only twelve years old. I held her tight to calm her down, but she didn't seem to hear me, she cried and looked into the void. When I tried to get her to stand up she couldn't move. We sat on the ground for a long time until I managed to get her to stand up and made her walk. We tried to get home, but there were tanks and soldiers everywhere and my sister trembled with fear. Suddenly some soldiers saw us and came toward us. My sister shrieked in terror. I don't know where she got the strength from, but she ran away without looking at anything in front of her. She slipped and... fell in front of a tank, which ran her over. She shrieked, she shrieked like a wild animal. The soldiers ran toward her, but it was useless, the tank had destroyed her, she was just a bloody scrap of meat. The soldiers seemed shocked, but my sister was dead. Does anyone know how many German women were raped? I was lucky because I survived. And now I have a little boy. His father is one of the soldiers who raped me. When I look at my son and see features that are not my own, then I know that they come from his father. The dark hair, the grey eyes, the wide forehead, the fleshy mouth... When I found out I was pregnant I wanted to die. I didn't want to have the child, I hated him. But he was born, and now... now I love him with all my soul, he's all I've got. He's two years old and his name is Walter."

We were all silent. I was very young, but I understood the drama of the moment. Amelia had not been able to stop herself from crying, Garin looked at the floor, and my father felt guilty for having provoked Iris into this confession.

"I didn't know you had suffered so much," Amelia murmured, taking hold of Iris's hand.

"Well, I don't normally tell anyone about it. I don't want Walter to grow up with the shame of not knowing who his father is."

"And what will you tell him when he grows up?" Amelia wanted to know.

"That his father was a good man who died in the war."

"Will you tell him... Will you tell him he was Russian?"

"No, why? Russian or German, he doesn't have a father, so it's better for him to grow up without asking questions for which there is no answer."

From that night on, Garin and Iris were welcome at our house. Amelia always insisted that Iris bring Walter with her, and although he was much younger than I was, we would play in my room while the grown-ups talked.

Albert asked Garin to join the Party, in the end, due to Soviet pressure, the Socialist Party had merged with the Communist Party. As Garin still had some Communist friends from university, he found supporters for his new activism without arousing any suspicion. He was a foot soldier, an unimportant party member, but Albert knew that Garin could win the confidence of the party hierarchy.

Once I heard Albert talking with Amelia about Garin.

"What do you think of him?" he asked.

"He's brave and clever, he's got authority in the group and we all listen to him and follow his lead in a very natural way."

"You know, sometimes I wonder why he's with us."

"He doesn't like the Soviets being here."

"Yes, but is that reason enough? He was a Socialist, he had Communist friends, he was a prisoner in a camp, and now, all of a sudden, he's anti-Communist, is that it?"

"You got hold of him for the network, if you didn't trust him, then why did you do it?"

"There's something... something, but I don't know what it is, it's just that every now and then I don't trust Garin."

"Do you think he's working for the Soviets?"

"Perhaps as a spy... You know, the Soviets prepare them for these activities."

"But he's giving you all the information that comes through his hands."

"Well, there's not been anything important until now, your group is not the most important one we're running here."

"And why do you make me work with them?"

"Because I want you to keep an eye on Garin."

"But if he works for the Soviets then you're exposing Max and Friedrich to great danger... ," Amelia complained.

"If my suspicions are ever confirmed then I'll get you out of here, you'll come with me to the other side."

"If you were right about Garin, then they wouldn't let us leave."

"We don't need to ask permission from the Soviets. You know that people are always coming over to our side and there's nothing they can do to stop it."

"And what about Otto and Konrad?" Amelia asked.

"I trust those two absolutely. I won't say why, but I know that they are loyal to us."

Otto was a translator for the Soviet military administration, and Konrad was a prestigious physics professor. They had both fought in the Spanish war. When it was over, Otto went to Paris, where he lived through the start of the next war. He didn't want to go back to Germany, and fought with the Allies who were opposed to Hitler. Konrad had stood out at his university for his confrontations with Nazi teachers. If they did not arrest him it was because his experiments interested Hitler, who ordered that he work in a laboratory alongside other scientists, although his passive attitude had been the despair of his superiors from the moment he arrived; they could not get more than the most basic contributions from him throughout the whole length of the war. But for neither Otto nor Konrad was the fact of being anti-fascists enough for them to be happy to see their country in the hands of the Soviets, and so, with the same conviction that they had possessed fighting the Nazis, they now fought the invaders.

Albert asked Otto, just as he had asked Garin, to join the Communist Party. No one suspected him, and he was made welcome.

The members of the group took microfilms of everything that came through their hands, whether or not it was important. Then they brought the microfilms to Amelia, and she in her turn gave them to Albert.

I still missed Cairo, although I never told my father so as not to annoy him. He wanted me to be a good German, even though it was the Communists who were responsible for my education.

"They are Communists, yes, but before that they are Germans," he said, "and they know what they have to teach you."

My father was wrong. The party members were Communists first and foremost, with everything else a distant second, including the fact of their being German, but he did not see it that way. He had made the idea of Germany into something sublime, and he thought it was important for me to be brought up as a good German.

Life was rather monotonous for me and for my father, but not for Amelia. At night, after sending me to bed, she would sit with my father and talk about the day's events. I listened to them talking, not because I was spying on them, but because I never managed to get to sleep before midnight, so I read until Amelia came in to turn out my light, and then I stayed awake thinking of fantastic stories.

I think this was at the beginning of 1950. One afternoon Amelia came back from work, she seemed very upset, and she sent me to bed earlier than usual. As soon as she was alone with my father, she told him what was on her mind.

"Iris will come round tonight, she called to tell me that we need to see each other. I don't know what's going on."

"I hope they haven't found her out," Max said, worried.

"If she thought that they might have then she wouldn't come here. No, it's not that, don't worry."

Iris arrived sometime after eight o'clock. She had Walter in her arms. The baby was half asleep.

"I wasn't able to come before," she apologized.

"Don't worry, have you eaten?" Amelia asked.

"I've fed Walter, and I'm not hungry."

"Leave Walter in our room," Amelia said, and went with her to get the child comfortable, so that he could sleep while we talked.

"I think that the Soviets are going to sign an agreement with the Chinese," Iris said.

"Are you sure?" Amelia seemed worried.

"Yes, I think so. One of the secretaries at the ministry was ill a few days ago, and they sent me along to give her a hand. This morning I heard the minister ask one of the girls in the typing pool to call our embassy in Moscow; he wanted information, and spoke about the 'Chinese visit,' and then said that the Soviets were behaving in a very mysterious way about the agreement they were going to sign with Mao Tse-tung. They don't know me because it was my first day there, but he didn't even look at me when he came out of his office to give the order. I carried on writing what I was being asked to write, and didn't even raise my head, as if I hadn't heard anything."

"I'll get in touch with Albert. I'll try to go to the American zone tomorrow."

"You have a pass, right?"

"Yes."

"Well, it doesn't seem strange that the Soviets would come to an agreement with the Chinese, they're all Communists," Max said.

"Yes, but what are they waiting for in Moscow? And if they sign a treaty, what will it say? It seems important to me, and I think we have to tell Albert in any case," Iris said, looking at Amelia.

On February 14 Stalin and Mao signed a Treaty of Friendship, Alliance, and Mutual Assistance in the case of aggression by any other power.

Iris's character led the bureaucrats in the ministry to pay attention to her. She worked without ceasing, she was efficient, silent, and discreet, the kind of secretary that everyone would like to have. These qualities made her open for promotion and she was passed to the department that dealt with the "other" Germany.

Otto had, in the meantime, started to work as an assistant to a member of the Politburo. The fact that he spoke Russian, as well as French and a little Spanish, had helped him to get a post.

Every now and then he wrote reports on topics that were bothering the Politburo, the power struggles between its members and the arguments that had taken place in the Central Committee.

As for Konrad, he was the indisputable leader of all the university malcontents.

Garin had also prospered, and Amelia along with him. They now worked in the Department of Propaganda at the Ministry of Culture, where they seemed to be as happy as fish in water.

Amelia kept a close eye on him, and would tell Albert that she could find nothing to concern her in Garin's behavior. If there was one thing she could reproach him for, it was taking too many risks, and sometimes he stayed working until most of the civil servants had left, when he could take advantage of their absence to get into other offices and take microfilm pictures of everything he found.

"He enjoys the risk. Sometimes I get angry with him and worry that we'll be discovered. It was about to happen the other night. We had stayed working in the department, and when we thought that there was no one else there, we tried to force the director's office door. We made so much noise that the night watchmen came. He told them that we had dropped a typewriter on the floor and that we were trying to repair it. They believed him, or at least I hope they did," Amelia said.

Although my father didn't like them holding meetings in our house, sometimes he permitted it. For me it was a welcome break in the monotony of daily life when Amelia's "friends," as my father called them, came round.

Garin was still my favorite, as neither Otto nor Konrad paid me much attention. I was just a little kid whom they preferred not to have around.

"We are 'planning culture.' They're crazy! As if it were possible to plan talent, or inspiration, or imagination," Konrad complained.

"Our department is trying to make sure that the whole of society soaks up 'the truth,' in order to achieve a new Socialist man.

This is a truth that is to be found in Marx and Engels, Lenin and Stalin," Garin said ironically.

"The only thing they really want is control, of everything including our thoughts," Konrad carried on.

"The role of the press is terrible," Otto added. "Isn't there a single journalist who can criticize what is happening here?"

"The ones who could have are already gone, and if anyone's left, then the authorities makes him see the error of his ways. People who criticize the party or its leaders are delinquents who are trying to destroy the triumph of Socialism," Amelia said, indignant.

But what scared her most of all was seeing how the Social Democrats were treated as enemies of the people. They were being removed, step by step, from any public role; many of them decided on exile, and others, the ones who did not want to give in, ended up in prison, or in labor camps.

"They want to impose one single variety of thought, one single ideology, so for them the Social Democrats are the most dangerous of all, because they dispute the Communist hegemony," Konrad complained.

"You have to be careful," Amelia said, "or you'll end up getting arrested."

"What I don't know is how you managed to gain their trust," Otto said to Garin. "You were a Social Democrat, weren't you?"

"Yes, but I have renounced my past. They accepted me in the SED, and now I'm a member of the party, I'm even going to the Third Congress in July," Garin said.

"I don't know how you can do it without your flesh crawling," Konrad insisted.

"We have a job to do. It's precisely because I don't deny my own ideology that I do what I do. I am copying their own infiltration methods; it's easier to fight them from the inside than from the outside," Garin said.

"I think that our President Wilhelm Pieck isn't like Walter Ulbricht or Otto Grotewohl," Iris said.

"You really think he's different? No, don't fool yourself, he's as Communist as the rest of them, only with a friendlier face," Amelia said.

In 1950 the most efficient secret service of all those involved in the Cold War, that of the German Democratic Republic, came into being. If controls over the population had seemed up until that moment to be exhaustive, from now on it was impossible for anyone not to feel that they were being spied on by the Stasi. No one trusted anybody. From this moment on, now that they existed, we all lived in fear. The Stasi had informants everywhere, even within people's families. They inaugurated a reign of terror that led people to inform on their own families and neighbors merely to shift suspicion away from themselves. Other people, of course, collaborated out of a sense of ideological conviction.

Albert James wanted one of his agents to infiltrate the Stasi, which at that time was known as the Prime Intelligence Directorate, but it was useless to attempt such a thing: The selection process was extremely rigorous.

In 1953 the protests against the new regime began. Obligatory "Socialization" crashed up against the desires of the majority of East Germans.

One night, Iris came to our house. It was late, and you could see that she had come running because her face was red and she was panting.

"They've arrested Konrad. His wife sent one of their sons over to my house to tell me. We have to do something."

Amelia tried to calm her. Then she told Max that she was going out with Iris to look for Garin. They had to do something to help Konrad.

"The only thing that will happen is that they'll arrest you too. What are you going to do? Turn up at the police station and ask for him to be set free?" Max asked, worried.

"The only thing we cannot do is sit and wait," Amelia replied.

The new regime was losing control of the situation. They couldn't stop the discontent, or the demonstrations and the strikes. Some party buildings, as well as the cars of party functionaries, were the object of the demonstrators' anger. The Soviets needed to intervene because the government was not capable of controlling the explosion of anger among its citizens, and they declared a state of emergency in Berlin.

The party hierarchy must have been scared, or else they were urged on by the Soviets, and on June 21 the Central Committee decided to instigate a program of improvements, but they didn't manage to prevent a new wave of Germans from leaving for the Federal Republic for good.

Amelia suggested to my father that we do so as well.

"I think that we should go, with every day that passes this is more like the Soviet Union."

"And where would we go? To the American zone? No, at least we have a house here, Amelia."

"We don't have anything, Max. This house does not belong to you anymore."

"Of course it does. The Constitution acknowledges private property."

"But the party acts in the name of the people, and decides what the people needs, that is, what each person is going to get. We are living in the caretaker's apartment, Max, and I don't care about that, we've turned it into a home, but don't let that fool you."

We still have time to change our minds, Berlin is not a closed city, we can move to another zone whenever we want."

"It will not always be like that, they can't let people keep on leaving. One day they'll do what their bosses the Soviets want them to do, and they will stop us from leaving."

"How ridiculous!"

"Max, I can talk to Albert, he'll help us, maybe we could be useful to him somewhere else."

"This building is the only inheritance I can leave to my son. They will not take it away from me while I'm here."

"They've taken your land, they've 'socialized' it, as they say... Max, don't you realize that this isn't yours either?"

But she could not convince my father. I listened in silence and was secretly in agreement with Amelia. I could not stand the indoctrination they were forcing me to submit to in the school.

I don't think it was that different from what children received under Hitler, except the uniforms and the insignia and the songs had changed.

Konrad spent six months in prison. He was such a prestigious figure at the university that even some committed Communist teachers stood up for him, not because they supported him, but because they realized that the damage he did to them by being in prison was greater than what he did out of prison. Konrad's students and many others would not stop calling for his release and that of the other teachers who had been arrested. I can still remember how excited Amelia was the day Konrad was released. Garin had asked us not to go and wait for him, because the Stasi would take note of everyone who did so. Amelia wasn't going to listen to him, but my father convinced her not to put herself in danger.

"It's a useless gesture, Amelia. One second and then you're on a list forever, so how are you going to carry on working for Albert? Garin is right. You must be discreet. Konrad won't want you to show yourselves, he knows what's at stake."

Amelia accepted this, reluctantly. She knew that Garin and my father were right. We stopped seeing Konrad. He was under observation, and every house he went to would become a target for the Stasi, so the group went under cover and started to meet in secret.

One day Amelia came home crying and handed my father an article from a newspaper. He read it and shrugged his shoulders.

"Do you know what it means?" Amelia said.

"Life goes on, that's what it means."

Amelia got in touch with Albert and asked him to come to see her urgently. Albert came to see us the next day and as soon as he arrived Amelia sent me to my room. I complained. I was sick of being sent to my room every time someone interesting turned up. Also, I wanted to tell them that it was useless for them to send me out, as I could still hear everything that they said. But I preferred not to, in case they ended up thinking of a plan that would stop me from hearing things for good.

"It's over, Albert, I'm pulling out."

He was surprised. He saw the emotion in Amelia's eyes and didn't understand why.

"What's going on? Tell me."

"No, I'm not the one who has to explain things to you. You have to explain things to me, to tell me how it is possible for Nazis to be given important public posts in the Federal Republic."

"What are you saying, Amelia! Don't tell me that you're falling for the propaganda too!"

"No, I don't believe Soviet propaganda. I believe what I read in the *Daily Express*." She held out the newspaper cutting, and Albert cast his eyes over it.

"It's an isolated case," he said, uncomfortably.

"Really? Do you think that I'm going to believe you? General Reinhard Gehlen, chief of German intelligence. The very distinguished general who was in charge of spying on the Red Army during the Third Reich, and now he's working for Adenauer."

"You think I like it? But we would be mad to reject the people who have information, useful information that we need. You knew Canaris, he wasn't a fanatic, many of his agents weren't fanatics either. Remember Colonel Oster. They executed him."

"Please, Albert! Are you going to tell me that just because Canaris and Oster conspired against Hitler that none of their agents were Nazis? From what I can see, anything goes: In exchange for a little information you can erase an individual's past. So what was the point of the Nuremberg trials? Just so you could tell the world that you had punished the bad guys while you were doing deals with them on the side? Is this why I risked my life In Warsaw, in Athens, in Cairo, here in Berlin? So that you can tell me that there are Nazis whom I have to understand, whom I have to learn to get along with?"

"That's enough, Amelia, don't be a child! The Nuremberg trials were enough to show the world the horrors of Nazism, to say that we would never let anything like this happen again, to show the wickedness of National Socialism."

"And once you've had your catharsis, turn the page and everything's back to square one. Is that what you're telling me?"

"You were in this business before I was, and you know that there's nothing innocent about it. You know that all too well. The German intelligence service was very efficient."

"And what does that mean?"

"That there is going to be another war now, a war without tanks, or planes, or bombs, but a war all the same. The relationship we have with the Soviets is getting more difficult by the day. They are building themselves an empire. Don't you know that that's what's happening? They have been installing Communist governments in all the countries that they had under their influence. In all of them. And they have put Communists in charge, Communist puppets who obey Stalin without complaint. Churchill has spoken of the Iron Curtain. The Soviets are now our adversaries, we need to be careful with them, to know what they're doing, what they want to do, what steps they're going to take."

"And you can use former Nazi spies for this. The end justifies the means. Is that what you are telling me?"

"You tell me, Amelia. Tell me if the end justifies the means. You are a field agent, you've had to take decisions on the go."

"Never in favor of the Nazis, they were our enemies, we fought to topple them. You have to get rid of all Nazis, wherever they are, wherever they are hidden."

"Do you really think we can do that? To put the whole of Germany on trial and get rid of everyone who cannot prove conclusively that they were fighting against Hitler? It would be crazy, and wouldn't lead anywhere. Do you think that the Soviets aren't striking deals with former members of the German intelligence service? Do you think the Soviets ignore the information they can offer simply because they didn't fight against Hitler? You didn't care when we captured Fritz Winkler, and you shot his son without a flicker of hesitation. Is a Nazi scientist different from a secret agent? Tell me, where's the difference? Tell me and I'll understand all your scruples."

"Albert is right." Max had been listening to them from his wheelchair.

He didn't normally intervene when Albert and Amelia met up, he would give his opinions later, when the two of them were alone, but on this occasion he did so.

"How can you say that after what we've suffered!" Amelia said.

"If we carried your argument through to its logical conclusion, what would you have to do with me? I was an officer in the Wehrmacht, I swore loyalty to the Führer even though I hated him with all my soul. I fought, I was at the front, I did what I could to win us the war. I wanted to see Hitler defeated, but without seeing Germany defeated. I wanted to defeat him politically, or even kill him, but I never betrayed my country. I don't know how many other Germans thought the same as I did, but I know that those of us who stayed, who didn't leave the country, don't have alibis for having acted as we did. We could all be accused of having participated in the horrors of Nazism. Me too, Amelia, me too."

When I heard my father's voice, I opened the door a crack and stuck my head out to see what was happening. Amelia was looking at Max and could not find words to rebut his arguments. Albert was looking at them booth and fighting against his desire to intervene.

A little while went by before Albert decided to speak.

"There will be more, Amelia, more hateful names that make your guts turn over when you read about the jobs they've been given."

"That's why you supported the Christian Democrats. The Social Democrats would never have let something like this happen."

"Are you sure? I don't know, but you're right, it is a relief to know that West Germany is in the hands of the Christian Democrats. Adenauer is a great man."

"If even you think so…"

"Yes, I believe it."

"Here they put the Social Democrats in prison."

"I know."

"So you have to know that I will not carry on working for you, that I will not risk my life for the information that I obtain to end up on some Nazi's desk."

"You work for us, not for the West German government."

"Yes, but the West German government is your ally, you help them and support them, as if there were no other way of doing things, and I myself understand that it has to be like that. And so it might be the case that the information I gather will be shared with them, lots of this information will have to do with plans connected to the Federal Republic. And... you know what, Albert? You're right. Yes, I have killed people, I have done terrible things in my life, but I will not do this. Albert, I will not do it, not for anything in the world."

"I respect your decision."

When Albert left, Max asked Amelia if she was really going to stop working for the Americans. Amelia said nothing, she only started to cry.

It would not be Amelia's only disappointment. The secretary of state in the Chancellor's office, Hans Globke, had been an official in the Interior Ministry during the Third Reich, and it was known that he had been an enthusiastic supporter of the Final Solution, the plan to exterminate all the Jews in Germany and in the countries the Nazis had occupied.

If Amelia had any trace of innocence left, she now lost it for good. She was also inflexible about no longer working for the Americans. She met Albert again to tell him that he could no longer count on her collaboration. He tried to make her change her mind, but it was useless; Amelia might have had many defects, but she was not a cynic.

After deciding on her course of action, Amelia told Garin to find a replacement for her. She said that her position should be covered by someone from an opposition group ready to work with the Americans. But Garin asked her only to think a little more and to take a few days off work. He would tell them that she was ill.

But Amelia did not go back to work, even though Garin and Iris and Otto and Konrad all tried to make her change her mind.

It was difficult to understand that a woman who had been willing to kill had been so affected by the idea that a few former members of the Nazi Party were working in West Germany for the Adenauer government.

Garin came to her house one day. He was worried.

"They are going to investigate you," he said.

"Why?" Amelia said indifferently.

"You have left your job and you don't seem willing to take another one... Some people are saying that you're not right in the head. You have to do something, or they'll send you to a hospital until you recover."

"A hospital? But I'm not ill." There was a note of fear in Amelia's voice.

"If you are not physically ill and you reject the chance to work, then it is because you are not right in the head. Let me help you, Amelia. Come back to work, please."

"I will tell them that Max is ill and that I cannot leave him. We don't have anyone to look after him, so I had to leave my work because of that."

"They could say that Max is a burden on you, that he should go and live in a hospital. There are no excuses, Amelia, don't fool yourself."

"I don't want to go back to work for Albert."

"I'm not telling you to work for him, but you do need to work. I can help you. Your job has not yet been covered by anyone else, but they have told me that they will send someone tomorrow. Please come back, Amelia, or you will trigger huge problems for this family. If they take you or if they take Max..."

"I don't want to work for the Americans ever again, or for the British."

"You won't have to, I'm not asking you to do that. I am going now, I'm going to Iris's house, but I will see you tomorrow."

My father and Amelia were speaking all through the night. I slept, but I woke with a start and they were still talking out in the room. I couldn't hear what they were saying, they were talking very low, as if they were afraid of their words passing through the silence of the night.

Amelia took me to school as she did every day. We were quiet and I only dared break the silence when we reached the school building.

"You're going to go to work, aren't you? You won't let them take you or my father."

She gave me a hug and tried to stem the tears that flowed from her eyes.

"My God, you're frightened! Don't worry, Friedrich, nothing's going to happen. Of course I won't let them take me, and I definitely won't let them do anything to your father! How could I!"

"So promise me that you're going to work," I begged.

She paused for a couple of seconds and then kissed me and whispered in my ear: "I promise."

I went into the school with more confidence. I trusted her.

2

Amelia didn't work with the British or the Americans for five or six years. She was still friendly with the members of her former group, but she didn't see them as often as before, although they came to our house to have dinner on a few occasions; they didn't speak about their work, just about politics and daily life.

Garin was her guardian angel. He had stood up for her and he kept her at his side, but he never asked her to help in his spy work.

In those years, from the mid-fifties into the sixties, Amelia lost a great part of her happiness. She woke up at six thirty every morning, made breakfast, cleaned the house, got Max out of bed, helped him to tidy himself up, and then we went out together: She took me to school and then she went to the Culture Ministry. She came back home at midday just in time to make my father eat something, and then she went back to work until six.

Her life was now running according to a routine, and this was a cause of unhappiness to her. For many years she had lived on the edge of the abyss and she had now lost the excitement that this brought.

My father was happy. He was no longer worried about what might happen to Amelia, and by extension to us. He preferred monotony, he preferred to grow old without anything more disagreeable than having to put up with the shortages that affected all East Germans, although now that Otto worked for the Politburo he would sometimes bring us produce that was not within our normal budget: Western items that were permitted only to the members of the Politburo.

As was the case in the Soviet Union, the *nomenklatura* of the Democratic Republic were given privileges that the rest of the citizenry were not allowed. Garin was extremely efficient when it came to getting hold of these products, which he generously spread out among his friends.

As I grew older, I grew to admire Amelia's solicitude for my father. She looked after him as if he were her most precious possession. I thought that she must love him very much for deciding to share her life with him when she could have a better one elsewhere.

Amelia passed the age of forty, but she was still so delicate that she looked younger. She had no gray hairs and was very thin. When we went out walking I saw how people looked at her, she was very attractive and I think that Garin was secretly in love with her. Even Konrad, who was married with two children, looked at her out of the corner of his eye when he thought she was not looking.

Amelia seemed unaware of the effect she had on other people, and this distance only served to increase her attraction. I felt proud that a woman like this could love my father.

I remember that in 1960 we all gathered to celebrate my entrance into Humboldt University in East Berlin. Konrad tried to convince me to be a physicist, so that I would have a great career, but I had decided to be a doctor, as my father had been before me.

"I will take care of him, even if he is not a student of mine," Konrad promised my father.

"Try to make sure he doesn't get into trouble like you," Amelia asked.

For the young students at the university, every day made clear the difference between West and East Berlin. Thousands of Berliners went to work in West Berlin every day; the Allies were transforming it into a shop-window of capitalist propaganda. Try to imagine the frustration, or rather the schizophrenia, inherent in living between two worlds, with two different currencies.

For the Democratic Republic, West Berlin was more than a shop-window, it was a military base where more than twelve thousand soldiers were stationed, American, British, and French.

And the East Germans did not like having these soldiers right at their front door.

Ulbricht's official policy was to propose the unification of Germany: In fact what he wanted was a federation with no foreign troops. In this way, he could seem like a man of peace who was making peaceful proposals that were not accepted because of Western imperialist intransigence. Pure propaganda, of course. His idea of reunification would be to incorporate the Federal Republic into the same collectivist system that the Democratic Republic was living under.

But he was aware of the constant bleeding away of brainpower and resources inherent in the continued emigration of many Germans from the Democratic Republic.

I will never forget the night of August 13, 1961. I was studying in my room when a noise made me look up and I saw a group of soldiers and Communist Party militants stretching out a roll of barbed wire. Our house, apparently, was on the "border" with West Germany.

"Papa! Amelia! Look out of the window!"

The three of us stretched and peered through the window as the soldiers carried on unrolling the barbed wire.

"The border," Amelia murmured.

"What border?" I asked, unable to believe that Berlin was not a single city.

"Churchill spoke of the Iron Curtain... Well, here you are, the curtain is being drawn across Berlin as well," she replied.

"But it's ridiculous. What are they going to do with this barbed-wire fence? The only thing they're going to do is make it difficult for us to get from one side of the city to the other, and there are thousands of Berliners who cross into the other side of the city every day," I said.

Amelia stroked my face affectionately, as if I were still a little child who could not understand what was happening.

My father was silent, with a look in his eyes that one often saw, a lost gaze, and his face twisted into a tense expression.

"We should go, it might still be possible," Amelia said.

"No, I'm not going, but I won't stop you," my father answered, visibly upset.

She didn't say anything. What could she say? He knew that we would never abandon him, whatever happened. But Amelia was right, we should go. What sense would our life make here? I never understood my father's insistence on our remaining in East Berlin. Sometimes I thought that he needed to punish himself for having been a member of the Wehrmacht and having sworn loyalty to Hitler.

The next day, Garin explained to Amelia that he had been told that the barbed-wire fence was merely the first step.

"They want to build a wall more than three meters high."

"But what help will that bring them? People are going to have to carry on going to work on the other side."

"It will mean the definitive partition of Germany. I think that they are going to make a proclamation that there is only one legitimate Germany, our own. And maybe they'll restrict the freedom of movement to West Berlin. We'll see."

Garin was right. Getting through to the West became a nightmare. You needed a permission document and to explain why you were going. It was easier to enter our side of Berlin, because the visitors had no intention of staying forever.

From our window we could see how the barbed-wire fence was followed by the construction of a concrete wall that was around three meters tall, and extended, we found out, for fifty-five kilometers. Now the only view from our windows was that block of concrete, patrolled day and night by soldiers. There was only a meter between our little garden and the fortifications: First came the barbed-wire fence, and then, the Wall. I felt like I was living in a prison, I felt suffocated, as did Amelia, but my father accepted it all without complaining.

"They can't cope with the constant exodus of people, it was putting the economy under immense pressure," he said in justification.

It was in the autumn of 1961 that Amelia met Ivan Vasiliev again. We went out like we did every morning and walked a while before going our separate ways, she toward the ministry, and me to the university. We spoke Arabic as we walked. We liked to do it when we were alone. Amelia said that she spoke it so as not to forget. Maybe it was instinct, maybe the man's insistent gaze, but Amelia suddenly slowed down.

"Amelia, Amelia Garayoa," we heard someone say behind our backs.

A man who must have been about sixty had said Amelia's name. She looked straight at him, trying to find in her memory the name that fit this face.

"Ivan Vasiliev," the man said in Russian, holding out his hand. "Do you remember Moscow? I worked with Pierre Comte."

"My God!" she exclaimed.

"Yes, it's a real surprise to see you here."

"What are you doing here?"

"Well, that's what I was thinking when I saw you, what are you doing in Berlin?"

"I live here with my family."

"Your family? Well, it's natural that you would have put your life back together after Pierre died."

"That's right. Are you still... ? Well... Are you still working in the same place?"

"You want to know if I'm in the KGB? That's a question you shouldn't ask me and I shouldn't answer. Who is this young man?"

"My son. Friedrich, allow me to introduce Ivan Vasiliev..."

The man looked me up and down, in a way that made me feel uncomfortable. He was taller than me, and stronger, and though he was wearing a suit, he seemed to have a military bearing.

"If you have time, maybe I could invite you for a coffee," Ivan Vasiliev suggested.

"I'm sorry, Friedrich has to get to class and I need to be at work in fifteen minutes."

"Where do you work?"

"In one of the departments of the Ministry of Culture."

"Maybe I could walk with you and we could talk about old times."

I was going to take my leave, but I thought that I would go to work with Amelia too. She was tense and pale, as if this man were a ghost.

"I always wanted to tell you how sorry I was about what happened. It was a mistake on Pierre's part to go to Moscow."

"He was ordered to go."

"He should have followed Igor Krisov's advice."

"Did you ever see him again?"

"Krisov? No, never. He may be dead. I don't know."

"What are you doing here?" Amelia insisted.

"Well, as you know, the Soviet Union is providing valuable help to our friends in the Democratic Republic. They have sent me here to keep an eye on things in the Security Ministry."

"So now they do trust you."

"Yes."

"They must trust you a lot, or else they wouldn't have sent you here..."

"Well, now that you know that I am worthy of the confidence of my people, what can you tell me about yourself?"

"Nothing special. I live in Berlin."

"Why in this part of Berlin? A young woman like yourself would fit in much better on the other side."

"You don't know anything about me. Don't you remember that I was a Communist activist as well?"

"You're right, we barely had time to get to know each other. It was very brave of you and that American journalist to try to save Pierre. You almost managed it."

We got to the door of the ministry building and they shook hands goodbye. He asked for our address so that he could come and visit us, and Amelia had no option other than to give it to him.

When she had gone inside, the man turned to me and looked me up and down again.

"So, you're Amelia's son..."

"Well, I suppose you could say that I am like her son, that she raised me. My father and Amelia have lived together for ages."

"And what does your father do?"

"Sadly he was wounded in the war, he's an invalid, he doesn't have any legs."

"I'll come and visit you one of these days, I hope you and your parents won't mind."

"Oh no, come when you want, Amelia's friends are always welcome."

When I got back home that evening, I found Amelia telling my father what had happened. This was when I discovered that Amelia had been in love with a Soviet agent named Pierre.

"Ivan Vasiliev behaved well toward me, but he was scared," Amelia explained. "When we went to Moscow, they put Pierre under Vasiliev's orders. He was very rigid toward him, but Pierre said that he seemed insecure, even though he was a good man. He told me that Pierre had been arrested because they thought that he had been one of the agents run by Igor Krisov, another spy whom they accused of treason after he deserted. When I met Ivan Vasiliev, he was extremely scared, now he seems changed, not just because he's older... It's like things were going well for him."

"I'm worried that he's with the KGB," Max said.

"Me too," Amelia agreed.

Two days later, Ivan Vasiliev turned up at our house. He brought a bottle of Rhine wine, a packet of sausages, and a piece of cake.

He was charming, he helped Amelia to cook the sausages and me to lay the table, and played a game of chess with my father. If he was surprised to find out that Max had been an officer in the Wehrmacht he didn't say so, but he listened with interest to how Max had been a member of a group opposed to Hitler.

"A single bullet could have stopped the war, but none of us would have dared to fire on the Führer," my father admitted.

"I don't think that the Russians can be very proud of the Molotov-Ribbentrop pact," Amelia said, trying to provoke Ivan Vasiliev.

"Tactics. Stalin avoided going to war at that critical moment," Vasiliev replied.

"He delayed it, and destroyed the morale of thousands of Communists all over the world who couldn't understand why the Soviet Union would make a deal with Hitler," Amelia replied.

"Hitler would never have been overthrown without us," Ivan Vasiliev said.

"Yes, but if the Führer hadn't invaded the Soviet Union, what would you have done? Would you have let him carry on with his atrocities?"

"History is what it is, it can't be something different. Hitler made the mistake of attacking us, as did Napoleon. And here we are."

I don't know why, but my father got on with Ivan Vasiliev and the Russian got on well with him in turn. They seemed to feel comfortable with each other. After that night, Ivan Vasiliev came round for many more evenings. Amelia was tense at first, but bit by bit she relaxed. It was clear that if he was one of the KGB agents who had been sent to Berlin, he must enjoy the absolute trust of his superiors. If he had survived Stalin's purges, he must be tough and intelligent.

Amelia told Garin that she had met Ivan Vasiliev and asked him to pass the information on to Albert James.

"You want to get back to work?" Garin suggested.

"No, not at all. If I'm asking you to tell Albert it's because we both met him in Moscow many years ago."

"So you've known each other for a long while..."

"Longer than you could imagine."

"It's a great opportunity to have a friend in the KGB..."

"An opportunity for whom? I've told you, I don't want to work for Albert or for anyone else. We are doing alright here, Max is happy, he sleeps peacefully and so do I."

But luck was not to be on our side. Walter, Iris's son, was now a young fellow of thirteen or fourteen, and he came to our house one night unannounced. It was nearly Christmas, although the party had removed the festival and substituted for it winter holidays. Anyway, there were no classes.

"My mother told me to come here and that you should speak to Garin. She thinks they suspect her and they're going to arrest her."

Walter was scared and was trembling. His face was red and he was making a great effort not to cry.

Amelia tried to calm him down. She sent me to bring a glass of water from the kitchen and made an effort to calm him.

"Now, tell me what happened," she asked Walter.

"I don't know. Mother has been worried for several days, she says she's sure that they've been following her. She spends the nights looking out into the street through the curtains. She doesn't want me to answer the phone, and she's told me not to bring any friends home. This afternoon, when I got back from school, I found her in the house with all the lights off. She gave me some money that she keeps hidden, American dollars, and sent me here. She said I shouldn't get in touch with Garin or Konrad or Otto, but that you should do it, that she trusts you, and that if anyone can save her it's you. Then she said that I should come here, but not directly, that I should take buses going in different directions, and walk, and that when I was sure that no one was following me then I should come to your house. I don't know what's happening, but she is very scared."

"He can't stay here," Max said. "If they're following Iris, then they'll come and look at all her friends' houses sooner or later, and if they find Walter, then they'll think that we know where she is."

"Well, he's going to stay here," Amelia said, standing up to Max with an anger I found surprising.

"I haven't said that we're not going to help him, just that he can't stay here," Max said, seriously.

"And where do you want me to take him?"

"Down to the basement," I said. "They won't find him there."

The basement was where our old furniture and the odds and ends of our neighbors' were stored. We had the keys.

"A good idea, Friedrich," my father said.

"But it's dirty and the light bulb is very faint," Amelia complained.

"But it's easy to hide there. I know of a place in the basement where no one will ever find him," I insisted.

"What place is that?" Amelia asked with interest.

"I liked to explore the basement when I was little. I went down there with my flashlight, and well… One day I nearly fell down a hole that I hadn't seen because it was covered with a very thin piece of wood. I found a space there, I think it's where they must have kept the coal because the walls were made of wood and are very dirty. I climbed down there using a little metal ladder that I found among the rubbish."

"You never told us that you discovered this place," my father said reproachfully.

"We all have secrets, and this was mine."

"But Walter won't be comfortable there… ," Amelia protested.

"We could make a little hidey-hole there, just in case the police do come," I insisted.

They accepted my plan and, without making any noise, Walter, Amelia, and I went down to the basement, each of us carrying a flashlight. Walter put on a horrified face when he saw the dark basement and the little hidey-hole I had spoken of. But Amelia sent us upstairs for cleaning equipment.

"We'll get it ready only for if you need to hide yourself."

When she came out she was completely black, but she seemed happy.

"Well, it's much better now. And with these blankets that I've put on the floor and this pillow you'll be comfortable down here if you ever need to hide. I don't know where it comes from, but there's some air that gets into the hole as well. We'll come down tomorrow to have a better look, but I think that the hole must lead somewhere."

The next morning, Amelia got up early to go to work, she wanted to get there as soon as possible to speak to Garin. She told me to look after Walter and not to let him leave under any circumstances.

"Garin, Walter came to our house last night. He says that Iris thinks that she's being followed."

"They went to arrest her last night."

"Good God!"

"A few days ago Iris told me that she thought her boss suspected her and that she was sure that she was being followed. One afternoon, when her boss had said he was going away for the day, she stayed behind, as was her habit, with the excuse that she was going to do a bit of filing. This was when she normally used the camera to photograph documents. But he came back because he had forgotten something, and she heard him and was able to hide the camera, but the papers she was photographing were still laid out on the table. Her boss asked her what she was doing, and she said that she was trying to find a document that she thought she had filed in the wrong place. He didn't believe her, even though he pretended that he accepted her explanation."

"Where is she? Tell me where they've taken her!"

"Nowhere. She had a cyanide capsule, like we all do, for if they arrest us. You know, you have one as well. She wouldn't let them arrest her. She always used to say that she wouldn't let them torture her. When the police came to her house, they knocked the door down and found her dead."

"How do you know all this?"

"I've got a friend in the Foreign Ministry, who works near Iris's department. It's an open secret what has happened. Now they're looking for Walter."

"He's in my house, but I'm going to hide him."

"You have to get him out of Berlin. It's what Iris would have wanted, she always said that she'd leave to start a new life with Walter one day. She was saving to be able to do it. She dreamed of living in the other Berlin, you know, so near and yet so far from where we are."

"But how are we going to get him out?"

"I don't know, I'll have to get in touch with Albert. It's not easy to get out of here, you know that."

"But you must have some escape route..."

"You know how all the attempts at jumping over the Wall end up."

"We might be getting ahead of ourselves, they can't have anything against Walter, he's just a little boy."

"An orphan, whom they'll lock up in a state institution and treat as the son of a traitor. Can you imagine what that means? It's not what Iris would have wanted, and you know that very well. If it's a problem for you, try to get him out of your house this evening and we'll sort it out." Garin spoke bluntly.

"You know how much I love Walter! I love Iris as well, I'll do whatever it takes."

"In that case, hide him until I tell you what to do. When I've worked out how to get him out of Berlin, I'll tell you. At least we're lucky and they won't miss him at school, because it's the winter holiday."

"But the police will be looking for him, and they'll be going to all the houses of Iris's friends."

"Yes, it's possible that we'll be getting a visit, or some of us in any case. You know that we're trying to be discreet and not let them see us together, but it's inevitable that someone has seen us, so we have to be prepared for everything. You too."

"I haven't seen Iris for a long time..."

"I know, but that won't stop the police from searching your house. Where are you going to hide him?"

"I can hide him in the basement. Friedrich found what used to be an old coalhole. I think they won't find him there."

"Try to act naturally, carry on with your normal life. I'll get in touch with you when I know how to get Walter out."

"He could jump over the Wall, you know it goes just in front of my house."

"Don't try to do anything. Wait until I tell you what to do."

My father asked us to put his wheelchair by the window so that he could keep an eye out for anything out of the ordinary.

Walter barely left my room. I tried to be with him as much as possible, but Amelia insisted that I go out and spend time with my friends. She didn't want them to miss me and for someone to come to my house looking for me. She went to work punctually every day, impatient for Garin to tell her what she had to do. She asked him every day, but he didn't yet have the answer.

Sometimes Ivan Vasiliev would surprise us by coming to the house unannounced. He used to explain his presence by saying that he was just passing by, and that he had decided to come and pay us a visit. My father always made him welcome; he liked playing chess with him and sharing a glass of cognac from a bottle that Ivan Vasiliev had brought him. And Ivan never came to visit emptyhanded. The special shops where the upper echelons of the party were allowed to buy produce were well stocked with Western goods, so it wasn't strange for him to come with Dutch butter, Spanish wine, Italian oil, or French cheese. These were luxuries we could not afford, and we were sincerely grateful for them. I think that we were the closest thing that he had to a family.

But in those days, Ivan Vasiliev was the person from whom we would least like to receive a visit.

We were shocked by the doorbell. Amelia was making dinner and Walter was laying the table. I pushed Walter into my room; there was no time to hide him in the basement.

Ivan Vasiliev gave me the bottles he was carrying with a smile.

"Ah, Friedrich, I couldn't resist the temptation to come by and give you this little present for Amelia!"

They were two bottles of Spanish olive oil, and Amelia was truly grateful.

"Will you stay and have dinner with us? I'm making a tortilla, and now with this oil... Well, you'll see, the flavor will be much better."

"Thank you for having mercy on this poor bachelor," Ivan Vasiliev replied as he sat down and made himself comfortable next to Max.

Amelia seemed comfortable, as if this were just any normal night, but my father and I were nervous, and it was difficult for us to hide it. I still remember how nervous I was that Walter would make some noise that would give him away, and I wondered what would happen then. Would Ivan have us arrested?

"Max, my dear friend, you look very worried. And you too, Friedrich. Is anything wrong?"

"Nothing important, but you know what parents are like about their children and their children's future. Friedrich wants to become a general practitioner, and Max says he should be more ambitious."

"Well, I think your father is right. You are a brilliant student, and you could aim to be more than just a family doctor. A good surgeon, a neurologist, a specialist of some kind... Something with a bit more heft to it."

"Why? I want to do what I like doing, and I want to be like my father," I replied, following Amelia's lead.

"He won't listen to me," Max complained.

"Maybe I've come at a bad moment..."

"Of course not! The argument can't carry on while you are here, so we can have a peaceful dinner," Amelia said, smiling at him with apparent innocence.

The tortilla was excellent, and Ivan Vasiliev promised Amelia that he would get more bottles of Spanish oil on the condition that she would invite him to share whatever she cooked with it. Then he played a game of chess with my father, but Max was distracted and couldn't concentrate, so Ivan didn't insist on giving him a chance to get his revenge.

"I'll come back soon, my dear friends. And look after yourself, Amelia."

"Of course I will."

When Ivan Vasiliev had left, we wondered why he had said this last phrase. My father suggested that this had not been a casual visit, and that Ivan's last words had not been merely accidental either. But Amelia wouldn't let us speculate too much.

Poor Walter had not had any supper, and he had to make do with a mug of milk and a bun.

"We have to be more alert. Today it was Ivan Vasiliev who caught us unaware, but what if it had been the Stasi?" my father said.

"Our house is over the basement, so maybe we could make a hole and connect the two," I suggested.

"You're crazy! The whole neighborhood will hear if we start to bash on the floor to try to make a hole through to the cellar, and also, we don't know how solid it is, or what we will find," my father objected.

"I think that Friedrich is right," Amelia said, unconvinced by Max's objections. "If someone turns up unannounced then there won't be time to get Walter out of here. And we can't keep him in the cellar the whole time. Let's knock a hole through to the basement, we can do it ourselves if we're careful, trying not to make too much noise. If the neighbors ask, we can say that we're doing a little bit of work because the house is falling to pieces."

"When shall we start?" I was pleased that Amelia had accepted my proposal.

"Right now, but we'll make the hole from the basement upwards. That way we'll know if you can hear the noise from up here."

Walter and I went down into the basement with a flashlight and worked out where we thought the kitchen was. We started to hack away at the roof of the basement. Amelia came down after a few minutes to tell us that you couldn't hear all that much noise, but we should still be careful. We wrapped the tools in cloth to lessen the noise of the blows, and worked for a while until Amelia sent us to bed.

After a couple of days we had managed to make the hole. We could have finished it on the night that we started, but Amelia wouldn't let us. She preferred for us to work slowly so as not to attract attention. The hole into the kitchen came up into a little cupboard where Amelia kept the dustpan and brush and the iron, and other household utensils. We hid the hole as best we could, but first of all we checked that Walter fit through it, and we put an old mattress in the basement so that when he slipped through the hole he didn't break a leg. I almost wanted Ivan Vasiliev to come back so that I could see how effective my idea was.

Garin told Amelia that Albert was on top of the situation, and that he had promised to take charge of Walter.

One afternoon, Amelia took the bus back home and a strange man sat down next to her. He looked like a factory worker. Gray-haired, with a moustache, a hat pulled down over his ears, glasses, thick gloves, and a worn-out overcoat.

"Don't speak or move."

It was difficult for Amelia not to do either. She recognized Albert James's voice coming from this unknown man.

"We've checked that no one is watching your house. You haven't seen Iris for a long time, and it might be because of that, or else because they wouldn't dare watch the house of anyone who was a friend of KGB colonel Ivan Vasiliev."

"I asked Garin to tell you that Vasiliev had turned up."

"And he did. I remember Moscow well, but you said that he was a coward back then, a scared shadow of a man. And now he's a colonel, with a medal that he won at the front for bravery. And he's one of the most dangerous men there is. We know that he's got moles in strategic points in the West, but we don't know where they are. But there is some very sensitive information that's getting into his hands. He's a friend of yours, and so maybe you can help us."

"Help you to betray him? No, I'm not going to do that."

"It's strange, you didn't care about betraying Max, and you have scruples about doing so with Colonel Vasiliev."

"I know that the line between lying and betrayal is very fine, but I never felt that I was betraying Max. I knew that we wanted the same thing, to finish with Hitler. But I'm not going to argue about this with you. I don't work for you. I thought we were here to get Walter out of Berlin."

"Yes, I'm here for that, but also to ask you to help us to find a mole that Vasiliev has managed to infiltrate somewhere. We don't know where, but he has access to American and British information."

"So you still share everything with the British."

"Of course, they're like our cousins."

"I've already told you I'm not going to work with you any-more."

"Think about it. I'll come for Walter tonight."

"How are you going to get him out?"

"You'll have to allow me to refuse to tell you that."

When Amelia got home, she asked Walter to get ready.

"You're going tonight."

"I... I want to stay here, with you."

"That's impossible, and you know it. You'll be fine, don't you worry, and you'll be doing what your mother wanted you to do. You're going to have a great life, I promise you."

But Walter burst into tears, he couldn't hold back the tears that he had repressed so often since his mother's death.

Max watched the street and didn't see any suspicious cars or people. But suddenly he thought he saw a shadow coming to the garden that led to the building.

"It might be Albert. I hope so, because the watchmen are going to turn their searchlights on in two minutes."

My father had recorded how long the searchlights were trained on our area at night, and how long it took the patrols to pass by.

Amelia went out to the porch and opened the door. She hoped that it was Albert and she waited for him in the darkness.

It was him. He came quickly into our house. Just as had happened with Amelia, it was hard for us to recognize him.

Walter had hidden in the cupboard and had the trapdoor open, in case he had to jump quickly into the basement.

"Most ingenious," Albert said when we showed him what we had done.

Amelia explained that we were the only ones who had the key to the basement and that we had found a little hole where some-one could hide.

"There's air, but we don't know where it comes from."

"Will you let me take a flashlight and have a look?" Albert asked.

"Yes, of course, but isn't it a bit late?" Amelia asked, worried that time was passing and that it would only get more difficult to get Walter out of there.

I went down to the basement with Albert, slipping through the hole that we had made in the floor. I helped him to examine the space that there was in the floor of the basement. He lit a match to see where the air came from, and we found a crack in the wall.

"It's a thin wall that leads somewhere, maybe even... I don't know, but I can hear noise, as if... Perhaps there's a tunnel for the underground trains that runs near here."

"It could be the sewers, there's a drain cover in the garden, hidden under the plants. You can't lift the cover; I tried a lot when I was smaller, when I liked to play at treasure hunting, and thought it would be a real adventure to go down into the sewers. But I never managed to lift it."

We climbed back into our house, and Albert asked how many meters we were from the Wall.

"Two meters away from the fence and twenty from the Wall itself, but if you're right and the air in that hidey-hole comes from the drains, then you should know that they've covered all the gates that lead to the other side of the city, and that the sewers are constantly patrolled. I imagine that if Friedrich is right and there is a way down to the sewers in the garden, then it must be watched even more closely, because we're so close to the Wall," my father said.

"I'd like to come back and have a look around. I'll see if I can get a map of how the sewers were in Berlin before the war. If there were a way through... then maybe we could get people out of here."

"I've told you, I do not work for you anymore," Amelia said in a voice that was low but furious.

"You refuse to save lives? Because sometimes that's what it boils down to, saving someone's life. You can't imagine how difficult it is to get people out of here, and it's getting more difficult all the time. We've used all our wit to work out ways, but no more than the Russians or the Stasi. Don't you read the papers? A fortnight ago another man died trying to jump over the Wall. How many more do you think are going to die?"

"It's getting late," my father interrupted.

"Yes, you're right. Thank you for looking after Walter."

"Don't thank me, we love him," Amelia said.

They left the house and were lost in the shadows. I don't know if Amelia ever found out how they got him out of Berlin. And if she did, then she never told us.

The possibility that our basement was somehow connected to the sewers sunk its hooks into Amelia. So much so that when she could she went down to the basement herself and tried to make a hole in the wall, to see where the air was coming from. I helped her, in spite of my father's protests: He told us we should leave things as they were. It wasn't hard to make a little hole, but it gave onto absolute darkness, so we stuck a flashlight through the gap and lit up the darkness, worried what we might find. We heard running water and could see through the hole that the coal cellar led to another space, which in its turn must lead onto the sewers.

"You can't hear anything from up there, so let's make the hole a little bigger and I'll go through it with a flashlight, I want to see where it leads to," Amelia said.

"You heard my father, the soldiers patrol the sewers and they're even more vigilant the closer you get to the Wall. It's dangerous."

"Yes, I know, but while I'm out there, I think about how we're going to hide the hole. If the soldiers come past, I don't think they'll go into this little space that leads onto our basement, but even so, we should hide it as well as we can."

"But why do you want to do this?" I asked, nervously.

"I don't know, we may need it some day."

"Let me come with you, there may be rats."

"No, I'll go alone. It's not the first time I've been in these sewers. I know what they smell like and what I might find here."

We took the bricks out carefully, until Amelia could go through to the other side. I saw how she disappeared into the Berlin underworld with only a beam of light accompanying her. She was away for almost an hour and I got scared, because I thought that I heard footsteps and voices in the distance. I didn't breathe easily until I saw her coming back. She smelled of filth, her hands were grazed and her shoes were wet, but she seemed happy.

"Did you think of a way to hide the hole?"

"Yes, we'll make a block with the bricks we've taken out, then we'll put it back in, like a piece of a puzzle, so that it will be easy for us to remove it the next time. But tell me, what happened? I heard voices."

"Me too, I nearly died of fright. I had to turn off the flashlight. It was a patrol, five or six people, talking to each other, they came close to me but they didn't see me. I stayed quiet until I heard them leave."

"So my father was right, and there are soldiers patrolling the sewers..."

"Yes. Now let's go home, and tomorrow I'll come down again."

"Why?"

"Who knows, maybe we'll find a way to get across to the other side…"

"It's impossible, my father said that they shut all the sluices."

"Yes, but there is water flowing there…"

"You're not going to get into that water!" I said in horror.

"We'll see, we'll see…"

A few days later, while Amelia was in the archive organizing some files, Garin came up to her. They were a long way away from the rest of the department, so they could talk freely.

"Walter got through alright, I just wanted you to know."

"Thank God!"

"Albert took a lot of risks for him."

"How did they get him out?"

"I don't know."

"Come on, Garin!"

"What Albert did tell me is that he will be coming to see you. Apparently you have a very interesting basement."

"I told him to forget about me."

Garin smiled, shrugged his shoulders, and walked out of the archive.

Neither my father nor my mother knew that I belonged to a group of students that met regularly with Konrad. We spoke about politics and organized activities at the university in which, very carefully, we tried to get various things past the censor.

Readings, plays, music… Everything allowed us to think that we were offering firm opposition to the authorities of the Democratic Republic. There were obviously police informants in the university, but we were sure that our group was impossible to infiltrate.

No one was allowed to join without Konrad's approval, so when he turned up with two young women to the rehearsals of a play we were going to put on, no one mistrusted them.

"These are Ilse and Magda, two of my best students."

As well as the play, we were organizing a day of protest at the university. We were going to ask for more freedoms, and also for the release of a history professor who had been arrested and accused of activities against the Democratic Republic.

We thought that we would organize a silent march across the university campus, carrying placards with the single word "Liberty" written across them. We wouldn't shout slogans, we would just march in silence. We thought that a silent demonstration would be much more effective. We were also putting together a pamphlet calling for the professor's release, which we planned to distribute over the whole area.

I was taken by Ilse as soon as I saw her. She was like a Valkyrie: blonde, tall, thin, with dark blue eyes... She was a real beauty. Magda was one as well, but different from Ilse. Magda's hair was black, and her skin was very white, and she had green eyes. She was not as tall as Ilse, nor as thin, but it was impossible not to notice her either.

The date of the demonstration grew closer and Konrad had organized a meeting in the little print shop where we printed our clandestine material. None of us knew where it was, but the most important thing was that all the ringleaders of the opposition at the university and the intellectual circles that supported the underground movement would be there.

"I think that Ilse and Magda should come to the meeting. That way they'll meet the rest of the people. Friedrich, you will go and pick them up," Konrad said.

"But I don't know where the print shop is," I said.

"I know, but once you're with the girls, you'll go to the park and there you'll meet the other group. Don't worry, someone will turn up to show you the way."

Ilse and Magda were pleased to accept. They wanted to meet the rest of the group.

That night I slept badly, and in the morning Amelia noticed the bags under my eyes.

"Haven't you slept well?"

"I suppose I must be worried about my exams."

We left the house as we did every morning and walked toward the bus stop, where we said goodbye. When I got to the university

I met Ilse, and we spoke about the meeting that afternoon. She was waiting for Magda to be able to go to class, but Magda was late.

When I left at midday to go home, Ilse came to find me. She was pale and nervous and seemed out of sorts.

"Something's happened... I... I don't know if it's important, but I'm worried... I'm looking for Konrad but he's left and I don't have his home telephone number, or his address, I don't know what to do..."

"Calm down and tell me what's happened."

"Magda came late this morning. She said that she had felt a little ill and that she'd stayed in bed a little longer than usual. She didn't seem ill, but I thought that maybe it was just something that she'd gotten over. But we met a friend who said, 'Hey Magda, where were you going so fast this morning? I called you but you didn't say anything... Of course, I go fast when I walk past the Stasi... but it looked like you were actually headed there...' and then he laughed and so did she, but I know her and I could see that she'd gotten nervous."

"How long have you been friends?"

"I've known her since we started at the university, but we've only really become friends this year. She's very intelligent, Konrad's best student."

"And you think..."

"I don't know, Friedrich, but I'm scared. There are informants everywhere, we know that we shouldn't trust anyone... Maybe I'm being unfair to Magda, that's the most likely thing, but I wouldn't be happy if I didn't tell anyone, and as I haven't found Konrad... I... I should never have got caught up in all this, I don't know, I don't think that things are going as badly as Magda says, but even so... Well, I wouldn't like anything to happen to anyone..."

"And I need to go and pick you both up at your house this afternoon... ," I said.

"Well, Magda said that maybe we would go alone, she said I should come to her house instead."

"And how were you going to get there if you don't know where the print shop is?"

"She wants you to go to her house as well. I don't know, Friedrich, I don't know, but I'm not feeling well... I don't know what to think..."

I didn't know what to think either, and even less what to do. I called Konrad, but they told me that he wasn't expected at home for lunch. I didn't dare talk to other comrades and maybe spread unjustified doubts about Magda. I didn't know if Ilse was paranoid, or if she was envious of Magda, or if her suspicions were based on fact.

I made a decision that turned out to be the correct one. When I got home, I made a sign to Amelia and shut the kitchen door. My father was drowsy and didn't pay us any attention. I told her everything that had happened, and I could see how upset she was when she found out that I was involved in clandestine activities at the university.

"You shouldn't go to this Magda's house, it could be a trap."

"Or it could be nothing."

"Do you have the address?"

"Yes..."

"And when should you be there?"

"Six."

"Let's go earlier."

"Let's? Us?"

"Yes, you and me."

"But..."

"No buts! You'll do what I say."

I didn't protest and accepted what Amelia said. We left the house as soon as we'd eaten.

We walked to where Magda's house was and Amelia watched it from a distance to see if there was anything strange going on. There were three hours to go before we were meant to be there and she seemed to be prepared to stay there all that time. I was already bored when we saw a car stop close to Magda's house. I saw her getting out of the car, followed by a man, and they both headed to the house: She seemed worried. The man was not there for very long; he came out after half an hour.

"Stay here and don't move," Amelia ordered.

"And where are you going?"

"Look and keep an eye out for anything suspicious, I won't be long."

The time seemed to drag on for an eternity, and my mind had wandered when I heard Amelia's voice next to me.

"You weren't paying attention."

I looked at her, but it didn't seem like her. She wore thick glasses that covered the top half of her face, and a gray cap covering her hair that I had never seen before. I didn't recognize the coat she was wearing either.

"But..."

"Shut up and wait. Don't move, whatever happens. Give me your word."

"But..."

"Give me your word!"

"Yes, I give you my word, but I don't understand... You're dressed up and... where are you going?"

"I'm going to Magda's house."

"I'm coming with you."

"No, don't move from here or you'll put me in danger, and not just me, but you, and your father, and all your friends."

I saw her go in through Magda's door. She didn't come out until half an hour later.

"Call your friend Ilse and tell her that you've fallen ill, and that she should rest too because she had a bit of a cold this morning. I hope she'll be clever enough to realize that she shouldn't go out this afternoon."

"It would be better for me to go to her house..."

"No, don't go to tell her personally. You will call her and you will tell her that it is best if she stay in bed this afternoon and tells everyone else that she is ill. Do you understand?"

"Yes, but..."

"Do as I say! I have to find Konrad, the meeting cannot take place."

And she disappeared. She got caught up among the crowd. I did as she had said. I got home and called Ilse. I could see how stunned she was when I told her that she had to go to bed until her cold cleared up.

"But, what about our date?"

"Do what I tell you and we'll talk later."

I went to my room to stop my father from seeing how nervous I was.

Amelia came home later than usual, and my father was anxious.

"What kept you?" he said as soon as he heard the door close.

"Lots of work, you know how we're organizing a Peace Conference, and our department is overwhelmed. Garin can't cope with everything and he asked me to stay and help him."

I had come out of my room and I looked at her in astonishment. She was entirely back to normal. The glasses, the woolen cap, the overcoat... It had all disappeared.

When she went into the kitchen to make the dinner there was a ring at the door. We both jumped, but it was she who opened the door.

"I hope this isn't a bad moment... ," Ivan Vasiliev said, giving us his best smile.

"Of course not! Come in, Ivan, you're just in time for dinner."

"Thank you, Amelia, if it weren't for you, then I think I'd have forgotten what a good meal really means. I haven't had time to get anything today. These kids at the university have been giving the Stasi a lot of trouble," he said, looking at me straight in the eyes.

"Oh really? What have they done?" Max asked with interest.

"The Stasi are extremely upset. Someone has murdered one of their informers and they're putting everything behind the investigation. Nobody will stop them until they find their culprit."

"And what's this got to do with the university?" Max was interested to hear what Ivan Vasiliev had to say.

"The youngsters were preparing a demonstration... By the way, hadn't you heard anything about this, Friedrich? No? Anyway, the youngsters were preparing a silent demonstration asking for freedom and for one of the professors who has been arrested to be released. You know, the normal student concerns. The police knew all about it, and were prepared to swoop and round them all up. They'd got hold of a dozen youngsters and nothing more. But apparently the mob had also organized a meeting with all the higher-ups among the university activists, professors included. Anyway, a good occasion to get hold of these people who are filling the heads of our youngsters with rubbish. But the informant must have made some mistake, and ended up dead, and the meeting, strangely enough, didn't take place. So, I've been working all afternoon."

"So now you spend your time running after students?" Amelia's voice was filled with irony.

"No, my dear, not at my age, but although it is none of my business I would like to know who shot the People's Army's informant. It was done with a Western gun, a Walther PPK, small caliber. A woman's weapon, as the experts say. But a weapon is a weapon, no matter how big it is. What matters is how you use it. The murderer had good aim, got the informer right in the heart. Dead, instantly. I'm telling you it must have been a professional. Which makes us think that these students in revolt and their teachers have good friends in the West, don't you think?"

"But anyone could have a gun like that," she replied.

"Anyone? What do you think, Friedrich? Did you go to the university this afternoon? I don't know if you know that there was a roundup... I'm glad that you weren't arrested."

"And why would he have been? My son was here with me, and Friedrich knows that you should never get involved in politics, not ever; he gave me his word and he's keeping it," Max interrupted opportunely.

"But young people are so contrary, and have their own ideas, although I am glad that Friedrich was here, and doesn't have anything to do with the rabble-rousers."

"Anyone could have something to do with them; everyone knows everyone in the university," Amelia said.

"Why not let Friedrich talk?" Ivan Vasiliev said.

I must have been pale. I felt the colonel's gaze passing over me as if he could read all my thoughts.

"I... Well, what you just said makes me very nervous. It's not a good piece of news to know that there's been a roundup, and that maybe they've taken people I know... I... if I can be sincere with you I should say that when one is young one dreams of building a better future, and that cannot be a crime."

I don't know where I got the strength to produce that little speech, but it seemed to impress Ivan Vasiliev.

"Well, you are a brave lad to come out in defense of your friends like that. You know what? You're right, when one is young one wants to change the world, but the world has already been changed by the people of my generation. The people now govern and it is the people's children who go to university; we're all equal, and we're building a better world for everyone. The only thing you young people need to do is walk in the same direction."

I didn't say anything, it was hard for me to hold Ivan Vasiliev's gaze, as well as my father's.

"There's a professor, Konrad, his name is... He has disappeared, and they're looking for him. Apparently he's the main agitator. You know him, don't you, Friedrich?"

"He's one of the best-regarded professors at the university."

"We know him as well, he's even come to dinner here a couple of times, but that was several years ago," Amelia said naturally.

"And how come you know him, my dear?"

"When we came back to Berlin a friend introduced us, the Wall wasn't yet up... and one night he brought him round to dinner. He was very friendly, I didn't think he was a dangerous revolutionary. But that was more than fifteen years ago."

"And who was this friend who introduced you?"

"Someone who's sadly dead now. But he lived in West Berlin. Things were different so many years ago, the Berliners weren't separated by any wall and people went from one sector to another with no problems... How people thought wasn't so important. Back then the Germans on this side of the border hadn't all become Communists."

"Well, Professor Konrad is now the most sought-after man in Berlin..."

"They'll find him, I'm sure they'll find him," Amelia said firmly.

"Well, I'm glad that Friedrich had nothing to do with the troublemakers. But I should go now, an exquisite dinner as always, Amelia, my dear."

"Thank you, Ivan."

"Look after yourselves, my dear friends, look after yourselves."

I couldn't breathe calmly until Ivan Vasiliev had left. My father seemed disconcerted.

"How strange! I don't know, I've got the impression that Ivan wanted to tell us something... Friedrich, I hope that you have nothing to do with what's going on at the university..."

"Don't worry, Papa."

"And you, Amelia... I don't understand you. Why did you tell him we knew Konrad? We haven't seen him for years."

"Because he already knows it, and if he doesn't know it, then he will know it. It's better for him to see that we've got nothing to hide. They must be investigating everyone who knows Konrad, and someone could remember at any moment that we know him too."

As I did every night, I helped Amelia put my father to bed, then I offered to help wash the dishes.

"What happened?" I asked her when we were alone in the kitchen.

"Nothing, you just have to be careful."

"He said that they killed Magda... Although all he said was an informant... It must have been her, I'm sure."

"That's none of our business."

"With a little gun, a woman's gun... That's what he said."

"Neither you nor I know anything about this and I have no interest at all in knowing anything about it."

"You went to Magda's house..."

"No."

"But I saw you going into the house disguised and it took time for you to come out..."

"I was scouting out the house, I wanted to know if someone we hadn't seen was going to come out. I left because I didn't see anything suspicious."

"You didn't go up to her apartment?"

"Of course not, how ridiculous!" she lied to me.

"And where did you go next?"

"To look for some friends who might be able to warn Konrad."

"You found them."

"Apparently so. They're looking for him and they still haven't found him."

I didn't sleep at all that night. I didn't know until a few days later that Konrad was in our basement. And it was years before Amelia told me what really happened that afternoon.

3

For a few days neither Amelia nor Max would let me go to the university. However, they suggested, forcefully, that I call my friends to tell them that my father didn't want me to go. We all knew that the telephones were bugged, so nobody said anything more, they just asked me when I would be coming back.

One night, when my father was asleep and I had the light in my bedroom turned off, I heard a noise in the kitchen. I got up, thinking that Amelia might have gotten up for a glass of water. I found her opening the trapdoor in the cupboard.

"Where are you going?"

"Go back to bed."

"Tell me where you're going," I insisted.

"Don't get involved in this. Go to bed."

"Please... trust me."

"Alright, come with me."

I followed her down into the basement through the trap door. Then we went to the hidey-hole and Amelia shone a little flashlight into it. Konrad was there. Amelia put the little ladder in place and we climbed down. I hugged him with relief.

"You were here all the time!"

"Yes, here I am, turning into a mole, I think I'm going to go blind from being so much in the dark."

"I came to tell you that tomorrow we're going to try to go over to the other side. Garin will help us. Albert has looked at the plans. If everything is as he says, then we're about five or six kilometers from the other side, that is, from the exit to a drain in West Berlin. He'll be waiting for you there."

"If anyone sees Garin coming into this house..." Konrad was worried.

"We work together, it's not so strange that he could come to have dinner with us. We'll try to make sure no one sees him come in. There will be people watching. They've been watching us for days to see if the Stasi or the police are on our trail. They haven't seen anything suspicious. Apparently we're not among their top priorities."

"Maybe the fact that you're a friend of that KGB colonel is helping you."

"I don't know, in any case we'll try it tomorrow. Now eat what I've brought you and try to rest."

I was cross when we got back to the kitchen.

"So, you've got Konrad hidden away here and haven't told me anything."

"Friedrich, shush! This isn't a game. You and your friends have got us into a very big mess here. You know that some of them have been sent to labor camps. Do you think they've said nothing? Of course they have, and they've named names, including your name. That's why Ivan Vasiliev came here that night. He has saved you. He thought that your participation wasn't important, that you were just one more member of the group of rebellious students. But he warned us. No more pranks from you."

"They didn't arrest Ilse either, and she was Magda's friend."

"How could they arrest the niece of a member of the Central Committee? Anyway, Ilse didn't know anything; she'd only met you the day before when Konrad brought her and Magda to your group meeting."

"Her uncle is a member of the Central Committee?"

"Yes, didn't you know? You've got away with it this time, but you can't tempt fate again. They think that Ilse got cold feet at the last minute and decided not to go to the meeting. That's what her uncle says as well. Also, there was nothing against Ilse in Magda's reports. Magda used her as a bait to get close to Konrad. The Stasi infiltrated Magda into the university, knowing Konrad's weakness for pretty women, but he wasn't interested in her, only

Ilse, so Magda made friends with Ilse. She tested her out to see what her opinions were, but Ilse didn't seem too interested in politics, her family's doing alright, they're a part of the *nomen-klatura*. But Magda insisted so much that Ilse let herself be convinced to get closer to Konrad. He didn't mistrust them, Magda was very convincing about her rejection of the values of the regime, so he lowered his guard and committed a great error by inviting them to this meeting at the print shop where the senior figures in the opposition movement at the university and in intellectual circles were to meet."

"And how do you know all this?"

"Via a friend."

"Does my father know anything?"

"Your father knows nothing. Do you want to give him a heart attack? No, don't say anything to him."

"Have they interrogated Ilse?"

"They've given her a warning, nothing else."

"Tomorrow I'll help you to try to find the way out of the sewers."

"No, it's better for you to stay at home. If your father woke up or if someone came..."

"Why did Magda betray us?"

"She didn't betray you, she was doing her job. She was a Stasi agent. She had been trying to infiltrate herself into opposition circles in the university for two years. She wasn't in any hurry, she wanted to catch all the upper echelon of the organization, and she was about to manage to do so. If Konrad hadn't been so sloppy... But pretty women like Ilse have always turned his head."

I was scared, very scared. Suddenly I realized just how close I had been to the abyss, and I admired Amelia even more for her cold-bloodedness. I had known ever since I was a child that she was special and that she did special things, but now I was aware of just how far she was willing to go, and I was struck by her coldness.

Amelia carried on behaving as if our life had not left its regular tracks, so my father suspected nothing.

The next day Garin came for supper. He had not been for a long time.

I opened the door and he smiled at me.

"Hello Friedrich, long time no see. You're quite a man now!"

My father greeted him and, while Amelia made the dinner, challenged him to a game of chess. It was not Garin's favorite activity, but he accepted.

When we finished eating, we spoke for a while about the Peace Congress that Amelia and Garin were organizing at work.

"Young people will come from all over the world. Poor things! They think they're working for peace, but they are really puppets of Moscow, as we all are," Garin said.

"But they are acting in good faith," Max defended them.

"Yes, and they stage demonstrations in their countries for everything that they would never be allowed to demonstrate in favor of here or in the Soviet Union. The agitators and propagandists are masters of their trade: They've convinced all these left-wing movements of the intrinsic evil of the bourgeoisie. But they are attaining their objective, which is to control the thought processes of these collectives and drive them toward the ultimate goal, which is a fully Communist society. That's why they don't trust intellectuals, that is to say, everyone who thinks for himself and doesn't toe the Moscow line. The party will not allow artists or writers to decide what the State needs in terms of cultural material. The State needs to decide what is to be done, and how, and when," Garin explained.

"It's a perversion!" I couldn't stop myself from giving my opinion.

My father said he was tired and I helped Amelia put him to bed while Garin cleared the table and took the plates to the kitchen.

"Don't stay up late, you've got class tomorrow," my father said.

"Don't worry, I'm going to study for a bit and then I'll go to sleep."

I shut the bedroom door and followed Amelia to the kitchen, where Garin had made a start on the washing-up.

"Did you see any of our neighbors when you came in?" I asked Garin.

"No, and there wasn't anyone in the street either, no cars, nothing. My people have been watching the house and its surroundings all day, they say that they haven't seen anything suspicious, so we can be calm."

"It would be stupid to be calm," Amelia said.

I helped them open the trapdoor down to the cellar and saw them slide down and heard the soft thud as they landed on the mattress we had put down there. They told me later what happened down in the cellar.

Konrad was drowsing, but he woke up at once and helped them to remove the block of bricks that gave access to the sewers.

They had flashlights and a rope, and were also carrying pistols just in case. Amelia had a bag with tools slung over her shoulder.

She led them through the sewers, following the map that Albert James had given to Garin. There were a couple of occasions when they were about to meet patrols, but they managed to hide.

"This is the point where, according to the map, the sewers run across to the other side," Amelia said.

"But the wall is blocked and they've put up a grille in the water... I don't know how we're going to get past."

"If we make a hole in the Wall, the soldiers are going to hear us," Konrad said.

"Yes, that's why I think the best thing to do is for us to cut through the grille and swim through," said Amelia.

"Swim, in this filthy water?" Konrad seemed scared.

"It's the best option. We've brought tools to try to get through the grille," Amelia said.

Garin pushed against the wall, trying to see how solid it was.

"I think that Amelia is right. Help me, I'll see if I can move the grille."

Amelia tied a rope to Garin's waist and took some swimming goggles out of the bag.

"Put these on, you might need them."

"Where did you get them from?" Garin asked.

"They're Friedrich's, they'll fit you."

"Is it deep?" Konrad asked.

"I'm afraid so, at least my feet don't touch the bottom. I think I'm going to throw up, the smell is unbearable."

He put the goggles on and ducked his head under the water. After a minute he came up again.

"How disgusting! Give me the tools, I'm going to try to cut through the grille, but it's a narrow gap and I hope we don't get stuck when we try to swim through."

"Do you want me to help you?" Konrad asked.

"Yes, it will be easier if we try to break through together."

They were trying to break through the grille when they heard the voices and the footsteps of a patrol.

"They're coming straight here, and there's nowhere to hide," Amelia said.

"Come here!" Garin held out his hand and Amelia didn't think twice, but jumped straight into the black water.

"When we hear them getting closer we'll put our heads under the water," Garin said.

"I won't be able to," Konrad complained.

"Either we do that, or they find us and kill us right here. And let me assure you that it won't be a glorious way to die. We'll keep our heads up until the last second, then we'll duck under until they've gone," Garin insisted.

Without saying a word, Amelia went over to Konrad and tied the rope that was around Garin's waist to his belt, and then also to her own waist.

"What are you doing!" There was a hysterical note in Konrad's voice.

"It's better for us to be together; if one of us wants to come up, then the others won't let him."

They stayed still, in silence, with the flashlight turned off, and heard the footsteps getting ever closer. A shaft of light swung toward them and they ducked their heads under the water.

Garin had the swimming goggles, but neither Amelia nor Konrad had anything to protect their faces.

They couldn't last another second under the water. Amelia thought that her head was about to explode, and Konrad was trying to struggle to the surface, but Garin and she held his wrists and wouldn't let him go up. Suddenly Garin let Konrad go and they all pushed to the surface. Darkness had fallen again, and they trod water in silence for what seemed like an age. They didn't want to turn the flashlight back on, in case the soldiers were nearby. When they finally did, the three of them were trembling with fear and disgust.

"We have to try to break through the grille however we can." Garin put his head back into the water. It took them more than an hour to cut through a couple of bars and make a hole that was big enough to pass through.

"Who knows what we'll find on the other side." Konrad was worried.

"Whatever it is, we have no option but to carry on. I hope the soldiers don't realize that there are three bars missing," Garin answered.

They swam for a while until they reached an islet. Amelia looked at Albert's map.

"Ten meters to the right should be an iron staircase that goes up to the drain cover. I hope we haven't made a mistake and come up in front of Stasi headquarters," Amelia joked.

They walked the last ten meters in silence and found the old iron staircase that led to the surface.

Garin came up first, followed by Konrad and then Amelia.

As they had agreed, Garin knocked four times on the drain cover, which began to lift up.

"Thank God you're here!" they heard Albert James say.

Some men were waiting next to two cars parked by the drain cover, and one of them came up with a blanket, which he put over Konrad's shoulders.

"We have to get back," Amelia said, looking at Garin.

"Was it difficult?" Albert wanted to know.

"It was disgusting more than anything else," Garin laughed.

"Thank you, Amelia." Albert's voice was sincere.

"You don't need to thank me. If it were up to me, I wouldn't let anyone fall into the hands of the Stasi."

Amelia and Garin gave Konrad a hug and wished him luck.

"Imagine how the sons of bitches are going to feel when they find out you're here." Garin seemed happy just thinking about it.

"I think that you should be prudent and not announce too soon that Konrad is with you, or else they'll go crazy and start arresting people," Amelia suggested.

"Don't worry, we'll be careful and... Well, I'll come and see you one of these days," Albert said.

They shuddered as they saw the manhole cover closing over their heads again, and they began their descent into the darkness of the sewers.

"You know what, Amelia? I'm surprised that this place doesn't give you the shivers, I've wanted to scream several times," Garin said.

"It's not the first time I've been in the sewers... I got to know the Warsaw drainage system very well. Some friends taught me not to be afraid."

"You always manage to surprise me. Looking at you... well... No one would say that you were capable of doing what you do."

They were lucky and didn't meet with any patrols, although it took Garin longer than they had expected to fix the bars back across the grille so they didn't look like they'd been cut. I breathed more easily when I saw them come back up into the kitchen.

"It's six in the morning, I thought something had happened to you."

"Why don't you make us coffee while we try to get clean?" Amelia asked.

I gave Garin a towel and he went into the bathroom, telling us not to make too much noise or we'd wake up Max. I had to go in myself after a while to tell him to hurry up and get out of the shower so that Amelia could come in. She was exhausted.

"I think it's going to take years to wash this smell off me. I'll come out now."

While Garin drank a cup of coffee, Amelia went into the shower.

"The most difficult thing is going to be for you to leave without anyone seeing you," I said, worried, looking out of the window.

"If there were anything suspicious outside, I would have been told. My people had orders to be around all night until they saw me come out."

He left a little while before Amelia and I did.

"You're exhausted, you shouldn't go to work today."

"What excuse could I give them? It's better to behave normally."

The path from the sewers to our basement was too important a route for Albert James not to attempt to use it on further occasions. So it was that not a month had passed since Konrad's escape when Albert came to see Amelia.

She left the ministry building and an old man in dark glasses, walking with a cane, bumped into her.

"I'm sorry... ," the old man said.

"Don't worry... It's nothing..."

"Could you help me to cross the road?" the man asked. He appeared to be blind.

"Of course, which direction are you going?"

He explained and she offered to walk with him a while until they got to a place where he could walk more safely. They hadn't crossed the street before his voice turned into that of Albert James.

"I'm happy to see you."

She gave a start and would have let go of his arm, but she managed to control herself.

"I see that you have become a master of disguise."

"Well, you've been known to use them yourself."

"What do you want?"

"I want you to come back."

"No, I've told you, don't insist."

"You helped Konrad."

"Konrad is a friend, I had to help him. How is he?"

"Happy, as you can imagine. He will appear in public in a few days and will be welcomed by our university."

"I'm happy for him."

"We need to be able to access the sewers."

"It's very dangerous, they'll discover that the bars on the grille have been removed, and when they do, they'll set a trap to catch us, you know that."

"It's a risk we have to take."

"But it's not a risk I want to take."

"You could save people's lives..."

"Come on Albert, don't try to make me feel guilty."

"Help us, Amelia, we'll pay you well, double what you are getting now."

"No, and don't insist."

"I have to insist."

"Don't, and now I've got to go, I think you can find your own way from here," she said ironically.

"I need your basement, Amelia."

"And Max and Friedrich need me. And I'm not keen on helping your friends in the West, not while they're working with people who worked with Hitler."

But in the end Amelia gave in, not because of Albert James's insistence, but because of Otto.

Otto had become a close friend of the assistant to a member of the Central Committee, who said that he no longer shared the goals of the Democratic Republic.

He was a man with certain privileges, but he could not cope with seeing how some of his friends had ended up in labor camps simply because they had offered dissenting opinions, which had been picked up by the regime's spies. He was scared and had information, which was a useful combination to allow Otto to convince him to go over to the Federal Republic.

"He has been working in the Central Committee for several years, he knows all of its ins and outs, and he has strategic information which could be very useful for us," Otto explained to Amelia.

"And what does this have to do with me?"

"Garin told me that you could help him get out of here. Albert is waiting for you to decide what to do."

"For God's sake, Otto, you're not giving me many options here!"

"Look, he's a very special man, he has an artist's soul in spite of working as a bureaucrat. He is... well, he's a homosexual, although very few people know it; it's an inexcusable weakness for a party member. He had a writer friend who disappeared one day. He's been able to find out that he was sent to a labor camp where they are re-educating him. He's afraid that not even his job will save him from the Stasi. Help me get him out of East Berlin."

"And what if it's a trap? What if they're testing you to see how large the network really is so that the Stasi arrests you all?"

"No, it's not. Anyway, I haven't promised him anything. I've just said that I'll introduce him to a friend who may be able to help. We'll get him out without him knowing where he's going. By the time he realizes it, he'll be on the other side."

"It's not so easy to get to the other side."

"I know, but in any case he won't know when it's going to happen. Amelia, I think he's being followed. His friend the writer was not discreet with his criticisms of the regime, even though he did so in restricted circles, but you know that the Stasi has eyes and ears everywhere."

"I'll think about it."

Amelia was upset to think about going back on what she had said to the journalist, that she would never again work for any secret service. After going over it many times, she came to an agreement with Albert and with her own conscience.

"I will not be paid a pfennig for getting people out of East Berlin. I will do it when I want, and I will direct each operation myself, from deciding the day and the hour down to choosing the people who will work with me."

Albert tired to convince her to accept at least some payment, but she refused, flat out.

After helping the Central Committee bureaucrat cross over, other men went out through our basement. This went on until Amelia decided to close this escape route after a visit from Vasiliev.

I think it was at the beginning of the seventies that Ivan told us he was going back to Moscow.

He had turned up unannounced, laden with bags filled with farewell presents.

Two bottles of cognac for Max, a bottle of vodka, olive oil, soft soap, butter, jam, jeans for me... It was like Grandfather Frost bringing his New Year's gifts.

"I've come to say goodbye, I'm going back to Moscow."

We asked him, worried, what had happened to make him return.

"It's age, my friends, I have to retire."

"But why? You're still young!" Amelia said.

"No, I'm not, I'm going to be seventy-five, it's time to rest. I should have gone back years ago."

"Comrade Brezhnev is no spring chicken either," I said, upset that Ivan Vasiliev was leaving. I had grown to like him, even though he was in the KGB.

"Ah, my dear Friedrich! Politicians are not subject to the same laws as the rest of mankind. Our leader is at his zenith; after Nikolai Podgorny's removal, he is the first leader to be head of state and general secretary of the party at the same time. All power is in his hands. I hope to be back in Moscow to celebrate the sixtieth anniversary of the revolution. They say that Comrade Brezhnev is preparing a truly extraordinary celebration."

He played his last game of chess with Max, as was his habit, and praised Amelia's tortilla. After we had eaten and were each drinking a glass of vodka, he looked at Amelia.

"You know what? Our friends in the Stasi are worried about some of the recent escapes to the West. They're wondering about possible escape routes that they have not discovered, which the Americans are using to get traitors out of the city. There's a young major who thinks he knows what's happening. Maybe he does, maybe he doesn't. Young people are so ambitious, but even so they sometimes get things right. You know what he thinks? That they are using the sewers to smuggle people out. Imagine that. So they are going to put them under guard day and night until they have found out if the major is right. Do you know how the major has managed to come to such a conclusion? I'll tell you: There's a popular journalist, a German, who has discovered, reading between the lines, that there has to be a very effective escape route between the two Berlins that has only one problem: the smell. We found out years ago that it's not necessary to have too many agents in the West, all you have to do is read their newspapers. The Western journalists think that their sacrosanct obligation is to tell people everything they know. And I'm grateful to them. Anyway, they'll find this foul-smelling secret passage very soon, if it exists. If it were up to me, I think that I could have flushed out this rat a long time ago. But our friends in the Stasi are self-sufficient, they accept our advice and our collaboration but they don't need us. They're the best spy service in the world... with the exception of the KGB, of course. But the truth is that Germany is a good platform for us to have, a springboard to the rest of the world. That's not a secret to anyone, don't you think?"

"Do you really think you could have caught that rat?" Amelia said, making me nervous.

"Of course, but sometimes our friends are too proud and don't want us to stick our noses into their business. Although I think that this major is going to start taking the steps I would have taken myself."

"And what would you have done with the rat?" Amelia asked.

Ivan stretched out his hand and then made it into a fist, before bursting into laughter.

"My dear Amelia, in this game it is the duty of the rat to try to avoid the cat, and the duty of the cat to try to eat the rat. Both of them know it, it's the reason they exist. Yes, I would have eaten the rat."

"Whoever the rat turned out to be?"

They looked at each other for a few seconds. Amelia held Ivan Vasiliev's cool gaze, waiting for him to reply.

"Yes."

"I understand."

I had sat stock-still, terrified by the direction the conversation had taken. I didn't understand what Amelia was doing. My father also looked at her in surprise.

"You're still a good Communist."

"I never stopped being one."

"In spite of Stalin?"

"He made mistakes, he persecuted innocent people, but he made Russia great, and he'll be remembered for that."

"And for his crimes, Ivan, and for his crimes."

"Not even he managed to make me stop believing that Communism is the truth."

Ivan Vasiliev said goodbye to us affectionately. I think that he really felt that this was a permanent separation.

"I didn't understand that little duel you had with him about the cat and the rat." Max was asking for an explanation.

"It wasn't a duel, just idle curiosity."

"It was as if... I don't know, as if one of you were the rat and the other was the cat... I didn't like it... I don't know..." Max was worried.

"You don't need to worry, it was just a game."

"And the sewers... I couldn't help but remember that you got into the Warsaw ghetto through the sewers, so it's not a crazy idea to think that someone else might have come up with the same plan."

After we had got Max to bed, I made a sign to Amelia for us to go and talk in the kitchen.

"Do you think he knows something?" I asked, nervous.

"Maybe he does, yes, or maybe he's only suspicious."

"But he said that he wouldn't have hesitated to put an end to whoever it was who was taking people out through the sewers."

"Yes, he would have, and it would have been his right to do so."

"Even if it were you..."

"Yes, of course. He has to do his duty, just as we have to do ours. Everyone works according to their own principles."

"I was terrified... I don't understand how you could have had that sort of conversation with him."

"It was something that we both had to say to each other. You know what? I'm going to miss him a lot."

Amelia spoke to Garin to tell him that she would never use our basement again as a way into the sewers.

"It's over, or else they'll discover us. Friedrich is going to cover up the hole in our basement that went through to the sewers. I'm sorry, but I'm not going to put my family in danger."

Albert James had no option but to accept Amelia's decision; in any event, he didn't have strength to fight with her. He had been diagnosed with lung cancer, and he was retiring.

He came to our house one afternoon. When we heard the doorbell we couldn't imagine who it might be.

He was dressed as a Lutheran pastor, and wore a wig that covered most of his forehead. I opened the door and stood stock-still, not knowing who it was.

He asked my father and me to let him speak to Amelia alone. I took my father to his room and shut the door, but I left my door ajar. I couldn't bear not to hear what he had to say to Amelia.

He described his illness, the sharp burning pain in his chest, and he said that the doctors were not optimistic about how much time he had left.

"I don't know if it will be years or months, but whatever time I have left I want to spend with Lady Mary."

"Lady Mary?"

"My wife."

Amelia was silent for a few seconds.

"You didn't tell me about her... I didn't know you were married."

"I didn't tell you, why should I have? Your life and mine took different paths. I should thank you for having left me for Max. I don't know if I'd have been able to deal with everything I've done here without Mary's support. She gives me strength, and before every operation, every dangerous action, she said that it had to go well so that I could come back to her."

"Your parents must be happy, it's what they wanted for you."

"And they were right. You and I would never have been happy, and not just because you didn't love me enough."

"You know something? I've wanted to ask you this for years now: What made you change so much?"

"The war, Amelia, the war. You were right, it's impossible to be neutral, I admitted as much to you a few years ago when we met after the war. I got involved in this, and when I wanted to step away from it, I couldn't, and I realized that I shouldn't either."

"And you've come to say goodbye..."

"We've worked together all these years, but our relationship has been tense, as if we were confronting each other about something. I've never known why. You were with Max and I was with Mary, we'd both of us made our choice, and even so we weren't able to be friends. Now that I know my death is close I don't want to go without reconciling myself with you. You were very important in my life, before I married Mary, you were the woman I had loved the most and I thought that it would be impossible to love anyone the way I loved you. Then I found a superior kind of love, a different kind of love, and I was grateful to you for having abandoned me. But you are a part of my life, Amelia, I cannot tell my story without you being a part of it, and I need to reconcile myself with you in order to be able to die at peace with myself."

They embraced. In each other's arms, Amelia was crying and it was clear that Albert was making a great effort to hold back his tears.

"We're older now, Amelia, it's time for us to rest. You should rest too and... I know I shouldn't say anything, but haven't you ever thought of going back to Spain to be with your family?"

"Not a single day goes by when I don't think about my son, my sister, my uncle, my aunt, Laura... But there's no turning back. The day I left with Pierre... That day put an end to the best things about me. Of course I miss them now, Javier will be a man, he'll be married, he'll have children and he will have asked himself why I abandoned him..."

"If you want, I could try to get you out of here; it would be dangerous, but we could try."

"No, I'll never leave Max, never.

"You have sacrificed your life for him."

"I took his life, it's only fair that he should have mine."

"Don't carry on blaming yourself for what happened in Athens, you didn't know that Max was traveling with that convoy, it wasn't your fault."

"I set off the detonator, it was I who set off the detonator as he came past."

"There are innocent victims in any way; thousands upon thousands of them, men and women, who have lost their lives. At least Max is alive."

"Alive? No, you know he died that day. I took his life from him. How can you say that he's alive? He's stuck in that chair, he can't leave his room. He hasn't got any family left, and he didn't want us to look for any of his old friends. I know that most of them will be dead, but maybe someone is left... But he didn't want to, he didn't want anyone from his past to see him reduced to a lump of meat in a wheelchair. And it was I who put him in that wheelchair."

Amelia went to get my father so that he could say goodbye to Albert, and then called me. I made an effort not to show my feelings. I was in a state of shock: I had just found out that Amelia had caused my father to be in his current state. I knew that he had lost his legs in an act of sabotage carried out by the Greek Resistance, but it was not until now that I found out that the person who had set off the detonator had been Amelia.

It was hard for me to shake Albert's hand to wish him farewell. When he had left I shut myself in my room and gave way to tears. I hated her, I hated her with all my soul, and I loved her, I loved her with all my soul, and I hated myself for loving her.

4

I made a decision. I had finished my studies some time ago and I was working as a doctor in a Berlin hospital. Over those years I had established my relationship with Ilse, who insisted that we should marry, or at least go live together. I had resisted because it seemed to me that leaving Amelia and Max would be like a desertion. He was an invalid whose health worsened by the day, and Amelia gave him every moment of her life. Until that night I had thought that it was a boundless love that tied them together, but now I knew that what connected them was something even stronger and more painful than love.

Ilse had stopped living with her parents some time ago, and I decided to go to her house that very night. I found a couple of bags and put some clothes in them. I left the house without making any noise.

The next day I went with Ilse to get the rest of my things. My father didn't understand why I'd made such a sudden decision.

"It's a good idea, but to do it like that... without saying anything," he said, regretfully.

"Either I should do it like this, or I'll never be able to leave."

"Friedrich has the right to look for his own way through life, to have his own life. We've been lucky to have him with us for more time than we could have imagined," Amelia said. "But we will miss you."

I didn't say that I would miss them too, because at the moment I needed to get away.

"We'll come often enough, won't we, Ilse?"

"Of course we will. Anyway, my apartment isn't too far away from here, it's not more than half an hour's walk."

But my visits grew ever more spread out and I felt guilty because of it. I needed to find myself, put my feelings in order. I knew that my father was suffering because I didn't go to see him, and that this was affecting his health, but I couldn't change the way I felt. Even when our first child was born, I didn't do anything to help my father enjoy being a grandfather.

One night, Amelia called me in alarm. Apparently, my father had suffered an attack and he wanted to see me as soon as possible.

When I got there I thought he was dying, he was having a heart attack, but we got him to the hospital in time.

My colleagues in the cardiology department had told me that there wasn't a great deal of hope, but they didn't bank on my father's desire to carry on living. He was in hospital for a month before they let him go home. From this moment on I decided that I wouldn't let him suffer more than I had suffered, and I made it my habit to pass by their house every evening on my way home after I left the hospital.

My relationship with Amelia had changed since that night when I heard her talk with Albert, and I was somehow annoyed that this change was not something she condemned, or felt offended by. She accepted it, as she accepted everything that happened to her over the course of her life.

My father was extremely happy that Ilse and I started to bring the children round more frequently. He liked reading them stories and teaching them to play chess. Amelia was the very best of grandmothers. But she was something more than a peaceable old lady.

Ilse worked in a research institute, and some of her fellow scientists were opposed to the regime. She knew of and sympathized with many of the members of the opposition, but she kept herself distant from their activities.

Until one day, when she found herself caught up in a situation.

It was early one morning, because Ilse always liked to arrive before the rest of her colleagues, she said that in this way she was able to organize her day. She thought that she was alone, but then one of her colleagues came into the room.

"Hello Erich, what are you doing here so early?"

He didn't reply, but fell to the floor in a faint. Ilse was scared, went up to him, and saw that he was bleeding. She sat him up as best she could and tried to rouse him.

"Don't tell anyone," he said in a faint voice.

"You're wounded, you need a doctor."

"Please, don't call anyone!"

"But..."

"Please! Help me to hide, I'm begging you!"

She felt nervous, and didn't know what to do. She thought about telephoning me at the hospital, but she knew that the telephones were all tapped and that if she told me to come straight away then it would arouse suspicions.

Without knowing how she managed, Ilse got Erich to a storeroom.

"I'll have to find someone who will help us to get you out of here. Can you tell me what happened?"

"A roundup... they shot at us... but I got away."

Ilse didn't know what to do, she didn't want to get me involved, but she didn't trust anyone enough to ask them to help. But she did know of one person whom she could trust, who wouldn't ask any questions, who would help her.

She locked Erich into the room and ran out of the Academy of Sciences to go to Max and Amelia's house.

Amelia opened the door and saw the despair and fear in Ilse's face.

"Help me! I don't know what to do."

She told Amelia everything that had happened, and Amelia told her to calm down and give her a few minutes to get ready.

She went to the Academy with Ilse; at that time of the morning, scientists and other employees were beginning to arrive.

They walked in calmly. Amelia asked Ilse to pretend as if nothing was amiss.

They got to the storeroom and Ilse unlocked the door.

She was surprised to see Amelia take a bandage out of her bag, examine where Erich was bleeding from, and bandage his torso extremely tightly.

"Can you walk?"

"I don't know..."

"You'll have to try if you want to get out of here."

We started to hear noise and shouting.

"Go and see what's going on, and when you've found out come back here," Amelia told Ilse.

Ilse left the storeroom trembling, she was scared half to death. In the corridor she ran into her boss.

"Ah, Ilse, there you are! It's a right mess here. We all have to go to the lecture theater. Apparently the police are looking for someone who could be hiding here."

"Here?"

"Yes, there was a meeting last night, you know the sort of thing, people talking out about the government. Of course, there was a Stasi informant who had infiltrated the whole thing and there was a roundup. Someone shot at and killed a policeman, and so you can guess the kind of mood they're in. There have been hundred of arrests."

"But here..."

"Apparently a woman saw a man who could hardly walk around the Institute early this morning, and she told a watchman and he called the police, who are about to get here. The director of the Institute has told us all to go to the lecture theater and be identified."

"Alright, I'll be right along. I was in the bathroom and I came out when I heard the noise, but I've left my bag there."

She went back to the little storeroom and when she told Amelia and Erich what was going on, Erich said that he'd give himself up.

"No, you can't, they'll kill you," Amelia said.

"There's no other way out."

"We'll see."

The loudspeakers announced that all employees had to go to the lecture theater to identify themselves before the police arrived.

"We have to get you out of here, and you're going to need to stand up straight even if it hurts."

They left the storeroom, Ilse and Amelia supporting Erich one on either side. There was no one in the corridor. They heard footsteps approaching and almost ran straight into one of the building's watchmen, a man whom everyone suspected was a Stasi informer.

"You... Why aren't you with everyone else?" the watchman asked.

"We're working..." Ilse was about to take her ID card out of her bag.

The watchman looked at Erich and saw that blood was seeping out through his jacket. Ilse was looking for her ID card in her bag, but the watchman must have thought that she was about to take out a gun. He took his pistol out of its holster and aimed it at them, but a second later he collapsed to the ground, to the astonishment of Ilse and Erich.

There was a silencer gun in Amelia's hand.

"My God!" Ilse cried out.

"Shut up! If I hadn't shot him he would have killed you, he thought you were going for your gun. And now, let's walk."

Ilse was terrified, as was Erich, but they obeyed her. They were on the third floor and got down to the second floor, and saw in the street the first employees who had been identified and were now standing around by the door.

"What's on the ground floor?"

"Laboratories..."

"Is there a door that leads into that garden?"

"Yes, yes..."

"We'll go down, we'll try to find an exit or else leave through a window, I don't see any policemen down there, we'll try to mingle with the crowd of people who have already had their papers checked, then we'll go to your car. Do you understand?"

Erich and Ilse nodded. They did as she had said, they left through a side door into the back garden and walked around the building until they could join the crowd of employees.

"Smile, Erich, and try to cover that part of your jacket with your scarf. You're still bleeding, in spite of the bandage."

Ilse still doesn't know how they were able to get to the garage. Amelia took them home, and as soon as they had got Erich into bed, he fainted. They had to explain to Max what had happened.

"You have to help this man, you're a doctor," Amelia asked him.

"I can't, you know I can't. I haven't been a doctor for more than forty years. Anyway, I don't have anything to work with."

"Improvise, Max, tell me what you need, I'll look in the first aid kit, there must be something..."

"He's bleeding to death..."

"Look at the wound, at least see if the bullet hit any vital organs."

"How am I going to do that from the chair?"

"Max, if you don't do it, then this man will die. You swore to save lives, so save his life."

Ilse and Amelia between them helped my father to get close to Erich. He examined him and said that the bullet had gone right through him, but that he couldn't be certain that there were no vital organs affected. He told them how to clean and cauterize the wound, but he told them that Erich would need a blood transfusion as soon as possible, or else he wouldn't make it.

"That can't happen," Amelia said, "or at least not now."

Amelia sent Ilse home to look after our children.

"When Friedrich comes, tell him to come over. Don't talk to anyone in the meantime; if someone calls from your office tell them that you got scared and went home."

"But the police will find that man..."

"Of course they'll find him."

"And they'll look for us."

"No. No one saw us. You have to be calm now and when you go to work tomorrow you need to behave like everyone else, be curious and horrified by what happened."

968

"I… I'd like to thank you, it's my fault that you're in this mess."

"Don't thank me, Friedrich would never forgive me if I didn't look after you."

"The pistol… Why did you have a pistol? I didn't know you…"

"It's better to prevent things from getting nasty. And now get out, I'll look after Erich."

My father could scarcely believe his ears. When Ilse left, he looked at Amelia furiously.

"Again… Will this ever end?"

"Would you have preferred me not to help Ilse, or let her get killed? I didn't have a choice."

"Of course you had a choice! You've spent years justifying whatever you do with the phrase 'I didn't have a choice.' There's always a choice, Amelia, always."

"Not for me, Max, not for me. Do you think he'll die?" she asked, indicating Erich.

"He's lost a lot of blood and needs a transfusion, and if he doesn't get one then his heart might fail."

"We can't do anything apart from wait, maybe Friedrich will know what to do when he comes."

"It's dangerous for him to be here, they must be looking all over Berlin for him."

"But nobody connects him to us."

"Are you sure that none of the neighbors saw you come in?"

"No, I'm not sure. I think not, but I'm not sure."

"We're too old to be tortured or sent to a labor camp. If they discover us, I imagine they'll kill us," Max said in despair.

"They won't do anything to you, it's obvious that you couldn't have helped this boy escape, I'm the only one responsible."

"Do you think I'd be able to live without you?"

"Yes, of course you could. You've got Friedrich, and Ilse, and your grandchildren, who love you. You don't need me as much as you think."

"My life is you; you are my life."

"Well, if that's so, it was me who cut your life down so small."

I was scared when I got home and saw how nervous Ilse was. I had been hearing rumors all day about what had happened, and I had even called her at home to see if she was alright. She seemed scared, but I thought that it was because all this had happened in the building where she worked.

Ilse insisted that I go to my father's house. Erich was in an extremely bad state, in spite of the efforts that Max and Amelia had been making. When I arrived, I gave him an injection and a painkiller that was much stronger than the one Amelia had been able to find for him.

"We should take him to a hospital, or I don't know what might happen," I told them, although in fact I knew all too well.

Erich opened his eyes a little and tried to speak, even though he was very weak.

"Tell my friends, they..."

"Impossible. You and your friends have behaved like amateurs. If we call them we'll end up in the hands of the Stasi," Amelia interrupted him.

"So what are we going to do?" I asked, worried.

"You keep him alive, I'll try to think about how to get him to a safe place."

"He won't survive in the basement," I said, worrying that she wanted to take him downstairs.

"No, I don't want to take him there. It's not that late, I'm going to call a friend."

Garin arrived at my father's house half an hour later. It was years since I had last seen him, and I was shocked to see him turned into an old man, although he still stood upright and had kept his moustache, even though it was now entirely white."

Amelia told him what had happened. He laughed, and then he slapped her on the back.

"You're unpredictable, you always have been. You've been

retired for years, and then all of a sudden you up and shoot a security guard and take a fugitive into your house. What do you want me to do?"

"Save him, and if possible get him out of Berlin."

"You're asking me something that can't be done from one day to the next, I have to get everything sorted out and it's not easy. I need to talk to my people, we'll be risking a lot."

"It's not just his life that's at stake," Amelia said, pointing at Erich, "but the life of my family: Friedrich, my daughter-in-law, my grandchildren. If it weren't for them I wouldn't ask you. You have to do me this favor, Garin, you owe me."

They were silent for a few minutes. Then Garin shrugged his shoulders in what appeared to be a gesture of resignation.

"I'll do what I can, I don't promise anything. But you have to hide him until we can get him out of here."

"For how long?" Amelia asked.

"I don't know, two days, three, maybe more."

"He may not last that long."

"Well, if he dies, then there's no problem; it's easier to dispose of a body than get someone out of Berlin alive."

"How can you talk like that?" Max couldn't contain his fury.

"Come on, my old friend, there's no room for sentimentality in my line of work. I'll do what I can to save Amelia's neck, because she's killed a security guard to protect your daughter-in-law and her friend. And she's reminded me that I owe her a debt, so I'll pay it and we'll be at peace."

I couldn't sit around waiting for Erich to die, and I couldn't let Amelia take all the risks either. I went back to the hospital with the excuse of examining one of my patients who was in intensive care.

I stole a couple of bags of blood and some hypodermic needles, as well as other supplies that I thought might be useful, and then got ready to go back to my father's house. I was just about to leave when I ran into the medical chief of staff who was on duty that night.

"What are you doing here?"

"I came to see a patient, I've been treating him for years and they operated on him this afternoon. I promised his wife that I'd try to see how her husband was doing."

"You look worried..."

"I am, my father's not very well himself, he's very weak. I was with him a while ago and he wasn't doing so great, so I might go to his house and see how he is."

The blood transfusion gave Erich a boost that he needed, but his temperature was still high. I gave him another injection of antibiotics. I couldn't do any more, there was no way of telling whether he had an internal hemorrhage or a collapsed lung.

Erich hovered between life and death for two days, until Garin finally showed up.

"A friend of mine will come in half an hour with a truck, but how are we going to get him out of here?

"I've thought about that. We'll take him down to the cellar and put him into an old trunk. I've got it ready, I've put in a mattress, and I've made a couple of holes in the roof for him to breathe through."

"You've thought about everything." Garin seemed to be impressed by Amelia's preparations.

"I think so. Friedrich will help me to lower him down through the trapdoor that leads to the basement from our kitchen."

We followed Amelia's instructions. If any neighbor came to snoop around, all he would find would be some men taking some old furniture up from the cellar.

I couldn't resist the temptation of asking Garin how they were going to get Erich out of Berlin.

"I shouldn't answer that question and you shouldn't ask it."

"We should at least tell his family that he's safe..."

I couldn't finish my sentence. Amelia and Garin were furious and seemed about to hit me.

"You're crazy! You'd put us all in danger. We save his life, we take him to the other side, and then he lays low for at least a year. His family will stop suffering when they know that he's safe and sound. But you mustn't be seen with anyone who knows him, not his friends, not his family. Tell Ilse the same, or else..." Garin's voice was threatening.

Ilse still shudders when she remembers what happened. If Amelia had not pulled the trigger, she would be dead. So she is always grateful to Amelia for doing what she did. It was the second time that she saved us both, because if anything had happened to Ilse... I don't know what I would have done.

A few days later I went to see my father. He was in bed, and didn't feel too well.

"He didn't want to get up," Amelia said.

He had had two heart attacks, and had circulation problems, and his eyes showed all the tiredness of a long life confined in a mutilated body. I thought that my father was giving in, that he was losing the will to live.

While I was dozing next to him, I felt Amelia's eyes boring into my face.

"You heard my last conversation with Albert James." It was not a question.

"Yes." I didn't want to lie to her.

"I know. You like to listen at doors, to try to understand some of the strange things you see. Your father and I know it and we try not to talk too much when you're awake. I knew that you were listening to us that night. And it was a great relief that you did. I needed you to know what I did to your father, you can't imagine the number of times I asked Max to tell you the truth, but he refused, said that it would hurt you to know the truth. You know, I felt like an impostor with you for a long time."

"I hated you for what you did to my father."

"It's right. You couldn't do anything else."

"And you don't mind?"

"I care more about not paying my debts, and about dragging this imposture around with me on my conscience."

"You are a strange woman, Amelia."

"We're at peace now."

Life continued monotonously, day by day. I had another couple of children, and my father died a little more every day.

At the end of the eighties, the East Germans felt that something was going to change, perestroika was altering what had previously appeared to be a monolithic and unchangeable order of things.

In October 1989, when we were getting ready to celebrate the fortieth anniversary of the foundation of the Democratic Republic, protests and demonstrations burst out onto the streets. As if that weren't enough, Gorbachev said that he was only going to carry on supporting East Germany if a reform program was put into place. That day we realized that we were at the end of an era.

The party leaders started to get worried; so worried that they even published a document announcing reforms. They were trying to control the people's desire for change. But Erich Honecker did not agree and maintained a hard line, using the police to suppress the discontent that could be seen in the streets.

A group within the party leadership decided that the time had come to retire Honecker and take control of the country. On October 17, 1989, the Politburo held a meeting in which they decided on the reasons for removing Honecker. In the end he had to present his resignation for what where euphemistically called "health reasons." The Central Committee named Egon Krenz as general secretary of the party, president of the State Council and of the Committee of National Defense.

However, Krenz's election was not seen as sign that things were opening up, and although he offered to begin a new era in the relations between the party and the people, he did not manage to make people trust him.

We all followed the news with a great desire for change, and we started to dare to talk with less care and attention.

My father seemed indifferent to all these events. Some days, after having breakfast, he would stay caught up in the foreign broadcasts from the shortwave radio that Amelia kept like a treasure. But neither her comments nor ours seemed to interest him.

On November 1 he collapsed and we took him to the hospital, but my colleagues said that there was nothing we could do for him, and that it was best for him to be allowed to die at home, quietly, so we took him back to our apartment.

Amelia never left his side, not even for a minute. I think that she grew old very fast in those days. Even though she was seventy-two, she had seemed younger, she was always well dressed, with her white hair tied back in a bun.

On the afternoon of November 9 Amelia called me to come to my father's house straight away. My father was starting his final agonies.

This lasted several hours, with periods of lucidity when I was able to say goodbye to him and tell him how much I loved him and how happy I had been by his side.

"I couldn't have wanted any life other than the one I had with you," I told him.

Night had fallen, and hundreds of people were in the streets. The authorities had announced that after midnight special permission would no longer be required to cross the border.

I looked at the wall that stretched along in front of our house. I was used to its presence, and I thought about how strange fate was. My father was dying, and thousands of people were in the streets celebrating something.

It was round about midnight when Amelia beckoned for me to come to the side of the bed. He had opened his eyes and grasped hold of Amelia's hand, I saw his eyes filled with love, then my father took me by the hand as well and brought the hands of the three of us together on his chest, and died.

Amelia and I stayed still, without moving, with our hands on his chest, my father's chest. His heart had stopped beating and ours were beating faster because of the emotion of the moment. Shouting from the street pulled us out of ourselves. Amelia kissed him gently on the lips.

We heard more commotion and went to the window. We couldn't believe what we were seeing. Thousands of people were going up to the Wall, carrying pickaxes and hammers and chisels, and they started to beat at it in front of the soldiers. We stood silently looking at this spectacle, and then Amelia looked me in the eyes.

"You're going," I said, knowing that this is what she was going to do.

"Yes. There's nothing left for me to do here."

"I understand."

She took a bag and put some clothes into it. Then she opened one of the drawers of her bedroom cabinet and took out a box, which she gave me.

"Here is all the money I earned working for the Americans. It's dollars, they should be useful. The documents of ownership for the possessions your family had are here as well. Who knows..."

She went up to the bed and knelt down next to Max's body. She stroked his face and put her head on his chest. She shut her eyes for a few seconds, then got up. We hugged, and I felt her tears on my cheeks and mine on hers.

She left without saying goodbye, although both of us knew that she was going forever.

I saw her walk out of the door and approach the Wall. She joined with the thousands of Berliners who were beating at it and tearing chunks of concrete and brick away with their bare hands. They had made a large hole, and a goodly part of the Wall was broken down. I saw how she stepped over the rubble and walked with her back straight to the other side of Berlin, where other Berliners were shouting and singing with joy. She didn't turn back, although I'm sure that she knew that I was looking at her. I didn't move from there until I saw her lose herself among the crowds.

Friedrich fell silent. He was obviously moved, and I was as well. I realized that Ilse was looking at us from the door, I don't know how long she had been there.

"And she never came back," Ilse finished.

"No, never."

"But didn't she say where she was going, or what she was going to do?"

"No, she didn't say anything, she just left."

"Did she ever write to you, or telephone..."

"No, never. And I didn't expect her to. That night she recovered her liberty as well."

I had dinner with Friedrich von Schumann and his wife Ilse and we speculated about where Amelia could have gone but, as Friedrich himself said, my great-grandmother was unpredictable.

"I have no idea where she died or where she is buried. If I knew, I would go and put flowers on her tomb and say a prayer," Friedrich assured me.

I thanked both of them for having been so kind as to receive me, and above all for what they had told me. I promised them that if I found out where Amelia's tomb was, then I would tell them.

I couldn't do much more in Berlin. No one could tell me where my great-grandmother had gone, so I went back to London, convinced that if I insisted with Major Hurley and Lady Victoria, then they would tell me what had happened to Amelia. I was sure that they would know.

Major Hurley seemed surprised when I called him.

"I've told you, I can't tell you anything else. I can't reveal official secrets."

"I'm not asking you to tell me any state secrets, just to give me an idea about where my great-grandmother might have gone. As you can see, I hope, no one cares about what a seventy-two-year-old woman who is already dead did in 1989.

"Don't insist, Guillermo. I don't have anything else to tell you."

Lady Victoria was friendlier, but equally firm in her refusal.

"I assure you, I do not know what became of Amelia Garayoa, I would like to help you but I cannot."

"Maybe you could convince Major Hurley..."

"Oh, impossible! The major will stick to the rules."

"But I just need to know where my great.-grandmother is buried, I don't think it could be a state secret."

"If Major Hurley doesn't want to tell you anything else, then he will have his motives."

I couldn't arrange a new meeting with either Major Hurley or Lady Victoria. The major told me that he was going fox-hunting for a few days, and Lady Victoria was planning to go to a golf tournament in California.

5

Over the next few days, back in Madrid, I called all the people who had helped me find out about Amelia's wanderings, but no one seemed to know anything about what happened to her, it was as if the ground had swallowed her up.

I decided to get in touch with Washington to get permission to look in the National Archives there.

I remembered that Avi Meir had told me about a friend of his who was a priest and who had been in Berlin in 1946, and who now lived in New York and was an expert on the Second World War.

Avi seemed happy that I had called him and gave me the address and telephone number of his friend.

Robert Stuart was an old man who was just as charming as Avi Meir, as well as being a walking encyclopedia.

He did as much as he could to help me, he even got me in touch with a retired CIA operative whom he had known in Berlin in 1946. But it was useless. If the British were extremely cautious about their secrets, the Americans were even more so. Although they had declassified some of the documents that contained the names of people who had worked for American intelligence, there were other names that were still secret. The most that I could discover was that a friend of this former agent confirmed for me that during the Cold War there had been a Spaniard collaborating with them from East Berlin.

In despair, I decided to try my luck with Professor Soler. I turned up at his house in Barcelona without warning.

"Professor, I'm at an impasse, I can't go any further without your help."

"What's happened?" he asked me with interest.

"Amelia disappeared from East Berlin on November 9, 1989. Does the date say anything to you?"

"Of course, the fall of the Wall..."

"Well, it's as if she were swallowed up by the night, I can't find any trace of her from that day onwards. I think I'm a failure."

"Don't be a pessimist, Guillermo. You should talk to Doña Laura."

"She'll think that I'm a failure."

"Maybe, but you do have to tell her that you can't carry on with the investigation."

"I tell you, I'm trying everything. There's not even a trace of her on the internet," I said.

"Well, if something's not on the internet, then it obviously doesn't exist," he said, ironically.

"So what should I do now?"

"I've told you, call Doña Laura and tell her that you've reached a point where you can't continue any further."

"After so much time and money... I'm ashamed."

"Well, it's better for you to tell her the truth as soon as possible, unless you think you can find another clue."

"If you don't help me..."

"I don't know how to, I've already put you in touch with all the people I know who can help you."

I had to have a couple of drinks before calling Doña Laura. She listened to me in silence as I gave her an account of my wanderings and of how I had lost track of Doña Laura on November 9, 1989.

"I'm sorry, I would have liked to have told you where she is buried," I said apologetically.

"Write down what you've found out, and when you're done, give me a call."

"Write it down? But the story isn't finished..."

"I'm not asking for the impossible. If you've got to 1989, then that's good enough. Write it down and try to be as fast as you can. We can't wait very long at our age."

I hadn't seen Ruth for a very long time: What with her traveling and mine, there hadn't been a time when we coincided in the same place. And I went to see my mother as soon as I arrived in Madrid, but she was so cross with me that she didn't even invite me in to dinner. I told her that I had finished my investigation, but not even that moved her.

"You've spent so much time acting the fool that I don't care if you do it a bit more. At least my sister has given up on the idea of giving us some absurd storybook for Christmas."

In fact, I had spent these months not just investigating, but also writing up all the episodes in Amelia Garayoa's life as I had been told them, so I almost had the story ready and written out.

It took me three weeks to put it in order, to correct it and print it. Then I took it to a printer who made it into a book with a leather binding. I wanted it to be presentable, and not too much of a disappointment for the two Garayoa women who had been so generous to me.

Doña Laura was surprised when I told her over the phone that I had the story all written down.

"How quick!"

"Well, I've been writing it up as I've been going along."

"Come round at four o'clock tomorrow."

I felt satisfied, and a little melancholy at the same time. My work here was over, and once I'd handed in the book I would have to find my own life once again, and forget about Amelia Garayoa.

Epilogue

I brushed down my only suit. I wanted to be presentable when I saw the two old ladies. I even went to the hairdresser in the morning.

The housekeeper who opened the door took me through to the salon and told me to wait.

"Madam will be through shortly."

I didn't sit down. I was impatient to give the two old ladies the report that had cost me so much to put together.

Doña Laura came in, leaning on a cane. She had grown older, if that is something one can say about a woman who had passed ninety some years ago.

"Come on, Amelia is in the library."

I followed her, walking at her rate, ready to meet her sister Melita.

"Amelia, Guillermo is here."

"Guillermo? Who is Guillermo?"

She looked lost. She was so thin that she looked as if she were about to break.

"The boy we asked to investigate... He's finished, and he's written the history you wanted."

"Guillermo... yes, yes, Guillermo..."

Her eyes seemed to flit back to the present day and she looked straight at me.

"Have you written it all down?"

"Yes, I think so..."

"Come closer, Guillermo, and tell me who I am."

I was struck dumb and didn't know what to say. The old woman's eyes were begging me.

"Guillermo, tell me who I am, I've forgotten, I don't know who I am."

I looked for Doña Laura, who had stood up and was leaning on the cane, looking at the pair of us.

"I... I don't understand," I managed to say.

"Tell me who I am, tell me who I am," the old woman insisted desperately.

I held out the bound book and she took it in her arms and hugged it tight.

"Now I can find out. I remember lots of things, but there are others that have grown cloudy in my memory. There are days when I don't know anything, not even who I am, isn't that right, Laura?"

Suddenly, the old woman sounded perfectly lucid, although she wasn't talking to me but to herself, or her own ghosts.

I didn't understand anything, or else I was starting to understand it all, but I didn't dare move, or speak.

"Is it all in this book?" Doña Laura asked me.

"Yes, up until November 9, 1989. That's the day Amelia disappeared and... ," I said.

"Yes, that's what happened," Doña Laura said.

"But..."

"Everything finished that night, there's nothing else to look for, Guillermo."

"Do you know who I am, Guillermo? Will you tell me?" the old woman asked, still hugging the book to her chest.

"I don't need to, I've written it all down, you can read it for yourself."

"I don't want to lose my memories, they're being taken away, Guillermo, they go away and I... I don't know where to find them."

"I've found them, and they're all here, and no one can take them away from you."

The old woman held out her hand to me and smiled. I took her hand: She felt firm and fragile at the same time.

Doña Laura made a sign and we left the library.

"She is... she is... Amelia," I babbled.

"Yes, she is Amelia."

"But isn't she Melita, your sister? I thought she was Melita... I've thought she was Melita all this time, you made me think she was her."

Doña Laura shrugged indifferently. She didn't care what I might have thought.

"So, she's my great-grandmother?" I was just about capable of saying this without stammering.

"Yes. But now you must forget about her. Remember your promise: You would do this work for us, not for your family, and you would keep secret everything that you found out. Those conditions still apply, alright?"

"Of course, of course. But why did you trust me?"

"Fate brought you to us, and Amelia, in her moments of lucidity, decided that she trusted you, that you would find her secret and be able to keep it. She believes in you."

"And I will not betray her. I won't tell anyone that she... well, that she is alive."

"There wouldn't be any sense to it. It would be a shock for her family to discover that she was still alive, and for her... Well, Amelia would not be able to resist meeting her grandchildren. It's too late now."

"When did she come back?"

"In November of 1989. She turned up without warning. Edurne opened the door and screamed the house down. We all ran to see what had happened. I recognized Amelia as well. Just imagine! She was twenty-something when we had seen each other for the last time, and she was more than seventy when she came back, but we recognized her at once."

"And... well, what about... explanations?"

"She didn't give us any. And we didn't ask her for any. It was hard enough to tell her that Antonietta had died shortly after she left. Or that Jesús my brother had died in a traffic accident along with his wife. And as for Javier, your grandfather, he was still alive but he was ill."

"How did you know?"

"We never stopped getting information about him, gathering it in case Amelia came back one day. We knew about his wedding, his successes, his children, everything, even though we never got close to him. When Santiago died we went to see Javier, I went with my sister Melita, but he made it very clear that he preferred to have nothing to do with us. He was right, what could we say to that?"

"So you have always been here, knowing everything about us, but we have known nothing about your side of the family."

"That was your great-grandfather Santiago's wish, and your grandfather Javier's; he could never get over the knowledge that he had been abandoned by his mother. She didn't blame him for it. The terrible part is that Amelia outlived him. We went to his funeral, no one saw us because we were up in the choir. Amelia cried out of despair."

"And you, didn't you have family: children, grandchildren?"

"My sister Melita died two years ago, shortly after losing her husband. Her children Isabel and Juanito are married and live in Burgos, but they come to see us very often. My brother Jesús and his wife died a year and a half after they had married and had a son. I took charge of my nephew, and brought him up as if he were my own. He died of a heart attack. He was the father of Amelia María, my niece who lives with us. My great-niece, I should say."

"So you gave up your own life..."

"No, I didn't give up anything, I chose the life I wanted to live, the life I have lived, and I have been happy."

"I can't understand how you stopped yourself from asking her questions, or how she stopped herself from telling you where she had been all this time."

"I know it's difficult to understand, but that's how it is."

"How long... well, how long has she had... problems with her memory?"

"How long has she had Alzheimer's? It started a little more than two years ago. One day she told me that there were things she couldn't remember. We went to see the doctor, and although he never said the word 'Alzheimer's,' he led us to understand that the process would be irreversible. Amelia started to worry. She was in despair thinking that her memory was gradually being erased. And I couldn't help her because I didn't know anything about what had happened in her life. And then you appeared, out of the blue. She had the idea of asking you to recover her memories. I tried to persuade her that this was a wild plan, that you were after all a stranger, but she's always done what she wants... So we asked you to investigate as much as you could. I was surprised when you called me to tell me that you had managed to get as far as 1989.

"And why didn't you ask Professor Soler?" I asked.

"Pablo... We love him, he's another member of the family, but Amelia insisted that it had to be you."

"I suppose you'd rather I didn't come back here."

"Do you think it would be necessary? In my opinion, everything's all been said now, and you have done something of immeasurable value for your great-grandmother. She couldn't hope to recover her memory, and here you are, giving it back to her. I think that this is the end. You always need to know when the moment comes, and to accept it. Don't you think?"

And I left their lives forever, becoming one of the last lines in Amelia's story.

Printed in the United States
by Baker & Taylor Publisher Services

Printed in the United States
by Baker & Taylor Publisher Services